The
Salmon's
Run

D.F. HIGHBERGER

ISBN:1480244589
ISBN-13: 9781480244580

DEDICATION

To Alexis:

This book was conceived as a chronicle of my life from my earliest memories, so I could describe my relationship with my mother for you and show you how that guided me to raise you differently. I've certainly never been a "traditional" mother. By the time my journey through this book ended, I learned who I had become. This is the story of my mistakes and my triumphs. I have gone through life with an open mind and a free heart and real courage. While I have been afraid of many things, I have tried to face each and every one. Sometimes I have had success and sometimes not. For my failures, I beg your forgiveness; as to all of my successes, while they rewarded me, everything I did was always for you. You were my reason for living, my drive to be the best, and I want to thank you.

I have been cognizant of others in this book and have made changes to protect their privacy. My perception of events may be different from others, but this was written from my heart, with the most honest of feelings.

I love you, Lex,

Mom

PREFACE:

You know me. We have never met, but you know me. Well, my life at least...it is a life like many others. We are products of our own unique circumstances. We don't have a choice of who our parents will be...where we will live...We are riding on the coattails of our parents' existence. We are all raised in this similar yet exclusive environment. Up to a certain age, we believe their way is the only way. We are born into this world. We learn the difference between good and evil. We try our best to get through another day. Many people will live and die and never question any of it. They will be the unprivileged few who were born without aspiration. For others it is more than that. It is about living life to the fullest. And sometimes, when you are young, the pulse that runs through your body is like the rush of a river driven by conditions that are out of your control. In these cases, alongside this rush lives desire. And sometimes that desire can take you to places, both safe and unsafe. Some will make it; others won't. Those who do are the people who achieve the salmon's run.

ACKNOWLEDGMENTS

I would like to thank a number of the people who touched my heart and made this book what it has become. I include the nameless strangers who appeared to me at times of need in my life: the hurried girl on the streets of Lynn, the convention men who reassured me they would get me to my destination, the German policeman who helped me find my way home, the soldier who carried me to the hospital, the elderly woman from the Salvation Army, and the countless other souls who are far too many to list. This book was written because of a promise to show your good deeds and to acknowledge the human spirit and its virtue.

Eleanor Buras: I would like to express my deep love and gratitude to you, my high school child development teacher. You guided me when I couldn't find my way. The result was in the ripple of lives that were touched in my own wake from your direction.

Jack Highberger: You have always been my creative mentor and my friend, my parent, my husband. As my creative consultant on this project, you were indispensable. Thank you for the years of reading and discussing certain passages that wouldn't have been written so well if it weren't for your ability to keep me focused.

Nancy Satin: You have painstakingly edited this book more times than one should have to. You amaze me for all that you can do, in art and life. You are a true friend, and I am honored to have you in my life.

Bob Donovan: You were a stranger when asked to be my location editor, but you jumped in with both feet. You were my unconditional voice of reason, when I questioned my own ability to pull this off. Now a friend, I will always cherish the exchanges we have had.

Alexis Baliotis: Thank you for being the family I had always wanted, for putting up with a crazy artist for a mother. You took care of me when the wolf had his claws in me. You are so wise beyond your years. You have allowed me to be who I am, even if it meant altering your own life. I love you

JeanMarc Dykes: You are the son I never had...I should have had. Thank you for insisting with all your might and making me go back into this chronicle to make it a novel. Thank you for being there when I was most sick and needed to laugh. This Mom loves you.

Angel Johnson: You have has helped me through many things, wolf -related and otherwise. Thank you for your computer expertise in formatting. You are a true friend.

CHAPTER: 1

I grew up in a New England town north of Boston, along the eastern coast of Massachusetts, where summer embraces you with its warm sea air kiss and winter assaults you with a biting cold. It was this seed that first germinated inside me that created the thick skin that has come to be known as a "New Englander." I came by this sturdiness naturally. I was born into a Yankee family that was here long before the rest of the country thought the need to declare their Independence. It was a time when life was more difficult and the winters were just as hard...although I didn't realize it until I was much older; my internal destiny of stubbornness and success was laid before me long before I was born. Environment can also set the stage for the adjectives of one's life. Famous in its own right, my town is where people accused of practicing witchcraft were tortured into submission centuries before me. They, of course, were not witches, but merely people trying to live through yet another difficult day in a confined Puritan existence. It is a lesson that most have never fully digested. When I was growing up, the witches were merely a story in our history books. And yet today, they are a part of the past that walks beside me every time I see injustice and prejudice in the world.

The town I grew up in was actually considered a city. But to me, it will always be a town. It was a place of neighborhoods, where everyone knew each other by name and children looking for adventures owned the streets. It was a time when your friend's parents had jurisdiction to discipline you as much as your own, and the secret lives of youth were never disclosed. Adults didn't get involved in children's activities, and dirty hands were encouraged. If your hands were clean, then you must have been sitting around doing nothing. The world of the child back then was a world filled with exploration.

When I was growing up, we didn't have the herds of tourists flocking to see all the gory details of our "witch" heritage. But years later, this same gruesome history brought the masses and left its mark. It is now a place where practicing, witchcraft is actually encouraged. As a teenager and only an onlooker observing this new practice I soon realized, as did everyone else, that the surface of what you see isn't necessarily the whole truth. The older woman in her orthopedic shoes, working the perfume counter at the local department store could be a practicing witch, and you may not know. Life is strange like that. It can hold a secret disguise. Where I grew up was Salem, Massachusetts.

I started my life in a lower middle class family. I had a mother, a father and two older brothers. My first memory is of the color green. It was a warm spring morning. The birds were foraging in the sand along the gutter, and the sun was painting a pink glow on my cheeks. It was the kind of spring morning that makes you realize just how long the winter has been. I must have been about two. I know it was spring because of the jacket I wore. My mother always dressed me in Easter coats back then, over frilly little dresses. I wore black patent leather shoes that were stiff and unforgiving. I remember the ground beneath my feet being unstable. It taught me to walk carefully. I know I was two because of the place we were living and the limitations of my mobility. Because I was so small, my visions of the world consisted of ladies knees, nylon stockings, and the interesting textures to the undersides of tables. Chairs were actually the surface on which I played with my toys. During that time in my life, everything was bigger than I. To keep up, I had to be carried.

We were on Allen Street in Salem. It was one street over from the power plant. It was during a time of innocence, and no one knew then what they do today about its cancerous effects on women and children. On this particular morning, my mother had me in her arms, and we were walking next door to visit a neighbor for coffee. Pressing my head against her chest, I could smell her Chanel #5 perfume competing with the stench of the leather factory on the other side of our house. The sun was warm on my face that morning, and I remember feeling safe.

The green I saw was the fresh coat of paint on a picket fence that bordered our neighbor's property. It was the most beautiful thing I had ever seen. The shine from the sun dancing on its glossy surface blinded me. The color was a perfect emerald. Reaching out to touch it as we glided quickly past; I was surprised by it smooth surface. Laying my head on my mother's shoulder as I looked back and peeking around the nape of her neck, I somehow knew I would remember it forever...and I have.

That morning had started like many others, in the warm kitchen of my home. My mother was my world back then. As I sat at our aqua blue kitchen table with silver and gold glitter imbedded in its surface, I watched daily as she fluttered between counter and stove. Stirring this and washing that, she was a whirling dervish in high heeled pumps and an apron. She was making homemade jars of jam from grapes that we picked in the yard that morning. I loved the smell of the grapes boiling in the kitchen. It filled the room with a warm mist of sweetness and earth.

"Don't get up from that chair, Barbara," she said, as she poured the hot paraffin on the top to seal the lids. When she was finished, she lined them up on the windowsill to cool. They looked like a row of jewels dancing in the sunlight. Loading them into a basket, she would distribute the jars to the neighbors. That is what we were doing on that spring morning.

My mother was a devout Catholic. She served fish on Fridays and taught me to say my prayers before bed. Yet in other ways, my mother was a lady of contrasts. When we worked in the kitchen together, she was so tender and sweet. But often I would catch her sitting alone at the table smoking a Pall Mall cigarette with a look of sadness on her face that I didn't recognize or understand.

She was a striking woman, and men always noticed her, yet she seemed to be unaware of her beauty. She had long auburn hair past her shoulders, full of massive curls. They felt so soft and smelled so good. My mother's attire consisted only of dresses, and every day she wore a single strand of pearls. In my eyes, she was the most beautiful woman that ever lived. She was the oldest and wisest mom anyone could have. I had no idea that she was only 21.

Our neighbor Marge opened the door and greeted us with a huge smile. "Well good morning, MaryJane, isn't it a beautiful day?" Taking me from my mother's arms, she hugged me and placed me on the kitchen floor next to an aging dog that had the look of dread at the sight of me.

"I have some news ", my mother exclaimed excitedly," We have bought a house in Peabody and will be moving at the end of the month."

Marge looked first at my mother and then back to me, "Are you sure that is a good idea?" The atmosphere in the room suddenly became as thick as the oatmeal I had refused to eat that morning. The dog quietly stood up and left the room.

Back home, my mom started putting all our precious possessions in boxes. It confused me as I sat quietly watching her. A tear rolled down her face and fell freely onto her best linen table napkins.

I wasn't an only child in this house of disparity. I had two older brothers: Jake was two years older than I and Doug was two years older than he, but for some reason, all I remember from that time on Allen Street are moments with my mother. It was 1963, and the world was changing rapidly.

As my mother had promised, my parents, brothers and I moved to a single family home on Lowell Street in Peabody. The house, white with black shutters, was very old and set back on a busy street. Behind it were rolling woods that went on for miles, where my brothers and I would play and explore. Forbidden to venture near the street, we spent many hours in those woods, always within reach of my mother's eyes.

"Stop following us, Barbara! Girls aren't allowed."

My reply was simple and direct with the conviction of an old soul, "When I was a boy, I always let girls play with me!" Turning around, I crossed my arms and stomped away. Sitting the allowed six feet from them I would hunt for caterpillars and butterflies or just sit under the trees and listen to the language of the leaves. I felt warm and safe there. I thought my life would go on like that forever. I was three.

It was in that house that I learned a lot of truths. There was no such thing as Santa Claus. Danger was in the world, and sometimes people got angry. In this house, I saw the Vietnam War on TV and watched, with the rest of the country, the shooting of a president. But I understood none of it. I only knew it upset my mother.

Our house was filled with fireplaces and floor grates. Every room had one. The grates were large holes in the floor to allow the heat to rise from room to room. They were circular in shape and had iron filigree inserts. My brothers soon realized that not only could they hear everything going on downstairs from these holes, but if they also removed the iron inserts, that I was small enough to be lowered into them and report back what I could see. I learned a lot from this ritual. One New Year's Eve party my parents held proved to be most entertaining.

"Barbara, it will be ok; I won't drop you; just tell us what you see." It was Doug who was telling me this and of my two brothers, he always seemed like an adult to me. I loved him and trusted him in that way. Although I was frightened, I would do anything back then to be a part of Jake's and Doug's adventures. Doug grabbed my ankles around my Dr. Denton footie pajamas and slowly lowered me into the hole. The living room was filled with fancily dressed men and women sporting silly, glitter-covered hats. I was surprised by what I saw. People were laughing and dancing. Some were blowing horns. There was even a couple in the corner, kissing. "Hey the hotel is down the street!" one man said as everyone began to laugh. The scene was strange and awkward for me. I didn't see my mother. She was more than likely in the kitchen. My father was sitting with a group of men toasting to a better year. Soon my head started to ache. I thought it would burst. The floor below seemed so far down, and I became scared. I panicked. I started wiggling my feet for my brothers to lift me back up. They didn't get the hint, so I yelled to them.

"You're hurting my head!"

The crowd below looked up with horrified faces. My father and another man grabbed an afghan throw off the couch to use as a net, in case I fell. My mother who suddenly appeared from nowhere started heading for the stairs to the second floor. That's when we got caught and were never allowed to do that again...at least while my mother was looking.

The grate in the floor was my first form of entertainment, not unlike television or computers are for children today. I was mesmerized by the images below. Every day at nap time, with my brothers off to that place they called school, my mother would sit in the living room and fold laundry or do some other domestic chore that required her to sit on the couch. My room being above the living room gave me a great opportunity to watch the domesticity in action. Carefully, I would sneak over to the hole and peer in. It was during those times that I watched my mother sew and clean and cry. I was afraid to go to her when she was crying. The one time I did, she pretended she wasn't. I figured then that all mothers cry when they put their children down for a nap, but no one is suppose to mention it. So I didn't. This was me and my mom's secret.

My room was also a magical place for me. In the early morning, when the sun came up, it streamed across the floor and sat in my unused fireplace. Actually, the fireplace was used, just not by fire. I took all the doll furniture out of my fancy doll house and set it up inside it. I could climb into the fireplace, but I could never fit in the dollhouse and be a true part of my dolls' lives. This was something I loved to do. Sometimes I was a friendly giant, but mostly I was just the Mom. I loved my fireplace doll house. Being the youngest and, heaven forbid, a girl, I found myself playing alone in my room a lot. My brothers had each other, and to my mother's chagrin, all they wanted to do was play war games like the ones they saw on TV.

Night time was a different story. At night, my room became an absolute chamber of hell. It was in this room that I first experienced night terrors and saw my nightly visitor, who would be with me my entire life. He only came at night, which is why I was never afraid during the day. Some children called him the "Boogie Man." I called him "Shadow Man." Sometimes I would feel the pressure of him sitting at the end of my bed, next to my feet. Pulling the covers over my head, I would want to scream but couldn't. The air under the covers became as hot as the kitchen, when my mother boiled the grapes for her jam. I sat there for what felt like an eternity, until I was sure if I didn't get a breath of cool air, I would perish. Then after seeing a glimpse of his form sitting there, in one swift motion, I would jump from my bed and go tearing down the hall in what could only be described as an Olympic feat. The whole time I was screaming at the top of my lungs.

On other occasions, the sight of him would grip me with such fright, that I was immediately paralyzed. I could not move even my little finger. I could not scream. All I could do was move my eyes around the room. But worse than all that was the sounds of the bees I heard. The buzzing was so loud, it made my teeth chatter and vibrate. All I could do was close my eyes and pray for sleep.

I have hardly any memories of my father back then. He left us when we lived in that house, and my mother changed. There were fewer and fewer jars of jam, and her skirts became shorter and shorter. She still cried a lot, but afterwards she seemed better. Eventually, even the crying stopped. I remember the night he left very clearly. We were all having dinner in the dining room. I hated to eat. From the time I could remember, the thought of putting something into my mouth...chewing it to oblivion...and swallowing it, repulsed me. I would gag and eventually vomit on the floor. I never made it to the bathroom; I never even tried. The bathroom was also a scary place for me. That big porcelain thing that always took a piece of me was too much for me to take. Not to mention the noise it made when you flushed it. Getting me to eat was always a trial at my house at dinner time.

"I think this is the best meatloaf I have ever made," said Mom, placing it on the table. "Mmmm, it looks good," said Jake.

"If we eat it all, can we have dessert?" chimed in Doug.

My family would make over-exaggerated comments about how good everything looked and smelled. I knew it was a game, and I wasn't buying it. I hated to eat, because if I ate, then I would have to go to the bathroom. Somehow, at that age, I knew they were connected. There were times I had to be hospitalized for it, and that was worse. On that fateful night, the tension in the room was thick. My father, who was rarely in good spirits anyway, was in an awful mood. He barked at me, "Barbara, we are not going to play this game tonight!" Being the age I was, I thought that he meant the exaggerated comments about dinner and proceeded to make a castle with my mashed potatoes. Suddenly he got very angry and walked over to me to try and force feed me.

"If you are not going to feed yourself, then dammit, I will do it for you! I am sick of paying hospital bills for something that can be prevented."

My mother started yelling at him to stop, and I began to cry. Potatoes were smeared all over my face as if someone had "pied" me. My brothers pretended they weren't there. Dad stormed off into the kitchen and began to throw things around. My mother ran after him. "You coddle her too much!" I heard him say. I asked Doug why it was bad to cuddle, as he quietly wiped my face with a napkin and tried to reassure me. I wanted to go to Dad and apologize for not eating my potatoes, but my brothers told me not to. They lowered their heads and quietly resumed eating. The screaming got worse. I couldn't stop myself; I had to do something. After all, it was my fault.

When I entered the kitchen, they were at opposite ends of the room. My mother was dressed in a beautiful flower print dress that cinched at her waist. She had her hands on her hips with her feet planted firmly apart. When she screamed, she bent forward, making her pearls roll slightly up her long, slender neck. Her auburn curls that I loved so much were flying freely from their pins and bouncing wildly in the air with every shout. I ran to her and wrapped my arms around her knees. I begged her to stop. I didn't want to see her upset; it scared me. I told her I was sorry. Even though I questioned my own ability, I promised to eat my potatoes. I tried to scream as loud as I could to make them stop, but that just angered my father even more.

He was at the other end of the kitchen. With every shout, an item in reach would sail across the room. I wanted to go to him but was afraid. The next item was the sugar bowl. I loved that bowl. I made funny faces in the reflection on the side of it and would laugh. It always laughed back. I wondered why he was angry at the sugar bowl. It was a silver one that sat prettily on its own little perch. Only now it was dented and leaned to one side, and sugar was strewn across the floor. In a split second he was gone. I climbed up the length of my mother's body until I reached her chest. She was sobbing uncontrollably and had a hard time holding on to me. In one last- ditch effort to hang on, I accidently grabbed her necklace. Pearls went streaming across the room, each making its own individual clatter as they fell to the floor and rolled quickly away; like cockroaches scrambling under the refrigerator from a kitchen light turned on in the middle of the night. My memories of my dad after that incident are few. I still have that sugar bowl fifty years later. It is one of the only things I do have.

The next house we moved into was on Spring Street in Salem. My father didn't come, but Shadow Man did. I was four. It was a small apartment in a two family dwelling, and I hated it. A tall narrow structure situated between two others like deli meat in yesterday's sandwich, it felt perfectly like the life we now were about to lead. Cramped, hot and sticky, it had the smell of another family still lingering in its viscous linoleum floors and its tattered papered walls. The house was actually between Spring and Pickman Streets, with Pickman being the true address. I always thought of it as Spring Street, because that's the side I played on. I had to share a room with my brothers. It was tight quarters, but fortunately, we each had our own bed. It was odd seeing my dolls sitting on the floor next to their toy guns. Shadow Man visited me more in this new, strange place. My Shadow Man drove both of my brothers crazy. After Jake and Doug fell asleep, I could still be found waiting in terror for his visit. Sure enough, in he would come. But this time, instead of screaming through the house looking for my mother, I would jump in bed with Doug and scream in his ear waking, both him and Jake in the process. They complained all the time to my mother that I was keeping them up.

"Don't you see him?" I would shout with tears running down my face. "He is right there!" pointing in the direction of my bed. I couldn't figure out why, but they never could.

In this new strange place, I no longer had my doll house, my fireplace or the holes in the floors. The yard was made of black tar that skinned my knees when I fell. I still had my imagination, and that's where I played all day. At nap time, when it was storming, I would watch the raindrops race down my window pane, creating watery and undefined images of the world outside. On sunny days, I would dance with the fairy dust in the sunbeams, pretending I was the queen of the fairies. I never did sleep.

There was a clothes line in the yard of that house that was supported on pipes cemented to the ground. I loved to hang by one hand with my body extended and swing around it. The rust on the pole burned my hands but made a funny sound. When I stopped, I would sit on the ground and watch my house whirl past me. It felt like my short lived life up till that point was on fast forward. I tried real hard to focus in and stop the image...sometimes I would reverse direction and pretend I was at my old house...but it never worked. I loved to make myself dizzy and did it all the time. My mother thought it was a weird obsession. She always got upset when she saw me do this; she would scream at me from the kitchen window.

"Barbara, stop that! Your eyeballs are going to cross or, worse, pop out of your head!" To me it was worth the risk

This was the house in which I experienced a lot of "first," one being making my first friend. I don't recall his name, but I do remember what his penis looked like. We had made a deal to see each other's private parts. We were the same age and hiding under the porch when he presented his to me. "Wow!" was the only thing that I could think to say at first. Then I added, "The top looks like a jingle bell!" and I giggled.

"Hey, it does," he said, as we both laughed. "Ok, your turn," he said with a smile. An image of my mother flashed before my face, and I got scared and ran away. "Wait, that's not fair!" I heard his muffled voice say from under the porch.

I was sure that I had a black mark on my soul from the incident. That's what Mom said happened to sinners. If you had too many black marks, you weren't allowed in Heaven. Knowing I had a lot of years ahead of me, I figured I was sure to be rejected from that holy place. Unfortunately, I wouldn't see another penis until high school.

I also learned to ride a two wheeler bike that summer; the mailman taught me. I would wait for him every day promptly at eleven. I sat on my hand-me-down boy's bike, precariously balancing myself on the curb. My brothers always rode their bikes every day after school. I wanted to be just like them and prove I was as big as they were.

"Mr. Mailman, Could you give me a push?"

Rolling his eyes, putting down his huge sack, he did every time I asked. He hated seeing me there. I could tell by the look on his face. He never said a word to me in all the weeks he taught me. But he always pushed me. I could only ride up the street. My mother let me go that far because my grandparents lived at the top of the hill. I was too afraid to try it going down. When my brothers came home from school, I would ask them to help me, but they refused. Mom was too busy trying to pretend she was still domestic. Then, one day, I had a long talk with myself and thought, "If I don't try to ride downhill by myself, no one will do it for me." It took me an entire afternoon to get the nerve; I sat at the top of the hill for hours. The mailman had gotten me up there, and, by golly, I was going to get myself down. It was finally my mother's call for dinner that made me do it. Suddenly, for the first time in my life, I was controlling my own fate. It was an exhilarating experience. No one had told me about the air blowing past my face like a warm, late summer storm front and the feeling of flying like a bird free in the sky; I had only known the struggle. When I arrived at home, I quickly threw my bike on the hot top with a clang and ran into the house. Everyone was sitting there, lost quietly in their own worlds. Jake's face was sitting in his hands and supported by his elbows on the table. Doug had his nose in a book, as usual. Mom had her back to us all, stirring something in a large pot with an aroma I couldn't identify. How is it that they weren't feeling this happiness I was feeling? Didn't they realize what had just happened? It was a big day for me. I knew it was a turning point in my life. Didn't they see that I looked different? I know I felt different. I was no longer a baby.

The beach was across the street from our house. Although I couldn't swim, Mom let me go, if my brothers were with me and I was covered from head to toe with clothing. No one could figure out why, but I always broke out in a rash at the beach. My skin would blister and itch. I didn't mind being covered. When the sun touched my skin, it felt like I was on fire.

"I don't want you taking off those sneakers until you get to the beach," my mother would yell to us as we slammed the door. The minute we were out of the driveway and out of sight, off they came. The hot top burned under our feet. We had to run on tiptoes to get there.

The street to the beach was worn away in parts to the cobblestones from earlier times in Salem. In the middle of this was the exposed iron trolley tracks that brought beach goers during the 1920's to their destination. It was common knowledge in the neighborhood to never step on the trolley tracks. Rumor had it they were hotter than the tar. I couldn't tell you if they were, because I never stepped on one. "Oochie, auchie, oochie auchie! " The words echoed out of the mouths of a half dozen children all at once, as we hobbled across the road in a gangly, awkward dance. Our arms were flailing madly in the air, with our shovels and pails flying in all directions, barely able to hold on. When we reached our destination, in one choreographed movement together, we would jump into the sand with both feet.

"Ahhhhh, that's better, shhh, listen, do you hear the sizzle of your soles cooling down?" asked Doug. I would always stop to listen; I never did hear it; but I did feel it.

Once at the beach, I would build in the sand, while my brothers swam. It was ok that I couldn't go in the water, because there were plenty of things to keep my imagination busy. I would build sand dragons and teddy bears. Carefully gathering water in a pail from the ocean's edge, I would begin to drag it up to my destination. The uneven sand losing ground beneath my feet made me waddle like a penguin from the weight of my burden. Scraping my legs with the edge of my plastic pail with every swaying step and the whole while getting my pants legs wet in the process, made the effort all that more heroic. The sand felt like a warm soft clay, and the water was my glue. Meticulously patting my way along the form, gathering the drips as I went with my tiny fingers, the image would take hold. I never built castles. That would be too ordinary to make; anyone could do that. I wanted to be different. And then with the turn of the tide, it was gone. That was never an issue for me. It was the process I enjoyed and did it every day of the summer.

Another thing I did while at the beach was search for pirate's treasures. These usually consisted of sea glass and shells, with an occasional periwinkle and crab thrown in for good measure. If you sang softly to a periwinkle, you could entice him from his dark, cavernous home. A few of them would sit on my hand. Lying in the warm sand and singing to periwinkles is one of my fondest memories. I would try to bring them home as pets. I named every one. I saved them in cups that I would hide in our room until the flies came. Mom always made me throw them out.

"Hey look!" I shouted one day, "baby minnows! " "You better not take them home to our bedroom," insisted Jake. "Yeah, that would really smell, and then we will all get in trouble," Doug added. The rocks were another place to explore at the beach. I was not allowed to climb them, because that's where the rats lived. The neighborhood kids would compare stories as to who saw the biggest and meanest looking ones. I never did climb the rocks. That tidbit of information kept me from ever having the desire to do that. Instead, I looked upon them as the place where the monsters lived.

Our summer continued like that in a most uneventful way. When fall hit, it was filled with carving pumpkins and Halloween costumes. And then, on November ninth, nineteen sixty-five, in the late afternoon, the strangest thing happened. All the power went out in the whole North East. This power outage not only affected all of New England, but it also included parts of Canada, New York and other points to the Midwest. I didn't understand geography back then. But I did understand one thing. No power… meant no stove. No stove… meant no chicken soup, my only staple until first grade.

"Barbara, you have a choice. You can eat it cold or have a sandwich like the rest of us."

Sitting at the table with my head hanging low and a pouty bottom lip, I refused to respond.

"She is such a baby. You should just make her eat it, Mom," said Jake, suddenly sounding like my father. MaryJane was not going to get into this fight with her son…it was too familiar. Instead she sent me up the street to get some candles from my grandmother. Our transistor radio that ran on batteries was saying this outage was going to last all night.

Making my way up the street, grumbling to myself that I was going to starve by the time I got back down with the candles, I didn't fully understand that this lack of ability to cook my soup was out of my mother's control. My grandmother was expecting me and greeted me at the door. She had heard of my refusal to have a sandwich and offered me a banana.

With my pouty lip still firmly in place, I said, "No thank you." "You need to eat something, Barbara; an empty stomach will give you dreams at night."

Somehow, I never saw the connection…but in her own way, I think she was trying to convince me it was why I always saw Shadow Man.

My grandmother was a very voluptuous woman. She was so well endowed on top that she was a wet nurse for half the neighborhood, when she had her own babies. Her thick, black, curly hair had a white streak that extended from her widow's peak and sat delicately in the waves on top of her head. She was wearing hot pants and go-go boots on the day she died at 62, eight years later.

My grandfather used to say, "Maria, you are built like a brick shit house, with every brick in the right place!"

That was his way of giving a compliment. He and my grandmother were similar in age. His image in their wedding picture reminded me of Clark Gable, when I got older. I remember him to be a funny guy, but usually it was with jokes at my grandmother's expense.

"Maria, why are your feet always purple?" "Oh, Leo, stop that," she would retort.

I would carefully look under the table when no one was looking to see them for myself. All I saw were delicate little feet in stylish pumps. It wasn't until years later that I realized the foot joke was in reference to her being from Sicily and, therefore, a grape stomper. For years, I heard of stories about my grandfather having a terrible drinking problem. I never saw him drink, not even once. But those stories were forever fresh in everyone's mind. They were only spoken of in whispers between my mother and her three other siblings. To me, he was kind and loving and made me feel special. Once, when I was a bit older, he called me into the living room.

He hoisted me on his lap and whispered in my ear, "This is something I want you to see, so you can tell your grandchildren." Together we watched the first man land on the moon.

I was still too young to realize the significance of this event. The picture on the black and white set he had was fuzzy and faded in and out. I don't know if this was because of his TV or from the poor images transmitted from space. Either way, he kept hitting the top of the set, saying, "Come on, dammit," as if it were his own secret code, telling Cape Canaveral that the connection was not reaching Salem.

My grandfather always called me "Babe." I don't remember him ever using my real name. We called my grandmother Grammy. I always felt that was a silly nickname; I never liked the sound of it. I wanted to call her Grandma, like my friends called their grandmothers, but of course that would have been even sillier, if everyone else in my family called her Grammy. So I didn't call her anything. This was easy to do, because she was a person you didn't speak to, unless you were spoken to first. At least that's how I felt. She had a thick Boston accent that mingled with a hint of broken English. My grandmother was from Sicily and didn't tolerate any form of nonsense. Needless to say, I didn't eat dinner there. Sometimes I would have to stay with her, when my mother had to run an errand. I hated that, because it seemed like it was always at that time when my grandmother would do her cleaning and run the vacuum. She had a closet under her stairs in the hall, where I would hide when she performed this daily ritual. I thought that if I hid in there and screamed at the top of my lungs, I wouldn't hear the noise. I always hated loud noises. If the loud noise was coming from me, it gave me a sense of control. My grandmother would get impatient with me on this issue. I remember the first time it took her a minute or two to find me. Following my screams, she discovered where I was. "Barbara, what on earth you doing there?"

"I don't like the noise, please don't do the rugs." "That is the silliest thing I ever heard! Of course I will do the rugs. Be a big girl."

She kept vacuuming, and I kept screaming. Eventually, she did her vacuuming after I left. That's how I knew she loved me. My mother's sister, Tina, lived with my grandparents as well. Although I am not sure, I believe she was in her late teens. I say this because she had a boyfriend named Evan, who had a wonderful white convertible car. My mother didn't have her license, so driving in a car was a treat for us. Evan knew this and would let us go for a ride once in a while. On the dashboard of his car, Evan had a statue. It was a plastic, cream colored icon of a very young pregnant girl. She was wearing a short dress and looking down. She was cupping her swollen belly with her graceful hands, looking very angelic and serene. I thought she was beautiful and couldn't take my eyes off her, whenever I was in the car, never noticing that "Kilroy was here" was written on the base. The only things I remember about Tina and Evan during those times were that statue and driving in his car with the top down and the wind whipping my long hair straight up in the air. My grandfather had a similar icon in his car. It was plastic and cream colored also, but his statue was of the Virgin Mary. A few years later, Tina and Evan would get married. I don't recall the wedding or how old I was. But I do recall running to Grammy's house one day to see a brand new baby. Her name was Kerry, and she was so small.

The day of the power outage, after refusing the banana from my grandmother and listening to her reasoning behind my nightmares, I finally got the candles to bring back to my mother. My grandmother couldn't have just ordinary candles, she had to have the kind that were stuck in Italian wine bottles and covered with wax. Granted, from a child's perspective, they were a sight to behold when lit, but they were also heavy, and she gave me two of them.

Stepping out the door, she said very sternly to me, "Keep your eyes on these so they won't break."

Holding them up close to my face, that is exactly what I did. It was difficult to walk with them. Taking a lesson from Mrs. Jean's Romper Room TV show, I put one foot in front of the other, heel to toe. With my head held high and my eyes fixed on the candles, I didn't notice the stairs I was approaching. In a movement so fast I didn't understand what was happening, I proceeded to fall up the cement steps that lead the way out of the sunken garden. Tripping on the first step, my face hit the third one. So focused on the candles, I spread my arms wide to protect them. My face took the full brunt of the fall, lodging my two front teeth deep into the roof of my mouth. What I remember from the incident are random clips of images. I remember my grandmother screaming and searching for my teeth. I remember me and my mother in an ambulance with the siren blaring. The worst image of all was the ether they gave me at the hospital, so they could surgically remove the teeth that were imbedded in my head. That was a headache you never forget. Then, all of a sudden, I was at my grandmother's house again, and the candles were all lit because the blackout was still going on. I could have all the ice cream I wanted, but all that my grandmother had was maple walnut. I didn't eat. I didn't have front teeth from the age of four until I was about eight.

My world back then consisted of one street and the beach, a half a dozen friends I could call on and the endless rides up and down the road on my bike. But soon the world outside was going to enter my life in a way I had never expected.

I was coloring in my room, when the phone in the kitchen rang. Whoever was talking to my mother was making her very upset. In a split second, she scooped me up, and we were out the door. We were running to my grandmother's house. I had never seen my mom run before. I was bouncing violently in her arms and cried for her to stop. She was too upset to answer. When we burst through the door, the scene was total chaos. My Aunt Cheryl, who was another of my mother's sisters, who lived on the other side of town, was pounding on the refrigerator and screaming. My grandmother was crying and praying. My grandfather was also crying, but he kept saying over and over, "Let it out, honey, its ok." I was wondering what was in the refrigerator that made her so mad and needed to be let out. I don't recall seeing Tina and Evan. Cheryl's three young sons were sitting on the floor, crying as well. Little Sam was her oldest. He and I were the same age; Steve and John were younger. I sat on the floor and began to cry with everyone else. My family was out of control. My mother ran from person to person trying to calm them down.

"You don't know this has happened for sure. Why are you all so hysterical?" She was saying this through her own tears. But Mom knew and so did my grandparents. Cheryl had a way of knowing things before others did.

Then two strange men in uniforms knocked on the door. Somehow Cheryl knew what they had to say before they arrived. She had had a dream they would come, and they did. No one would open the door for the military men. They knew we were in there; they could hear all the commotion. So they slipped the paper through the mail slot. Big Sam was dead. The Vietnam War came home in a way we never could have imagined.

When we lived on Spring Street, I started school. A nursery school program had opened in Salem, funded by the state and in its first year. It was called Project Head Start. It was a program designed to prepare underprivileged children for kindergarten. I didn't know what those words meant at the time, and I didn't care. All I knew was it meant that I would be spending less time with my mother. I was picked up by a big orange bus at the top of the street. I hated that bus. It was too bouncy, and I couldn't see over the seat in front of me. Every day I would try and hold on, so I wouldn't fall off. At Head Start, we were fed breakfast and lunch. Both were hot meals. Breakfast usually consisted of your choice of powdered eggs and toast or oatmeal. The lunchroom smelled as if they boiled everything that could be plus things they shouldn't have. The stench used to make me sick to my stomach. I tasted that smell in my throat all day. I tried to keep my eating rituals a secret by pushing the food around on my plate. I had no friends and talked to no one.

One day, while out in the school yard, I was standing next to a brick wall. It was a beautiful day, and all the children were running and playing. As bad as lunch was for me in this place, recess was worse. I was afraid to join in on the fun and felt everyone was looking at me. The truth is none of the kids even knew I existed. I started looking at the texture of the bricks. Running my finger across the rectangles, I felt that indestructible surface. I wanted to be the bricks, to sit outside all day and be unnoticed.

I was jealous of that strength and felt sad. Denied that, I tried to be invisible, but it didn't work.

Soon I was found out about my eating rituals, and my mother was called. The teachers didn't seem to mind that I didn't have any friends just that they never saw me eat. I did have two staples in my diet back then: chicken broth and black coffee with lots of sugar. The next morning, my mother sent me to school with two thermoses. It became almost impossible to hold on to my seat on the bus after that. The black coffee became an issue with my teachers. They refused to give it to me until my mother told them it had liquid vitamins in it prescribed by my doctor.

The only time I remember enjoying myself was around St Patrick's Day. We were each given a piece of paper with a big shamrock on it and one very fat green crayon. All we had to do was color it in. I was so excited about this project that, at that moment, nothing else mattered. When I started coloring, I discovered that my desk had hollows and dents in it from years of past students bored with their daily lessons. It made coloring very difficult, because my crayon kept getting caught in the grooves. I had to color slowly and press down hard to achieve this task. I always colored carefully, even at home, so this did not bother me. It did, however, bother my teacher. When the rest of the class was finished, I wasn't even half way done. When the bell rang, and it was time to go to lunch, I didn't want to go. The teacher told me that I had been given plenty of time to complete this task and that it was my fault it wasn't finished. She said I could finish it at home, but I never saw it again. I felt so alienated at school. I missed my mother so much. I cried every day. Instead of me getting used to school like most shy children do, I was getting worse. I would try really hard not to cry, but the lump in my throat would always get the best of me. It would start out as a tickle. I tried to cough to make it go away. Failing miserably, I would give in and let the tears flow. I would work myself up to such a frenzy that even if I wanted to stop crying, I couldn't. It was hard for me to catch my breath. Finally, the school called and told my mother that I wasn't ready for nursery school, and I never went back.

I loved being at home with my mother again. We were very poor, but I didn't notice. The only job she could get and still take care of me was doing other people's ironing. My father apparently gave her money every week, but not much. Several times she had to take him to court for what little he did give. He was allowed to pick us up on weekends, but I don't recall him ever doing it. My brothers said he did, maybe two times. Between the ironing and Dad's checks, we got by. I would sit on the floor below her when she ironed. Tented by hundreds of men's dress shirts, I found a replacement for the fireplace doll house in which I would escape. I loved to look at the patterns in the linoleum. It was white with gold flecks. Every day I would search for a different image I had not yet seen there the day before. I would see the outlines of dragons and knights rescuing fair maidens. An entire story can be built on the images of a linoleum floor, if you just took the time to see it.

"Down, you ferocious beast...stay away from that innocent girl!" "Barbara, who are you talking to down there?"

I didn't answer her. Just like Shadow Man, I knew she wouldn't see them.

The work was tedious for her. In order to make enough money she had to iron a lot of shirts. After a while, she began ironing day and night. She no longer smelled of Chanel #5; instead, it was replaced with the odor of fresh hot cotton and Niagara Spray Starch. Even her hair lost its curl. She started to become distant with me. We didn't play anymore. One day, to get her to play with me, I took all the canned goods and cereal boxes out of the cupboards. I set them up in an elaborate display in my room. I was going to be the storekeeper, and she would be the customer.

Coming out of my room, I held one hand in the other in front of me, bowing slightly, and said, "Our special today is canned peas, six for one dollar." She turned away from her duty and looked at me with a helpless blank stare.

The words she spoke were barely a whisper. "Barbara, please put those all back. Don't make extra work for me."

On those rare moments when she did take a break, she would often gaze into space and smoke a cigarette. Sometimes I would catch her whispering to herself. But I never understood what she was saying. I no longer recognized this woman I loved so much. Her curls became stringy and lifeless; her pretty dresses were replaced with nylon pants and a sleeveless cotton jersey. Around her neck she hung a damp cold cloth that she rewet every half hour to wipe her sweaty brow. She no longer wore her pearls.

When we lived on Spring Street, my mother also cleaned the house of an elderly woman who lived across town. My grandfather would drop her off there, and I would join her. I never knew what my mother did in that woman's house. I was told to play in her back yard. To my delight, she had a grape arbor filled with juicy delights. Sitting under its canopy, I would smell an aroma of a time long forgotten of boiled grapes and paraffin. On that first day, I ran into the house, all excited, to tell Mom of the treasure trove of the past I had found.

At the sight of me, she turned abruptly and put her finger to her lips, "Shhhh, Barbara, Mrs. Robertson is not feeling well. Don't wake her...she is sleeping."

Looking past my mother, I saw what looked like a pile of delicate laundry lying on a bed. It was filled with lace and satin and smelled of Vicks Vapor Rub. On further investigation, I realized that the laundry had a head and wasn't laundry at all...but Mrs. Robertson. A few months later, Mrs. Robertson passed away...and my mother had to look for another part time job.

CHAPTER: 2

When I was six, I was old enough for kindergarten. We moved to Forrester Street in Salem. It was only four blocks from Spring Street, but to me, it was a million miles away. It was a three family home that rose straight up to the clouds, when I stood at the base of the front steps. It felt like the biggest house on the street. With ornate wood trimmings, it sat regally on the corner. We were on the top floor. My bedroom was on the far right curve at the front of the house. There was a big, walk-in closet that my mother let me use for my dolls. The room had a bay window that sported views of the harbor in the winter, after the trees lost their leaves. Once again, I had my own room. The first night I slept there, Shadow Man tucked me in.

At this house, I found some normalcy. This time I could walk to school and was relieved I didn't have to take a big orange bus. I was supposed to walk with my brothers, but they didn't want their friends to see they had to watch their little sister. So we all pretended we didn't know each other. Instead, I walked behind them with other girls from my neighborhood. In September I enjoyed this voyage. There were lots of kids laughing and joking, and the scenery along the water was beautiful.

"Hey how much will you give me if I can pitch this rock far enough to go over the hill and into the water?" yelled Jake. He was always challenging someone for something, and usually he won. I knew better than to ever take him up on one of these offers. Jake was a strong kid who could do most anything.

"I bet you my ice cream from the ice cream truck after school," said Thomas. Thomas was our downstairs neighbor.

Standing with his feet perfectly steady, Jake stuck out his tongue as he closed one eye to aim. Making exaggerated movements with his arm for good measure, he lobbed it right over the hill and into the water.

Turning to Tyrone, he said confidently, "Make mine chocolate."

I giggled to myself. I knew he would do it. It was a nice way to start the day. This was a big change from my last school experience. I was growing up, and my world was expanding.

Soon the warm walks of September turned into the cool walks of October. Leaves falling off the trees that lined this New England shore were strewn about in patterns on the sidewalks.

Inconceivable shapes and pictures were laid before my feet, as every step I took to school became a journey of a thousand lands. My brothers would become impatient with me, as I lagged behind, picking up one leaf after another. Putting them in my pocket, I was planning on reproducing the pattern I saw when we got home. Like the sea shells before them, my room became filled with various kinds of leaves in color and species. Mom, being of better spirits and not having to work so much, showed me how to iron them between wax paper, so as to preserve them in a scrap book. I think it was her way of trying to help me organize my obsessions. I meticulously arranged each preserved grouping on a black page, so that the spaces between the leaves made shadow characters that interacted with each other.

"Barbara, doesn't that look so much neater now that they are all together?"

"Yes," I said, not trying to explain what I was really doing. As with all the images I saw, I knew she wouldn't see them.

In the winter, the walk to school was a cold one. Because more than half the way was along the ocean near the beach, we were exposed to the elements. The street was a wide open expanse, with no houses on the ocean side. The route was windy, no matter what time of day or year. I prayed it wouldn't snow or worse, be freezing rain, because if it was then by the time I got to school, my braids would be a solid chunk of ice. It would take a half hour to thaw them, only to leave me a dripping mess the rest of the day; drying up just in time for the walk home. The wind was biting and felt like hundreds of tiny needles hitting my face. My tears in my eyes would feel like they could freeze in their sockets. I never cried for fear this would actually happen. Fortunately, I was never alone in this agony. Every child of New England who lives on the coast knows this feeling. Once inside the school, the entire troop of walking frozen children, with their wool mittens and hats with earflaps, would kiss the floor for having made it yet another morning without turning into a Popsicle.

My new teacher was my mother's friend, whom I had seen quite often. She would come over to our house in the summer and drink iced coffee on the back porch, trying to catch a sea breeze or two. They often talked about the war protests that were now all over the TV and the latest fashions of micro miniskirts pared with just darling go-go boots. My teachers name was Miss Twombly; she was only a little older than my mother, and I, of course, was her pet. The attention she gave me made me feel a little uncomfortable, but only a little.

There was one girl in the class that the other children were mean to. It upset me to see her so sad. She cried a lot, and my heart ached for her. I remembered the feelings of hating school. I wanted to tell her it was going to be all right, but I never did. Even the teacher would get frustrated with her outbursts.

"Ok, children, gather around. Sally, you get in the middle; we are all going to sing 'Alligator Tears' until you stop crying." I didn't want to do it. I was afraid to speak up about the horrible treatment of this child.

"Miss Twombly, I think I am going to throw up," I said.

Knowing full well I had a history of this, she sent me home. I wanted to tell my mother about it, but I knew with Miss Twombly being Mom's friend, this behavior would only make her feel awkward, too. I didn't want that for my mother, so I never said a word.

That year, on picture day, I was the first in my class to get the mumps. I was standing in line feeling god awful hot and trying not to faint. The cold cement blocks that made up the wall in the hallway where we stood in line felt nice on my face. I loved having my picture taken. I was always told I was a beautiful child, and this was my way of sealing it to fact. I had waited all week for this day: one step at a time, one inch closer to the photographer, one more bead of sweat staining my dress, one more strand of hair falling moist and stringy from my braids. It seemed like it was taking forever for it to be my turn. Placing my face once again on the cold cement, I thought about the conversation I had had with Mom that morning.

"This is the dress you will be wearing, Barbara, and we will have no more discussion about it." "But, Mom, it looks like I go to a Catholic school in that dress." "And you would, if I could afford to send you to one; so put it on and stop whining." "Why can't I wear the pink silky one? It is my favorite."

"Because that is only for special occasions; now go get dressed." Stomping off in my tights and slip, I muttered under my breath, "This is a special occasion."

When the time finally came, the photographer lifted me onto a carpeted box. He looked me in the eye and said, "Do you feel ok, sweetheart?" His voice was tender and concerned. My reply was a wary nod, yes. I wasn't going to spoil the moment. He snapped the picture, and I collapsed on the floor. "Miss Twombly...Miss Twombly...come quick!"

The photographs from that day were always a good source for laughter in my family. I have to admit, they were funny. My face was beat red, and my checks were three times their normal size. My smile was toothless and pathetic. All the excitement I had for that day, and it took me years before I let anyone see that picture.

On Forrester Street, my mother came "into her own." She no longer did ironing and seemed to be happy again. I don't remember her working back then, so my father must have been giving her money. She made lots of new friends: one was a woman by the name of Pam, who lived downstairs and had a lot of children. Like my mother, she was a single parent. Because Shadow Man visited every night, my sleeping rituals didn't change. After Pam inquired one day about the screams she heard coming from my room in the middle of the night, Mom made me sleep with the light on.

This house didn't have a yard, but the Salem Common was right up the street. It was so big and had a playground with all the amenities. There was a black wrought iron fence that surrounded the entire area. It was Victorian and reminded me of the park in the movie Mary Poppins. But the best part was that it had a tree I could climb. It was a big, old one with really low branches. Back then, I could always be found up a tree. Its bark was rough and scaly feeling. It smelled earthy and comforting. Every day I would climb up and pretend I was riding a dragon. I was brave and strong; I was the rescuer...that is, until the park monitors would come and tell me to get down. By the end of the summer, they were so tired of yelling at me that they stopped policing me altogether. I remember there was a boy my age there who would always bring dog biscuits and eat them. He offered me one, but with my eating history, I wasn't going to go there.

Pam, our neighbor downstairs, had two daughters close to my age. Their names were Maureen and Darleen. Darleen was exactly my age, and Maureen was older. We became very close and played together everyday. Mom and Pam became good friends and were together a lot as well. Many times our families would go on vacations together.

That summer, my mother got me a piano. I'm not sure how she was able to afford it, but my mother was amazing like that. It was quite a sight to watch the big, burly moving men try and get this huge monstrosity to the third floor. The piano was an old wooden upright, and it clanged out awful sounds with every jerking motion. They tried both sets of stairs, but nothing worked. I sat and watched the calamity from across the street on the curb. With my elbows on my knees and my chin in my hands, I was sure I was going to witness a death. This frightened me so that through most of it I closed my eyes. Eventually they decided that the only way in was through a window. The problem was the window was three floors up. This news spread throughout the neighborhood in a flash. All the kids on the street came out to watch. The next thing I knew, I was a kind of celebrity.

"Who is getting a piano?" asked Benny, the freckle faced tattletale that lived three doors down. "It's Barbara's piano," responded Maureen with her hands planted firmly on her hips. When I saw Maureen in that stance, I was certain Pam was her real mother.

We all watched in horror as they removed the large bay window that was in my bedroom. I was hoping they wouldn't break it. As they were hoisting the piano up, I scrambled as fast as my

listen to music, and when she put the stereo on, I knew she was back. Her album collection was vast. She danced when she cleaned, always an expert at multi-tasking, even before someone thought to come up with this phrase. The atmosphere she created was contagious, and many times I found myself jumping up and joining her. We would laugh and hold hands while twirling each other around the room.

I liked it most when she would lift me into her arms, and we would slow dance. "Come on Barbara I need a partner!"

Jumping into her arms, I felt more at home than I had in any house we ever lived in. The music she listened to the most was Diana Ross. Her soulful melodies about love lost seemed to strike a chord with her. She made me her backup singer, and the two of us would laugh at the pure enjoyment of it. She taught me to swing my hips and do the twist.

When we lived in that house, my mother bought us a fish tank. It held ten gallons and had plastic plants, beautiful pink rocks and a fake cave where the fish could hide. She purchased seven small black guppies, and our undersea world was complete. When we first got the fish tank, my brothers and I were mesmerized by its perfect little world. We would sit and watch the fish for hours, as if we were watching an epic event.

"Doug, you are crowding my view, said Jake." "No I am not, you are."

I just let them fight it out till they got tired of watching them and left to torture each other with a different game. Once they left, I would sit in front of the tank in blissful peace and quiet.

Each fish had its own personality. Following in the footsteps of Snow White and the Seven Dwarfs, we named them accordingly. My favorite was Bashful. He liked to hide in the fake rock cave. He seemed so fragile in his social skills, and I understood that. There was also one that was mean. He would bite the fins of the others. They ran from him. Another one seemed more athletic. That one was Jake's favorite. He could swim faster than any of them. It was funny to me that their little community was called a school. Their combined personalities were not unlike the children in my class at my own school. In my head, they were those children. I watched with intensity how they related to each other. It felt like I was given a secret opportunity to figure out how to relate to others and get through the day, even if I was too young to verbalize it at the time. After a few months, my brothers got tired of the fish and paid no attention to them. I, on the other hand, never tired of watching these marvelous creatures. One day when my mother was talking on the phone, I noticed something different in the tank. Bashful was hiding as usual, but emerging from the cave were tiny little guppies. They were so small that had I not been looking at them with such intent, I would have missed them. When they started swimming, I realized just what it was that I was looking at.

"Mom come quick; bring the net! Hurry they are getting eaten!"

It took three shouts and a tug on her clothing before she acknowledged my sense of urgency. She quickly hung up the phone and ran into action.

"Oh my goodness Barbara, how on earth did you see these little guys?" Scrambling to get the proper equipment for housing two dozen baby guppies, my mother, as always, knew what to do. For weeks after, I watched as our new additions to the family swam, grew and died. In the end, we were able to save about four. No matter how hard I tried, I couldn't save them all.

A few weeks into the first grade, my mom decided to move again. I didn't want to go. I was happy where we were. But, of course, I didn't have a choice, nor did I know her reasoning for moving in the first place. Mom always made moving sound like an adventure, but for me, it meant more change, another school, new friends and a different bedroom that Shadow Man could haunt. My last day at the Bentley School, I was sitting in my class. The secretary from the office buzzed our teacher on the new fangled toy they called "the intercom."

"Could you please send Barbara to the office?"

"Hello...Hello? Are you there?" My teacher had no idea how to use this new device. Unfortunately, there were five girls with the name "Barbara" in my first grade class. The secretary was very surprised when we all showed up at her door. She was actually looking for another Barbara and not me. I had been hoping it was my mother picking me up early. On my way out of the office, I heard one secretary say something to the other that confused me.

Pointing in my direction, she said, "That one comes from a broken home, and she is moving this weekend."

When I got home that night, I asked my mother what was broken in our house. "Is that why we have to move?" When she questioned me further, she became angry with what the secretary had said.

"Barbara, don't listen to ignorant people. They will never understand and refuse to be taught." Her words made me feel I could be smarter than a grown-up, or, at least, that grown-ups weren't always right. It was an empowering feeling. The next day we moved across town. Although my mom did, I never saw Pam and the girls again, until many years later in high school.

CHAPTER: 3

Our new house was on School Street in Salem. The day we moved in, I had no idea that my childhood of pure innocence had been left behind. It was a brown two-family with a wonderful wraparound porch in the front. We lived on the first floor, and an older woman lived on the second. The street I lived on was called School Street because my school was on it. Actually, it sat across the street from our house. My bedroom window looked directly at my new first grade classroom. I thought that was strange. Who wants to look at their classroom on Saturdays and Sundays? When I was sitting at my desk, I would in turn, look at my safe room across the street and long to be home.

That year I had the worst first grade teacher known to man, and I am not afraid to say it. Her name was Mrs. Durham. She was a very large woman with wiry black hair and glasses. When she spoke to you, she would peer over her spectacles with her beady eyes. When she did this, her eye brows would meet at the bridge of her nose to form a perfect "V." Every time I saw that "V," the word "vicious" would cross my mind. I was certain it was a secret code, branded on her forehead, that allowed her entrance into an evil cult. Behind her back, the children referred to her as Mrs. Dumbham. Not only was she mean, but she was also abusive. She would think nothing of letting someone pee in his pants, if he had to go to the bathroom during one of her long winded lectures. She would also pick us up and shake us if we angered her. I don't know what her normal speaking voice was, because she always yelled. A day in her class was filled with emotional harassment and physical abuse.

When I entered the class, it was already into its fourth week. On my first day of school, after I had completed writing my spelling words, she got angry and tossed me down a small flight of four stairs with my paper in hand.

"Show this to the principal...let her see the type of students they are giving me these days. How on earth I am ever going to be able to read this writing? It is too light." It was the way my last teacher insisted we do it. She thought it was ridiculous to teach a child to write this way. Fortunately, I didn't get hurt by this unexpected trip down the stairs. But a precedent was set for me in that class. I was frightened of her. I was too scared to tell my mother about the daily abuse.

On the weekends, I would look upon the window of my classroom from my own window with disdain. I wondered what God would say to her on the day that she died. How many black marks did she already have on her soul? Would she apologize to Him for the heartache she gave to children over the years? Would He forgive her? Throughout my life, at quiet times, these questions of this teacher would find their way back into my head. And, eventually, I would feel sorry for her. While I was still in the thick of it, I had other ways of dealing with it.

"Mom, I have a belly-ache. I feel like I am going to throw up."

"Oh Barbara, we aren't going to start this 'dance' again are we?"

"But I can't go to school. Please don't make me go." Because of my nerves, I actually did have stomach aches. Once again, I hated school.

The winters at this house were always bad. There were several large storms in a row. Despite my daily complaints of a stomach ailment, my mom sent me to school every day. She just thought it was me being my neurotic self again and didn't make the connection, until one day after school, when she witnessed my teacher holding me by one arm, shaking me and screaming in my face.

It must have been quite a sight, but I couldn't tell you, because my eyes were closed. That afternoon the snow banks were tall, and Mrs. Durham was afraid that if we climbed them, we would fall in the street and get run over by a car. She had made specific rules when class was over, as to how we were to leave the school. Upon exiting the building, I soon noticed I had a unique dilemma. With my house directly across the street and the driveway and walk not yet shoveled in front of it, how was I to get to my front door? Crossing the street, I tried to scramble quickly over the bank before she saw me. Unfortunately, Mrs. Durham also had a keen eye. She didn't know my house was across the street. She immediately ran across and grabbed me.

"BARBARA, WHAT DID I SAY ABOUT CLIMBING THE SNOW BANKS!?" Holding me by the crook of my right elbow, she raised me two feet off the ground. Shaking me violently, she added, "YOU ARE GOING TO GET HURT, IF YOU FALL!" When my mother saw her from the window, she came running outside.

"LET HER GO! WHO THE HELL DO YOU THINK YOU ARE?" Climbing awkwardly over the bank, Mom started speaking very sternly to her. This was something no one did to Mrs. Durham, and I was worried for my mother. I soon realized I had nothing to fear. Mrs. Durham was no match for my MaryJane.

At first, Mrs. Durham tried to explain, but Mom wasn't listening. My fears then were directed towards my teacher. Grabbing me around the waist with one hand and wagging her finger in Mrs. Durham's face with the other, she screamed, "You are going to be so sorry you ever laid a hand on my kid!" I thought my mother was going to hit her. Mrs. Durham was apologizing profusely to my mother and me.

"I'm sorry...I'm sorry, I was just trying to..."

"I don't want to HEAR what you were trying to do," my mother interrupted her. "If you ever touch her again, I will have you fired!"

That afternoon, over a bowl of chicken soup, in the warmth of my kitchen, I told my mom the whole story of Mrs. Durham and her behavior. She was shocked. She tried to get her fired, but it was impossible. Mrs. Durham had tenure, which protected her. My mother was frustrated, yet I learned a lesson that day. If you stood up to a bully, he or she would turn into a coward.

My mother got a new boyfriend when we lived on School Street. His name was Gil, and he was a roofer. He was tall and slender with white hair. He was Irish and twenty years older than she. He loved Saint Patrick's Day and sang Irish songs every day of the year. At first I wasn't sure about my mother seeing him. I had liked many of my mother's boyfriends in the past. Then she would break up with them. I would be upset when I didn't see them anymore; I became so attached. I would ask why we didn't see them. She never knew how to answer this question and stuck with her old standby," Because I said so, and what I say goes." But her relationship with Gil was different from the others. I thought Gil was funny, because to me he looked like a handsome leprechaun. Of course, Lucky Charms had just come on the market, so I had leprechauns on the brain. He was charming, and, after a while, I learned to love him. He was around all the time. The first day I met him, I was wearing a fairy dress my mother made me. It was pink and green with layers of soft nylon tiers. It was complete with crown and wand. My mother had made it for me a few years prior to this, occasionally letting out the seams to keep up with my growth. I wore that outfit every day, until it was tattered and had no more give to accommodate my natural development. I only wore it in the house.

"Barbara, I want you to meet Gil."

He stood there in front of me with a stupid crooked smile and his hand extended in a warm gesture; he didn't say a word.

Holding my wand in the air, I tapped his outstretched hand and promptly told him he was now a toad. He played along with me and plopped down on the floor and started hopping around.

Pointing to his cheek, he said, "You now have to kiss me, so I can be a prince again." Scared, I ran into my room. For months after, every time I saw Gil, he would give me a sorrowful look and point to his cheek. Eventually I kissed him, because I was tired of the game. He was madly in love with my mother. It was the kind of love you only see on TV. He told her everyday that God outdid Himself when He made her.

He was a very Catholic man and took us to church every Sunday. For some reason, this was the time when my mother stopped going. She stayed home on Sundays now and made Irish boiled dinner to serve upon our return.

I always hated going to Mass. The hour it would take seemed like three. I also didn't like what being in church did to Gil. He would suddenly become serious and quiet. We were never allowed to ask any questions of him when we were there. If we did, he would shush us sternly. My mind would wander whenever I was in church, because I rarely understood anything that was being said. I couldn't understand why children were forced to go, if they only spoke to grown-ups. Out of desperation, I would sit quietly and stare at the murals on the walls, the pictures in the windows or the sculptures of the holy ones. Organized religion never made me feel devout, but it was in this sacred house called church that I began my commitment to the love of art. The paintings were my favorite. Week after week, year after year, I studied those paintings, trying to figure out how they were made. I vowed to God that someday, when I grew up, I too would make beautiful art for His house. After all, it was the least I could do for all those years of not paying attention. Every day I would look at pictures in our incomplete set of encyclopedias and try to draw them on left over paper bags. All the other paper in our house had lines. One picture was of the Mona Lisa. I must have drawn her a dozen times. I started getting good at this, and in a short time my family was noticing this unusual interest I had. For the first time in my life, I could do something my brothers could not. I kept hanging my drawings on the refrigerator. After all, isn't that the honored place for children's art? Mom would let them stay for a day, and then she would take them down, to my disappointment. She said it made the kitchen look messy.

"Mom for Christmas can I have a real oil painting set, one with brushes and canvas?"

"We will see Barbara," she said in a distracted voice. She was looking at the manual for the new washing machine like it was written in a foreign language.

When Christmas came that year I realized she had misunderstood me. She bought me paint by number instead. I used it anyway and actually learned a lot about line and value, although I was too young to verbalize it. I also realized that if I were careful with the amount of paint I used, I would have left over paint to make my own pictures. Unfortunately, this paint was always sticky and stringy, compared to real artist paint. I tried putting water in it, but that didn't work. Somewhere along the way, I figured out that my mother's nail polish remover would thin it out. She got angry with me one day when I spilled it on my dresser. The next day she tried to surprise me.

"Here Barbara, look what Gil brought you. It is a water color set, so you don't have to deal with the mess and smell of the oil paints and still make your pretty pictures."

I hated them. Instead, I just drew on the paper that came with it. I knew that for me to ever have real oil paints, I would have to be old enough to buy them myself. And that was a long way off.

My mother started showing self confidence again. She was the strong one in the relationship. She called all the shots. If she decided that she didn't want to see him that day, she wasn't afraid to tell him. She was her own person in that way. She protected herself as well. He was always compliant and never gave her a hard time about it. It was because of his easy going manner with this subject, that he started a joke about it. "MaryJane (he always called her by her proper name), even the President of the United States would have to clear things through you." Then he would laugh. In a short time she just became known to him as Head of the War Department. I always thought back then that he was calling her the Head of the Water Department and wondered, "What does she care about people's water?" I often mixed up words and phrases that I heard. On the radio, there was a song that kept saying "Big Fat Girl." I was too young to know who sang it, or if that was even the title. I just remember the chorus said it over and over. I thought, "What a terrible thing to say!" It took me almost five years to realize they were singing "Dig That Girl."

I began to like having Gil around. He slowly stepped into my father's shoes. He was especially good to have in Jake's life. They had similar interests in sports and carpentry. He took Jake on job sites and taught him a lot about swinging a hammer.

Gil and Jake would often have power contests. They used to wrestle a lot, and it always made the rest of us roar with laughter, because Jake always won. But Gil never gave up. Every day he would try again. I was too young to realize that Gil let him win. This would go on day after day, until my mother would get fed up with it and yell at them.

"Ok!...enough you two...someone is going to get hurt!" "Yeah, like Gil," piped in Doug, as he nonchalantly peered over the top of his book.

At those moments, Gil might have been just another one of us kids. He would jokingly hang his head in mock shame. He was in his late forties at this time in our lives, but I never thought of him as old. He was an agile man, and he never seemed to tire.

With Doug, he was respectful. He understood how smart he was, and I think, in his own way, he was awed by it. They didn't do much together, although Gil joined Jake sometimes when he would tease Doug. But it was all in good fun, and Doug laughed and seemed to enjoy it. In Gil's eyes, I was a princess. He called me that every day. He told me often that I was as pretty as my mother and that God had decided to be generous to two beauties. My mother had a spell on him. This would be the first time I realized that women could do that to men. He touched her a lot. He always had a hand on her butt. He would make some comment about its firmness, and that would make me laugh. I'd struggle in my room to see my own butt in the mirror and wonder if it, too, was firm.

One night, when Shadow Man wouldn't leave me alone, I broke free and ran screaming to my mother's room.

"MOM! MOM! HE IS THERE! HE IS GOING TO GET ME! COME QUICK!"

To my surprise, Gil was with her in her bed. They had no clothes on and had been asleep. The scene was horrifying for me. My first thought was, "My mother is going to join me in hell." Gil immediately tried to comfort me. He struggled in the dark to find his clothes. I closed my eyes so I wouldn't see his jingle bell. Mom threw on a night gown and brought me back to bed.

"Mom I can't go back to bed...he will get me." She told me that from now on I had to knock before entering her room. I realized then that sleeping in Mom's bed was no longer an option for me. For the rest of the night, I laid perfectly still. With the covers over my head, I was breathing fresh air from a small opening in the folds.

A family lived next door with lots of kids. Their last name was O'Neil. Over the course of two and a half years, the relationship I would have with this family would once again chip away some of my innocence. They had six children in total, four girls and two boys. Of the girls, two were younger than I was, and the other two were older. Lynn was one of the older girls, but we were in the same grade, this now being second. She had stayed back in first. Chris, the oldest of the sisters, was my brother Jake's age. Her brother Peter was exactly my age and also in the same grade as Lynn and I. He was actually in my class, while Lynn was in the other class. Walter was Doug's age. The two younger sisters were only a few years younger, and they were thrown in the mix with everyone else and tagged along everyday. With this family living next door, we all had someone to play with, if we chose to. Their mother's name was Sharon, and she became best friends with my mother. It would be a friendship that would last until Sharon's untimely death. They smoked cigarettes, drank coffee and talked at the kitchen table, always at our house. At the O'Neil's house, the atmosphere was affected by lots of kids with high energy. Her husband, Walt Sr., worked nights and was always asleep on the couch. The few times I saw him awake, he was grouchy. When I would knock on the door to see if the girls were home, he would be bellowing and was always rumpled, as if he just got out of bed. The O'Neil's house in general was different from what I was used to. Chris's friends consisted generally of boys, and they were always hanging around. It was a large family; the atmosphere often got loud and emotional. Even their parents would get caught up in it. It was their only recourse. This would be the first time I had seen such behavior, and it was unsettling for me. I learned a lot of things from the O'Neil's. At the tender age of eight, Lynn sat me down and explained to me all about the birds and the bees. I was appalled. I knew grownups kissed. But to do what Lynn was telling me sounded outrageous. Besides, who would want to? That must have been what Gil and my mother were doing that night! The thought of it was both intriguing and disgusting to me. In a strange way, I knew it was good to have the O'Neil's next door. They were a constant reminder of how comforting it was at home. When the atmosphere of dysfunction over there would get to me, I would retreat to my room and spend some peaceful time alone, drawing. Eventually Mom got wind of the goings on over there, and, although she didn't forbid us to play with them, she did limit our time at their house. Somehow she was able to pull this off without disturbing her friendship with Sharon.

I was, however, not unaffected by these influences. How could I not be? Boys took on a whole new meaning to me. I suddenly realized their jingle bell had a purpose, albeit not a purpose I wished to ever see firsthand. I did, however, find myself attracted to Peter. He was really funny. He had a great sense of humor and always made everyone laugh. He was like Jake in that way. Yet at school, unlike Jake, he didn't know how to turn this off. He was in trouble with the teacher every day for something, but it was, at all times, harmless mischief. And the class thought, as I did, that Peter, being so witty, was somehow superior. Because we saw each other everyday in class and lived next door to each other, Peter and I were together more than the other kids. We became good friends, and he would often look in my direction to see if I laughed at his jokes. I began to become enamored of his presence. Because Peter was so clever, he realized very soon how I felt about him and capitalized on it. In class, if I had to walk by his desk, he would pretend to grab my legs. This bothered me, and I would yell at him, wanting to hide my true feelings. He just fed off this type of reaction, but I was too young to realize that. After school was worse; there was no place to hide. Without any of the other children noticing, he would try and touch my hand. Eventually, I gave in to my feelings and let him do it. It became an innocent game. Where would we hide, so that all the other children couldn't see us hold hands? Eventually we found the perfect spot.

"Pssst...Barbara, come here!" Peter was motioning me from the back side of the garage that sat on the other side of the yard.

The rest of the kids were arguing about the proper rules for Hide and Seek. Their voices were pretty loud and emotional. Each one was trying to make his point known by screaming over the others. This made slipping off with Peter very easy. Stepping through the back door of the garage, we slid carefully into its darkness unnoticed. The smell was a tinge of musty dirt mixed with motor oil. The air was surprisingly cool to my hot sweaty skin of summer. Putting his finger to his lips, he motioned me to be quiet. The excitement I felt from this was making my body tingle from my head to my toes. He took me by the hand and led me to an armoire in the corner. It was a cedar armoire, and when we stepped inside, the smell was captivating. With no shelves and too tall for us to even touch the rod at the top, we fit in there perfectly and could close the door. It was so dark I couldn't see a thing. Reaching up, Peter stroked my long hair. He placed his hand on the back of my head and guided my lips to his. It was my first real kiss. When we were finished, we sat in there for hours. We laughed. We talked. And we kissed some more. The whole time we held each other's hand. When we were together, he was a different person. He was quiet and at peace. Sometimes I pretended he was Tom Ellis. It was fun, exciting, and made me feel so grown-up, even though I was only in second grade.

Our yard was a fairly good size and surrounded by trees. One was a pear tree that we could climb. The pear tree was actually in our neighbor's yard behind us but hung over our fence. She was an old lady who lived alone and would yell at us constantly about it. I never actually saw what she looked like. It was only this quivering voice from behind a lace curtained window.

"Get out of my tree, you degenerates! Trees have feelings you know. They feel your grimy little feet all over them!"

We thought she was crazy. But I have to admit her words of wisdom stuck in my head. In the fall, my brothers and I would eat pears with the other children in the neighborhood until we were sick. I had been eating solid food for a few years now, and, as long as it was crunchy, it was ok. I still hadn't tried anything soft. That's when my gag reflex went haywire. Years later, a doctor told me that if a baby doesn't eat solid food before the age of one, his gag reflex is screwy for some time after.

During February vacation, my mother decided to take us to see her brother Joe. Uncle Joe was in the Navy and stationed in Virginia at the time. He was married and had three children who were similar to us in age. Although Doug was around eleven at the time, he was still older than all of us by a few years. My mother and her brother talked often on the phone, and their relationship was a very close one. It was a closeness that I did not share with my own brothers. I wondered if something magical happened on the day you became a grown-up that gives you a sudden love for your siblings. For this, I was hopeful.

We only knew my mother's brother as the uncle with the funny accent who would sometimes make small talk with us, if we answered the phone before my mother did. I realized from these little snippets of conversation with Uncle Joe that children have a strange power over adults who don't know them. We make adults nervous when they have to talk to us. They become tongue tied and don't know what to say. Are we that much of a mystery? Do they forget what it is like to be a kid? I decided then that I was going to be different when I grew up.

Despite the fact that this trip would be our first encounter with this side of our family, the most memorable moment of the visit happened before we ever landed in Virginia. We were to fly out of Boston on a snowy day at dinner time. Never having been on a plane before, I was looking forward to it. My mom, on the other hand, seemed nervous. The weather outside was starting to get bad. The plane was small by today's standards. It was a propeller plane and only had one aisle down the middle. Because it only had seating for two people on either side, my mother chose to have me sit next to her, and my brothers were behind us.

"Isn't this cozy?" she said, trying to sound normal. "Are you boys ok back there?"

"YUP!" my brothers said in unison. "Look, Doug, the snow is making swirls on the runway like little tornados!"

The plane was so small that from my seat that was on the aisle, I could see practically everyone on board. I began watching their faces to see if they were feeling the same fear I knew my mother was feeling. We sat on the runway a long time, because of the snow getting worse outside. At one point I was wondering if we were ever going to leave. My mom was trying to ease our worries by telling us funny stories about her and our Uncle Joe when they were young.

"Did I tell you kids about the time that Uncle Joe and I used to have to collect the coal from the cellar? It was a big heavy bucket, and he used to make me carry it, and the whole way up the stairs he would be tickling me. Boy that was fun times."

I didn't understand the joy in her story. I thought about my mother as a child. If we met on a playground would we be friends? Maybe my need to always play alone would have been a barrier. After all, if we were the same age, I certainly wouldn't have looked upon her as my mother. How does one choose a friend anyway? The captain came down the aisle a short time later and gave me and my brothers a pin that was in the shape of bird wings.

"Wow!" said Jake, all excited. "He says we are junior copilots now!"

I had my favorite stuffed animal with me on that trip. I had him for years but rarely let my friends see him. His name was Squeaker. He no longer squeaked from years of love and the weekly bath that my mother gave him, but I loved him just the same. He was white and soft and hung like a rag doll. I purposely took him on this trip, because Mom said he would make a great pillow on the plane. The captain, back in the cockpit at this time, announced over the loud speaker that we were all to keep our seat belts on for the duration of the flight. I glanced down the aisle to check the reaction of the other passengers. They didn't look happy.

"We will be taking off soon, and turbulence is expected for the entire flight."

This bit of information made my mom more nervous than before. Sure enough, we hit a pocket of turbulence right away. The plane felt as if it were bouncing. As soon as we dropped, we would rise right up again. I was so glad I didn't eat my dinner, because I was sure I would have been seeing it again. I grabbed my mother's hand and held on tight; I was so frightened. She tried everything she could think of to reassure us.

"Isn't it nice the captain has decided to give us a rollercoaster ride? What a treat!" "Mom tell him to stop it. I don't like rollercoasters!" "I can't tell him honey, he is too busy flying the plane. Just hold on tight."

When it started getting really bad, I was practically in her lap. She kept yelling to my brothers over the loud banging that was caused by the dropping of the plane.

"You boys ok back there?" "Yup," their unison response this time was not very enthusiastic.

Suddenly there was a big bang! The luggage compartment that was holding everyone's things fell off the ceiling and was sitting in the aisle! The personal contents of the passengers were strewn across the plane, casual things of intimate lives. The plane then tilted to one side and started to descend. It felt as if we were falling out of the sky. My hair was flying straight up in the air, and this strange contraption fell in front of me from the ceiling above. It looked like a toy I had called Romper Stompers. The toy was simply two cups attached by waist length tubing. Standing on the cups made me feel four inches taller. Holding the tubing, I was able to walk with them on. But this contraption was not a toy. It had a big cup also attached to long hoses, but this time my mom put it over my head.

"Here honey, Put this on; it will help you breath. Boys, put your masks on, ok?"

I didn't like it. It reminded me of the cup the dentist had put on my face when I knocked my teeth out. I had to hang on to Mom to keep from falling out of my seat. People were screaming and praying. The smell of vomit was strong in the air. Then the lights went out, and we were suddenly all in the dark. We were still falling, and at that point my mother seemed to lose it altogether. In the dark, I kept hearing her voice. It sounded like she was trying really hard to sound happy when I knew she wasn't.

She kept saying over and over, "It's just a rollercoaster. Wheeeeeeee! Say it with me kids!" I knew then, even as young as I was, that she couldn't help herself. The captain came over the loud speaker again and said that we had lost an engine and would be landing in New York instead of Virginia. This caused the screaming lady next to me to scream louder.

"We are all going to die!" No one could get to her because of the luggage compartment being in the way. The next thing I remember was hitting the ground hard. Although my head was between my legs as instructed, it bounced back up and hurt my neck. The plane was turning again, and I heard sirens in the distance. When we finally stopped, the quiet was deafening, except for the murmur of prayers that could be heard. It was as black as night, and I wondered if Shadow Man had come. It was very cold. I heard a swooshing sound, and suddenly, a door in the distance was open, and snow was coming into the plane. Someone had a flash light and was trying to lead the passengers to the exit. It appeared that no one was hurt. The next thing I remember was being picked up by a strange man.

"Come here little one; it is very cold outside." His voice was one of calm and reassurance. It was the tone that children understand as: this is a grown-up trying to make me feel safe. He tried to zip me into his coat to protect me from the wind and snow. For the most part he succeeded. He was wearing Old Spice after shave. I realized years later that it was Old Spice, when I found a bottle of it and remembered the smell. I was hanging on to him so tightly that my fingernails hurt. I was afraid he would drop me. My mom had told me not long before that that I was now too big to be picked up; I could hurt her if she tried to. That statement was in my head at that moment. I felt like a monstrous clod. I didn't want to hurt this kind and gentle man, and I could see he was struggling. The snow was whipping wildly at the entrance near the door. I tucked my head deeper into his armpit.

"It's ok, sweetheart, just hold on. I won't drop you." My mother and brothers were behind us the whole time. The snow outside was swirling in circles and blinding me; my eyes were stinging. It was impossible to see, so I just closed them. An ambulance was checking to see if anyone was hurt. We were all standing on the runway; it was before they had the portable devices that connected to the planes. Then someone asked if anybody was heading to the Naval base in Virginia. My mother raised her hand.

"We are, over here!"

They told us that if we hurried, we could catch a plane that was a few terminals down. We began to run. Seeing sailors boarding a plane in the distance, my mother told my brothers to run and catch up with them and tell them to hold the plane. They did better than that; they brought a few sailors back to help my mother and me through the snow. We eventually arrived in Virginia, shaken but safe. A week later my mother exchanged our return tickets for seats on a brand new 747 jet.

That was also the time I first developed what would end up being chronic pain. A few times I would wake up in the morning and complain to my mother that my legs hurt. This had been an issue for me now for at least a year.

"Mom, it hurts when I do this with my leg," I said, as I lifted my knee to my chest. "Life is simple, Barbara. Don't do that." "Mom, I am serious. This is a new kind of hurt compared to the other leg pains."

"Well, if it is still hurting when you get your physical next week, I will mention it to the doctor." I knew that was useless. Every time I mentioned my sore feet and legs to the doctor, he either grunted some kind of noise that was an indication that he was only half listening, or he called it growing pains. I decided to ignore it. Mom didn't seem concerned.

That winter was also a bad one. Once again, we had several huge snow storms. One was especially big. It was so exciting. The electricity went out, and we had to eat by candlelight.

"Remember the last time the power went out? Mom, is it going to be like that again?" Jake always loved to talk about the "great power outage of "65." I, on the other hand, still didn't have teeth. The power did return that night, but next day school was closed. Since we had the bigger yard, the O'Neil's came to our house to build a snow fort. It was an elaborate construction made by children. It was an entire city complete with all the necessities. It took us all day and two changes of clothing to build it. There were tunnels and rooms and stores. We were lucky we didn't get trapped inside. I ran the general store. I made can goods and cereal boxes out of snow and sold them with snow made money.

"Our special today is canned peas," I yelled with a devilish grin. No child likes canned peas, and that is when the snow war inevitably broke out. My food store suddenly became the ammunition warehouse.

Jake was the guy you always wanted on your side. He could throw snowballs better than anyone. "Just call me GI Jake, the grenade launcher!"

Eventually we got tired of that as well, mainly because we were no match for Jake. We soon realized that our neighbor's garage that abutted our yard had a low roof. There were large drifts from it that overhung our yard. In an instant, we were in an amusement park. I sold the tickets. We slid from the roof to our yard for hours.

I made my First Communion that spring. Peter and Lynn were making it with me. I was still eight. Just like the prom, it was all about the dress! Lynn and I were so excited showing each other our dresses. They made us look like mini brides; they even had veils and white gloves.

"Look," said Lynn. "See what my mom bought me?"

Sitting on her bed wrapped in tissue was a pair of white fishnet stockings. It was the rage at the time, and many girls wore them to school. I wanted a pair, but Mom said they weren't appropriate for church.

We were given missalettes by our Sunday school teacher. These were little white books that had our prayers in them. Mom bought me a white purse to put mine in. I felt so special in that outfit and wanted to pretend I was marrying Tom Ellis. Peter had a white suit that he had to wear. He felt uncomfortable in it and looked out of place.

In order to make our First Communion we all went to Catholic Christian Doctrine, or, as we called it, CCD, every Tuesday night. For years, I looked back on it as the Tuesday night terrors. It was a cold, dark walk to the church. Again, I was supposed to walk with my brothers and again, I tagged behind. I would imagine Shadow Man lurking in every dark corner of all the driveways I passed. Peter, knowing I was afraid, took advantage of the situation once more.

"Barbara, what is that over there...is that a man?!" "Where?" I would shout, looking around quickly.

Everyone would then break out in laughter at my expense. Once we got there we would to have to sit and listen to the wrath of God for an hour.

"It is important to be good Christians," the Nun said, "no lying or swearing. Listen to your parents and be good boys and girls. If you don't, you will not go to Heaven and instead spend all of eternity in Hell." She ended with, "This is God's will."

She said my guppies that died were not in heaven, and if we kissed a boy we would get pregnant. Now I was really scared. Peter and I glanced in each other's direction with fear. We both looked at my belly that I was now holding with my hand. When it came time for our first confession, the nun gave us a piece of paper that had spaces for ten sins. We were to take it home, and every time we committed a sin, we were supposed to write it down. That was a mixed message for me. Weren't we suppose to try not to sin...especially after they told us how many things God didn't want us to do and what would happen to us if we did them? Our first confession was that Saturday night, and she wanted to see the paper filled. When Saturday afternoon came around, I had nothing written down. I had agonized all week about it. I made sure that I didn't go anywhere near the armoire in the garage. Of course, being conscious of my behavior, I had been extra good. An hour before I was to present my wrongdoings to the priest, I came up with the perfect solution to this dilemma. I quickly fabricated ten sins on the paper and ran out the door. The confessional was dark and scary with a musty kind of smell. The velvet on the knee rests was worn away by years of confessed sins. The priest opened his cut out window, and the ritual began. I read from my paper as best as I could from the dim light that was coming from his side. "Bless me Father for I have sinned," I said.

"I had a fight with my brothers." "I spoke back to my mother." "I didn't clean my room, when I was told to." "I cheated on a paper in school." "I stuck my tongue out at Susan, who sits next to me in class." "I didn't wash the dishes when I was told." "I didn't make my bed on Saturday." "I played with my brothers' toys when they weren't home." "I tattled on Jake when he told me not too."

Reading the first nine sentences, I was heading for the home stretch.

When I got to sin number ten, I paused, and, with a beating heart, I stated, "And...Father O'Malley...I lied."

He forgave me, and I was struck with a sudden sense of relief, except the part about the kissing. I figured my baby and I would take that one to our graves, after my mother killed us. He made me sit at the altar and say twenty Hail Mary's. I could never remember that prayer. I was always too busy trying to memorize the Act of Contrition. Because I couldn't remember the Hail Mary's, I said BLAH, BLAH, BLAH in my head and felt guilty. I was sure that I was going to be struck by lightning, so instead, I just talked to God. I told him I was sorry.

Although we didn't move, the third grade brought me to yet another school. It was old and creepy and was built in 1910. It was called the Pickering School. It was a tall mammoth of brick and mortar. The steps had recesses from years of use, and the floors were so bad, in some parts of the building, the rooms were condemned. The cafeteria still smelled like everything boiled. Its only saving grace was that I met my friend Cherri while standing in line waiting for the bell to ring. She would become my friend all through high school. The mere chance of being in front of her in line and the happenstance of the question she was to ask me shaped our bond for many years.

She turned to me and said, "Spell I cup."

I burst out laughing, while I spelled I-C-U-P, and our fate was sealed. Our third grade teacher was Mrs. Pendleton. She was warm and loving. It was a drastic change from my last teacher. Mrs. Pendleton was very old. She was what TV said a grandmother should be. In this grade, we were classified. Cherri and I were in group two for average students. Peter and Lynn were moved down to group three. Group one was for the smart kids. Cherri would be moved to that class halfway through the school year. That year Sharon divorced her husband, and the O'Neil's moved away. They moved to Irving Street. It was on the other side of North Salem, still in our district, yet too far to visit them if you were just a kid. A couple with small babies moved into their old house. The O'Neil's now lived next door to Cherri on Irving Street. I was not allowed to go that far on my own, so we only saw each other in school. Cherri and I did join the Girl Scouts together. We would meet at the library once a week on North Street. Right off the bat, we became the comedians. The other girls did enjoy our bantering. We were often in a good mood, and that atmosphere was contagious, even if we did annoy the troop leaders. We did charity work and went on field trips. I enjoyed the hay rides and Christmas caroling we did every year. Cherri and I would be Girl Scouts until eighth grade.

I had the most special Valentine's Day of my life in Mrs. Pendleton's class. We made Valentine sacks out of brown sandwich bags. I spent a long time on mine and decorated it more than anyone else's. The day of our party, we pinned them to the black board. One by one, we went to the front of the class to distribute our cards in the appropriate bags. Then it was Norman's turn. Norman was an unusually tall boy with wild, black, curly hair. His head was large and shaped like a rectangle, which unfortunately caused him to be called Frankenstein by some of the kids in the class. I felt bad for Norman and smiled at him once to show him I was not like them. (I began to have a low tolerance for meanness at this age.) When Norman went to put his cards in the bags, he slowly passed every bag and didn't distribute a one. There was a slight gasp in the room followed by a deafening quietness. That is, until he got to my bag, which was near the end of the row. He lifted the large pile of cards he had in his hand and poured them all into my bag. The whole class gasped and looked at me. Then they all burst into laughter. My face turned beet red. They continued laughing until Mrs. Pendleton made them stop. She didn't say a word to Norman, but after class she took me aside.

"Barbara, do you have any idea the amount of bravery it took for Norman to do what he did? The way you react to his act of endearment will have a big impact on him. Please think about that carefully."

When I got home, I ran straight to my room to look at all my cards. I tore open the bag I had so painstakingly made. Separating Norman's cards from the rest of the class I opened all 21 of them. Every one said simply, "I love you, your friend, Norman." February vacation was that week. I wasn't sure how I was going to act around Norman when I got back to school. I didn't get the tingly feeling when I saw him, like I did with Tom Ellis and now Peter. And I didn't want to be mean to him. How was I going to look at him now? Could I look into his eyes at all? The first day back at school, I realized that Norman had had it all figured out.

"Class, listen up. I have an announcement to make. Norman has moved away and will no longer be with us." There was a murmur among the kids. I wondered if he moved because they were all so mean to him. The lesson he taught me that year was two-fold. He made me feel special and taught me how to say goodbye.

Mrs. Pendleton told us one day that our parents were invited to visit our classroom. This was oddly exciting for me. I had never heard of such a thing and pictured everyone's mother sitting in our assigned seats with us on their laps. How on earth were we all going to fit? I was excited because I was proud of my mother and wanted to show her off. When the day finally came, it was snowing outside. The air was dry and crisp. I asked my mother if she was going to walk with me to school. She still hadn't learned how to drive. She told me that the parents were going to visit in shifts. Her time was after lunch.

Mrs. Pendleton set up chairs at the back of the class for this glorious event. Parents were coming and going all morning, some covered with snow and wearing boots, most in their work uniforms. It was funny to see the parents of some of the other kids: how they looked and if they resembled their children. What was even more noticeable to me was how differently the kids acted when their parents were in the room. You could tell the parents who were strict; those students immediately became different people. I was relieved I didn't feel that way about my own mother. I couldn't believe I had to wait almost an entire school day for her to arrive. When the time finally came ...a goddess walked through the door. I was surprised at how nervous I was. She was wearing a black maxi coat with matching black high heeled leather boots that went past her knees. Her hair and makeup were perfect. None of the other mothers could hold a candle to her, especially since she was about ten years younger than they were. Quickly, whispers started circulating among the students. They were good whispers; I know this, because one got as far as me. The boy who sat in front of me turned around and said, "Wow, whose mother is that?" I proudly stated loud enough for others to hear... "She belongs to me." Mrs. Pendleton approached her and asked if she could take her coat. To myself, I thought, "Wait till they get a load of this." Sure enough, my mother was wearing a beautiful wool mini skirt she had made herself; it was a red Samina plaid. Her top was her best cashmere sweater, the soft one that I loved to touch, the one she only wore on special occasion dates. Her nylons were sheer and black. When I saw the sweater, I knew she had dressed this fancy for me. When she took off her coat and tried to hand it to my teacher, Mrs. Pendleton hesitated. Seeing how short my mother's skirt was Mrs. Pendleton whispered to Mom with a voice of concern, "Maybe you should keep the coat on." Mom just smiled confidently and sat in her seat. This caused a pleasurable giggle among the students, and, once again, for a split second, I was a star.

Life had already shown me so much at such a young age, some of it unsettling, yet always adventurous. It was because of this I would crave for more. I would often think of all the complexities of my past and the possible ones of my future. On a Saturday afternoon, I was sitting alone in my back yard and thinking of all the houses I had lived in---- the friends I had made ----- the goodbyes I had never said. I thought of the Salem Common and how much I enjoyed it. I missed having the Salem Common to play in. It seemed so long ago, even though it really wasn't. With the O'Neil's having moved away and my brothers refusing to play with me, I found I had a lot of time on my hands. I was invisible to those around me and knew it. Taking advantage of this new form of freedom, I would often go for a walk. One day I decided to explore past my immediate neighborhood, something I wasn't even allowed to do a year before. At the end of my street was a large sign. It said Moody Square. Moody Square was a large intersection where the main street in town, North Street, crossed my street. I always knew crossing North Street was an adventure in itself. It was a four way intersection with only pedestrian lights between you and death. I stood there for a long time, wondering if I was doing the right thing. Like Alice through the looking glass, my only want was for adventure. My heart was pounding in my chest, excited with anticipation of the discoveries I had yet to make. Pressing the light, I waited patiently. And, like Alice, I stepped off the curb. To my amazement the cars all stopped. One had a bit of a squeak to its brakes that made me jump slightly in my shoes. Holding my head, high I put one foot in front of the other, never looking in any other direction but straight ahead. Safely on the other side of the street, I noticed a beautiful wrought iron gate that led to a wide expanse 0f trees and grass. Hoping I would find another inviting place to play, I stepped inside the open entrance. This was the Greenlawn Cemetery. The attraction that first brought me to its front door were the trees I saw from the outside. They reminded me of Salem Common, and once again I was homesick for a place that was never really my home.

Although cemeteries in general can be creepy places, this was never an issue for me there. The Greenlawn Cemetery was truly an oasis, frozen in time by unseen, caring individuals. It always seemed out of place in this blue collar neighborhood. With so many varieties of trees, I couldn't imagine anyone from around here planting them. Some had little plaques on them with exotic names, such as Kentucky coffee tree. I was in heaven. This adventure was just what I needed. I walked around and collected fallen leaves from different ones to put in my scrap book and to draw. Feeling nostalgic, I tried to climb some of these beautiful creatures, but they were so well cared for and pruned that only a few were low enough to even attempt. Mostly I just lay under them and looked at the patterns the leaves and sky painted together. It was as moving an image to me as the murals in the church. With a gust of wind, in a split second it would all change, and a new pattern would emerge. I started thinking about how other people view things. I realized I was seeing the mural that no one bothers to look at, the landscape that no one paints. It was a painting without a horizon, having God as the artist.

That same day, I stumbled across a greenhouse at the far right hand entrance. It was filled with citrus trees! I had never seen Florida fruit trees before, except for those in an orange juice commercial on TV. I pressed my nose to the glass and peered in. There were orange, lemon and lime trees. They even had grapefruit! I didn't know that grapefruit grew on trees. I had never thought about it before. This room, built by someone I had never met, spoke volumes for me inside its walls, certainly because of its beautiful site, but also because of its protective environment, unchanged and isolated from the rest of the world in order to sustain life. I wanted to go inside, but the door was locked. I sat there a long time wishing I was among them, but knowing it would never be.

Eventually I decided to finish my exploration. Although I didn't know it yet, there were still more wonders to come. The roads throughout this place rolled up and down, bending right and left. Every turn was a new landscape. Every hill had another tree more magnificent than the last. I vowed next time to bring a pencil and paper. In a short while, I came upon a pond. It was about as long as our house. A moss-covered cement bridge spanned the middle of it. I walked out to the center of the bridge and peered over the edge. Circling the pond was the biggest gold fish I had ever seen. I had fish once, but this one was bigger than any of the guppies I ever had. Two small fountains were on either side of the bridge, throwing a fine mist and circulating the water. Lily pads floated delicately from their stems and sat on the surface with pink and white lotus flowers cupped in their hands. Although I had never seen a lily pad, I knew from my coloring books that frogs sat on them. So I proceeded to make myself comfortable and waited for the frogs to arrive. After ten minutes, I heard a cadence of quacking sounds. These sounds weren't coming from where I was sitting. They were coming from the other side of the hill behind me. I stood up and ran towards the noise. Cresting the hill, I was once again thrown off my feet in disbelief. There before me was another pond. This one was six times bigger and seemed more natural than the last one. Willows lined its edges, dropping their graceful arms onto the water's surface. Cat o' nine tails dotted its perimeter. The sky was so open above it. Everywhere you looked, there was life. The ducks were swimming slowly, without a care in the world, unaware of the charm they had. Fish were making bubbles on the pond's surface. I was certain there must be frogs, although at the moment I didn't see any. But despite all this glory, the most amazing sight I saw that day was the snapping turtles. They were sunning themselves on rocks at the water's edge. Once again, everywhere I looked there were majestic trees.

One particular willow had a fallen branch I could climb. It extended from half way up the trunk down to the water. Straddling it at waist height, I began to shinny myself to the top. It was a strong main branch, so I wasn't afraid of it giving way, but I knew that this tree was probably not going to be around much longer. The bark was different from other trees I had climbed. This was textured with hard inlets and channels running its length from top to bottom. It scraped the undersides of my legs, as I inched my way along. I studied it and wondered how many beautiful days like this it had seen. When I reached its apex, I sat in awe and watched nature's performance. I made a promise to myself that day. When I could buy my own paints, I would come back and paint this spot. I never realized it wouldn't be until I was forty that I would fulfill this promise. On this perch, I felt invincible. No one could touch me. I knew this view would never leave me. I was on top of the world.

I would sit on that branch a lot that spring when I visited the cemetery, until the day they eventually hauled it away, tree included. Being older now, my world and life were expanding. My thoughts became more serious, even though I was only at the tender age of nine. My imagination began to share time with wondering. I would speculate about who I would be when I grew up. What would I do for work? I knew one thing. I was not going to get tied down with kids like my mom did. I was beginning to see the limitations we put on her. I felt bad about it and knew I didn't want that for myself. I also knew I was going to be an artist. I was drawing almost every day now. Sometimes I would set up a still life from things I found in my kitchen. Other times I would copy pictures from the encyclopedia. I wanted to have choices in my life. I was selfish in that way. On several occasions, I tried to apologize for the restrictions we made on my mother. The fact that we were a family that didn't communicate feelings combined with my age made it hard for me to express it. She never did understand what I was trying to say.

Another thing I thought of a lot when I was on the branch was how I would be at the age of twenty. I would wonder if I came back to this spot at that age, would I remember these moments? Would I still be a day dreamer? Would I be caught up in the everyday grind of work? Would I be an artist with my own paints? I closed my eyes tight and repeated over and over, "Remember this feeling...remember this feeling." It was as if I were trying to lock it away in a file cabinet in my brain. Sometimes I would imagine a grown up lady next to me. She was tall, beautiful, and smart...and was me. She would gently put her hand on my shoulder and tell me she loved me. She would never go away. She was like the mother I used to have. She would constantly be loving and caring and she would never change. I didn't realize then that the age of twenty was still in many ways your childhood. It was only my particular mother who had missed that option.

I hated to leave that day, but the sun started to go down, and I realized I wouldn't hear my mom's call for dinner. Besides, it was a cemetery. Who wanted to be there after dark?

When I got home, I was all excited about my new discovery. I was leery about telling my mom, because I knew she wouldn't approve of me being in such an isolated place. But I was so amazed by what I had just seen; I wanted to share it with her.

"Mom I found the most beautiful place on earth! And it is right around the corner from here! It has trees and birds, turtles and fish!"

"Barbara, what are you going on about?"

"It's the cemetery Mom...it's right down the street and beautiful!"

Just as I thought, she told me I shouldn't go there alone. She did, however, inform me that Uncle Sam was buried there. I was so surprised, but I tried to act indifferent. Of all the possible places to be buried in Salem, he was there! Poking at my never to be eaten mashed potatoes, I devised a plan.

CHAPTER: 4

Disregarding my mother's rule, the next day I made it my quest to look for Uncle Sam's grave. With Aunt Cheryl and the boys now living in California, Sam had become the forgotten dead relative. I was going to change that. I searched for an hour. Being nine years old now, I could read the names on every headstone I saw. The task was a tedious one. I started by looking for stones that didn't seem so old. To my surprise, there were more of those than I thought. Despite the old look to the place, this cemetery was very current. Mingled with the stones from the 1800's were graves that read 1968. That's this year! When I got to the small pond, the stones lining it were very old. I realized that some were for entire families who had died in 1918. "I wonder what happened then that caused so many families to die all at once? I'll have to ask Grampy, he was alive then." I thought. I searched for an hour, until I couldn't look anymore. Defeated, I felt I would never find him.

Walking back with my head hanging low, I came up with an idea. Maybe there was an office in this place. They must have a directory! Renewed, I went to search for it. This was a big step for me. Unlike the mailman whom I saw every day, it took all the bravery I could muster to ask a stranger for help. Next to the greenhouse were two beautiful small brownstone buildings with gothic detail. They were very old looking and surrounded by big trees. They looked like they were right out of a fairy tale. One, I quickly learned, was a chapel. I figured the other building was my best bet. Walking around its perimeter, I found an old wooden door with big, fancy iron hinges. Upon the door was a sign. It read OFFICE. I knocked on the door, but no one answered. I tried again, and soon a bent over lady, much older than my grandparents slowly emerged. She stared at me with squinting eyes, as if the sun were something she had never seen before. If this place is made of candy inside, and she asks to squeeze my finger to see how fat I am, then I am going to run! My palms were sweaty, and my throat was dry. I could barely speak. When I did, it was merely a whisper.

"I am looking for the graves of the soldiers. Could you tell me where they are?" Of course she could not hear me, so I was forced to repeat it. She seemed unmoved by my obvious fear.

In her crackly voice that sounded like years of cigarette smoke trying to escape she replied, "They are on the far side of the cemetery, next to the fence near the new school they are building." Pointing with her bony shaking finger, I knew exactly what school she was talking about. It was a school I would be attending in a few years, when it was done. She then shut the door with a loud thud and went back to her task of boiling children, I presumed.

Immediately running in that direction, I wanted to get as far away from her as possible. When I reached the small pond, I raced across the bridge to the other side. At the far end of the bridge was a staircase that rose up to the sky. I say rose to the sky, because you couldn't see any ground at the top of it when you were standing at the bottom. Climbing the large steep, stone steps that were roughly carved out of granite, I found another plateau at its summit. This was the back end of the cemetery. Looking back down the stairs, I was suddenly struck by their age and the odd angles. Covered in moss and dried leaves from many autumn days, I wondered how long they had been there. And when was the last time anyone had used them? Taking a right, I began my search. A short way down the path, I came across a grouping of white headstones. They seemed out of place. They were so bright compared to the rest of the old, greenish grey ones. Unlike the other stones, these were all the same, with no ornamental sculptures or angel carvings. They sat alone and isolated. They reminded me of a set of white dentures forgotten in a glass. Some had flags, some had lit candles, and others were just empty and plain, except for the names and dates. Most of the dates were from the last six years. Uncle Sam was one of those. When I found him, I got this sudden feeling of inadequacy. I felt bad that everyone had forgotten him. From what I understood, even his parents couldn't bear to come. "What am I suppose to do now?" I thought. I only met Sam once as a child, and all I remembered was that he held his small pinky finger in the air when he drank tea. Certainly that was not a springboard for starting a conversation with a dead man. Besides, I had always thought he looked silly holding his tea cup that way. Coffee was still my drink of preference. Maybe I should say a prayer? How do you pray? Mouthing the words the nuns had taught me didn't feel right. For the first time I was confronted with a real reason to pray, and I couldn't. I looked at the date on the stone. After doing the math, I realized he was only twenty-four when he died. "What a waste," I thought. I started remembering the stories my mother and Sharon would talk about over coffee. The story of Cheryl and Sam had become legendary. Growing up next door from one another, they were the only boyfriend and girlfriend each of them had ever had. They ran away together at the age of fourteen to North Carolina. Apparently, back then a couple could get married there without parental consent. Their parents weren't consenting in this state. Somewhere along the way, they had three kids. Then the war came. I always thought they had more time together. Quietly, I stood up and walked in the direction of the willow branch at the edge of the pond. There was nothing I could say.

CHAPTER: 5

This was the year that Mom made her first chore chart. "You kids are all getting older. It is time you pulled your own weight," she said.

The chart was made of thin white cardboard and hung on the refrigerator. All our names were on it, along with every day of the week. She felt that it was time we learned responsibility. Of course we always had had to make our beds and clean our rooms every day, that was a given. But this chart was something new that added to our room responsibilities. With these new rules, my brothers were in charge of the trash. I was to do the dishes. Mom, as always, still did the laundry and vacuumed. I felt my having to do the dishes was unfair, since the dishes were every day and the trash was once a week, and, besides, there were two of them. I knew this was really about the dishes, and the trash was an afterthought.

"Hold on a minute! Why do I have a chore to do every day and they only have one once a week? And they share a room, so there is always someone to help them clean."

"Yeah, and always someone to help mess it, too," said Doug, looking in Jake's direction.

"What... I don't make a mess," said Jake, as he aimed his toy gun at an invisible intruder, planning on taking him out in one shot.

"Enough...all of you! Barbara you are not strong enough to take the trash out. Besides, they also have to take it to the barrels outside daily and then, once a week, to the curb. I think this is more than fair."

"And you are a girl, and girls do dishes," said Jake as he stuck his tongue out at me. All I could do was glare back at him with my best "you are an idiot" face. My complaints were settled on deaf ears. This was how I became the official dishwasher for years to come.

The first time I washed them, I was so small that I had to stand on a kitchen chair to accomplish this task. It wasn't that I couldn't reach. I sort of could. It was because my arms would get so tired from the angle they were locked in by the time I finished the last dish. Washing dishes also meant pans. I would beg my mom to let them soak. The first day she agreed. But then, I forgot about them, and she put an end to that. So I filled them with soapy water first, before I did the plates. I hated doing the dishes. It was always at the time when "The Courtship of Eddie's Father" was on TV. I loved that show. I thought Bill Bixby was cute. My family would tease me about it. They thought I was in love with Eddie, the son. I didn't dare tell them it was the father. I would crane my neck to see the TV from the kitchen. Sometimes, during a good part, I would run into the living room with soapy hands, so I wouldn't miss it. I always got yelled at for that. Dishes also meant wiping down the table, counters and stove. Jake's side of the table was always a mess, and I called him a slob everyday for it. I felt like a maid to my brothers. I didn't realize it then, but this would begin to put a wedge in our relationship that would only escalate as the years went by.

Bedtime was still a time of fear for me. Shadow Man could be found sitting across from my bed, poised on my toy box in the dark. He watched my every move. To distract me from this, I would spend much of the night in absolute stillness. The only thing I allowed myself to move was my hands. With the covers over my head and a flashlight lighting my encampment, I found my fingers took on a whole new role. Mostly they were dancers; at other times they were soundless singers in a choir. Using my imagination for distraction gave me peace. This is how I fell asleep most nights.

After about a year of this, my night time routines changed. I was getting used to sharing my room with this entity. Suddenly Shadow Man became less scary for me. It was also a time when my leg cramps began to get worse. Somehow, they now seemed to be connected to unusual nightmares I was having. Every night I would find myself being chased by a wolf...always in the dark and in the middle of an unidentified forest. The dream always ended the same way. I would trip over a root, and the wolf would pounce on me and start gnawing at my legs. I would wake up in such pain and horror. It forced me to jump out of bed in an awkward and gangly way. The first few steps, my feet seemed to forget how to work. Holding onto the tall bed post, I would will my brain to connect to them and remind them how to move. I would limp around the room, trying to get feeling back in my limbs. When I was finally successful, it was Shadow Man who could be found facing me with a feel of sympathy in his posture. With his head cocked to the side and his outstretched hand in a gesture that could only be described as caring, he was always there. As I walked past him, he would never speak. He would look down at my feet to acknowledge I had a problem. He began to become my only companion in this time of anguish and pain. Every night I could count on him being there.

The next morning, when I went to the kitchen for breakfast, I was still limping. My mother asked me what was wrong with my leg. I told her about the incident the night before. I told her of my dream. I chose to leave out the detail of Shadow Man. She told me I just needed to eat more bananas. She rambled on about potassium and the fact that I didn't eat right. After a few minutes, I just blocked her words out of my head and poured my Raisin Bran into the bowl. By the early afternoon, the pain would subside, and it would be life as usual.

This became such a nightly occurrence that my sleep pattern was changing drastically. I found I no longer needed the 8-9 hours most kids did. I was always awake at least 2-3 hours in the middle of the night. It was at this time, with a new found bravery, I decided to confront Shadow Man. Since he was my new confidante, I wanted to know who he was.

On one particular night, after my walk around the room with him watching me, I got the courage.

"Who are you, Shadow Man? Why do you sit with me all the time?" Holding my stuffed dog, Squeaker, in my arms, I continued, "You frightened me when I was younger. But now I know you won't ever hurt me. Are you ever going to talk to me?" He said nothing. Although I couldn't see his eyes, I always could tell he was looking at me. I couldn't see details that defined him, only the outline of his silhouette. He seemed well dressed with perfect posture for a boogie man. I decided to show him he could be my friend. I did what any child of that age would do. I challenged him to a staring contest. The next morning, I woke up lying sideways on my bed, with Squeaker still tight in my grasp. Sitting upright with a jolt, I looked at the toy box in the corner of the room...he was gone.

After a few months of limping to the breakfast table, my mother decided to take me to the doctor. I had been to the doctor before for this, but every time he said the same thing...growing pains. This time he asked me a lot of questions. I tried to explain the best I could for a child. He asked me to walk across the room. He measured both my legs and the sizes of my feet. He then sent me for a series of x-rays of my feet, hips and knees, as well as blood work. A few weeks later we went back to get the results.

"Now, Barbara, I don't want you to be a whining baby to the doctor. You are a strong girl, and you don't need to complain." I wasn't sure what she meant by this remark. Was I suppose to tell him it was ok, I didn't mean to take up all his time? I chose to only answer what was asked of me. While waiting in the examining room, I looked at the child enticing posters on the wall. One was Winnie the Pooh. I loved that story. I had always thought Christopher Robin and I would have been great friends, if we had only been given the chance. After a short time, the doctor entered the room and closed the door.

"Well, I was sure after the last few times I had seen you that what we were looking at was growing pains. Sometimes children get them from the lengthening of their limbs. But since I have seen you every year for the past three about this, I wanted to examine it further. I have the results of the x-rays, and I think I know what is going on. But first, Barbara, I want to ask you some questions. Does this pain happen all year round or just sometimes?"

I had not thought of that before. "Well, it seems to be worse in the winter." "And how do you know that?" he asked.

"Well, when I step on the floor the wood is always cold, and for some reason that seems to tell my legs to wake up."

"Hmmm...and you don't have these issues as much in the summer?"

"No, I can climb and jump and run in the summer. But sledding in the winter hurts me for a whole day after."

"Well," he said, turning towards my mother, "according to the test results, it appears that what we are looking at is JRA. That is short for Juvenile Rheumatoid Arthritis."

"Really? What do we do for it?"

"At the moment, unless it becomes completely debilitating and changes the quality of her life, let's just sit back and watch it. The medications to control this can sometimes be more harmful than the original problem. Warm baths may help and baby aspirin before bed in the heavy winter months." He continued on with jargon I didn't understand, and in a short while, he left. Taking my hand as I limped out the door, I asked my mother what it all meant.

"Well, Barbara, it means you are going to be ok."

"But, Mom, don't old people get arthritis?"

"Honey, everyone has arthritis, just some more than others. All you have to do is know that this pain when you feel it is just that. Pain... and it isn't going to kill you...you just need to deal with it." And so began my life of ignoring any illness or ache I would get.

I didn't let this new challenge stop me from doing all the things kids love to do. Knowing what it was actually made dealing with it easier. Being just a child...and an artist, I began to visualize the source of my physical pain. He was an entity like Shadow Man, yet this entity had the mask of a wolf on his face. One day, my brothers and I got up early. It was one of those rare mornings, when we were all in a good mood and actually getting along with each other. It started with Jake. He was the funniest person I knew. His sense of humor would always bring the rest of us up. He was the important element of comic relief in our family unit. As usual, he was kidding my brother Doug about everything. It was so funny you couldn't help but laugh. Doug was always a good sport about it, despite his two year seniority in age, and would laugh along too. Jake was always bigger and more athletic than Doug. And, jokingly, he would use it against him. He could physically do anything, and I was proud he was my brother. In our family, Doug was the brain, and Jake was the brawn. It was because of my brother Jake that I wanted to be brave. I wanted to be able to do all the things he could. It was because of Doug I wanted to be smart. In their own way, they were good for me to have around. Secretly, I knew this but would never say it to them. On this particular morning, we decided to go to the cemetery and play explorers. I was so thrilled that they let me tag along. We immediately went to the large pond to hunt for snapping turtles. That was going to be our food, since we were trapped in this foreign land. There were turtles everywhere.

"Hey, look, a turtle nest!" Jake was pointing to a pile of mud and sticks on the ground next to the embankment.

"How do you know it is a turtle nest?" I asked. "Because look, it has eggs in it!" "Maybe it is a duck's nest," I continued. Doug came over to investigate. "Nope, that's a turtle nest."

I didn't question him. Why would I? He was Doug, he knew everything. The mother turtle was not with it, and we were amazed by this stroke of luck. We had heard how badly a bite from one of these creatures could be. We scooped up the eggs, there were about five of them, and headed home. We wanted to hatch them and raise them as our pets. When we got to our backyard, we sat down and tried to figure out what our best course of action would be.

"How do we hatch them, Doug?" I asked when we all sat down on the top of the picnic table.

"Well, we will have to keep them warm at all times, I guess." "How about a blanket?" I said. "No, that still might not be warm enough," said Doug.

Jake wasn't saying a word. He was staring off into space and thinking. Doug was usually the leader of decision making, but it was Jake who got a perfectly brilliant idea: "Let's put them in the laundry room next to the dryer! Mom does the laundry every day, and if we hide them on the window sill behind the curtain, she won't find them." Somehow we knew Mom wouldn't approve. So we did. We hid them beautifully and then proceeded to make a chore chart like Mom's for whose turn it would be to keep an eye on them. We hid the chart in the boys' bedroom. Mom always referred to their room as the air raid site and never went in there. Soon the "checking" went from every hour to a few times a day. Eventually, it became once a day, until finally, with the many adventures a child has in the course of a week, we forgot about them.

"What is that smell? Do you kids know what is causing that smell in the laundry room?" She kept complaining about it and searching for the source. We didn't pay any attention to her complaining. She was always on the hunt to destroy some germ or other, so we just figured it was her usual rant. Then one day we heard a horrific scream.

"ARRRGGGHHH!!! Who put these things on the window sill? Jake, Barbara, Doug... get your fannies in here. Someone has some explaining to do!"

We were all sitting in the living room, watching LOST IN SPACE, when the banshee reared her ugly head. We looked from one to the other. Doug summed up the situation with one word, "Shit!"

When we ran into the laundry room, Mom was holding the edge of the curtain with two fingers as if it were diseased. In her other hand, was a can of Lysol ready to assail. Sitting on the sill in the warm stream of morning sun were our turtles. They were halfway out of their shells and petrified in time. All dried up and looking like mini dinosaurs, it was an amazing sight that I will never forget. Even in our incomplete set of Golden Book Encyclopedias, I had never seen an image like what I saw that day. They had such a look of pain on their twisted faces and bodies. Their mouths were opened wide, as if screaming. Their eyes seemed to be glued shut. Their skin looked shriveled and burned.

We all stood there, at first, in disbelief. No one said a word until Jake broke the silence..."COOL!" This upset my mother immensely, and she sent us to our rooms, after we cleaned up the mess.

With the warm weather now upon us, I found myself outside in the air and warmth more than indoors. My bike was my mode of transportation. Unfortunately, I had outgrown it that spring. Besides, the girls in the neighborhood were making fun of me for having a boy's bike. It had been a hand me down from Jake, who would outgrow everything he owned every six months. My friends all had pretty pink bikes with flower power stickers, banana seats and sissy bars. I wanted one of those.

"Mom, I think I need a new bike."

"Oh, really, and what made you come to that conclusion?"

"Well, for one...I am a girl." Long gone were the homemade clothes she sewed for me and the cooking together in the kitchen. Replacing them were my brothers' left over jeans, tee shirts and mud pies. Somewhere along the way, "the kids" became "the boys," and I was thrown into the mix. I never really knew where I fit in this family dynamic. When my brothers got to wrestling and teasing, it often overwhelmed me, and I would retreat to my room and lay down. When I wanted to spend time with Mom, she was always with Gil.

I ended our conversation with," Gee, all I want is a girl's bike," as I stormed off to my room to pout (Something I became a master of by the age of 7).

Turning to Gil, she said, "How on earth are we going to afford a new bike?" "Don't worry," he said, "I will find her one."

One morning, he came by with a half dozen bicycle parts, all stacked in the back of his truck. Some were pink, others purple and blue. There was every color you could imagine. He brought me a basket, a banana seat and even a sissy bar.

"Look, Barbara, the base of this one is built for a girl," he said. It was blue. My brothers weren't jealous that I got to have this monstrosity of metal and paint. But they did want my banana seat and sissy bar.

"Gil, can we put it together right now? I want to help. I will pass you the tools!"

"Sorry, Miss Muffet, I have to get back to work right now. We will put it together on Sunday." Gil always called me Miss Muffet when he had to tell me "no."

I asked Jake to help me, but he wouldn't; he was too busy playing with his friends. I knew it was useless asking Doug. He wasn't mechanically inclined in the least. It was such a beautiful day; it was killing me that everyone was riding, and I was not. It was summer, and the June bugs were out singing in unison. I wanted to ride so badly. I became agitated, and nothing would hold my attention. Finally, with no one around to help me, I decided to build it myself. Using my old bike as a guide, I carefully placed the pieces I needed on the ground. I made sure to use the pink and purple parts. And, of course, I had to use the girl's bike base, even if it was blue. With tools my mother kept in the garage, it began to take shape. I was so nervous, I was afraid I was going to fail, and everyone would laugh at me, especially my brothers. It was times like these, when I felt something was beyond me, that I would get the shakes. What did that to me? It was hard to keep my hands steady. But worse than that, I was afraid of what Mom would do to me when I got hurt. And I knew I would. It was difficult for me to tighten the nuts and bolts. I did the best I could. The hardest part was the sissy bar. It kept falling backwards, every time I tried to sit on the seat. The sissy bar was a curved piece of metal that sat in the back and rose above my head. It was meant for leaning back and relaxing when you rode. I found some black electrical tape and secured it the best I could. I figured when Gil got there, he could tighten it up for me. I placed the only flower power sticker I had prominently on the banana seat, and I was off! My feelings of accomplishment were only slightly clouded by the wobbliness I felt when I left the driveway. I put the wrench in my basket, just in case.

CHAPTER: 6

By the beginning of the fourth grade, Mom made plans for us to move again but this time failed to tell us. This move always felt like it was a last minute decision on my mother's part. I was nine. My mom was working at a sub shop on North Street, owned by a man who was to become our new landlord. My mother didn't want to tell us the actual day we were to move; she felt it would be easier if we were not around. After it was all done, she thought she would surprise us. So on moving day, my brothers and I were in school when the van pulled up. With our school now a few streets over and not across from the house anymore, she was able to pull this off quite easily, especially since we still only had a few possessions. Despite this, the movers apparently took all day to accomplish their task. By the afternoon, my mother, Gil and my grandfather were sorting furniture and boxes, when my mother realized that we had gotten out of school an hour earlier. In a panic, she raced back to find us.

When my brothers and I had arrived home, we found the door wide open and the screen swinging freely on its broken hinges, from years of abuse by excited children with adventures to tell. The house was empty. In shock, we walked quietly through all the rooms, it was so big and open. It looked like the day, not too long ago, when we had first moved in. The familiar smell that we knew to be ours was there, but there was nothing else in the rooms that confirmed it. The linoleum creaked loudly beneath our feet in the kitchen. The hum of the refrigerator was no longer present, and the sun was streaming through the windows, no longer trapped in our curtains like a fish in a net. We were mesmerized by the sight; none of us said a word. Walking slowly into the vast expanse that used to be our living room, we were struck by its size. It looked lonely and vacant. The rug was neatly vacuumed, and all the walls had awkward nails left on them, retired from their duties of supporting our family treasures. In a panic, I ran into the room that I had come to love and know so well: my bedroom.

The minute I stepped in, I stopped short from the hollow sound my feet made on the hardwood floor. My beautiful bed and throw rugs were gone; my clothes and toys were no longer there. The life I had known to be my own had disappeared, as if it had never existed. I walked back to the only connection I had with the things I owned, the only tie left: my brothers.

Standing in the center of the kitchen again, we were afraid to speak the words that were running through our minds. We had all experienced these feelings before, long ago, in a house in Peabody. Only that time my mother was with us, and she shared in our abandonment...this time we were alone. The parallel was so familiar, that we didn't dare look at each other, for fear that we would know what the other was thinking. I was remembering the night my dad had left, when we stood in that house a few weeks later, to say goodbye to its beauty, safety and comfort. I sobbed the day I had to let go of my fireplace doll house and the holes in the floor, knowing I would never see them again. And now I was feeling it all over again, with this house.

Suddenly, breaking the silence, Jake said, "Echo, echo, echo." His words vibrated and bounced from wall to wall, only to return to us as a reminder that what we were seeing was really true. Laughing, Doug followed suit. I did the same, never liking to be left out and wanting to join in the fun. Soon, the echoing banter turned to whatever word or sound that entered our heads. We said, "Hello, hello, hello." Jake even yodeled. Then we yelled our names. It was like a confirmation to the empty house that we were still there and alive.

Finally, tired from the game, we broached the unspoken subject. It was I who spoke first, "Where is Mom?" I said in a whisper, because somehow it felt like we would get in trouble if it were spoken out loud. "She obviously decided to move today," Doug responded in return, with the voice of reassurance, as he went and sat on the empty window seat. Although only 13 in years, in my eyes, Doug was already an authority on such things, and his words eased my fears. He always knew what to say and had the answers, sometimes even when Mom didn't. When the newness of playing in an empty house started to wane, we decided to sit on the porch and wait. Doug made us free from worry, he told us she would be back.

Mom, having felt the guilt of a thousand mothers, was in an especially good mood by the time she arrived. Having now gone back inside the empty house, we were all in the living room when she burst through the door.

"I am so sorry," she said, grabbing us around by the neck and holding us tight "Mom, where were you?" I said, with one hand on my hip, tapping my foot on the hard wood floor that echoed in its chambers.

"Oh I am just a little late. Besides, wait till you see the surprise I have for you. She picked me up and twirled me around, and suddenly all was right with the world. Jake was jumping up and down with excitement. "What is it? What is it?"

Doug sat across the room on the window seat with his arms crossed, waiting for what he was sure was the other shoe to drop.

"You will see," was all she said." Now stop asking questions, or you will ruin the surprise."

She wanted to make it up to us, so we stopped at McDonald's on the way to our new house.

She had other motives for this treat as well; the new kitchen was not set up yet. Once we got to McDonald's, we could have whatever we wanted. This being pre "Happy Meal" era, the one true pleasure on the menu was French fries. They were amazing and were only 15 cents.

"Barbara, must you insist on autopsying that hamburger?" This was Doug's way of trying to be clever. "What? I don't like bread."

"Or cheese, or pickles, or ketch-up and mustard. "Is there anything about a hamburger that you do like," asked Doug.

"Don't forget the onions; she hates onions," said Jake. "Hey, can I have your pickles?" "I like the hamburger," I said with a smile, as I whipped ketchup off the tip of my index finger. Mom interrupted, "Finish up, guys, I still have that surprise for you. "Please tell me it contains a bed," said Doug in his best Bob Newhart imitation

When we pulled up in front of our "big surprise," it was 4:00 PM. Our new address was now Dunlap Street and was only five blocks away from the house we had just moved from. The sun was just beginning to retire for the day, and I'm sure my mother was ready to as well.

"Oh my, looks like someone has a chore ahead of him, cutting down that hay, otherwise known as a lawn," said Doug, turning to Jake. I have to admit the grass was very high. I had never seen grass that tall that wasn't growing wild in a field. Its only saving grace was that It had an orange glow from the sun that danced on its tips when the wind blew. A rusted chain link fence surrounded the property. Grass poked through its holes at odd angles. The back yard was dust. It was a three decker house, and the first floor was ours. The paint on the front porches was peeling in three inch curly strips along the pillars and railings. The house was sided with dirty, green vinyl siding. The lattice on the side of the stairs had been broken in places the size of an angry foot. My heart sank. This was a disaster site. What was Mom thinking? This is a place where poor people live. I had never met a poor person. Then reality hit me, "We are poor people." My hands started to tremble, and the feeling I had experienced so many times before but was too young to identify came flooding into my soul like a familiar face; it was insecurity.

I searched for a sign of something about this place that was good. On the rest of the street the houses didn't look as bad as this one. Some looked even kind of nice. Maybe, we would be the only poor ones in the neighborhood. The trees that lined the front of our house were monsters; they reminded me of the ones that tossed apples at Dorothy, in the Wizard of Oz. I knew they would be difficult to climb; there was not a single one in the yard. I would no longer climb and hunt for pears.

Entering the house, my mother was chattering, "We just need a little paint and wallpaper, that's all. I know it is a mess," she said, "but together we will fix it up." She was using that not so convincing happy voice again. Her attempt to rally us was not working. Gil was talking to Jake about paneling. "I am going to need your help, big guy...this is man's work." The expression on Doug's face was the same as mine. "You have to be kidding."

With every move we made, my first interest was always my bedroom. This move was no exception. When my mother told me which one it was, I opened the door to a barrage of pornography and profanity hitting me in the face. It was written all over the walls, from floor to ceiling, in Crayola crayon. And there were my bed, clothes and toys sitting inside it. I was afraid to have my mother see it, because swearing and vulgarity was something she never tolerated. Then I realized, it was obvious she had seen it. How else would my stuff get in there? I was shocked she had let me walk into it. When I turned around, I noticed a name written on the inside of the door. It said, "Greg Baggett's Room." It seemed to me that any hope of ever calling this room mine was suddenly destroyed. This was a disgusting boy who was in my class at school. He always made farting sounds with his armpit when the teacher's back was turned. He constantly looked like he needed a bath and smelled really bad. In the school yard, he was the one who had the loudest mouth with usually unpleasant things to say. He was basically the guy that everyone feared...the bully. And now I was going to have his old bedroom. The thought repulsed me and panic set in. What was I going to do? I couldn't sleep in that room this night. There was no doubt in my mind that Shadow Man was going to be with me, but to have the aura of the devil's spawn hanging out was too much for me to take. Interrupting her ritual of spraying Lysol, I made a plea for my mother to give me a different room.

Walking over to her without making it obvious to my brothers, I whispered in her ear, "Mom, I can't sleep in that room. Can I have a different room... please?"

"Oh, I know, Barbara, imagine the young boy that had to endure that room before you." I tried not to let it but his face kept popping into my head.

"Mom, you don't understand. Please can I have a different room?" She had a better idea. She handed me a bucket of paint.

The next morning was Saturday. At first, when I opened my eyes, I didn't know where I was. Then all the terrible realities flooded back. I pulled the covers over my head.

Over the course of the next few months, my mom, with the help of us children and Gil, began the transformation of our apartment. The atmosphere of the apartment went from a rundown dump to a place that felt familiar, and we would eventually call it home. In all the years we lived there, I longed for the other places that had been our home. This place always felt temporary; but unfortunately it was reality.

In the late winter of the fourth grade, I turned ten. I was in Mrs. Hine's class at the Pickering school. Although not an abusive teacher like the one I had had in the past, Mrs. Hine was impatient. The fact that we were a huge class didn't help. The class was so huge, because there was another class sharing the same room with us with the same number of kids we had, due to the condemned rooms in the school. That meant forty kids in one classroom, with two separate teachers governing twenty kids each. When one teacher was lecturing her class, the other class was working quietly on assignments at their desks. In theory, this seemed to work, but if you were a daydreamer, like me, the distractions from the other teacher talking made it very difficult to concentrate. It was a bad year for me to be in a class like that. It was the year that school became difficult for me and led to my downfall in math. It was partly due to Mrs. Hine being a poor math teacher, but my inattention played a major part in it as well. I couldn't help myself. A pattern in the room would catch my eye or the other teacher would say something that drew my attention, and I was off. I could never look Mrs. Hine in the eye. I felt she was the one true person in this world who knew just how dumb I was.

Despite my difficulties in learning, I still had my imagination to occupy me outside of school. One morning, I got up early and decided to go exploring this new neighborhood. What I was looking for was my replacement for Greenlawn Cemetery. Mack Park was up the street a few blocks, the biggest park in Salem. It didn't have the beauty of Greenlawn, but in a pinch to satisfy the need to be alone, it would do. It had rolling hills and lots of places to be by yourself and sit. It also had what we referred to as the gully. This was a large area at the lower right hand side of the park. In the winter, it was filled with water, and we would ice skate on it. I was good at ice skating. I would watch Peggy Fleming on TV and try to do everything she could. I became good at jumping and spinning. I especially liked the spinning. This was an activity I longed for every winter, despite the fact that I had to go home and rest my legs after every occasion. I was learning how to push myself, even with my sporadic limitations. In the spring, we would hunt for frogs and tadpoles before the water dried up for the summer; that's when the older boys used it to practice football. At the peak of the park was where we converged for sports events. It also had swings, a slide, monkey bars and a twirling merry–go–round. I loved that. I didn't care what age I was, I always twirled on that thing to make myself dizzy. The best part was that it was placed near some trees, so when I stopped twirling I could watch them whiz past me in shapes and patterns. During the summer, activities were run by park instructors, usually college kids looking for summer employment. It was the place where we spent time making gimp rope and playing baseball. There were a lot of sport teams we could join, and I enjoyed them all. I especially liked baseball and a game we called squash ball. Unlike traditional squash ball, this game was played like baseball. But instead of a baseball, the pitcher threw a soccer ball, and instead of a bat, the hitter used his arm that was wrapped with an ace bandage. Mack Park became my replacement for Greenlawn, which was my replacement for The Common, which was my replacement for Collins Cove, which was my replacement for the forest behind my house in Peabody.

I would go to the park year round, whether it was open or not. On one particular day that I was visiting the park, it was off season, and there were no park instructors at the time. I was on a mission that day, and I wanted to be alone to accomplish it. I was going to teach myself how to climb the monkey bars! These bars were simply a set of three squared-off ladders. There was one on each side and a third that ran parallel to the ground and connected them at the top. The top was well over six feet in the air. All the last summer, I had watched as other kids climbed the ladders to sit on the top. They would be up there for hours, talking. At Mack Park, if you were at the top of the monkey bars, you were a part of the in crowd. I knew I could climb them; that wasn't the real problem. After all, I had been climbing trees for years. It was the kids at the top who intimidated me. They would goad anyone on who tried. Many would not succeed, and these kids were just downright mean. It was because of this that I was too embarrassed to try it when others were there. What if I fell? Besides, there is nothing worse than seeing a nervous kid awkwardly trying to climb something. I didn't want anyone to see that image of me. Climbing the monkey bars, for me, was not about being with the mean kids; it was about sitting at the top. I was struck with the wonder of the images I would see from up there. The monkey bars sat on a large hill that overlooked the far right side of the park. You could see the gully from up there; I just knew it. I wanted to know if I would be able to see my house. It was about 9:00 AM on a Saturday morning, as I sat in front of the structure and decided this was the day. Getting up was not as easy as I thought; it was different from climbing a tree. I had no traction, nothing to grab onto. There was a big space between the last bar of the vertical ladder and the first bar of the horizontal one. I could reach it, but it took all the physical strength I had to hoist myself up. The key was to swing your legs like a monkey and slip them into a square at the top. Timing was everything. I did it on the first try! I pulled myself through the square at the top and enjoyed the sight. The view was amazing. I could almost see the entire park. Although I couldn't see my house, I didn't mind. Instead, I pretended I was on top of the crow's nest of a gallant sailing vessel. I was off to explore a new world. I sat there for awhile, since the park was empty except for the groundskeepers. They were busy with their fall clean up in the gully down the hill and didn't even know I was there. After a while, two teenage boys I had never seen before showed up. They had a volley ball in their hands.

"Hey kid, get down. We are going to use this as our net." Now there was something I had never thought of. How would I get down? Jumping was out of the question----it was too far. I chose to ignore them; maybe they would just go away. They didn't.

"Hey idiot, are you deaf? I said get down."

The other piped in, "I know how to get her down."

Once again, I turned away. Of course, they didn't know that I didn't know how to get down, and I wasn't going to tell them. Suddenly, without warning, I was hit by their soccer ball. I fell over backwards and hit the ground hard. When I got up, I ached all over. Then I looked down at the worst pain I was feeling; it was my wrist. My hand was turned around and facing at an odd angle. I thought I was going to vomit. I was slowly going into shock, as I looked up at the perpetrators.

"Oh, my god, come on, let's get out of here!" Gathering their ball they ran from the park, they left me all alone to figure out what I was going to do next. I did the only thing I could; I headed for home. With my right hand supporting my mangled left, I headed down the hill in the direction of my house. My mother was working at the sub shop, and I knew she wouldn't be home. To get to her would take another ten minutes to walk, and she didn't have a car or her license. I started to cry. The pain was unbearable, and I was beginning to feel light headed and thought I would faint before I got to her.

"Hey, are you all right? Do you need help?" It was a man who was a groundskeeper for the park. He was driving a city vehicle and pulled up next to me. He was about 50 years of age. His hair was ruffled with pieces of cut grass stuck in it. He smelled like fresh, tilled earth. I looked into his kind eyes and didn't know what to say. He got out of the truck as the earth beneath my feet began to sway.

"Come here sweetheart, I need to take you to the hospital". He supported my back slightly so I wouldn't fall.

"But I can't, I protested. You are a stranger." I was practically delirious from pain. I didn't know what to do, so I gathered my strength and kept on walking. He didn't give up. Standing in front of me, he put his hands on my shoulders so I couldn't walk any further. In a soft voice, he said, "I will take you to your mother, and then I will take the two of you to the hospital." He seemed so concerned and kind that I gave in and let him lift me onto the front seat of the truck. Pulling up to the sub shop, I was afraid to go inside. How was I going to explain to my mom that I let this stranger give me a ride? Seeing my hesitation, he said, "Don't worry, honey, your mom won't be mad. You did the right thing." I thought to tell him she was the Head of the War Department, and then I thought maybe I better not. Seeing my wrist as I walked through the door, my mother let out a wail like I have never heard uttered from her mouth. Composing herself, she took charge. She began asking all sorts of questions, as she reached for her purse and coat. Without even saying a word to her boss, who was standing right there, she was out the door. The man who brought me to her then took us to the hospital. He sat with us the entire time we were there. We were lucky, in that they took me to a room right away. My mother and the kind man made small talk about raising children and how these were the battle wounds a parent has to face. It was unavoidable. After the x-rays, the doctor entered the room and tried to talk to me calmly. He was acting like I was 5 instead of 10. Then he smiled. Looking at my wrist, he told me to look away. With a pull and a twist, he popped it back into place." It was mostly dislocated," he said, turning to my mother, "but there was a hairline fracture as well. We will have to cast it." I was so happy it wasn't my drawing hand. After getting my cast, the kind groundskeeper took us home. He was a person in my life for many years after that. When I saw him mowing the lawn at the park, he would stop and ask me how I was. It wasn't until I was in high school that I learned his name was Mr. Sullivan, and he had a wife and five kids, all older than me. I saw his picture in the paper under his obituary.

CHAPTER: 7

One day, my mother got a call from my uncle Joe. He was calling from a ship out in the middle of some ocean that was unknown to me. He said that the Navy had called him from Texas to inform him that they had his children in custody, because his wife of many years had abandoned them two weeks earlier. "Jane, I need your help with this one; I have no one else to turn to. The kids have been raising themselves for two weeks. A neighbor noticed and called the authorities. If I don't find someone to take them while I finish out this tour of duty, they are going to take them away from me. Jane, they are my kids. I can't lose them, and I would be stupid to throw away 30 years of service, when I only have the last few years left."

"What do you want me to do Joe? You name it." "Take my kids for a few years. I will send you money for them every month. I know this is a lot to ask, but I don't know what else to do. Jane I don't even know how they were feeding themselves."

"Don't worry, Joe, I will take care of everything." MaryJane was true to her word and got all the paperwork settled and arranged for their arrival. After all, she was the Head of the War Department; she had the power to do anything. The kids were in Texas and were immediately brought to Massachusetts. That is how, in the darkness of the night, my family went from a family of three kids to a family of six children, and I suddenly had a sister.

"Barbara, sweetheart, move over, you need to make some room in your bed," my mother whispered in my ear. In a semi-conscious dream state, I rolled over without question.

She was placed beside me, this stranger who was my age. When I woke up the next morning, I was surprised to see this unfamiliar person sleeping peacefully next to me and realized it wasn't a dream. Although we had met one time previously, it had been a long time ago, and we had both been very young. There was nothing about her looks that gave any hint that we were related. She was fair skinned with thick, short, blond wavy hair. I, on the other hand was dark skinned with long, straight black hair. I would soon learn there were a lot more differences between us than just our looks. "What if she doesn't like me?" I thought. "What if I don't like her?" Her name was Veronica. I thought about all that this girl had been through in the past month. To see her sleeping so peacefully, one would never suspect that she had just been thrown away.

That first morning, my mother sat Veronica and me on my bedroom floor and separated all my clothes into two piles: Veronica was to get half of everything I owned. A lot of my clothes had been matching outfit hand-me-downs from a set of older twins who were in our family. With Veronica being blond and me a brunette, my mom felt that I should have the blue outfits and Veronica the matching pink. We looked like Daphne and Velma on Scooby-Doo.

"I am so glad you two are the same size. This makes this task so much easier," said Mom.

"Easier for you," I thought. No one even sat me down to tell me I was going to lose half of everything I owned. Seeing Veronica sitting there, not saying a word, I felt guilty even thinking that. She had lost everything...including her mother. I tried not to show my disappointment. I sat there saying nothing and watched my belongings slip away. We had to share all of my toys as well. My world had changed drastically in a split second. Suddenly, I went from being an only girl with a lot of time on my hands to imagine and play to a girl with an instant sister, whom I had to get to know. I no longer had the freedom to escape to my room when I felt the need to be alone. I no longer had my own room. I no longer had my own bed. We shared a twin bed. Veronica slept at the bottom, and I was at the top. Her feet came to my shoulders that first night; before long they would be sharing my pillow. "Hey! Your breath is tickling my toes!" "Your toes are giving me bad breath!" We then would start to giggle. "No talking in there," Mom would call from the other room. Walking the house in the middle of the night to loosen my joints became trickier. I didn't want the others to know I had an issue. Shadow Man just sat in the corner watching me. I never told Veronica about him. I think he preferred it that way. So did I; he was all I had left that was all mine.

Of course, having a new sister also meant I now had two more brothers as well. It was awkward at first, having new siblings. Our natural pecking order had changed and, subsequently, how we related to each other on a daily basis did as well. I was no longer the youngest: Dylan, who was "the wild man" and a few years younger, stepped into those shoes. Doug was in high school and found it easy to never be at home or, more to the point, never be missed. He walked away from the whole mess and became a part of his friends' lives instead. Jake changed the most. He lost his sense of humor and became quiet and withdrawn. We no longer relied on him for comic relief, because he didn't have it in him. He was also entering that time in most boys' lives, when they become internal and distant. Stuart and Dylan were now my new added brothers. They were younger than Jake, and he never let them forget. Stuart was older than both Veronica and Dylan, but somehow he didn't act like the oldest. He was a very sensitive boy and was easily riled by the littlest things. He was a nervous child, who always felt uneasy around everyone. Veronica and I were the same age. Although I tried to hold on to my two week seniority, with this new pecking order, it was a losing proposition.

We all had very different personalities. Veronica came to the table with a survival instinct; she was emotionally stronger and more adventurous than I was. She had a will that made her feel she could do anything, even at the expense of others---a natural talent of a child who had been abandoned and uprooted. She was a warrior. She didn't talk much about her mother, and I didn't ask. I never saw her cry in all the years we knew each other. I admired this about her, even when we were young. She also had a sneaky quality to her personality. She was funny and often in a good mood, but there was always a side to her that she kept close to her vest, a facet of her personality that didn't trust people, and, in turn, others around her didn't trust her. At times she made me feel inadequate in front of our friends, whom I also had to share. I realize now it was just her way of protecting herself. She was, after all, just a child. But for me this was a huge changing point in my life and affected how I would learn to relate to others. Everything I now wanted in life not only had to be negotiated but also had to reflect a type of fairness to others around me. I had to develop a strategy. I now needed to learn how to compete for my mother's attention. I was confronted with a sister who had learned to lie to get what she wanted. It took me awhile to see this and then to learn how to deal with it. I never wanted to tell my mother of this. I figured she had enough to handle. I also felt that Veronica would eventually realize she didn't need to do this to get what she needed. I was wrong. The biggest change was the loss of my solitude. The sudden overload of reality caused my imagination to burrow deep inside me and not resurface till much later.

I remember Veronica getting impatient with my naiveté. She was always coming up with adventurous things for us to do, never bad, just secretive somehow. She always had to talk me into them. "Let's go to McGlew Park instead of Mack Park today," she whispered to me one morning during breakfast. I couldn't respond, because others would hear me, and she knew it. After we cleared the table, I waited for us to be alone in the kitchen. "Who do you want to see at McGlew Park?" I knew instinctively this had to be about a boy.

Her reply was accompanied with a sly grin, "I don't know; I haven't met him yet." That Saturday morning we trekked the seven blocks to get there. When we arrived we found ourselves to be alone. Turning around we headed to Mack Park.

There were a lot of kids in our neighborhood, at least twelve of us. Being outside, away from the closed confines of the house, was always more preferable. Indoors, we were constantly in each other's way.

We were a creative bunch, and our play reflected it. We would put on shows and hold carnivals that no one would come to but us. One of the girls in the neighborhood had three beautiful prom dresses that had belonged to her mother. We would take turns dressing up in them and pretending we were damsels in distress. We would urge the boys to play along, but they thought we were crazy; so many times, the girls would have to play the male parts.

With none of us having enough money to take classes like gymnastics, we taught each other to do cartwheels and round-offs. When the Olympics were on TV, we would hold our own events. Never feeling we were deprived, what our parents couldn't give us, we would improvise. I think we were better off in that way than children who have everything handed to them.

One day, we decided to play volleyball, since there were enough kids in the neighborhood to form two teams. We played this game a lot. None of us had a backyard big enough, so instead we just used the width of the street. We also didn't have a net, so we just imagined one. For some reason that was ok, and we never fought about the boundaries. We irritated the other neighbors on the street with this game. They constantly had to wait for us to move, in order for them to pass with their cars. This was more evident when hockey season rolled around, and we did have a net. Then they would call the police on us at least once a week. We played all the traditional games like Red Rover and Giant Step, games I fear have been lost today in this world of organized sports for children. The game we liked the most was the one we had to wait all day to play. Ghost Hide and Seek, as we called it, could only be played at night in the summer. It was played like traditional Hide and Seek, but, because it was dark, you could hide in plain sight. On one occasion, it was Veronica's turn to be the seeker. I was hiding behind a fire hydrant. I was so scared, crunched up in the dark, hanging on to a protrusion of the metal. I became uncomfortable from all the lemonade I had drunk at dinner and began to wiggle. Trying not to squirm or move, I was practically holding my breath and awkwardly crossing my legs, when Veronica came up from behind me. Knowing I had this issue every time we played this game, she suddenly grabbed me with both hands on my shoulders and yelled, "BOO!" Falling over onto the street, without warning, I wet my pants. Looking up I noticed Shadow Man leaning against a tree. He just shook his head.

"Hahahahaha...look at Barbara. She got all wet sitting behind that fire hydrant! Did you lift your leg first, Barbara? Oh, that's right, you're a girl; you were squatting...hahahaha"

Getting up and waddling back to the house, I looked over my shoulder and mumbled under my breath, "That's the last time I eat your beets when Mom isn't looking."

Every day for us was a new beginning. All the arguments of the day before seem to magically disappear from history. In the mornings during the summer, Mom would give us each a dime to go to the store at the top of the street and buy penny candy. At that time, penny candy actually did cost a penny. To go to the store, I always put on my roller skates. My roller skates had metal wheels and soles. They had clips that clamped onto my shoes. I had to use my leather school shoes for this activity, because the clamps would pinch my toes in my soft canvas sneakers. I always wore the key to tighten them on an old shoe lace that hung around my neck and shared space with my house key.

"What are you going to buy with your money? I'm thinking of 10 pieces of bubble gum," I said, as we struggled to roll up the street.

"I like the paper dots," said Veronica with a huge smile. Paper dots were dots of hard sugar candy, all in rows of different flavors and colors, on a roll of thin paper similar to the kind found in an adding machine.

There were certain surfaces that were more pleasant to skate on. A house at the top of our street had a cement driveway, instead of the rough hot top that was everywhere else. Each time I approached that house, I would swing halfway up their drive and enjoy a pleasant roll down.

"What did I tell you kids about roller skating in my driveway?!" The lady who lived there often yelled at us for it. We didn't care; it was worth the pleasure. When my skates rolled across the hot top, the graveled tar would vibrate between my toes. It would slowly work its way up my legs, until eventually it settled in my teeth. When I would remove the skates hours later, the vibrating would change into a tingling sensation in my whole body that lasted for a long time.

The candy store was a free standing building, approximately fifteen feet square with hard wood floors that creaked when you walked on them. They were often dusty from dirt that was tracked in from the neighborhood kids. In the winter it was always covered with puddles from our boots. The entire room was filled with the fragrance of packaged bread. Over the years, it had seeped into the wood of the building and was a permanent aroma. Homemade bread was a wonderful smell, but packaged bread smelled different; maybe it was the plastic wrapper mingling with the preservatives. I wasn't sure I liked it. On one side of the wall was a glass display case. Over in the corner was a deep chest for cold drinks. I had to stand on tippy toes in order to reach the treasures inside.

The owner of the store was Mr. Pipper. He was a nice enough man, but his wife ran a tight ship. She never let me enter the store with my roller skates on. She said they would mark the floor. In the summer, we always had to be wearing a shirt and shoes. In the winter she would yell at us to wipe the snow from our boots. If we pressed our faces against the glass display case or in any way leaned on it, Mrs. Pipper would speak to us about it in a very stern voice. She frightened me, and the first thing I would do when I arrived at the store was check to see if she were there. It was hard for Mr. Pipper to hear our orders, so we had to speak loudly. This was so uncomfortable for me. If there were other people in the store at the time, I would wait for them to leave. I did this because I hated to be the center of attention. Sure it was nice to pretend, but never in real life! I think Mr. Pipper knew this about me, but maybe he just thought I was shy. He never forced me to order before the others.

The candy selection was huge. One whole side was filled with bins of loose candy. The visual symphony was astounding in color; it opened the irises of my eyes with a sparkling sensation. There were a few staples in my candy choices that were a must: one was Squirrel Nuts. This was a small, rectangular, chewy candy that was filled with nuts. The juicy caramel that surrounded them left a velvety feeling in my mouth. Another candy was called Mary Jane's. I liked this one, because that was my mother's name. "How cool," I thought, "to have a candy named after you." It had a sweet taste of honey. My favorite of all time, though, was a coconut candy that I don't recall had a name. I used to just point when making that selection. It was a thinly sliced, gelatin-based candy that was pink, white and brown. It looked like a watermelon slice but had a taste of coconut and sugar. I loved to let one melt naturally in my mouth, until all the sugar coating was gone. Then I would eat the chewy leftover. There was also a variety of wax lips and vampire teeth, and every Halloween season, you could purchase marshmallow pumpkins. Around Thanksgiving, Mrs. Pipper would make home-made candied apples. She had the best candied apples for miles around. At Christmas, there were candy canes. After making our purchases, we headed home. Sometimes we would beg each other to trade what we got, but we rarely did. We would try to make our candy last all day, but we would always fail.

Gil was still dating my mother at the time. At first, this extension to our family was too much for him. He no longer slept over, and they pretended that they were just friends. The touching had stopped, but we all knew the truth. They would go out sometimes and leave Doug in charge. One night, when Doug was watching us, Stuart and Dylan got into a playful wrestling fight. They were laughing and bouncing on their bed.

"I can touch the ceiling, and I bet you can't," said Stuart.

"No fair! Only because you're taller!" yelled Dylan back at him. The bed protested under their weight. Dylan, holding the stuffed bear that was the only possession he brought from Texas, was trying his hardest to jump higher than Stuart. During this war of might, Dylan accidently hit Stuart in the head with the bear. The eye of his bear, which was made from glass, put a two inch gash in Stuart's head. Blood began pouring down his face. We all thought Stuart would faint. Stuart was one of those rare people who could faint on command. He used this tool when ever things got too much for him to take, or, and I always admired him for this, if he didn't want to sit through a long Mass at church.

The night Stuart got hurt and had blood oozing from the gash, Doug, always fascinated with medicine, decided he could handle it. He put ice on it and a bandage first thing, but the bleeding wouldn't stop. Then he put Stuart in the bathtub, so as not to get blood all over Mom's carpets. While Stuart was sitting in the tub, the rest of us were cramped in the bathroom with him to get a good look.

"Oh gross! Look how dark the blood is," said Jake.

"Oh, man, that has to hurt," we all added as we craned our necks to see. None of this, I'm sure, was making Stuart feel any better or Doug feel more confident. Stuart, trying so hard to be brave, began to cry. When it was apparent that Stuart needed stitches, Doug decided he could handle that too.

"Barbara, go to Mom's sewing box and get me a needle and thread. Jake, fill a small pan with water to boil." Grabbing a disposable razor my Mom had on the side of the tub, Doug began shaving Stuart's head. I was so impressed that he knew what to do. Watching as Doug took my mother's sewing needle that had darned a sock the day before, I was awed by the precision he had. The sound of the needle pulling through Stuart's skin was only masked slightly by Stuart's screams. As each stitch was set in place, the skin pulled together, and in no time the open gash on his head was replaced by a neat mound of black thread and drying blood.

It was an exciting evening compared to the homework and bickering that we were used to. When Mom and Gil got home, she went frantic. Gil, with the quiet demeanor of a layman who was just shown a great work of art for the first time said, "Shit, that's pretty good!"

"Are you serious?" she said, turning to Gil in disbelief. "My 16 year old son just sewed the head of my 13 year old nephew!"

Gil just smiled and shrugged his shoulders. Patting Doug on the head, he said, "Good job, Dr. Doug." Mom didn't think it was funny and insisted they take Stuart to the emergency room, despite the protests of Doug. The doctors were amazed with what Doug had done and told him so, but they replaced the thread with real sutures anyway, just in case. Poor Stuart had to endure not only a second round of stitches...but several
shots as well.

CHAPTER: 8

Doug became our official babysitter after that. I'm sure Mom figured if he could handle blood, he could handle anything. On the other hand, we didn't like Doug watching us, because he was bossy. This new found power was going to his head. It must have been difficult for him to feel responsible for all of us kids, and we didn't make it easy for him. There was one thing he did enjoy about it. He loved to cook and would make us elaborate meals out of nothing.

"Ok everyone...come and get it," he yelled in the direction of our bedrooms, where a sock fight was just getting underway. Being just kids, we never liked his dinners.

"What on earth is that?" said Veronica.

Holding the platter as he glided it just under our noses, he triumphantly stated, "It is Chicken Dijon Doug."

"I thought you were suppose to just stick it in the oven at 350...I heard Mom say that. She didn't say to put all that stinky brown stuff on it," I protested. As you can imagine, I was not pleased.

When it was meal time, there were so many of us at the table. Veronica and Dylan were left-handed, so we had to have assigned seats, in order not to topple things over on to the floor, or worse, accidentally bump into the person next to you and start a food fight. On nights that Doug was in charge, after each meal he would make us clean up the mess and do our homework. Veronica and I hated the clean-up. There were always at least five encrusted pans, and someone inevitably put bread in the sink. Not having a automatic dishwasher, this was always a concern with Veronica and me. Soggy bread was hard to pick up and felt soft and squishy between your fingers, when you attempted to do it. It was the absolute pet peeve Veronica and I had about the chore. We decided to band together and protest.

Veronica spoke first, "All right who put the bread in the dish water?"

"Yah, fess-up," I added. It didn't help. No one confessed. And besides, the boys said, because we were girls, we had to wash the dishes. Woman's Lib was becoming a catch phrase in households back then; it just hadn't reached our house yet. So we brought the issue to a high court... the Head of the War Department. She had an easy solution. She brought out the chore chart again. Veronica and Barbara were boldly printed under dishes.

I was still in Mrs. Hines' class, but finally our new school was finished. It was called the Bates School. My class was group two, the group that was average. We weren't smart, but, supposedly, we weren't dumb either. Veronica was in the class that used to share a room with us, in group three. I never understood this. She was always so much quicker than I when it came to puzzles and things, but for some reason, they felt she belonged there. We walked to school with Cherri, my best friend since third grade. She was in group one. It was a long walk to our new school, past our old house, past the Greenlawn Cemetery, and three more blocks after that. Our classes rotated that year: Cherri was ahead of me, and Veronica was behind me.

There was a boy I liked in Veronica's class. His name was John Holliday. Veronica thought he was gross, and I was crazy, and Cherri agreed. At Christmas, I wanted to tell him how I felt. Taking a lesson from Norman, I made him a Christmas card.

"OK, Veronica, here it is." Using red construction paper, I painstakingly drew an image of the Virgin Mary on the front. I got the likeness from my misselette. Inside, I decorated it with hearts and wrote the inscription "Merry Christmas, Love Barbara." It was Veronica's job to give it to him. Against her wishes, she did. He opened it and realized what it was. When the teacher unexpectedly left the room, he stood up on a chair in the middle of music class and read it out loud. He then proceeded to rip it into a million pieces and scatter them in the air. When the teacher came back, Veronica told her she had to go to the bathroom. From the hallway, she peered into the door of my class and motioned me to join her. Using the same excuse, I was out the door.

I was all smiles when I asked her, "So, did he open it?"

"Barbara, I told you it wasn't a good idea!" She told me what had happened. I was devastated. It was such a feeling of betrayal by another human being bestowed on to me. My face became red with embarrassment. The image of Veronica's class laughing at my expense flashed in my mind. I wanted to go home, but I knew everyone would know why I did. At lunch time, I snuck back into the music room and cleaned up the mess. At home, I put the pieces in a paper lunch bag and hid it in my treasure box. I vowed from that day on, no boy was ever going to do that to me again.

At night our house was crazy. The apartment was only a three bedroom, so the boys all shared a room. This made the living quarters very tight and uncomfortable. We argued a lot, mostly about territory, and it often came down to the boys versus the girls. There were so many boys that Veronica and I didn't have a chance. This was especially true when it came to the bathroom, since there was only one. Out of necessity, my mother had it all down to a science: yup, another chart. This time it had bath times written at the top of it. Veronica and I bathed together, as did Stuart and Dylan. Doug and Jake got to bathe alone. I'm not sure about the boys, but I do remember that Veronica and I used to "buck up" to see who had to sit at the faucet side of the tub. Because we were both tall, when we sat in the tub our legs had to be crossed, in the Indian style of sitting, and someone always had the faucet in her back. One time we tried sitting back to back but found we preferred to face each other instead; it felt more civilized, and we could talk and play. We loved to play in the tub. Mom would put dish soap in the water so we could have bubbles. We would try and find the perfect bubble and pick it up gently, so it wouldn't break. I remember our eyes would feel bright when looking into the perfect world inside of them.

"Don't you wish, Veronica, that we could shrink down and live in this beautiful bubble? It would be like living inside a house with walls made of diamonds."

"I think it would be sticky and slimy," said Veronica. She always had a practical way of seeing things, unlike me. After that, we would give ourselves beards with the bubbles and laugh at how each other looked. Sometimes, we would spread them all over our bodies to design the perfect bathing suits. Mom would then call to us from the other side of the door and tell us it was the boys' turn. A few times, we would get so caught up in playing that we would realize that we didn't even wash. On those occasions, we would grab the soap to get it wet, so the boys wouldn't tell on us.

It was understood between Veronica and me, that whoever had the faucet in the tub had the luxury of standing next to the heating register to dry off and put on their PJ's. The bathroom was too small for both of us to stand near the heat. The heating registers are another fond memory. Our house was heated by forced hot air, from registers that were on the floor. The heat was fueled by oil, so it was a pretty powerful blast of warm air when it came on. On winter mornings, when all six of us were waiting for the bathroom, we could be found standing in a lethargic state, on top of a register somewhere in the house with the heat blowing up at us. Jake started this unusual ritual. And because some of the rooms had more than one, there were enough to go around. My mom would call our names. One by one, we would emerge from our comatose state of early morning brain fog and leave our protected warmth, as we would tread reluctantly in the direction of the bathroom. Sometimes we would plead to have another take our turn. But of course we couldn't do that, as it would mess up the whole system of the morning bathroom chart.

The sleeping situation wasn't much better. Veronica and I seemed to be able to work it out, but it was another story for the boys, since their room was so small. Gil made bunk beds that were built into the wall for my brothers, and there was also a queen-size free standing bed for Stuart and Dylan to share in the same room. The kitchen table was yet another issue, because, as we grew, there was no way we could all fit around it. Sitting down to dinner at separate times was not an option; it would have been considered absurd. So a bar was constructed in the kitchen that ran the full length of one wall. It was complete with stools and felt as if we were at a diner. As kids, we loved it. Uncle Joe came home on leave to help Gil with all this construction. He, too, was very handy with a hammer. I was unsure of Uncle Joe; he was strict. Every morning, he would insist on us kids lining up for inspection. Our shirts had to be tucked in, and there was to be no dirt on our shoes. If there were, he would make us wash them. Veronica and her brothers were very different when he was around. They were timid around him as well. He was always to be addressed as "Sir." My brother Doug was not going to have any of this, so he fought with him constantly. Doug had long hair at the time, and this bothered Joe. Because my brother's hair was very curly, it became an unruly afro. He had a lot of hippie friends, as Joe called them, and one time Joe found a pipe in the boy's bedroom. This brought the whole situation to a boil, and my mom had to step in. At first she didn't say anything to Joe about the disruptions he was causing. She felt he wouldn't be around long and why make waves. But now the family was feeling the effects of his presence in a very uncomfortable way. Soon they, too, began to argue. I think this was the first real fight the two of them had ever had. Joe was the older sibling, so it was interesting for me to see my mother stand up to him. Of course she was the "Head of the War Department," and everything had to be cleared through her. Joe eventually succumbed to her requests, but not without a fight.

"Joe, they are all just children, they are not your subordinates." "Jane, I found a pipe in Doug's room!"

"Doug is my son, not yours! I will say what he can and can't do!" She left out the part that it was her Christmas gift to Doug last year. It came with a hand scrolled note: "This is only to be used for tobacco." We all had laughed that morning when Doug, who was well into high school at that point, read it out- loud. Throughout this entire exchange between MaryJane and Joe we kids watched from the other end of the room. Doug, Jake and I were relieved; Stuart, Dylan, and Veronica were amazed. They learned the true power of MaryJane that night. As far as the pipe was concerned, I never heard it mentioned again.

Despite this dispute between the adults, it was still nuts in our house. The craziness always started as mindless teasing that would escalate to something further. On the rare occasions that Doug was home, he and Jake used to gang up on Stuart. He was an easy mark, the runt of the litter. One day my mother decided that Stuart needed to spend time on something that would focus and relax him.

"Stuart, honey, come here, I have something for you." Pulling the surprise from behind her back she handed him a large bag. She was smiling from ear to ear. We all just sat and watched.

"OH AUNT JANE!!! THANK YOU!!! " In his hands was a huge box that contained all the pieces to construct a five foot model of the Apollo13 space rocket. Opening the box, he spilled the contents out on the table. There were hundreds of tiny pieces and looked impossible to put together. I sat across from him and watched in amazement at his organization of the task. He separated the pieces into categories to make it easier. This rocket occupied our dining room table for months, but Mom didn't seem to mind. I thought this was out of character for my mother, the chart maven and Lysol queen. She was the ruler of organization, who hated anything left on her dining room table. But for Stuart, she had a soft spot. This was good, because he needed someone like that in his life at that time.

He wouldn't let anyone help him, including me. But every day I would sit at the table across from him and marvel at his progress. It was this protectiveness of his project that drew attention to him and made him a target.

"So...what do you think there, "Captain Kirk," is the ship going to be ready in time for us to leave this godforsaken planet we are all on?"

Egged on by Doug's comment, Jake added in a deep solemn voice, "Houston, I think we have a problem." The teasing began to turn nasty, and every day they would tell him they were going to throw out three random pieces. Eventually it just turned into a chant: "We're going to break your rocket. We're going to break your rocket." This would put Stuart into a tizzy, and he would cry and complain to my mother.

"Aunt Jane, please make them stop!"

"OK, boys, that is enough!" These were my mom's famous last words. She tried the best she could do to control my brothers on this issue, but nothing seemed to work. Even Veronica and I would tell them to stop, but of course that was useless.

It took Stuart about two months to build the model to its full height. There were still a lot of pieces left to complete it. It stood about five feet tall, and anyone who saw it could tell that it was fragile. It was hard to find a safe place to keep it from harm's way. Behind the door in the boy's room was where it lived, when Stuart was not working on it. On one particular night, my brothers were being overly mean to Stuart; they tormented him horribly. Stuart was trying to work on his rocket and getting more and more agitated by their antics. Finally, he gave up. He couldn't work under those conditions. The tiny pieces he was putting on as finishing touches kept falling out of his hands with the chanting going on behind him. Putting the rocket in their room, he went to seek out my mother and complain. The race was on, with Stuart going in one direction to get my mother, and my brothers going in the other to pretend to break the rocket.

Veronica, Dylan, and I were yelling at them to stop. I could see them from my own room, and they weren't touching it. Standing in the middle of the room and holding their stomachs, they were laughing hysterically. Suddenly the heat came on, forced hot air from floor registers. Unfortunately, that's where Stuart had placed his model. Slowly, we all watched as the rocket rose then fell to the ground and smashed into a million pieces. Jake and Doug looked at each other and burst out laughing even harder, just as Stuart and my mother were entering the room. I hated the way my brothers teased Stuart, but it was out of my control to stop this injustice.

"I swear, Mom, we didn't touch it!"

"It was from the heat," added Jake.

"I don't care how it happened; you boys are going to work together to pick up this mess! Stuart, after you put that back together; you can store it in my room. Doug and Jake apologize to him, and if I hear one more thing out of your mouths on this subject, you're both grounded." I could never tolerate meanness at school, but at school I could escape it by going home. From this there was no escape. I wanted to cry, but I didn't have to; Stuart cried enough for all of us. I saw the new dynamics in the house change my brothers and my mother in a way that was disturbing for me. My brothers seemed to have had a gang mentality, on this issue with the rocket. My mom never seemed to want to address this important chance to teach acceptance to them. Instead, she would act like nothing was happening around her. More and more, she would withdraw to that place inside herself that I had seen her go so many times before. Only now she was there more than she was with us. I would often retreat to my room and try to block out the words that I heard coming from the other side of the door. I would hold my hands to my ears, shut my eyes tight, and try to listen to the sounds of my own heart beating in my chest. I would then sit near the window and look at the world outside and think...someday I am going to walk out there, walk down that street, and never come back. I looked over at Shadow Man for his approval. He just stared at me. It was a pronouncement that I didn't realize at the time was really a prophecy.

After months of dealing with this kind of behavior, my mother was losing her patience. She was sitting at the kitchen table starring into space, when she announced in a very compelling tone, "I'm going on strike." It was not an emotional statement. As a matter of fact, because it was so unemotional, it concerned us. "I am no longer doing laundry, cooking your meals, or doing any other motherly duties. I need a break." We knew she wasn't kidding, and at first we didn't know what to do. But she had forgotten...Veronica, Stuart, and Dylan had lived on their own before. We met in the boys' room to plan our course of action. We made our own chore chart. Doug, naturally, would do the cooking. And, once again, Veronica and I were expected to do the dishes. Dylan was to clear the table and pick up any mess. The funny part was watching Jake and Stuart try their hand at laundry: all the underwear turned pink the first day, even the boys! We were able to pull it off for two weeks. And funny, the better we were at it, the more Mom got mad. Working together suddenly stopped all the bickering. But Mom's issues were deeper than our fighting. Her real issues we never found out about. Finally, she couldn't take it anymore. On the bar in the kitchen sat our canisters, various kitchen tools and other supplies; in one fell swoop, Mom ran her arm along the bar and pushed all the items to the floor. We were all in the other room when we heard the crash. We ran into the kitchen to see if she was hurt.

"I want you kids to pick all this stuff up and throw it all away. I don't want to see it anymore." "Mom, are you OK?" asked Jake. "DON"T ASK ME ANY QUESTIONS, JUST DO IT!!!"

I began to cry under the pressure. I wanted my old mother again. Just like in the incident on the plane, I knew she had crossed a threshold and couldn't return.

"Barbara, pull it together," said Doug in my ear. We dutifully and quietly did as she had requested.

That night we stayed as far away from Mom as we could, so as to not upset her. The next day, I was working on an art project for school and needed to use the scissors. When I went to retrieve them in their usual spot, I realized that they, too, were in with the mess that we had had to throw out.

"Mom," I said with a soft voice, "I need the scissors for something I have to do for school." "Too bad," she said, as she continued to stare out the window at the empty driveway.

"But, Mom, I will get in trouble if I don't do it!" My pleas became desperate. My voice began to shrill. I started to cry. "Please let me get them from the trash." I was breaking the code we children had set, and I knew it. I was feeling helpless and didn't know what to do. I melted to the floor and sobbed onto the linoleum. My world, as crazy as it was, felt even crazier. Mom began to realize what her actions were doing to us...she went and got the scissors for me. For a short while, she was back.

CHAPTER: 9

Dylan's story was a different one from Stuart's. He was like a wild, untrained pony. If something was amiss around the house, it was unanimously assumed it was Dylan's fault. For instance, he woke up early one morning and was cold, so he set the heat to ninety degrees.

"Why is it so hot in here?" said Mom as she entered the living room and found us all standing there. We were sweating and emerged from our rooms wondering the same thing. It was 6:00 AM. We all turned at the same time, looking in the direction of Dylan. He was sitting in front of the TV, content. He was wearing his superman cape, eating a bowl of Cocoa Puffs and watching Scooby-Doo. When he realized how quiet it was, he turned to the mob that was forming behind him, and said, "What? I was cold." Dylan had the energy of a thousand children. He was the fastest runner and the most agile of all of us, as well as the youngest and the smallest. If we were all playing together outside and we needed someone small who could fit into a compromising area to carry out our deeds....Dylan was it, and he was always willing and excited to do it. If the other children in the neighborhood ever dared us to do something dangerous, Dylan was our man, our own personal daredevil. He loved Evel Knievel and would emulate him daily with his bike. Dylan got to have my old bike with all the colors; he didn't care that it was a girl's bike. Dylan was the first one on the block to set up jumping ramps for our daredevil contests, and he was the best at it.

"Hey, everyone, look over here. Watch what I can do!" We all cringed at the thought and looked in his direction. He had the front wheel high in the air. Sitting with his weight on the back tire, he rode the length of the street in a wheelie. He was heading down the road towards a ramp that was set up in front of a barrel he had laid on its side. Before we could protest, the bike sailed in the air and hurdled the object. He cleared it by a mile, as we all ran towards him.

"Are you crazy!?" It was Stuart who spoke first.

"Bet I could do that," said Jake, as he went to grab his own bike and another barrel. Veronica and I took a seat on the curb to watch what we knew was going to be a great show. As both cousins competed, we began to cheer them on, that is, until Mom heard the commotion and yelled from the window.

"You kids better put those barrels back right now! And there better not be any trash on the ground or else. I am going to be checking!" Since the incident of the "Strike," my mother's voice had seemed to change drastically. Her tone was more impatient. Her octave was lower and more of a shrill. It was a tone she would have the rest of her short life.

Despite my mother's protests, Dylan pursued his daredevil career. If anything, the success of his jumps that day propelled him even further into the world of taking risks. He begged my mother all the time to buy him a unicycle. She thought that was going too far. He had a sense of immortality like no other child. We always worried about his safety, because we were never sure what he would do next.

"Hey guys!" We were all playing Red Rover in the street, when we heard the distant voice. Looking in the direction of the back yard, we saw Dylan climbing up the back of our three story house with a rope had he found in the cellar. Hand over fist, he was already past the second floor porch, which was about 25 feet in the air. We all ran into the yard and stood underneath him to coax him down.

"Damn it, if Mom sees this, she will send us all to our rooms for the whole day. Dylan, get down from there, you idiot." It was Jake, voicing these concerns and giving him orders.

"I thought it was your turn to watch him," said Stuart, as he turned in my direction.

"No it wasn't I had him yesterday. It was your turn. Just check the chore chart; you will see." Dylan had made the chore chart months before; the line below trash.

"Hey, look, I am a mountain climber!" It amazed me he had no care in the world of the possible consequences of his actions. When he reached the third floor successfully, we raced up the stairs to join him. Jake took the rope from his hand with a violent tug. "You have to be the dumbest kid on the face of this earth!" Untying it from the post, he continued, "You pull a stunt like that again, and I will pound you into the ground myself!"

"It would save us on funeral expenses," said Veronica, as she and I headed back down the stairs since the excitement was now over.

One day at the height of the summer Olympics, we decided to hold our own competitions. Each family of kids on the street was a team. We, of course, had the biggest team, but no one seemed to complain. We started with gymnastics. When it came time for the cartwheel segment, we were graded on how straight our backs were and whether our final hand left the ground before or after our first foot touched. I remember the pain in my wrists from this feat. Once again, I ignored it. When it was time for Dylan to do it, we advised him to go slow. He had other Ideas. He did one without hands. Because we were performing this on the hot top of the street, we were forced to give him points off on it. Later that day, after the competition we were all trying it.

Dylan was the main focus of our outdoor play time. This was not by choice. You often heard my mother saying in that new tone of hers, "Where's Dylan?"...or... "Whose turn is it to watch Dylan?" He left us all exhausted. One day, Aunt Tina and Uncle Evan were watching us kids at their house. I can't remember why, but we were all there. Tina had two little girls of her own at the time, and they were under six. Gil had thrown all our bikes into the back of his truck to bring over there.

"I want you kids to stay outside and ride your bikes until Jane gets back." I think Tina was thinking that if we were all in the house at the same time, it would be chaos. And she was right. She checked on us often and, at one point, was sitting on the front porch watching us. At the time, there was a constantly run commercial on TV that had a child riding a bike and mimicking the words, "Look Mom, no hands!" I don't remember what it was advertising, but everyone knew the phrase. Dylan, always liking to impress others with his bicycling expertise, yelled to her from the street, "Look Aunt Tina, no handlebars!" Lifting the handlebars up in the air, he proceeded to hit a tree. No one knew why he had unscrewed the handle bars from his bike. With Dylan, you didn't need a reason. He was Dylan. What a mess he was; the screams could be heard for miles. An ambulance had to be called, and, not unlike Evel Knievel, Dylan broke both his legs, one in two places. We were all really worried. He was in the hospital for a week. Although we never verbalized it, we all felt this new found feeling of being able to relax. Veronica wanted to go see him, but, at the time, the hospital didn't allow children to visit. She always felt like a mother to Dylan, a role, I'm sure, that was a leftover from their days in Texas. When he came home, he was in a full length body cast. To get him home, Gil had to put him in the back of the truck, with Jake riding back there with him. In the cast he didn't fit in the cab. We all sighed with a bit of relief, because he couldn't possibly get into mischief in a body cast. How wrong we were!

Dylan's cast started at his chest and went down both legs, with only his toes exposed. His legs were spread wide and had a bar joining them that read, "Do not lift with bar." The hardest part was figuring out where to put him. Although he was small, with his legs spread so wide and in such an awkward fixed position, it was hard to find a comfortable place for him to be. If we put him in his bed, Stuart wouldn't fit at night to sleep. With the expanse of his legs, he didn't fit on the couch. The floor, he complained, was too hard. The only place to put Dylan was in my mom's bed. She had a queen-size bed, and for the six weeks that Dylan was in the cast, Mom slept on the couch. Fortunately he was small, and we could lift him. Veronica and I could do it together, as could the combinations of Doug with Mom, or Stuart. Jake could lift him alone. Dylan being in a body cast was the comic relief this family was looking for. Sometimes we would forget about him. At dinner, always a time of confusion in our house, we would hear a lonely plea, "Hey, what about me?" coming from the other room.

Mom would say, "Oh shit, somebody grab a plate and go eat with Dylan." If we were all watching TV, we would hear the same sorrowful little voice. Only this time, Mom would say, "Somebody go get Dylan and put him on the floor." His bathroom routine was another story. The poor kid had to use a bed pan and urinal for the entire time. Mom fastened a towel as a makeshift diaper around him because, for privacy, the cast didn't cover his crotch area. He didn't like that.

After the first two weeks, Dylan, the hyperactive hellion, was getting bored. Lying in Mom's bed, looking at the ceiling for most of the day was getting to him. Mom tried to find things to amuse him, but there was little one could do, because he couldn't bend at the waist. One day, he somehow got a hold of a straw and paper. Dylan, always the improviser, decided to make some artwork. The ceiling became his canvas, and spit balls became his paint. He tried to write his name by painstakingly spitting them on the ceiling. He was pretty good at this, yet we didn't notice until one day, bored even with that, he decided to use anyone that passed by his door as target practice. He hit me first. I didn't know what it was but knew it felt gross. I wiped it off and ignored it, like any ten year old would do. When the other kids walked by, they did the same. It was quite a covert operation he had going, constantly hiding his weapon when we turned around. Then he did the unthinkable...Mom walked by. You would have thought he would know not to hit her. But then again, this was Dylan.

"What the hell was that?" Wiping the residue of a wet paper wad off her face, she realized what it was. Turning to Dylan, she said in a voice that was about to boil, "You have to be kidding me." The Lysol queen was completely appalled. Dylan pretended he was sleeping. He was making exaggerated snoring sounds. When she entered the room and saw what he had done on the ceiling, I thought she was going to kill him. Instead, as usual, she came up with a better plan.

Opening up the living room window, she yelled, "Stuart, come in here right now." We all looked at Stuart who was waiting his turn for hopscotch, and said, "OOOOOOH, someone is in trouble." Stuarts face turned white, as he headed to the house.

"Lift him up," ordered Mom, as she held on to the upper half of Dylan. "I am putting him on the floor in the living room." I am sure Stuart was relieved that it was Dylan and not he who had angered the Head of the War Department. With the help of Stuart, she put Dylan on the carpet in the middle of the living room. Placing him on his stomach, she then handed him the hose to the Electrolux. She said, "When you finish vacuuming what you can reach, call me, and I'll give you a push." There was that tone again. She went back into her room to clean the ceiling. My mom was a very creative punisher. Dylan officially vacuumed the floors every day after that.

This time in my mother's life was a real challenge. I remember one day when the weather outside was bad, and we were all trapped in the house. I'm sure days like that were nightmares for her. She had long since quit her job at the sub shop; she needed to be home with us. As would be expected, Uncle Joe was sending her his paycheck. Out of his cast, Dylan was revved up and raring to go. We were all feeling the effects of cabin fever as well. By about three in the afternoon, we were bored with all the activities Mom was forcing on us. The puzzles were mind-numbing, and the hide and seek game was just not the same indoors in such a small apartment. As usual, this was when the teasing would start. But this time it was, once again as in years past, really just for fun.

Dylan started it. "Boy, you sure can smell the North River today, huh? Oh, wait, that's Jake's feet."

"Shut up you little twerp!" said Jake. Dylan then threw a rolled up sock at him, hitting Jake in the head. It was our weapon of choice back then. This naturally made Jake grab one and start chasing Dylan around the house with it. Dylan was never a child who tattled, so he was the perfect one to play this with. I think he enjoyed the opportunity to release some energy. The rest of us, excluding Mom, started to laugh hysterically at the scene. Dylan was so fast, yet Jake was really strong. It was a sight to behold, watching these two Olympians. In a split second, Dylan hurdled the couch and slid under the dining room table. Once he would reach him, Jake would "shot put" him into the kitchen. The entire time that they were running around and chasing each other, Stuart, Veronica and I were clapping and chanting, "Go go, go!" When the chairs in the kitchen started to get overturned and the items on the table tumbled to the floor, Mom decided she had had enough. As a matter of fact, that was a phrase she used a lot. "That's it; I have had enough! Now you are all going to your rooms!" she would bellow. She always punished us at the same time. If one person did something wrong, we all got in trouble. I wasn't sure if this was a tactic she was trying to use to have us learn how to govern each other or if she just wanted to feel, for a short while, that she lived alone. By the time we got settled into our rooms, we were in that state that children so often get into when they can't stop laughing, no matter how hard they try. Our rooms were across the hall from one another. Our doors were actually two doors that split down the middle with handles instead of knobs. The boys, being all together, kept up the ruckus. Not wanting to be left out, Veronica came up with a great idea.

"Quick, take these," she said, tossing me a handful of rolled up socks. "At the count of three, fire!" With each of us holding a handle to the doors, we could hardly contain ourselves as we counted: "One...two...three!" The door was flung open and the barrage of girly socks went flying across the hall into the boy's room and "beaned" them all on the head. With the sounds of bombs we were making with our voices, they knew we meant business. This started an all out war: the boys against the girls. Then Jake's jock strap came flying into our room. This had to be the work of Dylan. Girly screams could be heard from blocks away. We were repulsed by it, and neither one us wanted to pick it up. Finally, it was Veronica, the brave one, who skewered it with a Barbie doll head and tossed it back. If you were sitting on the couch in the living room, you could see the onslaught of items being tossed back and forth. You could hear the whooping and hollering of children, yet you couldn't actually see us. The whole time this was going on, Mom once again went to that place that all mothers go to; she just stared at the TV and didn't acknowledge that we were there.

It was hard to find a place in this house to be alone; no matter which room you were in, there were always at least one or two other people in it. Reading was out of the question. First of all, there were no books in my house, except that old incomplete set of children's Golden Encyclopedia. Even if there were books, the atmosphere had always been that strength was displayed by might, not words. As a child who cherished my down time, having this many people under one roof would often cause me to become stressed. It would show itself in various ways. Usually, I became quiet and withdrawn. Out of necessity, I found a solution to this problem. I would lock myself in the bathroom in the middle of the day and pretend it was my own apartment, and if I didn't want any visitors, I didn't have to let them in. Sitting on the edge of the tub, I would close my eyes and be taken to this daydream, that is until inevitably, someone would rap on the door.

CHAPTER: 10

Eventually, the stress of raising six kids alone was too much for my mother. She was at the breaking point. She knew what we needed was to have a man in our lives, so she gave in to Gil and had him move in with us. I'm not sure where Gil had lived before he lived with us. It's funny, the questions kids don't ask. But I do recall one thing: I was thrilled about the idea, and I know Jake was too. Doug didn't care one way or another. The rest of the kids saw this as sinful at first but only spoke of it to us.

"Aunt Jane is going to go to hell," said Stuart.

"Shut up, Stuart," said Jake. "What about your..." He stopped short of mentioning their mother. The room got strangely quiet. Veronica stood up and stomped out of the room. I ran after her. Alone without the boys, we sat quietly on our bed. I thought this time I would see her tears. But I didn't. Instead I just put my arm around her and whispered..."I saw a boy's jingle bell once...I'm not going to heaven either." She pulled away from me with a surprised look on her face; a smile began to emerge on her lips. In a few seconds, we both broke out into laughter.

Gil did bring calmness to our lives. Because he could drive, there was always a car at the house. He and Mom always did food shopping together anyway. Now we found we could go more places and do more things. Once he took us all to the movies to see "Coal Miner's Daughter." It was playing at the old Salem Theater. Veronica and I loved it. We sat next to each other and cried at the end. Having Gil around meant another income, and that gave us more opportunity in general. When the landlord announced one day that he was going to put the house up for sale, Mom went into a panic. She knew that there was no way on earth a new landlord would let six kids and two adults who were not married live in a three bedroom apartment. Our apartment was also the biggest of the three, and there was a good chance that a new landlord might want to live in it. Then MaryJane did what she had become so famous for: she somehow figured out how to get something that there was no way we could afford. She bought the house. She had heard about a credit union in Peabody that was giving house loans to lower income families. She applied and got one. This was something she did herself. Having lost the last house that she had shared with my father to the bank, she was not going to put anyone else's name on it but hers. No one argued with her. Once a week, my mother and I would go to the Hellenic Credit Union to pay the mortgage. Her rents upstairs paid for most of it. She always paid in cash, and I was awed when she pulled it out of her purse. She became empowered. For the first time in her life, she felt that because she owned something, she now meant something. Years later, when I was out of high school, that same credit union had to close down for making mortgages below the prime interest rates. A lot of men went to jail for it. This upset my mother very much, not because anything would happen to her house, but because she knew she would never have had a house if it hadn't been for those men.

Gil became a new element in our family dynamic. He was never the authoritarian that Mom was; everything still had to be cleared through her. He would joke about being angry with us, but he never was. I can still hear him say, " (insert child's name here), get my belt," and then, once it was in his hands, he would fold it in half and make snapping sounds with it. Sometimes he would take us in the other room to do this, and we would play along, making fake crying sounds. Everyone would laugh. My mother, on the other hand, had a stick. The first one was one of those toy paddles that had elastic and a ball at the end of it. Once the elastic broke, it became her weapon. It bothered Gil when she did this. I think that is why he would try and calm her by making a game of the whole situation. One day the stick went missing. No one was sure who took it, but we all suspected Dylan, since he was the one who was visited by it most often. This didn't stop Mom. She got a bigger stick. It was a small piece of lumber twelve inches by two. She pulled out of Gil's truck one day. When she wasn't looking, we would graffiti it with words that said "Ouch" and "Watch Out!" One day, Jake angered her. She yelled at him to get the stick. She, too, always made us get it ourselves. He had a sheepish look on his face, and at first we thought it was because he knew he was going to be hit. When he came back with a small paper bag and poured it on the table, we were all in shock. Jake, tired of the stick, had taken matters into his own hands; he had hacked it into tiny squares.

What Gil did the most was bring meaning to Mom's life and make her feel there was more to living than just taking care of us kids. When Mom was happy, we all were happy, including Gil. Around this time, Mom got a job at Parker Brother's Games. It was down the street, and she could walk there. The pay was good, and she seemed to enjoy having a place to go and be with other people besides us. This was heaven to us, because she would come home sometimes with defective toys. They were never ones that could hurt us---she wasn't that stupid. Instead, they were Nerf balls that didn't have the proper imprints on them or Monopoly games with a box that was missing a color in the printing. Because Mom's job started before we went to school and, on good weather days, so did Gil's, Doug had to make sure we were fed and dressed and had all our homework done. We gave him such a hard time in the morning. We didn't like him bossing us around, especially when we were all half asleep and waiting for the bathroom to do something as simple as pee. Doug, of course, took this opportunity to cook us breakfast. He would make eggs or pancakes or French toast, none of which I liked at the time. One morning I was very hungry, but I knew I was not going to eat what Doug was making. When he was not looking and no one was in the kitchen, I pushed a chair up to the refrigerator, so that I could reach the cookies in the jar on top. Even with the chair, I still had difficulty getting to them. The jar was heavy, and I thought I would drop it. I stepped on the stove, which was next to the refrigerator, to give myself more leverage. Accidentally, I stepped on the handle of a frying pan that was melting hot butter. The pan flipped into the air and poured the hot butter down the entire lower half of my body. Doug heard the thump when I hit the floor and the screaming when the heat became trapped in my flame retardant pajamas. Without a second thought, he scooped me into his arms and put me in the tub. Immediately turning on the water of the shower, he soaked me from head to toe. He practically drowned me in the process. He kept me there for what seemed like a life time. I was freezing and uncomfortable, but the burning feeling was gone. Every one came running to see what the commotion was. Slowly pealing off my pajamas with the help of the others, we were all amazed that aside from having a few red marks, I didn't have a burn on me. We never told Mom. We were all late for school that morning. Doug wrote the excuse notes.

Joe called one night from the ship he was on. He had an announcement...He had enlisted for another three years. This bothered Stuart, Dylan and Veronica. They had a mother who had abandoned them and now a father who didn't seem to want them either. I have to say, none of us were thrilled by the prospect of it. My mom tried to keep it light, although I knew she also felt that it was a terrible thing for him to do. She told the kids that if he added three more years, he would be able to get a better pension and therefore be able to buy them a better house. Then everything was going to be perfect. We weren't sophisticated enough to express it, but we all felt it: if you had never had anything in your life, how would you know what you missed? All they had ever wanted was their mother and father, the two people they couldn't have. Meanwhile, our family was growing and changing. We were getting older, and we had always been a tall family. It is one thing to have a bunch of children running around in a small apartment; it's a whole different story having adult sized people all living under the same, small roof. The little things that we had taken for granted, we could no longer do. Because there were so many of us, and we now each bathed alone, we would run out of hot water before the eighth bather had a chance. We had to do this in shifts, both morning and night. We no longer fit all together on the couch to watch TV. Because we were not all yet teenagers, we still did many things like this together. That Christmas, we all got beanbag chairs. They had to stay in our rooms, unless we were all together in the living room. It went on like this for months, but somehow we made it work.

Another night, Joe called again; he was expected home on leave for a few weeks and had a surprise for his kids. He wouldn't tell any of us what it was, not even Mom; at least, that's what she told us. The day he was expected home, we were all excited...about the surprise, that is. We still remembered the last time he had been home on leave. For weeks, we children would congregate in one of the bedrooms and try to guess what he was bringing. Jake always acted as if he didn't care, and he probably didn't. We made lists and held lotteries to see who would guess correctly. Dylan was certain it was a unicycle. We hid this list from Mom, because she would have gotten irritated if she knew we were obsessing about this. Of course, the gift was meant for Joe's kids and not us. I didn't care; I was just getting caught up in the excitement. We waited for him on the porch all day. At about 2:00 PM, a cab pulled up. The gift walked out first...it was a new mom.

CHAPTER: 11

She was average height with brown wavy hair to her shoulders. She wore glasses and looked like a librarian to me.

"Who do you think that is?" I asked.

"I can tell you," said Veronica. "It is our new mother."

"Would he really get you a new mother without you guys meeting her first?"

"Barbara, stop being so naive," said Veronica. "In his eyes, if she is comfortable, reliable, and is good for the long haul, then we don't have a say."

"You make it sound like he is buying a used car." "In a way...he is" Turning to Dylan, she added, "You'd better be on your best behavior."

My mother was already out on the sidewalk to meet them. She threw her arms around Joe, first, and then turned to the new mother and welcomed her to the family. We all watched the awkward hug exchange between the two women.

Martha was her name, and she was from Maine. Joe had been stationed there, and that's how they met. Martha was a nice, subservient type of woman.

"Veronica, Stuart, and Dylan, this is Martha. We are getting married in a few weeks, and I want to take you guys out to dinner, so you can get to know one another." I had learned over my little contact with Joe, that everything with him was either a statement or a command. The kids quietly went to get their coats. No one said a word. I sat back on the chair in the far corner, watching this entire scene play before me, as if I were watching one of my mother's soap operas. I didn't say anything either. After they left, I went to my room for some long needed alone time. I took out my sketch book and began to draw. I used to draw lions a lot back then. I had this fascination with their strength and pride. This time I drew a lioness and her cubs.

When they arrived back home, an hour and a half later, I was waiting anxiously at the window. I wanted to see the attitude that walked through the door. I knew that what they said wasn't always what they felt. I wanted to see their faces to find the truth. Everyone was smiling and seemed happy; I was glad. She was kind to the kids and understood that Joe was boss. My mother evicted the tenants upstairs, in order to give Joe and Martha the apartment. The day they moved in was filled with enthusiasm. Everyone helped. A feeling of joy was in the air. We were all laughing and joking and teasing. My family was returning to normal again; whatever that was, we no longer knew. By evening, my cousins were all moved in on the floor above us. That first night we spent alone again in our own apartment felt odd and empty. Something was missing. It was so quiet. No longer was there activity in every room. Gil, Jake and my mother were in the living room watching TV. Doug was working late at the hospital. We found we could choose wherever we wanted to sit. The bean bag chairs stayed in our rooms. My mother was sitting on the couch. I cuddled up next to her as close as I could; she wrapped her arm around me, neither of us saying a word. Later that evening, I filled the tub with hot water and bubbles. I didn't emerge until two hours later. Veronica's bedroom was above mine. I could hear her moving her belongings around the room. She was listening to her new record player (we both had a collection of forty fives back then). The song she was listening to was by Creedence Clearwater Revival. I felt lonely. Shadow Man returned that night to keep me company. I talked to him all night.

Over the course of the next few weeks, the two apartments melded into one, and Joe went back to sea. It was hard for us kids to understand the boundaries. Our moms knew this was going to take time and let us float between the two. The cousins called Martha "Mom" right from the start, at Joe's insistence. Having failed at this once, Veronica and Dylan were reprimanded, so it was easier to just call her Mom. I called her Aunt Martha. The two mothers seemed to get along ok. I wouldn't say they were real close, but they did coordinate this melding of families. It was not unusual, back then, to be asked which kitchen you were going to eat in each night. And if the program that was on our TV set didn't appeal to us, there was always another choice just a staircase away. Martha loved to knit and would often be seen making one project or another. Veronica and I would sit with her, and she taught us how to knit and crochet as well. My first knitting project was a poncho. It was hot pink and purple and took one long curved needle to produce. The pattern was always hard for me to read, but Martha had an infinite amount of patience in that area. I could never get the tautness of the stitches right. When it was finished, and I put it on for the first time, it hung to my ankles. The fact that Martha was teaching me to knit as a left-handed person may have had something to do with it, because I was right-handed. We won't even get into the matching mittens I tried to make after that. Eventually I stuck to embroidery.

Veronica and I still walked to school with Cherri and our other friends. And we were still in different classes. We shared lunch together, always saving each other a seat. At recess, we froze together in the school yard in our flimsy tights, waiting for the bell to ring, craning our necks to find the boys we secretly loved. For me, it was Mark. He wasn't a boy we had known since first grade, like we did the others. He had moved to Salem from Beverly at the beginning of that year and lived on North Street. He was different from the boys we grew up with in other ways as well. He was short, with a massive mane of thick soft hair. He didn't try to impress the girls by being loud and obnoxious, a trait I was soon learning I didn't like in my "boyfriends." I was attracted to the quiet types. They intrigued me. What was going on in their heads? To me, that was the attraction.

One autumn day, while walking home from school, I was carrying an armful of books. My book bag had ripped earlier that day in math class, so I had thrown it out. My arms were piled six books high, with the middle one wanting to escape. My papers were tucked helter skelter among each one. I was also holding a treasured drawing between my thumb and forefinger, hoping against all hope that the wind wouldn't pick up, when all of a sudden, an unsuspecting rock crossed my path. I stepped on the edge of it with my right toes. This caused me to tumble and twirl in an awkward dance, with my books slipping and sliding from my grasp. My feet were finding it difficult to keep up with the upper half of my body. Cherri tried her best to catch me, but her arms were filled with books as well. I put up a good fight with this unfortunate circumstance, but in the end I lost. My books went flying in all different directions and landed on the ground. They flew open from the impact and all my papers were escaping and flapping wildly throughout the neighborhood. I followed their descent shortly after and found myself flat on my stomach. My precious drawing, still pinched between my fingers, was ripped down the middle.

"Oh man, are you ok, Barbara?" Cherri, putting down her books, grabbed me by the arm to lift me to my feet. While she was doing that, some boys from our class started to laugh very loudly, as they stepped over me and all the debris. Looking back at us, one said, "What an idiot." That just brought more laughter. I was so humiliated. I didn't even have the emotional strength to retrieve my papers. Then, out of nowhere, Mark showed up.

"Forget about those morons, Barbara. They are just being mean. Here, I found some of your papers." Gathering the rest of my fallen books, he looked me in the eye and smiled the friendliest smile. With my gravel pitted cheeks, I smiled back. He walked home with us that day and every day after. Sometimes he would hold my hand. He wasn't ashamed of our friendship, like boys usually are with girls at that age. My relationship with Mark was a very innocent one. We never even kissed. Before the sixth grade was over, when we would be going back to the Pickering school for seventh, he moved back to Beverly. I felt his absence greatly.

Cherri was the smart one in the group. She read all the time. She had every Nancy Drew book ever written. Between Veronica and me, we were lucky if we could come up with a complete set of encyclopedias. Reading was not my mom's strong point. I never asked Cherri to borrow one of her books, although I wanted to many times. I was afraid my family would make fun of me, if they saw me reading. Cherri was also good at math, dispelling the myth I had believed that no one can be smart at everything. The sad part was that I wanted to do well in school. But when my homework got hard, my mom didn't know enough about it to help me. I would spend hours on my homework, only get to school the next day and realize I had done it all wrong. Even though I got B's and C's on my report card, I felt the school was making a big mistake, and maybe I should stay back. Art was a different story. I could draw anything I saw. It was the one thing I could do that no one in my class could. With this, I was a star. And with this, I would escape.

Later that night, Veronica and I realized that we had a hole in our closets that gapped my ceiling and her floor. It was left over from when a pipe had been removed years earlier. At night, we would write secret messages and pass them through. They were innocent writings about boys we thought were cute and injustices of parents. One night the message got caught in the hole, and we could never send another. I'm sure that message is still there today.

We cohabited like this for months; then Joe retired from the Navy. Although Martha was not the stronger of the two in the relationship, she did develop a sense of concern for the children. She enlisted my mother to help her speak to Joe about the way in which he spoke to them. Soon they no longer had to stand at attention and be inspected. He was still very strict, something she would learn she could never change. During this time, Joe and my mother became very close again. One of their common bonds was dealing with my Aunt Tina. Tina's family was everything it should have been and, even as a child, I felt this sense of tension between the three of them. The stress went far back, long before any of us children were ever born. Joe was the oldest, and then came my mother and Cheryl. Tina was the youngest in their family and more fragile than the rest. They all seemed to agree that she had been spoiled by my grandmother. At times she often felt afraid. When my grandmother and grandfather passed away, years later, this seemed to escalate. She began to have trouble going out of the house and doing simple tasks like grocery shopping. When she would attempt these rituals, she would find herself in a panic attack and needed to call someone. She would require reassurance with this and would seek out our family for help. My mom and Joe would become impatient with her, and not unlike Stuart had seemed to my brothers, would consider her weak. Weakness was never tolerated in my family. It was a sign of defeat, something they were ashamed to have others see. They often said she was crazy and suffered from some emotional illness. I don't know where the truth lies in all this; I only remember her being kind to me. She couldn't have been too crazy; I spent many days at Tina's house playing with her girls, who were younger than I was. She would make the best homemade apple pies and was tolerant of my eating habits. Everything that Tina made was from scratch. This was a big difference from my mother, who only knew how to open a can. It was sad to see their relationship, and many times I would feel torn. When Tina would feel her siblings were being mean to her, she would call them on it. She would repeat her case, over and over, in a kind of mantra. This only convinced them more that she was a fanatic. It had never occurred to them that perhaps they should have listened to her. They were in desperate need of counseling, this extended family of mine. But to admit this would also be a sign of weakness. So instead, they let the situation fester until, finally, they were no longer talking at all.

CHAPTER: 12

When Veronica and I entered the seventh grade, I went back to the Pickering school that had now turned into a junior high school, and she and her family moved to New Hampshire. Our long talks about boys were over, as well as the stress of having her in my life.

Their new house was in Rochester. I remember seeing it only once. The images of it are blurry to me; I couldn't tell you what it looked like. When we did see the cousins, it was only on holidays, and they always came down to see us. With each turn of the calendar, the relationship between Veronica and me began to wane. In the first hour of our meeting, we felt like we were total strangers, instead of the cousins who had shared a home. I felt an awkwardness that stemmed from what I saw as my own inadequacy. She somehow seemed more developed than I and looked more like she was sixteen than twelve. Suddenly, there was a silence that had never been there before. It was difficult for us to push past these feelings, but we never stopped trying. After awhile, we would find ourselves sitting on the bed we had once shared, laughing and talking about boys, just like old times. This usually was when they were about to leave, once more giving me a sense of what I'd lost. Because I needed this connection with another girl my age, Cherri and I began to hang around with each other more and more.

In seventh grade, I found myself getting into a lot of unwanted fist fights with other girls. The first one was the history making one with Phyllis Blaisdell. She was a girl who had moved upstairs when the cousins moved out. The Blaisdells were a large family. My mother had met their mother at Parker Brothers, where she worked, a woman with seven kids and a reclusive husband, who didn't work. I couldn't figure out what my mother had been thinking when she rented them this apartment. Three of the kids were teenagers. Phyllis was a year younger than I was, and her brother Tim was a mentally handicapped boy who was my age. They also had a set of twins who were really young. The teenage girls always had a different boyfriend every week and drove very fast in their cars up and down the street. They were bullies, and I stayed away from them as much as possible. They were loud and obnoxious, and my mother had to constantly call them on the phone to stop them from banging on the floor. Tim, the mentally handicapped boy, was a strong kid who had trouble controlling his urges. He was bigger than I in both weight and height. The first day I met him, I was coming out of the house, and he grabbed me by my waist length hair and started biting it in a very sexual way. I was traumatized!

"MOM! MOM! HELP ME!" My mother was at my side in a flash.

"Oh my God, Tim, let go of her!" My mother tried to act as calm as she could, but I could still hear the quivering in her voice. Putting her hands on his stubby unformed ones, she tried to force him to let go. They were grasped tightly in my hair, close to my scalp; she tried her best to pry him off. I could feel his mouth on the back of my head; I could smell his breakfast. His saliva dripped down my neck. His teeth grazed my mother's hands, and she started bleeding onto my hair. He was making growling sounds of pleasure. I tried everything I had in me not to faint.

"Linda! Come help me!" she screamed to his mother, whom we hoped was in ear shot. Linda was at our side in a second. I instantly got the feeling that this was something she had to control on a daily basis. Talking to him sternly, she was able to free me from his grasp. I didn't look at him or anyone else. I ran to my room in tears and hid in my closet. I was afraid to go out after that, without looking first to see if he was outside.

Phyllis was another problem. She stood only five feet tall, if she was lucky. I was five seven. She soon became the meanest kid on the street. At school she also had this reputation; she teased and tormented anyone she came upon. She would harp on various issues with people and not let up until they wanted to pound her or, worse, break down and cry.

"That is the ugliest hair cut I have ever seen. I hope you didn't pay for that." Phyllis was tormenting Monica, who lived next door. Monica had tried her hand at being a hairdresser that morning and had ended up with a misshapened bowl on her head. She had been trying to give herself a "pixie" cut.

"I kind of like it," I said, with a smile. "It shows a daring sense of individuality."

Phyllis just looked at me with her penetrating eyes. "What do you think you are, a dictionary? Who talks like that?" I put my arm around Monica and said, "Come on, let's go to my house and play in my room." We left Phyllis sitting by herself on the steps. I was hoping she would eventually get the hint and change her ways.

When Phyllis did fight physically, she usually won. She was small but incredibly strong. When we were outside, she would force herself upon us and join in with our games. Not wanting to create any friction with her, most of the kids in the neighborhood would allow it. I found myself always trying to divert attention, so that arguments and fights wouldn't happen when she joined us. It was a difficult time, and not very fun and relaxing. Despite my efforts, it never went well. She couldn't help herself; she would start in on someone, and the next thing you knew, everyone went home. She had a tendency to target certain kids. These were usually ones who couldn't defend themselves. It was at this point in my life that I became empathetic to kids that were being picked on. It reminded me of the pain I had felt when I watched Sally being teased by everyone in my kindergarten class. My mother thought it was an unhealthy obsession of mine, this vigilante streak I was developing. She said it would land me in trouble. I would argue with her that someone had to do it. To stand back and do nothing would be wrong, and besides, two wrongs never make a right. I started to stand up to Phyllis for the sake of the others. I was the tallest on the street and always the negotiator. If there were an injustice, I couldn't stand around and do nothing. Phyllis was half my size and a year younger, so I kept my hands to myself when I spoke to her and just defended everyone to her with my words. This made me a target. She started teasing me, calling me names every time she saw me, pushing me from behind in front of the others. I told her I was not going to fight her, because I might hurt her. She only laughed in my face and told everyone I was just a big chicken. I knew if she kept tormenting me, my anger and strength would overpower her, and she wouldn't have a chance. Every day she kept it up. I was able to hold back for about two months. Then one day, Cherri and I were walking home from school:

"I know you have explained it to me a million times, but Cherri, I just cannot wrap my head around word problems."

"Why? What did you get on the test?"

"I got a 34%! Who gets a 34%? ME! I DO, BECAUSE IN MATH I AM STUPID!!!!" I was beginning to get all worked up. I felt so beaten, with nowhere to turn on this subject. I felt like my back was up against a wall, and like a caged lion, I had no way out. My defeatist attitude was turning more and more to anger, as I tried to plead my case. "WHY DO WE NEED TO KNOW THIS CRAP ANYWAY? I DON"T CARE HOW MANY MILES IT TAKES BOB TO USE UP TEN DOLLARS WORTH OF GAS!" I could feel it. I was beginning to peak. Any minute now I knew I would cry, especially since I had to show the Head of the War Department my test, have her sign it and bring it back tomorrow. As Cherri was about to try and reassure me, out of the blue came a fist that hit me square in the jaw. I fell over backwards, not knowing what had happened. When I looked up from the pavement I was now sprawled on, it was Phyllis' smiling and condescending face I saw.

"What's the matter, chicken? Are you going to cry?"

The anger began at my toes. It felt like a tingling, itch sensation that I couldn't scratch. All of a sudden every injustice I had ever felt or witnessed came flooding into my mind. There before me was my father throwing the sugar bowl, the house that had a hot top yard, my first grade teacher shaking me by the arm, Veronica taking half of everything I owned, and there, in the midst of it all, stood Phyllis, with her grinning face egging me on.

I was on my feet in a flash. I grabbed her by the arm and twisting it, I tossed her in the air and onto her back. Before I knew what was happening, I straddled her and started punching her left and right in the face. Blood was everywhere. We were both covered in it. Two black eyes were starting to emerge. It was obvious I had won the fight, but I wouldn't stop. That's when Cherri tried to bring me back to reality.

"You're going to kill her!" she yelled. Cherri pulled me off her, and we stood there for a moment, looking at the damage I had done. She was a bloody heap on the ground and crying. I had never seen her this vulnerable, and I felt awful. I was the one who didn't like bullies, and now, in my eyes, I was one.

My first instinct was to help her up. Her arm, that I had initially twisted, was pointing at an odd angle. I knew what that meant. I had been the victim of that before. I tried to talk to her and tell her I was sorry. When I tried, she just yelled at me as loud as she could.

"GET AWAY FROM ME!" Then she said something I had not thought of until that moment: "I'm going to get my sisters after you!" My blood ran cold. Her sisters were big and twice as mean as she was. Cherri said, "I think we should get out of here." We started running down the street, separating at the end of the intersection to reach our individual homes. The last thing I heard was Cherri's distant voice yelling to me, "Call me tonight and let me know what happened!"

When I arrived home, no one was there. I immediately locked all the doors and ran into my room. Frantically pacing back and forth, I felt there was no place to hide. With this violent family only a floor above me, I knew it was going to be a fruitless effort. I was sure her sisters were going to kill me, or, worse, I was going to jail for having killed Phyllis. I did the only thing a child could do. Grabbing my faithful stuffed dog Squeeker, I hid in my closet. Despite the tight quarters, Shadow Man sat with me. I couldn't see him. This time I could only feel him. I cried into the darkness that I was sure was his shoulder.

"Shadow Man, I want to be a good person. Am I a failure?" A warmth settled around me, as the rapid beating of my heart began to slow in its pace. I stayed in the closet until I heard my mother's key open the front door an hour later. When I slowly emerged from my room, I burst into tears.

"Mom, I think I hurt Phyllis real bad." I felt bad for what I had done and knew I couldn't change it. For the first time in my life, I felt like a bully, the one thing in this world I couldn't tolerate. I had lowered myself to their level and didn't like it. I tried to explain to Mom about the fight and my lack of control. It took my mother a few minutes to understand what I was saying.

"You? What do mean, you hurt her? What did you do?"

I was getting more hysterical with every word. "I was talking to Cherri...then a fist...and then the blood. I was shaking so bad!" She began to get impatient with me and started yelling.

"BARBARA, PULL IT TOGETHER! TELL ME RIGHT NOW WHAT HAPPENED!" This brought me back to reality, and I calmed down enough to tell her what had transpired. I told her the whole story about the two months of torment. She seemed to understand. I remembered her outburst at Mrs. Durham and knew I was not at fault in her eyes. I felt I had an ally, and that made me feel safe once more. She picked up the phone to call upstairs. She was informed, with attitude, that Phyllis was with her mother at the hospital and was not home yet. Mom looked at me and said, "What exactly did you do to her?"

"I think I broke her nose," I said.

My mother's voice was barely a whisper, as she stared off into that unseen place she sometimes went , "Barbara, they said you may have broken her arm."

Meanwhile, back at the fight scene an hour earlier, other kids had started to happen upon Phyllis as she was trying to make her way home. Whether they actually helped her, I don't know. She was a mess, and everyone saw it. Word spread quickly in the neighborhood. The wicked witch was dead. And I was the hero, but the news had not gotten back to me yet. Instead I sat all night on my bed with Shadow Man and counted sheep.

The following day Phyllis was out of school. Rumors were spreading like crazy; one even said she was still in the hospital, but she wasn't. Even the teachers heard about it. They all gave me a look of both surprise and bewilderment but kept their thoughts to themselves. I was dreading lunch time and shared my concerns with Cherri. "You don't get it," she said. "Everyone is glad you did that. She has tormented enough people around here, so that no one is crying any tears over her." I knew I should have felt empowered, but instead I felt like a large ogre. At the lunch table, kids were coming up to me, wanting all the juicy details. Kids who had never given me the time of day in the past were patting me on the back. I thought of Phyllis and wondered if she had ever realized this many people didn't like her. My heart was aching; it must be horrible to go through life with so many people thinking badly of you. That kind of atmosphere I knew must be somehow contributing to who she was. I felt sorry for her. In the meantime, people were staring at me in a way I had never seen before. It was called respect.

The next day Phyllis came to school with two black eyes and a large bandage on her nose. Her arm was in a sling.

For a few months, against my wishes, I found myself in the middle of several fights ... some were with bullies who didn't like the idea that others thought I could beat them. These were always the same. They would catch me off guard to try and get the advantage. In all the fights I was in, I never threw the first punch. I fought either in self defense or in defense of someone else. Out of fear for my life and with the benefit of pure adrenaline, I always won. No one ever realized this and most became afraid of me. These fights were always off school grounds, a fact that all kids secretly knew was best. My science teacher started calling me slugger. He would smile when he said it, because he knew I wasn't starting these fights, only defending myself. The faculty turned a blind eye to all this violence. I felt there was no use trying to get adult support, because that would label me in a different way. In reality, I hated to fight. The few times I knew I was going to fight after school, I would have a horrible day of stomachaches, sweats, and the ever constant hand trembles. After three such fights, I became a kind of crusader. It was a role I had never asked for. If someone were picking on another kid, I would be expected to step in and stop it. I was pressured into it by people I thought were my friends. Sometimes this resulted in another fight, but mostly the bullies just backed down.

Then Lauren moved to our district and started attending our school. She had a difficult time adjusting. Overcompensating, she would do and say things that irritated the others. No one liked her. I naturally felt bad for her. I could see she wanted friends but didn't know how to go about it. She was in my group in school, so I befriended her. At lunch she sat with Cherri and me. I don't think Cherri approved, but she said nothing. After school, Lauren walked halfway home with us. Then, one day, she angered the last tough girl I had not yet fought...Sharon. Sharon was someone I was really afraid of. She was strong and tall like me, but unlike me, she was mean, a combination of traits that I was sure would work to her advantage. Sharon approached Lauren and said she was going to "kill her" after school. Lauren, naturally, approached me. Everyone assumed I would fight this fight. It felt like the fight of the century to the others, and they were anxious with anticipation. To back out then was impossible. If I went home with complaints of an ailment, the fight would still be waiting for me the next day. I was stuck. I wasn't mad at Lauren, though I probably should have been. I was angrier at the injustice of cliques. By lunch time, the whole school knew what was going to happen. After lunch, I was called into the office alone. To my surprise, my mother was there, and she and my principal wanted to know what was going on.

"Barbara, what on earth is all this I hear about you fighting?" My mother led the conversation, as my principal sat back in his chair.

"I didn't start any of these fights, I swear. The kids in this school are really mean, and the teachers just sit there and let them bully people. Well, I can't just sit there. Everyone is counting on me to stop it."

I saw a look of pride cross my mother's face. Turning to the principal she stated, "What are you going to do about this? My daughter should not have to feel she is the one policing your school."

Looking me directly in the eye, the principal said, "I promise to take care of all future bullying, if you promise me that you won't fight anymore."

"I promise not to get into any fights, if you promise I am not put in a position to feel I have to." So began my habit of talking to teachers as if they were my equals. Sharon and I never did fight that afternoon, to the chagrin of all the others. After school, we were called into the office to settle things. I was surprised to find out that she was as afraid of me as I was of her. The matter was resolved, and we never spoke of it. When asked by our peers why we didn't fight, we simply said we all sat down and talked about it and decided it was a bad idea. Then we told them that the principal had said that if we fought we would get suspended. This was the dialogue the principle said we should use, even though he didn't mean it. The next day, to back up our story, he called an assembly. He told the entire school that if anyone was caught fighting both parties would be suspended immediately. It worked. That year, the students never fought again.

CHAPTER: 13

In seventh grade, I had my first official boyfriend. Mark, who had walked me home from school in sixth grade, was just a friend compared to this new relationship. This boy was in high school and harmless compared to most boys my age. He was the paper boy in our neighborhood and lived in the next town, Peabody, close to Cherri's house. His name was Gary, and he was tall, blond, and a sophomore in high school. Our relationship was an innocent one. We would often go to Mack Park to sit, talk, and kiss. The talking never got too serious; after all, we were young. Mostly he talked about cars and magic tricks. He was a paid magician and one time used me in his act, when Cherri and I unexpectedly went to see him perform at the Willows. I didn't like being the center of attention and told him not to call on me again. The Willows was an amusement park in Salem. It had ski ball, rides and food. It was situated on the water, and at night they had concerts. Gary and I would often ride our bikes to the Willows. For very little money, it was a place to have fun. One time, when we were there, I saw a bunch of girls from my class at school. The next day everyone knew about Gary by the time the first bell rang.

"Barbara, who was that blond guy you were with at the Willows last night?" asked Polly Perkins, a nosey busybody at school.

"Oh he is just a friend," I said. "Just a friend...then why did I see you holding hands and kissing?"

"Because, Polly, that is the type of friend he is." I walked away to show that this was the end of the discussion. The last thing I needed was to have her blabbing my business all over school. Too late, the damage was done. I heard the giggles behind me fade as I turned the corner in the hall. Cherri walked next to me and didn't say a word. I liked that about Cherri; she always knew when I wanted to talk about something and when it was best to leave it alone.

As usual, I was a bit out of the loop on what makes a person popular. Before I knew it, I was a kind of celebrity among adolescent girls. To the boys, I became somewhat intriguing. Well, for a week anyway, then it went back to the way it was before.

I enjoyed being with Gary. We spent more time at his house, because it was bigger and had a nicer yard and was more private. I was embarrassed to tell my family about him. It would be difficult, but I knew I had to do it. At first, my family teased me about this relationship, including Gil and my mom. They would make kissing sounds at me whenever he called me on the phone. I would turn red, face the wall and talk to him in whispers. Even with all the bantering at my expense, Gil and Mom never made a big deal about his age. How could they, when Gil was twenty years older than Mom? Gary began to hang out with Cherri and me on Irving Street. Cherri was the oldest of three kids and often had to stay close to home to keep an eye on them. She lived with her mother and grandmother. Like me, she hadn't seen her father since she was very young. Unfortunately my relationship with Gary wouldn't last long. After awhile, he and I drifted apart. Our interests were changing, and we had no room for each other in our lives. He no longer came to Irving street.

The O'Neils, the family who had lived next door to me on School Street, now lived across the street from Cherri. Although the parents had divorced, the kids' behavior had not changed. Cherri only hung around with the younger girls; I think the older ones were too advanced for her liking. I didn't blame her. They were too advanced for me as well. They weren't bad kids, but they were certainly living life to its fullest. They were so alive, in fact, they were pushing life to its boundaries. Peter, in the meantime, acted like I no longer existed. That was ok for me; I wasn't interested in him anyway. My mother was still friends with Sharon, but she didn't see her that often. One morning when I was walking into my house, my mother was crying. I had not seen her do that for a long time. She asked me if I had heard the news. I said, "What news?" She said Donna, Sharon's oldest daughter, had gone for a drive with some boys in their car and had gotten into a terrible accident. I asked if she were dead. She told me no but said she might die. She was at Salem Hospital, and my mother was heading there as soon as she could pull herself together. She told me they had hit the chain link fence at the Bates School, and the pipe had gone through her chest. It had missed her heart by less than an inch. She said the boys had just left her, because they thought she was dead. When the fire department arrived, she woke up. They couldn't believe she was still alive. They cut the bar on the front and back of her and brought her to the hospital with it still inside her. They had to remove part of her lung and her left breast. The last thing Mom said before she left was, "I never want you to get into a car with a boy." Then she closed the door. Donna lived through that, but the outcome of her poor judgment was a strong lesson in my life. It removed any of the young notions that most kids have about their own immortality. For the first time, I saw how precious life is.

Cherri lived in a predominantly Portuguese neighborhood. There was a beautiful girl who lived on her street and was a year younger then we were, named Adelia. She had thick, waist length auburn hair and spoke with a delicate voice. She was the type of girl who was so perfect in so many ways that you had to evaluate yourself. She came from a strict family and often had to do the things that were normally reserved for mothers, like food shopping. This made her very mature. She would play street games with us if she weren't expected to do some family chore, like cook dinner. At times when she was with us, she was just one of the kids. She liked that and needed that connection. One day after all her work was done, she emerged from the house with a strange look on her face.

Putting my arm around her shoulder, I asked. "Adelia, are you ok? What's the matter?" She burst into tears and could barely speak. When she did, we were all shocked by what she said.

"I have to move to Portugal. I am to be married to a man there who is waiting for me." "WHAT? YOU ARE ONLY THIRTEEN!" I was outraged by this news. "Have you ever met him?" asked Cherri. "No, he is twenty years old." Her voice quivered as she spoke these words. "I leave next week."

We couldn't believe it! All this time she was being trained to be a wife. Over the course of that week, we tried to think of ways to stop this event. We thought of having her live in Cherri's cellar. But what kind of life would that be, and how would we keep it secret? Adelia was so distraught; out of desperation, I went to my mother and asked for help. She couldn't believe that people still made arranged marriages and was upset by it. She also knew there was nothing we could do and told me so. The day of Adelia's exodus, we sat on the curb and watched. Sitting in the backseat of her father's car, she gave us a tearful wave goodbye and was gone. We never saw her again. It felt like a huge injustice, and yet it was arranged by the ones who loved her, her family. Although I already lived in a diverse community, it wasn't until this event that I learned its true meaning.

That was the summer the O'Neil's moved away, and a Portuguese family moved into their old house. They had lots of kids and the oldest was a boy our age who didn't speak English. Robbie became Cherri's boyfriend. I, in the meantime, became friendly with Aaron. He was also Portuguese but was born here and spoke only English. Aaron was very handsome and shaved by the time he was nine. Aaron was the community boyfriend. Eventually, everyone had gone out with him. It was, at that time, my turn. He was a great kisser and must have spent a long time practicing on a mirror. We didn't mind that we were all his girlfriends at some point; none of us were serious anyway. He was funny and would always make us laugh, especially with his impersonations of Cher. In the summer, we would all sit on the steps of an abandoned house at the top of Irving Street and talk about what we would be when we grew up. I immediately thought about the imaginary woman sitting with me so long ago at Greenlawn Cemetery. Aaron jokingly got down on one knee and proposed to me. He said we could live in this house---we would fix it up. Then he proceeded to explain the décor we would have. He had it down to the minute details, including the curtains we would have in our kitchen. I laughingly told him to stop. It was too much for me to hear about decorating from a boy his age; it scared me.

Together, we spent that summer teaching Robbie to communicate. It wasn't organized, like it would have been in a classroom setting. Instead, we taught him English by playing innocent games like Red Rover and Spin the Bottle. One day, we found a deck of cards and decided to play Strip Poker. Cherri and I were pretty good at this game. At first it looked like we weren't going to have to remove anything, while the boys were down to their underwear. After we lost a few rounds and had already removed our shoes and socks, we girls changed our minds and wouldn't play anymore. They just laughed at us, and called us "chicken." We were all together constantly. We spent many rainy days listening to Aerosmith and Led Zeppelin. Music was an important element in kids' lives. Aaron and I had a short lived fame that at the first school dance we were the first to slow dance together...the song playing was Lynyrd Skynyrd's "Freebird." Cherri had a room in her cellar that had black lights on the wall and psychedelic posters. It was our own little home away from home, a place for teens to escape, a place where the music became our world.

The Monroes were another family in the neighborhood who were our friends. They had two girls our age. Tony was my age, her sister Jenny was older. The Monroes came from a horrible home environment. Their mother was a passive woman, who worked many hours and was rarely home. Their father had a terrible drinking problem and worked nights. He was also abusive and would often beat them horribly. We would all be playing outside, when he would bellow one of their names from the top window. Our blood would run cold, and the poor victim of his anger would slowly go and see what he wanted. It was always the same. We would then all sit sullen and helpless on the curb and listen to the cries of one of the Monroe girls as Mr. Monroe let out his anger violently. The sounds of the beatings were horrible. Sometimes it sounded like he was throwing furniture at them. Most times they didn't have to have done anything wrong; he just had to be in a bad mood. Afterwards they would come back out of the house with brave looks on their faces, usually sporting a bruise.

"Tony, you need to tell someone about this. This is just not right." We were all pleading with her after her last beating.

"I can't, he will hurt me more."

"But you can't live this way. What if we tell the school?"

"NO! THEN THEY WILL MAKE HIM MOVE OUT, AND MY MOM WILL GET MAD, BECAUSE WE WONT HAVE ENOUGH MONEY!" She was so adamant about this that she would cry, so we never did...we should have anyway...but we were only kids.

There was another evil that lurked on Irving Street for the Monroe girls. His name was Mr.

Goodhue. He was a man who was in his late sixties, and lived in the neighborhood. He saw what Mr. Monroe was doing to his children and took advantage of the situation. He befriended the Monroe girls and allowed them to spend time at his house. He would make them lunch, let them watch TV and showed them a kindness they had never felt before. Over time, Mr. Goodhue, using his loving kindness, convinced each Monroe girl to pose naked for pictures and perform oral sex. For this he would give each of them a quarter. When he would request these acts, he would stand in his doorway and call to the girls, pulling them away from our street games. After a while, we became suspicious of this relationship he had with them and insisted on knowing the truth. Tony was the one who caved in first.

"Tony, where are you going? It is your turn."

"I have to go. I will be back in a minute." When she returned, we pressed her for answers. Eventually, over a period of months, she told us everything. The details were of the likes we had never heard before. I thought I was going to vomit when I heard it. My heart in my chest tightened with fear for her. Cherri and I were appalled. We told her that it was wrong, and he was evil. I wanted to report him too, but Tony said her father would kill her if he found out. We all knew this wasn't just an expression she was using. He probably would have. Instead, Cherri and I made it our mission to convince Tony not to go there anymore. With her we succeeded, but unfortunately, with her sister, we could not. I agonized about this dilemma; I wanted to go to my mother. I was afraid that if I did, she wouldn't let me play on Irving Street anymore. So I never did, and no one ever told.

Other things were happening in my family life as well. Gil and my mother began to have difficulties with their relationship. Gil had a history of a drinking problem, although, until this point, we had never witnessed it firsthand. When it did start to emerge, it escalated rapidly. At first he would come home late, and then he would not come home at all. I could feel my mother get more and more agitated as the night wore on. She would call the local bars looking for him and never believe them when they said he wasn't there. This would frustrate her, and she would rant and rave about it, but mostly to herself. When she was in this mood, Jake and I would hide out in our rooms. We never spoke of this situation with each other, enduring it silently in our separate quarters. Doug would just leave the house---that is how he would deal with it. When Gil eventually strolled into the house, at all hours of the night, he would be drunk and apologetic. He would trip over the furniture, toppling candy dishes and figurines and slurring his speech. It was pathetic to see him look this helpless. My mother wouldn't let up on him and would needle him for hours, until finally she would reduce him to near tears. He was a man with a serious problem, and she emasculated him every time he slipped up. But I'm not sure which came first. Did she emasculate him because he drank, or did he drink because she emasculated him? In time, I'm not sure even they could have answered that question. I always felt that Gil could not control this behavior. Although he was never mean and abusive, I didn't like it when he drank. I didn't like how it upset my environment. Regardless, drinking was always an issue for my mother; an issue I'm sure that was left over from her own childhood. This behavior went on for months, until one day, after a night of celebrating; he came home with his son. Jimmy was in his thirties and was his son from a previous marriage which had dissolved long before he met my mother. The two of them had been drinking all night, and, by midnight, Gil was afraid to face my mother by himself. He thought Jimmy would soften the blow. It was odd for me to see him do this, because, as a kid, I had done this many times with my own friends, when I had to deal with my mother.

I was up late in my room working on a painting, when the men came through the door and the fight began. My mother, having paced the floor all night, had already made a decision about their relationship. She had decided that she would throw him out. I heard Jimmy pleading with her that it was his fault, not Gil's. Jimmy was happy about something that had happened that day, and they were celebrating together.

"Jane, Dad wanted to leave. It is my fault I wouldn't let him."

"He has a mind of his own. He still could have left. It doesn't matter anymore, because he doesn't live here." Taking his clothes, she threw them out the front door. This angered Jimmy, and, in a split second, he snapped. He was screaming at her about how unreasonable she was being. Then he started throwing furniture around the room. I stood in the doorway that led to the living room and watched as all our precious belongings were being destroyed. I was afraid for my mother. She didn't let up. She was yelling at Jimmy, showing no fear. Meanwhile Gil was pleading with him to stop. He was genuinely upset and was apologizing to everyone, even me. What we saw that night was horrific. Jimmy reminded me of a large gorilla let loose in my living room. He stood six feet five inches and weighed over two hundred and fifty pounds. At one point, he lifted up our dining room table and threw it through my mother's china hutch. Glass went flying everywhere. Gil was pleading with him to stop. It frightened me terribly. Jake and Doug, knowing they were no match for Jimmy, called the police. When they finally arrived, it took six policemen to get him down on the floor and handcuff him, toppling more items in their wake. Dragging him out, he managed to put both feet through the solid oak front door.

After they were gone, the quiet in the room was only disturbed by the hushed sobs of my mother. The boys righted the table. Jake went to get some tools to fix the door. I made her a cup of coffee. Doug sat with her at the kitchen table while she cried, between fits of anger. She loved Gil very much. When he wasn't drinking, he was good for her. He brought balance to her life.

After the dust settled, I went to my room and closed the door. Shadow Man was gazing out the window, when I walked up to him and said, "Why must our life be this way? Why can't it be normal? Why does it take a crisis for my family to be civilized with each other? Why do we seem to need these crises in order to feel our love?" Turning to me with his head resting on his hand and his elbow still on the sill, I got my answer. In my head, I heard, "It is what it is meant to be." Pulling a chair up next to him, I wanted to rest my head on his shoulders. Instead I just sat real close. He stayed with me the rest of the night.

MaryJane threw Gil out that night, but their love never waned. He would come by periodically over the next few years and beg her to let him return. He told us he was sorry and acknowledged he had a problem. I saw a genuine look in his eyes when he would say this to me. I don't know if he stopped drinking that night, but he never lived with us again.

Eighth grade that year had seen me reach maturity, along with getting breasts and my period. I had been developing for several years now, but my breasts would stop growing in eighth grade. It was a very awkward time for me. I was always taller than the other girls in class, and now, with breasts, I felt uncomfortable about my appearance. I developed a slouch that took years for me to get rid of. I noticed the boys were constantly looking at my chest. Mine weren't overly big; the boys just looked at everyone's. My slouch drove my mother crazy, and she was in the habit of nagging me about it. She would imitate my posture when she spoke to me; I always felt awful afterwards. It made me want to be around her less and less, because she never let up. She had an awful look on her face when she did it. It was a sour look that she had developed to go along with the tone that had appeared a few years earlier. Both these facets of her personality would be with her until her death. She was lonely and unhappy again, and she took it out on me. Doug was a junior in high school. He also worked at the hospital, and we rarely saw him. Jake was a freshman, and that was the year he turned into the handyman. He would help my mother with odd jobs around the house and became indispensable in that way. He also became somewhat reclusive and could often be found just hanging out at home. A year prior to this, he had experienced a back problem that was related to his rapid growth. It had caused him to be in bed and in pain for months. He wasn't able to play any sports, the place where his talents showed the most. It was during that time that Jake and my mother became very close. Meanwhile, I was showing my independence. I was always a person who didn't tolerate meanness and unfairness, when I started feeling like it was directed at me and coming from my own home, I fought back. I felt that Jake and Mom didn't like me. Although Jake ignored me most of the time, it was that lack of interest combined with his own sour looks that made me feel that way. They were both unhappy, and it was awful to be around them. As a result, I stayed away as much as I could.

I learned that year that through the desperation of despair comes hope. Sitting in my last class of the day, I was listening to Mr. Perry drone on about social injustices that we put on the Native Americans. Injustice was a powerful word; it said so much. Mr. Perry was a great teacher. He had been teaching for many years and had every wrinkle to prove it. He was to retire at the end of the term. He was an enlightened teacher. He respected us and insisted on respect in return. He had a lot of old sayings that would make us think. If someone were trying to talk to you in his class, something Mr. Perry did not tolerate, and you said you weren't talking, he would bellow at the top of his lungs, "REMEMBER THE STORY OF THE SMOKING GUN!!!" In other words, you were guilty by association.

The whole lesson on injustice was making me feel lonely. Sitting with my elbows on the desk and my chin in my hands, I felt a weight on my soul. At a time when my family life had finally gotten back to normal, I felt that my family had disappeared. But worse than that, I felt I was losing respect for all of them and didn't want to be around them either. For that I felt guilty. I wanted it to be a happy time for me. I tried to think of when I had last felt joy. I immediately thought of Mark...the one who got away.

Glancing at the front of the room, I noticed that Mr. Perry had a series of roll down maps. They were as ancient as he was, and he took pride in the fact that he had had them his entire teaching career. I got a perfectly brilliant idea, but I would have to wait until the bell rang. Once it rang, and everyone had exited the room, I stayed seated at my desk. Seeing me sitting there, Mr. Perry asked me, "Miss Barbara, is there something I can help you with?" (He always addressed us this way.)

"Well, Mr. Perry," I said, "There is. I was wondering if you had a map of Beverly."

"Why I think I do," he said, excited to finally have use for his precious tools. "Why do you want to see it?"

"I need to find Glidden Street. You see, a friend of mine moved away a few years ago, and I miss this person very much." I tried to sound mature and grown up.

A smile crossed his face. He stated in such a knowing voice it even surprised me, "And does this boy know you are looking for him?"

"Well not exactly," I said, slightly embarrassed at my own admission, "but I think he would be glad to see me if I found him."

"Let's hope, for your sake, he is." Then he pulled down the map. Together, Mr. Perry and I combed the map of Beverly. It was old, he said, and it might not be all that accurate. In ten minutes time, he found the street for me and helped me draw out a route. I was so excited, I couldn't contain myself. I threw my arms around him and gave him a big hug.

"Thank you Mr. Perry!" I cried, over my shoulder, as I was running out the door.

I heard him yell back, "Does your mother know you're doing this?" I pretended I didn't hear him and ran to meet Cherri for our walk home.

I was so motivated when I caught up to Cherri and Aaron. Aaron, having moved on to his next girl, was now just my friend. We liked it much better that way. "How would you both like to go on an adventure with me?" I asked.

"Is it legal?" Aaron questioned. "Of course it is!" I said, hitting him in the arm. "Ok, we're in," he said. "Wait a minute; speak for yourself, I want to know what it is first." said Cherri.

Sometimes Cherri had to be talked into things. I got down on one knee and held my praying hands in the air. "Cherri, I want to go see Mark. Mr. Perry helped me find out where he lives, using one of his wall maps. We drew a route and everything, but I can't do it alone. I need my partners in crime!"

"Wait a minute," she said, "You want to go to Beverly to see a boy? Your mother will have a fit if she finds out. But as crazy as that sounds...Mr. Perry drew you a map!" She burst out laughing.

"Let's do it," Aaron said, all excited. "Come on, Cherri, please!!!!!" We both gave her our best doe eyes.

"Ok, but when can we do this, and how do we know he will be home? If we leave after school, it will be too dark by the time we get there. Besides, your mom always wants you in the house by 4:00 PM."

"I have it all figured out; you can count on me," I said in a devilish tone.

The next Wednesday, we had no school. It was a teacher-in-service day. I was sure that Beverly still had school since it was a different town. That's the day we made our move in the hunt for Mark. For days prior to this big event, I had been getting nervous. What if he didn't want to see me? What if he laughed at me? Or, worse, what if he had a girlfriend and was walking home from school with her like he used to with me? I forced myself not to think about it. I closed my eyes and jumped.

When the infamous day arrived, we were in luck. It was beautiful outside, and the noon time sun felt warm on our faces. We met on Irving Street. Taking our bikes, we headed to the Kernwood Bridge. The bridge was only just past the Bates school, a ten minute ride from Cherri's house. The bridge was a white wooden structure, left over from the early New England past. It was a quaint bridge that looked like it was right out of one of my mother's jigsaw puzzle collections. When we approached the beginning of the bridge, we saw the open expanse of the Beverly-Salem harbor, with seagulls circling around a fishing boat and squawking. When we reached the center of it, the gate came down. It was a metal fence that stretched across the width of the bridge to stop the traffic and allow boats to pass under it. Two men emerged from a small wooden office with a large metal rod in the shape of a "T." Placing the long end into a hole with one man on each side, they ceremoniously began to rotate in a clockwise direction. It was a wonderful sight to see, a dance of some kind. With creaking and groaning sounds, the bridge began to rise. Only the very center of this structure was adjustable. This gave us a perfect view from the side on which we stood. Gliding in the water before our eyes was a beautiful wooden sail boat. It was forest green with gold trim. It was so close, it felt as if we could reach out and touch it. On board were handsome men and women enjoying a beautiful day of sailing---a world none of us had ever seen. Aaron turned to Cherri and me and said, "Someday, when I'm famous, I'll take you girls for a sail, when I get a boat like that." We both laughed. Aaron was always referring to his ultimate future fame. With the bridge back in place, we straddled our bikes and crossed over into Beverly. Stopping at the first intersection we came to, we took out our map. The steep hill that was ahead of us was the first road we should take.

"There is no way we can pedal up that hill." Cherri said very adamantly.

"Sure we can," said Aaron. "Besides, it might just give you some muscles in those scrawny arms of yours."

Cherri was frail in stature yet strong in opinion. Huffing and panting, try as we might, we couldn't bike our way to the top. We all collapsed in the street half way up. Looking at each other all in a heap on the road was just the recipe we needed to start a laughing fit that we couldn't stop. I had a funny laugh that everyone said sounded like a cartoon. Aaron and Cherri, still tangled in their bikes, started pointing at me, holding their stomachs as best they could in the hysteria when they heard me do this. Then Aaron started snorting with his laughter, and we were all no good after that. It wasn't until a honk of a horn brought us back to reality that we realized we were still in the road and had to move. Walking, our bikes at our sides, we continued our journey.

At the top of the hill, we had a problem. We were looking for a street that was on the map, but at the intersection, in this rural neighborhood, the streets had no signs. Always the comic, Aaron started doing an impersonation of the Scarecrow in the "Wizard of Oz." Making his body go limp, placing his arms clear across his chest pointing in opposite directions, he said in a silly voice, "Some people go both ways!" This started the laughing all over again. When we finally calmed down, we decided to use the scientific "eeny meeny method." Luck was on our side that day, because the next street was clearly marked with a sign. While riding our bikes down it in triumph, I started getting nervous with anticipation. All my doubts were entering my mind again. This time I had a new fear, the fear of rejection by a boy in front of my friends. Suddenly, without warning, the road came to a dead end.

"Are you sure we are on the right road?" Cherri asked. "I'm positive," I said, "it had a sign."

Standing dumbfounded, we didn't know what to do. In front of us was a hill that reached way over our heads. Hearing the sound of a whistle, we watched as a train crested the top of the hill and was gone.

"Wait a minute...Aaron, scramble to the top of that hill and see what is on the other side." "Can I wait till we are sure the train is gone first? I wouldn't want to die an untimely death." "Well, ok," I said. "Besides, we would miss you."

Aaron was never the athletic type. As a matter of fact, he was more like one of the girls than one of the guys. Struggling to reach the top, he was funny to watch. Cherri and I watched from the bottom, looking at each other and laughing. Once at the top, Aaron raised his hands in the air and exclaimed, "I'm king of the hill!"

"What do you see?" I yelled up to him.

"I see houses and people and civilization!"

"Very funny, do you see a street sign?"

"Yeah, it is the same street."

"I knew it," I said, "When they put in the train line, they cut through the street. Aaron, get back down here and get your bike. We are going over the hill!"

"I wonder how old that map was?" said Cherri.

Getting up the hill was tough. The dirt was soft, and with every step forward, we fell two back. With the bikes, it was almost impossible. With the laughing that soon took hold, it was amazing we ever did it. The hardest part for me was to try and not get filthy. That wasn't part of the impression I wanted to leave with Mark. Brushing ourselves off, we got back in the saddles and rode on. According to the map, Mark's street was the next one over. My heart started beating really hard in my chest. Rounding the corner, we read the sign: Glidden Street.

It was a beautiful, tree-lined street. The houses were all well kept. No one was around, so there was a deserted, quiet feeling. Slowly we rolled down the street; none of us said a word. Most of the houses were without numbers. Counting backwards from the few that did, we found the correct one. It was a brown house, one story, with a screened porch wrapped around it. The front yard was filled with fir trees; there were fallen pine needles and pine cones everywhere. The smell was wonderful.

Checking my watch, I realized that Mark had not gotten out of school yet. Looking at Aaron and Cherri, I said, "Let's sit here on the curb and wait."

"Shouldn't we at least knock on the door? Maybe he didn't go to school today." "No, I'm not ready yet," I said. I was scared out of my mind. In ten minutes time, Cherri said, "Look---someone is coming."

Walking down the street were two young boys who were our age. I knew instantly one was Mark. I had watched that walk for a year. "What do I do now?" I thought, as my palms began to sweat and my hands began to shake.

"Walk up to him," Cherri said, "You can't come this far and chicken out now!"

Slowly rising to my feet, I headed towards the boys. At first, I thought I would just walk right past. I still had time to chicken out. But when I got close enough for him to see me, Mark let out a shout.

   "Oh my God, I can't believe it," he said. "Barbara!?" We embraced, and he kissed me on the forehead.

CHAPTER: 14

Mark and I saw a lot of each other that year. Mostly it was I who went to see him. Because it was dark so early, and I had to be in the house by 4:00 PM, I only saw him on Saturdays. I would ride my bike to Beverly and meet him at his house. We spent most of our times together walking and talking. He never kissed me again. He always hugged me and led me to believe that we were going out. Our relationship was confusing for me and caused more pain than pleasure.

My mother hated to see me go to Beverly, not because of how I felt about this relationship, but because she felt it was too far away. In reality, when I walked to high school the following year, that would be twice as far.

"Barbara, I forbid you going to Beverly to see that boy!"

"He does have a name....Mark. Remember?" My mother's tone of voice was still one of distaste, no matter what she was speaking to me about. She could be describing the weather on a beautiful day, and yet it would come out like she was describing the fall of the Roman Empire. I also realized, at that time, that to have a tone in your voice like that would eventually give you a permanent scowl. It was really the only lesson she taught me in those formative years. It is a lesson I have kept close for the rest of my life...watch your tone and it will police your face. I tried to talk to her reasonably about the issue of going to Beverly.

"Mom, I have about a half dozen friends that live there. It makes more sense that I go see them, instead of all of them coming here."

"I don't care who your friends are. What I say goes, and I say you stay home and are in the house by 4:00 PM!" She was yelling at this point and I knew there was no arguing with her. That place she used to go when I was child, that place where she became quiet and withdrawn, now was a place of anger and resentment. I went to my room and tried to remember the last time she had had a kind word for me. Images of me in her arms, dancing to Diana Ross flashed through my head. I started to cry. I knew that Mom was gone forever. But my one real friend was here. He was sitting off to the side, very relaxed. I could tell he had been waiting for me. Sitting on the bed, he had one leg crossed over the other, his arms behind him on the blanket supporting him. "I guess it is me and you tonight, old friend." I sat next to him on the bed.

It was this lack of respect for my reasoning that caused me to no longer respect my mother. A wall was built that summer that would never be taken down. I went to Beverly anyway. Every time I left, I had to sneak behind her back; just leaving the house in general had become tough. She demanded more of me at home, and I was beginning to resent it. I was expected to be home by 4:00 PM every night, when my mother would arrive from work. This rule had been set long before I started seeing Mark. Before she got home, the house was expected to be clean. That meant every room had to be picked up. The kitchen had to be cleaned and wiped down, and there were to be no dirty dishes in the sink. If it wasn't done, then I was grounded with no room for negotiation. Meanwhile, my brother Doug would make elaborate meals for himself every day after school and leave a horrible mess. He never cleaned any of it up. Everything he cooked involved at least four pans. He would make sauces for all the meals he made. He enjoyed French cooking and that meant spilled flour, grease splatters and tons of mixing bowls. On average, it would take me at least an hour and a half to clean up. Because he got out of school at noontime, a perk for being a senior in high school, he would do his damage and be out of the house by the time I arrived home at 2:45 PM. I appealed to my mother about the unfairness of this, but she didn't listen. Her only response was that I was a girl; therefore it was my responsibility. I didn't realize then because I was too young, but as I got older and looked back on this time in my life, I knew she was too busy trying to get a handle on her own emotions and raising three kids at the same time; I wasn't making it easy for her. I think she just wanted to know where I was at all times, and housework was a great way to accomplish it. It meant that if I didn't go right home after school to pick up after Doug, then I wouldn't be done in time before she arrived, and I was grounded for it. It was because of this injustice that I began to rebel. I felt the only use I was to my family was as their maid. I knew this wasn't what I wanted for my life and thought once again about the imaginary woman who had sat on the willow branch with me in the cemetery and told me it was going to be ok. I put my life in my own hands after that and decided that although I had to live there, I didn't have to like it or them. I withdrew and became secretive. I no longer talked to them about my day. They never asked. Jake was no different from my mother and Doug. He often gave me dirty looks, whenever he saw me. When my mother was not around, he would make mean comments that were uncalled for and always made me feel angry. We got into huge fights about this, and often he would push me to show me he was stronger. In anger and frustration, I would throw things at him.

At night, after dinner, I would quietly retreat to my room. I had no TV or books, but I would draw for hours, or, if I was lucky, I might be called next door to babysit. With money I made from the babysitting, I bought my first set of artist oils and canvas. When I ran out of canvas, I would paint on palm sized rocks I found in my back yard or on my walks home from school. I turned these rocks into animals and funny little gnomes; I always said I was the first to invent the pet rock; I just never made the millions from this strange fad.

Soon I wanted to expand my painting skills. With babysitting money I had earned, I ran to the art supply store downtown and bought myself some Walter Foster "How to Paint" books. Using a half day at school, I found I had plenty of time to make my purchase and get home in the allotted time. One of these books was called "The Human Figure." It was an artist's anatomy book of the female body. It gave a step by step account of how to approach painting the female nude. When Mom saw that book, she gave me that sour look and said, "What does a thirteen year old girl want with a book of naked women? That's strange and unnatural." I knew I couldn't educate her on the importance of learning how to draw the figure. Instead, I just shrugged my shoulders and tried to ignore her meanness. Drawing and painting became my outlet for such thick headed ignorance. My only constant companion through all this was Shadow Man. I would often catch him staring at my drawings that I had pinned to my walls as posters.

Every Saturday I was on a kind of furlough. It became my only time off from my after school household duties. Somehow, my mother knew I was going to Beverly. To this day, I don't know how, but I always knew she did. When I would arrive home, she would ask me where I had been. "One day... (slap)...you...(slap)...are going to realize...(slap)....that I am boss! (slap)." I never lied to her. I told her every time I went to Beverly. I took my punishment with my head held high. I never once cried when she treated me this way. It was my only way of staying honest and true to me. She saw it as arrogance.

So every Saturday I went to Beverly, and every Saturday night she grounded me for a week. She only slapped me when she was in an especially rotten mood. I didn't mind being grounded. I had to be in the house after school every day anyway. To me, it was business as usual. To her, it had become a power struggle, this routine of mine of going to Beverly and being grounded. I never understood why she always let me out on Saturdays. Deep down I felt she enjoyed this game we were playing. When summer came, I would get up early and wait till she left for work; then, with my brothers still asleep, I would quietly leave. I would make sure I was back by noon, which was the time they woke up. By then, they would find me painting in my room. No one would be the wiser. Some may have thought this sneaky. I thought of it as a necessary component to my survival. I was growing and learning to separate myself from this family that I found no connection with. I wanted to be a good human being, but all around me was hatred and resentment. I enjoyed this control I had. I needed it as an essential part of growing and autonomy. Knowing I wasn't going to get it from my family, I found a way to get it myself. That is, until one day, my mother came home from work early. While I was sneaking quietly back into the house, she met me at the door. She was cooking lunch for my brother Jake and had a wooden spoon in her hand. Without warning, she hit me across the bare thigh with it. "Where have you been?" she screamed.

I wanted to cry from the pain in my leg, but I crossed a threshold at that moment. Looking back at it now, I see I was heading there all along. I no longer cared what she did to me. In a strange way, I wanted her to kill me. I wanted her to be arrested for it and spend the rest of her miserable life in jail. To me, it was worth my death. I looked her in the face and antagonized her. I told her I had been in Beverly, and she could hit me all she wanted and ground me until I was old and gray, because she would never have my soul, no matter how hard she tried. Anger swelled up inside her to a quick boil. She looked at me with hatred in her eyes; in a split second, she started beating me with the spoon and slapping me in the face. With every blow, I kept my cool. I was outside of myself again in that protective place. I was viewing everything as if I were standing next to my own body instead of experiencing it firsthand. I didn't fight back, except with my cold stare. I didn't look away from her. I didn't allow her the satisfaction. No one was there to witness this fury. No one was there to stop it. My brothers pretended that they were sleeping and ignored what they heard, if anything. She grabbed me by my long hair and dragged me to my room. Tossing me inside, she said I was grounded for two months. During those two months, my only companion was Shadow Man. My room became my asylum, my jail cell and, like the churches I visited as a child, my sanctuary. Out of canvasses, I began to paint the walls. I created a place I wanted to be. My entire room turned into a jungle with vines and animals. I even painted myself sitting on a branch. Shadow Man was in it too. He sat on the tree next to me. The entire time I worked on this, I would talk to him and asked his opinion. He never spoke back, but in the dim light of evening, I would find him standing there and touching portions of the mural with his dark, boney hand. Since I was kept away from the world outside, I was bringing the world to me, a world filled with wonder, mystery and peace. Stepping back and examining what I had done, I thought of the evening many years earlier when I had first walked into that room and seen the profanity on its walls. I wondered if the little boy before me had experienced similar injustices, and perhaps that was his art and his way of letting it out. My art gave me strength and got me through those lonely times, as it would prove to do for me later in life as well. Years later, I sat down and added up the time of these events and realized that in total, except for the few hours I would escape every Saturday and the other times that I would sneak out of the house in the summer, I had been grounded for my entire eighth grade year.

Eighth grade was a very difficult year for me. At a time when girls should be blossoming, I felt like I was just trying to survive. One day, I was sitting in my math class, always a tortuous place for me, when I was inadvertently hit square in the forehead with a chalkboard eraser by the teacher. There were two boys who sat directly in front of me who were always talking and fooling around. They were a great source of aggravation for this poor teacher. They were a great source of entertainment for us.

John turned to Eddie, who sat across from him in the first row, "So what are you going to be for Halloween?"

"I am going as a hooker," said Eddie with a smile. "I figure I will just steal some of my older sister's clothes, when she isn't looking."

"Hahaha, boy, you are going to make one ugly broad. What are you going to do about your hairy legs?"

Turning to me, Eddie said, "Barbara, can you give me lessons on shaving my legs? We can make a night of it."

"Yeah," said John. "He hasn't even had to shave his face yet." I wanted to laugh, but I chose to ignore them, looking straight ahead. These boys were always getting in trouble for talking and disrupting. On this particular day, they were especially noisy. The teacher, a male by the name of Mr. Devlin, was constantly telling them to quiet down. Of course, they didn't listen to him, and every time he turned around to the blackboard to write, they started up again. Wanting to surprise them in the act and put them in their place, he quickly turned around and, in one fell swoop, whipped a blackboard eraser at them with all his might. They were bent over low in conversation at the time, and I became the prime target in range. The result was that the eraser's wooden back hit me hard, right between the eyes. I saw stars, and an egg was forming on my forehead immediately.

Having been the butt of physical attacks by my own mother in recent weeks, I surely wasn't going to take anything from a teacher, when I wasn't involved in the first place. I stood up in my seat and demanded an apology. He wasn't totally convinced that I wasn't involved and refused to give me one. Still standing, I told him that I wasn't going to sit down until he did. He then yelled at me to go to the office. I told him I would do better than that. I was not going to stay in a class in which the teacher could not control himself, and I was going home. And so the power struggle began. I walked out of the class, to the surprise of the rest of the students, and he started following me down the hall. Picking up speed, I ran to the nearest exit. Passing the office, I caused enough commotion to bring the secretary and principal out into the hall.

"Barbara, where are you going?" the principal yelled. "You need to stop this instant young lady." I yelled back, "My math teacher is a maniac, and I'm going home!"

The chase was on: me, my math teacher and the principal. But I was the fastest. Out the door I flew. I ran three blocks and didn't stop until I reached my house. I didn't know what I was doing. I wasn't thinking straight. I just snapped and knew I had to get away. Looking back on it now, I can see why I did it. Everyone was controlling my life, and I had to get it back. When I reached my back door, I fumbled with the lock; my hands were shaking so badly. Once inside, I locked the door behind me and immediately pulled down all the shades in the house. Pacing back and forth, I didn't know what I should do. The reality of the situation was beginning to set in. I did the only thing I could do; I called my mother at work. By the time she got on the phone, I was hysterical and in tears. I told her what had happened. She told me to calm down and go to my room; she would call the school and handle it. She didn't have to. Before she hung up with me, the school was on the other line looking for her.

I spent the rest of the afternoon in an anxiety driven whirl. By the time my mother arrived home from work at 4:00 PM, the house was spotless, but I was a mess. I stuck to my beliefs and said I was not going back. I said that Mr. Devlin had always been a ticking time bomb, and I was not going to be subject to that kind of behavior. Once again, I was watching myself say this, but I didn't recognize that it was me. How was it that I could protest my concerns about him but was helpless when it came to my own mother? To my surprise, Mom seemed to understand how I felt and wasn't angry at me. The more I stated my case, the angrier she became with the school. She wanted to go down there and show them who was boss. The thought of her hitting me with the spoon the week before crossed my mind. Is this what it means to be an adult--- having your emotions so close to the surface that you have no control over what you do physically? I kept my thoughts to myself. She said we couldn't ignore this. It was illegal for me to be out of school. I had to face the principal in the morning and tell him how I felt. I didn't sleep the whole night. Shadow Man sat in the corner and watched over me.

The next day we went to the school together. We arrived late, so I didn't have to deal with the stares and finger pointing from the other kids. This was at my request, and everyone agreed. We sat in the nurse's room of all places, and I was able to explain my side of the story without my teacher present. In conclusion, I added, "Even if I were the one who was talking, violence is no way to behave to another human being." I hoped my mother was listening, because I was secretly talking to her too. No one could argue with this, and they asked me what I wanted. I said, "I want Mr. Devlin to apologize, and I refuse to go back to his class." Seeing he was the only eighth grade math teacher the school had, I was not in a position to negotiate, but I wasn't going to take no for an answer. Mom let me do all the talking, I said, "Fine, I'll take math, but I refuse to step foot in that room." I had my math class in the nurse's room for the rest of the year. The nurse gave me my assignments, but only after Mr. Devlin had said he was sorry. This situation, of course, increased my struggles in math.

CHAPTER: 15

In late August, Cherri, Aaron, and I agreed to walk together to the high school on the first day of school. Happy to be starting with a clean slate, I looked forward to this day with anticipation. I would meet them on Irving Street, and we would go on from there. Unfortunately, right before school was to begin for the year, Aaron's parents informed him he would attend St. Johns Preparatory School, two towns away.

On the first day of school, I was taken aback by its very size. Sitting on a large hill, the high school peered down on me like an old relic, forgotten in time. The building had been built in the early 1900's. I am sure that if we had decided to eat any of the peeling paint that was found everywhere, we would have all been immediately struck dumb. The entire place smelled of a mixture of chalk dust, mold and worn out floor pine. And the cafeteria still smelled like everything was boiled, with some things that shouldn't have been. Once again my graduating class was too big for the school. There weren't enough lockers to go around, so many had to carry all their books and coats. A new high school was in the process of being built down the street, but it was not ready yet. So for the first semester and a half, we all had to cram into the old school. There were so many kids in our school that we had to change classes on different bells in order to fit in the corridors. Even then, it was an art just to get to class on time. The girls learned really quickly that it was important to hold your books close to your chest, or the chances of getting accidentally groped were great. Some of the guys took advantage of this situation. There was a whole group of boys who lived down by the Beverly Bridge who thought it was great fun to grab a girl in the hall and kiss her unnoticed, before slipping back into the crowd. This happened to me. By the third time, I was ready for him, whoever he was, and introduced him to my knee. His friends just laughed.

My A period class, on that first day of high school, was a science class. When I arrived at the room, I found I had to squeeze in, just to get through the door. The noise in the class was from freshman chattering away. There was not one familiar face in the crowd. A group of girls sitting on the left side of the room was trying on lipstick. An epic game of paper football was happening in the back. Everywhere you looked were coats and books. The science class and the lab were held in the same room. This only complicated things more, with the large lab desks. I was praying no one lit a Bunsen burner. I was sure we would all perish in a flash. There were so many students that in order to walk down the aisle between the desks, you had to look first to see if anyone else was coming from the other end. The only empty seat I could find was in the middle of the class. I slid my books under it and tried my best not to meet anyone's gaze. I wanted so badly to disappear, to go unnoticed. Trying my best to make as few movements as possible, I realized that my pencil was in my book bag. As I bent down to retrieve it from under my desk, my long hair fell in front of me. Flipping it around my head so that I could see, I wound up in a disastrous situation. It just so happened that a male student was walking by and adjusting his fly at the exact same time I was flipping my hair. Needless to say, my long hair got caught in his zipper.

"Ouch," I said, as I tried to grab my hair.

"Oh shit," he said, stepping back, and pulling me from my seat in the process. Before I knew it, I was on my knees in front of him. Closing my eyes, I was so embarrassed at the compromising position this put me in. The sound of the laughter was making my head spin. Struggling, in a panic, he tried to free my hair, but in the end, he only made it worse.

"Hey, does anyone have any scissors?" he yelled through the room.

"You are not cutting my hair!" I screamed in protest. With the realization of what was about to happen, I found the strength to demand, "Pull down your damn fly!" This, of course, drew the attention of the whole class, and everyone turned around to find out what was going on. Finally, out of anger, he tore my hair loose from its hold in his pants. I didn't talk to anyone in that class the entire year. And, by the way, I sucked at science.

That first year of high school, I was an awkward target. One day at lunch time, while heading to the cafeteria, I was met with another uncomfortable outcome. The cafeteria was on the bottom floor. Walking down the crowded stairs, I pushed past people and craned my neck as best as I could to hunt for Cherri. "What is it with a school cafeteria smelling like everything boiled?" I thought. Having brought my own lunch, I wasn't worried about there not being something I liked. Instead, I was worried about not being able to find my friends. The cafeteria was so crowded that it took two days before Cherri and I realized we had the same lunch. The lunch room was next door to the boy's locker room, an architectural oddity, I'm sure. Seeing no one I knew in the cafeteria, I stepped back towards the direction I had come from and ran into Cherri, who was standing in line. I stood with her and began eating my peanut butter and jelly sandwich (jelly on top). The line for the hot meal spread out the door and covered the front of the boy's locker room. "Who designed this school?" I said to Cherri. She just shrugged her shoulders and laughed. Anytime you got a group of kids together in close quarters, mischief was bound to start. The boy I had kneed in the groin was standing outside the locker room, towel drying his hair. He was obviously in gym class. Noticing me, he gave me a big smile and headed back to the showers. Cherri asked me, "What was that all about?" I told her about the hallway incident and the groping. She was appalled. A little while later, the same boy came out, but this time he had a friend. They were heading towards me. I knew I was in trouble, but I never would have guessed what was going to happen next. With the swiftness of two secret service agents, they each grabbed me by an arm and dragged me into the locker room. My sandwich fell helplessly to the ground. They laughed as they pushed me towards the middle of the room and left me with all the naked boys. I quickly raised my hands to my face in horror, trying to find my way back to the door, but not before seeing at least a half dozen jingle bells.

In February, the new high school was finished. In February, I turned fifteen. In February, Rosanne's husband said he would kill us.

My mother got a job working at an electronics factory that made heating units for home appliances. She spent day after day, hour after hour, welding wires under a microscope. She loved this new job, and I never understood why. I felt sorry for her for not wanting something better in life. Rosanne was her boss. The two women became close. With no man in her life and both Sharon and Pam now dead from cancer at a very young age, my mother found herself alone. Rosanne and my mother were inseparable. They went shopping together and frequented yard sales. They were both still young and beautiful, and Mom had started paying attention to her appearance again. Their relationship was as innocent as two teenage girls, always laughing and joking and sharing secrets. For a while, I thought this was good for her, because when Mom was happy, we all were happy. Sometimes they would take me along with them. During those rare times, I felt honored to be let into their world. I tried really hard to act grown up and not cause them to suffer from any of my teenage angst.

Rosanne was good for my relationship with my mother. She was a go between... a sounding board... an impartial judge. She was always honest in her opinion and never favored sides. But Rosanne, however, strong in character she was, was married to a violent man. He would often beat her, and this upset my mother tremendously. Once again, my mother took it upon herself to be a savior, with total disregard for her own children's needs. I would like to think that she was too ignorant to ever realize the danger she put us all in.

She encouraged Rosanne to leave him and move in with us. Although we did not have a spare bedroom, this was of no concern to my mother. We had no say over the matter and, as usual, kept our mouths shut. She had been talking to Rosanne about this for months without our knowledge. When we did find out, I didn't want her moving in; I was tired of my mother always picking up "strays" and letting them live with us. At first Rosanne had refused, until one night she showed up at our house, all battered and bruised. I initially thought it was temporary, because Rosanne slept on the couch. Every day her husband would call and beg her to return home. Sometimes these calls would go on for hours in one night. Rosanne pressed charges against her husband for all the abuse he had given her over the years, but with laws the way they were back then, she could never get the charges to stick. He would be back out on the street in twenty- four hours and back into her life. And now he was in ours. When the phone calls became excessive, Mom called the police. She never let Rosanne do this, because she was too vulnerable. The police were sympathetic, but there was little, if anything, they could do. Then Mom developed her own ways of dealing with Bill's annoying phone calls. She bought a whistle, and every time he called, she blew it into his ear. She also refused to let him talk to Rosanne, which angered him more. What my mother did to Bill was the equivalent of taking a stick and constantly poking it into a hornets' nest. Soon Bill lost his home to the bank, and, at first, we thought that would be the end of it. Then within weeks, the phone calls started again, this time from Iowa. Mom started using the whistle again. The few times he did get through to my mother, he would give her an earful.

"If I ever get my hands on you, I am going to make you suffer! I am going to kidnap your children, starting with the youngest. I am going to cut them up and send them back to you in tiny packages." Mom hung up the phone as if it were a foul smelling, rotten piece of meat. She then called the police. This time, some detectives responded to my mother's call. They were sitting at our dining room table, plotting to get Bill arrested, when I walked into the room.

"Jane, as long as he is out of state, we can't do anything."

"You came all the way over here to tell me that!" My mother was getting that shrill tone in her voice again. Rosanne was trying to calm her down.

"Jane, let the man talk."

"The only way we can get him is if he sends something in the mail. Then it becomes federal. Jane you need to get him to put it in writing and send it through the US Mail."

"How on earth am I going to get him to do that? He isn't stupid. As a matter of fact, he is very intelligent!"

This time Rosanne spoke, "Yes, but he is also arrogant enough that it just might work. We need to play on his arrogance."

"How will that change things if he does this?" asked Mom.

"It means we can call the FBI." The words hit the living room floor like a huge, granite bolder. My mother was finally quieted. I turned and left the room.

When Bill called again the next night, she and Rosanne had it all rehearsed out. Jane was going to go into a whole dramatic dialogue about how he wasn't smart enough or brave enough and that he needed to put it in writing before she would believe him. But when it was time to deliver her lines, all she said was, "Prove it in writing; I don't believe you." That's all it took. The next week, after the letter arrived, so did the FBI.

Bill not only sent one letter, but, with this new found form of venting, he sent hundreds. Every week Mom would receive handfuls---he must have been writing ten a day. Each one was more gruesome than the last, but all we needed was one. There was no doubt in anybody's mind that this man was serious. The next step for Rosanne was to file restraining orders against him. They were state-wide restraining orders, so he was no longer allowed in Massachusetts. The minute he passed the state line, he would be arrested, the FBI reassured us. Rosanne, having worried that she should leave so as not to endanger our lives, did not have this choice any more. The FBI wanted this man.

Once again, our lives were turned upside down. The FBI was planted everywhere. Two men were stationed in a car across the street from our house. One was at the bus stop, where we waited for our ride to school. I could no longer walk to school. Several men were at the high school, although I didn't know which ones they were. I couldn't tell any one, not even Cherri. I didn't want to. How do you tell someone a story like this? Although I felt safe, with a child's naive sense of the situation, for weeks I couldn't help but look over my shoulder. Once again, I was restricted to the house, but this time it was for altogether different reasons. One night we were all watching TV, when the phone rang.

"Jane I want you and the kids to get away from all windows and get as close to the floor as possible." It was the FBI man across the street; his voice sounded concerned. Somehow, Bill had gotten past the border of Massachusetts and was in the area. The FBI knew this because he had used a credit card at a local store, but they didn't know where he was at that time. It felt so unreal, like playing a game with the neighborhood kids when I was little. I guess that's the way my mind protected me from the realities of the situation. We weren't on the floor long, when we received another call. They had him. I don't remember where he was when they caught him, but I do remember that he had a known assassin with him. They found sawed off shotguns and other ammunition in the trunk of his rented car. One of the guns had a scope on it. He could have killed us from a far distance, if he had ever gotten the chance. It was a scary night. None of us slept after that. Shadow Man spent the night at the foot of my bed. I could feel the pressure of his hand on my feet. It felt comforting.

As would be expected, the story was all over the news and in the papers. Although they didn't use our names, they gave our address. Kids at school knew it was me. I was met by stares from the neighborhood kids. By lunch time, everyone knew it. Teachers were concerned and asked me if I was ok. I didn't know what to say to these people. I chose to keep it brief. Cherri was shocked that I hadn't told her, but, like a true friend, she supported me and figured I would tell her the whole story eventually. When the newspapers got a hold of this story, they implied that Rosanne and my mother were lovers. Homosexuality was not widely discussed at this time in history. It was still considered taboo and wrong.

"So, Barbara, your mom is a lesbian?" It was a girl I had gone to school with since first grade, a girl I never really liked.

"What the hell are you talking about?" I was completely dumbfounded and thrown off guard. I hadn't read the papers.

"That's what the newspapers are saying. Your mom and her lover got some guy mad and he was going to kill you."

My reply was simple and monotone, "Don't believe everything you read in the papers."

When I got home, I told Rosanne and Mom what people were saying. Instead of reassuring me, they laughed it off, actually, not shocked at all by it. I didn't know if that was because it was true or if it was because they had read the articles and were ready for this question. They had been sharing a bed for some time now. It was a huge, king size bed and it made sense; Rosanne couldn't sleep on the couch forever. I was suspicious of their relationship after that. When they were alone in their room at night with the door closed, I often stood and listened outside it. I wanted to know. It ate me up inside. I never heard anything remotely sounding like love making. The question haunts me still. If it were so, I would have preferred they had been honest with me.

CHAPTER: 16

The August before my sophomore year of high school, I asked my mother if I could fly to California to visit Aunt Cheryl. She lived in a town which was just outside of San Francisco. She had given birth to a little girl after her new marriage two years before, and I wanted to meet her child. Although my mother was leery, she agreed. I was nervous about the plane ride for obvious reasons; my last plane flight ending the way in which it had. This time I would be staying for a month. My mother didn't help much by showing her fears before I left. But like many times in my life, I just closed my eyes and took that first scary step. The plane arrived on time with no incident. Cheryl and her daughter met me alone at the airport. Seeing her for the first time in a long while, I noticed a resemblance between us that was uncanny. I asked her where the boys were. She just responded, "You know boys."

When we arrived at her house, no one else was there. When they eventually did come home, Cheryl reintroduced us. They gave a noncommittal hello and went to their rooms. Her oldest sons, Sam and Steve, ignored me the first week, waiting for me to show my worth. Without being overly conscious of it, I tried my best to win them over. At times, I didn't even recognize myself. They were outgoing and boisterous, and I tried to show them I was like them. It worked; eventually they let me tag along with their friends. It was at this time that I was introduced to marijuana. I knew it was wrong but found myself wanting to fit in so badly that I threw away my morals as if I were discarding a rag. We would all go to a beautiful park to commit this unlawful act. At the time, we were just fifteen and felt we were above the law. I liked the way it made me feel. Without boundaries, the funny thoughts that were forever circling in my head would let loose, and I would often fall into fits of laughter. They would all laugh at my enthusiastic joy at every palm tree I passed. I became closer to Steve than I was to Sam. We would often talk for hours in a stoned state of mind about random facts we knew. We had many conversations about who came up with the names of things and why they got the privilege to name them. I remember I once asked Steve who decided four equal lines were to be called a square. Then we would come up with our own names instead and laugh. It was dumb, but it was fun. It got to the point where we couldn't even look at each other without bursting into laughter. We also talked about what we would change in this world if we could. The first thing, of course, was war. I asked him if he remembered his father. He said he didn't. He was surprised when I said that I did. I told him I often visited his grave. Steve was movie star handsome. He had long shiny blond hair, blue eyes and sparkling white teeth. He seemed to have a bunch of girls all hanging around him when he walked into a known hang out.

I was in a different world, and I knew it. There were huge hills all around us, and I wanted to climb them constantly. Steve told me it would take the entire day to do so, so we never did. Cows were grazing on them, and I wondered how they got there, and why they didn't ever run away. The sun was hotter than I had ever felt. It made my skin burn and itch, I worried for the cows. At night it got cooler. We would put the heat on in the pool and go for a dip. I still didn't know how to swim, but half the pool was shallow with stone benches that lined the edges. It took weeks for him to do it, but Steve talked me into jumping off the diving board. He said that he would be in the water on the deep side to help me to the shallow end. He told me to relax, and I would naturally float to the top. The depth of the water was something I had never felt before and was surprised at how it wrapped around my body. He did as he said he would and led me to shallower water. Holding each other, we laughed and jumped up and down at my success of overcoming my fear.

One afternoon, we were all in the back yard. Natasha, the two year old, was walking around the pool. She had been swimming since she was about six months old, although she was never allowed out there by herself; we were not overly concerned with her toddling around. I was sitting in the shade reading a magazine, and the boys were playing volley ball in the deep end. Suddenly, we heard this shrieking cry coming from the kitchen window. While doing the dishes, Cheryl had glanced out the window and noticed Natasha had fallen in the pool. We didn't understand what Cheryl was saying at first; her hysteria was making her difficult to understand. When we glanced over to where she was pointing, all we saw was the top of Natasha's head bobbing in the water. Her body was perpendicular to the pool. The water had an eerie kind of stillness; not even a bubble could be seen on the surface. The second thing I noticed was Shadow Man standing off to the side by the fence in a very casual way. I was confused by everything that was happening all at once. Someone save Natasha! Why is Shadow Man here? These were split second thoughts racing through my head. All of a sudden, I heard a splash. Sam, who had been standing on the diving board perched to jump on Steve in their horse play, was the first to react. In one huge dive, he reached clear across the pool and lifted her in the air. It was a miracle he didn't bump his head on the shallow end. Cheryl, out of the house by this time, grabbed her from his arms and started hitting her on her back. Turning her over she performed a type of Heimlich maneuver, and water started pouring out of her mouth. We all held our breaths, until we heard her cry. I looked back at the fence just in time to see Shadow Man fade away. I was very shaken by this event. I felt guilty on many levels. Why didn't I see or hear her fall in? I felt terrible that I froze when I finally did see her. I felt helpless knowing that even if I had wanted to, I wouldn't have been able to save her. I never dove off the diving board again that summer.

John, Cheryl's youngest son, who was two years younger than we were, wanted Steve and me to take him everywhere we went. The few times we did, I felt he was fun and enjoyed him very much. Cheryl took me to the big shopping malls and bought me very hip clothes for school in the fall. She had very different taste in clothes from my mother. She bought me platform shoes and a tight denim halter top jumpsuit. Mom never let me wear that one to school. Cheryl was very beautiful. Everywhere we went, men would look at her. She had a power that was more enticing than even my mother had had in her younger days.

On a sunny afternoon, Steve and I found ourselves alone at home. We decided to go into the pool, because it was a particularly hot day. I was sitting on a stone bench at the shallow end. Since the incident with Natasha, that was the most I could do at that point. Steve was jumping off the diving board. The water felt so good; the air was so warm. I leaned my head back with my arms supporting my body and let my feet float to the surface... I closed my eyes. Hearing the phone ring, Steve went into the house to answer it. With my eyes closed, I started thinking about the difference between the East coast from the West coast. Having lived on the water my whole life, I would often sit on the rocks and let the waves wash up on my legs. Lying there with my eyes closed, I felt a tiny ripple wash over my chin and hit my nose. Surprised, I opened my eyes and saw that the entire pool had tiny, vibrating waves breaking the surface. I was confused; I didn't know what I was looking at. Steve ran out of the house and stood with his feet apart, arms outstretched and perfectly still. "What is it?" I asked.

"An earthquake," he replied. "Just stay where you are." Before he could finish the last word, it was over.

Cheryl talked to me a lot that summer. We would sit by the pool, sharing a pitcher of lemonade. Our talks were mostly about her and Uncle Sam. I think her almost losing Natasha brought a lot of her feelings to the surface. She spoke about the unfairness of the war and the short length of time they had had together. I was surprised at how freely she talked to me, as if I were her best girlfriend. This was something I did not have with my own mother. I started realizing what I was missing. Feeling comfortable doing so, I told her that I remembered the day we found out he was dead. She was amazed when I recounted the events. It was at this time that she told me about the dream and how real it had been. In it, he had been in her bed that night and put his arms around her. He told her that he had died and wanted to tell her himself. She cried in his arms that night, and he told her not to worry and to take care of the boys. She said he was with us all in that kitchen that morning. Even in her infinite grief, she could feel his presence. A chill went down my spine. I believed her. She asked me to do her a favor when I got home. She said that she had never had closure with his death. She felt he wasn't buried in his grave, although she knew he was no longer alive. She didn't know where he was, and she needed to find out. She had been too upset at the time to make sure of such things. My mother had apparently made all the arrangements with the funeral parlor for her, but I never realized that Cheryl had never seen the body. But I knew then that in her heart, he wasn't in his home soil. Was that why no one had ever visited him? I told her that I went to see him a lot. I placed wild flowers on his grave. She was so certain he was not there that it left me feeling uneasy. If that were true, then there was such a thing as a soul mate---and somehow he was letting her know.

When I got home, I asked my mother about it. She seemed to pale at the question. I asked her again and again, until finally she told me the truth...he had been blown up in a fox hole with six other men. By the time they got to the bodies, they couldn't tell whose parts belonged to whom. They just assembled complete human bodies and attached dog tags to each one. My mom said she never saw the body either. There was no use, it couldn't be identified anyway. Somewhere in this world, Uncle Sam was buried, and we buried someone else's loved one in return. I urged my mother to call Cheryl and tell her what she had told me. She was afraid to at first. I didn't let it rest. I told her Cheryl was a tortured soul and needed to know. She called her that night. This was the first real sign I had ever had that there was something greater than us controlling our destiny. It gave me a comforting feeling.

Shortly after returning home, I noticed that Rosanne had started developing a drinking problem. I knew that my mother was repeating the same patterns that she had followed so many times before with other people in her life. I started wondering if she had kicked my father out for the same reason. Why did she find herself drawn to people with these issues? Rosanne was not an obnoxious drunk. As a matter of fact, she could control herself very well. What she did do when she was drunk was to say all the things she felt should be said. I have to admit, she was pretty insightful. Her insights were usually directed towards my mother, about her issues and how she needed to deal with them. Rosanne was not mean about it, just overly concerned. They didn't fight, although my mother, being in denial, did defend herself. Rosanne was a stronger debater and better educated, and my mother was not used to someone being her equal, never mind craftier. The only hold Mom had on Rosanne was that this was her house. In the end, the drinking was too much for her, and she asked Rosanne to leave. I know the drinking was an issue, but I'm sure she felt backed against the wall as well. Once again, we were left alone with just our immediate family to have to relate to. As always, we never did that all that well.

CHAPTER: 17

I had begun seeing a boy by the name of Martin before I had gone to California. We had first met in September of my freshmen year of high school, and he became one of my friends. By the end of that year, he was my boyfriend. The summer between freshman and sophomore year was a wonderful time for me. I had visited California, and I had made many friends at school. Martin was a mechanical wizard. He drove several different broken down cars, all of which he fixed up himself. One was a Volvo that had to be started with a screwdriver. When I asked him why he didn't get a key for it, he said it was more fun to start it that way. That was Martin, always looking for a challenge. His other car was a very old Mercedes that had bench seats. During my sophomore year, I gave him the "gift" every teenage boy dreams about. We were parked on a secluded street. It was a warm dark night."The Chain," by Fleetwood Mac, was playing on his new cassette player. The air outside was soft. I felt relaxed and safe. We weren't talking, but the world around us was speaking volumes. With my head on his chest, I could feel the life beating inside him. I slipped my hand between the buttons of his shirt. Traveling along his curly hair I found his breast and held it gently. He smelled so good.

"Barbara?" "Yes?" "Never mind," he whispered in my ear.

Sitting up, looking him in the eyes, I whispered back, "What?" Our lips were so close. When I spoke, they brushed his like a soft butterfly landing gently on a petal. He put his hand on the back of my head and led me to his mouth. We had kissed before, but this time was different. The stress I had felt over the past few years was lifted from my spirit. I drank of him, like a stranded soul lost in the desert, and he my oasis. The gentleness turned to a fiery passion I had never felt before. With both hands, he cupped my backside and lifted me to his lap. My skirt fluttered in the air and lay back down gently on his thighs. I pulled away from his lips and looked into his eyes. I wanted to see his heart. Still fixated on his gaze, I reached down and undid his pants. Gently, I lifted him from that protective home and guided him inside me. When we were finished, we didn't move. We held each other for a long time, still coupled together. I cried softly into the nape of his neck, as he rubbed my back.

That spring and into the summer we spent a lot of time in his car. The Mercedes was a classic that turned heads when we drove down the street. My mother liked Martin a lot, although she didn't like me being in his cars, obviously, for good reason.

Martin came from a different world from mine; his family had more money, and he was a major part of his parents' lives. He lived down by the Willows, in a beautiful house. His mother and father were both college graduates and had great dreams for Martin. They should have; he was very smart. Education was a priority in his house. His father was a professor at a college in Boston. His mother was my old librarian at the Bates school. She was an Italian woman like my grandmother, and like my grandmother, she frightened me. Because of this focus on school work that had been ingrained in him, Martin was a good influence on me. He helped me with my math homework and taught me what it meant to be a student. On summer nights we went to the Willows, and he taught me how to play ski ball and win the most tickets. It seemed to me that there was nothing this guy couldn't do. We had an ideal relationship, and we never fought.

Together, we hung around with Cherri and her boyfriend, Dana, from Beverly. Often this was at the Willows or at Mack Park. There wasn't much to do in Salem after September. That's when the Willows closed for the season. It was at this time that Cherri took up drinking. She was a very small girl; standing five feet six, she only weighed ninety-five pounds. Although it was only a glass at every sitting, Cherri began to like drinking and so did her boyfriend. Soon they began drinking at least once a week. Martin didn't do any drugs. I didn't like to drink, but I did smoke weed occasionally. That night was no different. Cherri took some vodka from her mother's liquor cabinet and added it to a large, half empty bottle of fruit punch. She and Dana met Martin and me at Mack Park. It was a beautiful autumn day, and the sun was setting; the leaves were golden but had not fallen yet. We went into the wooded area near the back stairs and started to party. Cherri and Dana shared the bottle. Because I didn't drink, I was smoking a joint. Martin, as usual, was straight and making sure we didn't get out of control. In a short time, Dana asked Cherri to go a few yards away so they could be alone. Martin and I stayed on the stairs and just talked.

"So, I am going to visit colleges next week with my parents." I thought you were supposed to do that senior year?" "No, junior year. Senior year you apply." "Where are you considering going?"

"I will probably end up at Suffolk. It is where my dad teaches, and tuition would be free. What about you? Are you going to go to college for art?" As he told me of his plans, I sat sullenly examining a leaf.

"No, actually...ummm. I'm not sure" I knew I was not going to be able to afford college. Doug was paying his own way through school to become a surgical technician. Being the only girl, from a low income family, I knew my chances were slim. It was the first time this reality was presented to me, and I realized that in this world, I was on my own. The talk we were having was starting to get to me, so I put out the joint.

A half an hour later, Dana came running over to us in a panic. "Come quick! Cherri has passed out and I can't wake her up!" Back then, I was Cherri's protector. We had a history of adventures that had resulted in me pulling us through. She had always been slight in stature and somehow seemed frail. Once, traveling to Nantucket with the girl scouts, we hit an unexpected storm when we were on the ferry, the outer edge of a hurricane. When the winds hit first, we were on the top deck. Cherri was slammed against the rail and almost went over the side. It was me who was strong enough to grab her and pull her below deck. From then on, I watched over her. Through the rough years in middle school, when the girls were fighting a lot, I made sure no one touched her. If a guy was bothering her when we were at the Willows, I put a stop to it. When she needed an excuse for her grandmother, I never said no. We were true friends, and now she was in trouble.

When I got to her, she was lying on her back with her arms and legs spread wide. My first instinct was to turn her on her side, in case she were to vomit. I yelled at Dana, "What did you give her!?" He claimed he had given her nothing but that she had been drinking before they had left to meet us and that she had drunk almost the whole bottle herself at the park.

"Cherri...Cherri...wake up sweetie." I tried to wake her by screaming her name. When that didn't work, I lifted her eyelids, but all I saw was white. I checked for a pulse. It was faint, but it was there. I was never any good at that, so I didn't trust just how faint it was. I was in denial. The fact that I could only see the whites of her eyes told me she was in a deep unconscious state and in a lot of trouble. The words "alcohol poisoning" would not be spoken at school assemblies for another fifteen years; we had no idea, at the time, just how serious a state she was in.

"Let's try and stand her up," said Martin. "Maybe we can get her to walk it off." He was grasping at straws. I knew it wasn't going to work, but I didn't know what else to do. When that failed, I did the only thing I could think of. She had too much alcohol in her, and I had to get it out. Fortunately, she was light enough to pick up. Lifting her with her back against my body and facing away from me, I stuck my finger down her throat. She immediately vomited at my feet.

"Barb, wait, let me help you," said Martin.

"No, she is my responsibility; I can handle it." I did it again, several more times. She didn't wake up, and her eyes were still white. With the sun having gone down twenty minutes before that, I realized we had to get her out of there. I knew I couldn't take her to her house. Her grandmother would have killed her. She was as frail as Cherri and in her nineties; she would never have been able to physically deal with the predicament. None of us had ever even been allowed into Cherri's house; we had never seen the inside. Her grandmother was eccentric in that way. No... I couldn't bring her home. The only thing I could do was bring her to...MaryJane. Martin lifted her in his arms, and we started heading for his car, which was located on the far side of the park.

"Martin, lift her onto your shoulder, in case she vomits again. I don't want her to choke." I had heard of people dying from choking on their own vomit, and I was afraid it might happen to Cherri. It was a good thing I knew this, because she vomited down Martin's back. This grossed him out, and I thought about why God had given the job of childbirth to women.

When we got to the entrance of the park, the car was still three blocks down the road. (We always parked far away, so that no one knew we were in the park when we were there.) As we were heading to Martin's car, our friend Mike pulled up next to us in his brand new Mach 1 Mustang. Mike was a twenty year old senior at our school. He was the nicest guy. One time at lunch, he told us his parents were in their seventies. In amazement we asked him how that could be. He said that he was a menopause baby, and the first five months of his mother's pregnancy, the doctors thought he was a tumor. We all burst out laughing, but he was a good sport about it. Mike always had had feelings for Cherri; he asked her out every day, but she never returned his affections. When he saw her in the condition that she was in, he jumped out of the car and took over. Putting her on my lap in his car, he instructed the boys to go to Martin's car and just go home. They followed his advice.

My house was just a few blocks away. When we pulled up to the curb, he wanted to carry her in for me. Knowing that Mom had never met Mike before, I didn't want to have to deal with that too. He understood and helped me lift her onto my back. She vomited again. Maneuvering her through the door was difficult. I wanted to get her to my room before I told Mom what was going on. Cleaning the vomit off both of us would have been ideal, but I knew it would be impossible to do that and not have her see us in that small apartment. Mom was in the kitchen, and we were coming through the back door that led to it off of a small hallway. She smelled us before she saw us. Of course she would; no smell ever got past MaryJane. Seeing the two of us covered in vomit, she hit the roof! She was screaming and yelling at me and demanding to have an explanation. It was then I realized that I was no longer stoned. When did that happen? I couldn't recall coming down from the high.

I yelled back at my mother, "Now is not the time to for explanations! Cherri is in a bad way, and we need to help her." My words angered her, and she slapped me across the face. Cherri was still on my back. She said, "If you think you are old enough to talk to me that way, then you are old enough to handle this yourself." She went to her room and didn't emerge until the morning.

The first thing I did was put Cherri on my bed. Grabbing pajamas from my dresser, I then lifted her again and headed for the bathroom. I laid her on the floor face down and removed my vomit covered clothing. Taking her clothes off was awkward for me at first; I had never seen another naked girl before, other than in my drawing books. For a second, I wondered if I should close my eyes. In desperation, I put us both in the shower. She became heavier when we were both wet and slippery. Vomit was encrusted in our hair. It was hard to wash us both at the same time. I sat her in the tub, away from the running water, so that I could wash myself first. When I was done, I lifted her once more, this time with her head on my shoulder, away from the streaming water. Our bodies were pressed together. With one hand cradling her, I washed her long, fine hair with the other as best as I could. There were bits of food that were tangled in it. It was surreal, and suddenly, it felt as if I were outside myself watching the chain of events unfold. I remember thinking that this should wake her up, but how was I ever going to explain to a drunken person who was my best friend how we ended up together in the shower? I didn't care; I thought, I'll figure that out later, but I didn't have to...She didn't wake up.

Now I was really scared. What should I do? I sat naked, cradling her on the bathroom floor, and started to cry. I made sure I was quiet, so that my mother wouldn't hear me from the next room. I knew I had to control my emotions. I didn't have time to feel sorry for myself. I brought her to the toilet and put my finger down her throat again. Again she vomited...again she didn't wake up.

Putting her back on my bed on her stomach, with a pan under her, I called her grandmother. I told her Cherri was staying with me that night. I said it was a sleepover and that my mother was home. She naturally became suspicious and demanded to talk to my mother.

"Mom, Cherri's grandmother would like to talk to you."

"I'm not talking to anyone. You handle this." Mom refused to get on the phone, so I lied and said she was in the shower. Unhappy with my excuses, her grandmother drove to my house. Being old, she just sat outside in her car and leaned on the horn. I went outside to confront her.

"Hi, Mrs. Connelly, Cherri is in the house upset. She refuses to come outside. My mother is comforting her. She had a fight with her boyfriend," I added as I rolled my eyes. "You know how awful boys can be, don't you Mrs. Connelly?" I promised that she would see her in the morning and asked her to please let me calm her down. She bought the story but was still very angry with me. As she drove away, she called me a kidnapper and said she was going home to call the police.

Returning to my bedroom, I looked down at Cherri lying there, and limp. She looked so young and helpless. Her skin was pale, and her lips had a purple hue. Her wet hair, so stringy and clinging to her face, made it look like she was dead. I checked her pulse again, but this time I couldn't feel anything. In a panic, I grabbed a hand mirror and placed it under her opened mouth. I cried again, when I saw the moisture form on its surface. That mirror would be the tool that kept my sanity for the rest of the night. By the time I laid her down in my bed after the shower, it was nine o'clock in the evening. My brothers weren't home and wouldn't be expected for hours. I was exhausted, but my heart was beating hard in my chest. I sat on the floor next to her and thought of all the possible scenarios that I would experience by morning. She could sleep it off and wake up with a horrible headache. She could vomit on my bed. I'd have to change and wash the sheets in the middle of the night. My best friend could die right before my eyes, and there was nothing I could do about it. I felt helpless. The thought of calling an ambulance crossed my mind, but I knew this would upset my mother, and, besides, would they respond to a teenager if her mother was being unreasonable? I began to hate my mother. How could she turn her back on this? Why couldn't I count on her? Who was this woman? I thought about the time so long ago, when I had searched for her under the couch. I realized, then, that she had left me a long time before this. A seed was planted that night that would grow a hatred between my mother and me that would never die.

I didn't sleep that night. I didn't even allow myself the luxury of lying down. I propped myself against the side of the bed and held Cherri's hand. I could feel Shadow Man's presence; he always came when I was vulnerable. That night he gave me peace. He was a familiar face in this room of desperation and despair. He did not intervene. As always, he said nothing and just watched. I turned to him and said, "What am I to you, a damn movie you are watching? Help me!" He came closer to me and sat down beside me. It was all he could do.

Every hour I tried to wake her. Every hour I held the mirror to her mouth. Every hour I tried to make her vomit into a pan. After the third hour, even that was no use...she wouldn't wake up. I toweled her head with damp cloths and spoke gently to her. I was convinced she was in a coma and we would never laugh together again. Seeing her look helpless, I felt certain she would die. I cried alone that night, with no one but Shadow Man to hear my sobs. I vowed if I got through this, I would never allow Cherri and myself to be put in this position again. I knew from this I would become stronger. I grew up that night.

I talked to Cherri all night long, but she never heard a word I said. I reminisced about the times we had had, talking about boys and looking for adventures. I told her about California, the places I saw and the people I met. It was hard to believe that only four weeks had passed; California and my time spent there seemed so long ago. I told her how much she meant to me and that I loved her. When I said all that I could think of, I sobbingly told her I would make sure she was cleaned up and looked pretty when they came to take her body away.

At six in the morning, I tried to wake her again. This time, to my relief, she responded. It was a faint moan, but to me it was life. Elated and renewed by this glimmer of hope, I grabbed her and began to cry. This made her stir more and, with her eyes still closed, she said in a faint voice, "What the hell are you doing to me?" I replied, "Nothing, are you ok? How do you feel?" She said her head hurt and that she was tired and wanted to sleep. I told her we were at my house, and her grandmother had said it was ok. Although it was hard for me to do so, I said, "Go back to sleep and I'll explain it all in the morning." She said, "Ok," and dozed off again. I looked over at Shadow Man and said, "Thank you." He nodded in response.

I slept only a few hours after that. I lay on the floor next to the bed. I had horrible dreams of death and dying and was pleased when the sun fell across my eyes to tell me it was a new day. I woke her and gave her some clothes to wear. She looked silly in one of my dresses that was too big for her. I walked her home at nine thirty. On the way home I told her the whole story. I don't think she ever understood the complexities of it, how close she had come to death and how that night had changed me forever. I'm not sure what she told her grandmother when she arrived at home. Her grandmother never did call the police that night, but deep down I wished she had. Cherri and I never talked about that night again. There was so much that Cherri never knew. Instead, we talked about boys and hunted for new adventures. Although she didn't realize it, I kept my promise that night about being responsible for her...Cherri never drank again.

CHAPTER: 18

The new high school was huge and a comforting relief from the last one. We moved into it after February vacation, and at first everyone was lost. The right hand side of the building was separated into three different sub schools, depending on your level of ability. Each floor had a different color; every student was assigned to a floor. This meant that all your classes and your lunch room were on that assigned floor. But in practice, it never seemed to work that way. When we first got there, a student who was assigned to the green floor was not supposed to be seen on the orange or blue floors. That rule didn't last long. With everyone split up, it was rare to be on the same floor as your friends. Because the school was so large, with several different stairwells, it did however, become easy to find a way to join a friend at any of the three cafeterias. The lunch rooms were attached by an open atrium that we called "the courtyard" in the center of that wing. It became easy for a student to go through his cafeteria and back into a different lunch room, using the stairs that allowed access to the courtyard. We were all required to have our student ID's with us, which included our floor assignments, at all times. Several times in the first two months of the enforcement of this rule, I was sent back up to the orange floor. I wasn't the only one who was driving the corridor ladies crazy with this; no one followed this rule. In two months' time the rule was overturned.

As with all schools, the students would govern where the cliques would congregate. The orange floor was for all the average students. The blue floor was where the high honor students met, and the green floor was called the burn out floor. The green floor was actually the most diverse. It had its fair share of pot smoking burn outs, but it also had all the Spanish and Korean students for whom English was a second language. The green floor housed the classes for the automotive and industrial arts, and the art students were part of the industrial arts. My first year of high school, I wasn't allowed to take art. I was told that if I took honors courses, art courses weren't allowed. But for some reason, I still ended up on the orange floor. No matter how hard I worked, I still couldn't get past group two. Cherri was on the blue floor; although I did take some honor classes, we didn't have any together. It was difficult for me in those classes. I felt like a fish out of water. I thought I didn't belong there, and I didn't know how I had gotten there. Once again, I felt that the school system had made a mistake.

I struggled in math and science; the hardest part was not letting the other kids in the class know it. I went for extra help with those classes every afternoon, but it seemed that nothing I did ever helped. It was hopeless; additionally, the teachers were all tired and impatient at the end of the day. By the end of the first semester, I knew I was in over my head, with no support to help me through. I spent hours each night on my homework in tears. I did extra credit whenever I could. In the end, I passed each course with a mercy grade of "D." I don't think the teachers wanted to see me in their classes again the following year. During my free periods, I spent my time in the art room. It was a large room that was big enough for four classes to be held at once. Because of its size and constant commotion, it was easy to slip into unnoticed. I sat in on figure drawing and painting. One day, I tried my hand at clay. Not knowing what I was doing, I proceeded to make a large bust and, subsequently, blew up everything in the kiln. This happened in the middle of the last quarter. That is when the teachers realized that I wasn't in any assigned class.

"Excuse me, Miss, who are you? What art class are you suppose to be in?"

"My name is Barb. I don't have a class here, but please, please, don't make me leave." "What are you doing here, Barb?" "Sitting in a place where I belong?" I said with a sheepish grin. "Are you a freshman?"

"Yes. And they wouldn't let me have art classes, because I am taking a stupid honors math class. God knows how that got on my schedule. If they really knew me, they would put me here." I then learned that the art teachers were different from the others. After I told them of my struggles with my classes and my desire to make art, they became my advocates. Although it was too late for me to transfer, they asked me to bring in all the art work I did at home, so they could see it.

I was so excited to comply; the next day I brought in everything I had. It was awkward to do this, causing quite a commotion in the morning on the school bus. I enlisted Cherri and Tony to help me, and together we managed. When the art teachers saw my work, they scolded me for not coming to them sooner. They wrote a letter to the principal that day asking to relieve me of honors classes the following year and advance me into an art two major. But, first, I had to pass my freshman year honors classes.

This was the first time in my life I had ever received emotional support from an adult, the first time anyone had ever told me I was good at something I did. I had always felt I would find my way out of my low income, low self esteem existence, but that day, I knew my art teachers had handed me a map. I took every art course I could in sophomore year, overloading my schedule. My academic courses suddenly became disappointing; back then, school systems made the assumption that if you were an artist, then you were not bright. My new math classes were now about balancing checkbooks and understanding percentages, in case we came across a sale item at a store. I felt that this type of class belittled me and made me feel stupid and embarrassed. I never discussed it with Cherri. My English class was bad also, only to get even worse in junior year, when my only option was to take a class called "Reading for Fun." That class was filled with the school derelicts, and we read comic books. I told the teacher that I wanted to read the classics. She was thrilled to hear this and assigned me books on my own that I picked up at the library. I talked to her after school, and she would give me quizzes to take home. The rest of the class had no quizzes or tests at all. I got an "A" in the class, but only she and I knew I was actually doing a higher level of work. History was always my favorite class of all, and junior year was no different. I loved hearing about the beginnings of civilizations and the struggles of mankind. I felt a strange kind of connection to it. My history teacher that year was Mr. Tobin. He was a brilliant teacher. He was so knowledgeable about the subject that we never had to use a book. Instead, he would explain parts of eras in history to us, and we would have an open discussion about it. Sometimes these discussions would come down to an all out debate that would then seep into current events. I knew what he was doing, and I was impressed. He involved us and gave us a passion for learning. We were expected to take notes constantly, and those were what we studied from for our tests. If you wrote your notes incorrectly, you could fail the test; understanding the discussion was the key. His tests were the most difficult I had that year. They would have been rated difficult by most standards. I got an "A" in that class too.

There seemed to be no happy medium for a student like myself. I had difficulty in math, but I certainly was not dumb. I would learn later in college, after receiving an "A" in math, that my real problems were my math teachers. No one was more shocked than I when I got straight "A's" that first term of college and was put on the honor role. High school just had never provided the proper place for me.

At lunch, Cherri and I hung around the green cafeteria. I would like to say we ate lunch, but usually the line was so long that we just got snacks. Although we were still friendly with each other, Martin and I had broken up. He liked to go to the library at lunch; I needed space and fresh air. The green cafeteria, on the ground floor, had the easiest access to the court yard. The group we sat with consisted of approximately seven kids, mostly from the lower to middle class income bracket. Some were artists; others were musicians and theater people. Some were waiting for their sixteenth birthday, because that was when the law stated they didn't have to be there.

We hung out with a boy named Alex. He was majoring in theater and had dreamed of being an actor in New York. He was of average height and build with a huge mane of brown, curly hair. He was a lead singer and played the harmonica in a band. He was so good at this that he could imitate any harp solo he heard. I was with him the day he bought his first harmonica at Ted Coles' Music Shop in Salem. By the time we made the two mile trek to my house, he had figured it out. He was very talented, and the music he wrote was beautiful. Alex was also a very funny person. He was the clown of the table. Being in theater, he was out going and boisterous. It was noticeable at lunch when he was out sick and not in school.

Unfortunately, Alex did have one flaw: a drug issue. It happened to him innocently enough, which, I'm sure, is the story with most kids. Because he was so active in many things, including the lead in the school musical, he took speed to keep up with his grueling pace. At first it was just to stay up all night to study, then it was to keep from falling asleep during class, after he had stayed up all night. He was riding a cyclone that was out of control; the worst part was that he knew it. I would talk to him about this abuse he was putting on his body, particularly concerned for his heart, as well as about the inevitable time when he would have to quit and get off this locomotive he was riding.

One day at lunch, I noticed him sitting by himself across the room with a sad, distant look on his face. He was not his usual self, and I was immediately concerned. I had never seen him this way in the year that I had known him.

Approaching him, I asked, "Alex, are you ok?"

"Oh, hey, Barb. It has been a tough week. And on top of it all, I am questioning the friends I hang out with at my dad's house. He lives in Lynn, you know, the drug capital of Massachusetts." Alex's parents were also divorced. "Why don't you just hang out with us? We smoke a bit of weed, but that's all."

"You know, that's the thing, I don't know what defines a good friend anymore. I decided to sit over here and see if my true friends would show themselves to me. I am glad it was you."

For many months we remained just friends. We would talk for hours about the careers we wanted in art, and I encouraged him to quit the drugs. I told him he would go nowhere with them in his life. He started to listen to me; he was ready. He encouraged me with my art. He believed in me and thought I could draw better than anyone. He asked me to duplicate an album cover for him in pen and ink. He showed it to a guy he knew at the local "Head Shop." The man asked me to put some of my art work in his store. It became the first time I had ever made money at what I loved doing.

One Saturday morning, we were sitting at the light house on Derby Wharf. It was a sunny spring morning, and the promise of summer was in the air. We were drinking coffee and eating a donut, talking about life and how complicated it was and wondering how complicated it would be after high school.

Turning to me, Alex said, "I want so much from life...is that bad?' I smiled and said, "Actually, I think it is bad when you desire nothing." He was quiet and searched my gaze for approval. When I said no more, he leaned over and softly kissed me.

"Alex," I said, "For this to become anything, you need to get off the speed." And he did.

At first it was difficult; he was in a constantly agitated state. When it was really bad, he stayed home from school and told his mother he didn't feel well. When he did that, I knew why he was out. I would worry about him all day and had difficulty concentrating myself. I would call him on the payphone in the cafeteria at lunch time.

"Alex? How are you doing?" "I am ok. I just feel real sick." "Hang in there. Do you want me to talk to you for this entire lunch? I brought enough quarters." "That would be great. I would rather listen to your voice than the one in my head." "Alex, you are doing the right thing, and you are not alone. I am here for you."

He became quiet. Then he replied, "Thank you." I told him how strong he was. It was amazing, the resilience he had; I was proud of him. Without the help of an outside source, he became completely clean. What Alex and I experienced in that short time when he was kicking the speed was empowering. Again, I found myself on my own, without an adult to guide me. Our relationship was bonded from this experience, a feeling more powerful than either one of us realized. We became inseparable. He met me at the door of every class I had, so he could walk me to the next. He would hold my hand every chance he got. After school, we would go to his house, which sat on the edge of the woods near the high school. We would talk and dream and tell each other of our love. We spent many hours walking in the woods; I would draw in my sketchbook, and he would play his harmonica or sing. We talked of houses we would build in the woods and the fact that we felt so grown up; yet we were trapped in the years of adolescence, and we knew it. We had a standing date every Saturday night for pizza and a movie; afterwards he would walk me home in the dark, always my protector. I told him about Shadow Man and my tormented nights of joint pain. I also told him that it was ok, I knew that Shadow Man loved me. He was always there when I needed him most. Alex was the only person outside my family that I had ever confided in about my nightly visitor. To make me feel safe, many nights, he sat in my room until he was sure I was asleep; then quietly, so as not to disturb my mother, he would slip out the back door. The only time we did not see each other was when he was working on Friday nights and Sunday afternoons at one of his uncle's many restaurants in town.

One day after school, about a month into our relationship, he told me he had a surprise for me.

"What for? It isn't my birthday," I said, as I began jumping up and down. When it came to pleasing me, Alex didn't need an excuse. It was the first time in my life I had ever had anyone be this thoughtful towards me...I was beginning to like it.

"Well, it is because I love you so much!" In the heat of the moment, with great enthusiasm, he bent down grabbed me by the knees and threw me over his shoulder. Smacking me on my backside, he called out to the cars that passed, "Free spanks if anyone is interested!"

"NO!" I squealed in protest, laughing. It was the happiest I had ever felt. On the way to his house, still on his shoulders, I said, "Give me a hint. I want to know what it is!"

"Well"...he said. "It is something I have been thinking about all week. And because it has taken me a while to plan this and make sure everything was perfect, I am not going to give you any hints to spoil it." Taking me down from his grasp, he placed me gently in front of him. Looking into my eyes, he asked in a tender voice, "Do you love me?"

I answered, "Yes, I love you more than I thought I could." I then added, "I always thought I was alive, but now I know I was just living. Thank you."

Walking into his house, he made me wait in the kitchen while he silently stepped into his bedroom and closed the door. Sitting at the table, studying the pattern of dried flowers on the wall paper, I was alone with my thoughts. Only with the ticking of the clock, in unison with my own heartbeat, did I realize that this life was not a dream, but reality. I felt every nerve ending in my body right down to my feet. It was a feeling I had never had before, a wholeness I had never known. "Is this what love feels like?" I wondered. I heard my inner self answer, "Yes, it is called peace." Returning, Alex emerged from behind the door and said, "Ok, stand up: take my hand and close your eyes." Without saying a word, he opened the door. The shades were all drawn, and the room was dark. In various locations around the room were tiny tea candles, casting a soft glow of light. Handing me a bouquet of fresh wild flowers he had picked not more than three minutes earlier, he gently kissed me on the neck as he placed them in my long hair. Little Hershey kisses were strewn across the bed; unwrapping one carefully, he placed it in my mouth. Incense was burning in the far corner; a faint scent of patchouli filtered the air.

"I will love you forever. I hope this day never ends. I am living for the first time, because you gave me my life back." His next token of thoughtfulness was something I never forgot. Placing an album on the stereo, he said, "I listen to this when you're not here, because it makes me think of you." It was "Lady of the Isle," by Crosby, Stills and Nash. The words encircled my soul, as he slowly undid the buttons of my blouse. Revealing my breasts, he leaned over me and softly kissed them. Traveling up to that place where my jaw meets my ear, he lingered slightly, brushing his lips lightly on my lobe. I turned my head and met his mouth, as my hands reached for his belt. Rolling over on his back he took off his pants, as I removed mine. My body was reacting to him, as he let his hand wander down between my thighs. Stretching his leg to the other side of my body, he effortlessly covered me and slid inside. We made love the whole afternoon.

Although I didn't think it possible, our relationship became even stronger after that. Other than Cherri and her boyfriend, we hung around with no one but each other. We became the couple that other couples talked about and referred to as one name. They were certain that the minute we could, we would elope. We thought so too. I auditioned for musicals with him, and we both got parts. Mine was always minor; his were always the lead. He walked through museums with me and looked at the paintings. He told me every day that someday my paintings would be on those walls. I couldn't tell you what was happening in the world at that time, because at that time the world that was happening was between us.

My mother wasn't sure of Alex at first, and he knew it. He was more affectionate than my family was. To soften her up, he kissed her on the cheek every time he saw her. He said, "I love you, Mom, and I know, someday, you'll love me." Eventually, she did fall in love with him too and told him so. My relationship with my mother was better when I was with Alex. She trusted me more when Alex and I were together; maybe it was he who she actually trusted. He opened a door for us, a door I never knew existed. Unfortunately, it was a door that only opened when he was around.

One day, soon after my surprise, Alex announced, "Barb, there is someone I want you to meet, someone who is very special to me."

"I thought I have met everyone in your life."

You haven't met this person." I thought I knew everything about him, so I had no warning of what I was going to see. I had already met his mother and her new husband and his little brother; the only one left would have been his father, but that wasn't right either. We went to his house around two on a Saturday afternoon. The sun was shining and we sat on the porch and waited. His mother and the rest of the family were gone.

"So, seeing the rest of the family is not here, I am assuming the person we are to meet is your father?"

"This person will be in my life forever, I am responsible for her. If you and I ever get married, you will be responsible for her too." Within a half hour, a small van pulled into the driveway. It had one passenger and a driver. It was a wheel chair van, and the driver hopped out and ran to its side door. "Hi Alex," he said, "She's in great spirits today. Get ready."

Alex introduced the driver to me, and I shook his hand. Opening the door, the driver went inside to maneuver the wheel chair to the opening. "Barb, I want you to meet my sister, Debbie. Debbie, this is Barb," said Alex, giving her a big kiss that was met with her squealing delight. He lifted her out of the chair and carried her to the house. She was a year younger than we were.

Debbie visited Alex once a month. She lived in a facility for mentally handicapped teens. He had asked his mom a few months back if it was ok to have her for the day, once a month, and he would watch her the whole time. . She could not walk or talk. She had beautiful, thick, waist-length hair and wore a pretty dress. Around her neck was a diaper fastened like a bib. Somehow she was always able to express her feelings, a trait my own family didn't have. When she was happy, she would smile from ear to ear. When she was excited, she would squeal. When she was sad, she cried. It was interesting to watch, this girl with no voice, who could express herself so clearly. It was uncomplicated and primal, refreshing and honest. Alex was always genuinely happy to see her, and she knew it. They had a wonderful relationship. She was never a burden for him; he felt responsible for her but loved her dearly.

One day, Alex and I were walking down the street. We were in a long, drawn out discussion about cliques at school and the way that people in society generally treat one another. As usual, I was ranting about the injustice of it all. And as usual, Alex was saying that change can happen with an individual, with you and with me. I was doubtful that I alone could make a difference. He said, "You can't necessarily to the world but you can to someone's life." I told him he was spouting clichés. He said, "No I'm not; watch." Just passing us was a bent over old lady walking with a cane. She looked tired, with the weight of years on her shoulders. Slowing down to fall into step with her, he struck up a conversation about the beauty of the day. I walked behind as an observer. She responded positively and returned his small talk. When they reached the curb, he gently, unthreateningly, took her arm and continued across the street, pleasantly chatting all the way. At the intersection, they parted ways; she thanked him for his kindness, patting him softly on the shoulder. Her demeanor had changed, somehow she seemed taller. That was only one of many things Alex taught me that year.

At the end of my sophomore year, I had a worry that was on my mind. I didn't tell Alex, because I didn't want to worry him too. He could tell something bothered me and asked if I were having nightmares again. I told him no, these fears were real. I said I would tell him after school, when we were alone. I wanted to go to the woods where I felt safe, in his arms. All the way there he kept asking me what it was. He was genuinely concerned, and I was scaring him.

He asked me if my mother was giving me a hard time, because whatever it was, he could talk to her. I simply said no.

When we arrived at the woods, I sat on a rock; sitting next to me, he put his arm around me and waited patiently in silence. I wasn't afraid to tell him, because I feared his reaction. I was afraid to utter the words out loud that I had never even spoken to myself, even when I was alone. Finally, I had no choice; it had to be said.

"Alex, we are going to have a baby." His reaction was surprising, even for Alex. He calmly hugged me and wouldn't let go. With his lips so close to my ear, he softly stated, "Now they have to let us get married. Don't worry; I'll take care of everything." How wonderfully naive he was and I, for believing him. "Does your mother know?"

"No," I said. "I'm afraid to tell her." "Don't worry; we will tell her together." That night, we sat MaryJane down and told her our plans.

"Jane, I have something to tell you. Barb and I are going to have a baby." He just stated it outright, as if he were telling her what the weather was to be tomorrow. Meanwhile I was cowering in my room. I didn't want to see the look on her face, when he broke the news to her. I listened with my ear to the door, but I heard nothing. Stepping out of my room, I was certain I would find her on the floor from having fainted and Alex fanning her frantically with a magazine. When our eyes met, she was staring at me blankly. Her eyes were glazed over with a sparkle of a tear. Her expression was filled with defeat and despair. In that moment before she spoke, I saw her love. After a while, she said, "What about school?"

"Well, I am going to drop out, work full time for my uncle and get my GED high school equivalence test. Barb will go to school as long as she can and then do the same thing. Jane, I am going to be a responsible husband and father, you'll see."

"But what about your futures; what kind of life is this going to be for the both of you?"

"I am going to sign up at the local vocational school at night to become a chef. Who knows, maybe I can do the GED there too."

"Where will you all live?" "We will move in with my parents." "Well, it looks like you have it all worked out then."

"Yes, and after a while I hope to buy my own restaurant." In his innocent mind, he did have it all worked out, or was he just trying to convince himself?

It was so much information at once, that it took my mother a few minutes to grasp what she had just been told. I hid, slightly behind Alex, as she let it all sink in. I thought she was going to scream and yell. I was sure she would ground me. I was certain she hated Alex at this point. What I didn't expect... were the tears. Alex put his arm around her and told her it was going to be all right. She hugged him back. She knew he loved me. She said, "Ok." I was thinking about all his dreams he was willing to throw away.

For the next few months, we told no one. It was a scary, wonderful secret we kept to ourselves. The thoughts of being together forever were sinking in. We were happy. My mother gave me my grandmother's engagement ring.

We decided that Alex wouldn't leave school, until it was absolutely necessary. We decided not to tell his parents, until I was four months along: my mother's idea. She must have known something I didn't...at two and a half months, I lost the baby. I cried in Alex's arms. My mother turned back into her old self again, with her looks of disdain and biting comments about my life. When I was pregnant, she had seen a bond between us. She had been a young mother too. Although I am sure on many levels she was relieved, now I was just her teenager again.

CHAPTER: 19

January, 1978, was to be the beginning of a memorable winter that would provide stories around dinner tables in eastern Massachusetts for years to come. Also that January, my grandfather was dying of lung cancer. He had smoked unfiltered Pall Malls for forty years or more, and it was finally catching up with him. My grandmother had died suddenly of a cerebral hemorrhage several years before. Although the suddenness of her death was a trauma we all felt, like an unexpected blow to our heads, nothing compared to the drama that surrounded the expected death of my grandfather. My grandfather had married a woman by the name of Lorna, right after my grandmother's death and before he was diagnosed with his illness. She was a tolerable woman of his age, who was very naïve and often got on everyone's nerves with her insistent clamor of useless dialogue and uneducated questions about everyday life. As teenagers, we all saw her as his toy, something to distract him from the loss of my grandmother.

At the end of January, we received two feet of snow. Although, at the time, not a common occurrence for the coast of Massachusetts, it did happen every so often. School was never called off in Salem, because at that time, the policy was that a parent had to use his discretion as to whether to send his children to school or not. The school buses were always late on snowy days, if they even showed up at all. One time, we had waited an hour, only to find they had failed to tell anyone that they had planned on not coming. Because of that incident and the long walk I had to get to school, I never went to school on days that snowed more than three inches. This particular day was no exception.

My grandfather was staying with us off and on that week. He was uncomfortable and found it difficult to sleep at his own house. He complained about his bed and the coughing attacks he would have when he laid down. I'm sure the constant chatter of Lorna wasn't making it any easier. At our house, he slept on a Lazy Boy overstuffed chair my mother had purchased for him. This seemed to ease the coughing spasms, and he was able to feel comfort, even if it was for short moments at a time.

The morning of the snow storm, I got up early to check out the weather. To my surprise, my mother was still asleep. Walking into the living room where my grandfather was seated, I saw him stir slightly in his chair. The room was dark, and I gently walked over to him to ask if he were ok. He said he had to tell me something. He said he wasn't sure if he was allowed to. Sitting on the couch next to him, I waited for him to continue. It took him awhile at first, and, as

I sat there patiently, I noticed beads of sweat developing on his brow in the glow of the street light outside the window. He was obviously concerned, and I wondered if I should wake my mother. Before I could do so, he spoke again. His voice was as soft as a whisper, and he was staring past me, as if I were no longer there. He said, "I saw Cheryl last night." It was a flat statement that didn't ask for an explanation.

Knowing Aunt Cheryl was in California, I simply asked, "You had a dream?"

"NO!" he said abruptly, turning his head in my direction, as if he had noticed for the first time that I was still there. "I was sitting here, unable to sleep and thinking of her. I miss her. Then all of a sudden, I found myself lifting out of my chair. I was so light in weight, and the feeling was exhilarating. When I looked back to where I was, I could still see myself sitting in the recliner. I wasn't scared; I just wanted to see Cheryl. The next thing I knew, I was gliding over the house and across the entire country. I saw Niagara Falls and the Grand Canyon. It was dark, but I could still make out what was in front of me. Then I saw Cheryl's house and wondered how I would get inside. Before I knew it, I was standing next to her bed while she slept. I wasn't surprised; it felt natural to be there. I wanted to touch her and tell her that I loved her, but I was afraid I would scare her---so I didn't." He then turned to me and asked, "Do you think she knows?"

I was struck by what he had just told me. I wondered, too, if he were supposed to tell. The wind was whipping up the snow outside, and the street lamp had cast our shadows on the far wall of the room. The shadows, long and lean, danced on the walls like scary figures and reminded me of my early days with Shadow Man. I looked for him. I was sure he was there. At first I couldn't find him, and then, as if he knew I was looking for him, he stepped out from behind the dark corner of the room. I was not scared, but I knew this wasn't a good sign. I tried not to look at him and instead focused my attention on my grandfather. I placed my hand gently on his cheek and said, "Grampy, I'm sure she knew you were there and that you love her. Cheryl is special like that."

In a short time, I went to the kitchen to make him a cup of coffee. I sat with him that morning until he finished his drink and fell asleep again. The snow from that storm was a compacted two feet. It was heavy and wet, the worst conditions for removal. Storms were unpredictable back then, compared to now. Streets weren't plowed as neatly, and everyone had a hard time getting around. I stayed in the house for two days; my grandfather's words played over and over in my head, like a skipping record.

Within a week, he was put into the hospital. He was attached to tubes and monitors that held his spirit from flight. We knew he would never come home again; my mom made the necessary calls daily to family members who were out of state. When it looked like the time would be near, she said she would let them know, so they could come. Timing a death isn't an exacting science, and the doctors were doing their best to keep her informed. A week after he had entered the hospital, my mother was sitting in his room watching TV, when the weather man predicted a small storm for the middle of the next week. Knowing that could shut down the airports, my mother chose to call all the relatives to fly in early. She wasn't sure how much time he had left. She called my Aunt Cheryl in California, as well as Joe and his family in New Hampshire. The storm was still predicted as only a few inches, but, as usual, my mother had been taking precautions. The family arrived all together on February fifth.

My grandfather had slipped into a coma, two days before they had arrived. The vigil that was kept at his bedside was quiet and oddly routine after the first day. We all sat in shifts to ensure he would not be alone when the time finally came. The night that Cheryl arrived, I was at home. She went straight to the hospital after landing at Logan. She walked into his room, and took my grandfather's hand. She started to cry, and through her tears, she quietly said, "I'm here, Daddy."

In what could only be described as a testament to the strength of the human soul, my grandfather opened his eyes, and with a strained low voice, he began talking to her. I don't know what he said, but my guess would be that it was how much he loved her and missed her. A few hours later, he died. The entire family felt he had been waiting to see her before he could go. The night he died, the storm started. The weather predictions began interrupting scheduled TV programming every hour with new updates on the expected amounts. Every hour, they seemed to add three more inches to the previous hour's projections. By eight o'clock that evening, they were calling it the storm of the century. We were relieved to realize that Cheryl and her husband, Jim, had flown in on the last flight to arrive at Logan, before they shut down the airport.

Apparently, it was more than one storm that was hitting the east coast of Massachusetts that night. A cold front had set in, and it was stalling it off the coast. This had caused it to become a full blown Nor'easter, a type of storm that New Englanders had come to fear over the centuries. The cities and towns were completely unaware of its seriousness; with the two feet of snow that was still left on the ground from the last storm, snow removal was at a standstill. Everyone became trapped in their homes.

Stranded at our house were Joe, Martha, Veronica, Stuart and Dylan as well as Lorna, my grandfather's wife. Added to the five people in my immediate family who lived there already, this meant we had eleven, full-grown adults trapped in a three bedroom apartment. We also included a Great Dane, who had been a birthday present for Jake several years earlier. We were eleven people in the throes of loss and grief, with no room to endure it in private. Cheryl and her husband stayed with Tina and her family across town.

We all gathered around the TV to keep abreast of the latest updates and inches of the storm. It was now raging with such force, it sounded like someone had a jet airplane idling outside our front door. The windows were rattling so hard in my old drafty house, it felt like a Hollywood disaster film that you couldn't turn off, no matter how many times you tried to change the channel. When the governor declared a state of emergency, I knew we were in this for the long haul. Having given up my bed, I was now on the floor. Tired of being stepped on by unsuspecting visitors to the bathroom in the middle of the night, I declared the area under the dining room table was to be mine, to the disappointment of the dog.

My brother Doug was working in the emergency room of Salem Hospital during all this. After graduating from college, he had gotten a job there, working as an OR technician. He was called in the night the storm started, shortly before midnight. I can't imagine how he drove himself there, with the snow blowing in front of him and the torment of grief that he had just left behind, but he did. He called us once he had arrived and said the roads were so bad that he would be stuck there for some time. The news was predicting the storm to last for several days. It seemed there was no end in sight. When you looked out the window, all that could be seen was a weak glow from the street lamp fading in and out. The whole time it was snowing, the wind was howling. Its intensity didn't wane the entire time. Boots, our Great Dane, and I slept cuddled together under the table to keep warm. The floor was cold, and, no matter how many articles of clothing I had on, I felt a chill. Blankets were at a premium, hard to get with so many people under one roof. The warmth from the large dog next to me and three pairs of pajamas were the only comforts I had.

During the day, the house seemed unusually flooded with light. I realized it was because of the brightness of the snow that was still coming down in bands. No other color could be seen when you looked out the window. Visibility was five feet, which meant you couldn't see past our front porch. It was an eerie sight. No matter how advanced in technology, we were still at the mercy of Mother Nature. Plans had to be made concerning my grandfather's funeral. We soon learned that all arrangements for such things had been postponed indefinitely. I knew the funeral parlor had his body; I wondered where they were keeping it. I learned later that he had been in a garage at the back of the funeral lot. They apparently didn't have cold storage. Cheryl wanted to see my mother, whom she hadn't seen in over twenty years. Jim, having never seen snow before, was driving my grandfather's car to get her there. On the second day of the storm, he walked through the door, visibly shaking. At first, I thought it was the cold; but when he threw himself against the wall, clutching his body as if to reassure himself that he was in one piece, I realized he was just downright scared. The car had been all over the road the entire way. He had witnessed six accidents and gotten stuck in the snow four times. He couldn't believe they had been able to get there. Jim didn't want to go back out in it, but he knew he had to. He seemed uncomfortable with this weather. Considering the fact that this was the first time that most of the family had ever met him, he made an unforgettable first impression. Cheryl, on the other hand, was taking it in stride. She said, "I told you New England weather was unpredictable." Somehow they were able to make it back to Tina's house, after an unfortunately short visit.

In previous years, my mother had been teased about having a hurricane room in the dusty, dirt floor place we called a cellar. It was a room Gil had made, with shelves that she kept canned goods on. For many years she meticulously rotated the cans with food she bought every week. Since our area of Massachusetts hadn't seen a hurricane in as long as we kids could remember, we took the opportunity every week to harass her about this, until eventually, a year before this storm, she had stopped rotating them. When it became evident that we were going to run out of food during this storm, with no relief in sight, and stores running out of supplies, my mother proudly reminded us of the hurricane cellar. Sending us kids down into the bowels of the house, she made us fetch as much as we could carry. I hated going into the cellar. The third step from the bottom had been broken long after Gil had left, and no one had fixed it. Stretching the distance between the two remaining ones hurt my hips. But I never told anyone. It was cold, dark and damp down there. It was a party fest for spiders and cobwebs, and I always wondered why it never scared my mother to be down there. I had made a perfect path to the laundry area. Every time it was my turn to do the wash, I ran to the machines and did it as quickly as I could. I was probably the fastest laundrywoman in the East, without a crown to show for it. It was the perfect playground for the unsuspecting, active mind I had, even as a teenager. When we entered the hurricane room, we were all dismayed by what we saw. In the dampness of the cellar over the past year, all the labels to the cans had fallen off onto the formidable, untouchable, spider-haven dirt floor. There was no way to know what each can contained. Jake, of course, chose this time to have some fun with us and started making howling noises that only added to the already scary sounds we were hearing outside. Grabbing whatever we could in haste, the rest of us scrambled our way back to the stairs in fright. Stuart, naturally, slipped through the broken step and let out a howl of his own. Yelling at us to stop fooling around, my mother stood at the top of the stairs to retrieve the loot. That night we sat down as a family and ate chicken noodle soup with baked beans and condensed milk.

On the last night of the storm, Doug was informed he could go home, if he wanted to. He called us at five in the evening and said he was headed home on foot. His car was completely buried to the roof, and he couldn't find it in the parking lot. He said walking seemed safer, anyway; the emergency room was filled with casualties from accidents. My mother wanted him to stay there. She was worried that he wouldn't make it. The storm had already dropped another two feet of snow, and the drifts were well over ten feet tall, according to the news broadcasts. The worst was the wind chill. There were warnings on TV and radio that no one should be outside for any length of time. Reports were coming in that over a hundred people were trapped on Route 128 in their cars. Elderly and children were also reported missing. They had ventured out into the storm and not been seen since.

My mother was pacing the floor the entire time that Doug was walking home. I sat vigil at the one window in the house that showed any sign of visibility. It was the one in the living room that had cast the shadows of my grandfather and me in the early morning of our last conversation. After several hours, I saw a figure making its way up the street. His camel hair, full-length coat was covered in snow. On top of his uncapped head sat at least six inches of snow in his Afro. I screamed to my mother that I saw him coming. She ran to the door with a towel, yelling to me to boil some water.

Through this whole ordeal, I don't recall losing power. Alex and I kept in touch over the phone. He said he missed me, and it felt like we were never going to get through this. He was living in Peabody at the time, a mile away from my house. He surprised me the day the snow finally stopped by showing up at my house. It took him two and a half hours to get there, and he was frozen from head to toe. My mother made him some hot chocolate, another item she had uncovered from an unlabeled can. He stayed for only a few hours and then headed back. Two days after the storm had stopped, the governor declared it to be unlawful to drive on the streets. My mother had declarations of her own. With the four shovels she found in the cellar, she sent us teenagers out in shifts. When I stepped out onto the porch for my first sight of the devastation, I was blinded by the glare. The sun was shining, causing it to be impossible to see. The snow that lay before me stood four feet tall. Where there were drifts, it was past our second floor porch. How on earth were we ever going to shovel out from this? My cousin Stuart looked at me with a big smile and said, "This is going to be fun!" I thought he was crazy.

We had to shovel two hours at a time, removing the snow in painfully slow layers. To shovel a foot's distance took at least five shoveled layers. Even then, we never saw the pavement. Because we lived on a corner lot, we had at least forty feet of sidewalk to shovel, not counting two driveways. Rotating through the kids in the family, my mother figured we would be cleared out by dinner. After every shift, I took a hot shower. It was the only way to warm up before I had to go out again. Stuart decided to take this opportunity to make some money. On his shifts off, he shoveled out as many neighbors as he could. He was smart; he chose ones that had the least amount of frontage first. Eventually, we just let him do that and took his shifts at home ourselves. Word got around he was doing this, and for two weeks that was all he did. I think he single-handedly shoveled our entire street.

After a week, even my mother's hurricane food started running out, as well as any available cash she and Joe had on hand. We had heard that a store, a mile up the road in Peabody, had received a shipment from the National Guard. Once again, it was Stuart who came through. He said, "I have enough money. If I take the toboggan I saw in the cellar, I'm sure I could get there and back." Feeling the excitement of the moment, not to mention the ever present cabin fever, "I'll go with him," I stated.

And that is how I became to have the most fond and memorable moment of Stuart and my relationship. My mother made us bundle up in two layers of clothing. Long before cell phones, she had to set us free into the snow-covered tundra with only her blessing. The snow on the street was packed down in some places and not in others. The plows, although still trying to clear them, could only realistically remove a few feet of it. There was just nowhere to put the rest. The mounds on the side of the road were well above the first branches of every tree we passed. The trek to the store was uphill all the way. Coming back was an anticipated joy ride that kept us steady on our journey. We were sure we were going to experience the sled ride of a lifetime going home. Along the way, we were struck by the amount of people who had taken to the streets. They were joyful and talkative to one another, an aberration I had never witnessed in this neighborhood before. Some of them knew Stuart from shoveling and were thanking him for the job he had done. Before we knew it, we were one of them, chatting away about the storm and the store that was now supplied a mile up the road. It took us almost two hours to get to it. Together pulling the sled, we never let the other down from fatigue. We had a job to do, and others were relying on us to get it done.

When we finally arrived, the place was packed. Pandemonium was everywhere. It was hard to even step foot in this small, mom and pop store. The line was out the door and around the corner. We soon learned that the supplies were being rationed by household. Stuart calmly went to the owner and told him we had two families trapped under one roof. He said we had had a death in the family and that his family was from out of town. The man took a shine to this straight forward teenager and gave us rations for two households. We purchased tuna, milk, bread and peanut butter. Stuart, always thinking, grabbed cereal and as many boxes of pasta he could carry. While we were waiting in line, I noticed they also had skeins of yarn for a very cheap price of three for a dollar. Stuart noticed me looking at it and put six skeins on the counter. He smiled at me and said, "Knit me a blanket, we could use more of them, too." I smiled and gave him a big hug. The thought of doing something with my hands through this long, drawn out ordeal was like a gift from above.

The projected slide back to the house was disappointing. Because the snow was so uneven, we found we were only allotted a few yards at a time for this joyous endeavor. It didn't matter; we were having fun and would be hailed the heroes when we arrived home in a few hours. The minute I stepped into the warmth of the house my mother was already drawing me a bath. I laughed when I saw her do this without me asking. It was a wonderful reward for a job well done. My nose was so red and hurt; I thought it was going to fall off. Slipping into the tub, I immediately fell asleep. I did knit that blanket Stuart had suggested. It took me two weeks to do it. It was warm and cozy with crazy colors.

The day of my grandfather's wake, the National Guard had to bring us to the funeral parlor. They had been driving my brother Doug to the hospital daily, so they knew the route easily. It was a strange experience seeing the army trucks as the only vehicles on the streets. When we reached the downtown area, the place was a vast desert of snow. All the stores were closed, and the cars had been replaced by people in sleds and cross country skis. If a person viewing the scene had to put a date on the year, it would have been difficult to do so.

The whole ordeal lasted two weeks. During that time, Salem and its surrounding communities were at a stand still. If it weren't for the fact that my grandfather had died, it would have been a wonderful time for all of us. The news was still reporting horror stories from the storm. Many people who had been stranded in their cars on route 128 that first night were dead.

CHAPTER: 20

High school to me never meant the glory days that a lot of people talk about. It was about getting in, getting it over with, getting out, and then getting out of the house. It felt like my life was filled with crowds of people, all with their own agendas, and I was merely there for the ride. Everywhere I turned, someone was telling me what to do and how to think. The world was beginning to change with a liking towards prepackaged conveniences; high school was no exception to this new way of American living. It had become a life of making things simple: everything was categorized for the sake of saving time and money. Each student was prepackaged in the new tracking system. They passed judgment and pigeonholed you as to how smart you were and how well they felt you could handle certain information. If you were put into group two...that's where they felt comfortable leaving you. You were considered average, not smart...not dumb...just a flat line. Once in this tracking system, it was where you stayed. For some it was a label they would hold the rest of their lives. Well, not me...I wanted more. I was craving intelligent conversation and debate. I wanted independence from the chains of both the institutions I was a part of: school and home. Alex felt the same way I did, but, unlike me, he saw no way out. In the beginning of my junior year, I found an escape. Because I had crammed my schedule freshmen year, I soon realized that I could graduate at the end of junior year, that is, if I kept up the pace and received all my credits. Back then, you only needed two years of math and science, and foreign language was not a requirement. All I had to do was take an extra gym and English, and I was all set. Tensions at home were getting difficult again, and I knew I needed to get out. I was required to fill my junior year schedule with courses that I had not yet taken. By chance, I took a course in child growth and development. The teacher was extremely boring, but the subject matter was very interesting to me. The class not only discussed the physical development of a child but also the emotional one as well.

One day, I raised my hand in class and asked the teacher, "What does it mean when an individual doesn't outgrow his childhood fears?" I was thinking about my Shadow Man who was still with me after all these years.

She simply stated, "In a child of normal development, he more than likely was not nurtured in a way to overcome them and conquer them. Sometimes it can be because his environment was unpredictable leaving the child not knowing what to expect."

This was a confirmation for me, an understanding that my fears were normal; it was because my environment was unpredictable. I realized these night time fears must be common for someone in my situation. This new found information was just another example in my life that made me stronger and allowed me to become more of an individual. I became obsessed with the subject of development. I took every course on it the high school had to offer, and I got straight A's in every one. It was as enduring for me as my art.

One day, my teacher in child psychology approached me to be a part of a new program called "The Child Care Program."

"Barb, we are opening a new program here at the high school. I think you might be most interested in taking it. It is going to be a nursery school class setting. The teachers will be high school students. They will make lesson plans and chart the children's development. There will be a high school teacher to monitor the learning of both the preschoolers and the high school students who are in attendance."

"Oh, wow! I would like to do that. Let me see what I can do with my course list for this semester coming up."

"Well, here, I wrote up the details. Tell your guidance counselor to fit it into your schedule."

"Thank you for thinking of me," I said with a huge smile. I was so excited about this new program. It was in its first year, and I was going to be in on the ground floor.

The high school teacher I had assigned to me was a woman in her sixties by the name of Mrs. Buras. She was a soft spoken, kind-hearted individual. Her demeanor and heart told me that she was fulfilling a calling. I didn't know it then, but this woman would change my life, and in turn, change the lives of many children in the future who would cross my path. She was the nucleus of the ripple in that wave. I loved her dearly and always will. On the first day, Mrs. Buras made a statement that is at the core of how I think today. She said that in order for all children to learn and grow in a healthy way, they must ultimately feel safe. To make a child feel safe, one must first make his environment safe. She was, in fact, making reference to the class room; I, however, saw it on many different levels, all of which were personal. Suddenly, the inadequacies of my home life and my various school environments were being made clear to me. The struggles in math were not because I was dumb, they were due to the unusual circumstances surrounding those important years, the over-crowded and noisy classrooms. More than one year, I had to sit in a room shared by two classes with two separate teachers; a teacher who hit me with an eraser caused me to refuse to return. It was an unfortunate chain of events. At home, a similar story was happening; I was being moved constantly to a new house every year until the age of eight. My mother would subject the family to the huge issues of other people's problems under our own roof. She would force us to live with them and make them our own problems. As a result I was robbed of my security, the true core of what every child needs.

I decided that day that, although I couldn't take back what was so nonchalantly taken from me, I could ensure that it didn't happen to other children. I left the class that afternoon and went to see my school guidance counselor. My guidance counselor was an older woman who was in the home stretch before retirement. She was leaving at the end of the school year and, as a result, had not been much help for me in the past. She was rarely in her office, and this day was no different. Out of frustration and disbelief at the inadequacies of her performance, I knocked on the counselor's door next to hers. A middle aged man by the name of Mr. Byron opened it.

"Yes, may I help you?"

"Hi, my name is Barb, I am wondering if you could help me?" I looked him in the eyes unflinchingly. He looked back at me with curiosity. Stepping aside from the open door, he gestured me to take a seat. I sat down and put my books on the corner of his desk. I confidently made myself at home.

"Mr. Bryon, I would like to enlist you as my new guidance counselor. You see, there are things I need to do in my life, and I first need a guidance counselor in order to achieve them. The counselor I have is never in her office, and every time I want to speak to her, I need to do it with a note under the door. Well this time it isn't going to cut it....so I am firing her, and I want you." He was both surprised and impressed by this audacious girl he had never met. I was bold, determined and needed some answers.

"Who is your counselor now?" he asked.

"She is the woman next door. I hear she is retiring soon." Leaning forward, I added in a softer tone, "Hell, I am not even sure I know what she looks like."

"Well, Barb, I can't just take you away from her as one of my students. But why don't you start at the beginning and tell me what is on your mind. Maybe there is something that I can do."

"You can't just talk to her and tell her that you are going to be my counselor now?" I was still stuck on his words that told me I had to stay with her.

"Barb, it is somewhat unethical."

"Isn't it unethical that she is never there when I need her?" Although he didn't say it, I could see that he agreed with me from the look in his eyes.

"What is it that you want?" he asked me.

"I want to drop out of all my art classes and work towards finishing all of my child care courses, so that I may graduate at the end of junior year and go to college to become a teacher."

"Do you want to become an art teacher? Because if you do, then you will need a portfolio."

"No, I want to become a nursery school teacher. I want to work with children at the most important time in their lives."

"Well, right off the bat, you have one major problem. They have discontinued the early graduation program this year. No one is allowed to graduate early anymore."

In a split second, all the blood drained from my face, and I thought I would faint. I sat there in silence and stared at the floor, trying to swallow the lump in my throat, no longer the fired up girl I had been one minute earlier. All you could hear was the ticking off of the clock that was keeping time with the slow, sad beating of my heart. After a minute of silence, while Mr. Byron waited patiently, I found my voice again, but the tone was different.

Looking down at my feet, I said, "You don't understand; I have to get out of my house." It was more a statement that escaped my lips and fell softly onto the floor. He wasn't sure if I was talking to him or to myself.

Mr. Byron immediately stood up and closed the door. Without warning, I burst into tears. For a while, I couldn't stop. He handed me a box of tissues and stated firmly, "I'll do whatever I can to help you. Let's start from the beginning."

I told him about the lack of support I was receiving at home, the unfortunate and sometimes dangerous situations I was forced to live in, the feelings of being simply the maid for the family, the violence I had to endure if I didn't comply. I told him the thing that bothered me the most was that my family didn't even know me. They saw my drive for something more out of life as selfish and uncompassionate. He told me that people sometimes do that; they see their own faults in others unfairly. Many times those people never change, because to do so would require them to look inside. I felt better after he told me that. It brought definition to actions that had no meaning. Next we talked about my future and how he would help.

"Wait here; I am going to go get your school records out in the hall." I got confused. I had always imagined them in an iron, underground vault at an undisclosed location somewhere in town. Now I found out they were in the hall? It was hard to believe that my complete school history was in a manila folder inside a file cabinet drawer five feet away. Children hear about these records all the time, usually as a warning to curb bad behavior, and here mine now sat on his desk, in his office. Except for my name, the file was free of markings. It looked cold and sterile, filled with facts stated without feeling. What did it say about the fights I had had in junior high? Did it explain that I didn't start them? And the eraser incident, was that in there? How on earth could a school system explain such a horrible injustice? I was sure it wasn't in my favor. I began to get nervous, and my hands started to tremble. I wanted so badly to see that file and vowed to myself that it would be the first thing I took when I graduated.

If it was all in there, Mr. Byron didn't care. He turned to my high school pages.

"Barbara, there is nothing I can do about the early graduation, but there is something else that you may find interesting and more to your liking. They have started a new program called Dual Enrollment. Simply put, you are still in high school, yet you take classes at Salem State College. You could do that next year, when you are a senior. The courses you would be taking will be similar to Mrs. Buras' class. The requirements will force you to drop all your art classes. There is only one glitch: you have to take a course in child health at the high school that year, and they are all full. I will talk to the nurse who teaches the class and find out if she has any suggestions around that. Come see me tomorrow, and I will tell you what I have learned.

He let that sink in for me, and after a while, he said, "Maybe this will give you the respect you are looking for."

"Well it still doesn't get me out of the house. But you are right, it might gain me some respect. OK, I will do it. What do I need to do?"

"Nothing, I will work it out with your real guidance counselor." Then he smiled at me with a knowing grin, as I left his office. I had entered his office as a child, but, thirty minutes later, I walked out of it as an adult.

When I left Mr. Byron, I ran to meet Alex. He had been concerned, because I wasn't where we usually met, and it was getting late. I was so excited when I told him about the meeting. I was jumping and skipping as we talked, and it was hard for him to understand what I was saying.

"You cancelled all your art classes?" was all he could say in his disbelief.

"I had to," I said. "I needed to make room for the other child care courses."

"But what about your art?" he asked.

"What I want to do is more important than art."

"It sounds admirable, but will you be happy?" "I guess I'll just have to find out," I said. We walked the rest of the way in silence.

Over the next several weeks, I was surprised by the reactions to my plans that I received from people I knew. My art teachers were concerned that I was throwing away all my dreams on an impulse. They talked to me for an hour during my lunch time. My friends became distant, as if I were no longer one of them. When I would catch up to them, they would be discussing their own projects and art assignments. No one asked me about my decision. I never spoke of it either. Maybe I had changed that day, and they could see it better than I could. I was going to go to college, while they would still be stuck in high school. My mother's only concern was whether I could handle it. She felt I was too young to be in college, and maybe I was in over my head. Those were the only words she ever voiced to me on the subject. My relationship with Alex changed most of all. This new glimmer of hope in my life gave me confidence and direction, so that I no longer needed a protector. He felt it right away.

CHAPTER: 21

When school let out for the summer, I decided to get a job. I knew eventually I would be paying for college, and I wanted to save some money. I applied at the hospital to work in the kitchen. Within a week, I was employed; I would be working on both the breakfast and lunch assembly lines. I had to be at my station by 6:00 AM. Since I didn't drive, this meant I had to leave my house by five for the three mile walk. I wouldn't finish work until 2:30 PM, but in the afternoon, I could get a ride with a guy I went to school with, and he went out of his way for me. That gave me plenty of time to get back and clean the house before Mom arrived at home at four.

"So I hear you got a job." "Yes, I did. I want to save for college, and babysitting wouldn't be enough." "Well, you do realize that this means you have to pay "room and board" now?" "I figured...how much?" "What are you making per week?" "I take home sixty dollars."

"Then you need to give me forty." I wanted to tell her that, at that rate, I would never get to college. I knew arguing with her would only cause a huge fight, so I chose to be quiet. She gave me that sour look and asked, "Do you have a problem with that?" "No," I said and headed to my room to read. I was not surprised; she had asked this of my brothers as well. It was just one more kick in the head, as far as I was concerned. What I was surprised about was the amount she wanted. I had never asked her to pay for my college, because I had known it would be pointless. I knew she would just shrug her shoulders and say, "Oh well." I was also sure she would have told me that if I was old enough to be responsible and get a job, then I was old enough to be responsible to pay for where I was living. There was no use talking to her. As far as she was concerned, college was a luxury, a pipe dream. I kept my opinions to myself, but I thought she was an idiot.

Alex and I broke up that summer. We were going in two different directions. We were outgrowing each other. He was still talking about going to New York to try his hand at acting; I had plans to live with Aunt Cheryl in California. Once I was there for a year and had established residency, my education would be free. It was the only way I saw myself being able to go to college. Montessori schools were widespread out there, and that was the direction I wanted to go in. It was a sad day when Alex and I decided not to see each other anymore. We were in the courtyard at lunch time, when it happened. It was mutual, and we were sitting very close. He had both his arms around me in a sitting embrace. Our heads were touching, and we were looking at the ground during the whole conversation. To an outside observer, it would have looked like we were talking about our undying love. In a weird way, we sort of were. We were letting each other go, so that we could each follow our dreams. I wanted to feel what it was like to be on my own, without attachments, before I left. I had a lot of work ahead of me, and I knew our relationship would get in the way.

Without Alex to buffer the blows, my relationship with my mother deteriorated rapidly. I was beginning to dislike her so much and resented her for the torment I had to put up with. When I got out of work, once the housework was completed, I went to the library. I would stay for hours alone in the stacks and read. I liked to read about great figures in the past, mostly child psychologists, like Piaget and Maria Montessori. I read every book I could find about Maria Montessori and the work she did with "The Children's House" in Italy. Working against the tide in a man's world, she accomplished great things. She became my idol.

I developed a lot of new friends after Alex and I broke up. One was the brother of Cherri's boyfriend, Edward. Every one called him Emilio, because he looked Mexican, but he was really full blooded French. Emilio was twenty-one and had already graduated. He was in school to become a computer programmer, a new job field that had just opened up. He and Edward lived together, because their father was elderly and in a home, and their mother had died. Edward was nineteen. It was a sight to see, these two boys trying to make it on their own. Edward was going to Salem State to become a teacher and worked at a local after-school program for children. Although they both worked, it was difficult for them to make ends meet. They had monthly rent and tuition that they were both responsible for. To supplement their income, they sold pot. It was purely a business venture. We did party on the weekends together, but because we were all so tied up with our own career interests, those were the only times we got together.

On the weekends, I met a lot of their friends. They were all nice people. Some were seriously going places, while others were clearly not. Those people were just there to buy dope, and I tried to stay away from them as much as possible. Emilio and I started seeing each other. He would take me to a bar downtown to listen to his friend, Jay, play acoustic guitar. Jay was very talented and sang popular folk songs, as well as ones he wrote himself. He could play any instrument he was given. He and Emilio were the same age and had gone all through Catholic school together; they were best friends. Jay was married to a girl by the name of Denise, and they had a five month old baby, named Jenny. Denise and I became very close. She was a year older than I, and we spent a lot of time together. I became very attached to her daughter and would baby-sit for them, whenever they needed it. I never thought to take money from them for this service; they didn't have it.

School, in the meantime, was getting hectic. Now in my senior year, I was cramming courses again. Mr. Byron came through for me like he had said he would. He was able to get the school nurse to give me lessons independently on Child Health and counted it as a class. Unfortunately, because of her schedule and limited time, the only time I could see her was 6:30 AM, a half hour before school started. After I saw the nurse, I would go to my homeroom and report in. My college class was not until noontime. A mini-bus was provided for me and three other students to get there. They were in a different department at the college, so we only saw each other on the bus. Because I had this time between home room and college, I asked if I could take Mrs. Buras' class again that year. Mr. Byron worked it out. I enjoyed all my classes, and, after school, I worked the night shift in the kitchen at the hospital. My hours there were now 3:30 to 8:00 PM. It was a rotating schedule that included some weekends; usually I got two days off, but not always. When I got home at night, I did my homework for health class and made my lesson plans for my nursery school classes. I was relieved of my household chores at home, because I was rarely there. Walking to school required me to leave the house at 5:30 AM and didn't return until 8:00 or 8:30 PM, depending on whether I had gotten out of work early. Fortunately a friend always drove me home.

Everything was going smoothly, and I was able to keep up the pace, until the day I walked into Mrs. Buras's class, and it was total bedlam. Preschoolers were chasing each other with toys. The high school students were clustered together with their hands in their pockets, hoping they could go unnoticed and looking a bit lost. Mrs. Buras was out sick, and we were informed that she would be out for six weeks. She had to have an operation but was ok. The teacher who was giving us this information was the substitute. He was about twenty-five years old, not married and no children. He had majored in history in college. He didn't seem to care what was going on around him and was angry at the administration for putting him in such a predicament. He verbalized this to us as well. In my opinion he was the worst person to put in this position. I thought of Mrs. Buras and how disappointed she would have been at the unsafe environment this was creating in her classroom. I went into action.

"Where is Thumbkin...where is Thumbkin...here I am." As I got the children's attention, I purposely began lowering and softening my voice to bring down the energy of the room. Walking from one section of the room to the other as I sang, I found myself to be The Pied Piper. By the time I reached the carpeted area where we held our morning gatherings, all the children were sitting quietly and waiting for my next song. I handed a book to one of the high school girls to read to them. Seeing me take charge, the substitute came over to me.

"Are you Barbara?" I said, "Yes."

"Good," he responded. "I have a note here from Mrs. Buras that says if I have any difficulty, you know what to do." "You do realize that teaching this class requires two separate lesson plans: one for the high school students and one for the nursery school children?" He was surprised by my directness. "I figured that, but I know nothing about early elementary education. It wasn't my major in college." "Well, I have all my notes and tests and lessons from last year. Let me see her lessons, and maybe we can figure it out. If I know Mrs. Buras, she is pretty organized. Are you going to be the substitute for the duration of her absence?" "What do you think? They got me because I was desperate for the money and they couldn't find anyone else."

That day was tough. We were working on the fly. The substitute told the high school girls that I was basically in charge, along with him, and they had to listen to me. At first I thought that was going to be a problem. I had known some of these students since grammar school, and I wasn't sure how they would take to me being their boss. What I soon realized was that, in many ways, they were like the four year olds. Although they didn't verbalize it, they wanted a comfortable, safe environment for their class too. The chaos was too much for them to take.

When I got home from work that night, I took all of Mrs. Buras's lessons and tried to sort through them. Using my own papers from the last year, it became easy to figure out the lessons she had planned for the nursery class. The tough part was the high school students' requirements. Making a chart, not unlike my mother's chore chart, I plotted my course. The easiest way for me to do it was to figure out how many tests were expected of us for the time in which she would be gone and then work backwards from there. Basically, I would be teaching from the tests. This, I knew in my heart, was not the best way to have a student totally comprehend what they were learning, but I felt, under the circumstances, I didn't have a choice.

I was up all night, making lessons for a three day stretch. Shadow Man sat diligently next to me. It was a comfort to know I wasn't alone. Along with the children's lessons, I also had to go over the information the high school girls would need to know in order to do their jobs accurately, with understanding. Because it was September, the focus was on autonomy. This involved teaching the children how to write their first names and do basic daily rituals like zippering their coats. I remembered some children's books, in the class from the previous year, which were used to support the lessons at story time. Using the theories I had learned independently about Montessori, I took the whole plan one step further. I decided to give the small children their own chore charts with their names and gave them simple tasks, such as passing out snacks and cleaning the table. At project time, I had them glue squares of sandpaper onto a separate piece of paper, spelling out their names. According to Montessori theory, the tactile experience they would receive from the sand paper would aid them in remembering the letters. Montessori was not listed on Mrs. Buras' lesson plan, but I saw no harm in incorporating something new for the test. So I wrote a lesson on those theories too, for the high school girls, and added them to the tests. The biggest dilemma I had was whether I should also take the test. Because Mrs. Buras always scaled the grades, I felt this would not be fair. Besides, I soon learned that I would receive no help from the substitute, and I would be administering them as well. Mrs. Buras had given us a test every Friday. In a few weeks time, I was feeling the effects of my schedule, and Mrs. Buras was not due back for three more weeks. Most nights, I only got a couple of hours sleep. In my head, I knew this was good training for me. I also knew there was no one else to do it. The substitute sat at Mrs. Buras's desk and didn't participate in anything. He felt he was the adult body in the room that was required by law, and that was all he was there for.

One day, I was late for my meeting with the nurse. This caused a domino effect on my time constraints for my other classes. Although there were still fifteen minutes until homeroom bell, there were a lot of little things that had to be done in the nursery before the class started. Racing down the deserted corridor, juggling all my books, the hallway started to spin in my head. I stopped and tried to support myself on one of the long banisters. I was dizzy, and I knew it was because I had skipped breakfast that morning. I was doing a lot of ritualistic things with my eating habits back then. I would often not eat for an entire day. If I did, I would only grab a package of crackers at the hospital. It was a strange kind of control I was having with my body. Although I was five foot seven, my weight had plummeted to 105 pounds. It was all about control and my lack of it. When the books dropped from my hands and made a loud crash on the floor, a science teacher that I knew came out of his class to investigate what the commotion was. Seeing me sitting on the floor, bracing myself, he came to my aid. He asked me if I was all right and helped me to my feet. I told him I was fine. He said he saw me every morning, racing down the hall before school, and wondered what I was up to. Without getting into detail, I told him I was helping the substitute with Mrs. Buras's class. I think he understood more than what I told him, because every day after that, when I passed his door, he asked me how it was going. It felt good to know that someone was keeping an eye on me, a sign that I was still just a kid myself.

Somehow I got through those six weeks. I always felt that if it had been even one week more, I myself would have ended up in the hospital. No one was more excited than I was to see Mrs. Buras sitting at her desk, when I arrived one morning. She had never been an overly demonstrative person. I greeted her with a polite "Welcome back." She thanked me for all that I had done and stated firmly, "From the looks of the lesson plans, you did more than your share." I wondered if she understood that her substitute had been, in fact, me, but I never mentioned it. It wouldn't be until she had written me a letter of recommendation for college a few months later that I realized that she had.

Working at the hospital was fun, and I enjoyed it very much. Basically, there was an assembly line of trays that rolled down a conveyer belt, each tray with a menu on it. All the menus were different; most were special diets. Along the line were stations that matched up with various sections on the menu. For instance, the first station was the milks, then the desserts, next was the entrées, and so on. There were approximately fifteen people who worked the line. Almost all of us at night were high school and college kids. In order for the line to run smoothly, we all had to be in sync in a type of rhythm. The supervisor would let us off a half hour early, if all our work was done. We were rotated through every station in the course of the week, so that we could perform them all. The toughest one was the "hot side." This was the station with the hot entrees, and the degree of difficulty depended on what was being served that night. Some of us were better at this than others, and we knew it. When the entrée was a difficult one, such as fish, we would change the schedule on our own to improve the efficiency of the line. The person who was removed from the hot side was usually relieved. The person put on the hot side usually felt honored. The supervisor was an older woman, a motherly type, and was just glad that we all worked so well together. When the cooks set up the stations, we were all poised and ready. Looking down the line, we all gave each other the official nod and a grin. Down came the trays from the far end of the line, like a well timed symphony. The first person put on the menus according to the floors. The silverware and condiments came next. Milks and juices followed, with over fifteen to choose from, then desserts, with as much of a selection. The hot side, holding the entrees and pureed meats and vegetables, was next, immediately followed by the cold side, with the sandwiches. Our eyes were fixed on the menus; our hands flew in time with the music on the radio. We were so well trained as to where all our items were, that we didn't lift our heads until the line was through. Our entire job for the night consisted of supplying the trays with the right menus and food, then delivering them all to the proper floors of the two separate hospitals that were side by side in location. We had a twenty minute dinner break ourselves, and then we had to do the whole thing in reverse. We picked up the trays from the rooms and brought them back to the kitchen for washing, putting away and prepping for the morning breakfast. When I worked the day shift in the summer, it took the line an hour and a half just to get the trays on the carts for delivery. At night, this same job took us kids forty minutes. Fortunately, there was a dietician checking all the trays before they were delivered, but we rarely made mistakes. The incentive to leave early governed us to work together as a team and perform the most efficient line that hospital probably ever saw. This was another life lesson for me that I would use in the future: having a common, purposeful goal makes everyone work more efficiently.

One Saturday before work, the entire crew went to Crane Beach. We did things together like that a lot. Somebody brought half a sandwich bag of dope; others were in charge of the picnic food. It was September, but the weather was warm. Because the water was cold, no one went swimming. We sat and talked, ate and got high. It was civilized, and no one bothered us. The beach was deserted. At around 2:00 PM, we all loaded up into several cars and headed for work. We had a great time and were in good spirits, laughing and joking. When we got to work and looked at the roster, everyone started laughing.

"Hahaha, Barb, you have hot side, and the entree is fish!"

I said, "Well this should prove to be entertaining!" I laughed with the rest of them. Fish was the hardest entre to serve because it broke apart so easily. It was the one dish that could break our perfect rhythm and keep us from leaving early.

Standing on the line, ready to begin, I noticed the person doing desserts was staring into space with his mouth hung wide open, in a haze of drug induced euphoria. Poking the person next to me, I motioned him to look at this funny spectacle. All the way down the line, people were drawing attention to desserts. We started to giggle, and, before you knew it, we were all roaring in laughter. Our supervisor made a comment about how good it was to work with young people who all got along and were so happy. That was it; we were no good after that. When the trays started rolling down the line, our rhythm was off. At times, it was going so slow, it actually stopped: a first for this crew. In a panic about not getting it down in time to get off early, we would try to speed up, but none of us were in sync. This caused laughter again, which by now was irritating the dietitian.

The fish was just not cooperating with me that night. Every time I tried to pick it up with the spatula, it kept breaking into pieces. Because the rhythm was to scoop a plate at the same time in one horizontal motion, I found myself more than once sending the fish flying across the room. Desserts got hit with it a few times, and because of his delay in reaction time, couldn't get out of the way. He got it square in the face. The laughter would start all over again. Then the worst thing happened. I was scooping a ladle of pureed meat into its container and missed. It went down my bare leg and into my shoe. To fully understand this atrocity, you would have to know about pureed meat. It looked and smelled like vomit. How anyone could eat this stuff was beyond me. I spent the rest of the night slipping and sliding, not to mention my foot was burning from the hot meat.

When it came time to retrieve the trays and wash the dishes, we weren't any better at it. Coming down now from our high, it felt like it took a lifetime to complete the task. We all worked in silence, only to be broken by an occasional, "Are we still here?" That would start the giggling all over again. We didn't get out until 8:30 PM that night, a half hour past our pay time. After that we vowed to not do our partying before work.

That spring brought me new promise. I was going to be graduating in a short time, and I was making plans with Aunt Cheryl for the move. My mom was not thrilled with me making such a drastic decision and came home from work at the factory with what she thought was good news. She was working at a new place in Woburn, doing a job similar to her old one.

"Barb, I talked to my supervisor, and I was able to get him to give you a job next to me on the assembly line! Isn't that great? You will be starting at just under three dollars an hour. But if you do a good job, you will get a twenty cent raise in three months."

"Mom, I am going to be in California for college."

"I wish you would stop with these aspirations of college. I have this job waiting for you, and you're just going to throw it away?"

"Wait, let me get this straight. You want me to throw away my chances to go to college instead? I want to become a teacher. Besides, why would anyone want to do such a degrading, manual labor job that is going to go nowhere?" She slapped me across the face.

A silent cloud hung over us for days, neither of us saying a word, and then, when I thought things couldn't get any worse, the sky fell down on top of me. Aunt Cheryl called from California, concerned and wanting to talk to me. She told me my cousin Sam had gotten his girlfriend pregnant, so she had moved in with them. When the baby arrived, they would need the spare room for a nursery.

There was no longer room for me. I heard the words she was telling me echo in my ears. It was as if I were in a tunnel, deep down below the ground. I was trapped, and there was no way out. My dreams were shattered. All my hard work (that I still hadn't completed) meant nothing.

When I told my mother what had happened, she was glad and sarcastic.

"Well, see, the only person you can truly rely on is me. I will talk to my boss in the morning."

"Mom, I am not going to go and work with you. Please don't push it." For the first time, I wondered if she were jealous of my ambitions. We fought constantly and began to truly hate one another. When we weren't fighting, we didn't speak; we couldn't even look at each other. I was still giving her most of my pay. Doug had moved out of the house, and Jake and I were supplementing her income, under the guise of making us responsible human beings.

A few months prior to this, I had gotten a call from Jay and Denise. They were planning a surprise thirtieth anniversary party for Denise's parents, to be held in New Hampshire near her parents' house. They had wanted to know if I could watch the baby in Salem overnight. This was scheduled for the following week. I had told my mother about this event when I was asked to sit and reminded her of it that week. She said, "Well, I made plans to take a trip to Washington State for a week, and Aunt Flo will be staying with you."

This made me furious. My Aunt Flo was my grandmother's sister and was nastier than my mother. She was in her sixties, unreasonable, with no room to bend. When she would visit us, she always asked me embarrassing personal questions about my home life and my physical development. She was a person who loved to argue and would hunt out topics to do so.

"You'd better tell her I am babysitting for Denise on Saturday or she will throw a fit. How could you do this to me?"

"Why do you always feel I am doing something to you? Maybe I just want to know that everything will be ok when I get home!"

"Because you don't trust me and treat me horribly!" I screamed. "It has always been about control with you." This comment was met with a slap.

The first hour that Aunt Flo arrived her grilling began. She, as usual, was trying to get me to say something bad about my mother. This was a complicated position for me to be in. Over the years, Flo and my mother had never trusted each other and would badmouth each other behind their backs at every opportunity. My mother, somehow, knew she was questioning me and would grill me in return, always ending with a reminder to tell Flo nothing. My way of dealing with it was to take no sides and not tell either of them anything.

When the interrogation about my mother didn't work, Flo asked me if I had my period. This was the icing on the cake for me. In a very irritated voice, I said, "What does that have to do with anything? And besides, that is none of your business." So we got off on the wrong foot right from the start. My schedule was still crazy at school, and she didn't believe that I was where I said I was. She would call all the places I went to during the course of the day to see if I were lying. At night when I was trying to write my lesson plans, she would tell me it was bed time and to put out the light. By the end of the week, I was ready to kill her, and she knew it.

I had told her the first day she came that I was planning on spending the night at Denise's house that Saturday to watch the baby.

"Aunt Flo, did mom tell you I am going to babysit for Denise and Jay on Saturday? I will be staying overnight, and I will give you the phone number."

"Who are Denise and Jay? Are they married? How old are they? Did they have to get married because she was pregnant? I don't think I want you hanging around with such a promiscuous girl. How come Jay is so much older than she? Does she like older men?" Some of these questions I had never even thought of, never mind knew anything about. She told me Jay was too old to be hanging around with, and Denise was a bad influence. When I told her Denise was my age, she said, "I don't care, you can't go." I couldn't win with her. And I was furious at my mother for not telling her my plans.

I was determined to go. Every day I told her in a non-threatening way that I was still going on Saturday night, so she wouldn't worry when I didn't come home.

Every day, she matter of factly stated, "No you're not."

And so went our week, until Saturday rolled around. Fortunately, I had had the insight to switch my hours at work for the day shift. I would get out at 3:00 PM, and I had planned for Denise to pick me up from work. That would give her plenty of time to drive to New Hampshire. I left my Aunt Flo with the phone number and address, so she wouldn't go crazy on me and could call to confirm I was there... big mistake. She had already called Denise at noon time to grill her. She was asking her when she had gotten pregnant and how old the baby was. I was so embarrassed by my aunt's behavior; I was apologizing profusely to Denise. She took it in stride. Jay chose to just tease me about it. From that day on, Flo became known as Aunt Blows.

Jenny was in an awful mood when we arrived at their house. Denise told me she wasn't feeling well, because she was teething. Jenny was always a difficult baby to put to bed; I knew this was going to be a long night. I had brought all my school work with me and intended on making lesson plans the whole time. I was looking forward to catching up on my work and, hopefully, doing extra. The minute Denise and Jay left, the phone calls started.

"Hello," I answered the phone. "Barbara, it is Aunt Flo. I want you home right now."

"Aunt Flo, Jay and Denise left; I am here with the baby. I can't come home." I kept my voice calm. I knew that if I raised it, she would too.

"Then pack up the baby and bring her here, right now!"

"That is ludicrous, where on earth will she sleep? Besides, she is a cranky baby who is teething right now, and I just got her settled down, not to mention that I don't have a way to get us there, since I don't drive, and I am four miles away." As I spoke to her, it felt like I was watching it all play out on a TV show. I was so detached from myself that my voice remained calm. Even then, I knew it was my way of protecting me from what I was really feeling. Then she said something so shocking, I almost fell off my chair. She said, "I know you are at a party, doing drugs and having sex with boys, and I'm going to tell your mother." I hung up on her, but that didn't stop her; she called me every fifteen minutes. I tried to disconnect the phone, but it was an old-fashioned wall phone, and I couldn't. Besides, if Denise called, she would be worried sick, if she couldn't get through. Flo called me all night long, until about midnight. Every time I picked up the phone, I'd say, "You're being unreasonable; I'm hanging up." Not once did I raise my voice. I had learned this from Mrs. Buras: when dealing with children, you state the facts as simply and clearly as possible about your next action, then follow through. To make matters worse, every time she called, she woke the baby. Jenny didn't get any sleep that night, and I didn't get any work done.

When Denise and Jay got home the next morning, I told them what had happened. In the dawn of the new day, I realized that I had crossed a line, and I couldn't get back. My mother was expected back by 1:00 PM, and I knew she was going to get an earful from Flo about partying, drugs and sex. I knew she would believe her and be twice as upset having it be Flo who knew what I was supposedly doing. In her eyes, this would be the ammunition Flo needed to badmouth her. In reality, my mother was just watching her own back. Denise and Jay thought Flo was bluffing and that my mom would never think that of me. They didn't know my Aunt Flo, and they didn't know my mother.

As the day wore on, I became more and more nervous. My hands started to shake at round 11:30 AM and got worse as the clock ticked away every minute. By 1:00 PM I was a basket case. Denise and Jay knew this and asked me what the worse was I thought would happen. I said, "My mother is going to beat the crap out of me, and unless I hit her back this time, I will be defenseless."

"You're not defenseless," they said. "We are going with you. If she sees the baby, she won't get violent." I still wasn't convinced, but I wanted them with me anyway.

When I walked into the house my mother was in the dining room. I tried to act like everything was fine, but I could tell by the look on her face that it wasn't. There we were, squared off for battle, three of us on one side of the room, my mother holding a dinner plate at the other. She was apparently in the middle of emptying the dishwasher. I didn't have a chance. I tried to make small talk. I said, "You remember Jay and Denise and the baby." She didn't respond in kind.

"Who the hell do you think you are, causing all this trouble!? Right now, Aunt Flo is calling everyone she can think of and telling them what a whoring drug addict you are!"

The words hit me like a ton of bricks. Composing myself, I said, "Then she is a liar."

At that moment, she threw the plate at me. It sailed past me, hit the wall and broke. Jay immediately took action. He told Denise to take the baby outside. He approached my mother and tried to calm her down. She threw some nasty remarks at him and turned to me. "As far as I'm concerned, you are just a boarder here. You are no longer my daughter, and I'm raising your rent $15 more a week!"

"What do you mean; I'm not your daughter?" The words I spoke were barely audible.

Then it was Jay who spoke next, "Come on Barb, you can live with us. You don't deserve this. Where's your room? Let's get your things."

My mother was screaming from behind us as we entered my room, "You can't take anything. I bought you all those things; they belong to me!"

Ignoring her, I took my art supplies and whatever clothes I could fit in my back pack. My school books were still in the back of the car. All the way to Jay and Denise's house, I cried and shook.

CHAPTER: 22

That first week was spent in a haze. Somehow I got to school and completed all I had to do. Jay and Denise were great and gave me all the space I needed emotionally. I lived with Jay and Denise for only a week. I realized I needed my own place. I was a wreck emotionally and didn't want to burden them. So many people over the years had told me what to do; I needed to control my own life. College was out of the question, and I knew it. I now had to use the money to survive. I had managed to save enough money over the years to rent a room to get me through the rest of the year of high school, but just barely. I only had to get through a few months, but those few months felt like a lifetime. I didn't tell anyone I was on my own. I was afraid, for some reason, that it might be illegal, even though now I know it wasn't. When I knew no one was at my mother's house, I would sneak back and get more of my things.

The apartment I rented was a one room studio, downtown. It was on the third floor of a rundown apartment house on Summer Street in Salem. It was completely furnished with all utilities included and cost $80 per week. The building was filled with drug addicts and bikers; it was noisy and violent, but the apartment was all I could afford and still finish school. I moved in on a Saturday. It had a couch that folded down into a bed that smelled. I tried not to think about the events in the past that this couch had probably seen. There was a small kitchen table with one chair that wobbled. The kitchen area consisted of a sink that was actually a bathroom sink, a hot plate, a toaster oven and one cabinet, which was actually a bathroom cabinet. The bathroom was off the kitchen area. It had a good sized tub, and soaking in it was where I spent most of my time, when I was there. Denise gave me two towels. The carpet that spanned the entire room was stained and looked like the previous tenant had changed the oil in his motorcycle on it. It was a disgusting place, but it was mine.

The day I moved in, I put my backpack on the floor and threw a sheet that Denise had given me over the couch. Laying my frail body on it, I tried to rest. It was two in the afternoon. I fell into a semi conscious state, my only form of sleep since I had left my mother's house. I missed my bed and wanted to cry. I had dreams of a large, menacing man opening my door and walking towards me sleeping on the couch. I wanted to scream but couldn't. I woke up paralyzed with fear, until I realized it was just Shadow Man checking out our new quarters. He made himself comfortable across the room. I smiled at him and fell back to sleep. When I woke up a few hours later, my door was wide open. I realized the lock was broken, and, more than likely, it was the tilt of the building that allowed the door to slowly creak open. The only thing I bought for that apartment, while I was still in school, was a deadbolt.

I didn't go out anymore with my friends. Emilio and I broke up. I couldn't handle being emotionally tied to anyone when I had to emotionally heal myself and find the strength I wondered if I had. I lived on Raisin Bran with milk and plain peanut butter. I couldn't afford the luxury of bread. I chose those items because the vitamins and protein I knew I needed were in them. The Raisin Bran had a lot of iron. With my eating rituals, I was constantly anemic and knew I wouldn't be able to get through the day if it became a problem. I couldn't afford to be sick or miss work. At the hospital, we were allowed to have all the food we wanted for free. I stocked up packages of crackers to have as a treat with my peanut butter before I went to bed. I ate hospital food for dinner on the nights I worked. I only thought of the day at hand. I no longer thought of my future. My future was only about how I would get through to the next day. With the dish soap I bought, I washed my clothes in the tub and hung them up daily to dry.

I never went to the senior activities that were going on at school. I missed the banquet, luau and prom. It was hard for me to be with the people I had grown up with, to hear their plans for college and their trivial problems. I did go to my graduation; I felt I deserved to, after all the struggle. It was a blur. My saving grace was the library. When I wasn't soaking in the tub, I was reading in the stacks. I enjoyed reading nonfiction. I took strength from hearing about others who had survived adversity. From this, I found my own strength. I felt at peace when I talked to myself. I would do this at night, when I was alone and scared. I became my own coach, mother and advocate. I became the woman I had met by the pond at Greenlawn Cemetery; I kept my promise.

When summer came, and I was no longer in school, my money began to run out. I knew I needed to get a full time job and fast. I applied for the day shift at the hospital, but, unfortunately, there were no openings. I did the only thing I could do, the one thing I said I would never do. I applied to Thermal Circuits, my mom's old factory. I earned $98 a week. It was degrading, monotonous work. For hours a day, I, too, welded tiny wires. Fighting off thoughts of failure became my daily battle. When I was disappointed in myself and the position I was in, I would have random thoughts about history repeating itself and being no better than my mother. It was the kind words of Mrs. Buras that would get me through these tough times. Although I never saw her after high school, her voice was forever in my head. I knew I needed nurturing. I knew it was up to me. With the little money I had, I went to yard sales and bought the few necessities I could to try to make myself a home. The first thing I bought was a set of sheets and towels for a dollar. For another dollar I bought a throw rug to cover up the oil stains on the carpet. Denise bought me a spider plant that had lots of new shoots. One day while walking to work, I found plastic flower pots in the trash. I couldn't believe my luck! That night I took dirt from the back yard and replanted the new shoots, scattering them in various locations around my tiny room.

I no longer had the free food from the hospital, which became a problem. I was hungry and thin, so I gave in to what I didn't want to do. If a guy asked me out for dinner, I would say yes, even if I had no interest in him, just so I could have something to eat besides Raisin Bran and peanut butter. A lot of men were asking me out. I was young, beautiful and thin. Some of these men I liked, but I didn't want to have a serious relationship. I didn't trust myself. I was afraid I might fall into the trap of wanting one of them to take care of me, and I knew that would be the wrong reason to start a relationship. I was fighting the way of life my mother grew to know. It was a constant effort on my part to keep my head straight about this matter.

At one point I was seeing seven different men at the same time. It is interesting to look back on. It was kind of like being involved with an online dating service today. Each man in my life back then fulfilled a different need for me. I couldn't name any of them now; I just remember my wants. I knew I was changing, and I didn't care. One guy was a truck driver and rode a motorcycle. He was in his mid twenties and was a sweet man. He would take me for rides on his motorcycle and in his rig. The open air experience made me feel free, and he always took me to lunch. There were a few guys that took me to dinner and a movie. Without them, I never would have been able to afford these luxuries. One man was an outdoorsman. We would go hiking and fishing. One was an educated man. He worked in an office. Lucky for me, he loved art and would take me to Boston to go to museums. Another one took me dancing and taught me how to disco. I wasn't crazy about it, but I did it anyway. He was actually gay. With these men, I felt like I was in the real world again. They gave me adventure and made me feel my life was normal. I never had sex with them. They did not fill me with that desire; and then I ran into Ben. I saw Ben in the parking lot of Crosby's, the local grocery store. He and I had gone to high school together and could often be often found sharing a joint in the courtyard. He was small in stature, yet large in personality and heart. One hot spring morning, I watched him leave school as I sat on the rocks across from the parking lot. His shirt was open, letting the warm breeze sail it majestically behind him. He was walking with two other guys, yet all I saw was him laughing and smiling with the most beautiful teeth. He stood 5'8" with the tightest body I had ever seen. His chest was smooth, with a teasing hint of things to come. I had never told Ben in high school how I felt about him...the timing had never been right.

After our short conversation at Crosby's, we agreed to get together. We spent a wonderful two months of boating, talking, and making love. The passion was intense. All the pent up feelings of the past six months in both our lives was left behind on the sheets. Ben was a boy from my past, a shadow of my childhood that was inevitably slipping from my fingers. Desperate to hold on to something that was familiar, I asked him to move in with me...the next day he was gone, and once again I was alone.

I did have female friends as well. One was a girl I worked with. One night, she asked me to go to a club with her. Although I was eighteen and legal now, I still didn't drink. I told her I would love to go, but I couldn't afford it. She said, "What is there to afford? You walk in, and a man will buy you a drink." I had not thought of that until she said it. We went out that night to a place in Rowley called E.J.'s. That's where I met the man who would become my lover. His name was Anthony. We were attracted to each other right from the start; the chemistry between us was powerful. Anthony was the type of guy that women only fantasized about. He was tall and handsome with girls constantly around him. Of all the choices of women he had that night, he wanted me. I knew I didn't want a steady relationship, I told him this the first night. That made me different from the other girls. It gave me a power I didn't even realize I had.

He came to my apartment, and we talked and kissed. I told him things about my life that I had never told anyone. I was surprised and angry at the effect he had on me. Up until this point, I had kept my personal life to myself. I was embarrassed by it. To cover up my feelings, I had started to develop a cocky attitude towards men. I told him about my fight with my mother and my shattered dreams. He listened intently but made no comment. I immediately felt exposed and built a wall inside myself that night, a wall that has never been completely destroyed. It protects me. It would be the same barrier that held my inner thoughts to myself for years to come. I became more protective of my feelings and knew I no longer had to worry about falling in love. I understood the game Anthony was playing; I was a willing participant. He wasn't interested in me as a person. When it came right down to it, I wasn't interested in him that way either, so how could I blame him? He just wanted sex. I, too, needed a physical relationship in my life. I realized that was the one area I had been fighting. I needed to be held and to feel someone cared, even if I knew in my heart that he didn't, even if it were just for a few hours. We became lovers that night.

I had been damaged by my upbringing, although, as I began to realize that night, there was nothing I was able to do about it. I had conflicting feelings of wanting someone to help me end this nightmare I was living, but I was afraid to trust and enjoyed the control I now had. I was feeling a true sense of freedom for the first time in my life, and I didn't want it to end. I vowed that no one would ever tell me what to do again.

I told Anthony he was just my lover. We were together to fulfill each others needs, and that was it. This was the only way I could protect myself from the inevitable pull of wanting more. My sense of expectation had been so damaged; I didn't even trust myself to recognize that what I really needed was a companion. I knew that is why I became too attached to Ben and wanted him to move in with me. I vowed not to fall into that again. During that time in my life, I refused to let myself fall in love with anyone. I knew I had had love with Alex, but that, too seemed to be gone. My family, who was supposed to give me unconditional love, never even knew the meaning of the word. I knew that love had failed me in every aspect of my life. I became hard and cold about the topic. I was convinced that it didn't exist. As a result, I kept seeing the other men I was dating, and Anthony knew it. I was open and upfront; I never lied to him about this. I told him he was the only one I was sleeping with, and it was the truth. He didn't seem to care; I always wondered if I were the only one he was sleeping with as well. I was afraid to ask, so I never did. We saw each other late at night, once a week, but it only lasted for a few months.

As would be expected, the men I was seeing wanted more, but I wasn't willing to give it to them, so I found myself alone. I needed to make more money. I looked for a weekend job. I walked downtown in search of some weekend employment, but I soon realized that the only job I could get was that of a cashier. With the feelings I had of my math skills at the time, I was afraid to do that. I decided to try the hospital again. They told me that they didn't have any openings in the kitchen, but that Shaughnessy, the rehabilitation hospital that we also used to serve meals to, had just gotten their own kitchen, and I should try there. I did and was able to secure a weekend position. It was new, small and not well designed for functioning. The job was difficult, and the boss was always in a bad mood because of the disorganized atmosphere. I hated it. The only job I did like was delivering the meals. I felt bad for the patients that I saw. Many were forgotten and alone, and I understood how they felt. I began to call them by name, when I would hand them their trays, even if they couldn't respond in return. The ones that were aware began to know me as well. I would ask them how they were doing and soon got to know small details about their lives. They were in desperate need for some company, which affected me. Sometimes on my break, I would sit with some of them, and we would talk. What I was doing was perfectly fine. Sometimes the nurses would need some help, and I was more than willing to lend a hand. What they didn't know was that I, too, needed human contact, someone to talk to, although I had never told them my own story. They would ask me questions about my life, but I would just stick to my dreams of someday becoming a nursery school teacher. After a while I began to believe that maybe, someday, it would still be possible. This gave me hope. What I didn't realize at the time was that the nurse who was in charge of the fourth floor was watching me. Her name was Sherry, and she only stood five feet two inches tall. She was small but strong and ran a tight ship.

At home in my apartment, I felt as if I were dodging bullets. The people who lived in my building were always out of control. This was a scary environment, especially when you realized that they were full grown adults. I was the youngest in the building, something that worked to my advantage most of the time. The other tenants mostly left me alone, except for the people who lived next door to me. They were bikers who sold drugs for a living, bringing a lot of undesirable people past my door. The walls were thin, and I could hear all that was going on in their apartment. Mostly I heard the beatings from the guy named Rob, who lived there. He often beat his girlfriend Debbie or would fight with those who were buying something from him, if he felt they were trying to rip him off. He was a very violent man, so I tried to stay away from both of them as much as possible. This was difficult to do, because they would open their door on numerous occasions and ask me to join them, when they heard me in my own house. The first time I said no, but they started giving me a hard time about it. They said that I thought I was better than they were and called me a snob. I was really just scared out of my mind. I went over to their apartment and smoked some pot occasionally to be polite. Many times I just pretended I was smoking, so I could always keep my wits about me. There were lots of guns in their apartment, and when Rob would get too stoned, he would brandish them in the air and try to scare people in the room. I felt trapped and didn't know how to get out of this situation.

One day, Sherry, the head nurse at the hospital, asked me if I would be interested in working weekends for her at a private rest home that she owned. It was in Salem on Lafayette Street, a half mile south from where I lived. I would be a nurse's aid and an activities director, and I could start whenever I wanted. I jumped at the opportunity! I told her I would start after Christmas, which was only a few weeks away. I had to give my notice at the hospital and didn't want to leave them in the lurch.

Meanwhile, at the factory, I was becoming very fast at the machine I was working on. It was different from the first one I had done. I had to take a series of six long wires and staple them to a fiberglass panel. The large stapler was operated by a hydraulic pump that was activated by a foot pedal. It was an old machine that broke down often. It was frustrating to work at, because I had a quota that I had to keep up with. The mechanic who worked on the machine was frustrated with it as well. He was constantly taking parts from a similar one and putting them on mine and vice versa. He complained the whole time that it just needed to be thrown away and that they needed to buy a new one, but no one would listen to him. On Christmas Eve day, he proved himself right. I was working really fast that day, because I was behind in my quota. It was the fastest I had ever worked, and I was enjoying the challenge of it. For the first time, I had seen why my mother had felt her job meant something, yet I still couldn't understand the lure of wanting to do this forever. Because I was going so fast, my manager decided to time me. This made other employees on the same type of machine angry, because it meant that our quota would be increased. I didn't have a choice by then, the damage had been done. I had dug my own grave. I didn't know that the reason why I could go so fast was because the mechanic had taken the safety switch off. That had been the reason for it shutting down in the past. Standing behind me with a stop watch, the manager set a new quota and went on his way. The people around me made nasty comments to me after he left. I felt awful and afraid that they might try to hurt me after work. Some of the people I worked with were uneducated and street wise. They would think nothing of taking revenge at my expense. I began to lose my concentration and, as a result, the rhythm that I needed to keep up with the machine. At 1:00 PM on the afternoon of Christmas Eve, I stapled the top segment of my index finger to a fiberglass panel. Because the panel had ripped in half, at first I didn't realize what I had done. I saw the blood before I felt the pain. I couldn't figure out where it was coming from for the first five seconds. My hand wasn't stuck to the board, so I kept working when the next panel was lifted. Then I felt it. Looking at my finger, I couldn't believe I hadn't passed, out. Standing up, I realized that I was splattered in blood and had to go to the hospital. I cupped my finger with my good hand and walked slowly to the office. I was in shock and could barely speak. I was afraid to look at it, but from the first glance I got of it, I knew that I no longer had a nail, and the finger was split like the letter "Y." By the time I got to the office, which was on the floor below mine, I was angry and crying. I knew the safety must have been taken off, because they were too cheap to replace the machine. All they cared about was their damn quotas. A meeting was going on in the office, when I entered it. There was no secretary, so I barged right in. Seeing me covered in blood, they got me a seat. Because I had put my hands between my legs when I first felt the pain, most of the blood that was on me was on my crotch. They thought I was having a miscarriage. Out of frustration, I yelled at them that it was my finger and that their damn quota was what had caused it. Looking at my finger, they began to panic. In a split second, they were pulling out papers for me to sign. These were papers saying that it was my fault, that I had taken the safety off the machine. I refused to sign. They refused to take me to the hospital unless I did. My finger was throbbing, and my whole arm hurt. In anger, I signed the papers, but at the same time I purposely smeared them with blood. They were almost unreadable. They took me to the hospital and left me at the front door.

When I got to the emergency room, it was packed, but the nurses took me right away. That's when I knew how serious this was. They told me I was in luck. A plastic surgeon was on call that night and coming in. They gave me a valium for the pain. By the time the surgeon arrived, I was feeling the effects of the medication. My finger still hurt, but the pain of the previous ten months was on the surface of my feelings, and that was worse. I began to cry. The doctor was concerned about both my finger and my emotional state of mind. He started questioning me about what had happened. I not only told him about my finger, I told him everything. He told me not to worry about my finger, which he could save. I was lucky, and it had only grazed the bone. He spent the whole time trying to convince me that I shouldn't be alone that night. It was Christmas Eve, and here I was, this teenage girl alone in the world and hurt. I had been injured while working a horrible job on a machine he felt I was too young to be operating and hurt from the people who were supposed to be my family. His heart went out to me. He gave me some aspirin to take home with me. He wrote me a generic prescription he said would be cheaper to fill, along with the name of a lawyer. After he fixed my finger, he gave me some money to get something to eat at the cafeteria. He was kind to me; his kindness gave me strength. He would become the first of many strangers who would reach out to me at times of need. After I ate, I walked a mile back to my apartment. It began to snow.

When I arrived home from the hospital, I laid down on my couch. I didn't remove my coat; I stayed there for an hour. It was about six o'clock in the evening but felt like ten. My pajamas were lying next to me; I had left them there in my haste that morning. That morning seemed like a week ago. The medication was wearing off, so I took the aspirin he had given me. It didn't help. My whole arm was aching; it felt like it was going to fall off. The bandage was so big that it looked like I had three fingers in it instead of one. I started to cry again. I began to miss my mother. I thought about the times we had danced together, pretending to be Diana Ross. I thought about the love I used to have for her and wondered what had happened. I was sinking lower and knew I couldn't stop. I started pacing around the room. I was out of my mind with pain. I needed that prescription filled, but I knew I would never get it, because I didn't have the money. Shadow Man stood casually on the other side of the room. With his arms folded across his chest and his feet crossed at the ankles, he cocked his head in a gesture towards the door. Even without words, I knew what he was telling me. I went for a walk. Without intending to, I was headed for my mother's house. It was difficult to walk in the snow. My feet were throbbing, and my fingers were numb. Taking off my mittens to look at them, I was surprised by their color. They were white. When I got halfway there, I was nervous but knew I couldn't stop. When I reached the front door, I stood there for awhile, not knowing what to do. Would she not let me in? I was saddened by the fact that I wasn't sure. My mother and I had not seen each other since I had left. She hadn't tried to see me. In my eyes, she hadn't cared.

My mother must have sensed that someone was in the hallway. She opened the door, and I burst into tears. She put her arm around me and asked me what had happened. When I told her, she was surprised that I was working where I was, but she didn't throw it in my face, like I had thought she would. To me, that was a good sign. I told her I needed the prescription filled and didn't have the money. She said she would give it to me, but the drugstores would be closed for two days. I hadn't thought of that, and my heart sank. She pulled out some money from her purse and handed it to me. I thanked her and asked if I could go lay down in my old bed. All I wanted at that point was to feel its comfort. She said I could. Passing the Christmas tree that was set up in the living room, I noticed there were presents for me under it. The whole scene seemed ironic; instead of being pleased by the sight, I was sad and confused.

I went to my room. It was exactly as I had left it. My bed, calling me from the corner, was a comforting sight. Laying down, I closed my eyes. My finger wasn't any better; if anything, it hurt more. I tried not to think about it, but the thoughts I was having were worse. In what I thought was the safety and comfort of my own bed, I realized that I was sitting in a house where I had never felt safe or comfortable. I was not the same ambitious girl I had been when I had last slept in this room, less than a year ago. Eventually, I fell into a tortured sleep. The next morning was Christmas. When I awoke, everyone was asleep. I made myself a cup of coffee and returned to my room. I wanted to talk to my mother, and I knew she would be up before Jake. Doug probably wouldn't arrive until later, so I figured that would be my best chance. The biggest issue I had and wanted to talk to her about was that she really didn't know me. I was falsely accused and convicted the day I left, and I wanted to set the record straight. I wanted the relationship we had had before all the trouble started. I knew it was my pregnancy that had pushed her to her limits and caused her to think of me in a way that wasn't true.

When I heard her in the kitchen pouring a cup of coffee, I knew that would be the only chance I had to speak to her alone. What I didn't count on was that her stubbornness would be joining us in the discussion.

I walked into the kitchen and sat next to her at the table. She asked me how my finger felt. I told her it still ached, and I hadn't slept much. We sat there for a while in silence; I was sure I was going to chicken out. I knew I would be angrier at myself if I did, so I began where I felt it was most important.

"Mom, I want to tell you something. I am really not the person you think I am." "Barb, I don't want to get into this now."

"But Mom, I have to. I feel I need to explain. I am a person with ambitions and dreams. I want to go somewhere in my life." I didn't tell her how I was forced to live these past ten months, and she didn't ask. I said, "I want more from my life than you have had in yours." It was the wrong thing to say.

"Your problem, Barb, is that you have never respected me!" She got angry and began to yell. Her words rang true to my ears. She was right; I didn't have any respect for her. I realized that I had lost that several years earlier, when I had witnessed the poor decisions she was making in her life. She had put us in danger more than once. She had struck me when she felt I was wrong. I had been like the maid. Then there was the personal side of her. She had never read a book and refused to see that there was more to life than just working in a factory. The one man she had fallen in love with was a drunk. In all the years that we had lived together, I had never stopped telling her how I felt about all that was going on. In her eyes, I was a problem, a reminder of all her faults. I didn't know what to say.

I was confused, because I still loved her. She was the woman who had brought me into this world. She had clothed me and fed me. She had fought for me at school when I needed it. She had made sure we had all the necessities for living...except one...a safe and nurturing environment. I gave up that morning. I no longer felt I needed to have her know who I was. We were different people, and that would never change. I knew I couldn't go back. Calming down, she asked me where I lived. Looking at my feet, I told her. She suggested we could go out to dinner, maybe the day after Christmas. I nodded my head in response.

I left that morning before Jake got up. I didn't take my presents. I didn't even open them. When I got back home, Rob and Debbie were celebrating Christmas in the only way they knew how. They were completely wasted. Hearing me come in, they asked me to join them. I was in too much pain to even deal with them and told them what happened to my finger, showing them my bandage. I was hoping they would sympathize and understand why I wanted to be alone. Instead they gave me a Christmas gift, sensimilla Thai stick, rolled into a joint. They said it should ease my pain and offered me prescription drugs, as well, but I refused.

I entered my apartment and sat on the couch. Making a cup of instant coffee with water that I had heated in a sauce pan, I tried to calm my nerves from what had just happened with my mother. My finger was aching, so I made a sling from a dish towel and tied it around my neck. I had several days off before I had to start my job at Ivy Manor and was hoping the pain would subside by then. That Christmas day I read, wrote and drew; I tried to clear my head.

When I woke up the next morning, I sat and waited for the drugstore to open. The store was across town, but I think I was the first one at the door, when they unlocked it. Getting my prescription filled, I asked the pharmacist for a glass of water and took a pill on the spot. It was only aspirin with codeine. By the time I got home, twenty minutes later, I realized it wasn't going to help much. I stayed in bed most of the morning. At noon time I remembered the dinner date with my mother. I began to get edgy. The more I thought of it, the more my finger hurt. Finally, at 2:00 PM I decided I had to do something to calm my nerves and reduce this pain. I smoked the joint. The last thing I remembered was looking at the patterns in my room. Just as I had done in my childhood, I saw pictures in everything I looked at. The ceiling had a series of cracks which reminded me of roads. I imagined I was in the heavens, looking down on someone's world. In reality, I was lying flat on my back on the floor in a drug induced fog. My finger felt better, and I drifted off to a peaceful, deep sleep.

At six o'clock exactly, I awoke to pounding on the door. It was a heavy hand, and I knew it couldn't be my mother. When I opened it, a policeman was standing there. My first thought was that he was looking for the people next door. Then my mother stepped out from behind him. "What is wrong?" I asked. "Did something happen?"

"I was worried about you," she said. "Where have you been?" "I have been here. What do you mean? I was waiting for us to go to dinner." "Barb, we were supposed to have dinner yesterday. I have been knocking on your door every hour since six o'clock last night. I thought something happened to you. I had to wait twenty-four hours before I could call the police."

My first thought was that of shock that she had been so concerned. My second was...how did I lose a day? That was the last time I smoked pot.

CHAPTER: 23

It was a cool, brisk January morning, as I walked down Lafayette Street and headed to my new place of employment. Despite the crisp winter air, I was hopeful with a bit of a spring in my step. It was a feeling of optimism that had been buried in me and was now emerging again, not unlike the first crocus after a long winter, poking through the snow. This new job, I was sure, was going to give me some purpose and expose me to people who needed me. It was just the distraction I was craving to divert me from the things going on in my own life. I didn't realize it at the time that it would become the place I would think back upon as home for many years to come. As I approached the Victorian brick building, I was struck by the beauty of the ivy growing up all four sides. It was a sea of green, surrounded by freshly fallen snow. This place looked alive, warm and welcoming. Sporting a white uniform with matching nylons and shoes, I walked up the steps. I was fortunate that the uniform I had for working in the kitchen at the hospital was the same requirement for Ivy Manor. With my hair pulled tight in a long cascading French braid down the middle of my back, I looked very much the part of a professional caregiver as I rang the bell. An elderly woman poked her heard from behind the curtain of a room on the left and watched my every move. I smiled at her, as she quickly pulled away from the window with the realization of having been caught. After a minute or so, I heard the shuffling of hard soled slippers on a hardwood floor, slowly, with rhythm, approaching from the other side. With a moan and a creak from its heavy oak panels and iron hinges, the door gradually opened to reveal a woman around the age of seventy wearing a house dress. Her name was Nora. Extending my hand, I said, "Good morning, my name is Barbara. Is Sherry here? She is expecting me." A trembling hand returned my gesture. With her eyes lowered like a dutiful servant, she said, "Right this way." Stepping into the foyer, the first thing that greeted me in this massive old estate was the winding mahogany staircase cascading down from the second floor. Four people could descend it comfortably side by side. An image of Scarlet O'Hara, from "Gone with the Wind," seeped into my brain as I walked past it slowly, refusing to let go of its sight. My senses immediately became alive. Glenn Miller's "In the Mood" was playing softly from a distant room upstairs, and the air was filled with the aroma of poinsettias that were placed everywhere. I felt an immediate peace coming from this home. I felt as if I had just walked into a mansion from 1943, untouched and welcoming.

It was 8:30 AM as Nora led me to the kitchen. The kitchen to this place was huge. Although it also looked untouched from 1943, it did have all the modern necessities it needed to support the facility. Martha, the cook, was loading the dishwasher. Sherry and Gloria were sitting at a small table against the wall and chatting. Gloria, a woman in her fifties, I soon found out to be a nurses aid. When Sherry saw me, she rose to her feet and greeted me. "Barb, I am so happy you are here." Introducing me to everyone in the room, she led me around the house to give me a tour. Out into the hallway again, she suddenly noticed my bandaged finger.

"What happened to you?" "Oh, I work at a factory during the week, and it got crimped in a machine." "That's awful! It must be a tough place to work." "Yes, it is a bit monotonous, to say the least, but it pays the bills." "Pays the bills? How old are you?" "I'm turning eighteen next month." I then added, "I'm on my own."

She put her kind hand on my shoulder, as we turned the corner to the library and added, "Well, I will take you full time, if you want to leave that awful place. I would have offered it to you right from the start, but I thought you were only looking for part-time work." I stopped and looked at her and said softly, "Thank you, I would like that." A lump in my throat began to grow. It took all I could to compose myself.

Ivy Manor had seventeen women, all over the age of seventy, living there. They were all ambulatory and, for the most part, could take care of their own personal, daily needs. The reason why they did not live alone was because many were at the beginning stages of dementia and would sometimes get confused. A small handful came to the Manor as a result of the deinstitutionalization of the Danvers State Hospital. That was a state run facility for individuals of varying degrees of mental instability. But even those ladies were happy and harmless. Sherry wouldn't have taken in any women that were potentially dangerous.

Sherry and her husband lived upstairs, in an apartment on the third floor. Her niece Tori, who lived with them, was the head nurse. Gloria was the nursing assistant. I was to be the jack of all trades. My positions consisted of nursing assistant, gardener, housekeeper, and activities director. I mostly did the night shift when I was on for nursing. My job as night nurse was to assist the ladies with their bedtime routines and provide an evening snack and most importantly, to make sure they were comfortable, and understood where they were. At times, some would get confused and think they were just visiting and try to leave. After all my duties were done, I would watch TV with the night owls, who liked to stay up. When they eventually went to bed, there was a bed for me as well, and Sherry would let me sleep.

Nights in the Manor were always interesting. The ladies seemed to revert to their youthful and playful years, once the sun went down. One night I was feeding the fish located in a tank just below the circular stairwell when I heard..."Look out below"...followed by a couple of giggles. Looking up, I saw something I couldn't identify drift slowly down from the second floor. It wasn't until it surprised the fish in the tank that I realized, it was a large pair of ladies panties.

The cleaning woman part of the deal was the easiest job in the world. The home was a big estate with around twenty four rooms, but the ladies all regarded their rooms as their own homes and kept them quite tidy. So basically, all I did was sweep and wash the floors and dust. While I was doing those tasks, I kept the ladies company and talked to them as I went from room to room. I think that was Sherry's intent all along.

One spring morning, I was sweeping the floor on the first level in Lori's room. Lori was a cranky woman in her eighties. All day long, she would sit by the open window, watch the cars pass on the main street, and eat cheese doodles. She was very protective of her things and was suspicious of everyone. I would try to have conversations with her, but all she would do was grunt or yell at me to be quiet. Most of the staff made wide circles around her unless they needed to speak to her directly.

"Barb, I say you're wasting your time." The cook was always trying to give me advice.

"But I feel sorry for her. Imagine what kind of life she had to make her so bitter. I think if I show her some kindness, she will come around. After all, how many more years could she possibly have left? I can't sit back knowing that she has been so miserable her entire life."

"Ahhhh, to be youthful and full of hope...I still say it is a waste of time."

Picking up the broom, I headed to Lori's room. The Manor was a bit more dusty than usual. It had rained for weeks on end, and everything seemed to have had a musty smell. If I wasn't sweeping and dusting, then I was spraying Lysol and feeling a bit like my mother. As I entered Lori's room, she was in her usual spot by the open window, eating cheese doodles. Gracefully, sweeping past her, I beamed with a smile, "Good morning, Lori, isn't it nice the rain has finally stopped?" She did not respond. She didn't even look at me. I continued, "Did you know that we had so much rain yesterday that the train station down the street flooded to the top, and they had to close the line?" With my back now to her, I chatted away about the fact that the neighbors were complaining about all the "critters" that had emerged from the tunnel after the rains. I was about to interject another tid-bit of information I had heard on the streets, when Lori's voice caught me mid sentence.

"Here kitty, kitty. Want a cheese doodle?" My first thought was, "We don't have a cat." Turning around, I was horrified to see Lori feeding the biggest rat I had ever seen. It had climbed the ivy on the outside of the building and was sitting on her open window sill. Lori thought that somehow we had obtained a pet and that it was in need of a meal. I have to admit that hearing her speak so kindly to something had also stunned me. For the first few seconds, I froze. Then, with the stealth mind and body of a super hero, I sprang into action. I knew if I tried to explain to her the dangers of what she was doing, she would not listen to me. So instead, I chose to use a different tactic. "Lori, is this house dress yours? I found it in the laundry." I was holding up an article of clothing I had pulled from a basket at the other side of the room.

"Let me see," she said, as she got up from her chair and came towards me. In an instant, I dropped the dress on a neighboring bed and ran awkwardly towards the window. Holding the broom like a baseball bat I took two giant leaps toward it, swinging at the same time. The adrenaline that was racing through my veins let me hit that rat with such force, it flew clear across the street, just missing the oncoming traffic. The sound of screeching brakes and swerving tires were heard throughout the block. I looked up in time to see the creature land on its back, stunned. In a few seconds, it was back on its feet and scrambled under a bush across the way. I slammed the window down and turned to see Lori standing behind me. She seemed frozen in time; her mouth was wide open. She was still holding the house dress. The look of shock on her face worried me, until she spoke. "YOU KILLED MY CAT! CAT MURDERER!!! CAT MURDERER!!!" Then she started screaming and crying and carrying on like someone was hurting her. This caused the entire staff, as well as the other patients, to show up at her door. It took Gloria a while to calm her down...Sherry handed me the ivy clippers, and the rest of that day I was the gardener.

In the four seasons of the year, I took care of the gardens. In the winter, I shoveled. In the spring, I planted the seeds. In the summer, I mowed the lawn and tended to the flowers and vegetables. In the fall, I raked the leaves. While working the vegetable garden, I would recruit some of the ladies to help me. I would jokingly tell them I was the grounds crew and they were my helpers. Madeline and Nora loved it. In the morning, before the sun got too high in the sky, we would sit in the dirt and weed around the plants. At harvest time, we would hunt for our buried treasures of root vegetables. It was at this time that I would have the most interesting conversations with these two women. Having your fingers in dirt seemed to bring out the truth in people. Nora told me she was from Syria. She said she was brought to this country by nuns who were visiting on a humanitarian mission. They adopted her and brought her to America. They taught her to read and write and do math. She spoke very fondly of them and her face lit up at their mention. She said she had wanted to be a nun. When I asked her if she had become one, her face would turn to that of shame. She looked away and flatly said, "No."

Madeline was from Ireland and spoke with a heavy brogue. It took me a good two weeks of speaking with her, before I could understand anything she said. The fact that her voice would sometimes drift off to a whisper didn't help. She was statuesque in height. She had perfect posture. She had long thick waves of white hair draping her shoulders. Other than the bright red lipstick that covered her mouth and the surrounding inch completely around it, she was a beauty. The other interesting thing about Madeline was the fact that she was highly sexual and still very much a woman of desire. She loved the opposite sex, and no man that entered the Manor was safe from her luring glances and wandering hands. One of my unspoken jobs was to keep an eye on the clock, and know the schedule of all the deliveries. I was to distract Madeline, to keep her at bay. Unfortunately, Madeline had memorized the delivery schedules as well, despite her aging years. The UPS driver, a man of about twenty-eight, was terrified, whenever he saw her. She had cornered him in the back hall his first day on the job. The poor boy had no idea what he was walking into when this heavily lipsticked beauty, wearing only an under-slip, made highly provocative advances towards him. It was the first time I had ever heard a man scream with such a high pitch of volume. For the most part, Madeline was harmless. She would often flirt with the men and rub their arms. The mailman, a guy of about forty, knew this and would play along. Some people felt he was encouraging her. I thought it was a sweet gesture. After he left, Madeline was always in a pensive mood and could be found gazing out the window, singing Irish songs of great longing. Watching her from across the room, I couldn't help but hope that at her age, I would still have such desires.

The third job I had at Ivy Manor was activities director, the most challenging, not as clear cut as the other jobs. I had to find out what used to interest these women when they were younger and try to motivate them to get out of their rooms and do something. I found a dusty old Bingo game and rallied the troops to the dining room. Just to get them all out of their rooms and seated at a table was a challenge. By the time the first one was settled and I would leave to get the next...the first lady was back in her room. It took me a few tries to realize that this was not something I could accomplish singlehandedly. Enlisting the nurse, the cook, and any other able bodied being who was there that day, I was finally ready to call the Bingo cards. Sherry gave me a large jar of pennies she had upstairs, and our gambling was complete, that is, until I realized that more than half the woman were deaf.

"B-12" "What did she say?" "I don't know; it sounds like she has marbles in her mouth." "I said, B-12." "Three elves? What is this girl trying to do...confuse us?"

Eventually, I just held up a large paper with the card numbers written on it. It all worked fine, except for Kate...she was blind. After the first time she yelled bingo, and I checked her card...I realized that she was just placing her red chips anywhere she felt like. In the end, I would split up the winnings, and everyone went away happy.

I tried a printmaking class there one day. Taking potatoes from the garden, I carved pretty leaves on them. Using water based paint and paper, I set up the table. The colors I had were red and yellow. I knew printing on top of each one would make an orange leaf. How on earth could this project go wrong? It was fool proof...until one of the women thinking the yellow was mustard and the red ketchup, dipped a potato in them and took a huge bite. Spitting it across the table, she splatter painted everyone in its path. Standing up, she yelled, "This is a terrible restaurant, and I am not paying." Turning haughtily on her heels, she left the room, leaving us all sitting there stunned and speckled, not knowing what to say. The silence was broken with a comment two seats down, "I don't know about you, but I think that woman needs to see a shrink." Sarah was on the second floor. She was also in her seventies. She suffered from the beginning stages of Alzheimer's. Sarah was stuck in her childhood, the teenage years, to be exact. She often spent her day getting dressed. Sometimes she would forget she had already put on her dress and would put on another. One hot day, Sherry told me to go and see how many housedresses Sarah was wearing. On one occasion, it was well into the nineties, and she had on at least ten dresses! I always made a game of this, and we would count them in exaggerated delight. She would laugh hysterically when I did it and sometimes pretend she was doing a strip tease. Sarah thought I was her childhood friend Issy; she never called me by my first name.

One day I phoned my mother. I needed her to bring me a paper for my taxes. I had been a little leery about calling her, but she seemed obliged to help me. I decided to take this opportunity to show her who I really was, to show her I was respected and loved, to have her see me as a caring individual. I was really nervous the day she was to arrive. When she came, I took her around to introduce her to all the ladies. They were thrilled to meet her and told her how pleased they were to have me in their lives. When we got to Sarah's room, Sarah was acting very suspiciously. When I asked her why, she whispered very loudly in my ear, "Issy, I have met your mother many times...and that is not your mother!" A chill ran down my spine, but I tried to laugh it off. After that, I showed Mom our garden and invited her to stay for Sunday dinner. She refused. She said she found the place too depressing and wanted to go. I was amazed at how we both looked at the same surroundings and saw two totally different worlds. It was another contrast in our lives.

Not all the women were confused. There were two that I often went to for advice or just to chat. The first one was Laila, who was one hundred years old. She was ambulatory and spry. She had a quick wit and often made me laugh. I would spend hours sitting on her bed, as she told me about living in a time when automobiles didn't exist.

"Barb, sit right here." She patted the top of her bed, which was covered in an antique crocheted throw her mother had made. "I have an important thing I want to discuss with you." Putting down my dust cloth, I excitedly did as I was told. "You know, Barb, woman have not changed much in the one hundred years I have been alive. They get hurt from friends and family. They question if what they are doing is right...or lady like...but mostly they want to be loved. Do you have a love, Barb?" I thought of the various men I was seeing for comfort. I paused just a little too long before answering, and she knew. "Just as I thought; you are too busy taking care of us crazies to think about what it is you need. Well, let me give you some advice. When the door of opportunity knocks...answer it. It might not always be there the next time you open it. I have lived a long life. But most are not that fortunate. Remember my words, Barbara. You may never know when your time to leave this precious world will be. And if I can say one thing it is this...love hard and love often. Understand your desires and needs and fulfill them. There's nothing worse than realizing you haven't done that, when it is too late to do anything about it." Laila taught me a lot of things that year. We talked about appearances and how to dress. She showed me the proper way to flirt, so as to not look cheap. "Create a mystery," she would say. "Never show anyone all your cards. But always be honest to yourself. You are the one person you can never fool, the one person who can tear you down more than anyone else. When you put your head down on that pillow at night, only a clear conscience will let you sleep." She spoke the unspoken words of all women to me.

Rose was the other woman I loved to sit with. She shared a room with Kate, the blind woman, and could often be found reading to her. Rose had polio as a child and had been living in the Manor since the age of thirty, when her parents were both killed in a car accident. In that year, she was seventy-five. Rose, unlike the others, had all her faculties. It was physically getting around that she found most difficult. She had a great sense of humor and would often point out to me silly things the others were doing.

"Rose, one of these days I am going to spring you from this mad house, you and me girl, in the middle of the night. We'll go out dancing!"

"Hahaha, and how do you suppose we will do that? You don't even drive." "Hey you got wheels!" I said, as I pushed her in her wheelchair. "I doubt we would get far."

"Yeah, but you and I both know we are smarter than everyone else...and that's all we need. Maybe we will take Laila along for laughs." And so our musings would begin each night, plotting an escape. We always ended these talks with laughter and longing. I knew deep down she could never go, even if she wanted to. She was trapped here in her crippled body, having long been resolved to the fact that this was her destiny. She had never married. She had never even had a boyfriend. One night, after Kate had fallen asleep she asked me, "Barb, what is it like to have a man who loves you hold you in his arms?" I looked in her eyes and paused. I thought of all the men in my short life and replied, "Each one is different."

"What do you mean different?"

"Well some love you in a tender kind of way. They hold you like a brand new kitten they don't want to hurt. Others touch you in a way that is fiery and passionate, as if you are the last chance on earth they have for fulfillment. But the worst is when they hold you like you are a great burden, a sack of groceries that is necessary for their survival, yet not the food they like to eat. I hate that."

"What does it feel like to make love to a man?"   "It depends, if it is love that you are making...or just having sex." "I want to know what love feels like."

"It feels like everything is right in the world. Your heart and all your other parts are alive at once. You don't know whether to laugh or cry. Both seem to be of equal importance. When it is all over, you feel as if you have melded together in a special, secret kind of way, something that only the two of you share. And because it is different with everyone you are with...that specialness is always unique."

I sat on the bed next to her and put my arm around her. She put her head on my shoulder. I wondered what it must be like in a world without a tender touch. I held her until she fell asleep, then I slipped from her room. As I started to close the door, I noticed Shadow Man sitting in the corner. He gave me a familiar nod.

The next morning, I went to wake Rose first. I was still feeling the effects of our conversation the night before and wanted to make sure she was ok...When I opened the door, she was lying peacefully in her bed. Her lips were slightly parted, and her body didn't rise and fall with her usual patterns of breath...she was gone. I resisted running to tell the others. I knew it was too late. Kate, getting out of her bed across the room, said, "Boy, she must be tired this morning. It is getting late. Tell her I will be at the breakfast table." She shuffled out of the room. Pulling a chair up to Rose's bed, I held her cold hand. I prayed she had finally found someone to hold her with love.

Ivy Manor saved me. It was the nurturing environment I was looking for. The women mothered me, and I took care of them. They taught me about life and about how to die with dignity. If I myself got sick, Sherry helped me get a doctor and paid for my prescriptions. They fed me all my meals, which allowed me to save a little money on the side. It was the way one should be raised in a loving environment. I had found a new family.

CHAPTER: 24

I learned how to drive when I was at Ivy Manor. Sherry had a niece living with her when I worked there, who was the other head nurse when Sherry was not on. Her name was Tori; she was a year older than I and was originally from the Bronx in New York. Tori and I became really good friends. We went places together, and she helped me study for my driver's permit. She drove me to the registry the day I passed. When we got back to the Manor, there were celebrations all around. She insisted I attend a driving school, so I did. To my surprise, my mother was getting her license from the same school as well. Sometimes we would pick each other up, a common practice in a driving school. When one lesson was finished, that person drove to the house of the next lesson. The next student would then drive the first student home. This was the common thread we needed in our lives. It forced us to see each other every week, even if it were only for a few minutes. I have to admit though, I was a bit nervous when she drove me home. I had never been in a car with her before, when she was the driver. Soon we started talking to each other. In front of others, we were civil. One time after a lesson, she asked me to lunch. We went to the Pewter Pot in downtown Salem. We were in public, so I figured we were safe, as far as fighting was concerned. We sat and made small talk. It was a pleasant lunch, and we made plans to do it again. We saw each other once a week after that.

One hot summer night while I still had my driving permit, Tori and I decided to take a drive to Gloucester. She insisted I get behind the wheel. It would turn out to be a night I would never forget. It was the kind of memory you often refer back to and wonder...who would believe this?

It was about 11:00 PM, and the road we took was dark. We were driving on the scenic roadways up Route 127. It was a beautiful road that wound along the north coast of Massachusetts. Around every other bend was a spectacular view of the ocean. Tori wanted to take me this way because she said it was a difficult road to drive at night, and if I could drive it, then I could drive anywhere. We were in her beat up Volvo, and the night was clear, with a full moon.

"Tori, this is crazy. This street has such sharp curves; what if I hit something, and why are there so few street lights?" Despite the serenity of the atmosphere, my nerves were getting the best of me. Tori tried to calm me.

"It's ok, Barb, at least it is a full moon tonight. Look how pretty it is reflecting on the water." As I drove around the curves, through the trees, and then along the ocean's edge, we entered in and out of small New England towns that were lit only by a handful of street lamps. The windows were down in the car. The mix of salt sea air danced with the scent of pine through our long hair that was trailing behind us out the window, the essence of each aroma rolling over us slowly, like the beach waves we had just passed.

Beautiful boxes of draping geraniums and baby's breath framed the window sills of quaint book stores and dress shops. Since the moment we had begun driving this road, we had not passed one commercial franchise. Everything was privately owned by an individual with a dream. At this time of night, inside the windows were shimmering faint lights, illuminating its wares with a magical glow. Between these towns along their outskirts were houses dotted among the trees; most were dark. It reminded me of elf houses scattered in the forest. We passed a few of these towns before we reached our destination.

Gloucester was a contrast to the scenes we had just passed. The bars were hopping with life, and people were to be seen walking the streets. Couples could be found leaning against buildings, kissing and smoking cigarettes; lost in a world of passion and pleasure. A fairly large city known for its fishing industry and illegal drugs, it could sometimes be a rough place for two young girls that late at night. Tori, being from a rough section of NY, was not fazed by it. "Barb, do you want to pull over somewhere for a drink?"

I looked around at the local flavor and replied, "I think I would feel more at home at the artist colony down the road. Let's go there."

"Ok, and then we can go to Rockport." When we got to the artist colony, it was last call. I was just old enough to drink, but I didn't like alcohol, so instead I stood outside and smoked a joint. Once inside, I bought a ginger ale and listened to the last set from the band. Tori was getting cozy with a guy at the bar. In a short while, a man came up to me and started making small talk. He was a handsome man about twenty-five. He had long brown hair to his shoulders. He wore a Led Zeppelin tee-shirt and tattered jeans that were covered in artist paint. He told me he was an oil painter and belonged to the arts association. I immediately felt chemistry for him. I can't remember what we talked about, but I do remember the taste of his lips. They were soft and wet; the tip of his tongue was coated with the sweetness of almond liquor. I am not sure if it was him or the joint...but had the lights not gone on when they did, my hands would have been all over him. Tori showed up at that moment, seeing I was getting in real deep and said, "Hmmmm, this could get out of hand. Come on Barb, let's go to Rockport." Leading me out the door, I couldn't help but look back. I never saw that handsome face or touched those sweet lips again.

The ocean views on the road to Rockport were beautiful. When we got there, we were surprised to learn that Rockport was a "dry" town. No alcohol could be served in any of its establishments. Because of this, it was also closed up as tight as a drum this late in the evening. We decided to turn around and head back. The tide was very high from the full moon. Our conversation that night was about the effects the moon has on people, its reference to both lovers and the insane. If anyone ever doubted this theory, we knew they would become a believer if they worked at a facility like Ivy Manor on one of those nights. When the moon was full, the patients that easily cried seemed to cry more. Madeline always sang louder, with more enthusiasm. Nora became noticeably more agitated. Then there were the arguments. Little squabbles always seemed to pop up during the full moon. It was exhausting to work when the moon was full, and we were laughing about it as we made the turn along the coast that led us back to Route 127 and the town of Beverly Farms.

It was about 1:00 AM, and we came across the first cars we had seen since our journey began. One was a `74 blue Mustang, and it was filled with a bunch of boys. It was in front of us and driving erratically. Behind us was another car with two girls in it, having no choice but to drive as slowly as I was. Being sandwiched between those two cars made me nervous; I spoke of my concerns to Tori.

"Is it me, or are these guys in front of us on something?"

"No, I think you're right. The real question is, what are they on? Just go slow and make sure there is enough room between you and the car in front. Hopefully they will turn off down one of these rich people's driveways and head home to Mommy." The streets were so curvy, and I was unsure what the boys in front were doing; they were all over the road.

"Tori, maybe I should pull over and let you drive."

"Pull over where? There is no room. It will be ok, just go slow. Besides, this won't be the first time you have to deal with a crazy driver in front of you; it will be good practice." I did as she said, to the irritation of the girls behind us.

When we got to the main street of Beverly Farms, it was a narrow, well-lit road. The boys swerved their car sideways and stopped abruptly in front of us. There was no place for us to go; we were trapped. This caused me to slam on the brakes, despite the distance I had been keeping, and the girls behind us had to go off the road, so as not to hit us from behind. They ended up in a row of bushes. At first we were stunned and just stared at the car full of boys. I locked my door. Following my lead, Tori did the same.

Without warning, another car came out of nowhere from the opposite direction. All the boys got out, and there were now ten of them in the street, arguing. They seemed crazed, and I couldn't make out what they were saying. The boys from the second car were fighting with the boys who had been in the first car. They all seemed younger than we were and still in high school. Two of them grabbed one boy, as another started beating on him. The same thing happened to a second boy they were arguing with. The rest of the kids that were with them originally took off into the woods. We didn't know what to do. There were so many of them, all taking a turn hurting these two kids. It was hard to watch and left us feeling helpless.

Then the most visually bizarre event I had ever seen unfold in my life happened. One of boys they were angry with apparently had an artificial leg. They somehow got it off him and started beating him with it. At first, I didn't know what I was looking at. I could tell it was a leg, because it still had a sock and sneaker on it. My stomach churned, and I thought I would vomit. The second boy was being hit with a large piece of wood. Tori said, "We have to do something; these boys are going to die!"

All at once, Tori and I, along with the two girls behind us, got out of our cars. We started screaming at them to stop. I told one of the girls to go get some help from a police station three buildings down. She ran in that direction. When the boys saw us, they jumped in their cars and took off fast down the street, leaving the two beaten ones behind. Tori, being a nurse, knew something about artificial limbs and went to help the amputee. I went to the other one. The fourth girl just stood there in shock.

When I got to the boy who had been beaten with the stick, he was lying on the ground, face first. I picked him up under the arms and turned him towards me. He was dead weight, and it was difficult. I leaned him against my chest with his head resting on my shoulder. The smell of fresh blood encircled us. There was a truck parked on the side of the road right in front of us. Carefully supporting the back of his head, I laid him against the side of the bed. It was the first time I actually got to see his face. The image was horrifying. When I saw it, my stomach lurched, and I vomited at our feet. When I looked back up I saw Shadow Man leaning against the other side of the truck bed. His stance was not casual. He looked tense, as if he were ready to step up and help. The board the boy had been beaten with must have had nails in it. He had numerous five inch gashes running down the length of his face. Taking out a Kleenex I had in my pocket, I began to blot the blood that was completely covering his features. He started to regain consciousness and began to groan. He was bleeding badly; I knew he needed stitches. I asked him his name, but he wouldn't answer. Instead, he was getting irritated with me and wanted to leave. I told him he needed help and to let us drive him to the hospital. He refused.

Meanwhile, the boy Tori was working on was bruised but ok. With his leg back on as best as could be expected, he hobbled over to me and the other one and said, "Come on. We better get out of here." Together, supporting each other, they headed in the direction of the woods behind us. The girl who had gone for the police returned, angry and yelling. The police refused to respond to what they called an argument between kids. For a moment, we all stood in the street in bewilderment, not saying a word. Looking at Tori and me covered in blood, I said, "You're driving home." Pulling away from the scene, we passed Shadow Man walking into the woods towards the direction of the boys.

The incident in Beverly Farms left me feeling numb. For days, I searched the local papers for some confirmation that what we had seen had, in fact, happened. There were no reports. Tori and I spoke to each other of the event many times in disbelief. Despite the gruesomeness of the young man's face, it was the sight of the artificial leg that stayed with me the longest. I was beginning to feel so vulnerable with all these new experiences I was having. I knew that I was too young to emotionally handle it all at the age of eighteen.

CHAPTER: 25

Not long afterwards when I was walking downtown, I ran into Bobby McCleary on the street. He had been a friend of mine in high school. We had a genuine respect for each other, and I was thrilled to see him. Bobby and I had sat together in art with another guy by the name of James Clough. The three of us would laugh and fool around in the class. It was the only memory I have of ever having had fun in school. James confessed to me one day that he wanted to take me to the junior prom. Of course it was the day after the prom he told me this. Bobby had also said he wanted to go with me but had made plans with his ex girlfriend instead. Needless to say, I never went. Art class was fun back then. As complicated as my life was, it wasn't anything like it had been for me at that current time. The teacher we had back then was a bit spacey and always tolerant of our behavior. Bobby and I had dated a few times after Alex and I had broken up, but we were never serious.

When we saw each other that day, we started with a big hug. We were genuinely happy to see each other. For me, after all I had been through, he was a breath of fresh air. He told me he was home on leave from the army, and wanted to know if I wanted to go out for lunch. We went to a local pizza parlor and talked for hours. He told me about life in the army and I told him about my life. He was amazed that I had been on my own in high school; he had never known. I told him no one had, and besides it was only a few months. He said he admired me for what I had been able to do by myself. I told him I hadn't had a choice. When we parted several hours later, he left me his address in California. He wanted me to write to him, to let him know how I was doing. I promised I would.

I missed Bobby after he left. The short time we had together, that afternoon, was a nice reprieve from my day to day struggles. A week passed, and I knew I needed to forget about all the thoughts I was having about my childhood. Picking up my coat, I went to E.J.'s to go dancing with a few of my friends. There was a guy there that I had met at Jay and Denise's house. His name was Gerry, and I had never really liked him. He was tall with dirty blond hair. He drank a lot and always acted cocky. He had asked me out many times, but I had always turned him down. The last few times he had gotten angry with me and, in a drunken stupor, called me terrible names. I avoided this man as much as possible. When I saw him that night, I asked the girl I had driven with if we could go. She was having a great time with a guy she had just met and didn't want to leave. E.J.'s was almost twenty miles from my house. I had no choice but to wait it out.

After awhile, Gerry spotted me. Crossing the room, he walked a straight line in my direction. The loud music and flashing lights made his stature quite menacing. He tried to put his arm around my waist. His vodka breath crawled across my cheek as he tried to kiss my mouth. I backed away.

"Gerry, take your hands off me, I am not interested, and I never will be, so give up."

"LISTEN, BITCH, WHO DO YOU THINK YOU ARE, TALKING TO ME THAT WAY? YOU ARE GOING TO REGRET YOU SAID THAT!" He was drunk and stumbled over his words. The whole bar was looking at us. I felt humiliated. I walked away from him and hoped he wouldn't remember the incident by morning.

The rest of the evening I avoided him at every turn. He just glared at me with a look of disdain that frightened me. That night I got home around midnight. I took a shower and went to bed. At approximately 2:00 AM, I heard someone trying to enter my room. I had left the bathroom light on, and in the dim light of my room, I noticed I had failed to set the deadbolt. I darted across the room to set it before whoever it was came in. I wasn't fast enough. Gerry pushed his way into my room. Turning quickly, he latched the deadbolt. He was drunker than when I had left him hours before that, and I wondered what else he was on.

"Get over here, bitch; I am going to teach you that lesson I promised. All you need is a good lay, and you will come around." He grabbed me by my pajamas and put his wet slobbering mouth on mine. His hands that were pawing under my shirt felt sticky and slimy. I was struggling to get free from him when he slapped me in the face. Holding his hand in front of me to strike me again I could see the dirt under his nails. His whole hand was covered in filth, as if he had been crawling along a dirty, slimy floor. Now these hands were all over me. He put one hand over my mouth, as he backed me up against the wall. The other hand pulled at my pants. I started stamping my feet in an attempt to thwart his efforts. It didn't work. He found his way into my pants and between my legs. I was surprised by the strength his anger was giving him. He was a lot bigger than me, and with one arm around my waist, he lifted me up and threw me on the couch. I tried to escape, but before I knew it, he was on top of me fumbling with his zipper. I tried to push him away but couldn't. All I could do was scream. The next thing I heard was my door coming off the hinges. With Gerry on top of me, I couldn't see who it was. All of a sudden, Gerry's limp body rose in the air above me, with a look of surprise on his face. Sitting upright, I saw that it was Rob, my biker neighbor, who had him by the back of his pants and his shirt collar. He dragged him out onto the porch. I scrambled to my feet, just in time to see him lift Gerry practically over his head and hurl him three stories below on to the grass. Unlike the crazy fury that had been on Gerry's face, Rob's was an ice cold fury of determination. It was a face I had seen before on a Hell's Angel; it was a look I had come to know that meant I shouldn't speak. When Rob was finished with Gerry I leaned over the rail to see for myself that he had not killed him. The amount of drugs he had in him must have allowed his body to go limp; all he did was break a leg. He had some friends waiting for him in a car in the driveway, so they helped him hobble away. Rob was standing before me in his underwear with nothing else on. He followed me back into my room. Debbie came in right behind him, holding a robe. He was still angry and began yelling at me about the men I associated with. I tried to tell him that I didn't like this guy and didn't know how he knew where I lived. He wasn't listening. He just kept pacing the floor and ranting. One thing he said that night rang true to my ears. He told me I was too young and vulnerable to be on my own. If he had not been home, I could have been killed. This incident, combined with the violence I had witnessed in Beverly Farms, left me shaken and scared. He could see it. He told me to go back to my mother and try to make it work. This life would harden me. Shutting the door behind them, I turned to see Shadow Man sitting on the couch. Plopping myself down next to him, I curled into a fetal position and began to cry.

The next morning, I made a lunch date with my mother for later that day. I didn't tell her what had happened the night before or about the boys that I saw beaten. She would have just lectured me, and I knew it. Instead, I told her I was tired. I was sick of sleeping on a couch and missed my bed. I told her I wanted to go to college and was going to look into enrolling at Salem State. Then I asked her if I could move back home. She said yes, as long as I lived by her rules. I wasn't sure what she meant by that. I was afraid to ask, so I didn't.

That evening I packed up my things and headed home.

Being back in my old room felt surreal. I had only been gone for a little over a year, but it felt like a lifetime. Rob was right. What I had experienced in that short time had changed me. I'm not sure hardened was the word I would have used. It was more like withdrawn. I wasn't a girl anymore. I had become a woman, the hard way. I was an adult. I made my own meals and did my own laundry at my mother's house. Jake was still living at home but had a social life now, and we rarely saw him. I was making more money now than when I had last lived at home, so Mom upped my rent. She was still taking more than half. It was less than it had cost me to live on my own, which allowed me to save for college. I felt I was on the right track.

I wrote to Bobby and told him what had happened. The letter I received in return was sweet and caring. I started to disassociate from my friends. They were mostly girls and harmless, so I found this to be easy to do. I wanted to change my life completely. More and more women were dying at Ivy Manor. It was too much for me to take so I quit, and searched for new employment.

While going to the Hellenic Credit Union in Peabody to help Mom pay the mortgage one day, I told her I was going to walk down Main Street to look into some shops. I would only be a short while, and I wanted her to wait for me. At the end of the square, I saw a sign in the window of a collectibles store that read "Help Wanted." I went in and applied. It was a coin and stamp shop that also sold jewelry. The owner's name was Phil, and he hired me right away. I told him I could start the next day. When I got back to my mother and told her, she thought I was crazy to get a job like that and told me I should have applied at the factory where she worked. I knew I was growing up, when I was able to ignore that comment.

Phil was an Italian man from East Boston. He had a wife and family. He had a daughter who was my age; I remember her being spoiled and getting whatever she wanted. I remember realizing that if that was what happened to girls who lived the easy life at home, I didn't want any part of it. She was an embarrassment to watch. Phil's wife was suspicious of me. I was a young and beautiful girl whom her husband had hired with no experience. I heard them arguing in the back room one time as to his motives. This made me nervous and caused me to keep my distance and just do my job. Every day I cataloged stamps. Some were rare; others were just pretty and worthless. I loved doing this; the delicate art work on them was amazing. I also learned to buy and grade coins. It was during the time that the Hunt brothers had cornered the silver market, so I learned to buy scrap precious metals as well. One day as a type of game, Phil handed me five precious stones. They all looked like diamonds, and he asked me to pick out the real one. Without hesitation, I did it correctly. He tested me over and over every day, trying to trip me up. Every day I proved him wrong. He showed me how to buy them too, and soon I was heading to Boston to the diamond district, picking up stones he would purchase and selling ones he had bought. This was a far cry from playing Bingo with the ladies at Ivy Manor.

I enrolled in a night course in painting at Salem State. The teacher was a woman by the name of Lori. She was a lousy teacher, and you could tell she didn't want to be there. She criticized our work in a very judgmental way. None of this criticism seemed to have merit. Most was based on her own personal opinion. It was in that class I met Bruce. He was twenty one and very serious. He owned a two family home in Lynn. We would often go for coffee after class, and I enjoyed talking to him. He was an intelligent man who had a plan to make it in this world by buying and selling real estate. Years later, I found out his plan had worked; he had become quite wealthy doing just that. Bruce and I started seeing more of each other. He became my boyfriend. I wasn't afraid to have a relationship anymore. I felt safe and cared for in his company. We shared a common interest in art; we went to museums and openings; we lived an adult life style, complete with dinners and movies. He introduced me to his family, and I became a part of his world.

Meanwhile, back at home, Mom was still treating me like I was twelve. Every day she would have lists for me that were left on the table. This was her new, revised version of her chore chart. For some reason, she never realized that I was working as many hours as she was. Sometimes we would get into a squabble, if she felt I was slacking off. Once again, there was no reasoning with her. She wanted to know where I was every minute of the day. As my life began expanding with Bruce, so was my sense of being unable to tolerate my mother. Her sour looks returned in less than a month of my return; after I started seeing Bruce, they only worsened. She took every opportunity to insult him to me. To his face, she acted like she loved him. I didn't understand this side of my mother, and, instead of just letting it go, I confronted her with it. She said he was cheap, and she didn't like cheap people. The way she said it, she might as well have called him a murderer. Bruce was tight with his money. He wouldn't have been able to own a home of his own by the age of twenty-one if he weren't. It never bothered me. I always had the belief that everyone had their own thing that was eccentric and unique about them. For Bruce it was money. It was not like he didn't spend any. We certainly went enough places to prove that. It was more his ambition about it that irritated her, his plans of how to handle it correctly so as to get the most gain in real estate. He was very handy with a hammer and nail, and this he used to his advantage when buying rundown property.

In time, my mother and I began arguing again. I had only been home for three months. She would harp on me for every little thing, and my stubbornness wouldn't let it rest. Whenever she did this, I would point out her faults surrounding this type of behavior. A few times she hit me. My living at home was not going to work, but I couldn't go back to living the way I had been either. I scoured the ads for apartments, but none of them could I afford. Eventually, when I couldn't take it anymore, I moved in with Bruce.

Phil, in the meantime, began crossing boundaries with me. He would try and rub my shoulders and talk softly in my ear. This made me sick to my stomach, and I told him to back off. One day, he asked me to run away to Crete with him. I told him if he talked that way to me again, I would quit. When I related the story to Bruce he just laughed. He didn't understand how uncomfortable this was making me feel, how it upset me. I didn't necessarily want him to do anything about it; I just wanted him to acknowledge my feelings. He never did.

Bruce and I got along just fine. Together we redid his house. We took an entire room, stripped it down to the bare slats and dry-walled it again. Then we applied a textured spackle, and it looked beautiful.

We turned a spare bedroom into a studio, where I spent most of my days. I tried my hand at cooking for two, but I wasn't very good at it. Most of the things I tried, I burned. I was able to make a "mean" lasagna. This dish felt like art to me. It was a kind of sculpture. I hated eating lasagna, but Bruce loved it. Living with Bruce was like playing house. My mom didn't mind when I moved out; she never said a word about it. I guess she hadn't wanted me living with her in the first place. With the money I saved living with Bruce, I was able to buy my first car, a 1967 Cutlass. The thing was a tank. I bought it for a dollar from a man I knew at the coin shop on the same day I got my license. I think he was just glad to get rid of it. It had taken me six tries to get my driver's license. It was the dead of winter, and we had had a series of storms around the time I was taking my road test. The first time I failed, the registry inspector had asked me to pull over and show him that I could drive in reverse in a straight line along the curb. I ended up putting the car up on a snow bank, and we couldn't get it down. The second time, he asked me to do a three point turn on a hill. There was ice, so I rolled back and failed. The third time felt like a trick. I was so nervous by this time, and he took me near a school zone at about 2:30 in the afternoon. There was a sign on the side of the road that stated the speed limit was reduced to twenty at that time of the day. I was doing twenty-three, and the bastard failed me. Do you know how slowly you are going when you are doing twenty-three miles per hour? I swear the guy had it in for me. The last time I had failed was the winner. I was driving down Cabot Street in Beverly. The sun was shining really bright directly down the center of the road. There were huge piles of fresh snow on both sides of the street. The sun blindness was so bad, you couldn't see a thing. Unfortunately, there was a blind man trying to cross at a crosswalk that I also could not see. The registry cop screamed at me to stop. I slammed on my brakes, making an awful, screeching sound. This frightened the blind man, whom I did not hit, and made him fall into the crosswalk from the sheer fear of the noise the brakes made. When I arrived back at the registry the next day, the cop refused to get into the car with me. Another one did and only had me drive a little way before he said I passed. I always saw my passing the driver's test as a pity pass. Now here I was, the same day, buying a car.

The undercarriage of this car I had purchased was so rusted through, that if there were even two inches of snow on the ground, the floor of the car would skim across the snow's surface and blow snow into my face while I was driving. The first time this happened to me was quite a surprise indeed. The man I had bought the car from lived in Winchester. He was also a coin dealer. The day I bought it, he took me back in the direction of the registry to an insurance company that was next door. I was afraid to show my face in that neighborhood but knew I didn't have a choice. When we were finished, I had to drive him home. He showed me how to get to his house by back roads, so that I didn't have to take the highway. I had never driven on the highway before and was afraid to. After I dropped him off, I headed back to Lynn, where Bruce and I lived. It was about twenty miles away, and I became confused as to where I was going. In no time, I became lost. I kept asking random people how to get to Lynn. After an hour, I crossed the city line. By that time, it was getting dark. Since Lynn is a very large and complicated city, I knew I wasn't out of the woods yet. I drove around aimlessly for an hour. No one seemed to know the tiny street that Bruce and I lived on. I knew I was in trouble, when I saw people hanging out on the street exchanging money. It was the middle of the winter, and I realized they were drug dealers. I saw a young girl who was walking along the sidewalk. She seemed nervous and in a hurry. She kept looking over her shoulder to see if there was anyone behind her. When I pulled up next to her she reacted with a stumbling leap away from the car. I turned on my interior light, so she could see I was harmless.

"Excuse me, I am lost. Could you give me some directions? I know if I can get to Eastern Ave. I can find my home from there."

Bending over the window of my car, she said, "You shouldn't be driving in these parts of town." "Well, if I shouldn't be driving, isn't it also dangerous for you to be walking?"

"I don't have a choice. I live here and don't have a car." Her voice sounded depressed and tired.

"Tell you what; I will get us both out of here, if you just show me the way." After some hesitation, she said ok and slid onto the seat next to me. I tried to make small talk with her. I asked her what her name was. She wouldn't answer me; she just told me to take the next right. In ten minutes she had us on Eastern Avenue. She told me to pull over, she'd walk the rest of the way. I told her I would drive her, because it was cold, and it was the least I could do. She didn't answer me. With her eyes on the road in front of her, she quietly headed down the street and was gone. Turning the car in the direction that felt familiar to me, I couldn't help but think about this fleeting moment we had shared together. How many people share vignettes like this and never know each other's names?

When I walked through the front door, it was about 10:00 PM. I had been gone for fourteen hours in total. Bruce was in the living room, laughing about something he was watching on TV. I stood in the doorway and apologized for being so late. He said not to worry about it; he hadn't noticed. I lowered my head and turned towards the bathroom. I needed to take one of my famous three hour baths. The relationship Bruce and I shared was one of convenience. I needed a place to stay; he liked having help with the house repairs. We never fought, and we never talked about the future. We knew we would never marry, but we never spoke of it. We were living like this day to day, until the day arrived when I knew I needed something more. When we broke up, it wasn't a big deal. I told him I was leaving. He said ok. I packed my things up, and in an hour, I was gone. That day summarized our relationship. I went to stay with Jay and Denise, until I could figure out what to do next.

One day while visiting a friend in the hospital, I ran into a girl named Andrea, whom I had worked with in the kitchen. I spent her dinner break with her, and she told me that her sister, Jill, was looking for a roommate. Jill had broken up with her husband, and she had a five year old little boy named Henry. I agreed to meet her.

Jill and I got along right off the bat. She rented an apartment a few streets away from my mother's house. It was on the third floor of a very large apartment building. The apartment was huge. I liked this new home and began to settle in, when something terrible happened to another sister of hers. Her name was Cindy, and she was more street-wise and tougher than Jill and Andrea. She was older than they were and had just had a baby with cerebral palsy. The baby was terribly sick, right from birth. She couldn't breathe on her own and was severely brain damaged. The baby died at two months. It put Jill's entire family in turmoil. There were constantly people at our house. I felt like an outsider peering in at the very private dilemma this family was experiencing. Cindy always seemed to be looking at me, as if wondering why I was there. After a few months, Jill told me Cindy was moving in. Cindy couldn't afford the rent at her own apartment, because of all her daughter's medical bills. She didn't have insurance, and the whole situation had left her destitute. Once again, I was out. Both Andrea and Jill said it was probably going to be temporary, because Jill and her sister Cindy had a history of not getting along.

Meanwhile, I had to find a temporary situation myself. Once again, I was forced to go home to Mom, and once again I hated it. Mom didn't turn me down to my surprise, but she did make it known she was not happy every time she saw me. All this moving around was getting to me. In less than a year, I had moved to Mom's, then to Bruce's, then to Jill's and now back to Mom's again. I was still only nineteen. Once I moved back to Mom's, I wrote to Bobby and told him everything that had happened. He was a sympathetic ear. To my surprise, he called me one night at my mom's house. We talked for hours; we began writing to each other regularly after that.

I was still working at the coin shop. I liked this job and decided that I wanted to be a jeweler. I had a natural eye for diamonds and felt this would be a respectable job at which I would be able to find employment anywhere. I knew that I had the dexterity in my fingers to do anything, from repairing watches to making settings if I had to. The problem was that I didn't know where to go to school for this. One day at work, I had an idea. Looking in the phonebook, I called a jeweler in Beverly to ask him how one goes about being certified. I chose this particular one because he wasn't part of a chain. I wanted to talk to someone who owned his own place, someone who would give me the time to pick his brain. He was nice to me over the phone and gave me a lot of useful information. He told me to enroll with the GIA, that is, the Gemological Institute of America. This was a school which was located both in New York and Los Angeles. They had a correspondence course for people who lived far away. I talked to other jewelry chains at the mall and found out that with a certificate from the GIA, I could work anywhere. I signed up for enrollment the next week. The course cost me $700. My mother thought it was a scam. I told her I had checked into it on many levels, and everyone said this was the thing to do. She didn't believe me and gave me a hard time; that is, until they started sending me diamonds in the mail to grade. After that, she just left me alone; she didn't discourage me, yet she didn't encourage me either. We began to stop talking to each other, but I was beginning to prefer this. It made my life easier, as long as I could continue to ignore her dirty looks.

Jill and Andrea were right. Cindy was too difficult for Jill to live with. They had a big fight, and Jill threw her out. Jill called and asked me if I wanted to be her roommate again; I jumped at the opportunity. She said she had rented a new place. It was in the woods, off of Highland Avenue in Salem. The day we first pulled up to it, I was shocked to see that it sat right behind Alex's old house. I moved again. It would be my fourth move in less than a year. Somehow during all these moves, I was able to purchase my first piece of furniture. It was a canopy bed. Ever since Veronica had been given one many years ago, I had vowed I would buy one for myself. I kept that promise, and it was my pride and joy. I was never going to sleep on a couch again. The house on Highland Avenue was great. It was large, with lots of windows. The living room was huge. One day when I was sick and home from work, I sat alone in that living room and watched on live TV as President Reagan was shot. I couldn't help but think about that time, so many years ago, of Kennedy's assassination and my mother's reaction. This time, I was the grown up, yet no one was with me to see how upset I was.

I didn't have a boyfriend back then. I liked being alone and in control of my own destiny. I received three letters a day from Bobby, and I wrote him as many in return. Our letters became poetic. Eventually, and I'm not sure when or how it happened, they turned into love letters. He wrote beautifully and soon won my heart. He had a lot of dreams of someday becoming a writer. He often wrote articles for his local military paper. He would send me the clippings, and they were very good. Jill and I were getting along great. Her son Henry was adorable and sweet; I fell in love with him. She never asked me to watch him, but I would have done so in a second if I were given the chance. Jill was on welfare and was home with him until he started school.

One morning, I was sitting at the kitchen table, having my morning coffee. Jill was getting Henry ready for school. He was in the first grade at the time, and every morning it was a struggle to get him off. He would cry and complain of a stomach ache and was practically hysterical by the time they got out the door. The scene was all too familiar to me, and I knew I had to talk to Jill about it when she returned. When she walked back into the house after dropping him off at school, Jill looked tired and beaten. She was genuinely concerned and was on the verge of tears. I got up and poured her a cup of coffee. Handing it to her, I told her about my first grade teacher and the abuse I and the rest of the class had had to put up with. I told her that my reactions in the morning had been the same as Henry's. She was standing near the sink, looking at me in bewilderment; she was appalled by what I had told her and couldn't believe that they would let a teacher behave in such a manner. I said, "I'll never forget her name; it was Mrs. Durham." The minute the words left my mouth, Jill dropped her coffee mug on the floor. Looking at me, she said, "We have to go get him right now! That is his teacher!"

We immediately got up and headed to my car. When we got to the school, we went directly to the office. We decided the best thing to do was to say there was a family emergency, and we needed to take Henry. They didn't question it and told us where his room was. I told Jill that I couldn't go to that room. It had too many bad memories for me, and it would have killed me to see Henry in there. I went to wait for her outside. Standing on the steps, I looked over at my old house and my old bedroom window. It looked exactly the same, but I thought of how much I had changed. For a minute, I wished I could go back to those innocent times of my childhood, of exploring, eating pears and catching snapping turtles.

When we got home, I called in sick to work. We sat Henry down and asked him what was happening at school. The stories he related to us sounded like my own. I got my tape recorder which I used to send tapes to Bobby, and we recorded everything he said. Then I recorded my own accounts from childhood, as best as I could remember. That afternoon, Jill got a lawyer who said he would handle this case. She told him she couldn't afford a lawyer. She said all monetary gain would go to him; we just didn't want to see any more children suffer. We wanted her fired.

That very week she pulled Henry from that school and sent him to another one. I can't remember how she was able to do this, but the school system complied. The case went before the Department of Education. Others had come forward. Most were grown children who had suffered under the hands of this woman. As adults, we had a voice. We all wrote testimonies and won. Mrs. Durham was relieved of her duties, and justice was done. The reality was they forced her into retirement. It was a great day for me to see this. I thought of Alex saying that one person can change the world. He had been right.

CHAPTER: 26

Bobby called me almost every night. He would call collect and then send me money to pay for it. Eventually he just sent me checks every month and told me to use whatever was left over for my personal needs. Even though it wasn't much after the phone bill was paid, I felt odd doing this, so I just banked it. Despite the distance, I couldn't deny it; we were now a couple. We had been corresponding for a few years through the mail, when the letters became that of love and appreciation. That is when the phone calls began. He would tell me his hopes of a better world and how he would make my life easier if he could. I confided in him all that I was afraid to speak out loud. He would listen and comfort me. His voice was soft and romantic, when he spoke of his feelings for me. It wrapped around me like a warm breeze on a spring day. He kissed my soul. I felt safe and relaxed for the first time in years. I returned the feelings to him, as well as the tone. After many months of these exchanges, he called and asked me to marry him. I was stunned, to say the least. I had no idea he loved me that much. Maybe I just didn't know how to recognize love when it was presented to me. I didn't know what to say. I was tired of all the unpredictable circumstances in my life. I needed a stable environment. Even living with Jill was becoming erratic; she had started dating a guy named Lenny, who was abusive. I would often come home to her in tears sitting in the kitchen, usually sporting a bruise or a black eye. I told her she was crazy, especially after the success we had had with Mrs. Durham. I asked her how she could tolerate this in her life. When that didn't work, I tried to comfort her. Even that was not something she wanted. We began to fight about this issue often, setting a wedge between us. I was afraid for her life, as well as Henry's. But there was a part of me too that was afraid for myself. The night not long before that, when Gil's son tore up my mother's living room, was still fresh in my head. She defended him for some reason, and I never understood it. Finally, one night I told her in a very sobering voice that I was there for her if she needed me. If the abuse got to be much for her, and she needed someone to go with her to get a restraining order, I would be happy to do so. She heard what I was saying, but I could tell she was frightened of him. I let the topic drop.

The atmosphere in the house had changed. My heart went out to Henry. I was surprised that Jill allowed this behavior in front of him. Lenny had a drinking problem and was loud and obnoxious whenever he was there. I couldn't seem to get away from this type of behavior in my life. I was convinced that was why I never drank myself. When Lenny was at the house, I stayed in my room.

To feel a sense of peace, I bought myself a pair of baby finches. They were tiny birds who made a delicate sound. With nesting material, they began to make a home in the beautiful cage I also had gotten for them. I spent my evenings watching them; after awhile, I realized that it was familiar to me. They were trapped in their world trying to make the best of it. I took comfort in it, knowing I was doing the same. The comfort was short lived, once I discovered that my world was as small as theirs. The bars on my cage were just as confining. My bars were molded from the lack of opportunity I had experienced. Meanwhile, I was halfway through my courses with the GIA. And it came easy to me. I got A's on every test, including grading the diamonds and rating their monetary value. They weren't really expensive stones; most were a carat or under, with several flaws and poor color. Every night I talked to Bobby on the private phone line I had installed in my room. Between my school work and talking to Bobby, it felt like I had spent my entire non-working time in there. It soon felt like living there was the equivalent to being at my mother's house. I spent all my time in my room, so that I wouldn't have to face the goings on in the rest of the house. Bobby became my sanctuary. It is why, when he proposed, I said yes.

One night Jill came home early from a night out with Henry and Lenny. She was crying, and Henry was upset as well. Emerging from my room, I went to see if they were ok. Jill had a black eye and was in bad shape. Henry was just upset. I made her a cup of coffee and asked what had happened. She didn't want to talk about it, so I told her I would put Henry to bed. I calmed him down as best I could, reading him several books before he finally fell asleep. When I closed the door to his room, I realized Jill had also gone to bed. I went back to my room. The next night, Jill and Henry were out again. I knew they were with Lenny and worried about them. I did the best I could, trying not to think about it and working on my schoolwork. The phone rang; it was Bobby. When I told him what had been happening, he told me he didn't want me to live there. He felt helpless and expressed this to me. It felt good to me to know he cared. When we hung up the phone, it was two in the morning. I wasn't asleep long before the phone rang again. It was Jill, calling from a pay phone in Lynn. She was frantic, and at first I thought she had been beaten again. I could hear Henry crying in the background. She said I needed to get out of the house right away, because Lenny was on his way over. She sounded genuinely concerned; she sounded like the Jill I used to know.

Lenny had asked Jill to move in with him, and she had said she couldn't, because I would have no place to go. She was afraid of him and was just using me as an excuse. He knew this, and it angered him. He decided to tell me to move himself. He was going to remove me from Jill's life, that night, from the house. I was so scared; I didn't know what to do. I called my mother in the middle of the night, and she sent my brother Jake over with his truck. It was the only time Jake had ever been kind to me since we were kids. I thanked him over and over that night. Together we gathered up the few things I owned. The toughest part was my canopy bed. I knew if I left it behind, it would be destroyed. We were able to get it all out in a half hour. It was a testimony to how little I actually possessed in the world. Jake said not to worry about it; he would love the chance to pound this guy. I was afraid to tell him there might be a gun. When I look back on that event, my memory is of passing items through my bedroom window, frantically, in the middle of the night. We must have brought the bed through the back door, but I can't recall. When we got to Mom's house, we left everything in the truck until morning, since we were both so exhausted. For years later, Jake would bring up that night and throw it in my face. He would say I had been irresponsible to have put myself in that position. He always spoke to me as if I were beneath him. When I woke up late the next morning, I found myself in my old bed at my mother's house; the night before felt like a dream. My birds were chirping happily away, as if nothing had even happened.

I called Bobby first thing, so he wouldn't worry. He was unavailable and couldn't come to the phone; I left him a message. He called me collect that evening; it was the first chance he had. My mom was upset that he had called me collect. I told her he would pay for it, that he didn't have a choice; they were not allowed to have phones in the barracks. She was fine with this, once his monthly checks started arriving. It was that day that I told my mother we were getting married. Bobby was expected to be home on leave in September, and that was when we had set the date; it was six months away.

I had turned twenty in February, while I was still living with Jill. The day came and went without fanfare. My mom more than likely bought me a trivial gift, but I don't recall celebrating it with her. I don't recall celebrating any of my birthdays between seventeen and twenty. Living with my mother was a little easier this time. The fact that I was to be married and settled in a few months helped. Our plans were that it would be a small wedding, and then Bobby and I would move to Germany. That was where he was to be stationed next. I wanted to elope. Bobby, being a very Catholic man, wanted to be married in a church. This was my mother's wish as well. I wanted to elope, but no one was listening to me. To my surprise, Mom agreed to pay for most of it. It was a Catholic rule that a couple had to attend pre-Cana classes. These were marriage counseling sessions for both the man and woman, usually conducted as a class with other couples and a trained psychologist. This was a problem. With Bobby in California and me in Massachusetts, it was impossible. At first, I thought that this would support my argument to just get a Justice of the Peace and to elope. I was wrong. Bobby called the church he wanted for the wedding and made special arrangements. We were told we could see priests from different states. In the long run, I wound up going to counseling, and Bobby did not. The counseling was ridiculous. Here was a man of the cloth, who was not allowed to be married himself and pledged to celibacy, telling me about marriage and sex. I told him that I felt he was not necessarily an authority on such subjects, and it was making me uncomfortable. He sent me to a private counselor which cost me $75 dollars a session instead. This, too, was ridiculous. All he talked to me about was the difficulty of living on your own. I didn't tell him I could write a book on the subject. I was afraid if I told him what I had been through in the last few years, he would want to see me more and therefore cost me an arm and a leg. As it was, I only had to see him twice.

With Bobby's encouragement, I called his family. They had not yet met me, and with no time before the wedding for him to introduce us, he felt it was a good idea. His parents and I agreed to meet for lunch. Sitting in the restaurant waiting for them, I thought of how much I had aged in the last three years. I had lived a lifetime since the age of seventeen, and it felt good to know I was going to begin to settle my life. His family was very Irish. I fell in love with his mother right from the start. She was sweet and loving. His father was a quiet man of few words, yet he, too, was open and accepting of me. What surprised me was their immediate concern for me. They said Bobby was different and could be difficult to live with. I didn't pay much attention to this; I was sure my mother would have said the same thing about me. I wanted to show them his letters that I had been receiving for the last several years, show them the kindness in them, the concern he had for me, the good advice when I needed it and had no one else. Instead I just sat politely and listened to them. In the end, when they realized that they weren't going to talk me out of it, they put their arms around me and welcomed me to the family.

Bobby also had an older sister and brother. I didn't meet his brother until right before the wedding, when Bobby himself introduced us. His sister, on the other hand, lived in Marblehead, one town over from Salem. She was the same age as my brother Doug. Her name was Maureen. She called and invited me to her house; she told me to bring the wine. This seemed funny to me, because I knew nothing about wine. After we introduced ourselves, she handed me a corkscrew. Looking at it I didn't know which end was up; I didn't want to look naïve, so I didn't say a thing and did the best I could. I was tugging and pulling on the cork, just as she was coming back into the room with the glasses. At that moment, the cork broke free, and we both got soaked. It was a good thing the wine was white. She laughed about it, and I was embarrassed. In the long run, it was a good ice breaker, and we became immediate friends. Although it was not the first time I had tasted it, it was the first time I had ever drunk a whole glass of wine. It was enjoyable and eased my tensions.

We went out to eat at the Landing Restaurant that night. Her conversations with me were similar to those of her parents. Being prepared for this, I had brought along some of Bobby's letters. She was pleased that he seemed more mature than the last time she had seen him. I asked if she was making her judgments on him based on childhood difficulties. She said maybe she was, and she, too, accepted me with open arms. That night was the beginning of a friendship between two women that would last for years.

The months dragged on. Mom was busy making all the arrangements for the wedding. I soon learned I would have nothing to do with the plans. Unlike most women, that was ok with me. I hated the thought of a big wedding. I wanted something more personal. The plans and preparation kept Mom busy and off my back. I was happy for the distraction. We were to be married at the Immaculate Conception Church in Salem on September 20, 1980. The reception would be at a small restaurant that a friend of my mother owned. There would be no music or dancing, and only seventy five people would attend. I borrowed Maureen's wedding gown from a failed previous marriage.

Bobby was expected home three days prior to the wedding. We had a week long honeymoon planned in New York City, and then he was to be shipped out to Germany immediately afterwards. I would be joining him later, after he was able to get us an apartment. A week before Bobby was to arrive, Maureen asked me to go out with her and her friends. It was a Friday night, and I had thought nothing of this, since we were seeing each other regularly, and I had became part of her personal circle of girls. I liked the girls that Maureen hung around with. In total, there were usually five of us. They all had a great sense of humor. As a matter of fact, all they did was laugh and joke around. It wasn't a childish humor; it was more like a night long string of one-liners, based on the happenings around them. And it wasn't just Maureen who was like this; it was all of them. Every time I went out with them, I would arrive home at the end of the night with a sore side from all the laughing.

At first, this particular night seemed like it was going to be like any other. We would meet at a bar down on Derby Wharf in Salem called Brandy's. We would get a table and drink and laugh all night long. I was drinking at this time, but not nearly as much as the rest of the girls. I only drank white wine. I nursed the same glass for most of the night. Men would come up and flirt with Maureen and her friends, and they would toy with them, until they finally got fed up. Then they would all laugh. I always felt uncomfortable in that situation for two reasons: the first was because I was getting married, the second was because I felt bad for the unsuspecting victims. When this would happen, I mostly kept quiet. This wasn't a problem with the other girls; they saw me as just young. In fact I was. They were all four years my senior. Because of this age difference, they protected me and never gave me a hard time.

That night, though, was going to be different. The girls had other plans as well. Maureen picked me up at my mother's house that night at nine. She didn't let me in on any of the plans as we drove down to the wharf; when we arrived, there were more than the usual girls holding two tables at the back of the bar. I think there were about eight of us all together. When we approached them, Carla, the only married girl in the bunch, pulled out a hat that had a veil on it and stuck it on my head. I didn't know why she did that and asked what was going on. I was so young, and naive I didn't even realize until they told me that it was my bachelorette party. They all thought this was funny and bought me a drink. Everyone was toasting me, and our tables began to get loud. Soon the rest of the bar was joining us, and, although there wasn't a band, everyone started dancing. I personally danced with every man in the place. All night long people were buying me drinks. It was hard for me to refuse them without insulting anyone. They expected me to get drunk, and I knew it. With the images of Cherri and the night I almost lost her forever present in my mind, I let the drinks pile up. I felt bad that she was not there. She was, after all, going to be my maid of honor. The girls were very boisterous, and someone got an idea. Grabbing the hat off my head, they started passing it around for donations. I was shocked and embarrassed by this. It was obvious I was the only one with my wits about me. By the time the hat returned, it had four hundred dollars in it. I didn't want to take it, but the girls and the rest of the bar insisted I do.

We left Brandy's around ten thirty that night and headed to another bar down the street. I had left half a dozen drinks untouched on the table. The girls, on the other hand, were feeling no pain. I was ready to go home, but none of them would hear of it. Entering the next bar, the celebration began all over again. At this location, we ran into some guys the girls had graduated from high school with. These were men they respected, their friends. I was glad they were there, because they seemed to put a lid on the excitement. There was still a lot of drinking and congratulations all around. And, once again, the glasses started piling up in front of me. Everyone at this point was drunk, and I was able to get away with only having drunk one drink without being noticed.

The next stop, to my chagrin, was a bar in Lynn. The bars there were the last to close in the area and they weren't finished with me yet; one of the guys, named Terry, had decided to join us. We all piled into several cars and headed for Rockefeller's. It was a dive compared to the other bars we were in that night. This place had dancing and a band. It was filled with a lot of low life bikers, and we were fresh meat walking through the door. Maureen told the guy that came with us to stay with me. She wasn't sure I could handle myself in a place like this, and she was right.

The minute we got there I wanted to leave. It was dark and smoky, and I was sure we were going to get into trouble. If Bobby had known Maureen had brought me there, I knew he would have been upset. As it turned out, we didn't stay long. Terry, who was supposed to be watching me, had left to go to the men's room. While he was gone, a very large and disgusting man came up to me, put his hand on my thigh and said, "What a shame you are getting married; I could have shown you the time of your life tonight."

That was it for me! I went over to Maureen and said I had to go. We waited for her friend to emerge from the men's room and left. Maureen, Terry, Carla and I piled into Maureen's car. Carla and Maureen were in the front, Terry and I were in the back. I was real nervous about getting in the car with them. They had all had too much to drink, and I knew I should be the one driving, but at the time, I didn't know how to drive a standard shift. I was stuck and didn't know what to do. I asked Maureen if she felt sober enough to drive. They all laughed at me and said she had driven in worse conditions than these. It wasn't a comforting feeling. I should have called someone to pick me up, but I couldn't think of anyone to call. It took this particular incident for me to vow that I would learn how to drive a standard. I also decided that night that I would never let anyone else drive me to a bar. From that point on, I always took my own car. Maureen had planned it so that I was staying at her house that night.

She actually drove ok, considering the amount of alcohol she had in her. There was only one scary time going down Highland Avenue, when I had to remind her of the lane we were in. By the time we got to the abandoned old high school, Maureen decided she couldn't hold it any longer, she had to pee. Pulling into a wooded area along the side of the road, she got out of the car and squatted right in front of us. Carla said, "Now you know she has had too much to drink!" Carla then turned the high beams on her so that all the passing cars could get a good look. We all roared with laughter.

When we got to her house, I made a bed for myself on one of her two couches. She plopped herself down on the other, and we fell immediately to sleep. The next morning, when we woke up, still lying on the couches, I started talking to her about the bizarre events from the night before. She was looking at me funny for a short while and then said in a very loud voice, "Are you talking to me?" I started to laugh and asked her why she couldn't hear me. She said she had a hearing problem, and unless she had her glasses on, she couldn't read my lips. Herein were the adventures of Maureen.

The day came when Bobby was to arrive home. We hadn't seen each other in over a year. Maureen said she would go with me to pick him up at the airport. I had voiced my concerns to her about getting lost trying to find the right terminal at Logan. We got there early and sat down to wait. I was excited inside, yet a quiet peace also took a hold of me, and I sat there in silence. Maureen was rambling on about something, but I wasn't hearing any of it. I started watching the other people in the terminal waiting area and was wondering about their lives. They were generic airport people: some were trying their hardest to read; mothers were entertaining their toddlers; one man was sleeping in a sitting position, but I could tell he was still awake. Were they waiting for somebody they loved too, or were they going to get on a plane to start a new life? I was doing both.

I then started thinking about the fact that soon I would be in a terminal not unlike this one to fly to Germany. I had not allowed myself to think of this expectation until this point. The wedding and my mother's craziness about it had kept me from the luxury of dreaming about anything. At one point, the priest who was to marry us asked me if the prospect of going to Germany was why I was marrying Bobby. His question made me look inside myself and realize he couldn't have been further from the truth. The fact was, I didn't want to go to Germany. It frightened me on many different levels. The first was, of course, the plane ride; seven hours in the air over water was a scary prospect to me. Then there was the fact that I couldn't speak the language. Also, Bobby had said we would not be living on base. The waiting list for housing was a year long, and he didn't want us to be separated for that amount of time. I didn't either. The last thing he told me was that he would be expected to go on field maneuvers for three month stretches every nine months. That meant that I would be alone in this foreign place, waiting it out. It was because of all these worries that I had just pushed all the thoughts of Germany aside. I figured when the day came, I would just close my eyes and take the first step, like I had done so many times in the past.

I was lost in all this thought when Maureen tugged on my arm and said, "I think they just called the arrival of his plane." I bolted to my feet and looked around as if I had just woken from a dream. She laughed at me and said, "It will take him a few minutes to get off the plane, why don't you go wait by that door?"

I looked at her like a child who had just been handed a candy bar. A big smile crossed my face. I couldn't remember the last time I had felt so happy. Standing at the door, holding the rope that had been placed there to allow the passengers room to pass, I waited. When the door finally opened and the first people got off, I couldn't help but think how lucky they were to have seen him before I. Were any of these passengers sitting with him on the flight? I fought the urge to grab one and ask.

It seemed like it took forever for him to emerge. As I waited, my excitement was rising to the boiling point. When he stepped into view, he was looking around and looked right past me. He was wearing his military dress greens and was the most handsome thing I had ever seen. I wanted to call out his name, but I found myself mute. Instead, I just burst into tears and slowly walked to him with my arms outstretched and put them around his neck. He embraced me and whispered he loved me in my ear. I couldn't stop crying. It was impossible to let go. All the events from the last few years rose to the surface of my soul and were pouring out of my heart;

I wanted to stay in that position in his arms forever. I didn't want to go back to Salem. I didn't want to go to Germany. I would never have to eat or sleep again. I was where I wanted to stay for the rest of my life, in his arms at the terminal in the airport.

We must have been quite a sight, because everyone who was standing around us broke into slow, sympathetic applause. It was the clapping and realization that we were not alone that broke me from my spell. Bobby looked me in the eyes, laughing, and teasingly said, "Who are your friends?" I laughed and gave him a big kiss. Maureen was standing right next to us; until that moment neither one of us had noticed. She said softly, "Welcome home Bobby," and threw her arms around him as well. We went to the baggage claim and gathered his oversized duffle bag and headed to the car. All the way home, he stared into my eyes and smiled. I did the same; neither one of us spoke.

Maureen told him he could stay at her house until the wedding, which was three days away. His parents had moved to a town just outside the border of New Hampshire. Although it was only forty minutes away, we would be able to see each other more if he stayed in Marblehead. He thanked her and looked back into my eyes. We were struck by cupid's arrow that morning, and I thought nothing was going to change that. What I didn't anticipate was the real world and the complications of having a wedding.

CHAPTER: 27

That day was a whirlwind. Bobby took Maureen and me out to lunch. We talked about his time in California and the inevitable move for him in less than two weeks to Germany. He said it would more than likely take him a month or two to secure an apartment. That meant I would be flying in the winter. For a second I thought about rollercoaster turbulence and the smell of Old Spice; I immediately became frightened. I didn't say a word to Maureen and Bobby---I had never told anyone about that trip. As it was, I wouldn't speak of it until I was well into my thirties.

I hated to do it, but it had to be done. My mother had never met Bobby before. We got back into the car and headed for MaryJane's house. Maureen had other plans, so she left us at the door. Mom was waiting for us when we got there; she wore a big smile and gave Bobby a hug. I was wondering which side of her we were looking at: was it the phony one she had always shown Bruce or the genuine one that had greeted Alex? I wanted everything to go smoothly, these next few days to go off without a hitch. Bobby, on the other hand, wanted to have a little more control with the wedding and sat her down and started questioning her about the plans. I knew this was the wrong thing to do, especially since it was only three days away. Bobby, being naïve, didn't realize that everything was set in stone.

My mother was irritated; I could tell. He asked why there wasn't any dancing, and why his friends weren't allowed to attend. I should have spoken up at that point and said it had been my idea, even though it hadn't. I didn't want to make waves with my future husband. I didn't want to have our first fight in front of my mother. I wanted it all to go away, but it didn't. Bobby was not a man who knew how to be subtle; in less than ten minutes into their meeting, they got into a big fight.

I could understand both sides. Bobby wanted a traditional wedding; my mother was paying for it and couldn't afford that. Bobby offered to give her some money, but it was too late. He should have spoken up months before. I'm sure my mother would have complied if he had offered to pay. It wasn't like I hadn't told him the plans months ago. I knew he was not happy about them when we spoke over the phone, but I had no idea he would go to such lengths on such short notice. I thought he was eventually ok with it all; for me, it was about the act and not the day. I said, "This isn't going to get us anywhere. I think we should leave, so everyone can calm down." Bobby agreed, turning to my mother with the parting words "I need to buy my wife a ring."

Picking out our wedding rings should have been a joyous time; instead, I was worried. I knew my mother was calling Doug and Joe and ranting about the way Bobby had behaved. I knew Bobby had made more than one enemy that day, and I didn't have the heart to tell him. Instead, I said he should relax about the wedding. I didn't care about the details. He saw me as siding with her, but the thought of that was foreign to me. He said, "Your mother has been controlling your whole life. Why do you let her get away with it?" I asked him to just let her do her thing. I was her only daughter, and she was paying for it. He said, "This is the only wedding I'm going to have." I said, "We can throw a huge one for all our friends when we get back from Germany in a few years. For now, because of the limited time, let's just do it this way." That seemed to hold him on the matter.

That night, my mother had had a weak moment and called Gil. When we all woke up the next morning, he was still there. Bobby had no idea who Gil was and asked me. I didn't give him any details but told him he was a friend of my mother's. Without a second thought, Bobby felt he would be funny and try to break the ice a little with my mother. The minute he saw her alone, he went up to her, poked her in the ribs with his elbow and said with a sly smile, "So you got some last night?" I thought I was going to die! My mother just narrowed her eyes at us, turned to me and said, "Barbara, tell your rude husband to get the hell out of my sight." I took Bobby by the hand, and we left.

I had been right; my mother had called Doug and Joe. The tension in the house was awful. Jake never spoke to us, but that wasn't anything new. Doug, on the other hand, wanted to speak to Bobby alone. Bringing him into my bedroom, he told him in no uncertain terms that if he made my life miserable, he personally would make his life difficult. Once again, my family had only shown its love in the face of adversity. When I found out, this angered me; Bobby didn't tell me himself---Doug did when Bobby wasn't around. I yelled at him and asked him where he and everyone else was when I was living on my own and in danger. I told him he had a funny way of showing that he cared. He told me that I had never allowed them to be in my life, and anything that had happened to me was my own fault. I said the real point was that I didn't allow them to force me to be what they wanted. And so, the lines of battle for the wedding day were drawn.

In the meantime, Bobby and I were not getting along. He couldn't understand this awful attitude my family was projecting on us. He hated that my family acted like I was their belonging and told me so. He hated me for allowing it. He asked me to go for a walk with him because he wanted to talk. We headed to the park, the only place I could think of where we could be alone. Standing under a big beautiful tree he told me he was concerned. The wedding was to take place the next day, and he was having second thoughts. He said that maybe we were rushing into it---maybe we should step back. I looked at him with my mouth wide open; I couldn't believe what he had just told me.

The flowers were set to arrive the next morning. I knew the florist was working on them as we spoke. The church and restaurant were reserved, and all the guests were notified. Telling them the wedding was off would have to be done at the church the next day. It all sounded like a bad movie; was that what my life really was? But worse than all that was my mother; she never would let me forget about this. She would harp at me about the money until the day she died. I knew this, and it would have given me no choice but to walk out of her life. What Bobby was asking me was to alter my life forever. I slowly sunk to the ground and cried. Then I did something so out of character for me: I prayed.

As Bobby sat, silently watching me, I asked God for direction. I told him I needed to find a way. I said that I could no longer live with my family; I needed to be allowed to follow my dreams. I said that I was confused by this last chain of events and didn't know what to do. I realized at that point that my love for Bobby was actually a love of his letters. They had helped me through the last few years. I knew now that he would be difficult to live with; but nothing could have been more difficult than what I had just been through. I knew I could find the patience for him, but he wasn't giving me a chance. I stood up and quietly walked to the other side of the park. I sat on the steps where Cherri had gone unconscious so many lifetimes ago.

I sat there for half an hour. It was getting dark, and I was trying to figure out what I was going to say to everyone. I didn't know how I was going to face them. I was embarrassed by just one more thing in the string of poor decisions I had made in my life. The thought of just standing up and walking to California was the strongest urge of all. I wanted to walk away from it, to not tell a soul and just go. I wanted to be alone, to not have to answer to anyone. I could endure this part of my life that would soon be history, because no one I would meet in the future would know. I wanted to become a missing person who would never return.

I knew it was the coward's way out, and I didn't care. I also knew I was not strong enough to face my family. My decision was made; that's what I would do. I would go to California, where no one knew me. California, I knew, was a different kind of place, beautiful and sunny. I needed a different environment, one that felt safe (like Mrs. Buras had told me so many years before). I only had the clothes on my back; I didn't even have a purse. If I had gone home for anything, my family would have been able to tell by my face that something was wrong. They would have become suspicious and questioned me until I broke down. I knew I couldn't bear to see myself like that. I had no other choice but to run away and to do it right then. But I didn't have any money. How was I going to get to where I was going? I always liked to walk; I figured I had a lifetime to figure it out. When I got to California, I knew I wouldn't be able to look up Cheryl. If I did, they would find me and bring me back. I had four hundred dollars in the bank, but I had to get my bank book. Was it worth the risk of getting caught for only four hundred dollars? I knew I was a runner---I had been doing that for the past few years. Never had my life been stable in one place, and I knew I would be plagued by feelings of insecurity forever.

I stood up and started walking down the steps, heading to what I thought was west. Before I got to the end of the street, Bobby ran up to me. He apologized for what he had told me. He said that after he had thought it over, he knew he couldn't throw away all the feelings he had from reading my letters. I looked at him and didn't know what to say. I questioned whether I really loved him, but I didn't dare say a word. He put his arm around me, and we walked me back to my mother's house in silence.

That night I didn't sleep at all. Finally, at 6:00 AM, I gave up and made myself a cup of coffee. Mom looked like she was in the same shape; she was sitting at the kitchen table staring into space. Sitting down next to her, I asked her how she was. She said she was ok and asked me if I was nervous. I lied and said no. I told her that I knew she was feeling I was doing the wrong thing. I said, "This must be so difficult for a mother to watch when she feels this way."

"Barb, you have no idea, and I hope that you never will." I told her I felt bad that she and Bobby had gotten off to a bad start. "All I have ever wanted is for you to be happy, Barbara."

This could have opened up so many old wounds. My life was flashing before me at record speeds. I turned away from the images and replied, "Thank you."

The flowers were to arrive at nine in the morning, the ceremony scheduled for eleven. Cherri showed up at eight thirty, and together we dressed in my room. She was wearing her eighth grade graduation gown, something we both had agreed was fine. I was glad she was there. I felt safe knowing she would be a buffer for any problems that might arise. That whole morning I was waiting for the sky to fall on my head, and at exactly 9:00 AM it did.

The flowers came C.O.D. Bobby was supposed to pay for these, a compromise he had made with my mother when she was complaining to him about the cost of the wedding. He had every intention of paying for them, but in true Bobby form, he had failed to realize that I would need the money that morning. The flowers cost well over three hundred dollars, and, unfortunately, my mother had to pay for them. This put her in a horrible mood, and she nagged me about it the whole morning. My Uncle Joe was going to drive Cherri and me to the church in his brand new Mercedes. If it weren't for the fact that I was dressed in a wedding gown, it would have looked like we were just going to another fancy affair. After Cherri and I were settled in the car, Joe turned the car around and started heading in the wrong direction. I began to panic and asked him where he was going. He said he was taking me to New Hampshire, because I was making a big mistake. Cherri just looked at me in shock. By the time we got to Route 114 in Danvers, I was hysterical. He was kidnapping me, and I knew I was helpless. I was sweating profusely in the dress and veil, and my now short hair was beginning to look plastered to my face. My make-up was running from all of my tears. I was making such a scene in the back seat that he had no choice but to turn the car around and head back in the direction of the church. By the time we got there, I was a wreck, and we were twenty minutes late. Cherri had tried the best she could to clean me up, but I was a mess. Pulling up in front of the church, Joe turned to me and said, "Maybe you'll luck out, and he won't show." His words hit me like an anvil falling from the sky. No one had known the conversation Bobby and I had had the night before, but I wondered if Joe knew something I didn't.

When we entered the Church, we were asked to wait at the front entryway. Joe was to give me away, so he waited there with us. He said he needed to find a men's room and instructed us not to start without him. I asked Cherri to look through the door and see if Bobby was there. Like a true friend she did as I said without question. She said she didn't see him, that no one was at the altar. People were in the pews, and everyone was whispering quietly to each other. I started to sweat again. We had not had a rehearsal, there hadn't been any time. Never having been to a wedding before, I didn't know that the groom emerged at the altar just before the bride arrived there. Soon the organist started playing, and Joe, back from the rest room, took my hand. He looked me directly in the eyes and said, "You can still back out now. Just say the word." Cherri stepped in front of us as the doors opened, and I began to walk down the aisle.

There was Bobby, right where he had said he would be. His face broke into a smile when he saw me. The whole way down the length of the church, the thoughts of divorce were penetrating my mind. I was visibly shaking, as I passed the people who were friends of my mother. She was in the front row, crying. I couldn't help but wonder why. I knew she loved me and thought I was making a mistake. Deep down, I hoped it was because she had finally realized that the mistakes that were made were really between us. My marriage was really just a way to get out of her life.

The service went beautifully. The priest was serene. He spoke of Bobby's love for me and mine for him; his words even convinced me. The only problem was the ring. From all the tension I was feeling, my fingers had swelled; in the end, when we couldn't get it on my ring finger, Bobby put it on my pinky. It was another sign to me that a power stronger than we were felt what we were doing was wrong. When the service was over and we turned around to greet the guests as man and wife, I grabbed Bobby by the hand and practically ran down the aisle. Standing at the top of the church steps in the fresh air, his friends were all gathered. Most were boys we had known in high school. Someone had a portable tape player playing "Another One

Bites The Dust." We both laughed and got into Joe's car for the ride to the reception. Joe said we had to wait until the guests had had time to get to the restaurant that was just down the street. Bobby suggested we go to Alice's Ice Cream, only a few blocks away. So we did, in full wedding attire.

The reception went off without too much of a hitch. Bobby did have two friends crash, to my mother's disappointment. It wasn't Bobby's fault; he didn't know they were going to do it. They weren't even really close friends. It was kind of weird for him, and he apologized to my mother. There was music, but no room for dancing. Some of my mother's friends thought it was inappropriate for the bride and groom to have no dance as man and wife on their wedding, so they took it upon themselves to push back some tables and insist that we dance. I looked in Mom's direction for the ok, and she solemnly nodded to me. Through the entire reception, I couldn't wait to get out of there. I hated it. I didn't like to be the center of attention, especially when I knew that no one approved of the wedding in the first place. The minute we had the chance, I told Bobby I wanted to leave, and we did.

We left the reception that evening at around six. We borrowed his father's car to drive to New York, an old Gremlin. It was a funny and ridiculous little car. It literally looked like a mini space ship. It had a hatch back that we put our extra clothes in. Cherri and Bobby's best man had written "Just Married" across the huge back windshield. I could have done without that. The drive was wonderful. It was what I had wanted to do for years: just get in a car and go. A part of me wanted to keep driving until we got to California. With Bobby's commitment to the army, I knew that was out of the question.

He let me drive most of the way down. I had driven on the highway a few times, but it was still a new experience. For me, it was like a rollercoaster: scary, yet thrilling. I couldn't believe we were married. It seemed like it had taken so long to get to this point. I immediately felt that my mother no longer had control over me. I remember wondering at what point the world had accepted me as an adult. Was it when we said "I do?" The feelings I had had when walking down the aisle were gone. I no longer thought of divorce. I felt happy and confident that I could make this marriage work; I was actually looking forward to the challenge. My first test came at nine o'clock that night.

Bobby said that he had made reservations for us to stay at an inn in Connecticut. His plan was to drive into the city in the morning. When we arrived at the inn, they told him that he had never sent in the deposit, so they had rented the room to someone else. There were no rooms left at the inn. The first night of our honeymoon was spent sleeping in the front seat of a beat up Gremlin on a cold, late September night. The first time we were to make love was going to have to wait another day. I soon learned that this type of behavior was typical of Bobby. His intentions were always good, but his follow through was lousy. I just kept my mouth shut and pretended it didn't bother me; inside I was furious. As could be expected, we didn't sleep much that night. At around six in the morning, we headed into the big city. It would be my first time ever in New York City. I was surprised how easy it was to get there. From Salem, it felt like a straight shot all the way. We had taken the Mass Turnpike and then meandered our way south.

The minute I saw the hustle and bustle of New York, I loved it. We had no plans other than to drive around and see it; we seemed to have no plans at all for our honeymoon. After parking the car at the first available space I saw on the street, I stepped out of the driver's seat without looking and came very close to being clipped by a cab. I realized then that we were far from home. Immediately, I was aware of a symphony of sounds I had never heard before. Everywhere I turned was commotion and urgency. Every moment in time, with every turn of my head, was a celebration as important as the next. The pulse I felt was as if I was inside the beating heart of a celebrity yet to be discovered. We went to the Metropolitan Museum and walked all over the city. We went into shops on Fifth Avenue and walked down Broadway. I felt bad that we both had forgotten to bring our cameras. We were such kids. Bobby wanted to see a Broadway show and went in to enquire about tickets, but they were all sold out. He decided that we would watch an off Broadway production instead. We had dinner in Times Square and waited until the production began. It was in the basement of a large building with the seats right next to the stage. We watched a wonderful production that I don't recall the name of about a mentally handicapped girl and the obstacles she faced in life. She was played by a fabulous young actress, and I was certain she really was handicapped. When it was over, we walked back up the stairs to exit the building, and I noticed the actors' black and white head shots lining the hall. It wasn't until I saw hers that I realized what an incredibly good actress she was.

We left the show around 11:30 PM. Walking down Times Square, we passed all sorts of degenerate people. It was a very different atmosphere from our arrival. This was 1980, and Times Square was a dangerous place at night. I found it to be fascinating, but Bobby, on the other hand, just wanted us to get out of there. This would prove to be difficult, since we had forgotten where we had parked the car. We roamed around aimlessly for about thirty minutes. When we walked down one street, we found ourselves trapped in a huge crowd. We didn't know what was going on. People were all dressed in shiny disco clothes, and many of them were dancing in the street. News cameras were everywhere, and reporters were working the crowd. Walking up to the building that was the source of all this commotion, we read the sign; it said "Studio 54." I had never heard of it, but apparently it was closing, and everyone was having a last hurrah.

Our week went on pretty much like this. When we made love for the first time there were no candles, rose petals or chocolate Hershey Kisses. There was no music on the radio...there was no sound at all. We had no plans and just experienced the happenings that unfolded at our feet as every day passed. It was a good time, and Bobby and I were getting along. I was too young to expect more. When it came time to head back to Salem, we were both very sad. We had breakfast our last morning at a little coffee shop. By eleven, we were back on the road heading north. As every mile rolled by under our tires, my heart sank more and more. When we got home, we would spend the night at my mother's house; the next day he had to report for duty.

By the time we got home, it was early afternoon. I told my mother that Bobby and I were going to visit some of his friends, so that he could say goodbye. I was trying to keep Bobby and my mother as far away from each other as possible, and this seemed like the perfect excuse. When we finally went to bed that night, it was late. I told him I couldn't make love to him with my mother in the next room. I was sure lightning would strike me dead if I did. When we were together in my mother's house, I no longer felt married. The next morning, Maureen and I drove him to the airport. It was hard to believe that the time had gone by so fast. The goodbye was a tearful one, just as his arrival had been. No one clapped.

CHAPTER: 28

When I got home, I went to my room. Finishing up the last of my assignments for the GIA, I then brought them to the post office and mailed them off. That part of my life was finished, and it felt good. I didn't realize then that I would never actually use the certificate I had received as a gemologist.

It was difficult to live with Mom. Now the collect calls were coming from overseas. She nagged me about it all the time, despite the fact that I was giving her the money. Her sour looks returned as well, but I did the best I could to ignore her. She saw this as me being difficult and distant. I still worked at the coin shop. And Bobby's letters began to arrive, like an old friend. They were filled with the wonders of this new country he now called home. Every day he told me he wished I were there. He said he had picked up the language really quickly, and it surprised him; it was almost as if he had known how to speak German all along. He had had two separate leads right away on apartments, but both had fallen through. I didn't tell him of the difficulty I was having at home; I didn't want to pressure him more.

Christmas came and went as well as the New Year. It felt like I was going to be stuck living with my mother forever. Then, in February, the call finally came; Bobby had rented us the most beautiful apartment, and he was sending me money for a ticket. My flight was scheduled to leave the third week in February. It was the week of my birthday and the anniversary of the plane fiasco when I was little, almost to the day. To make matters worse, Bobby had said he might not be able to pick me up at the airport; he was called on a three month field maneuver. That meant I would be arriving alone in Frankfort, which was a seven hour bus trip from our apartment and the base. He told me to pick up the American military bus at the Rhein-Main American Air Force Base, located next to the Frankfort airport. That bus would take me to his army base in Neu Ulm. From there, he said he would make sure that someone was waiting to take me to our apartment. He never told me who that person was. Every fear I had of Germany was going to hit me in one day.

My flight was at six in the evening. It was a clear night at Logan, and I felt this was a good sign. My mother and brothers drove me there; I think it was my mother who had insisted that they come. Doug seemed genuinely excited for me--I was going on an adventure to new lands. Jake didn't say a word; that wasn't new at all. Over the years he and I had become distant. I wondered why he was there. Boarding the plane, I hugged them each goodbye. Turning my back on them, I walked towards the door and couldn't help but smile. I was getting away. I was flying on Lufthansa, and the plane was beautiful. It was the most luxurious one I had ever been on. I sat at a window seat and read all the precautionary manuals three times before the plane even took off, until I had them ingrained in my head. There was a group of about a dozen American men seated directly in front of me. They all seemed to know each other, and I soon learned from their conversations that they were going to a convention in Munich. The first hour I kept to myself, trying the best I could to read, sleep and do some needlepoint. Nothing held my attention. I ordered an Amaretto to calm my nerves. It seemed to help. I was sitting quietly by the window, looking at the black night, when the Captain said he had an announcement. Anwar Sadat had just been assassinated. I wondered if this would have an effect on Bobby's unit.

Eventually, the "Convention Men," as I started to call them, seeming unaffected by the news, became rowdy from what they were drinking. They were funny to watch, and, at one point, they caught me laughing to myself about them. Rule number one... never let a group of men see you laughing at them, especially in such close quarters as a plane. A few came over to me and introduced themselves. They were all from New York, older than I was, and seemed pleasant enough guys. They could tell I was afraid to fly and did their best to calm my nerves. They bought me more drinks, and soon I was feeling very comfortable in their presence. They helped pass the time for me. They were all gentlemen. I told them I was married, and they were fascinated when I said I was moving to Ulm. Several of them knew the city and told me how beautiful it was. They asked me how I planned to get there when I landed in Frankfort. They knew it was several hours away from the airport, and it would be a long drive. I told them my dilemma and how Bobby might not be able to meet me. I asked any of them if they knew how close the air force base was to the Frankfort airport. None of them knew the answer to that. They offered to drive me to Ulm. It was only a few miles away from Munich, and they were all getting rented cars. I decided to keep my options open and told them that I would use them as a last resort.

By the time the plane touched down seven hours later, we were all good friends. They reassured me that the reason I didn't see Bobby at the terminal right away was because he wasn't allowed to cross into customs. They showed me where to stand in line and helped me get my bags. It was a good thing they were with me, because I would certainly have gotten lost. Waiting for me to finish with the custom officials, they carried my bags to the door and the waiting area that Bobby was supposed to be in. When we passed through the door, there he was. I was so glad to see him; we immediately embraced. The men who were with me shook his hand as I introduced them. I told Bobby how they had helped me, and he thanked them sincerely. Walking away with my husband, I took one last look over my shoulder. The convention men all waved. As I returned their gesture, I couldn't help but think of that night in

Lynn when I met that hurried girl who helped me find my way home. I had collected another vignette of people for the scrapbook in my mind---people I really didn't know, but would remember forever.

The bus ride was the longest one I had ever taken. We stopped at every military base from Frankfort to Munich. This old school bus that was painted army green was uncomfortable and bouncy, and I thought I was going to go out of my mind before we got to our destination. During the entire trip, Bobby was telling me about our apartment and the small Italian neighborhood we lived in. He said the city was divided, like many cities, into ethnic groups. I was surprised by this. He said the man who lived behind us sits in his yard every day and has a chicken for a pet. He calls it by its own name, and, for some reason, he sits the chicken in a laundry basket next to his chair when they are out in the yard. I asked why he did this in the winter. Bobby's response was... who in his right mind puts a chicken in a basket? We both laughed.

He told me the German people were very particular. He pulled out a legal note pad and said he was going to write down some things I should know. He felt he should do this because he had to go back to Cass Site the next day for the next three months and didn't want me to feel lost. I was taken aback by his last statement and asked him why the military would just leave a new wife in an unfamiliar country for three months. He grinned and said the military didn't care about particulars like that. Besides, we weren't living on the base; as far as they were concerned, I wasn't even there. I would fall under the status of tourist. I asked him if I were allowed to go on base. He said there are a lot of "DW's" that were in my position, which had nothing to do with my privileges on base. He told me DW meant dependent wife.

We lived in a two family house. Our apartment was on the first floor, the landlord lived on the second. It was completely furnished with all utilities included in the rent. The rent was a little over four hundred marks a month. The U.S. dollar was doing really well at the time, so our rent only cost $280. Bobby was taking home a thousand from the army. I was in shock! That was less rent than I was paying for my one room apartment. And his income alone was more money than I ever took home, not to mention that all our medical expenses were now free. When I expressed this to him, he said, "Imagine if we lived on base. Then we wouldn't have to pay rent either."

The car he had bought us was at the motor pool, where he worked as a mechanic, fixing the military trucks that broke down. He hated the job and knew it had been a bad decision after he made it. He wasn't very mechanical and felt the army would teach him, but he never quite caught on to it. He said he had been trying to change his MOS, but, from what he understood, that was impossible. An MOS was a soldier's job classification. The car needed some work and didn't run at the moment. He had been able to buy it for fifty dollars from a guy who had ETSed. ETS meant left to go state side. He said all it needed was a new carburetor, but he hadn't had a chance to put a new one in before they were called to Cass Site. He said he had also purchased a bike for us. He told me he was going to take it to get to the base the next day, so he could catch a ride back to Cass Site. The buses didn't run early enough. I would have to go to the base and pick up the bike, so it wouldn't get stolen. He would leave it locked up outside the Laundromat, a building I should be able to find easily. To get to the base, I had to catch a bus at the military housing that was located a few blocks from our apartment. This bus would take me to the base for free. I then had to pick up the bike and ride it the five miles back to our house. Bobby pulled out a map, which he had made himself, of the route from the base back to our house. My head was spinning with all these new military terms, and now a five mile trip in a foreign country that I was going to navigate by myself. I tried not to think about it.

When the bus finally pulled into the army base at Neu Ulm, it was 11:00 PM. The base was dark and quiet, and I couldn't really get a handle of how it looked and where things were, as Bobby had described to me. We crossed the quad to the barracks that were occupied by his unit. Bobby was looking for a person he knew who had said he would drive us to our house, which was five miles away. After he located the guy, the two of them loaded my belongings in the car, and we were on the road again. We drove through the city of Ulm, which is located next to Neu Ulm. We lived on the outskirts of Ulm in a tiny neighborhood called Turmli. The night I arrived was also the last night of Fasching. Fasching is a German holiday that is kind of like our Mardi Gras. It is a celebration where people dress in outlandish costumes and parade around the streets. The spectacle of people dancing in the streets of the town was an amazing sight to see. The costumes were fantastic. A lot of them looked like harlequins and jesters. Although they were dancing with a lot of movement, none of them that I saw were making a sound. They reminded me of mimes, and it felt like I was watching a segment from a medieval movie. This would be my first introduction to the German people and their culture. I watched them in a kind of rapt amazement.

When we pulled up in front of our house, the neighborhood was quiet. Stepping out of the car, I turned and looked at what was going to be my new home for the next few years. Bobby thanked the man who had brought us, before he turned the car around and was gone into the night. It was a modern home, compared to others we had passed. It was a two-story stucco and sat at the corner of the street set on a small hill. There was only one entrance, and that was in the rear, along the end of a brick path that wound around the side of the house. When we arrived at the door, I was surprised that it was made of textured glass. Before we had a chance to use the key, we were met by Martin, our landlord, who had opened it from the other side. He was average in height and build with sandy blond hair. He was smiling from ear to ear and greeted me in German. I smiled back, and he helped us with my things. We walked up four small steps to our apartment, where we were met by another glass door.

The apartment was as beautiful as Bobby had said. Everything in it was brand new. The walls were freshly painted white, and the floors had new, tasteful linoleum on them. The kitchen was the best of all. It was all white with shiny, red lacquered furniture. The table had two chairs and a bench chair that sat on two sides of it and was connected at the corner and bolted against the wall. The features that struck me the most were the windows. They were huge! Every room had a window that was so big that it took up an entire wall. Bobby said they opened sideways. Because of the hinges that were on the inside, they opened freely and completely, causing you to feel as if the yard were a part of the apartment when they were in this position. In the bedroom was a schrank. This was what the German people used for clothes closets. It was free standing from the wall and made of white lacquer as well. The bed was a twin. Bobby said that as soon as he was home from Cass Site, we would purchase a double. The living room also had a schrank. It was for a stereo system, another thing we did not own. The couch was brand new. It looked like a modern Beidermeier sofa. It was all wood with olive green cushions. Unlike old Beidermeier, it was comfortable. There were also two matching chairs. There was no form of entertainment in the apartment, no TV or radio.

I was so tired by the time we put my bags on the floor, that all I wanted to do was sleep. I had been traveling for fifteen hours, and I was sure I looked a mess. I wanted a three hour bath. Walking into the bathroom, I was disappointed to find only a shower. Like the rest of the house, it was brand new. The entire room was covered in sienna tile and was beautiful. The shower was the size of a regular one, yet the basin it sat in was a foot and a half deep all around. I contemplated whether I could actually fill it with water. I was too tired that night, but I knew that I would try it at some point before we left this country. That night it felt so good to sleep in Bobby's arms. Unfortunately, the morning arrived way too soon; the alarm went off at five. I got up with Bobby and made him breakfast. When I tasted the eggs, I thought I had done something wrong. When I commented on it, he told me they were fine, they were just fresh from the farm next door. He had bought them that morning from the lady who ran it. He went over all his notes with me again before he left. He gave me emergency numbers I could call for people he knew on base, if I needed help. In an hour, he was gone.

After the door closed, I watched as his figure disappeared beyond the glass. Standing in the hallway, staring at the door's watery textured surface, I felt like a statue, unmoving in my spot. There were no thoughts in my head; my mind was at peace. The world around me was silent, except for the quiet ticking of the clock in the kitchen at the end of the hall. I stood there for a short while, not knowing what to do. In time, I turned and headed to the living room; sitting on the couch, I stared into space. Eventually I laid down and fell back to sleep. I woke up again at nine o'clock and made a cup of coffee. Sitting at the kitchen table, I took out Bobby's map and began to examine it. It seemed simple enough, but I was still apprehensive about the adventure.

I had sent Bobby three packages in the mail the previous month. They had contained my personal belongings. I had noticed two of the boxes in the bedroom when I arrived. As luck would have it, it was the missing third box that contained my winter clothing and art books. The good news was that my tape recorder and a James Taylor cassette was in one of the ones that were there. I looked out the bedroom window and noticed a light fluffy snow was falling. That meant it was at most 32 degrees outside. Nothing I had in the boxes was appropriate for this type of weather.

I went into Bobby's closet and pulled out the smallest sweater I could find. Putting it on, I realized it was still several sizes too large for me. I didn't have a choice; it would have to do. I wore the same jeans I had had on the day before and a pair of tube socks that were also Bobby's. All I had for shoes were what I was wearing. They were a cloth pair of Chinese Mary Jane's, with a strap and buckle. I could find no hat or gloves among his things. Pulling one of his civilian winter coats from the closet as well, I was ready to start my adventure.

CHAPTER: 29

Bobby had left me with some German money; although I didn't yet understand the denominations, I grabbed that as well as forty US dollars. With the map clenched tightly in my hand, I made my way out the door into the snow that was now gathering on the grassy surfaces. Following his map, I took a left at the end of the street and started climbing a narrow walking path to the park that sat at the top of the hill. It was such a beautiful sight when I reached the park---I found myself in a grove. The snow was falling lightly, and the air was so quiet and clean. Little red squirrels were running across the snow coated grass, leaving their tiny paw prints behind. The entire place was filled with trees. The magic of the snow and the crispness of the air made me feel as if I had walked into a Brother Grimm's fairytale. The trees were so dense in some parts; it felt more like a forest than a park. Snow and ice were clinging to every tiny branch and twig that arched over my head. Webbed together in a quiet sacred place, it was as if I had walked into a crystal cathedral. The path I was walking on wound delicately among the grove. How lucky I was, I thought, to wish since I had been a young girl to be in a place just like this...and now here I was. Standing for a moment, looking at the intricate snowflakes gathering all around me, I thought to myself, I've finally come home.

Just over the crest of the hill was a clearing. Beyond that, I could see the institutional look of the American Military Housing. It seemed cold and unwelcoming in contrast to where I had just emerged from. There was a pair of huge, stucco apartment buildings. The span of each of them had to be two blocks long. There were no flower boxes or ornamentation of any kind at the doors. From the second floor up, there were bars on the windows; I assumed that was so that children wouldn't fall out of them. If this was what the price of free rent looked like, I was glad that Bobby had chosen not to have us live there. Near the center of the buildings, at the edge of the sidewalk, was a sign that read "Bus Stop." I stood there by myself, watching American children with southern accents making snow angels in the street. In a few minutes, the bus pulled up. It was the same type of bus that had brought me to the base from the airport: a school bus painted olive drab green. There was no one on it except the driver, and no one from the housing unit joined me. The driver, a man of Turkish descent who didn't speak English, drove me in silence to the base.

Looking out the window as we made our way through the city of Ulm, I became aware that Ulm was perhaps as big as Boston. It was considered a very large city by German standards. The other reality that hit me as I sat there was the fact that I could no longer read. Unconsciously, I was trying to read every sign I saw. I wondered how many times in the course of the day do we read without realizing it. Every word was foreign to me, so this act of mindless reading was interrupted by the fact that I didn't understand the language. It felt frustrating. It was as if I were four years old again, and everyone around me was more aware and superior to me. I tried to stop myself from doing it but found that to be impossible. Meaningless reading, as I soon called it, would be a major part of my entire German experience.

The front gate of the base was guarded by German civilian men. They spoke very little English and carried no weapons. This was a disturbing thing for me to see, and I wondered why the US government allowed it. There had been a lot of recent talk of terrorist activity on US bases. A US embassy had been blown up not long before that, and the lack of security that surrounded our own military bases concerned me. After seeing my ID, they let the bus pass. They did not ask for credentials from the bus driver, and I hoped that it was only because they knew him. The bus stopped right in front of the laundromat. It turned out to be the actual bus stop, to my surprise and delight. The bike was locked up to a bike rack right in front. I could see the base more clearly, now that it was daytime. It was smaller than I had thought. Along with the laundromat was a cafeteria, a book store that was really just a trailer, and a hospital that had a sign on it that said "Dispensary." To the left of the quad was a small building that said "Child Care Center." The rest of the base consisted of barracks for the different units and another restricted area I assumed was where they did their army stuff. The Commissary, which was the military grocery store, and the American School, which was run under the Dobbs school system, were actually six blocks away, in a very inconvenient place on another base. Just outside the rear entrance of the base was more military housing.

I wanted to explore these new surroundings before I made my five mile trek back to the apartment. I decided the first place to start was to sample some military coffee. When I stepped into the entranceway, I noticed the cafeteria had two other buildings attached to it: one a store to buy everyday essentials that looked like a small department store, the other one was a small library. Turning to the left, I opened the door to the cafeteria. It was a busy place. Women were seated together with babies on their laps and toddlers running around. Everywhere you looked were men in uniform. It was a noisy place, and for the first time that morning, I could hear my own language. It was comforting. The tables were set up exactly like a school cafeteria, with the kitchen exposed to a tray area. Everything smelled wonderful and did not have the odor as if it had all been boiled. I stood in line to get a coffee to go. As I had expected...the coffee was awful. My next stop was the library. It was one room, approximately ten feet by twenty feet. There were no art books or books on Maria Montessori, which disappointed me. It had mostly reference books and encyclopedias, as well as paperback novels. At the book store, I found a better selection. They had sketch books and drawing books, the latest novels and The Stars and Stripes newspaper. They also sold batteries, which I picked up for my tape recorder, because the American plug I had on it didn't work in German households. I wanted to buy more things, but without a basket on the bike or a backpack on my back, I knew I wouldn't be able to carry them. I did purchase a news paper. It was small and took me all of ten minutes to read.

Finally, without anything left to do, I had to face the inevitable...I had to find my way home. I looked at my watch, and it was now 1:00 PM. I figured I would be home by three at the latest. Mounting my bike, I rode to the front gate and realized, for the first time, that my feet were cold in the cloth shoes. I was glad I had chosen to wear Bobby's heavy socks, instead of the flimsy ones I had. When I got to the front gate with my bike, there was a group of German girls standing just outside of it, smoking cigarettes and talking amongst themselves in German. They looked to be in their twenties and dressed rather provocatively for the weather. At first I didn't know why they were there, and then it dawned on me. They were waiting for American GI's to meet them for lunch and give them a pass to enter the compound. As I passed by them, they stopped talking and gave me a nasty look, the kind of look that someone gives another person if he feels that he is unjustifiably privileged. I avoided their gaze and continued on my way.

Out the gate and back into the German world, I headed to the next street on the map. It was the same route I had taken on the bus and soon realized that it led straight to the autobahn. There were pictured signs everywhere, showing a bicycle circled with a slash mark through it. I didn't have to know German to realize that I wasn't allowed to ride my bike on that road. I stood there and didn't know which direction to take. I tried to ask a man who was walking by, showing him my map. He pointed to a small path that was similar to the one that led through the woods near my house, the path I had taken that led me to the military housing that morning. This one had a sign that read "Fussganger." Not knowing any better, I went in that direction. I would soon learn that this entire country was cross hatched with these paths, and not unlike a labyrinth, could get quite confusing. The fussganger was beautiful. It wound through parks and forests and even past a small stream. Ulm is located on the Danube River; I used to play the "Blue Danube" on the piano as a child and began to quietly hum it to myself. It seemed like a lifetime ago when my piano was hoisted through the window. The snow outside was still falling, yet it didn't look like it was going to accumulate much. My feet were beginning to get numb, not to mention I now felt the cold on my head and hands as well. After traveling this small path for about an hour, I came to the conclusion that I was terribly lost. I saw no houses. There were no people anywhere. All around me were the trees of the forest and stillness. Occasionally, I would see a squirrel or a raven. Even they scared me, when one would surprisingly cross my path. What had begun as a pleasant ride through the woods, suddenly became a frightening excursion. The snow-flanked trees now looked cold and mocking. The sky grew gray and menacing. I had no choice but to continue in the direction I was going, until I came across some form of civilization.

Finally, after another hour came and went, I happened upon a clearing. It seemed more like the kind of park that I was used to than the last ones I had passed. It had swings and a slide and a merry go round like the one I had twirled on at Mack Park when I was younger. Unfortunately, there still was no one in sight. I searched for an opening off the path that might lead me to a gate and an entrance. If children came to this place to play, they must live somewhere close by. I passed under a stone bridge, and, to my delight, I saw an elderly woman walking a very small dog. With a new found hope, I coasted the bike in her direction.

Still straddling the bike, I inched up next to her. "Excuse me; I am terribly lost; could you help me?" I held my map out to show her I expected her to take it. I was desperate and tried my best not to show that I was on the verge of panic. The old woman narrowed her eyes at me, and in a very stern and mean voice said, "NEIN!" and began to continue on with her walk. Still straddling my bike, I inched my way next to her again. I couldn't believe she would be so cruel as to deny me the simple satisfaction of looking at my map. I begged her to please stop. "Wait--I am lost; please don't leave me here." I put my hand on her shoulder to stop her, as I pleaded my case. The next thing I knew, I was on the ground in the snow, completely tangled in the bars of the bike. I was stunned, and at first I didn't know what had happened. Her dog was barking as ferociously at me as he could, given his size. My cheek hurt and was beginning to swell. In one swift motion, she had turned and hit me hard with her fist. Now I not only was lost and cold, but I was also wet. Leaving me to freeze in the snow, she walked away ranting in German, as if I had done something to her.

I wanted to cry. I felt alone and incapable of helping myself. I was sure I was never going to find my way home, and I would be roaming this country for days. A lump was developing in my throat; it took all the strength I had not to let it get the best of me. I knew if I did, I would no longer be strong enough to get myself through this and find my way out of here. Untangling myself from the bike, I stood up and brushed off the snow. I should have been angry, but my feelings of fear were overpowering any other emotion. My cloth shoes were now filled with snow and freezing from the cold temperature. They began to stiffen around my feet. The fact that I had been diagnosed with Reynaud's, a few years earlier in a routine exam for my joints, didn't help. Reynaud's is a circulatory ailment that acts up under cold conditions. I knew without looking that inside my socks, my feet must now be white, if not blue. Seeing my hands confirmed it; my fingers were white and swelling.

A few yards away, I saw the gate I had been searching for before I had come across the elderly woman. I was proud of myself for having known there would be one. It was a small glimpse of power that showed me I was still in control. This gave me hope, so I quickly passed through it. It opened up to a neighborhood street. The houses seemed more like apartment buildings; they were clumped tightly together with little room for yards. The thought I had had earlier of knocking on the door of the first house I came across was now dashed, after the abrupt behavior I had received from the last person I had asked for help. Instead, I searched for any form of a retail shop---a butcher, a baker, a candlestick maker; god knew what they would have for stores in these small towns. At the end of the street, I noticed the crossroad seemed larger with a lot of traffic. Before I was able to get to it, I came across several teenage boys, obviously on their way home from school, heading in my direction. Bobby had told me the night before that teenagers knew how to speak English. They studied it in school from a very young age.

"Excuse me; can you show me where this road is on this map?" One boy turned to me and in my native tongue said, "Are you a lost American?" I was so surprised when he responded in a language I understood, that I couldn't contain my excitement. Bobby had been right. I eagerly said, "Yes!"

"GOOD!" he said, "We don't want you in our country anyway! GO HOME!" He then pushed me against the building I was standing next to. Laughing, he and his friends continued on their way, leaving me to stand there with my mouth wide open in disbelief.

That was the final straw...the tears I had been holding in came. Walking slowly in the direction of the main street with my head down, so as not to draw any more attention, I tried my hardest to pull myself together. By then, I was not only cold, wet, and exhausted, but I was beginning to get hungry too. Images of me starving to death on this God forsaken street were forcing their way into my head. I knew I needed to sit down and get my wits about me. I looked for a bench that was sheltered from the wind and cold, but there was none in sight. One block down on the right, I noticed a large stone building with wide steps under an overhang. Locking up my bike to the pole in front of it, I sat on the steps and tried to warm my hands. I couldn't believe how cold I was. I didn't know how far away from my apartment I wandered, but after checking my watch, I realized I had left the base four hours earlier. It was beginning to get dark. I could have been anywhere, and I knew it; that was the only thing that I was sure of. All I wanted was to go home. Was that too much to ask? Hearing the words spoken in my head, I thought of the feelings I had had when I walked through the woods that morning...I am home. The thought left me little room for comfort; I began to cry again. As I sat there wiping the tears from my hurt cheek, I hadn't noticed a man standing on the landing a few stairs above me. I was so lost in the world of my own misery and self pity that I didn't even hear him until he approached me. He was in a uniform, walking slowly down the stairs as if he didn't want to scare me off. When he realized I was not going to run, he planted himself next to me.

"Are you lost, young girl?" Guarded this time, I meekly said, "Yes, how could you tell? And how did you know I was an American?"

"I thought you were lost because I saw you crying. I thought you were an American because you locked you bike at the police station. A German never locks his bike, especially at a police station." He then gave me a big smile.

"This is a police station!" I said, in surprise.

"Yes," he said. "Look at that sign; it says POLIZEI; that is the German word for police station. If you ever find yourself away from the base and need assistance, look for that. How long have you been in Germany?" I said, "Less than twenty-four hours."

"I think you may have set a country record for getting lost in the least amount of time." We both laughed.

"Come, I will take you to your home here in Germany." I handed him my map, and he examined it.

He told me I had traveled nine miles away from the destination of my house. I was, in fact, three cities over from Ulm. I told him I followed a sign that said "fussganger." He told me that fussganger translates to "foot path," and, although they are very pleasant, they can lead you to places unknown very easily, if you don't know the way, like a maze. He looked at my map and said, "Let me do the equation. According to your map, you are nine miles away from your house in the wrong direction." I was shocked. I couldn't believe how easy it was to get off track. He loaded my bike into the trunk of his police car. "Don't worry, you will be home in no time. I hope you will learn to love our country." I chose not to tell him about the last two Germans I had just met. I sat next to him in the front seat. The warmth from the heater was like a gift from God. He directed it at my feet. After a fifteen minute drive, we pulled up in front of my apartment. I was never so happy to see the sight of it. I thanked him up and down, wearily lifting my bike up the steps to the brick path that led to my door. He drove away, and I never saw him again. He joined the girl from Lynn and the Convention Men in the scrap book of kind souls in my mind. When I walked through the door, even the warmth of the apartment couldn't stop my shivering. I went into the bathroom and filled the tiny tub under the shower with hot water in an attempt to take a bath. I sat in that basin for two hours, like an Indian; I was in heaven.

When I emerged from the bathroom, I made myself something to eat. Remembering the batteries I had bought at the book store, I listened to James Taylor over and over while I sat on the couch. Shadow Man joined me right on cue. "Where were you when I needed you?" As usual he didn't say a word. Instead, he sat with me until I fell into a deep sleep. I had torturous dreams of swirling snow and wind. I was Gretel looking for Hansel in the woods. We had run from our parents because we weren't happy at home. Somehow Hansel and I got separated, and I came across the witch, and she punched me in the face.

The next day, I was still a bit shaken. I began to do menial tasks around the apartment to get my mind off the day before. I went through the few belongings I had and organized them in the shrank. When all the work I could possibly do was done, I roamed around the apartment between the three tiny rooms for hours. I was too afraid to go outside and get lost again. I wished I had a book I could read so I could get lost into another world. Unfortunately, I had inadvertently left the only book I had had on the plane. Everything else in the house was in German. Bobby had a German/English dictionary, but I found it to be very dry and so it was difficult for it to hold my attention. I didn't understand the different genders that each German word had. Without that one vital piece of information, the book was completely useless. After awhile, I just gave up. I was in such a desperate need for something to read that when I noticed the tube of toothpaste I brought from the US in the bathroom, I brought it into the living room and read it over and over until I realized the ridiculous and pathetic nature of this task. I sat down and had a talk with myself, like I had had the day on my bike when I was too afraid to ride down the hill. Bobby was going to be gone for a long time. I couldn't stay in the house for the entire duration. I had to learn how to get back and forth from the base. One thing was certain; I was never going to do it by bike again. I talked myself into going to and from the base by way of the military bus. I wanted desperately to buy a book to read. Taking a small back pack with me this time, I stuffed some dirty clothes in it and headed out the door. I figured I should take the time to do some washing at the laundromat while I was there.

Climbing the hill, I meandered through the park... past the snow covered trees... past the squirrels that now felt like friends to me. At the military housing where I had been just the day before, I waited once again for a ride to the base. I soon learned from others on the bus that its last return was at 11:00 PM. Seeing that it was only two in the afternoon, I had plenty of time to get my laundry done and enjoy myself . Arriving at the laundromat, I threw my clothes in the washer. Then I went to the bookstore and bought myself a sketch book and some pencils, a German dictionary that seemed to make more sense, another news paper and a novel. After I made my purchases, I went into the cafeteria to have a late lunch. It was quieter than it had been the day before, and I sat alone at a table in the corner and read. When I finished my lunch, I crossed the street to check on my laundry. The laundromat was filled with men in uniform, and I felt uncomfortable. It was such tight quarters in there, I could barely move. I quickly threw my clothes in the dryer and stepped outside.

Hearing the delightful squeals of children playing in the snow, I turned to see that the sound was coming from the daycare center. I had seen my recommendations for college from my high school teachers that morning, when I had been unloading my boxes. I had packed them, knowing I would apply at the college on base that was provided by the military. I decided to bring them back with me the next day and see if the daycare center was looking for any help. I then crossed the street to see if I could buy a blow drier for my hair from the PX. I couldn't believe how cheap everything was at the store. Items that I would normally pay ten dollars for were only six. On an overseas military base, there was no sales tax, the only dollars were in the Susan B Anthony coin, and pennies were not allowed at all. Everything was priced in a way to make this work. All the items were priced with a dollar amount and no change. It made adding up your items so much easier, especially with my poor math skills. I roamed around the base for several hours and then bought a dinner to go from the cafeteria. Boarding the bus, I headed home. I felt in control of my life again and looked forward to soaking in the tub and reading my book. I also had clean clothes...always a plus.

The next day, I did as I said I would. I went to the child care center to apply for work. When I walked through the door, I was struck by the drab appearance inside. Every wall was painted olive drab green. I thought to myself that this might be a color these children knew too well, but they didn't have to have it everywhere. I was greeted by a woman whose name was Connie. She was a six foot tall, large black woman from Georgia. She spoke with a high pitched southern drawl, and I immediately liked her. She was the director of the facility and had an infant child cradled in her arms as she led me to a seat in her office. I told her that I had just moved there, had experience working in a nursery school setting and was looking for a job. I presented her with my packet, which also included a cover letter explaining the activities work I had done at Ivy Manor and some of my sample lesson plans, along with a full resume of all the jobs I had had since I was sixteen.

Juggling the now sleeping child on her lap, she tried the best she could to look through my large stack of papers. Quietly, I plucked the sleeping child from her hands and placed him over my shoulder, so that she could read. She smiled at me in return, when he didn't wake up. The first question she asked was my age. I said that I was twenty. She told me I had done a lot of things in my short life. I told her I had been on my own for a long time and understood the meaning of hard work. "Do you have any children?" she then asked. I told her no. "Well you sure know how to handle babies," she said, nodding in the direction of the child in my arms. I told her I had been babysitting since the age of twelve and that I loved children. When she read the letter from Mrs. Buras, she said it sounded like my teacher had had a great respect for me. She thought I had had a lot of responsibility put on me for just a kid. I remember thinking quietly to myself that I couldn't remember the last time I had felt like a kid. She told me I had to apply at the employment office next door, because they did all the hiring for the base. She said she was glad that I had given her the opportunity to see my papers; she would remember my name when she had to choose. I asked her how often the childcare facility hired people. She indicated the wait was usually only a month. Handing the baby back into her arms, I thanked her and left. As I was exiting the door, she said, "Barbara, don't worry; you'll get the job." I went next door and applied.

My week went on with no problems. I began to settle into my new environment and even signed up for a crash course in German that was held in the evenings on the base. I understood what Bobby had been talking about, because the language came easily to me, as well. It reminded me a lot of English. I began to understand the different genders for each word and why. After two weeks, I still had not made any friends, but I could now go to the neighborhood butcher and flower shop and order things in the native language. Sometimes during the day, I would sit by the kitchen window and watch the children upstairs build snow men in the back yard. I was amazed that both childhood itself and learning through play were so universal. I learned a lot of new words, just listening to those kids outside.

The children upstairs belonged to Martin, my landlord, and his wife. They had a ten year old boy who was also named Martin and his sister, Greta, who was eight. I don't recall their mother's name. I remember it was a difficult one that I always had trouble pronouncing. I had heard from my German class that chocolate chip cookies were not sold in Germany, that most German children didn't even know they existed. I couldn't believe that something that was so ordinary to us was so foreign to them. Knowing I could get the chips from the commissary, I figured I would make them the next day and surprise the kids when they were playing in the yard.

"Excuse me. Ich habe ein paar Kekse für dich gemacht." I was so proud that I could tell them I had made cookies for them. Seeing the plate in my hand, they imediately ran to sit with me at the outside table. You would have sworn I had given them a million dollars. "Mmmm diese gut schmecken, ist das, was es heißt? "

"Man nennt Toll House Cookies Chocolate Chip um genau zu sein." They were my friends after that and never tired of my questions about their culture and language. In return for their patience, I made them cookies once a week. Eventually, they joined me in the kitchen to bake them.

There were so many things that were different in this new world I now lived in, particularly the little things that you don't think about and are never told about in guide books, like the street venders that roamed the neighborhoods in the morning. In no time, I was purchasing bread, milk, eggs and flowers from them. They would knock on my window in the living room; I would open it and the transaction would happen without me ever having to leave the house. They called me Frau McCleary, and I learned their names as well.

One of the first mornings I was there, I awoke to the awful banging sound of trash day. The trash truck had perfectly round holes to fit the German's perfectly round barrels that were perfectly lined up neatly on the side of the road...one was not allowed to place a bag on the curb. These neatly dressed men in white uniforms then picked up these neatly styled trash cans and placed them on their pristine trucks, inserting them into hooks that were attached to hydraulic powered arms from underneath. These arms, when in operation, would align the perfectly round barrels to the perfectly round holes that were so strategically placed on the back of the truck. Then, with the flick of a switch, the arms on the truck that were holding these little gems would slam the barrels over and over again until all the trash was out of them ,and everyone in the neighborhood was up...it was the German way.

One afternoon, I was sitting in my living room, reading, when the phone rang. At first I did not recognize the sound, because it was so different from the one we had back home in the states. It was a succession of two quick rings, followed by silence and then two quick rings again. It was vaguely familiar to me, maybe from a movie I had seen, but I wasn't sure. There were so many numbers one had to use in order to dial out, I had never used it. It startled me, and I wondered who could be calling me. Suddenly, I thought it might be Bobby, and I excitedly got up to answer it. It turned out to be a wrong number.

Sitting at my kitchen table one morning, contentedly writing a poem about these strange surroundings, I heard another sound that was unfamiliar to me...it was my doorbell. Although I didn't even know I had one, I figured it was my doorbell because it couldn't have been anything else. I had been in this country for a month and had not heard it used. There was a small, very high window in the kitchen near the sink, that I knew had a view of the door outside. Pulling a chair to the window, I tried my best to crane my neck and have a look. It was at too much of an angle; I still couldn't see a thing. Meanwhile, the person at the bell was adamant and wouldn't let up. It was getting to be irritating, and all I could imagine was that it must have been a door-to-door salesman. How was I going to handle this? I had had a hard time getting rid of salesmen back home, when we spoke the same language. My first instinct was to ignore him, and maybe he would go away. That didn't work; the bell kept ringing, and he was not leaving.

Opening the window, I leaned out as best I could to tell him I was not interested. What a surprise it was for me to see an American girl standing there looking up at me. I knew right away she was American by the way she was dressed. She was wearing tight, Levi jeans and a blue sweater that was similar to one I had back home. She had beautiful, thick, wavy blond hair that was down to her chest. She was pretty with a perfect figure and was my age. When I asked if I could help her, she said, "Ah yeah, Bobby sent me to check on you; can I come in?"

All I could respond in return was, "Who are you?"

"My name is Felicia, and I'm from California. Bobby and my husband Tim are in the same unit at Cass Site."

She was still rambling on by the time I jumped down and ran to the door to open it. I had never heard anyone that could talk so fast with run on sentences and still keep up with conversation . The minute the door was open, she pushed past me and headed up the steps to my apartment. As she walked, she was ranting on and on about how long she had been in Germany, what a head trip it was to be in a foreign country all alone, shame on the military for not caring about young girls being stranded there when their husbands went on maneuvers and did I like my apartment. As we stood at the entrance to my apartment, I was gaping at her with wide eyes. She had said all that in the span of thirty seconds. I didn't know what to say to her, which question to answer first. The whole scene was surreal. I had not spoken English in three days, because there had been no one around to talk to, and here was this girl who just had given me a year's worth of conversation.

Seeing the dumbfounded look on my face, she burst out laughing and said, "What a trip huh?" I smiled and apologized, "I'm sorry, I haven't spoken much in the past month, and certainly not English, I am a bit overwhelmed." She put her arm around my neck and said, "Well, honey, I'm here to cure that, and besides, I talk enough for two, so just nod your head once in a while in response."

Opening the door, I didn't know what to make of this girl. I wasn't used to someone who was so outgoing. After the last month of spending quiet time contentedly alone, I wasn't sure I wanted a friendship with someone who was so in my face. I knew I was projecting these feelings and felt bad. I figured I would just give her a chance. Walking into my apartment for the first time, she was awed by the newness of it. "Wow, this place is great! Look how new everything is! My place has old tacky wallpaper that's pealing. Tim doesn't seem to care. It took us forever to get the apartment in the first place. Hell we don't even have a separate room for our kitchen. Don't you hate how small all the German appliances are? Where do you get your groceries? Do you know how to cook? I just give Tim cereal. He doesn't seem to mind. I get my milk from the milk lady that walks down the street with a huge metal vat of milk. Do you have that here?" Taking a breather, she turned to me and said..."Do you realize how lucky you are to have this apartment?" I tried to answer her, but she was off on another tangent about being from L.A. and how cold it was in Germany and how she couldn't get used to wearing a coat. I just smiled sympathetically and nodded my head.

"I hear you're from Bawwwston. Go ahead, say, `Park your car in Harvard yard.' Go ahead, I want to hear it."

I looked at her in disbelief. Instead I said, "There's no parking in Harvard yard. If you parked there, you would be towed." She thought I was trying to be funny and roared with laughter. She was such a spectacle, I started laughing too.

"Get your things," she said, "We are going to see the guys." "What guys?"

"The guys we are married to!" She started laughing again, "Girl you have to get out of this apartment. You've forgotten you were even married."

"I thought we weren't allowed to see them."

"Now that's funny. We can see them once a month. Didn't I say that? That's why Bobby sent me to get you, to bring you to him."

My head was spinning. "What should I wear? What should I bring? How do I look?" The questions were flying from my lips as fast as they had been from hers a few minutes before.

"You look fine to me, but if you want to get all dolled up, we have plenty of time; go for it."

I ran into the bedroom and put on a white lace skirt with a matching shirt. "What are we allowed to do there when we arrive?" I said from the bedroom.

"We can have lunch with them. But the food sucks. If he is in a double room, sometimes the roommates give the wives time alone with the husbands, if you know what I mean."

"And everyone knows what you are doing?" I asked in disbelief.

"Honey, you're married. It's ok. It's not like you're teenagers in the back seat of a car! Just don't let the LT see that you're doing it."

"Who's the LT?" "That's the First Lieutenant. Boy you are a "newfer" aren't you?"

"I don't think I'll be doing that today. But I do have some cold chicken in the fridge that I can bring for lunch."

Felicia laughed, and said, "Hurry up. The guys are waiting, and I'm still not a hundred percent sure how to get there."

I ran into the kitchen and put the chicken and other items into a pretty basket I had purchased the day before from the market down the street. Grabbing a white parasol on the way out the door, I turned to Felicia and asked how I looked.

"Like Mary Fuckin Poppins. Why do you have a parasol?"

"Because I burn in the sun, and will break out with a rash all over my body on a sunny day like this. I don't want Bobby to feel he can't touch me."

"Really, is it that bad?"

"Yeah, I have been to a million doctors about it since I was a kid. It seems to mostly affect me in the summer. But for some reason, it has been bothering me the past few weeks. They keep testing me for this weird disease. But it keeps coming up negative. I can't remember the name at the moment...lupie something, I think." We both laugh.

"Well, if you are lupie, than we will get along fine. Let's go."

She had an old, beat up Fiat that would only go forty miles per hour. It was a standard clutch, and she ground the gears every time it shifted. I wondered, for a second, what I was doing in this car. The thought of seeing Bobby soon dispelled all my fears. She headed to the autobahn and asked me if I knew any German, in case we got lost. I told her I had been studying it and knew a little. I then told her about my first day, when I was terribly lost and how I sat on the police steps. She couldn't believe that Bobby had left me to fend for myself that way. But then, she said she wouldn't put it past Tim, either, to do something stupid like that on her behalf. She said the only German she knew was "Vo est de bahnhoff?" We both laughed. It meant "Where is the train station?" and it was the first thing that everyone learned. In no time, we were lost. We were still on the autobahn when Felicia rolled down her window and screamed out "Vo est de bahnhoff?" I started laughing.

"Don't worry," she said. "One thing I have learned in this country is that if you're lost, just take the next right."

"That doesn't make any sense," I said. "Sure it does. All we need to do is find an aus farht! They are always on the right." "What is an aus farht?" I said, laughing. "It's an exit off the autobahn." It literally means "out drive."

Then she started yelling out the window, "Vo est de aus farht?" I rolled down my window and started doing the same thing. In no time, we were laughing hysterically. I said, "Wait a minute...does that mean to drive a car, you first must pass a farhting test?"

We took the next exit we saw and came to a fork in the road in the middle of nowhere. "I hope you brought your passport," I said, "because we are probably in Switzerland by now."

"Let's hope not," she said, "because it was stolen at the last concert I went to in Munich." "Didn't you get another one?"

"Not yet, it's one of those things I keep meaning to do." Taking a right, we found ourselves on a dirt road in a wooded area.

"I can't believe how many pockets of wooded areas there are in this country." I said. "I guess that's why they call it the Black Forest." said Felicia. "We are in the Black Forest? I've read about it---why isn't it black?" "Hell if I should know," said Felicia, and we both laughed again.

In ten minutes, we were deeper into the woods. Felicia thought it looked familiar, but I thought she was crazy. It all looked the same to me. Driving very slowly because of the rough terrain, she took another right. There before us was a barbed wire fence and a menacing looking gate. It looked like a prison. Standing at the entrance were two men dressed in field fatigues holding M-16's. Their faces were painted with multiple shades of green, and they had leaves sticking out of their helmets. They were a frightening sight.

One of the men approached the car, his machine gun still in his hand, and screamed through our open window, "NAME, RANK AND SERIAL NUMBER!!!" I jumped in my seat and almost peed my pants. Felicia became nervous and was searching in her pocketbook for her ID. I began to do the same. After pouring the contents of her purse onto her lap, she said in a meek voice, "We are dependent wives coming to visit our husbands."

He then screamed, "LET ME SEE YOUR PASSPORTS!"

Now Felicia was really nervous. Pulling out her ID she tried the best she could to explain her passport, rambling on about how fun a night it had been at the concert. It was a Simon and Garfunkel reunion. And that Paul Simon still had a voice, but Art Garfunkel she felt sang better, and wasn't it Simon who wrote all the songs anyway? She ended this long spiel with, "That's why I don't have my passport." She was talking in fragmented sentences about the music and was making no sense.

"Why don't you have a passport?" The solder was acting irritated, and a line of cars with other wives was forming behind us.

"Because it was stolen, silly. I thought I said that." "Yeah, that was a good concert, wasn't it?" said the soldier, with a smile on his face.

With a look of realization, Felicia leaned out of the window and punched the soldier in the arm. "You lifer dog, Homer Dusenberry, don't scare me like that. I thought you were serious!"

He laughed and said, "I just wanted to mess with your head." Opening the gate, he let us pass.

The entire facility was bleak, looking like a prison on the inside. We were the first wives to drive through the gates. Other than the guards, there was no one to be seen; the whole place had an eerie silence. The buildings were the usual military type: cream-colored stucco with barbed wire everywhere you looked. Stepping out of the car, I whispered something about how bad I felt for the guys, who had to stay in this lock-down place for three months. Felicia agreed. We headed to the front door of one of the buildings. Felicia invited me to join her with Tim, until we found out where Bobby was. I declined and said I would just wait for him at the front door. Holding my parasol and basket of chicken in this awful atmosphere, I tried the best I could to look natural.

I hadn't been standing there more than two minutes when a big Klaxon went off right above my ear. It was attached to the door behind me. It was the loudest sound I had ever heard. "AAH-OOGA, AAH- OOGA!" it roared. Men started emerging from every corner of the place and running around like crazy. Some were flying out of the door, nearly running me down in the process. Holding tight to my basket while trying to block my ears at the same time, I turned one way and then the next, trying to get a handle on what was happening and what I was seeing. Some men were even jumping from the windows of the second story building. They were all headed in the same direction to the right of me and disappearing into a hole in the ground. When the noise finally stopped, I found myself alone, standing in the same spot that Felicia had left me. I didn't know what to do or where to go. Opening a window, Felicia leaned out and said, "Get the hell up here! There has been an alert!" I wasn't sure what that meant, but by the sound of her voice, I knew it couldn't be good. Scrambling through the door, she raced down and grabbed me by the arm.

"Quick," she said, "I want you to see this. We probably won't get another chance."

Directing me into a men's room, she pushed a chair up to the high window. "Jump up and tell me what you see." I could tell by her voice she had seen this ritual before. Doing as she said, I peered through the glass and watched as three nuclear missiles emerged from their bunkers in the ground. Shock and fear gripped a hold on me like a boa constrictor around my neck. I wanted to speak, but all that came out of my mouth were undistinguishable sounds. With my eyes and mouth wide open, I slowly stepped off the back of the chair and landed on the dirty men's room floor: white dress, basket of chicken, parasol and all.

"WE HAVE TO GET OUT OF HERE! DO YOU KNOW WHAT THIS MEANS! NUCLEAR WAR HAS STARTED!!! WE ARE ALL GOING TO BE BLOWN TO PIECES!!!" I was completely panic-stricken.

Picking me up off the floor, Felicia tried the best she could to calm my nerves. "Relax," she said, "It's just a drill, It happens all the time."

"HOW DO YOU KNOW IT'S A DRILL!?"

"Well actually, I don't, and the guys don't know either, but I can tell you, it usually is." Then she said, "Are those really nuclear missiles?" There we were, two girls of the age of twenty, from both coasts of the United States, standing in a men's room on foreign land waiting to die. At least I was. Felicia just said, "Come on, I'll show you Tim's room." I followed her in the same dumfounded silence as a dog being brought to the vet to be put down. I sat on Tim's bed and waited for the inevitable to happen. Instead, fifteen minutes later, our husbands walked through the door. They were with several other men, and the atmosphere was as jovial as if they were entering a locker room after a football game. They were talking about how fast each of them had gotten to the pad. They seemed to make a game of this and were adding up the points to see who had won. I recognized one of the men who had jumped out the window. Bobby looked over at me with a big smile and said, "Do I smell chicken?" I wasn't sure if he was talking about me or what was in my basket.

CHAPTER: 30

Felicia and I became good friends after that. We saw each other every day and did our laundry together and our food shopping. It was much easier for me, since she had a car. The car was an unreliable one, though. It broke down often, usually due to her clutch cable. She always kept a spare in the trunk for just such an occasion. Tim tried to repair it and the damaged plate for her, but he said the plate was too far gone, and they had stopped making them for that year car. He was going to see if he could find one in a junk yard, but then he was called to Cass Site, so instead he showed Felicia how to change the cable herself and where to buy new ones, if she needed to.

Felicia showed me, and together we changed the cable on the side of the road every two weeks. We sure did look like a sight when we were doing it. I was always dressed in feminine dresses; she was always in tight jeans. She would climb under the steering wheel to pass me the cable through the hole made by the pedal on the floor board; I would bend over the open hood and connect it to the hook thingy next to the engine. Whenever we did this, German men always stopped and wanted to show us how to do it. It always amazed them to see how proficient we were at it. It became a game to us, and in no time we could change a clutch cable in less than five minutes and were on our way in search of more adventure.

One day, Felicia needed to buy new windshield wipers. Driving to a Fiat dealership with a German/English dictionary in hand, we decided that I would do the talking. When the sales clerk approached us, I opened the book and looked up the word for windshield wiper. Before I could get the German word out of my mouth, I was laughing hysterically. For some reason the word fenster wascher struck me as funny. Fenster being the German word for window and wascher being the German word for washer, I assumed it would literally translate. I thought it was a great word. I kept repeating it over and over to the bewilderment of the clerk. Every time I said it I burst out laughing. I liked the sound of it, and, in English, to the confused look on the clerk's face, I told him so. Felicia couldn't see why it was so funny. In reality, I learned later, that the true way to say windshield wiper is scheibenwischer. When I think back on it now, the whole scenario seems even funnier. As far as the auto clerk was concerned, I was just some nut case American.

A week later, the car broke down altogether. We were without a vehicle, and at first, it saddened us. We soon realized that we actually had more fun without it.

The toughest part was doing our laundry. Felicia lived the same distance as I did from the base, but in the opposite direction. The town she lived in was called Pfuhl and pronounced "fool." This always struck me as funny, and I would rib her about it all the time. In English the word translated to muddy water. Without a car, together we learned the German bus system. Using my ever-popular Berlitz German/English dictionary, and the little I had learned from speaking with the kids in the neighborhood, we figured it out easily. Once a week, we would get on buses from our own neighborhoods and meet at the laundromat to wash our clothes. Bobby always gave me his dirty ones when we visited. I carried his large duffle bag to do this, instead of the small one that I wore on my back. It was quite a task, carrying that thing full of laundry on a five mile bus trip. I constantly bumped into people and soon learned the word "entschuldigung," which meant "excuse me." Felicia had a similar bag, so together we took up all the washers on one side of the row. We were using the laundromat on the back side of the base, because it was bigger. We always had a great time when we did our laundry. I was soon learning that Felicia had a great time no matter what she did. On this day we were laughing at how embarrassing it was to have a bra get caught in the holes in the dryer when there were soldiers in the room. The bra would hang there for all to see, taking its own little ride while the rest of the wash tumbled away. When this happened, we had a secret code to alert each other.

One particular day, Felicia had brought her bike to the laundromat, because she had too much laundry for it all to fit on the bus. She had rigged up a wire, two-wheel grocery basket to the back of her bike and had ridden it the five miles to base. She was so funny looking on the thing that I laughed when I saw her. Awkwardly descending from the seat without spilling all the contents, she just looked at me and laughed back.

She asked me, "Hey, you want to sleep over my house tonight?"

"Sure, but how are we going to get there, with you on a bike and me on foot? It is already seven in the evening, the laundromat closes at nine. Besides we have so much laundry between us, I'm not even sure we will get it all done."

"You have to have faith, Barb. We will get it done, and then you take a bus to the Ulm stop, and I will meet you there on the bike."

"But that still leaves us four miles to your house!" "Once there, I will show you how to get a transfer ticket to go the rest of the way on another bus."

"Well, since it is such a nice night, maybe we could walk the last four miles," I said. She wasn't sure she wanted to do that and would talk about it when I got to the first bus stop.

When the bus stopped, Felicia was right where she had said she would be. It was getting dark, and I couldn't help but notice that she had a strange look on her face. There was a German woman, who looked to be about fifty, talking to her. I knew Felicia didn't understand any German, so the scene had at first looked comical to me. By the time I had gotten off the bus, the woman had Felicia by the arm and was pulling her away from my direction. Felicia was trying to get away and was yelling at her. When I walked over to investigate, I realized that this woman thought Felicia was her daughter. When I told Felicia this, she started to pull out her ID. She was screaming, "I'm an American!" I tried the best I could with what little German I knew to explain to the woman that she had been mistaken. The woman got angry and tried to strike Felicia. The two of us ran: Felicia with her bike and laundry basket, me with a huge duffle bag. It was a good thing she didn't try to come after us. We were so clumsy running with all our baggage, I'm sure she would have caught us. Instead, the woman stood on the sidewalk screaming something in German back at us. We turned the corner and were gone.

Felicia was understandably shaken from this event. We chose to walk the rest of the way to her house. While we were walking, she ranted about German people. She said that they were an odd bunch, and she had always had a hard time getting used to them. She asked me if I had seen the young German girls waiting at the gates everyday. I said I had. She said they stood there waiting for the GI's, not caring if they were married or not. She was convinced those women at the gate didn't have any morals, they disgusted her. "They are our enemy, Barbara. What lonely man, whose wife was back home, could honestly resist them?" And those women knew it.

We quietly turned the corner and took a fussganger that she was familiar with. It was dark as we meandered in and out of parks and along the road. I kept asking her if she knew where we were. She kept reassuring me she did. We walked for a very long time, at one point hitting a wide open expanse. The path was a straight shot for the next mile down the road. It was dark, and if it weren't for the moon, we wouldn't have been able to see a thing. To the left of us was a huge corn field. To the right was a road and beyond that another wooded area. In the distance, we saw a set of lights heading in our direction. We knew the path we were on was too narrow to hold a car. At first, it was quite a ways off, yet we could tell it was traveling at a good speed. As it started to get closer, we tried to determine what it was. It was rising up and down as it got closer, looking like it was suspended in air. "Maybe it's a UFO," I said. We stood there in silence and in fear. When it got really close, the light grew bigger and blinded us. We grabbed onto each other and screamed as we closed our eyes. When it was upon us, the lights divided and passed on either side, while we were standing there in the middle in a farewell embrace. It had been two mopeds, and the drivers were unaware of our fear. We looked at each other and laughed so hard we had to sit on the ground in order not to wet our pants.

Still in hysterics, we heard the distant toll of a clock tower. Felicia turned to me and said, "Its eleven o'clock. Do you know where your parents are?" We started laughing all over again.

Helping her up, I said, "If it's eleven o'clock, do you know what that means?"

Smiling, she said, "In an hour, you will turn back into rags, my bike will change into a pumpkin, and I will become a mere mouse."

"No, we have been walking for a really long time. Are you sure we are on the right path?" "I told you, I'm sure. Don't worry about it."

In a short while, we passed a guest house along the way. The laughter coming from inside suggested there was a party going on. I noticed a gumball machine on the outside of the building. I went over and got one. I loved the fact that the Germans felt that a gumball was of such importance that one had access to them twenty-four hours a day. They also felt this way about cigarettes. On every block, a gumball and cigarette machine was guaranteed to be mounted to a building. What was really funny was when they were on a regular house, not a retail establishment. Could you imagine being in your house, perhaps in the bedroom with your significant other, and suddenly, from outside your window you hear, "Look, honey, Frank got a cherry!"

Felicia was right. We were on the right road. In the distance, we could see a twinkling town of lights. By the time we arrived, it was well past midnight. We were so exhausted that we plopped down on her queen size bed after changing into our pajamas. The last thing I heard was Felicia saying in the dark... "Good night, John Boy." We giggled ourselves to sleep.

One snowy night in March, I was at home alone, working on an oil painting of Bobby and me. It was about nine in the evening, and the painting was going well. James Taylor was with me on my cassette player, and I was in my element. My easel was located right next to the large, six-foot square window in the studio. With no shades and only a flimsy curtain, I was in full view of whoever happened to pass by on the street. I didn't have a choice about this lack of privacy with the windows. All the German windows were like this in town.

I was singing along with the music when all off a sudden, there was a big banging sound coming from outside. It startled me, and I screamed involuntarily. I put my hand on the curtain to push it aside and see what was out there. When I did this, I found myself looking directly into the face of an angry man not much older than I. He was holding a shovel in his hands, trying to break my window with it. The windows were triple pane thick. They were a type of glass I had never seen before. I had realized this on my first night in the apartment, but I had never known just how strong they were, until that night. I only got a glimpse of him; with his face so close to the glass trying to look in as I was trying to look out, I immediately retreated from the window and ran into the living room. It didn't help that he followed me there.

He was screaming at me from outside. He was chanting, "AMERICANS GO HOME!!!" I had two larger windows in the living room, each with large, woven mesh curtains that were not wide enough to close completely. Standing in the middle of the room, I was now in plain view. He started hitting those windows as well. He was so angry and adamant about getting his point across. I couldn't tell from his accent if he were German or Turkish. I was convinced he was a terrorist, because at the moment he was terrorizing me. I ran into the kitchen. There was no place I could hide. I was sure he was going to get me. My heart was pounding so hard inside my chest that I was sure, if he didn't kill me, that I would die of a heart attack instead. I wasn't crying. My mind was racing too much to figure out a way to get out of this situation. My landlords were away on vacation up north, and there was no way for me to get out of the house without him grabbing me. I was trapped like a rat in a glass cage. He was now at my kitchen window. Without anything left to do, I ran into the hall and grabbed the phone. Practically pulling the cord out of the wall, I brought it into the bathroom and locked the door. The bathroom was completely covered by tile, and the window was very high. I knew that he would have to have had a ladder outside in order for him to see me. In case he did have one, I drew the shower curtain, so he couldn't, and sat myself on the floor. The first call I made was to the military police. Bobby had posted the number on the phone for me, in case of an emergency. My hands were shaking so hard that it took three tries before I got it right. Meanwhile, the man outside had become a group of men, who had figured out where I was and were chanting and banging on the side of the building, just below the bathroom window. They now sounded like a mob, so when the MP's finally answered, I had to scream into the phone to be heard.

At first I was hysterical, and the officer on the other end of the line could not understand me. He told me to calm down and to slowly explain what was happening. I tried to do as he said as best I could. I told him there was a mob of anti-American protesters outside my window, trying to break into my house and hurt me. He asked me if I were in military housing. I said no and told him my address and neighborhood. He told me he could not help me and that I would have to call the polizei. The MP's had no jurisdiction on non-military soil. I started to scream at him on the phone that these men were going to kill me and that I was an American. In a very stoic voice he said, "I'm sorry ma'am. You'll have to call the police in your district." I asked him in an agitated voice if he knew the number. He told me he didn't, so I hung up the phone.

Crazed, I dialed the number for German information; it was also written on the phone. Without a pen to mark it all down, I searched frantically in the bathroom for something to write with. I found a tube of lipstick and wrote on the tile next to me.

Before they answered the phone at the police station, I could hear the men outside, trying to pick the lock on my door. They were sticking something in it and rattling the glass. I couldn't believe that the neighbors were ignoring this entire racket they were making. When the German police answered the phone, I was again out of control. The racket from outside my door could be heard on their end of the phone line. Because I was speaking in English, they knew that I was American, and hearing the banging and the chanting from outside, they figured out quickly what was happening. The voice on the phone simply said to me, "Where do you live?" I told him, and the line went dead.

In less then ten minutes, I heard men outside talking. Then I heard my outside door open and wondered in a panic how they had gotten in. The next door was the glass one just outside the bathroom where I was hiding. The intruder started banging on it and yelled in English, "OPEN UP!" When I didn't answer (trying to be as still as a mouse) he said "IT IS THE POLIZEI, OPEN UP!" "What if they're fooling me?" I thought, "What if it were a trick?" I was paralyzed with fear. He became more insistent and told me he would break in, if I didn't open the door. I cracked the door of the bathroom to look out. What I saw was an image that would stay with me for the rest of my life. It was a figure standing behind the wavy glass, holding an Uzi machine gun. It took every ounce of courage I had to open that door.

The policeman who walked into my apartment that night couldn't have been much older than I. He was tall and blond with blue eyes and looked like he had only been shaving for a few years. Despite his appearance, he was all business.

"How do I know you are really the police?"

"Here, this is my badge. Do you have a passport?"

"Why are you alone? Where are the other officers?"

"My partners chased the men into the woods. They are trying to catch them. They had run into the woods down the street, when they saw us coming."

"Do you know who these men are?"

"I do. Come this way please." He directed me to the front of the apartment to look out the living room window. Pushing the curtain aside, he said, "See that guest house over there?"

I said, "Yes." The guest house was the neighborhood bar where all the locals went to socialize at night; I had never been in there.

"That is the local meeting place for the Green Group. It is a young, neo-nazi organization that is gaining power. They don't like Americans. They have just had many of their followers elected into the legislature. They are not your friends. How long do you plan on being in this apartment?"

I told him we had a two year lease.

"I will come by every night at nine thirty and park outside your house. That should make them understand. Don't talk to them or even look at them."

"What if they come back after you leave?"

"They shouldn't," he said. "The German police are not like the American. These men know the trouble they can get into." He then handed me his name and number at the station, if I needed more assistance.

His parting words to me were, "See if you can find another person to take over your lease. You are not safe here."

The polizei were parked outside my apartment ever night for three months, until, finally, the group found another place to conduct their meetings. The day they left the guest house, they gave me a parting gift. It was fliers that were left all over my front yard and on my car. These showed cartoons of a naked Ronald Reagan with a nuclear missile stuck up his butt. They were disgusting, and I snatched them up and threw them away before the children in the neighborhood saw them, when they came home from school.

CHAPTER: 31

Easter arrived in April that year; the Germans celebrated it on a Monday, instead of the traditional Sunday that we were used to back home. I was sleeping when I heard the soft sound of children laughing and giggling outside my window. Rising from my slumber, I peered out to see what was going on. The entire neighborhood was filled with children in their pajamas, holding baskets. Their hair was still mussed, and you could tell they had just awakened. They were collecting the colored eggs and candy that was scattered all over the yards. Watching the delight in their faces and the joy they were having brought a smile to my face. I watched them until every last egg was found, and they disappeared back into their homes.

The end of April brought many changes to the fun for Felicia and me, the biggest change being that our husbands were coming home. This meant that we would be spending more time with them and less with each other. The second change came when I received a call from the daycare center, wanting me to report for work in a week.

The countryside around me was also changing. The crocuses were up, and the flower boxes on every windowsill were in full bloom. This also meant that my allergies would soon follow. One night before the guys came home, I was sleeping at Felicia's house. My hay fever had been particularly bad that day, and I was sleeping with a Kleenex box beside the bed. At around three in the morning, I reached for a Kleenex and realized I was out. Getting up and stumbling to the bathroom in the dark, I flipped on the light over the sink. When I looked in the mirror, I screamed. I was covered in blood from my nose down to my waist. This brought Felicia to the rescue in a flash. She, too, screamed when she saw me. "Where is it coming from?" she asked.

"It's coming from my nose. It's my allergies." "Why don't you take something for that?"

"I can't," I said, "The last time I did, I was knocked out for a whole day, I'm super-sensitive to antihistamines." I told her about the time at Ivy Manor when Shirley had given me two Sinutabs. They found me passed out on the floor of the library, with drool all down my chest.

"Well, that has to be better than blood all down your chest."

I promised I would grab my dictionary and go to the German apothecary the next day. We cleaned me up, and I went back to bed with a towel.

The apothecary was two doors down from Felicia's house. Armed with the words I needed to use, I was ready. Before I had time to open my mouth, the pharmacist directed me to the appropriate aisle. Reading the labels for a non antihistamine brand, I discovered a whole section of herbal remedies for allergies. Picking out one, I purchased it and brought it home. I was getting at least one bloody nose a day now, yet despite how badly I was suffering, I didn't want to take any chances until I could completely decipher the words on the box. I had made that mistake with hair dye the week before, and I wasn't going to take a chance with an oral medication. It took me an hour to understand the words written on the box. Most of the ingredients were natural, so I was able to find enough of a derivative of the words to know what they were saying. The one thing that stumped me was the word "bumble bee." It was not only written on the box, but there was a picture on the front of it as well. From what I could understand about the dosage, I had to take four every four hours. This made me nervous, so I asked my landlord if I were reading this correctly. Martin and his wife were from a northern part of Germany, with a dialect very different then the one spoken in the south. It had always been hard for me to understand them. After ten minutes of sneezing and hand gestures, I felt confident enough to take the medication. I was so relieved, when it worked like a charm. I had taken the recommended dosage and was better after that. I was told later by a German who spoke perfect English that the bumble bee ingredient was actually bee pollen, and the medicine worked like a vaccine to help your body fight off the unwanted allergy. As far as I knew, we didn't have anything like it in the US; I stocked up on the stuff every chance I got and mailed it to my mother, in the hopes that I could use it on my inevitable return to the States.

The Germans had a lot of pharmaceutical products like this. One was a well kept secret called Kinder Tee. It was a drink that was given to babies to calm an upset stomach. On close examination of the box, I realized it had paregoric in it. That explained why every child it was given to fell peacefully asleep.

Another thing that became the rage was a vitamin drop called B-Stwolve. It was actually a form of B-12, but this lovely little potion had speed in it as well, to be taken if you felt tired all the time. You were supposed to put one drop of it in your morning coffee. The American girls soon realized it not only helped them keep up with the ever abundant babies they were having, it also helped them lose weight. After a while, they were taking up to twenty drops a day. The army tried to put a stop to it by fining anyone caught using it. They did it anyway. I never used it, because I could see these women were becoming addicted to it.

The first week of May, Bobby came home. I was waiting for him at the base when he arrived that morning. I was disappointed when I realized he would have to work that day and not be home until supper. I learned a lot about Bobby the first month that he was home. He was moody and prone to quiet spells that could last for days. When I tried to talk to him about this out of concern, he wouldn't answer me. He would just stand in the kitchen and watch the children play outside. After awhile, it only became natural that I felt his unhappiness stemmed from me. I tried to make things easier for him. I spit shined his shoes and ironed his uniform. If he was polished enough, he might be exempt from guard duty. I knew Bobby hated to do guard duty, so I did my part in trying to make him look his best, and it worked. He was exempt from guard duty at least once a month. Sometimes Bobby didn't even come home at night. Weeks would go by, and I wouldn't see him. I found out that he had been staying at the barracks. When I questioned him on this one day, he refused to talk about it.

I kept myself busy with the daycare center. There was a lot of work that needed to be done there, and they were more than happy to let me do it. On my first day of work, I was called into the office to speak to a woman by the name of Deirdra. She was a beautiful and elegant black woman, who reminded me of Diana Ross. She gave off an air of power whenever she entered a room. She was the main boss at the center, and she wanted to interview me herself. Sitting very erect behind her desk, she asked me what I thought of the facility. I decided to be direct and not lie. I told her that if this same center were in Massachusetts, it would be breaking many regulations. She asked me what they were, so I began to list them.

The first problem was the teacher-child ratio per room. This facility had too many children for too few teachers at one time. The second issue was the ratio of children per square foot. Sometimes there were over twenty children in a room that I knew should hold only fifteen. Then I touched on cleanliness. The diaper tables and the buckets that the teachers washed their hands in were disgusting. The hot meals that were served were never hot, and the dishes were washed by hand. She didn't make a move the whole time I was talking. Her face never changed expression. It intimidated me, and I wondered to myself if she played poker. She then asked me if there were anything else I would change. I told her I would insist that the women watching the children act more like teachers and make lesson plans to help with the children's growth and development. But the first thing I would do would be to paint the walls a different color and put some murals of happy things on them. "Quite frankly," I said, "This place is depressing."

"You know," she said, "You're not bad for a white girl. You have balls, and I like that." I was the only white employee at the place. I had hoped her remark was not a look at things to come. "What color paint do you want? You can start painting the walls tomorrow," she said.

Most people would have perceived this as her form of punishment for my being so direct. I, however, was thrilled with the idea and told her I didn't care, as long as it was a pastel...and I could enlist the older kids to help. She agreed.

That Saturday, I was asked to work the evening babysitting shift, from six in the evening until 2:00 AM. I was working with three other women. The children were split up in groups by age, until it came time for bed. We played games and made art projects and watched a kids' video on TV. Video had just been introduced, different from what we have today. The cassettes were long and thin, called Beta Max. At bedtime, we put the children on mats in the largest room, and I read to them, one book after another, until they fell asleep. Starting at around ten, the parents would arrive to pick up their sleeping darlings and cart them off to their own beds at home. Most never woke up, and I wondered if they thought their time spent with me was just a dream. I liked this idea of being a pleasant dream to a child.

That night, there were two children who were still with us at 2:00 AM. Their names were Mark and Tashia, two adorable black children who had just arrived from the ghetto in Chicago. Their father's name was Stick. A few months prior to this, he had had to make a choice between army life or prison. I knew none of this at the time. The other teachers had families of their own and needed to get home. I was the only one who was alone, with no one expecting me. I told them to leave and not to worry. I would wait for the parents. Once they left, I would lock up for the night. They felt bad, but I insisted, thinking they would be there shortly.

Another hour had passed, and Mark and Tashia's parents still had not arrived. I began to get worried and wondered if they had been hurt on the autobahn. I was about to call Deirdra to ask her what to do, when the father approached the locked front door and began banging on it loudly. He was obviously drunk, and their mother was not with him. When I asked him who he was, he started calling me obscenities. I was afraid to open the door, but, more than that: I wasn't going to let him drive in that condition with the children. I called Deirdra, who called the MP's. The children woke up from all the banging. They began to cry and call for their father. They didn't understand why I wouldn't let him in. I tried to calm them as best I could. In a short while, the MP's showed up, and I could hear fighting going on outside. The children heard it too and became hysterical with fear for their father. The MP's hauled him off to the MP station.

Deirdra showed up right after the police and unlocked the door. She entered the main hall and found me locked in her office with the children. When I realized it was she, I unlocked the door. She told me I had done the right thing; he had been in no shape to drive. She called their mother but found she was not at home. She left her a message that she was taking the children to her house for the night. She dropped me off at mine first. I had missed my last bus.

The next day, Deirdra brought me the paint, and the transformation began. I had the five year olds help me. The paint was pastel green. I should have guessed. We started in the hallways first, so that we didn't have to deal with the kids in the room. Mark was a big help to me when it came to painting the hall, though he was a source of frustration for any teacher who happened to have him in her room. He was a very bright child, and, despite the poor organization at the school, he had learned to write his name at the age of four. Every day he played pranks on the other children and teachers. He had learned very expertly how to pick a pocket; he was in trouble daily for this.

I enjoyed talking to him. He was street-wise and very advanced in his vocabulary. I was always frank with him, and he listened to me. I told him I knew how smart he was, even though he didn't think grown ups could see this. This made him respect me. He followed me everywhere. The other teachers didn't mind; they couldn't control him anyway. He had a habit of being in whatever room I was assigned to, even if I were with the babies. I asked him what we should paint on the wall for a mural, and he said he wanted a big marching band. I told him it was a great idea and began to draw it on a piece of paper first. I decided to make it multicultural. Although it would be fifteen years until this concept would become second nature in a school setting, I felt it was appropriate, considering the vast differences they would encounter in town. Mark told me the instruments he wanted to see being played on the wall; together we designed the mural, and together we painted it. Mark had excellent fine motor skills for a boy his age. I told him this and outlined areas I wanted him to fill in with paint. We worked very quickly on this project, and, one day, when it was two-thirds done, he became angry at me for not letting him play in the baby room, when it was time for him to take a nap. It was required that he sleep with the older kids, something that always irritated him.

The teacher who was monitoring his room thought I was in the hall. Mark started waking all the children, so she sent him out of the room. Sitting in a chair, he waited for me to come and work on the mural. When I didn't show up, he became angry and scratched away the paint we had worked on for weeks before that. When I did have the chance to sit with him in the hall, my feelings were very hurt. We talked about what he had done and why. Together we repainted it.

On a sunny day in May, I decided to take the four and five year olds outside to teach them how to play baseball. I had found a wiffle ball and bat in the back closet that looked like they had never been used. I took some paper plates from the kitchen to use as bases, and we were ready, Securing the bases to the ground with flat rocks, the children stood there, looking at me with anticipation. Many of the children were half German, because their fathers had married German women. Most of the others were American but had been born in Germany. The result of these circumstances was that none of them had even heard of the word baseball. I thought it was a sin that American children had never heard of such an American pastime. When Deirdra heard what I was planning, she roared with laughter from her office. She said, "This I have to see." She and the entire day-care staff lined up in the yard to watch the spectacle. They were all holding the babies, who couldn't be left inside. The toddlers were running around in a protected, fenced-in area of the yard, where they could also be watched. It was obvious that something big was going to happen; soon, several soldiers who were passing by stopped and leaned on the chain link fence that surrounded the yard. They wanted to watch, as well.

I lined all the children up behind home plate, thinking it was ridiculous to separate them into teams. What I wanted was for them to enjoy themselves and understand the rudiments of the game. I knew the toughest part would be for them to understand the order in which to run the bases, because children under the age of five do not have fully developed sequencing skills, if any. I tried to explain this as best I could by demonstration: I ran them myself. They just laughed at me, so I knew I was in trouble, especially with such a large audience watching me. Many liked the idea of trying to hit the ball with the bat, but some of them tried to run off with it, hitting random objects in the yard. My audience was laughing at the comic spectacle unfolding. Finally, through trial and error, the children realized the bat was meant for hitting the ball. I made the oldest children hit first, so that the younger ones could learn by observation. Mark turned out to understand all of it and proved to be an asset in my quest. Even though I told them over and over that they had to drop the bat before they ran the bases, many of them took it with them when they ran. The first few batters did as instructed, giving me a runner on first and second. Then it was Manny's turn. Manny was a four year old who was very tiny in stature. I moved in close to pitch the ball to him. On his fifth try, he hit it. He got so excited that he forgot the sequence of the bases and ran to third. This caused confusion with the runner that was already on second, and she ran across the mound to first, crossing paths with the runner already on first, who also ran past me on the mound and over to second.

The children waiting behind home plate were jumping in the air, clapping and shouting to urge them on. My audience was doing the same... and laughing. I was standing at the mound, dumbfounded by what I had just seen. The game continued like this for an hour. It was a funny sight to see. More soldiers gathered at the fence, and the staff was all in a jovial mood. The children never did learn the correct rules of baseball that day, but the concept of the enjoyment of America's favorite pastime was forever embedded into their souls. At nap time they all slept soundly, and I felt confident that I had shown them that there was more to life in their olive drab world.

There was another boy at the center who caused some concern for me. His name was Joseph. He was two going on three with white blond hair and big blue eyes. His father was a high ranking officer, and I had never met him. He was away from the base a lot. His mother was a beautiful statuesque blond, who was forty years old, always in a hurry and very stern with him. Joseph had been a surprise for his parents, who had given up on ever having children long before he came. His mother also held a high ranking government service job in an office somewhere on base. I worried about Joseph because he was violent to the other children and didn't speak. He expressed himself physically, usually frustrated, so the results were rarely good. He would take large, metal Tonka trucks and ram them into the ankles of unsuspecting passersby. He didn't discriminate in his choosing: he would ram adults as well as children. Sometimes these adults were parents, dropping off their own kids. We tried to remove the trucks from the room, but Joseph could turn anything into a weapon, even a crayon.

He soon developed a reputation as the boy you wouldn't want to play with. Parents complained daily of the effects he had on their children. I had been observing him quietly for a month, when I realized that Joseph's behavior was reaching a crisis. At first, I thought his lack of speech was the result of a hearing deficiency. It would be the obvious explanation and certainly the first thing that anyone doing intervention would look at. So I took a book, and when he was sitting alone, I slammed it shut behind his back. He reacted appropriately. Unfortunately, he also reacted inappropriately as well. He turned around and punched me in the stomach. I knew what he needed was nurturing, yet he was unwilling to accept it. Every time I tried to cradle him, he cringed and withdrew from my touch... and he hit me again.

One night, sitting home alone, I was thinking about this very complicated boy. He was not deaf, yet he did not speak. I knew the violent behavior was a learned trait he had developed to gain attention, so that his needs could be heard, but he was also very angry, because his needs were never met. Out of necessity, he had learned to live in his own silent world, a world that felt threatening and isolated. I also knew that Deirdra had tried to speak to his mother. From what I understood, she had dismissed the whole thing and refused to look at the importance of the situation. She claimed he spoke at home, so she wasn't concerned about his development. I had heard of voluntary muteness, but from what I understood of it, those cases concerned children who were really shy as well. That was not the problem with Joseph. No, Joseph's issues were about language or speech. And then it hit me. Why hadn't we all seen it? I couldn't wait until the next day, to see if my theory was correct.

The following day, Joseph arrived at 8:30 AM. He immediately went for the Tonka truck and was pushing it around the room, within minutes ramming it into the legs of children, so that it was taken from him by the other teacher in the class. I was about to speak to him, when Connie called me in to the infant room, because that teacher had called in sick. Standing up to comply, I knew my experiment would have to wait.

The baby room was at the end of the hall. Its doorway provided a direct view of all the other rooms. The babies slept a lot, because most were under the age of one. Some were even a few weeks old, which was the case on this particular day. It was a boring room to work in, and time always dragged for me when I was there. That afternoon, cradling a sleeping infant in my arms while the others slept soundly in their cribs, I watched the happenings of the rest of the center from the doorway. Mark was with me as well. I was teaching him his alphabet, and he was quietly tracing dots on a piece of paper that spelled out my name.

It was nap time, and I could hear Joseph putting up a big fuss. I could tell the teacher in charge was frustrated, because she didn't understand what he wanted. He started screaming at the top of his lungs and then hurdling over the two foot security gate that barred the room; he ran frantically down the hall, holding one shoe. He was running away from where I was standing. Without a second thought, I yelled, "Josef, kommen du heir!" To my delight, he stopped in his tracks and ran back in my direction. I placed the baby I had been holding into the crib next to the door and reached my hands out to him. He was crying and reached up to me, as I lifted him over the gate. With him sobbing into my neck, I stroked his beautiful blond hair and told him in German that he was a good boy. He looked into my eyes and replied in a very sorrowful voice, "Ich kann nicht finden, meinen schuh." (I can't find my shoe.)

Connie, having heard all the commotion, had entered the hall from the office, just as this conversation was transpiring. We looked at each other, and she said in a whisper, "I'll be damned." I asked her if she would watch my room so that I could find his shoe. She complied, and Joseph and I went back to his classroom. We searched the room for ten minutes and couldn't find it. I asked him in German, "Was hast du mit heute spielen?" (What had he played with that day?) To the amazement of his teacher, he answered me in the same language. I searched the toy box, found his shoe at the bottom and handed it to him. I asked him, "Willst du, es anzuziehen oder einfach nur halten?" (Did he want to put it on or just hold it.) He told me he wanted to hold it. I asked him if he would like to nap in my room that day, and he said yes. Walking back down the hall together, with Joseph dragging his mat behind him, I lifted him over the gate into the baby room. Laying him down with his shoe clenched tightly in his hands, I whispered in his ear, "Good job." I then rubbed his back until he fell asleep. I thought of Mrs. Buras and how proud she would have been of me. I felt her presence that day and quietly thanked her.

CHAPTER: 32

Life at home with Bobby began to improve. He seemed to be out of his depression and wanted to spend more time with me. One Saturday morning, we went to downtown Ulm to search for a bed. We ended up getting a flip couch that opened to a full size sleeping mattress on the floor. It was similar to the inexpensive flip chairs that you can purchase today, only it was much larger. We put it in the living room, and that's where we slept. We turned the bedroom into a studio for Bobby and me to do our artwork. I painted pictures of the German people and scenes peculiar to the culture. Bobby was really good with cartooning and soon developed a comic strip titled "Brats." It was a parody of military brats, and he used my funny stories about the children as a resource. I was a character in this strip as well; I was always portrayed as the sweet, unsuspecting teacher. I liked the fact that he seemed to be happy when he was doing this. Work at the motor pool was difficult for him. I had learned from Felicia that he was regarded as incompetent. It was difficult for me to see him endure this, because I knew that he was actually a very intelligent guy who could dance circles around the knuckleheads in the motor pool, if given a chance. He was still trying to change his job in the military. He wanted to be transferred to an office job in the headquarters unit. He sent out letters weekly to various people to help him in his quest. Most came back unopened.

Then one night, his prayers were answered. He was with a few of his friends at a German bar near the base. He was giving the GI's he was with a hard time for not being able to speak the German language. Several had been there two or more years, and Bobby thought that was awful. To tease them, he insisted on talking to them in German. Bobby was now fluent in the language, and I'm sure a part of him wanted to prove he wasn't dumb. When he refused to speak English, it irritated the other men. Bobby never seemed to pick up on social clues, which often got people angry at him. An officer who worked at headquarters was sitting at the next table and also speaking fluent German; he and Bobby struck up a conversation, ignoring the other men. Bobby told him that he had been in Germany for less than nine months. Asking what his MOS was, Bobby told him he was in the motor pool and said he was lousy at it. He said he had been trying to change his MOS, but so far had had no success. The officer asked him if he had taken any classes in German. When Bobby said he had not, the man became very interested. He told Bobby there was a test that he wanted him to take and to report to him the following Monday after formation.

Bobby came home all excited; I had never seen him so animated. He told me about the events that had just transpired and the test he was going to take. He was sure that if he did well, he would secure a position at headquarters. I asked him what that meant for a job. He said he wasn't sure, but he knew it would have to do with the launching of the missiles. I didn't say it to him, but I felt if it were up to me that would be the last job in the world I would want.

When he arrived home Monday night, he told me what he could about the meeting. He said the test was called E-Moss, and it had something to do with deciphering codes. He said they were allowing him to be relieved from the motor pool for a week, in order for him to take the test. I asked him if it took a week to take the test. He told me he couldn't tell me any more than that. Every day he left in a good mood and reported to a building that was located at the operations unit. I don't know what he did there, but whatever it was, he was happy and in his element. He told me that if he passed, he would have the option of attending the Presidio Language School in California after his tour in Germany, if he wanted to sign up for three more years. It sounded like our life was getting back on track, and the thought of finally going to California was very appealing to me. I was thinking about the college I had wanted to attend and being certified in Montessori theory. I was so happy for him. He was in such a good mood, and our life seemed to be perfect. One night I told him that after taking care of so many children, I wanted to have a baby of my own, and he agreed that it was a good idea.

Meanwhile, Felicia and I were still good friends. She sometimes hung out with me and the kids at the center during recess. And I visited her often at the bar she worked at on base, when Bobby was out with the guys. We never hung out all together. Felicia's husband, Tim, didn't like Bobby very much, and I knew from past experience that Bobby didn't do well in a crowd. The friends Bobby hung out with seemed to tolerate him more than others did. They were more intellectual, and their conversations were about education and culture. That was why Bobby had been giving them such a hard time in the bar that night about learning the language.

Bobby was very dedicated to this new project. He went on base every day and studied in the special library. In a week, he had passed the test with a 98%. Headquarters took him on the next day. He was right about launching the missiles. Although I never knew the details, somehow he was involved with it. I thought this meant that he would be happier. But he wasn't.

We were walking into the PX one day, when we ran into a woman whom I worked with. She was pregnant and had a history of many miscarriages. She had been home on bed rest, and when I saw her, I was genuinely pleased to see her on her feet. She was about four months along and looked great. We didn't know each other too well, because she had left work shortly after I had started, but we did know each other enough for me to acknowledge her. When I approached her, I asked her how she was feeling. She said she felt fine and was hopeful. Bobby had heard the story of this girl's plight from me, when she first got pregnant. Realizing who I was talking to, he opened his mouth to acknowledge her as well. He said, "So what does it feel like to have so many babies die? Did you have to bury any of them?" I yelled at him immediately, in front of her, and told him it was the most insensitive thing I had ever heard anyone say. The poor girl burst into tears, and I tried my best to console her. I told her that he hadn't meant it the way it had come out and to pay him no attention. It didn't help. The poor girl was beside herself and got angry at me as well. She never spoke to me again. Bobby and I had a big fight after that, and he refused to talk to me for days.

My saving grace was my friendship with Felicia. Summer came and was filled with picnics on the river and carnivals. Felicia and I went shopping in the German stores, and I bought a lot of pretty, feminine outfits. We explored different stores, forever in search of an American-style grocery store that was not the commissary. We found one in the center of Ulm. It had all sorts of exotic looking things that we couldn't identify. Strolling down the meat aisle, Felicia came across an open refrigerated chest that held every possible part of a pig. She held two cellophane packages on either side of her head and said, "Look Barbara, they have pig tails!" We immediately went into an entire dialogue, using other various parts, until a clerk approached us, and it looked like we were going to be thrown out. We left giggling, without buying a thing. One morning, Felicia showed up at my house to see if I wanted to go to a lake she had heard about. She was dressed in a bathing suit and carrying a towel. I told her that I would, but that I didn't know how to swim. She said, "That's ok; I'm just lonely for some California sun. I figured if we laid down on a blanket and closed our eyes, we could pretend we were on the beach." When we arrived at the lake, there was no one there. The lake was so tiny, it was even smaller than the pond in the cemetery, where I used to hunt snapping turtles when I was little. Felicia brought a large blanket. We both brought books. I was never one to sit in the sun, but it seemed like it was something that Felicia did a lot back home.

After thirty minutes, other people began to come: some families with small children and men and woman our age and younger. An ultimate Frisbee game was started right in front of us. Not paying any attention to it, we were both engrossed in our books. Suddenly, the Frisbee landed on our blanket. Reaching for it without taking my eyes off the page I was reading, I reached up to hand it back. When I finally did look up, I was staring into the crotch of a stark naked man standing directly over my head. I don't know how I was able to keep my composure. Looking at the rest of the lake-goers, I realized that Felicia and I were the only ones wearing clothing. I was actually wearing both long pants and a top. Felicia came to this conclusion at the same time I did. We looked at each other, and, once the Frisbee man left we burst into laughter. After another ten minutes had passed, we took off our tops. I knew this was a bad idea, but I did it anyway. Sure enough I soon broke out in a terrible rash.

The end of September came, the guys left for Cass Site again, and the Oktoberfest came to town. Felicia was all excited. She had been to the last one with Tim and had had a great time. The Oktoberfest was the only thing I had known about the German culture before I had arrived. I also had heard stories of how out of control it could get. Felicia and I decided the safest thing to do was to go to the local one that was gathering in Ulm. As luck would have it, it was set up in the field directly across from the base. It looked like a carnival with rides and booths. When we arrived, it was about seven in the evening, and the first thing Felicia wanted to do was go on a ride. Like me, she was a big chicken about this sort of thing, so we walked around, until we found what we thought was a safe and easy one to enjoy. As we soon found out, looks can be deceiving.

There were roller coasters and Ferris wheels. We both ruled those out. Then there were rides that dropped you at a great speed until right before hitting the ground. They were definitely a no. Then we saw one that looked like a large pirate ship. It only seemed to rock back and forth. It looked like it would feel as if you were in a large swing, and we thought that might be fun, so we stood in line. We were one of the first ones to get a ticket and pick our seats. We chose to sit on the last seat at the top of the ship. Strapped in by only a metal bar, we were ready to go. When the ride started, it went very slowly. Just as we expected, it felt like a swing. The view from this high point was so spectacular. We were able to see the entire fair grounds, as well as the entire city of Ulm, including the river that was lit up beautifully for the occasion. Then, with every swinging motion of the ride, the momentum began to pick up. Before we knew it, we were both sliding all over the seat trying desperately to hang on. With every plunge it took in the opposite direction, our bodies would lift off the seat and into the air.

Felicia started screaming. I was too scared out of my mind to make a sound. She grabbed on to me for dear life, and I did the same to her. We were practically crying. At one point, we made vows of friendship to each other, because we were both certain we would die. Meanwhile, I was wondering about the safety regulations Germany had for such a thing. Then, when we didn't think it could get any worse...the entire ship swung into a complete circle. Someone below us lost his lunch, and some other poor soul found it. Thank God it wasn't us. We were pleading with God by this time, selling our souls and promising a life of purity if he would just make it stop. It worked. When we exited the ride, we were so dizzy that we had to hang on to each other just to walk. I turned to Felicia and said that I would never go on an amusement ride again, and I never did.

Our next stop was the beer tent. Forgetting our vows to God, we figured we deserved a drink. There were three tents set up, and we chose the biggest one. Inside, the beer tent was exactly what you would picture an Oktoberfest to be like. Waitresses were dressed in very low cut dirndls with bustiers, most with at least four one liter mugs of beer in their hands. I couldn't believe they didn't drop them. The noise level in the place was extremely loud, with a German band playing traditional music at the end of the room. Everyone was singing along. There were several tables that ran the full length of the tent. German girls were hanging all over the American GI's. Felicia tapped me on the shoulder, pointed at a group of them and said, "Always know your enemy."

The thing that struck me right off the bat, that made the atmosphere different from anything else I had ever seen, was the sense of community. Everywhere you looked, people were swaying back and forth with their arms around each other's shoulders and singing. German waitresses, with their breasts nearly spilling out of their bustiers, were laughing and teasing the men as they handed them their mugs. Everyone appeared to be sitting together. Because there were only long tables and not groups of tables, there were no cliques or social classes congregated together. Because we were so close to a military base, a lot of the patrons were Americans mixed in with the German people. When we walked through the door, the entire place was singing a German prousting song with the band. "Proust" is the German word for "cheers." The floor was coated with beer covered straw. The smell reminded me of a farm just after a harvest. Many women were sitting on men's laps, where the men's hands were finding their way up their dirndls. Some were already in what could be considered a sex act. The room smelled of flesh and beer and rang with joy. The people were singing at the top of their lungs, and intermittingly throughout the song, they would tap their beers on the table three times, clink their glasses in the air to each other and shout, "PROUST!" It was a wondrous, joyful sight to see such a large group of people enjoying each other's company in spontaneous celebration, disregarding ethnic and social differences. It was a celebration by a community that was expressing such joy and openness, and I understood why this country had looked forward to this time of the year and had been doing so for hundreds of years. Felicia saw a guy that she knew and decided we should sit with him. Two of the men got up and gave us their seats when we arrived at the table. I don't recall the soldier's name, but I could tell that he liked Felicia very much and that they had known each other for awhile. Next to me were a bunch of German guys who were dressed in World War 1 German air force fatigues. The outfits were authentic and looked so cool. One guy named Deiter even had the leather helmet and goggles that the pilots wore when they dropped the hand sized bombs from the planes. I told him he looked fantastic, but he was really drunk and didn't speak any English. Deiter was very interested in me. I tried my best to tell him I was married. In the end, I showed him my ring. He didn't care. His wandering hand would find its way to the warmth of my inner thigh. I would smile at him and delicately put it back on his lap. He then would laugh in return. His hand would eventually find its way back there. After an hour of this exchange, I began to look forward to it, and again it would return. It never went any further than that, but it is something I never forgot. He insisted he talk to me all night long. At first it was only body language that we both understood from each other. With hand gestures and smiles, we seemed to communicate in a world all our own. He bought me a beer, and, after drinking most of it, my German was getting better. He put his goggles on me while I was in this state of intoxication. They were lopsided on my face. Felicia took out her ever present camera and snapped a picture of me. That picture had always brought a laugh to anyone who had seen it. After Felicia finished her beer, she became very animated, and feeling less intimidated, she joined the scores of women who were letting their guard down. With the coaxing of the guys, she got up on the table and danced the chicken dance down the length of it. Everyone in the place was clapping and cheering her on. I was clapping as well. We had such fun that night that when we arrived back at her place later, we still couldn't calm down. We talked most of the night of how we would never forget it. We lay down on her bed for hours, just waiting for the bed to stop spinning. I think we had drunk two liters of beer each. I made more vows to God that I would never drink that much again, if He would just see us safely through to dawn. I finally did fall asleep, with the help of having one foot on the floor.

When Bobby came home from Cass Site, we decided to try and have a baby. In two months, I was pregnant. The morning I found out, I ran to meet Felicia on base to tell her the good news. We met at the coffee shop, before I had to go to work. She jumped up when she saw me, because she had news, too. Standing in front of a table full of people we knew, we grabbed each other by the arms and loudly exclaimed simultaneously into each other's faces, "WE ARE HAVING A BABY!!!" The whole table started clapping, and a guy sitting next to us leaned over and said jokingly, "I thought that was impossible. Don't you ladies need a man to accomplish that task?"

We all started laughing. We couldn't believe we had gotten pregnant at the same time. I was ecstatic; Felicia, on the other hand, was happy but cautious. We made plans to see each other after I got off work at three. That would give us plenty of time together before the guys got home at six. Back at the coffee shop that afternoon, I was the one who was rambling on, and Felicia was the one who was quiet. This was a first in our history, and when I inquired about it, Felicia admitted she was scared. She said the more she had thought about it that day, the more she was unsure if she liked the idea. She had recently found out about an affair that Tim had had when she was still in the States. It had put a wedge in their relationship, and she was uncertain if a baby was going to make it any better. She also said she wasn't too thrilled about the idea of childbirth, not to mention what it did to your body.

I put my arm around her and told her not to worry, that I would be there for her as emotional support. "Besides," I said, "You're not going through this alone...I'm pregnant too." This seemed to relax her, and we started making plans about the items we would buy for the babies. I had already had a name picked out. I had been talking to Felicia about my future children since the day we first met. If it were a boy, I wanted to name it Bobby. If it were a girl, it would be Brianna. I wanted desperately to have a girl, but Felicia didn't care what she had.

Pregnancy for Felicia, physically, was a breeze. I, on the other hand, was sick every day. In the morning, before I would even raise my head, I had to eat a Saltine cracker in order not to throw up. I still went to work, but the stomach cramps never went away in the course of the day. My belly was bloated, and it felt like I had a parasite. My legs ached as well. My joints were all sore and swollen, and I felt like I had aged ten years. I developed a butterfly rash across the bridge of my nose, spreading to both cheeks. My face always looked flush. It was different from the "glow" people often refer to when a woman is pregnant. In general, I looked sick.

One day I was standing in a classroom, when a three year old girl named Tanisia threw herself on the floor in a tantrum. She was prone to this type of behavior, and I walked over to her to calm her down. I was feeling really awful myself and wished I had called in sick. Moving slowly, I bent down to talk to her. In the throws of a full-blown agitated state, she caught me off guard and kicked me in the stomach. The pain was so excruciating, that it brought me right to my knees. When the other teacher saw what had happened, she called for Connie. Connie and I had become close over the past month, ever since the incident with Joseph. She knew I was pregnant and brought me to the dispensary. They checked me out, and I appeared to be ok, so they sent me home.

When Bobby came home, he was concerned. He made me dinner and pampered me that night. He told me he wanted me to stay home from work the next day. I expressed concern to him about the fact that I had had a big day planned and couldn't change it. I had signed up months before to take my SAT's, so that I could enter the overseas college that was on base, the University of Maryland, European Division. I had been studying for months and didn't want to miss it. Besides, it was a four hour test, and I would just be sitting in a chair, anyway. He understood but added that he didn't want me to go to work afterwards. He wanted me to go straight home, so he would know where I was. This new form of responsibility and caring he suddenly possessed made me feel comforted. I agreed to follow his wishes.

The next morning, I arrived, barely on time. I had been vomiting that morning and missed the first bus. I wasn't rushing, when I realized that I was running late; I couldn't. I was feeling too ill. Sitting in my seat, I glanced around the room and noticed that I was the only female and civilian. The rest were soldiers. It wasn't until the test was on my desk that I remembered the importance of the day and how, once again, I had been given a chance to follow my dreams. I immediately began to focus and got lost in a world of questions and answers. I was feeling confident and doing well. My stomach was killing me, but I chose to ignore it. I knew the pains were getting worse, but I was in denial. The time seemed to go by rapidly. I had answered every question; it was only a matter of having answered them correctly. I was so driven by years of anticipation for this chance, that I didn't realize that I was gravely in trouble and in need of medical attention...fortunately, the man behind me did. I had finished the test and was reviewing my answers, when he tapped me on the back. Still under the spell of words and numbers, at first I didn't understand what he was so delicately trying to tell me. He pointed to the floor, and I saw the blood. Looking down at my lap, I realized it was coming from me. Suddenly, I felt the warmth and heaviness of my pants. They were sticking to the inside of my thighs and chafing my skin. The smell of fresh blood hung heavy in the air. My temperature started rising as beads of sweat formed on my forehead. I didn't know what to do; I was too concerned for the baby to be embarrassed. The rest of the class seemed unaware of what was happening; we were seated in the back of the room, and no one had turned around. I grabbed the coat that I had draped on the empty chair next to me, covering my lap with it as I sat there in shock. I knew what was happening to me. I had been through it before.

While the rest of the class was passing in their tests and leaving the room, the man behind me told me to stay where I was, and he would talk to the monitor. The monitor looked concerned, and they approached me at my seat. When they stood in front of me and told me they were going to call an ambulance, I burst into tears and told them I was pregnant. I told them I didn't want to go. I was adamant that I would not be taken out in an ambulance. I was not making sense. They became genuinely concerned. In my own head, I knew that if I went to the hospital, they would tell me my baby was dead. I wasn't ready to hear such news. If I just sat in that seat, I could pretend it wasn't so.

The soldier who had been sitting behind me took charge. He gently lifted me up to see if I could stand. Too weak to protest, I let him take control. Soon I became dizzy and faltered. The pain I had been feeling in my legs the past few months was even stronger. I couldn't support myself. Because the floor was so slippery with blood, we almost fell. Getting his balance, he lifted me into his arms and carried me out the door. I tucked my head into his armpit, beside myself with grief. It wasn't the first time I had been in need of a stranger's physical support. I smelled the cologne he was wearing; this time it wasn't Old Spice.

Out in the parking lot, the sun was shining, and people were going on with their day. We did draw attention from a few, and they offered to help. He told them he would handle it. He carried me to his car, a white Corvette, with white interior leather. I expressed my concern about ruining it, but he told me to be quiet and not to worry. He drove me to the hospital, while the monitor tried to locate Bobby. I had lost my second baby that day, and I felt sure I would never be a mother. In my mind, this soldier joined the girl from Lynn and the German Policeman. I added another helpful soul to the scrap- book. Someday, I thought, I would record all these wonderful deeds that strangers had performed for me. It would be my way of saying thanks.

CHAPTER: 33

Bobby had been relieved early from work and was with me at home. He had been walking around the apartment aimlessly, since he had arrived. This time it was me who was staring out the window. My legs were still aching from the past events, and walking had become painful. Sitting was just as bad. There was no position that felt comfortable. I found comfort in watching the children; I wished I had the ingredients to make cookies. The ticking of the kitchen clock and the soft footfalls from Bobby's socks were all that could be heard. He didn't know what to do or say to help me feel better. There wasn't anything anyone could do. I needed to come to terms with this on my own. He decided to call Felicia. She arrived at our apartment an hour later. She walked in silently and immediately felt the heavy atmosphere of the room. This was new territory for her. She had never been put in such an adult role before. She was concerned and yet awkward about how she should go about consoling me. Instead, she sat on the couch, biting her nails in silence. When I looked at her, she looked like a pregnant teenager, confused and scared. Bobby sat across from her. For the first time in a long while, he seemed a part of our world. But even that wasn't enough for me. I wanted them both to leave. There was nothing either of them could have said to make me feel any better. Without saying a word, I grabbed my umbrella from the hall basket to use as a cane and left.

I took a week off from work. The joint pain was getting much worse. I began a regimen of aspirin. Without anyone guiding me, I ended up taking more than the required daily dose. Soon I was covered with bruises on my legs. Connie found out I was having such a difficult time, so she came by to see me. She brought me flowers. I held them in my hands, looking at them as if I were seeing beauty in the world for the first time. I looked back at her and gave her a faint smile.

"Barbara, honey, you have to have faith. Without it, what is there?" She then added. "Barbara, you are so good with children. God is not cruel, and He will someday grant you that wish"

"Connie, this isn't my first miscarriage. I am not like other pregnant women. Something happens to my body. My body doesn't seem to understand. It has always been different from most. And now to make it worse, since the pregnancy, my arthritis has flared really badly. I am having such difficulty walking. It is almost as if my body has gotten angry at me for becoming pregnant and is punishing me. In the morning, it takes me at least a half hour to get my legs working. I have not had it this bad since I was a child. Look at my legs." Raising my skirt, I showed her the purple marks and the swelling.

She leaned over and took me in her arms. She quietly spoke in my ear. "Then we will have to make an appointment at the dispensary for you. You shouldn't be in this much pain." She was the person I needed at that time. She was motherly and comforting...she let me cry and held my head to her chest.

The supportive attitude from Bobby vanished within the week, as he slipped back into a deep depression. This time, it was worse than the others. He arrived home from work on a Friday night, took off his coat and immediately went to the living room and stared out the window for hours. Knowing I had to pull it together because he was not going to, I robotically started dinner. He didn't move. When I called him to tell him it was ready, he didn't respond. I walked up to him and said it to his face, but he didn't even blink. I ate alone. After dinner, I went into the studio to work on a painting. When I emerged at bed time, he was still in the same spot, standing in the dark. I told him I was concerned about him; I still got no response, so I went to bed. When I woke up the next morning, he was sleeping beside me. I got up to take a shower, and when I came out of the bathroom, he was in the same spot again, staring out the window. We had made plans the week before to go into town to shop. After I was finished getting dressed, I asked him if he were coming but still got no response. I went alone. The only thing I bought was a cane. When I got home later that afternoon and saw him still standing there, I got angry. I told him with a very steady voice, "If you are going to act like a hat rack, I am going to treat you like one." I then proceeded to take off my coat and hang it on his shoulder. His spell was broken several hours later, and he acted like nothing had even happened. He asked me how my leg was. I said, "Nothing I can't handle." These episodes of his, as I soon began to call them, occurred at least once a month.

When I went back to work, I was greeted by little faces that were happy to see me. My cane became a fascination to them. It took only a minute to get them to understand its importance. Once they did, they acted as if it were normal. It was one of the things I love about children; they are so accepting and adaptable. I was still grieving inside, but the business of my day helped me get through it. I asked that I not be put in the baby room; I wasn't sure I could hold back the tears. Connie understood. The most difficult thing for me to handle was how other adults dealt with a woman's miscarriage. In their eyes, it had not been a baby yet, so therefore nothing had been lost. They were mostly concerned by the way I now walked. The people around me didn't understand the complexities surrounding the emotions I was having or what my body was going through. I knew the miscarriage and the issues with my legs had to somehow be connected. Other than Connie, I didn't discuss it with anyone.

As is usually the case whenever anyone suffers a loss, there would always be people who would say the wrong thing. The toughest one for me was, "Don't worry. You can try again." I wasn't sure that was true. No one realized that I was not only mourning the loss of this child, but also the potential loss of motherhood altogether. I did call my mother after it happened. Bobby showed me how to work the phone, so that I could call the States. My wanting to talk to her was purely a primal instinct. I felt like a hurt child, and I wanted to hear my mother's voice. I chose not to tell her about the baby. I wasn't sure if she were going to be sympathetic or not. I couldn't bear it if she had lectured me. Her lecturing wouldn't have been about losing the baby; it would have been about trying to have one with Bobby in the first place. I didn't have to worry about that. She had big news herself, news she told me she had been planning to call and tell me that night.

"Barb, I am getting married and moving to Washington State." Her tone was flat. She might as well have been talking about a sale they were having at Almy's Department store.

"WHAT! WHO? WHEN? WHY? I haven't been gone that long!" "Do you remember John? I dated him when we lived on Forrester Street."

I mentally went through all the old photos in my mind and the games my brothers and I would play trying to guess the names of the men in them. Finally she said, "He is the one who gave you that giant doll that was the same size as you at the time."

"Oh, yeah, the one that if you held out its arm, its opposite leg would extend out as well, as if to walk?" "Yes, that's the one." "Oh, I liked him. I remember him being very quiet though. Seems kind of sedate for your liking." "I need sedate right now. How are you doing?"

"I'm ok, arthritis is acting up, but it isn't anything I can't handle." This had become my "go to" line. It would be a phrase I would use for many years.

"Well, I am glad you are not letting it get to you. I will mail you my new address. Talk to you later."

"Ok, good luck." I wanted to say,"break a leg," but although it seemed apropos, it also didn't seem right. I hung up the phone and limped to the couch to put my leg up. I had always thought the people and places back home would remain unchanged, frozen in time until my return. Now my mother was getting married, Doug would be moving into her apartment, and Jake and his wife, Justine, would be living upstairs. My mother had written to me of Jake's marriage, and I had met Justine a few times when they were dating. The times I had seen her she had been cold, so I figured Jake had poisoned her mind about me. He and I didn't stay in touch.

The only one who could truly understand what I was going through was Bobby. After all, it had been his loss too. Even Felicia didn't understand. I didn't blame her; she wanted the old Barbara back, but that girl wasn't there. It was harder to be around Felicia more than anyone else, a constant reminder of what I could have had. When she started getting a belly and had to buy new clothes, I should have needed them too. But I didn't. While she marveled at the new size of her breasts, mine were still small. I knew that over the years, I would look upon her child at different ages and wonder how mine would have looked. I would be reminded of the lost years of my own child every time I saw hers. I tried to not show that being with Felicia was difficult for me. We still had coffee every morning before I went to work. We still met after work for a few hours. She was usually with me when unsuspecting friends asked me the inevitable question, "Why aren't you showing yet?" This was always so difficult for me to handle, because it couldn't be ignored. I would have to tell them, but the words would always get caught in my throat.

One afternoon, when Felicia was about four months pregnant, she asked me to go shopping with her. She wanted to buy some things for the baby, and she wanted my opinions. She still was nervous about the prospect of becoming a mother, and she hoped this would give her some maternal feelings. Without verbalizing it outright, she was asking me for the support that I had promised months before to give her. Knowing this, I agreed to go with her. Inside, I was dreading it. I felt torn; the feelings of knowing this was going to hurt me were very strong. We went to the military department store. It was on a different base from the coffee shop, so we had to take a bus to get there. Because of the dread I was feeling, I was quiet on the bus. I felt Felicia was asking me to do something that would be difficult for me, without any regard for my feelings. She felt it would somehow help me get through this grief faster, like throwing someone in the water to teach them how to swim.

By the time the bus arrived at our destination, I was beginning to resent it. We strolled around the baby section at the back of the room, and Felicia suddenly became animated. She was picking up one tiny item after another, holding them in the air and exclaiming how adorable they were. "Can't you just see a baby in this?" she would say, forcing me to look and imagine. I would simply nod in response. Before long, we met two other pregnant women doing the same thing. Felicia, always outgoing, struck up a conversation with them. They were talking about their pregnancies and the changes that they had experienced, the names they had picked out and the inevitable birth. I just stood there among them, silently knowing I would never know this joy. I walked away; I couldn't stand it any more. I went to the ladies' jeans department and looked for a pair of tight jeans that would look good on me. I didn't find any.

After awhile, Felicia sought me out. The women had left, and she was ready to go as well. When she told me this, I realized that I had gotten myself through this difficult ordeal without breaking down in tears, something I had been sure was going to happen. I was proud of myself and wanted to share this with her. I said, "Well, I think I handled that quite well."

"Actually," she said. "I think you handled it like crap." Her words cut me like a knife. Anger boiled inside of me, surprising even me.

I said, "That's not true. You have no idea what it feels like to be me. I never would have asked you to do what you just asked me to do."

She said, "Look Barbara, if I could give you this baby, I would. I have even thought about it several times. Tim and I are probably going to get a divorce, and then I'm going to have to raise this child alone."

Her words should have made me realize how much she cared about my loss, but instead, it made me think less of her, that she could just give her child away to a friend, like a pair of unwanted jeans.

I said, "It's a good thing you are pregnant, because if you weren't, I would slap you right now!" I walked out the door to catch a bus home.

When I got home, I was fuming. I paced back and forth from room to room, ranting to myself for an hour. It was actually a good thing that had happened that day. It propelled my loss from grief to anger, an emotion that was important for me to experience in order to heal. Even when it was happening, I knew it was for the best. I started to experience the first stage of acceptance. Yet, when Bobby got home an hour later, I got upset all over again. I told him what had happened, and he didn't respond the way I thought he should have. He said, "Barbara, you can't fault Felicia for being pregnant, and you can't avoid every pregnant woman you see. We are on an army base for Christ sake. Every other woman is pregnant. You have to get over this."

I didn't say a thing; I grabbed my cane and hobbled out the door. I headed to the woods. Deep down inside, I knew he was right. I also knew that Felicia was the one pregnant woman I couldn't witness having her baby. Her baby would be too much of a reminder of mine.

CHAPTER: 34

Somehow life went on. I still worked with the children, and I learned to accept the fact that I was going to see women who were pregnant. Yet seeing Felicia was still difficult. Standing at the military bus stop up the street from my house one morning, I met a woman by the name of Karen. She was a few years older than I was, and she was holding a baby. The child's name was Stephanie. Karen and I struck up a conversation that morning. It felt good to meet someone who had no idea of the problems I had just been through, so I didn't tell her. We saw each other every morning, until we coasted into a kind of friendship. One morning, she invited me to her house when I got off from work that afternoon. She said she would have a fresh cup of coffee waiting for me when I arrived.

Karen was nice. She was from Texas and stood maybe five feet tall. She was tiny in stature and always looked like a child holding a child, when her daughter was in her arms. Her hair was pitch black, and her skin was creamy white. One day, I told her if she had been taller she would have been the perfect Snow White. She liked that idea and smiled. She and her husband, Levi, met in high school; they had gone to a school for the performing arts. I thought that was intriguing, because I had never heard of a school like that before.

It was at Karen and Levi's house that I saw my first computer. I was there the day it arrived as a present from her mother back in Texas. It was a keyboard that hooked up to your TV. Karen said it could do so many things, but all I saw it do was play "Pong." Karen was addicted to this game and played it day and night. It was sort of like tennis, with a white dot volleying back and forth from side to side. I understood how a person could get addicted to it, but, at the same time, I couldn't help but think what a waste of time it was. It was because of this game that Karen and I never became as close as Felicia and I had been.

One night, Bobby was with me at Karen's house, and she was showing him how to play the game. Levi was on guard duty, and I was holding Stephanie on the couch. Bobby was pretty good at this game, but Karen was better. She had had more practice. They were laughing and joking and having a good time. It was a rare moment when Bobby was actually getting along socially in a group. A small group, I admit, but it was a start. I felt happy about it, even a sense of pride. Stephanie and I were cheering them on. Karen asked me to go to the refrigerator to get everyone a coke. That was another thing she was addicted to.

Rising from the couch I said, "Come on, Stephanie, let's get the silly grown-ups something to drink." Still too young to really talk, she squealed with delight as I brought her with me into the tiny kitchen. Sitting her in a high chair, I hunted for drinking glasses. Because my hands were too full to carry both Stephanie and the drinks, I left her safe in the high chair, while I brought the glasses into the living room. When I got there, Bobby was not there. When I inquired about him, Karen said that he had gone to the bathroom. Setting the glasses on the coffee table, I went back to get Stephanie. She was delighted to see me and reached for me as I approached her. When we entered the living room again, Bobby was emerging from the bathroom. This time, however, he had a toothbrush in his hand and was brushing his teeth. We all caught sight of him at the same time in disbelief.

I said, "Bobby, whose toothbrush is that?" Karen said, "It's mine." She sounded as if she were disgusted, and I didn't blame her. I said, "Bobby, what are you doing? I wouldn't even want you to use my toothbrush!"

Karen got up and pulled it from his mouth without saying a word. The tension in the room was thick. I turned to Karen and tried to apologize for him. Karen still didn't say anything and went to the barrel that was in the room and threw it away. Then she stood there and turned to us with her hands on her hips and quietly said, "Bobby, I think you need to leave."

I put Stephanie into the playpen that was in the middle of the room. She began to cry. I headed for the door; I was so embarrassed. Bobby followed me, and we walked home through the woods silently. It was my turn not to talk to him for days, but he didn't seem to mind. I swore to myself that I would never bring him to another friend's house again.

Connie and I also started seeing a lot of each other. She never treated me like a subordinate, and I visited her often at her apartment on base. She had three adorable kids: two boys and a girl. Her husband's name was Willie Mayes. I always thought that was cool. He was six feet four inches tall, very large, with a sweet and inviting personality. He was a teddy bear. Connie's younger son's name was Mayes William. He was under a year old. The other two children were preteens. Her older son's name was Jamal, and her daughter was named Candy. Connie's family was perfect. It was the family I had always wished I had had: two loving and nurturing parents who made it their job to teach the importance of family to their children. The result was that the children played with each other daily and liked it. Connie was ten years older than I. She became the wise woman in my life. I looked up to her and respected her opinion on everything. She genuinely liked me, too. We never saw the differences in our skin color.

Bobby and I were beginning to have problems again. He was depressed all the time, and I couldn't get him out of these moods. Connie was the one who I turned to when I felt I had no one to talk to about this subject. She never really had any answers for me, no one could have, but she was always so supportive of my need to vent. When things got too much for me to handle, I always had a place at her house to get away. The children were a wonderful distraction. On one such occasion, I was spending the afternoon with them, when Jamal came running into the room with a video cassette. He was so excited, he could hardly speak. The rest of the family was all gathered there as well. I was sitting on the couch holding Mayes. Jamal had just gotten his hands on the new Michael Jackson "Thriller" video and wanted to put it on the TV to watch at that moment. Willie Mayes was watching a movie on the Armed Forces Network and didn't think twice about turning it off, so as to let his son enjoy his new gift. There was another difference between my family and theirs.

What we all witnessed was music history being made, and we all knew it. We were so isolated from the rest of the United States that we were behind the times, when it came to music videos. Even still, we knew this was something special. The entire family got up and started dancing. It was a wonderful sight for me to see. They were quite good at it. In no time, Jamal had down some of the moves that Michael Jackson was doing on TV. His sister, Candy, was trying to do her best to keep up. Their parents, Willie and Connie, were dancing very seductively with each other. The love between them was evident. Mayes and I were bouncing to the music on the couch and clapping our hands. We were all laughing and smiling and having a good time. I had never seen a family break into spontaneous enjoyment of each other before. I knew it was an important lesson I was seeing. After awhile, Connie lifted Mayes from my lap and started twirling him around the room. Her husband Willie grabbed my hand and started twirling me too. It is one of the happiest memories I have.

A few weeks after the toothbrush incident, Karen called me to see if I wanted to go to a party at her house. I told her I would, as long as I didn't have to bring Bobby. We both laughed. I had a lot of friends in Germany, none of whom liked Bobby, yet they didn't hold it against me. The men were away so much that it was as if the women had their own little community, separate from the military one. This was most evident with the women that lived off base like me. Karen's party was a celebration of her husband Levi's birthday. He was in the same unit as Connie's husband Willie. When Karen invited me, I was half expecting to see Connie and Willie there. I was surprised when I arrived, and they were not.

I didn't know anyone at this party. They were mostly men from Levi's unit. Karen admitted to me that she wanted me there because she didn't want to be the only woman. I wished she had warned me about this little fact ahead of time. Once the party started, I was feeling uncomfortable about being one of the only women among this large group of men. When I wasn't helping Karen with the refreshments, I sat by myself on the couch and didn't talk to anyone. There was a man standing near the door who was doing the same thing. He was just less than six feet tall, with golden, straw-colored hair and blue eyes. He spoke to no one directly. He scanned the room with his eyes, using the same poker face that many officers have. When someone did approach him to say hello, he merely nodded an acknowledgment. He was older than the rest of the men; my guess was that he was in his early forties. No one addressed him by his first name; they all called him "Sir." He wasn't in uniform, so I couldn't tell what his rank was, but the respect that surrounded this man was evident. He intrigued me, and I watched him from out of the corner of my eye.

On one of his scans around the room, his eyes met mine. He stared at me with the look of someone trying to make an evaluation. When he didn't turn away after a few minutes, a shiver ran through my body, and he noticed it. I noticed an ever slight smile adjust at the corners of his mouth and a tiny nod of his head in my direction. My face went flush, and I could tell he saw this as a victory, a point scored. I turned away from him and started to talk to Karen. I didn't ask her any questions about him. He frightened me. I wasn't afraid of what he might do; I was afraid of how he made me feel. I hadn't felt that kind of chemistry in a long time. His power was intoxicating. I tried my hardest to avoid eye contact with him, but I felt his eyes on me the entire evening. After awhile, it was too much for me to take, and I knew I had to leave. Saying my goodbyes, I made my way to the door. When I got to it, he quietly opened it for me and smiled. I said thank you, avoiding his gaze, and quickly exited the room. Out in the cold air, I tried my best to pull myself together. Scolding myself the entire way down the hill to my house, I knew I didn't want to do anything to jeopardize my marriage. I still wanted to make it work. When I arrived home, Bobby was where I had left him hours earlier, in the kitchen gazing out the window.

After a few days, Bobby once again came out of his foggy gloom. He was his old self again, and I thought everything was going to be fine. I always felt that his constant bouts with depression would someday end. It was another sign of how naive I had been back then.

One day, he came home from work with a surprise for me. He had bought us two tickets for a bus tour of Paris. His leave came through and we were to go that weekend. I was so excited; I screamed when he told me and threw my arms around him. That morning when the bus arrived at the base, there were ten other people with us, and the whole time I was concerned that Bobby was going to inadvertently insult one of them. I tried my best to occupy him, so this wouldn't happen. The bus first stopped for a day in Munich. We walked around the city, and I thought about the convention men and the time I had spent with them on the plane. This had been their final destination, and I wondered if they had had fun. Bobby kept insisting that we separate ourselves from the group, so that we could see more. I felt this was rude, because I didn't want to keep them waiting. He told me that if I didn't go with him, he would go himself.

He left me no choice; I dutifully complied. We found ourselves stumbling into a square in the middle of Munich at noon. There were a bunch of people gathered there. They were all looking in the same direction to the top of a clock tower that stood above the center of a wall in the square. It was very high in the air. Bobby asked the man standing next to us in German what everyone was looking at. The man's reply was, "Just wait, and you will see." At the stroke of the last noon bell, two mechanical knights came out from openings in the clock. They jousted each other, and one mechanically fell backwards. Other figures also emerged from the hidden doors on the clock. One was a boy and the other a girl. They curtsied to each other and went on their way. What we saw that day was the Glockenspiel. I had never heard of it until that moment. It was fantastic.

When we arrived in Paris, it was a beautiful day. We still hadn't gotten too chummy with the others on the bus. I had experienced the outcome of Bobby's rudeness too many times in the past, and now I was on the alert for it constantly. We went to see the Eiffel tower, but it was closed for renovations. There was a man selling pieces of it, and that made Bobby mad. He went up to him and told him so. They argued on the street in French; Bobby had studied the language on the bus with an English/French book he had purchased. Once again, he had caught on to it pretty fast, to my amazement. When he and the French man were fighting, I turned around and pretended I didn't know them.

The next stop was the Louvre. We were disappointed when we got there and realized that it, too, was closed. It would have to be on another trip for me to get to see the Mona Lisa. Once the guide realized that our tour was not going as planned, he said that we could split up and explore, but we had to be back in forty-five minutes. He asked that none of us be late. I knew this was too much freedom for Bobby and that he would keep them waiting when it came time to go. I spoke of my concerns to him, and it started a big fight between us. We went off in different directions. I ended up sitting on the steps of the Louvre the whole time, wondering what I was going to say, when he inevitably made them late for our next stop. Just as I had expected, Bobby was late. What I didn't expect was the rest of the bus wondering why I wasn't with him. They kept questioning me as to his whereabouts. After twenty minutes had passed from the time we were supposed to have left, the guide told me they were going to leave without him. I had a choice of staying or going with them. I wasn't sure what I should do. It would not be unlike Bobby to not come back at all. If he didn't, and I chose to stay, I could be stranded in Paris alone. I thought about calling Connie to see if she could wire me some money to get back, because Bobby had all the money we had taken with us on the trip. Before I had a chance to answer, Bobby emerged out of the crowd. He was smiling and nonchalant. He seemed unaffected by the inconvenience he had caused everyone and was commenting on the beauty of the city. The tour guide told him he was late by twenty minutes. Bobby's only response was, "Am I?" Some of the other tourists looked at me with pity. It was embarrassing and made me feel uncomfortable. Bobby and I didn't speak for the rest of the night.

The next day, it was raining. We had a scheduled trip to Versailles. Despite the rain, we were going. This weekend had been so bad that a little rain was not going to make it any worse. I loved Versailles; the gardens were beautiful. I roamed around the neatly trimmed hedges and took photographs of the statues. Bobby had bought me a zoom lens for my camera the previous Christmas. I took it with me everywhere. The pictures I took at Versailles would be the best I had ever taken in my life. This time I wandered off. Knowing how much time I was allowed, I checked my watch. Walking alone down a pea stone path with the mist and fog at my feet and cypress trees on both sides of me, I came to a small opening. The air was heavy with dew; the smell of pine clung to it like an ornament. When I pushed pack some boughs, I was met with the sound of trickling water. I stood in awe, still grasping the branches, when right before my eyes was a golden chariot being pulled by bucking golden horses. It was in the middle of a small pond. It was so huge in comparison to the circumference of the water, that it seemed to appear larger than it probably was. I thought about the genius in this design and slowly lowered myself to the moss covered ground. Once again: art was my God; nature was my church. I sat and gazed at its fine detail, recording every last fold in my mind.

When we got back to the hotel, I told Bobby that I wanted to go to the drugstore that I had seen down the street. He didn't answer me, so I just left. I had a suspicion that I was pregnant again, and I wanted to buy a pregnancy test to make sure. When I got back to the room, he didn't ask me what I had bought. I was relieved by this, because I wasn't ready to tell him. The instructions on the box said I couldn't take the test until the next morning. Hiding it in the bathroom, I figured if it were true, then I would tell him.

Around dinnertime, he seemed normal again. He asked me where I wanted to go to eat. I suggested a small café I had seen next to the drugstore. I had always wanted to sip espresso at an outdoor Parisian café. He agreed that it sounded like a good idea. When we got there, the outside tables had been put in for the night. Clearly, I was disappointed, so Bobby suggested we eat in a very fancy restaurant instead. So we did.

I don't recall the name of the place, but I do remember what it looked like. The main room was filled with gold and chandeliers, and I wondered if we were dressed appropriately. The maitre d` didn't seem to mind how we looked and gave us a table against a wall. It was beautiful and romantic. Bobby took my hand and told me that he loved me. I hadn't heard him say that in awhile, and it gave me hope. The restaurant specialized in fish. I ordered flounder; Bobby ordered snails. What he really wanted was New England steamed clams. He figured this would be the closest he was going to get to them. We were two kids from New England, longing for the taste of home. When our meals arrived, my fish still had the head on it. The sight of it almost made me instantly sick; I couldn't have my food watching me eat it. Bobby started laughing when he saw my reaction. I discreetly placed my napkin over its face. It didn't help. To me, it tasted awful, and Bobby's snails didn't look any more appealing. With every one he scooped out, my stomach flipped. I started feeling the familiar bloatedness and twinges, and I realized, sitting at that table, that I didn't need a test. I knew I was pregnant.

After dinner we went to a night club called "Yellow Submarine." It was located on the same street as the Arc de Triomphe, it was a strange place with a new form of music I had never heard of being played there. It was called punk, and everyone was dressed in outlandish costumes. The dancing was even stranger. I don't think I could attempt to describe it. We only stayed for one drink. Bobby thought the place was hysterical and tried to talk to the people who were there in French. I could only imagine what he was saying. But I figured it was about their clothes and hair, because they were getting irritated. It left me feeling uncomfortable, and, still feeling the effects of dinner, I wanted to go.

When we stepped outside, a light rain was falling. Bobby pulled me into an entryway of an old building to tell me he wanted to start our relationship off fresh. It was the closest thing to an apology he had ever given me since we were married. I couldn't help myself; I told him I thought I was pregnant. He grinned from ear to ear and carried me back to our hotel. The next morning, he was with me in the bathroom when I did the test. It was positive. He looked at me very seriously and told me I had to quit my job. I agreed I would until the baby was born, then he or she would go with me to the center. He agreed.

When we got home, I told Connie the good news. She was happy for me and told me to take it easy. If there was anything I needed, I should feel free to call her. She then asked me how it was going with Bobby. I told her he seemed happy, and I was sure everything was going to be fine. I knew the first three months were crucial. With so many pregnant women on base, you couldn't even see a doctor till after three months anyway. I spent my time at home, quietly reading and drawing.

As every day went by, I felt confident that this time it was going to work. I was warned by Connie not to buy any baby clothes, until I was at least four months along. I was able to hold out until three and a half. It was the longest I had ever carried a baby, and I knew it was a sign. Soon, I went to the PX that Felicia and I had been to several months earlier, when we had had our big fight. I ran into her in the baby department. Her belly was very big, and she was looking at cribs. When she saw me, she seemed glad. I was holding some baby clothes in my hand, and she asked me if they were for me. I was still angry at her, but I told her yes. She congratulated me but felt the distance between us and quietly said good bye. I felt bad after she left, but I made no attempt to go after her.

That afternoon I was tired. Lying down on the twin bed that was in the studio I fell asleep. I was awakened an hour later by a phone call. I stood in the hall, looking at the phone, and was afraid to answer it. Something inside of me told me it was bad news, so I let it ring. The caller was persistent and twenty minutes later, called again. This time, I knew it was from Bobby's father and, without a second thought, picked it up and said, "Hi Dad."

"How did you know it was me?" He sounded distraught. I ignored his question. "Dad I have great news let me tell you…" "Barbara, is Bobby there?" "No, but let me tell you…"

"Barb."

"Dad, you are going to be a grandfather!" The line went silent. I heard him sobbing softly. "Barb, Bobby's mother is dead." This time, it was me, who was quiet. I looked up and saw Shadow Man leaning against the wall just a few feet from me. I whispered, "I know."

"How did you know? Who told you?" "Some things Dad, you can just feel."

Bobby's mom, the sweet woman I loved, was gone. In an instant, she had been killed by a drunk driver. I hung up the phone and stood in the hallway in shock. How could this be? I had just talked to her a week earlier. I loved Bobby's mother; she was so kind to me when we had met. Bobby loved her very much too. It was his father whom he had difficulty getting along with. I had no idea where Bobby was or where to even begin to look for him. It was a Saturday, and he had been acting kind of funny when he had left the house at nine that morning. He didn't even return my goodbye, before he went out the door. More and more, he had periods of time that he would not come home. At first, it was just overnight, and then it was for a few days. I never knew where he was. There was no way for me to locate him. I thought of what this might do to him, knowing it would throw him into a depressed state. I was concerned it would do more. I had no idea how he was going to react, but I knew it would be bad, and I didn't want to be alone with him, when I told him the news. I called Connie and asked if she could help me.

Connie knew exactly what to do. She told me to stay where I was, and she would handle everything. Her husband, Willie, went to Bobby's unit to see if he was there, but he wasn't. He spoke to his commanding officer and told him what was going on. His commanding officer put out a search party for him as best he could with the few men that were still on base. Willie was a part of it, but they still had no luck. Then they all went into town to search the large city of Ulm and the smaller city of Neu Ulm. They still couldn't find him. It was like looking for a needle in a haystack. Knowing Bobby, he could have been in Switzerland, which was only a few hours away, and not planning to come back until the next day. He would do things like that and not tell anyone.

Connie arrived at my house in fifteen minutes time. She must have been racing to get there. To my surprise, she was alone. It was the first time I had seen her without any children in tow, and I asked her who had the kids. She said she had left them with the neighbors. She told me about the search party, and inside I was hoping one of them would tell him, so I wouldn't have to. The more I thought about it, the surer I was that he was going to get violent when he heard the news. In my pregnant state, I didn't want to be the one to tell him.

Connie helped me make the appropriate calls to people on base, in order to get us out of the country on emergency leave. Every person I talked to brought me to a dead end. Because I wasn't the active duty personnel myself and just the DW, I had no jurisdiction to request such a leave. Connie took the phone from me and tried to explain that we couldn't find Bobby, that there was a search going on for him and that time was of the essence. She also said that when we did find him, there was a good chance that he was not going to be in any shape to handle this end of the paperwork. They told her to call his First Lieutenant. I thought of calling my mother, but I didn't want her to worry; besides, she would have been asking me all sorts of questions that I didn't know the answers to yet. I didn't want to have to deal with that too.

While Connie made the calls, I was sitting in the kitchen. Looking around the room, I realized that I needed to prepare the house for our departure. I locked all the windows and threw out all the food that was in the refrigerator. I then grabbed my German dictionary and looked up the word for death. Taking the money that I was going to give my landlord the next week for the rent out of the strong box, I went upstairs to tell them what had happened. It was three in the afternoon. When I came back downstairs, Connie was making the bed I had been sleeping in before I had received the call. She told me to throw some of our clothes into one duffle bag, because we would probably have to do a lot of walking, and she didn't want me carrying it all myself. The only things that fit me were maternity clothes. I was wearing a maternity dress, and I packed only one other for the trip. I figured I would buy more in the States when I got there.

The only thing we had left to do was wait. Willie called us from Bobby's unit at four and told us they hadn't had any luck. Then the First Lieutenant got on the phone and said he had two tickets secured for us on a train out of Ulm to Frankfort. He said we could use them whenever we arrived. He also said that he would drive us to the train station when we were ready. Connie made us a cup of coffee and asked me how long it had been since I had been home. I told her it had been just under two years, that my mother didn't live there anymore and that I wasn't close to my brothers. I said we would more than likely be spending our time in New Hampshire with Bobby's dad. He lived in a trailer park out in the woods, where Bobby's parents had retired. She said it might be best to have Bobby surrounded by a lot of people when we got home, that she didn't trust his behavior in such an isolated area. I agreed. I was glad his dad would be there, although I wasn't sure what kind of shape he was in. He hadn't sounded too good over the phone. I looked at the clock. Connie and I had been talking for an hour; it was now five in the evening, and Bobby had still not come home. I told Connie I was afraid he wasn't going to. She said, "Don't worry. I'll be here for the night, if he doesn't. I'll stay here until he arrives."

At exactly 6:00 PM, he walked through the door. He seemed surprised that Connie was there without the kids. He looked at me and asked what was wrong. He put his keys on the table by the phone. I gently directed him into the living room, while Connie very quietly took his keys. He was standing ten feet away from me; I had purposely put this distance between us. Connie was closest to him, she was standing in the doorway.

"Bobby," I began slowly, "I have to tell you something that I never thought I would have to. Your mom was in a car accident." When he didn't respond, I said, "I'm sorry; she's gone."

The look on his face was that of a person I had never seen. In a split second, he lunged at me from across the room and had his hands on my throat. He was calling me a liar, yelling how cruel it was for me to say such a thing. He threw me against the wall, and I fell to the floor. Connie grabbed him from behind the back of his shirt. Spinning him around, she started shaking him and telling him that he was going to kill his baby, too, if he didn't pull it together. She was taller and larger than he and overpowered him easily. Then she lowered her tone and became the voice of reason, telling him the things that had to be done. He said to her in a quiet voice, "I need to get out of here." She tried to stop him, but he was adamant. Searching for his keys and not finding them put him in an agitated state of mind again. Turning to Connie, he shouted, 'Where are my keys?" Then he calmed his voice and said, "I just want to get something. I'll be right back." She looked over at me. I nodded to her to give them to him. He slammed the door behind him, when he left. Connie asked me, "Do you think he'll be back?" I said, "I don't know." I looked out the window and saw that he was just sitting in our car. He was staring straight ahead and trying to decide what to do. After a few minutes, he came back into the house. Without saying a word he went straight to the duffle bag that was half full. He started throwing every item we had in it, until it was so jammed tight, he couldn't fit any more. I asked him what he was doing, because there was no way we would be able to carry that. He turned to me and said, "We are not coming back." Although I didn't know it at the time, it would be the last words he would say to me for the next three days.

I looked to Connie for guidance. She led me to the kitchen. She told me to let him have his way right then; he needed to feel a sense of control. I went to the phone and called the First Lieutenant of his unit for a ride. When the LT pulled up to our house, Connie and I met him outside. Neither one of us had ever met him before. I told him that Bobby was in poor shape; we had left him sitting in the living room, comatose.

He followed us into the house to help us with our gear. A puzzled look came across his face when he saw what Bobby was taking. He lifted his head to speak to Bobby about it, but when he saw him, he chose to keep quiet. Connie and I each took one of Bobby's arms and gently led him to the door. Placing him in the car, I turned to her and thanked her for all that she had done for me. She patted my belly gently and said, "Just take care of that little baby. Don't lose sight of that." She got into her car and drove off. I wondered if I was ever going to see her again.

CHAPTER: 35

It was eight o'clock at night by the time we arrived at the train station in Ulm. The LT left us sitting on a bench, while he went to get our tickets. He had not spoken a word to either Bobby or me, and I wondered what was going on in his head about the whole situation. When he was standing at the ticket window, he motioned for me to come and speak to him. I knew then that he realized the shape that Bobby was in. Military officers never spoke to the wives of other men, from what I had witnessed, unless they were friends.

"Mrs. McCleary, I want to give you some instructions so that you can both arrive safely; they are somewhat complicated but I have written them down." Showing me the paper in his hand, he pointed to each entry as he continued. "You will board a train here in a few minutes. You will have to transfer to a different train, so you need to be alert. If you fall asleep you could miss it. The stop is about four hours into the ride; so stay awake. This is the name of the stop. That train will take you to Frankfort. Once in Frankfort, you need to report to Rhein-Main, which is located next to the civilian airport. It is a bit of a ways from the train station, so I suggest you take a cab. Here are some German marks, to help you do all this. Once you are at Rhein-Main, you are to report to the military hop building. It is a large open room that is generally crowded. Go up to the desk and sign in. They will tell you what to do from there. Mrs. McCleary, this could take a couple of days. Looking at my belly and then at Bobby sitting across the room, he said, "Are you sure you are up to this?"

I answered, "Yes Sir, I don't feel I have a choice."

"Well, take care, and try to get him to snap out of this state he is in. I am afraid you won't be able to do all this alone. There was an embassy bombing in Beirut and Rhein–Main may be a bit hectic." I wasn't sure what he meant by that. I knew from past experience of being associated with a Pershing Missile base that there were things you didn't inquire about. I was too afraid to ask, and he didn't offer any more information than that. The last thing he said to me was, "Mrs. McCleary, make sure he is back here in two weeks, or we are going after him." I silently nodded that I would. I was scared out of my mind, but I wasn't convinced that I could keep that promise. I walked back to Bobby to help load him on the train.

That was my first train ride in Europe. I was surprised when I noticed the trains looked like they had in every old movie I had ever seen. Nothing on ours was modern; it had wooden sleeping compartments. Walking down the aisle to the right of the compartments, with Bobby's arm supported under my left hand and dragging the duffle bag behind me, I looked for an empty one. They were all full. I put us in the corridor and sat us on the duffle bag. In ten minutes time, a train conductor came by to check our tickets. He told me we couldn't sit in the aisle and made us cram into a compartment which held six other people and a chicken that was in a cage. The seats were folded into the bed position, and everyone was sleeping when we entered it. Only the chicken noted our presence. The people we were sharing the space with were of Turkish decent. It looked like an entire family: a husband and wife with four young children. They had knapsacks tucked under their heads for pillows. I wondered if I was looking at all the possessions they owned. The room smelled terribly of body odor and spicy food. The smell coming from the chicken only added to the mix. My stomach began to flip; from the combination of the rocking of the train and the odors; I was glad I had remembered the Saltine crackers, right before we left the house. I wondered where the bathroom was, in case the crackers didn't work.

Bobby fell asleep the minute we sat down. His head was on my lap, where I sat leaning against a wall. It was the longest ride of my life. I was the only one awake. I was so tired, I wanted to join this band of sleeping strangers, but I was afraid to because of what the LT had told me. Periodically, I pressed my fingers into my eyes to keep them open. The train rocked back and forth into the night. At least two people were snoring; one of them I knew was Bobby. I was glad; I hoped that when he awoke from his slumber that he would also awake from his silent world. The ride went on for hours. I checked my watch every half hour, thinking an hour had passed. It made it feel like it was twice as long. Finally after four hours and with my stomach contents still intact, I woke Bobby. I gently stroked his hair and quietly brought him to consciousness. We stood up, and silently, I gathered our things, so as not to disturb the others. We left the compartment unnoticed. Other than the chicken, the Turkish family didn't even know we had been there.

I helped Bobby off the platform and sat him on a bench with our things. I tried to talk to him. I asked him how he was. He didn't answer and never met my gaze. I went to a ticket window and inquired about our transfer. The woman directed me to the correct location, and I was once again holding Bobby and dragging the duffle back down the aisle of the next train. My legs were hurting real bad. With my hands so full, I couldn't use my cane. I was wondering how on earth I was going to get through this and what kind of shape my joints were going to be in by the time we arrived. I didn't allow myself to think about the baby. When I did it was only to reassure myself that I wasn't alone. This time, I found an empty compartment. I was thrilled and looked to the heavens for a moment to thank God. I laid Bobby on a bench seat, and I sat across from him on the other, staring out into the black night. It was 10:30 PM, and I felt like I had been traveling for a whole day. When the conductor came to check our tickets, I asked him if Frankfort were the last stop the train made. He assured me that it was. When he left, I realized that I had forgotten to ask him how long it took to get there. By the time I got up to look for him in the hall, he was gone.

I was so tired, I was afraid that if I slept, I would sleep right through the stop. I had heard of people doing that from stories that were told to me from others on base. More than likely, the train would pick up other passengers in Frankfort and head back in the direction from which we had come. The conductors never monitored to see if everyone got off; that way they could fine you if you didn't. The thought of this happening to us and ending up back at our last stop was too much for my mind to grasp. Instead, I tried to think of the friends I had not seen from back home and wondered if they were still around. I tried to not think about the reason why we were going home in the first place; I had to keep myself emotionally strong to get us there.

By the time the train rolled into the station at Frankfort, it was about 2:00 AM. I woke Bobby. He had slept the entire way. Dragging him and the duffle bag outside, I was relieved to see several taxicabs lined up at the curb out front. I walked over to one, and the driver placed our things in the trunk. It was a five minute ride to Rhein-Main, just as LT had told me it would be. I don't remember much about how it looked. It was late, and I was tired. I do remember seeing the large sign outside that read "RHEIN- MAIN." It was a beacon of hope to me.

I went up to the front desk and waited in a long line. Even though it was such an early hour, the place was packed. Everyone was American, most were soldiers in uniform. The LT was right; it was chaotic. People were running around, and the place had a sense of organized confusion. The line to the information desk was at least forty people deep. It took twenty minutes until it was finally my turn. I said we were heading home on emergency leave, and I gave my name and Bobby's ID number. The attendant, who was a female military soldier, told me we had to report to another building that was two doors down. I asked her what to do when we got there. She told me we had to wait in another line, and they would put our name on a list.

At the other building, the chaos was worse. I walked into what looked like a mob. The noise level for such an early time of the morning struck me first. Everywhere you looked in the room, there was at least one screaming baby. The looks on everyone's faces were that of fatigue and helplessness. I was sure I looked the same. We were all here for the same reason; we needed to get home in a hurry. There were over tired children running around, and mothers and soldiers were doing their best to keep their wits about themselves. It was hard to distinguish where the line began. I had to stand there for a few minutes, just to figure it out. It was set up like a bank, with a desk that held a row of service people in stations behind it. They were all in uniform, and there had to be at least ten of them. The line was single file. It snaked around the entire room and was at least two hundred people deep. I knew I couldn't drag Bobby through this maze of people, so I propped him up in a corner near the desk, sitting him on the duffle bag, and stood in line alone. My legs were aching, and I began to get worried. I was in a state of profound exhaustion. Unlike the joint pain, this was muscular. It was the same type of pain that had always signaled that something was not right with the baby. I tried to convince myself it was because I was so tired. I stood in that line for hours. By the time it was my turn, the sun was starting to rise. I knew that in a little while, I would have been up for twenty-four hours. I was relieved to get a woman behind the desk. I explained the reasoning for the emergency leave, and she seemed sympathetic. She told me, however, that I was not allowed to do the paperwork myself, since I was not the person who was on active duty. I became desperate and started pleading my case. I told her I had been traveling for twelve hours with a husband who was in shock. I pointed to him in the corner and asked her if she would please let me sign his name. When she saw him, she asked me if I wanted to have her call medical personnel. I told her that I didn't, that he suffered from depression a lot and what I really needed to do was get him home. She looked around to see if anyone was looking and quietly slid the paper across the desk. She said the wait could be a day and wanted to know if I needed a room. I asked her what would happen if they called our name, and we were in our room. She said that we would miss the plane and start the whole process all over again. I told her we would just wait where we were. She said, "I'll keep an eye on you." I thanked her and went to join Bobby. I turned and looked at her face when we sat down. She was still looking at me. I smiled and placed her in the scrapbook next to the German policeman.

At four that afternoon, she approached me with the news that she could squeeze two people on a cargo freight. She said they usually didn't put civilians on this type of flight, but she had told them about our situation, and they had complied. She told me it would be uncomfortable, but it was the best she could do; otherwise we would have to wait at least seven more hours. I told her we would take it. Going to the transport that would take us to the plane, I was greeted by some Air Force men who were expecting us. One took my duffle bag and another helped me with Bobby. The scene was all too similar to the time long ago in New York, on that snowy night when my family was going to Virginia.

The plane was huge, without any seats inside. Along the two walls were long benches that held shoulder straps to buckle us in. There were no cushions on the benches, just cold wood. Everything was painted OD green. The walls were curved, with no insulation to speak of. The rivets that held the plane together could be clearly seen from the inside. It looked like what you would see in an old army movie, where the paratroopers would sit before they jumped to their destinations over enemy territory. The noise was so loud inside the plane that anyone talking had to shout to be heard. They handed me earplugs instead of the complimentary peanuts. I wished I had had some gum; my ears needed to pop for the entire flight.

It was obvious that I was pregnant, and the men were all so kind; besides Bobby and myself, there were only four other men inside the cargo bay with us. I was surprised by how few people were on such a very large plane. They told me if I had to go to the bathroom that they would help me to the men's room. They didn't have a ladies' room. The cargo bay was about 30 feet wide and 60 feet long. We never saw the cockpit. The bay was filled with boxes stacked to the ceiling and stretched from the front of the plane all the way to the back, strapped down by thick running cables, tying them all together, so they wouldn't move when the plane took a turn. The cargo consisted of the belongings of military personnel who were heading back to the States, but there also were wooden crates, which were directly in front of my feet. They had letters stenciled on them which said "The human remains of" and then the name. They were lined up along the edges of the other boxes. I inquired as to why there were so many bodies, at least eight of them. One of the soldiers told me it was because of the bombing in Beirut. I flew for eight hours with these poor souls at my feet. I tried not to think about them, but I couldn't help it. I wondered about their lives and what was lost.

During the flight, one of the soldiers asked me if I thought Bobby was ok. I told him that I wasn't sure and asked him where we would be landing when we got there, trying to change the subject. He told me the plane would land in Dover, Delaware, and I could catch a flight to Logan from there. I began to panic; I hadn't thought of how to get home with no money. Listening to my dilemma, he told me that they were flying to Pease Air Force base from Dover. Since that was near Bobby's parents' house, I asked if we could catch that ride as well. He told me he would check and left me sitting alone with Bobby and the dead bodies. Looking at the crates once again, I saw Shadow Man sitting on one comfortably in the darkness. A few minutes later he returned with the news that they wouldn't let me take the connecting flight because I was only a DW. I told him that I would call Bobby's father in the morning to wire us the money. The entire flight I was ill. They gave me a box lunch with a ham sandwich in it and some chips and a carton of milk. After I ate it I promptly lost it in the men's room. The guys felt helpless for me and expressed their concerns. I reassured them, "It's nothing I can't handle." I was actually talking to myself every time I used this phrase...in hopes I would make it so.

When we landed at Dover Air Force Base, it was four in the morning, because of the time change. We got on a bus that was provided by the military to take us to the airport. The first thing that struck me when I arrived on American soil was the fact that I could read again. We drove down a long street filled with businesses and neon signs. It was a comforting feeling. When we arrived at the terminals they were all closed. The entire airport was shut up tight with only access to the hallways. We were allowed to sit in the halls, so I once again propped Bobby up against the wall with the duffle bag and sat next to him. A man was sweeping the floors next to where we were sitting. I asked him when the airport would open, and he told me the terminals wouldn't be open until six. After awhile, I couldn't sit there anymore. My legs were hurting, and I was in desperate need of peeing. I went in search of a ladies' room.

Walking down the hall, my whole body began to shake. I knew it was from the lack of sleep and the fact that I hadn't eaten anything but a few crackers since lunch the day before. The sandwich I had was certainly not in me long enough to have been of any nutritional value. I sat down on a chair and began to cry. It was the first time I had felt I had the luxury to do so. I couldn't believe that I was back in the United States; my mind was having a hard time accepting it. The last time I had risen from my bed I had been on German soil. I had a humming in my ears that wouldn't go away. It was the kind of noise in your head you experience from a great fatigue. I knew I couldn't call Bobby's dad until much later, so the tears I was shedding flowed even stronger; I couldn't control them. At one point in my grief, I looked up and saw a door that had a sign that read "Salvation Army." I thought of the men who rang their bells at Christmas. Slowly I got up and knocked on the door. I thought maybe they had some coffee and crackers.

A woman around the age of sixty-five opened it. She stood five feet tall and had white hair and greeted me with an angelic smile. Before I could say a word to this woman, who appeared to have been sent from God, I fainted on the floor. When I woke up, I was lying on a bed she had in a separate room.

"Where is Bobby?" My voice was desperate and frantic.

"I didn't know there was anyone with you. What is your name, my dear?"

"My name is Barbara. My husband, Bobby, is in the terminal, sleeping on a duffle bag. He is in a bad way. Someone needs to help him." She made a phone call and told me not to worry; she would take care of him. Watching her shuffle out of the room, the last thing I heard was the scuff of her feet in her soft-soled shoes and the delicate ruffles of her cotton dress. I felt as if I knew her. She seemed familiar and loving. It was a feeling of home. In this state of confusion, I fell soundly asleep. I called out a minute later, "Sherry, come quick, I need your help. I can't find my way." Shadow Man sat at the foot of the cot. He reassuringly touched my feet.

When I awoke again several hours later, it was my sense of smell that had aroused me. Opening my eyes, I saw the older woman sitting very close to me in a chair. In her hand was a cup of freshly brewed coffee. She helped me to a sitting position by gently supporting my back. "It's decaf," she said. "I hope you don't mind. I thought it was best, considering the baby and all."

I eagerly took the cup from her hand and thanked her. "Where is Bobby?" I asked, concerned as reality started seeping its way back into my brain like a slow acting poison.

"He is in the bed in the other room. I wanted to call a doctor. He appears to be in shock, although he did get up and follow us when we told him to. I told him you were with me and had him see for himself that you were ok and sleeping. Where did you two come from?"

I told her about the events of the previous day: the phone call, the search for Bobby, his reaction when we told him, the train ride with the Turkish family and their chicken, the long wait at Rhein-Main, the military cargo flight that held the dead bodies of the Americans killed in Beirut, and about our arrival in Dover with no money to get to Boston. She listened to me intently, rubbing my hand as I spoke. I felt like Dorothy from The Wizard of Oz, talking to her uncles when she awoke from her dream in her bed. But unlike Dorothy, my nightmare was not yet over. Patting my arm gently, she told me to wait for one moment; she had to make an important phone call. Sitting on the end of the bed, I wondered what the Salvation Army was. I had seen the bell ringers, and I knew they collected money for charity, but until this day, that was all I knew about them.

Returning a short while later, she held up two tickets in her hand. "Here you are, honey. I reserved you two seats on a flight to Boston. It leaves in an hour."

I was in shock. Who was this kind lady? I said, "I can't accept your money; I don't even know you, and you have been so kind to me already."

"Oh honey," she said, "I am the Salvation Army. This is what we do---save people who are in need. It seems to me you are very much in need."

"How can I pay you back? What can I do to thank you?"

She looked at me with a warm and comforting smile and said, "The next time you pass a bell ringer at Christmas, just remember us."

I promised I would. Every December to the delight of the clueless bell ringers, I throw a large bill into their pot, repaying the price of those tickets many times over and remembering the kind lady who had helped us. My scrap book was getting bigger.

As I hugged her good bye and she closed the door, I knew my next step had to involve getting someone to pick us up at Logan. It was 8:00 AM, and the sun was shining brightly outside the terminal windows. I felt rested and had a new-found strength. I dragged Bobby to the nearest phone booth. I knew that it might be too much to ask Bobby's father to drive down from New Hampshire. I thought of calling his sister, when I realized that she was more than likely with her dad. My next choice would have been a friend of Bobby's, but I didn't know any of their phone numbers. Closing my eyes, I called my brother Doug. He worked the night shift at the hospital, and I knew he would be home and still up. When I got him on the phone, I was surprised he had not heard the news about Bobby's mother. I told him we were coming home and needed a ride from Logan.

"When will you be arriving?" he asked. "We should be there in a little under two hours." "Two hours!" he said in disbelief. "Where are you now?" "We are in Delaware," I said. "We have been traveling all night." "I'll be there" he said. He sounded tired.

I got Bobby on the plane. He sat in the window seat; I sat on the aisle. I couldn't believe we were on another plane, but at least this one had comfortable seats. I was really getting worried about Bobby. I wasn't sure how my brother was going to handle the fact that he was in the state he was in. I knew Doug would get angry at him, so my thoughts became centered on that. For the past two years, I had been Bobby's advocate. When he had been rude to people, I was the one who apologized. When he said things that were unintentionally cruel, it was I who made excuses for him. Now, my dilemma was that I knew that Doug would see his behavior as weak, no matter if Bobby's mother were dead or not.

The flight felt shorter than I thought it would. I couldn't tell if it was because I was preoccupied with the thoughts that were taking over my mind or the fact that every other mode of transportation we had taken in the last twenty-nine hours had been so long and tedious. As the plane taxied into the terminal, I turned to Bobby and said, "Ok, honey, we made it. I don't know how we did it, but we got here." I didn't expect a response; unfortunately, the one I did get threw me into another panic.

Bobby turned to me, as sober as the day he was born, and said, "I'm not getting off the plane."

Now I was the one in shock. I had just dragged his ass across an ocean for three thousand miles with dead bodies and no sleep, concerned about him every step of the way, and the whole time he could have talked to me and helped me, if he had wanted to. I got angry. As the entire plane was exiting, I quietly walked up to the nearest stewardess and told her my husband was being unreasonable, refusing to get off the plane. I made no excuses for him and did not apologize for him. I had had enough (from my mother's lips to mine). The stewardess went to get some assistance from the pilot and copilot. The three of them told Bobby that he had to get off the plane, because it was taking off shortly for Chicago. He said he wasn't moving. They turned to me and asked if there were anyone waiting for us who might be able to reason with him. I told them I would get him and be right back.

Running down the ramp and into the terminal I saw my brother talking to another stewardess from our flight. He had been worried when we hadn't gotten off the plane and was inquiring as to whether we had even gotten on the flight. She hadn't had time to answer him before I burst into view. We didn't have time for any airport greetings or hugs hello, because I immediately told him what was happening. The first thing I heard Doug say, after not having spoken to him in two years, was, "That immature son of a bitch." Not a good choice of words, I thought, considering why we were home in the first place. Then he said very sternly to me, "Sit in that seat and don't move. I'll be right back." He and the stewardess raced back into the plane.

In less than five minutes, they emerged. I don't know what Doug had said to him, but it had been effective. Bobby walked off that plane as if nothing had even happened. He still looked sad about his mother's death, but his eyes were blinking normally again, and he was looking around to see where I was. Meanwhile, Doug looked like he wanted to kill him. Although I should have thought of it earlier in our relationship, it was the first realization I had that perhaps Bobby was mentally ill.

CHAPTER: 36

When we arrived at Doug's house, Bobby called his dad. His dad was happy we had made it home safely and wanted Bobby and me to stay with him in New Hampshire. Maureen offered to come down and get us.

I knew it wouldn't take long for her to get there, coming from just over the border of Massachusetts in Salem, New Hampshire. I said, "Boy, I can't wait to see you."

When I hung up the phone, Doug told me to call Mom in Washington State, because she would want to know that we were home. I had thought of doing this myself but wanted to wait until Bobby had left the room to ask Doug if I could use the phone in his bedroom. Doug had moved into my mother's apartment when she had gotten married, which made it weird for me to call my mother's old bedroom his. It was strange to see Doug's things in my mother's house. When I reached my mother and told her what had happened, she was sympathetic. She told me to tell Bobby she was sorry; she was going to send flowers. She then asked how I was feeling, so I lied and said I was ok. Then I told her I was pregnant. There was a pause on the end of the line. Then she said, "Be careful, make sure you rest." I thought she was going to tell me that she would fly home to see me. She didn't.

When I returned to the kitchen, Doug looked at my belly and said, "So how far along are you?" I replied, "A little over four months." "Well, I think you should stay here and let Bobby go to New Hampshire. If you need to get to a hospital, you will be too far from Boston. Besides, I can take care of you." Doug was always nurturing like that. I really wanted to stay, but I knew my place was with my husband at this time. "How are your joints and legs? I see you are using a cane." "I'm ok, it's nothing I can't...."

"Don't give me that bullshit, Barb; I know you better than that. You are in hell. I see it all over your face and in your posture. I am going to tell you right now, if I hear that you are having even the slightest issue, physically or otherwise, I am coming to get you and drag you back here myself."

"Ok," I said slightly irritated. I should have felt his love but instead I felt like a child. Bringing myself back to reality, I asked, "Where is Bobby?"

"He is sitting on the front porch, waiting for Maureen."

"Doug I am sorry; if I felt I could stay, I would. I would much rather be here." He walked over to me and put his arms around me. "Barb, you are my sister. I love you and worry about you."

"Doug, there is something I need to tell you. I had a miscarriage earlier this year. I'm scared."
"So that's two now. You shouldn't have flown."

"I didn't have a choice. You see the shape he is in. He was much worse twenty-four hours ago." We talked this way for twenty minutes, and then Bobby came in to get me, because his sister was waiting out front. I said goodbye to Doug. I wanted to thank him for not harping at me about Bobby refusing to get off the plane, but I didn't know how. Instead I just kissed him on the cheek and closed the door behind me.

When we walked through the door of Bobby's parents' home, it was evident to me that this visit was going to be difficult. His father was in rough shape, and it was obvious he had been crying after Maureen had left to pick us up. The minute Bobby saw his dad, he burst into tears. The two of them were crying so hard that I wasn't sure what to do. Maureen had left to make some last minute arrangements for the wake, so I was alone with these men in pain. I knew that crying was good for them, so I left them alone in the living room and went into the kitchen to see if I could find some Kleenex for them and maybe make them a cup of coffee.

Bobby's parents lived in the woods. Looking out the kitchen window on that October tenth, I couldn't help but notice that the autumn leaves were at their peak, and the day was warm with bright sun. I had forgotten how beautiful it was around there in the fall. Hearing the sobs coming from the next room, I suddenly felt guilty for having been thinking of something other than the issue at hand. I found some tissues and headed into the living room, balancing the coffee. I placed it all on the table in front of the couch, sat next to Bobby's father and gave him a big hug. He was pleased to see me and told me that he loved me. I wondered when I had last heard that from Bobby and realized it was in Paris. The time we had spent there now seemed like years ago.

Bobby's father gave us the details of the accident. He said it had happened at 6:00 AM, right in front of Boston Hill on old Route 1. She had been driving to the Hogan Regional Center in Danvers, where she had worked with mentally handicapped children. That was where Alex's sister lived, and I quietly wondered if they had known each other. If they had, I knew that she would also be upset by this news. I felt bad.

He told us the guy who had hit her had been drunk at 6:00 AM! He said it hadn't been his first offense, and he couldn't believe that he had been allowed to drive. She had been killed on impact; there was nothing anyone could do.

Hearing the story, my head started to spin, and my stomach started to flip. I still hadn't eaten, so I asked them if they wanted me to make them some breakfast. They both thought it was a good idea, and I left the room. My legs were still hurting, and I was desperately trying to convince myself that it was just from the traveling. It was difficult for me to stand at the stove. Somehow I managed and got us all fed. After we had eaten, Bobby asked his dad if he could borrow his car. He didn't tell him he wanted to see where his mother had died. He wanted me to go with him. I felt torn by this, not wanting to leave either man alone. I told Bobby that we should stay with his dad and do it another time, but he was insistent, and his dad said he would be ok. So we left.

We drove slowly down old Route 1 until we finally found the spot. There were no skid marks on the road, no signs that anyone had tried to stop. Glass was everywhere from the broken windshield. There was a black stain on the ground, and I knew it had been blood. Bobby sat down on the curb at the side of the road and began to cry. I wanted to comfort him, but he said he wanted to be left alone. I walked to the other side of the curb. I looked up at the numerous trees that lined the road. They displayed a golden yellow, bursts of orange and a spotting of deep red. I thought it was a beautiful place to die. I felt the angels in heaven were still present in these surroundings. It was a spiritual moment for me, and I took a picture of it in my mind. Years later, I painted those trees and the image I remembered. I called it, simply, "October Ninth."

The next morning we all got up and were getting ready for the wake. I noticed that Bobby's dad was having trouble figuring out how to use the iron, so that he could press his shirt. I immediately stepped in to help but it was becoming more difficult for me to stand. My legs were getting worse. Bobby and his Dad were in the living room while I was in the bedroom ironing. Suddenly, I heard his father say, "Bobby, Jesus Christ, are you ever going to grow up? Don't start putting on that act with me... not right now!" I didn't hear Bobby say anything and wondered if he were staring out a window. I never found out, because I chose to stay out of it, remaining in the bedroom. After awhile, when it appeared that things were ok out there, I entered the living room and gave his father his shirt.

When we were all ready, we drove silently to the funeral parlor. I was wearing the other maternity dress that I had bought in Germany. It felt good to finally shower and change. When we arrived, Maureen and Bobby's brother, Patrick, were already there. It was the viewing for just the family, so we were alone. His mother looked awful in the casket, she was swollen twice her size. I thought about this gruesome ritual and wondered why people still did it, since I knew it would be an image that would remain forever in Bobby's head. It certainly stayed in mine. Everyone was crying and trying to support one another. I was most concerned about Bobby's father. The funeral director gave him a sedative, and we all sat down in a fog and waited for others to arrive. In less than an hour, the place was packed, including many people from where she worked. I couldn't believe how many lives she had touched; Bobby and his family expressed the same feeling. No one had realized that her circle of friends had stretched so wide. We were all touched by this comforting fact, most evident by the amount of flowers taking up most of the room. I noticed those that were sent by my mother were one of the bigger bouquets.

At noontime we all went out to lunch. The evening showing was later that night, and Maureen felt it was important to make sure her father ate something and didn't go back to the house. It was a good idea. After lunch, we went to Maureen's house instead, watching the clock tick slowly by as we waited for the time that we had to return.

That evening, a lot of Bobby's friends showed up, some of whom I had never met. They all tried their best to console him. I stood there next to him as the dutiful wife, not saying a word; most didn't even acknowledge me. That was fine; I wouldn't have known what to say anyway. As the night wore on, so did the pain in my legs. I was standing the whole time with the rest of the family in the receiving line. I wanted desperately to sit down but felt it would appear rude. I was shifting from leg to leg, when after an hour and a half; I felt an all too familiar trickle run down my inner thigh. I closed my eyes and said, "Please, God, not this one too." I whispered to Maureen to join me in the ladies' room; I was afraid I might be losing the baby. By the time we had pushed past the people and found the rest room, blood was running down my leg and stopping at my knees. I went into a stall to see how bad it really was. I didn't want to sit on the toilet, because I didn't want my baby to miscarry into it. Instead, I stood in the stall, closed the door and cried. Maureen felt we should get me to a hospital. I said, "It's no use; there's too much blood. They can't save him."

All at once, a pain shot through me. It was stronger than any other time I had lost a baby. It went straight up my legs and into my cervix. My uterus was contracting, and I knew I was in labor. I put the seat down and sat on the lid, bending over to try and relieve the pressure as best I could. It didn't help. I let out a gasp, and Maureen tried desperately to enter the stall, but I had it locked. She rattled on the door and told me to let her in. I knew that I had blood all over my dress, and I told her I needed to get to the hospital. Opening the door, I stepped out into the ladies room and immediately had another contraction. Maureen sat me in a seat and told me she would tell the others. When she returned, Bobby was with her, and they helped me to the car. Walking through the crowd of people, it was obvious what was happening to me by the blood that was now all over my dress. I tried not to look at any of them.

When we got to the hospital, I was immediately seen by a doctor, the bleeding having slowed a lot, after they laid me down on a stretcher. He examined me and said that I was, in fact, in labor. He said that the contractions could have been brought on by all the stress, and he wanted to give me an ultrasound. Ultrasounds had only been in use for a few years, and this was the first time I had ever had one. The technician turned the screen so that I could not see what she was looking at. I probably wouldn't have understood it anyway. When the doctor returned with the results, he said that the baby was not right: the development was off, and I was going to miscarry. He said it would have been inevitable in a few weeks, regardless of where I had been or what I had been doing. He said the entire process could take a few days, to go home and let nature take its course. When the bleeding got heavy, he wanted me to return to the hospital so he could check on me.

I told Bobby that I wanted to be at my brother Doug's house, that this would be too much for his father to have to handle. He agreed. I also told him that I wanted to be there alone. He needed to be with his father, and I would call him if I needed him. I knew that Doug would take good care of me. He had always taken care of our cuts and bruises when we were little. He was a surgical technician and had been through all the same training as a nurse and more. He assisted in heart operations at the hospital where they had just taken me, and I felt confident in his care. I asked the doctor if they could page him for me, since I knew he was at work that night. In seconds, he was there. Alone in the room with him, I cried into his chest. He rubbed my hair and told me not to worry; he would be with me the whole time. "Oh Doug, why does my body always seem to fail me?"

"I don't know honey, but it sure does seem that way, doesn't it? Right from the day you were born and a few days later you had to go back to the hospital for that operation."

"What operation?" "The one involving your intestines; didn't Mom ever tell you about that?" "No."

"It is why you had such trouble keeping food down as a kid." I sat there in silence. So much was going through my head. I wasn't ready to ask any more questions. I didn't want to know the answers. He took me home and placed me in my old bedroom. It was the only thing in the house that hadn't changed. The pain became more unbearable as every hour passed. It was impossible for me to sleep that night. I told Doug to put towels under me, so that I wouldn't soil the mattress on my canopy bed.

By morning, I knew that this was the day that I would lose another baby. I was just over four months, and the labor was stronger because of this. Doug showed me how to breathe and sat by my bed the whole morning. I thought it was weird that he was playing the role of midwife. He had always been more like a woman in that way, especially as he had gotten older and better at nurturing. This would be the first time I had experienced this. At 9:30 AM, the pains were getting worse, and Doug told me it wouldn't be long. I wasn't bleeding more than before, at one point stopping altogether. Doug was mopping my forehead with a damp cloth when Bobby entered the room. As soon as we saw Bobby, I was sure we both felt the same thing. We didn't want him to be there; we were both doing fine on our own. The last thing we needed to do was have to deal with him. When he saw the shape I was in, he said, "Ok, Doug, you can go now. I will handle this." Doug immediately started yelling at him, dragging him from the room. I could hear them arguing in the kitchen. They were at a standoff; Doug wouldn't let him in the room with me, and Bobby wasn't leaving.

Suddenly, a pain shot through my entire body. When I opened my eyes, all I was seeing was images in black and white. I let out a scream, and the two of them came running into the room. This pain wasn't going away like the other contractions had. It felt like the baby was stuck. I could feel it between my legs. I told Doug what was happening, ignoring Bobby altogether. He said he was going to bring me to the hospital, but first he was going to call the emergency room. Bobby stood in his way and said that the doctor had told him we were to go to the hospital when the bleeding was bad, and we would wait until then. Without saying a word, Doug threw him against the wall and out of his way. He went to the phone and called the ER. When he came back to the room, I could no longer talk. I thought I was going to faint, when he tried to lift me from the bed. My legs didn't work, and the room started to spin. I told Doug I wasn't going to make it, certain I was dying. My color vision had not returned. Doug yelled to Bobby to give him a hand, and together they got me into Doug's car. I fell in and out of consciousness all the way to the hospital.

When we got there, Doug told Bobby to handle the paperwork. He and another nurse got me on to a stretcher. Seeing the pain I was in, the doctor threw a sheet over me and examined me as they were wheeling me down the hall. He stopped the stretcher, turned to Doug and told him I needed an emergency D&C. They turned the stretcher in the direction of the elevator, as a nurse ran to alert the OR.

In the elevator, the doctor tried his best to explain what was happening to me. He said my cervix had opened but then closed again, trapping the fetus halfway out. The whole time he was talking to me, he was placing his gloved hand between my legs. With the same swiftness as a magician's slight of hand, he pulled at the fetus and removed it. In a second, my baby was rolled up in his glove and in his pocket. When the elevator door opened, there was a nurse waiting to give me a shot. In a second, my world faded to black. When I opened my eyes an hour later, my baby was gone, and my mother was at my side. Doug had apparently called her when I had first started losing the baby. She was a comforting sight.

"Mommy," I said through tears, "I am such a failure."

"No you aren't, sweetheart; God just didn't think it was time for you to be a mother yet." It was brief, yet it was the most tender conversation she and I had ever had.

The remainder of our two weeks at home was a blur for me. I was getting used to the idea that I was never going to be a mother, and more importantly, I knew that I didn't want to have children with Bobby. As a matter of fact, I finally knew in my heart that this marriage was not going to last. My mother just harped at me the whole time I was home about the bad decision I had made in marrying him. She kept telling me I should stay and let him go back alone. I needed to get back to Germany. I had made a promise to the LT that I would bring Bobby back, and I was going to do my best to ensure that this would happen.

One night, when Bobby seemed less fragile than previous nights, I asked him the inevitable question I had been dreading.

"Bobby, how should we get back home?" I felt calling it home made it seem more inviting and a reality. "I don't know Barb, I haven't given it much thought."

"Well, I was thinking, since I can't fly a military hop in the states, maybe you should fly hop, and I will go commercial, so as to save some money."

"No, we will both fly commercial. Don't worry about the money." There I had it... his acknowledgment that he was planning on going back.

"I am glad we will be flying together. I don't like flying alone." I thought to myself, despite the last time when we were together, I felt so alone. I decided to leave that thought to myself. Instead, I said, "I will call the airlines."

The flight across the ocean was uneventful. We were both quiet and lost in our own worlds or torment. The entire way I wondered how it would end. Would there be a big fight? Would he become violent? Would he stand in the living room and stare out the window? The fact that I had absolutely no idea as to how to judge his behavior only enforced in me that I was doing the right thing. Because of this uncertainty I knew the timing had to be just right. We pulled into the train station in Ulm, leaving behind the losses we both felt. Stepping into the German night air, I realized that it felt good to be home. 'Home" had always felt like a transitional word to me in the past. I knew now that no matter what happened between Bobby and me, this would be the place I would stay.

The next day was a Monday. Bobby went back to work, and I went to see Connie and all the children at the center; they were all so happy to see me; the sight of them brought joy to me as well. It wasn't hard to look upon their little faces; I was getting used to the idea of not being a mother. Knowing I would soon no longer be a wife helped me in that area as well. Connie and I sat together in her office. She wanted to know all about what had happened back home, but first she looked at my belly and could tell I was no longer pregnant. I looked at her and said, "Its ok. I guess, after awhile, you get used to it." All she could say was how sorry she was. That night, Felicia called me. She had run into Bobby, and he had told her that I had lost the baby. He asked her to call me; he felt bad that we didn't speak to each other anymore. I was cold to her when she called. She did most of the talking. After awhile, I told her I had to go and hung up the phone. It was awful of me, I know, but I just wasn't ready.

CHAPTER: 37

One day, when I was rummaging through embroidery floss at the PX, I met a woman on base, named Sara. Sara was married to a guy named Josh, who was in Bobby's unit. Sara was tall with brown hair, from the mountains of North Carolina. That's where she had met Josh; they had been high school sweethearts, as well. Every couple I had met seemed to have this same MO. They were young, had dated in high school and had found the military to be an easy way to get started in a life together. They all seemed to be handling it well; only Bobby and I were having difficulty. Sara was a few years older than I. Back in the States, she had been a home economics teacher. I admired her for having her degree and wondered why she hadn't used it here. Sara had other plans. Her job here was to get pregnant. She was pretty good at it; a short while after I met her, she was.

I became Sara's shoulder to lean on; with my history of difficult pregnancies, I worried about her all the time. She seemed to take it in stride. We were together a lot. She knitted baby clothes, and I, still not ready to walk away, talked with her about ways that I might improve my relationship with Bobby. I felt I had made a commitment, and until I was absolutely sure I had done everything, I needed to forge forward. Sara didn't have a car either, so together we would take the bus to base and do laundry. She lived in military housing, so she had laundry facilities, but she went with me anyway. Together, we shopped at the commissary, and she taught me how to cook. Sara also had a sewing machine and helped me make a dress. I wanted it to be a special one that would please Bobby. We had gone to the PX and bought everything I needed; I chose burgundy colored cotton. The dress design was simple. It had to be in order for me to be skilled enough to make it. It had a square collar with capped sleeves, was cinched at the waist and went down to my knees. It reminded me of the dresses my mother had worn when I was little. Subconsciously, I'm sure that's why I had chosen it.

It took me over a month to make it. Sara helped me every step of the way. She was good at her craft, and, if it weren't for her, I don't think I ever could have finished it. The whole time we worked on it, we laughed and talked, mostly about the baby. She was only two months along, and she wanted a boy. She already knew his name would be Danny. The entire time I was sewing my dress, she was knitting booties. At every stage, I would strip down in her living room and try it on. I was so proud of it, I could have burst. It was a wonderful way to pass the time, and Sara and I got along great. The whole time we knew each other, we never fought. But she wasn't Felicia, and I knew I was really looking for a replacement. One day I realized how unfair that was and began to enjoy Sara for who she was, a woman who was more mature in her marriage than anyone I had met so far who was that young. She was a good influence on me. One day, when we were working on our projects, we were talking about motherhood and what defines a good mother.

"You know what I always wanted my mother to do when I was a kid?"

"What's that?"

"I begged her all the time to make Rice Krispy treats, every time the commercial came on TV."

"Oh those are easy. Did she ever make them?"

"No."

Sara said in her thick southern drawl, "Well, honey, we are just going to have to do something about that, aren't we? Get your coat."

"Where are we going?" I replied, shutting off the sewing machine.

"To get a box of Rice Krispy's cereal, you silly girl. No child should miss experiencing that delight at least once in her life. And if you're really good, we'll also get the ingredients for caramel popcorn."

It took us two hours to catch the buses we needed to get to the commissary and back with our loot. By the time we were ready in Sara's magical kitchen, I was like a kid in a candy store. We baked long into the night. First we made the Rice Krispy treats, and they were even better than I had ever imagined. After that, we made the caramel popcorn. That night when I went home, my arms were filled with a pirate's booty of delectable treats you couldn't buy in any store in Germany.

Eventually, Sara helped me finish the dress. When I put it on for the first time after its completion, I wasn't pleased with it. It was sewn perfectly; it wasn't that. It just felt stiff, and there was something else about it I couldn't put my finger on. When I looked in her full length mirror with Sara looking over my shoulder, I asked her why it didn't look good on me. She told me it was because of the material I had chosen, it was too institutional looking. She was right; I never wore it.

In a month, the Christmas holidays were upon us again. Christmas in Germany was such a magical time. In the center of Ulm is a plaza called the Munster Platz, where a church that has the biggest steeple in Europe stands. This church is called the Munster, a Lutheran church that is incredibly beautiful inside. The altar featured hand carved ebony figureheads on every seat. At Christmastime, the platz holds its annual Christmas Bazaar. Merchants sell handmade German wares, and hot wine and cider is served.

Bobby and I were, surprisingly, getting along great and having a wonderful time the day we went. It was snowing, and the square was lit up with lights. Carolers were singing Silent Night in German. Bobby asked me if there was anything special I wanted for Christmas. I told him that I wanted a red dirndl, which made him laugh, so he asked me why. I told him that I wore dresses most of the time, so it would only be natural to want a dirndl. We made it our quest to find one, but it wasn't too difficult, since dirndls were a specialty at the Christmas Bazaar, and being Christmas, red was an easy color to find. I loved that dress. It sat high under my bust with a tight bodice. It flared at my hips and cascaded to just above my ankle. Bobby also bought me a goat wool coat.

Feeling the spirit of the season, I asked him if we could have a Christmas party at our house on Christmas day. I was confident about cooking, now that Sara had taught me a few things. I told him it would be nice for the friends that he had who didn't have any family. He thought it was a great idea, and we started making plans for it. He only invited six guys. I had him make the guest list, because I figured he would invite men who knew him well enough, and there wouldn't be any problems. I was so excited. I was going to bake homemade pies. We had a large Christmas ham and all the fixings to serve, while the guys were all going to bring the wine and beer.

When I went into the commissary to buy all the ingredients, I was in heaven. I had never had a party before, and this would be the first time I had ever made pies. When I was walking down the aisle, lost in a world of flour and sugar, I looked up, because I had felt as if someone were staring at me. It was the officer from Karen's party; the mysterious man at the door. He was standing ten feet away from me and holding a jar of cranberry sauce when our gazes met. I instantly became nervous and fumbled with the five pound bag of flour that was in my hand. I dropped it on the floor, but fortunately, it didn't break open. I smiled at him out of embarrassment as I picked it up, and he smiled back in return. He then turned and walked away. At the checkout line, he was nowhere in sight.

I spent most of the night in the kitchen, preparing the meal with Sara on the phone. She and Josh had other plans for Christmas: a romantic dinner for two. None of my friends came; they were all busy with their husbands. It was an unspoken rule among military women to never get angry with each other when they wanted to spend time with their families. Besides, this party was for the men who didn't have families to share it with. The next day, the men all congregated in the living room and talked. I called my mother, and we talked for a short while as well. She had sent me a package in the mail for Christmas; it was filled with the usual: a sweater, socks and underwear. I thanked her. Bobby was on his best behavior; it was another sign to me that he could control his rudeness if he chose to. We had Christmas music playing on the stereo that Bobby had bought at the PX, and the men helped me decorate the tree. It was German tradition to put the tree up on Christmas Eve, but we decided to push the tradition to Christmas day.

The food was a big hit. Then again, it was easy to please military men with old fashioned home cooking. I didn't feel uncomfortable around these men, like I had at Karen's party. They were all guys I had met previously, and we knew a lot about each other. The party went on into the night, and we were all so sad to see it end. I promised them that we would do it again someday.

Right after Christmas, Bobby said he wanted to talk to me.

"Barb, I am really sad about what happened between you and Felicia. I think you are making a huge mistake by not speaking to her." We were driving in the car when were having this conversation.

I told him, "I can bear the fact that she is due to have her baby soon. It is just hard for me to forgive her for the way she spoke to me at the PX."

"Barb, that is crazy. I have never thought of you as a person who holds a grudge. What is really going on?" Then he added, "If I could do one thing right in my life, it would be this." Turning the car around, he started heading for her house. When I realized what he was doing, I said, "This isn't going to work; I am not going to get out of the car." He didn't answer me but just kept on driving. When we pulled up in front of her house, he got out of the car. At first I thought he was going to knock on her door, but, to my surprise, instead he opened mine. He grabbed me by the arm and dragged me out onto the street. He then got back into the car and drove away, leaving me standing on the sidewalk. I was furious. He had just left me more than ten miles from home, and my purse, with all my money for a bus, was with him in the car. It was cold, and there was snow on the ground. My first thought was to call Connie, but when I searched my pockets I didn't even have any coins for the pay phone. Felicia noticed me standing outside her house and opened the door.

"Well, are you going to come in, or are you just going to stand there and freeze to death?"

I had no choice but to comply. Her belly was huge and looked like she was going to deliver any minute. I asked her how she felt, and she said she felt fine. "Feeling fine when you are pregnant is not a concept I understand," I said.

"I know," she said. "I'm sorry you lost the second baby." "Third," I corrected her sternly. "I lost one in high school too." She said, "I'm sorry. I didn't know."

"Barbara," she said. "You really need to get rid of this anger. It is not my fault you lost the babies."

"I never said it was your fault. I'm angry because you were not sympathetic to my feelings that day in the PX, right after it happened. Listen, I wouldn't even be here if Bobby didn't just throw me out of the car at your front door."

She responded, "And I wouldn't have let you in if I didn't care about you and wasn't sensitive to your needs." She stormed off into the bedroom, and I followed her.

"Did you and Bobby have this planned?" I asked. "I swear to God, Barbara; we didn't. WHY ARE YOU SO ANGRY?!" she shouted. "BECAUSE YOU DIDN'T WANT THE BABY, AND I DID!!" I yelled back. "THIS WASN'T MY PLAN!!" she said. "NOR WAS IT MINE!"

We were very close to each other's faces when we were screaming these words. I can't remember who started it, but one of us pushed the other. As a result the other retaliated with another push, and we both ended up falling on her huge bed. We were in shock from our behavior. I remember being concerned for the baby. I asked her if she was ok. I knew my anger was not making any sense. I knew she was right, but I couldn't get rid of it, no matter how much I wanted to.

"Barbara, I'll give you the baby." Her words were barely a whisper. We were still lying on the bed, looking at the ceiling while we were talking. To anyone who would have seen us, we could have been two teenage girls at a slumber party, talking about boys and our future husbands, but we weren't. We were two girls barely out of our teens, talking about our lives and motherhood: hers that was impending and mine that was lost.

"No," I said. "I want my own child, and I want you to want yours. I wanted us to be mothers together, and now I will never be a mother."

"Is that what the doctor said?"

"He won't know until I try again. Apparently, I had an operation when I was two days old, and my uterus was not right when they opened me up. It wasn't just the uterus; it was other things too. For years, it was difficult for me to eat without throwing up. My mother told me about it when I was at the hospital with the last baby. There was something wrong with my stomach as well. For years, she had led me to believe I was just a neurotic child." I began to cry.

Felicia rolled over and stroked my hair. Without realizing it, she had jumped into the role of motherhood at that moment. She spoke to me softly and tenderly. She told me everything was going to be ok.

"Your mother has always sounded like a non-caring person to me. Don't listen to her."

I put my face into my hands and began to cry. "You don't understand. I want a baby, so that I know I have someone who loves me. I want to be a good mother and not the person my mother was. I know how to do that, and I'm not going to be given a chance. It's more than just losing a baby. It is losing something I have wanted my whole life, and now I know I won't have that. What am I going to do? Bobby and I are not going to last. I'm going to be alone."

Felicia was crying with me. She told me I could live with her and Tim if I ever needed to. She told me I could move back with them to California. She said her own mother would take me in if there wasn't room at her apartment. She whispered in my ear, "Barbara, you have lots of choices. You are not alone in this world anymore, like you were when you were seventeen." Then she kissed me on the forehead and said she was sorry for the day at the PX. I rolled over and embraced her on the bed. We were both crying harder now and vowed we would never hurt each other again. We laid there for a long time; it was Felicia who broke the spell. She said, "Come on, I'm having a craving for a kinder egg. Let's go to the gas station down the street and get some chocolate!"

The next day, I came across a letter near the front door that must have fallen out of Bobby's pocket when he was leaving, addressed to his old girlfriend whom he had dated in high school. It was stamped and sealed and ready for the post. Taking the letter, I sat with it in my hand for a long time in the living room on the couch. I began to imagine all the things he was writing to her about. What was he saying about me? Was it a love letter like the ones he used to send me? I was faced with a moral dilemma and didn't know what to do. I knew that opening it would be wrong. I also felt that ignoring it would be stupid. I could confront him about it, but he might not tell me the truth. I placed the letter on the end table and went into the kitchen to make a cup of coffee. When I returned to the living room, it sat on the table, staring me in the face; it was mocking me and tearing me up inside. To open it would go against all that I believed. I went into the studio to try and paint, but that didn't work. I couldn't concentrate; the letter was calling me from the other room.

After two hours, I came to the conclusion that I had to open it. If it were a pleasant letter with no guilty contents from him, then I would simply tape it back up and mail it for him. Then I thought about what I would do if it did have things written in it that had crossed the lines of marriage. I knew I would have to confront him. My suspicions were right. At first, he was talking to her about the difference in the cultures. Then he spoke about the loss of his mother, expressing more to her than he had ever done with me during the incident. Next he started talking about me. He said that we didn't get along much and that I wasn't what he wanted in a wife. This was a kick in the head for me. I was thinking of all the things I had been putting up with: the fact that I had had to drag him across the ocean in a semi-comatose state (that he wasn't really in), the silent days that he would spend staring out the window, the many times that he just left me alone and didn't return, the apologies I had to make for him every time we were with other people, the fact that he wouldn't take me to the hospital when I had lost the last baby and was obviously in need of medical attention. Then he told her the unthinkable...that he was disappointed in me because I couldn't do something that other women did so easily...have children.

I placed the open letter on the table and started to cry. After an hour, I realized that I had found out what I had needed to know. I called Felicia at work and told her. When I got off the phone, I taped up the letter, brought it to the mailbox and dropped it in.

CHAPTER: 38

I spent New Year's eve alone. Felicia and Tim were spending time together, and Sara and Connie were with their husbands. Bobby was starting to get into more of a habit of not coming home for days. I never knew where he was. I called my mother when the clock struck twelve in Germany. I wished her a happy new year. Inside I was glad to be alone, our days ran hot and cold when Bobby was home. He was either the perfect husband or was a miserable person to be around. This flip flopping back and forth was getting to me. I'm sure I was becoming difficult to be around as well. I was less tolerant of his moods, and I let him know it. I told him that if he wished to live a separate life from me, then I would do the same. I no longer tried to console him, and I didn't yell at him, either. I just learned to live my own life.

I had been asked, when we came back from leave, to teach the nursery school program at the elementary school. I loved the job at the nursery school. It meant a lot more money and a higher government service ranking. Run like the nursery schools I had been in back home, it was more structured and not like a babysitting service at all. The teacher they had initially hired had become ill and had to take a long leave of absence.

I was really under-qualified for the job, but Deidra, the woman who was the head of the childcare center, wanted me to do it. She had a lot of pull in the school system and somehow was able to get it for me. I rode with the children in my class on the bus in the morning; we picked it up at the housing unit up the street from my apartment. It was a big bus, and there were twelve children. They were so tiny that I couldn't see all of them when we were sitting down, if I sat in back. Because of this, I sat in the front with the bus driver. On the first day, I thought of my first experience riding a big bus to Head Start. I wanted to make this experience more pleasant for them than the one I had had. Every day we sang songs and talked about the things we saw out the window, as we drove to school.

One day, a few weeks after I had started, we were singing really loudly when I thought I heard a funny sound. It was a high pitched whistling sound, and at first I thought there was something wrong with the bus. I got out of my seat, as the bus was making its way down the Autobahn. We were traveling fairly fast to keep up with the other traffic, so I kept falling from side to side, as I made my way down the aisle, checking each child. I never stopped singing, so that I wouldn't alarm any of them.

When I got to the back of the bus, I found the source of the noise. There was a little girl sitting alone, slumped over in her seat. The sound was coming from her mouth. At first I couldn't imagine what was making the noise, so I lifted her to me as we drove down the street. Because of the rocking of the bus and the fact that she couldn't have weighed more than twenty-five pounds, I almost threw her in the air. I frantically yelled to the driver to take us to the dispensary, when we got on base. He didn't understand what I was saying and kept trying to talk to me in Turkish. I surmised that she had something lodged in her throat and immediately administered the Heimlich maneuver. She was so tiny that I thought I might hurt her. My adrenalin was pumping hard. She was blue and unresponsive, passing out in my arms. The other children were watching me quietly and not saying a word. In a panic, I thrust one arm under her ribs, while I held on to the seat next to us with the other, so we wouldn't fall. It worked; she threw up all over me. Looking down, I saw a candy life saver sitting on the floor at my feet. I found out later that the whistling sound had been made by air escaping out the hole in the center. They were purposely made that way, so an adult could hear if a child were choking; that's why they called them life savers.

Still clenching the child in my arms, I sat us down on the nearest seat. She was crying and calling for her mother. We were both covered in vomit, but I rocked her back and forth to try and comfort her. When we arrived at the school, I called Deidra and then washed my hands and the child as best I could in the bathroom down the hall, while my assistant teacher read a story to the rest of the children. When we came back to the classroom, Deidra was there. As soon as I saw her, my whole body began to tremble. It was a release I was feeling that I no longer had to be the one in control. I broke down and began to cry. I tried to stop but couldn't. I just kept seeing images of that blue child in my arms. She sent for Connie to take me home. I later found out that I had indeed broken the little girl's ribs, a small consequence of saving her life. I also learned that the mother had given her child the lifesaver before she got on the bus, but when she found out what had happened, she just shrugged it off. She never thanked me.

I was going to college at night, taking under-graduate requirements that I felt would transfer easily if I ever went back to the States. But as more time had passed, it looked like I would never be going back. I liked going to college and couldn't believe I was finally doing it. I mostly took English courses. I had a teacher who was from England, named Thom. He taught me a lot about writing, and I never forgot him. My inner life was getting back on track, and my focus was restored. Unfortunately, my marriage was falling apart. As the center of my life was growing stronger and whole, my marriage, the outer shell of my daily living, was molting from my body like dead skin.

One day, I was getting off the bus in Neu Ulm, to meet Felicia on base for lunch. When I stepped on the curb, I fell flat on my face. I was embarrassed but ok. A kind man helped me to my feet. At first I thought I had broken my big toe. It was my right foot, and, every time I put pressure on it, a pain ran up my leg and into my groin. Ignoring it, I hobbled to the base and went on with my day. The next day, it hurt worse than the day before. It felt like all the joints in my toes didn't work. Add that to the constant joint pain I already had, and I was a mess. My foot started to swell and become quite red. My limp became worse, and by the end of the week, I couldn't walk at all without the aid of my cane. I had not gone to the doctor months before that, when Connie had recommended it. Now I knew I had to. I went to see an American orthopedic doctor on base. He took some x-rays and told me that I had a bunion that was surrounded by arthritis. Because of the arthritis, it was only going to get worse. He scheduled me to have it removed a few months later. I was scheduled for surgery at the beginning of March. I had been walking with a cane for months, and every day the level of pain was different. When it was really bad, I had to use crutches. The operation was to take place in Augsburg. This city was a few hours drive from our house. Bobby arranged to take me there and got time off from work. Our relationship was strained, at best. Most times we didn't even talk to each other, although there were sporadic moments when it seemed like we would be ok.

On the day of the operation, Bobby was late getting up, and because I was so nervous about it, I was hounding him. By the time we did get on the road, we were twenty minutes later than our expected departure and giving each other the silent treatment.

He was driving fast to try and make up the time. The Autobahn had no speed limit, so I wasn't concerned about getting a ticket. I was, however, concerned about the way he was driving. He was angry at me, so I chose to keep my mouth shut, despite the obvious fear I was experiencing. The roads were icy, and there was gently falling snow. Anyone in his right mind would know that this combination should encourage driving with caution. Unlike freeways and highways back home, the Autobahn was a series of winding curves. It was only two lanes in most areas. We had been on the road for an hour and a half, when it slowly bent to the right. We were doing about seventy-five miles an hour, when we hit the curve. Just beyond the bend, we hit ice and started to cross the lane slightly. I hung on to the dashboard and was grateful for the German seatbelt laws. After a few erratic sways of the car, Bobby regained control, and we thought we had narrowly escaped an accident. Then all off a sudden, we realized that the traffic fifty yards ahead of us was at a dead stop. I knew it was the ice and wondered if some other poor soul hadn't been as lucky as we had. Bobby tried to slow us down, but the ice was making it difficult to get traction on the road. Our tires were squealing, and I thought for sure we were going to pile into the back of everyone. The cars ahead of us heard us coming, because Bobby had his hand on the horn the whole time; they frantically began pulling over to the shoulders of the road. Fortunately, there was a slight straightaway, and they were able to do this, because the road was wider.

Bobby maneuvered the car to the center of the Autobahn and rode the white line, until we were finally able to stop, ten cars deep. I turned and started screaming at him for driving so irresponsibly. When we finally saw the reason for the cars being stopped, we were shocked. There had been an accident, and two people were badly hurt. The rest of the ride to the hospital was made in silence.

Augsburg hospital was an American facility. All the personnel were enlisted people. It was an old castle that looked like it was right out of a Frankenstein movie. For an artist, it would have been beautiful; for a patient, it was scary. The people who worked there were not very friendly. Similar to Rhein-Main, we had to wait in a long line to have our number called. When I got to the desk after a half hour wait, the girl taking my name looked at me very seriously and asked, "Are you the one getting a screw removed?"

I looked over at Bobby, sitting comfortably in a chair across the room, and turned back to the girl and said, "No, but if you offer that here, I have a husband who has a lose one that needs tightening."

She didn't even crack a smile, and I knew I was in trouble. I somberly told her I was not the one having that particular operation and gave her my doctor's name. She told me to sit back down, and she would call my name when my room was ready.

I was placed in a room with four other women. They were all enlisted military, and I was the only civilian and the only one who was white. At first they ignored me. I knew that the introductions were going to have to come from me. I introduced myself, and they asked me why I was there. I told them I had a bunion on my foot, nothing serious. Tania, one of the girls, said, "Yah, that's not serious, but man, what a pain in the ass that is to recover from." She was a nurse who worked at the hospital and had been admitted for abdominal pain. I tried not to think about what she had just told me. Rhonda and Becky were sharing a Glamour Magazine and laughing at the "Glamour Don'ts." It was a monthly column where unsuspecting woman in outlandish costumes were photographed in public.

"What was this girl thinking, going out dressed like that?" "Rhonda, honey, it is obvious." "What is?" "Why she is poor."

"How you knowed dat?"

"Cause she obviously can't afford a full length mirror!" Everyone in the room laughed, including me. I immediately fit in and became part of their little circle.

My surgery was scheduled for the following morning. The doctor came in later that afternoon and spoke to me about the procedure, saying the only problem he could see was my long hair. It needed to be tied back, but I couldn't use a rubber band. I'm not sure why they didn't just put it in a bonnet, but for some reason that option was not presented to me. The other girls in the room watched me as I put it into a long French braid down my back. I wasn't sure it would stay without a rubber band, so I wanted to try it out first. Just as I had expected, it fell out in two seconds. I tried it again, and this time I tried to tie the large end of it with itself. Once again, it fell out. In frustration at watching me, one of the girls in my room said, "Honey, you come over here. Me and my sisters, here, will fix you up."

I wasn't sure what they were going to do, but I went and sat next to them anyway. Three of them started working on my hair, while the last one became supervisor of the process. The whole time their hands were flying, so were their mouths.

"Mmmmm, girl, what I would do to have long silky hair like this," said Rhonda.

"Let me tell ya sister, you wouldn't know what to do with it," said Tania in response. "You would have to wash it every day. Wouldn't she, Barbara?"

"I'm afraid so, and when it is this long, it takes twice the time."

"That's ok...I don't mind, as long as it were this pretty." They moved on to the topic of the handsome new doctor on the floor and what they would like to do to him.

It was so funny to watch these women all having fun. With three of them working on me, it only took them twenty minutes to finish. One of them brought me a hand mirror to admire the beautiful work they had done.

"Get a looky at that, Barb. The only other place you will get craftsmanship like that is Jamaica!" They had corn rowed my entire head from front to rear, so that all my hair that was well past my shoulders sat neatly down the center of my back.

"What do you think?" asked Tania proudly, with her head cocked to one side and her hands on her hips. "I think it's amazing." I said out of honest delight. "Sheeeit, Honey, you look like Bo Derek."

"I wish," I said laughing. "How did you get the ends to hold?"

"We tied them in tiny knots, but for sleeping tonight, we'll put rubber bands in them, so they won't fall out by morning."

The next morning a nurse came in and helped me onto a gurney. She rolled me into the operating room where the doctor was waiting. An anesthesiologist injected the meds in my IV, as I started to lose consciousness. The last thing I heard was my doctor say, "Wow, her hair looks beautiful." Then my world went black.

When I was wheeled back into my room after the surgery, it was dark outside. I had vague memories of the nurse telling me something about being attached to something, but I didn't understand her. I drifted into a deep sleep. At 2:00 AM, I awoke from my drug-induced state. At first, I didn't know where I was. It was dark, and someone in the room was snoring. What I did know was that I had to pee desperately. Trying to swing my legs over the side of the bed, I suddenly realized what the nurse had been saying to me earlier. I was in traction, and the foot that had been operated on was over my head in the air and attached to a metal pole that ran the full length of the bed. "Oh man, I hope this doesn't mean a bed pan," I thought. The little experience I had had with those things told me I was no good at them. I looked around the room, but it was dark. I thought I could make out a portable commode to the left of my bed, if I could only get to it. In no time, I figured out how to maneuver the leg in traction down the length of the pole. Reaching with all my might, I caught hold of the arm of the toilet and dragged it to the side of the bed. I was half way there, but I found I had to rest a bit. I was still feeling the effects of the drugs, and my head was spinning from the exertion. I was hoping my bladder could hold on. After a short while, with both of my arms extended behind me, I held on to the rails of the toilet and tried with all my strength to hoist myself off the bed. Then, you guessed it... the damn thing started to roll. Meanwhile, I was still attached to the bed! Fortunately I was able to catch myself, before I completely fell off the side and was left dangling from the ceiling. Imagine wetting the bed in that position! Luckily, the momentum I used to save myself from going over the edge also brought the toilet back to the side of the bed again.

Locking down the only side of the toilet I could reach, I tried the whole process over again. This time the toilet moved only a little bit, and I was able to secure myself on the seat. "Thank God," I said out loud with a sigh of relief. Then, "Oh no!" was my statement of realization in the dark. I heard a giggling from across the room. I couldn't see her, but I knew it was Tania. "Miss Barbara, didn't that nurse bother to tell you that you still had your underwear on?"

"Very funny," I said in exasperation. I rang the call button for the nurse.

I was in the hospital for a week, but it seemed longer. I passed the time by playing cards with the other girls in the patient lounge and talking. Most of them were in for minor aches and pains. I was the only one who was immobile, and they each took turns wheeling me around the ward in a wheel chair, after I was taken off the traction.

"One day, Tania came up to us during our morning card game in the lounge and said in a whisper, "Hey, what do you ladies say we go out to lunch?"

"Out to lunch? Where," I asked? "Girl, I think you is da one dat is out to lunch," added Rhonda.

"Girls, now don't get your panties all bunched. If ya jest let me tell ya." She leaned over the table and whispered for us all to hear, lifting her head only once to make sure no one was watching. When she was done, we all squealed in delight. Several were banging the table and laughing.

"Quiet down over there." It was the nurse at the desk looking at us over her glasses. "What are we going to do about her?" I asked as I motioned over my left shoulder. "Don't you worry your pretty little braids about her, Miss Barbara, I take care o' dat one."

Tania walked over to the nurse's desk in a very nonchalant way and started complaining. "The TV in the lounge doesn't work no more. Some idiot took da remote and lost it." Grabbing the remote from our table, I threw it across the room. It landed behind the couch. The others started laughing, until one of them said, "Shhh, here they come." Becky grabbed my wheel chair as Rhonda grabbed our purses; we quietly rolled out of the room. When we were sure the nurse couldn't see us, we raced down the hall. The last thing we heard as we rounded the corner was Tania saying, "You wait here, Ma'am, I see if someone brought it to dar room by mistake." Wheeling me down the hall, we were excited and jovial; we all looked like prisoners let out on furloughs. The café was in the cellar. It was cold and made completely of stone, like the rest of the place. Standing in line, they placed me ahead of them. We were talking and laughing. Becky worked there and knew a lot of the people. Sitting there in my wheelchair while she talked to a guy she knew, I became fixated on the back of the head of a different girl, who was standing directly in front of me. She was a white girl, about my height, with short brown hair. She wore a military uniform, she was enlisted. I had seen the back of her head before, but where? It was driving me crazy, and I swore I knew her. Then it came to me, "Donna, is that you?!!"

She turned around, and sure enough it was! Donna had sat in front of me in home room for four years of high school. "I knew I recognized the back of that head!" I said in animated delight. We couldn't believe it. I was so excited to see her that I could have jumped up and down, if it were not for the fact that I was in a wheel chair and cast. She couldn't jump either, she was nine months pregnant. "What the hell are you doing here?" was all we could say. She was a glimpse of home, and I couldn't believe my eyes.

The girls who were with me were stunned at the coincidence. I introduced them to my long lost friend, and we all ate lunch together. Donna told us she was leaving the military soon, because single mothers were given that choice. I told her where Bobby and I were stationed. She couldn't believe we were married. I didn't tell her the days were numbered. We had a wonderful lunch, reminiscing and catching each other up on friends back home. After we were finished, we hugged each other goodbye and went our separate ways. She was only at the hospital for a prenatal check up, and I never saw her again.

The day I was to leave the hospital, I was so excited to go that I got up at six in the morning. Bobby had said he would pick me up at nine, and I wanted to have everything packed before he got there, so we could just leave. I was so sick of being there. The girls who had shared my room had all left two days earlier, and every extra day that I was there dragged on, as if it were a week. A new cast was put on me. It was shorter and sat just below my knee. I had to walk with crutches and found it awkward and difficult. After the first day on them, I developed cuts in my armpits that stung.

It was so boring at the hospital. The TV was now really broken, and I had read every outdated magazine they had. No one visited me the whole time I was there, not even Bobby. Felicia couldn't, because she didn't have a car. I was looking forward to going home and painting or doing some of my needlework. I missed my little apartment and wanted desperately to watch the children playing in the yard. When nine o'clock rolled around and he still wasn't there, I wasn't surprised. By ten, I was agitated. By eleven, I was mad. When he strolled through the door at one in the afternoon like nothing was wrong, I was furious. It was so typically selfish of him to be that late. It was the first time he had seen me since he had dropped me off the morning before the operation, and he never even asked me how it was. I doubt if he had even called.

All the way to the car, I refused to let him help me. Emotionally, I was disconnecting from him; I didn't want to feel dependent on him. If I had taken the time to think about it, I would have realized that he had never been dependable anyway. We made the same silent ride to Ulm that we had made a week earlier, a mirror image of my ride to the hospital.

When I got home, I went into the studio and painted for two days. Bobby and I still weren't speaking. Getting to the base was very difficult for me. I really didn't have a need to, other than for laundry, which I soon learned I would be dragging by myself in a cast. I no longer worked at the nursery school; there was no way I could. I was going to be in the cast for six weeks and then in a splint for six more. I couldn't have kept up with the kids, and school would be out in May, anyway. Besides, the woman I had replaced, who had been on sick leave, had returned.

After a week in the house, I was going stir crazy. I called my mother and told her that everything had gone well, but I left out the details about Bobby, because I was afraid she would go into a rant about him. I had an appointment at the Neu Ulm dispensary to see my surgeon. He visited the bases once a month, so his patients didn't have to travel so far to see him. Bobby never asked me how I was going to get to the base. I never discussed it with him, either. I figured I would cross that bridge when I came to it. That morning, I got up early and made the slow trek up the hill to the military housing. I decided to take the military bus, because there would be less walking at the other end when I arrived. It took me three times longer to get there, and when I did, I was exhausted, and my arm pits were killing me. I made the decision right there to ask the doctor to put me in a walking cast. Felicia said she would meet me on base, and we would have lunch in the café after my appointment.

When I arrived at the dispensary, the doctor took me right away, an oddity when waiting for military services. He did as I requested and put me in the walking cast. It was much more comfortable. I had brought my cane in anticipation of this and smiled as I handed him the crutches.

When I got to the café, Felicia was already there, waiting for me. We were happy to see each other, and she was filling me in on the news about the impending arrival of her mother. I was telling her of how I had had it with Bobby; she was sympathetic. She asked me if I would stay with her from then until the baby was born. She was having a hard time getting around and thought, since I was too, we could help each other. I said that I would, but I would need to get some things from home first.

Just then, the officer who had been at Karen's party walked into the café. He went straight to the coffee line and didn't see me. He was dressed in fatigues, and for the first time I saw his rank. He was an E8. A high ranking sergeant, he had to be in command of a unit. I understood now the respect he was getting from his men. He was a noncommissioned officer as opposed to a commissioned one. I had more respect for noncoms. They were the ones who really ran the army. I watched him walk across the room. My eyes were fixed on his physique. I studied the way he carried himself: the movement of his legs, the slouch of his shoulders when he reached into his pocket for his wallet. I was mesmerized by every last detail that gave me a hint of who he was. He didn't speak to anyone. He poured himself some coffee and continued to the cash register. When he had paid and turned around, he noticed me sitting with Felicia. He saw me staring at him. He stood about eight feet away from us, looking back at me and not saying a word. Felicia didn't notice him, and I didn't tell her. She didn't even know anything about him, because I had never mentioned it. Our eyes were locked in an embrace, until I felt the flush rise to my face. I turned to Felicia, who was snapping her fingers at me. "Wake up. Are you under a spell or what?" She turn around to see what I was looking at, but the room was now filled with people, and she couldn't make out which one it was. She looked back at me with a smirk on her face but didn't say a word.

Meanwhile, another girl, an acquaintance of ours who lived on base, walked in. She was very boisterous and always had the habit of singling me out and embarrassing me. It started the first week that I had arrived, and she hadn't let up since. She was from Peru, married to a high ranking commissioned officer. Her skin was the color of honey, her body painstakingly crafted from hours in a gym. Her daily dress consisted of clothing that was so revealing that it left one feeling as if he had had an intimate encounter with her by merely saying hello. Whenever she walked into a room, every head would turn because of her beauty, whether men or women. Then she would open her mouth, and all the unsuspecting onlookers would be overcome by her arrogance. It was usually at this time that I would try to hide.

Without fail, this woman would always seek me out in a crowd. When she would find me, she would comment very loudly, to anyone who would listen, about how beautiful I was. I never understood this coming from her. She was so beautiful herself, no one could hold a candle to her. She especially loved my eyes and would go on and on about them in the most embarrassing way. She also found excuses to touch me. Usually, she tried rubbing my back, or playing with my long hair, to the delight of any man within three feet of us. I found out a few months later that she was bisexual and would have outlandish parties that often turned into orgies. She was loud and obnoxious, and I did everything I could think of to avoid her. I couldn't believe the noncom from Karen's party was going to witness this. I tried to hide, but there was nowhere to go.

She walked into the cafe. Her cocky air trailed behind her like a rooster walking into a chicken coop looking for some action. Meanwhile, the anticipative dread I was feeling hung thick in the air that surrounded me like napalm in the jungle. I turned away quickly, as to avoid any eye contact. Felicia saw it all happening and laughed. "Here comes your girlfriend, Barb. I dare you to go up to her and kiss her, just to get this place rocking." I glared at Felicia with sharp eyes, whispering under my breath, "Quiet, I don't want her to know I am here." Sure enough, she saw me. She came to our table and started in with her usual bantering. She was stroking my hair and telling the man who had come in with her to look at how beautiful my eyes were. I looked over at my noncom officer, and he seemed to be enjoying it.

He was smiling at me. I realized he knew exactly who this woman was. I feared he thought I was in her circle of "special" friends. I just gave him a pathetic smile back and shook my head to indicate that I wasn't. He smiled in return and began to laugh. He still hadn't talked to me. In all this time we had never said a word to one another. This unspoken dialogue happened in the presence of everyone. But only he and I knew it. These constant run-ins I was having with him were driving me crazy. I was very attracted to him, and he knew it. But I also knew that he was attracted to me. I thought to myself that if he wanted me, he was going to have to work for it and wait until I wasn't married anymore. My thoughts surprised even me. Out of guilt, I quickly turned away from his gaze. When I looked up again, five minutes later, he was gone.

CHAPTER: 39

The next day, I went home to pack some things for my stay with Felicia. I thought of telling Bobby, but he was on one of his disappearing acts, so I shrugged my shoulders and thought, "Oh well." Instead, I called my mother, so she wouldn't worry if she tried to reach me for days, and I wasn't home. She told me to wish Felicia luck and that she was thinking about her. I told her I would.

It was fun living with Felicia. The anger I had felt before was completely gone. We were our old selves again. Not much older but a lot wiser. I was getting used to the idea that I would not be a mother and enjoying the thought of becoming an aunt. I told Felicia that I would be with her during the delivery, if Tim couldn't get there in time. He and Bobby were scheduled to go back to Cass Site right before the birth. Her mother was arriving soon, and I couldn't wait to meet her. Felicia spoke often about her mother. It sounded like they had an ideal relationship.

I was at the Laundromat, when they picked her up at the airport. I met her later that night, and she was just as I had pictured. She was as funny as Felicia, and we got along immediately. She felt like one of the girls to me, and we joked constantly. Poor Felicia was feeling really awful at this point. With her swollen belly, she could barely move. She tried her best to show her mother the sights around town, and the two of them often came home exhausted. I usually didn't go with them. I wanted to give them some time alone. Meanwhile, I had been put in a splint. It was large and looked like a very ugly shoe. It was better than the cast, but it was still difficult to walk. So many things were happening at once. In a week, the guys left for the site. Bobby never tried to contact me. Tim told me he had informed him I was with them.

The day Felicia went into labor, her mother and I were with her at the Frauen Klinik. It was a German hospital for women, where all the Americans had their babies. Tim was called, and he assured her he would be back. Felicia's mom and I waited in the waiting room, while they prepped her. Her mom told me that she couldn't watch the birth. She couldn't bear to see Felicia in that much pain. When it looked like it was time and Tim was not back yet, a little German nurse came to me in the hall and said that Felicia wanted to see me. She started putting the paper bonnet on my head and the little paper booties on my feet. When the backwards coat was on me, and I realized that this was really it, I started protesting, "Can't we just wait a little while longer? I'm sure Tim will be here." The nurse just laughed at me and said sarcastically, "Hold on; let me ask the baby."

They brought me to the room where Felicia was strapped to what looked like the most uncomfortable chair I had ever seen. It was a birthing chair, designed to ease the delivery by theory of gravity. It was at a forty-five degree angle, and the seat the mother sat on was shaped like the letter U, so as to allow the baby to slide right out the center of it without obstructions. Felicia was in labor, and I was not that much help. Every time she got a contraction, I tried to teach her the breathing that Doug had taught me. Felicia didn't want to hear it and just screamed. The whole scene was awful for me, and I wanted to get out of there. Fortunately, after a few minutes, Tim showed up. I said that I would leave them alone and sit with her mother. I was sure she was worried, and besides, I couldn't take it.

The minute Sophie was born, Felicia's mom and I went into the room. The baby was still wet and shiny, and Felicia looked like hell. Sophie was the tiniest thing, weighing only a little over six pounds. She had the blackest and longest hair I had ever seen on a baby. Her eyes were the most incredible of all. They were such a light shade of blue that they almost seemed white. Around the outer rim of them was a deep ultramarine. She was like a fairy child, and I instantly fell in love with her, holding her within the first hour of her birth. I wanted to squeeze her tight; the love I felt was so strong.

I was so happy for Felicia and Tim. I thought that if the sight of this precious beauty didn't give Felicia maternal instincts, nothing would.

The day Felicia brought Sophie home from the hospital, it was Oster Montag again. I thought about the kids in my neighborhood the previous year, gathering their eggs, and felt bad that I had missed the morning. We didn't celebrate Easter that day. Felicia was nervous around the baby, and her mother and I did our best to console her. She was afraid, at first, to hold her and often left that job up to her mom and me. Tim was back at Cass Site. I hadn't seen Bobby; in our heads, we were officially separated.

When it came time to feed Sophie, Felicia wanted to try to breastfeed her. She took her into the bedroom and sat on the bed. Her mother was with her, and I politely waited in the next room, so that they could have this time together. After awhile, with the baby still crying with hunger, it was obvious they were having trouble. I knocked on the door and asked if they needed help. Felicia told me to come in, because she didn't know how to do it. When I walked through the door, all three of them were very upset. Her mother kept saying that she had never breastfed her kids and didn't know what was wrong. Felicia was frustrated, because she didn't know what to do. Sophie was starving but, for some reason, wouldn't eat. She was wailing ---screaming at the top of her lungs. When I looked at Felicia's breast for the first time, I was surprised by what I saw. Her nipples didn't look anything like mine, and, other than Cherri's, they were the only other ones I had ever seen. They didn't seem to have a tip on them and were soft, despite how much she was touching them. I asked her why they weren't getting hard. She had no idea what I was talking about. I asked her if her nipples got hard when Tim touched them. Out of exasperation, she moaned, "I don't know!" I knew this wasn't getting us anywhere, so I asked to see the baby. We had to see if she had a bellyache and wouldn't eat or if it was Felicia's nipples.

Taking off my shirt, I held Sophie to my breast. She immediately latched on to me so hard that a pain shot through my chest. She started sucking away but found no satisfaction, so she stopped and began to cry again. When Sophie let go of my breast, I said, "See, that is what your nipple is suppose to do." Felicia said, "My nipples have never done that." "Mine haven't either," said her mother. They both looked at my chest with curiosity. "That's because you both have inverted nipples." I had read enough maternity books to realize what I was looking at. I also knew that there was no way Felicia would be able to breast feed without someone who could coach her through it. I was not that someone. Sophie needed formula.

Because it was Easter, the German stores were all closed, and the American PX and commissary were also closed. The only place I would be able to get some baby formula was on base at the dispensary, but that was five miles away, and we didn't have a car. Sophie was screaming louder now. The poor thing was hungry. I told Felicia that I would go to the base; I would take a bus to get there. We didn't have a choice. Her mother suggested they feed her sugar water until I got back. I thought that was a great idea and was glad she was there. She said she would stay behind with Felicia in case she needed the help. I went to the nearest bus stop to wait.

The buses were running on the holiday schedules; it took two for me to get to Neu Ulm. With each one, I had to wait twice as long as usual. By the time I finally arrived, I was anxious and running on adrenalin. The bus stop was two blocks from the front gates of the base. Because it was a holiday, I figured the back gates would be locked. When the gates were locked, even the guard who was watching them was not allowed to let anyone in. I figured my best bet was the front. With my foot still in a splint and my cane, I hobbled to the next destination.

When I rounded the corner of the first block, I was met by a spectacular sight. The street was closed, and there was a parade of some sort, walking down the center of it. The people marching were all wearing white sheets over their heads that draped to their ankles. Their eyes were exposed by holes that were cut from the sheets. Around their eyes they had on thick, black stage make-up. It made their eyes look like black holes. They were all carrying candles, despite the fact that it was daylight; no one was making a sound, not even the people on the side of the road who were watching them. They looked like the walking dead, and a chill went down my spine. This wasn't an ordinary parade. There were ten people across in rows. When I looked down the street to estimate how many there were, I realized that I couldn't see the end of the line; it went as far as my view would allow.

Making my way through the silent crowd, I felt like I was trapped in one of my own nightmares. I half expected to see Shadow Man around every bend, but he never made an appearance. It was hard for me to weave my way through the people; a walk that should have only taken me ten minutes, tops, took me twenty. The fact that I had a cane and a compromised foot didn't help. The parade wrapped completely around the base and extended on down the street toward Munich. There was a large crowd of protesters, just standing there, barring the gate and holding anti-nuclear protest signs. The signs read "AMERICANS GO HOME" and "NO NUKES." Along with the crowd, to my great surprise, were also all the network news stations that we had back home. I saw ABC, CBS, and NBC. The only sound that I could hear was the whispering of the reporters. When I approached the front gate, I had to push my way through the crowd to try and talk to the gate keeper. Fortunately, this was a peaceful crowd, and they let me pass.

The guard at the gate was German and spoke little English. I was trying to explain to him that it was an emergency, and I needed to get in so that I could go to the dispensary. He kept telling me that he didn't understand. I was getting angrier at the American military for having non-English speaking gatekeepers and subsequently putting me in this helpless position. While I was trying to talk to the guard, a newsman approached me; placing a microphone in my face, he asked if I were an American and, if so, how I felt about the silent vigil. I was so distraught from my conversation with the guard that when the reporter asked me this question from left field, all I could do was look him in the face with disbelief. He backed off from my expression and disappeared into the crowd. In German, I tried telling the guard about the issues we were having with Sophie, but I couldn't remember the word for baby formula, and I didn't have my dictionary. He told me to go to the back gate; that guard could speak better English. Looking at the miles of people stretched down the street, I wondered if this were even possible. I didn't have a choice; with my head bent down, I plodded through the blizzard of people once more. The back gate was approximately four blocks away. When I got there, the guard was expecting me. His English was quite good, and I explained to him about the urgency. He let me in. The dispensary, however, was located near the front gate, just inside the base; so, once again, I trekked approximately four blocks back inside the perimeter of the compound.

At the dispensary, I didn't have any problem getting what I needed. As a military health clinic, it was fully stocked. They did look at me kind of oddly when I said I needed baby formula, but when I explained that the child had just arrived home, and the nurses had never told Felicia she had a problem but had been giving Sophie formula in the hospital, they seemed to understand. They gave me enough cans to get her through a few days or until the stores were open and

Felicia could purchase them herself. Stuffing them into my back pack, it felt like I had the Holy Grail in my hands. Now all I had to do was get back with it. Going the same route in reverse, I got back to Felicia's house. I had been gone for over four hours in total. Sophie had missed three feedings.

In a few days, Felicia's mother had to leave and return to the States. That left Felicia and me to take care of Sophie. When she woke up for her 2:00 AM feedings, we both got up. When she needed her diaper changed, we both did it. One day, after a few weeks of this, I realized that, although I was helping a lot, it wasn't really good for Felicia and Sophie's relationship, if I were always there. When I told Felicia this, she panicked. She said she wasn't sure she could do it without me. She was still nervous and expressed to me that she felt she wasn't a good mother. I told her she was crazy, that she was doing a great job, and that all a good mother needs to be is nurturing, patient and understanding. She said that she wasn't the lullaby singing type. I told her that was ok, to sing the songs that make her happy, just in a soft voice. Although she protested, I left anyway. I knew it would be best for both of them.

Bobby was still at Cass Site, so I knew I had at least two months with the apartment to myself. I figured I would give Felicia two weeks with Sophie, and then I would go check on her. She had my number, in case she needed me sooner. Two weeks later, when I did return, I looked through the large picture window that was next to her front door. I caught a glimpse of Felicia, cradling Sophie in her arms and parading her around the room. She was singing to her in a soft voice, "I Love Rock and Roll," by Joan Jett.

At home, I painted and read. I had my splint removed, although I still needed the cane. Because of the transitional nature of living in a military community, there were some who had only known me as a person who walked with a limp and a cane. When they met me, I had had one, and when their jobs overseas were done, and they left, I still had it. It's funny for me to think that these people will forever remember me as someone who was partially lame.

I loved being back at my apartment and realized how much I had missed it. I called my mother, because I knew she would worry if she hadn't heard from me. I told her about the baby and the hard time Felicia had had breast feeding. I didn't tell her about the protest people. When I hung up the phone, I realized that I didn't have any clean clothes. I took my laundry to the base to wash it, and it felt similar to when I had arrived in this country and felt my first taste of freedom. I did, however, know my days were numbered. I had to make a decision about my marriage before Bobby came home. I needed to decide if I wanted a divorce and where I wanted to live.

When I only had a month left to go, I knew my mind was made up. When I had inquired on base about getting a divorce, I had found out that I had to do it back in Massachusetts. My plan was to fly home and do this. I would have to be home for three months to get this job done. I would more than likely live with my brother and get a job, so I could save some money. Then I would come back to Germany as a full civilian and find another job working on base. I knew they would hire me again at the school. I probably wouldn't be able to stay with Felicia, because I knew it would be coming up to the time when she would be going back to the States for good. I thought about her offer to go to California and quickly dismissed the idea. In my head, I had it all worked out...I was coming back here. I called Bobby and told him my plans. He thought it was a good idea and was actually civil to me and said he would meet me at home, after I had everything all set, so he could sign the papers. He seemed to want out as much as I did.

CHAPTER: 40

I went to the bank to get some money to reserve a flight home for three weeks later. The line, as usual, was long. Standing there for what seemed like hours, I let my mind drift off. I was thinking about what type of job I would get once I got home, when I received a gentle tap on my shoulder. When I turned around, it was the noncom officer from Karen's party who was standing directly behind me.

"I don't think we have been properly introduced," he said, extending his hand. "My name is William." His voice was velvety and smooth. He had a confidence I had never seen in a man before. He smelled so good that a part of me just wanted to stand closer to him so that I could drink him in.

I shook his hand with my trembling one and said, "My name is Barbara." In a split second, my heart was racing, my breathing felt labored, and my whole body tingled from head to toe. "Oh please, God, don't let me faint at his feet!"

"Would you like to go and get some coffee," he asked, "after your banking is done? I know a quaint café about 10 miles outside of town, where no one will disturb us." He was still holding my hand and stepped closer to me. I hesitated. This man had a control over me like I had never experienced before in my life. I smiled as I looked at my feet and said, "I would like that." Standing in line, waiting for my turn, I tried hard not to look at him. Turning back around, facing the front of the line, I took a step closer to the teller. He could tell I was nervous and tried to ease my anxiety. Speaking softly into my ear from behind, he asked, "Where are you from?"

"I am from Boston," I said looking straight ahead. "I thought I had detected a New England accent." Turning back to him, I smiled and blushed. "I am actually going back in three weeks." "And why is that?" "I have some unfinished business to attend to." He didn't ask me what.

When we finished at the bank, we walked to his vehicle. It was a brand new custom racing Porsche. It was white with a black leather interior. It had spoilers running around the entire perimeter of it, as well as on the back. It was sparkling clean and shiny; I had never seen such an elegant sports car before in my life. He drove extremely fast, but for some reason, unlike when I was with Bobby, with him, I was not afraid. I estimated that he was at least forty-five years old. That would make him twenty-four years older than I. He was so much more experienced with all of this. I felt like an apprentice following his lead. He was so handsome; I couldn't take my eyes off him. He knew I was looking at him, and he just smiled a knowing smile and winked at me as he drove. My heart skipped a beat at his boldness.

He took me to a guest house with a wine cellar in a town I had never been in. The place had low ceilings and exposed beams. It was dark, and, although it was early afternoon, it was lit by tiny candles. We sat alone at a deserted table in the corner of the room. I asked him how long he had been in Germany. He told me it was his fifteenth year. I was amazed. I could tell by his uniform that I had been right; he was a non-commissioned officer, which meant his rank was granted by virtue of years in service, not a college degree. He was an E-8, the highest rank for a non-commissioned officer. I asked him if he had been in Vietnam, and he told me that he had. I didn't ask him any further questions on that subject; it was an unspoken rule not to.

"Barb, I have to tell you, you have put a spell on me. Ever since the first night I saw you at Karen's house, I needed to know who you are. I know that you are married. But I have never seen you with him. This intrigues me." When he spoke, his voice was soft, with the slightest hint of a Midwestern accent. He was smiling at me in the familiar way that I had come to know. "Your eyes are so beautiful, and apparently I am not the only one who thinks so." We both laughed, remembering the day the Peruvian woman was carrying on in the café.

"Yes, it is true, I am married." After a short pause, I added, "And the business I have to take care of is a divorce." He smiled and extended his hand to me across the table and held mine for a long while, just looking into my eyes. I was under his spell as well, but I tried to fight it.

"Which state are you from?"

"Originally I am from Iowa. I grew up on a farm. But I own several houses in Oregon, so technically I guess I am from there."

"When were you last home in Iowa?" "Twenty years ago, when I visited my mother. So, how old are you? You seem so young, yet so mature."

"I am twenty-one." When I said this, he didn't even flinch. He was so confident and in control. I had figured right; he was in his early forties.

I then asked him what he did for a job. He told me he babysat grown men. I laughed and said, "No, really." Then he got very serious, and, with no expression, he glanced ever so slightly around the room and said, "I can't tell you." I had never met a man like him before. He was so mysterious and intriguing. I was immediately attracted to him, and I wanted to kiss him. He knew it. He leaned across the table and placed his lips gently on my mouth. My whole body responded in a way that I didn't think it knew how to anymore. I was alive. I said, "Let's go for a drive."

I was glad to be back in his car. It felt safer to me than such an intimate setting. I didn't trust myself; I didn't trust my body. I was fighting it. As we raced down the abandoned streets of this tiny town, he straightened each curve the car met by crossing the imaginary center line, in order to keep up with his speed. He was a man with his own rules, a man who was used to having his own way. Although I wouldn't admit it to myself until years later, I fell in love with him that day.

We drove for an hour. It was a clear day, and the Alps were forever in our view. He asked me if I had ever skied. I told him I had not. He turned to me and very confidently said, "You will." I believed him.

After awhile, we drove to a tiny town called Oberelchingen. It looked like it had been carved out of a hill, with streets winding up it like a snake. We even drove under a church that crossed the road with an arch. Halfway to the top, we stopped in front of a tiny house. It was two stories high, and it had a plum orchard for a back yard. Since it was just shy of spring, you could see anticipation in the buds. I asked him where we were. He said, "This is my home." I became nervous. My body was awakening from a deep winter as well. I hoped I could be in control with this man who was used to having his own way and telling others what to do, especially since I was having feelings that had been gone from my life for so long.

When we entered the house, we were met by a kind and animated old woman. Her name was Frau Hirsch. She didn't speak English, but I could tell by her reactions that she loved William and was glad I was with him. She left me with the impression that he had rarely brought women home. The house belonged to her and her family. She had a disabled husband and seven young daughters, the oldest two years younger than I.

The house is difficult to describe. It was a single family home, yet there was a wing on the second floor that had a kitchen, living room and bed room. It also had its own balcony that overlooked the orchards and, in the distance, the Alps. The bathroom was shared. This was where William lived. He had a glass door like mine. It was a small apartment compared to mine but just as nice. An orange tiger cat sat quietly on a chair in the sun, disinterested in our arrival. The living room had a built-in glass cabinet that ran the length of the room. It was filled with a collection of very tiny trains. There had to be at least thirty of them, each one not more that two inches long. They were beautifully crafted with fine detail, and he told me they actually worked. I could tell the artistry was German. Next to the trains was a collection of porcelain tea balls that sat in their own tiny cups. There were about a dozen of them. They were hand painted, each with different blooms of delicate flowers. They looked French. Sitting next to the tea balls was a set of long stemmed Bavarian wine glasses. They were hand blown, and the stems were twisted from the base to the cup of the glass. Each stem was a different color. I had seen this set in a window of a shop in down town Ulm. I had wanted to purchase the set myself, but they were too expensive. William also collected movies; he had at least a hundred. It was an impressive amount, considering video was only a few years old. Most of them were classic old movies. He had one painting on the wall, an antique one of a German wine cellar. It was a dark painting that had a light shining through a high window and onto a man who was holding a glass of wine up, as if to check its color. On the other wall were two old movie posters. One was "The Maltese Falcon," with Humphrey Bogart, and the other was "Gone With The Wind." It was an odd, eclectic array of objects. I learned more about this man by walking into his house than by anything he had told me that day. He was a quiet man who spent time alone and loved beautiful things. His mystery was actually his inner understanding of who he was. He was happy and was at peace with himself. It was a trait I had never seen in Bobby.

When I was sitting on the floor checking out his movie collection, he sat next to me and didn't say a word. After awhile, I turned and looked into his eyes, and he kissed me again. This time it was a slow rhythmic motion, causing my whole body to rock in response. Without intending to, I let out a moan. His arm embraced my back, as he slowly lowered me onto the oriental carpet. Lifting himself gently on top of me, he held me close, as his lips traveled down my neck. It felt so good to be in a man's arms again. Between Bobby and me, the act of intimacy had become just the means to make a baby. With this man, I knew it would be something more.

"Are you ok with this?" he asked, as he kissed the top of my chest.

"It depends on which part of me you are talking too."

"How about this part?" He cupped my breast and lowered his lips to it. My breath caught in my throat and I moaned louder. Losing all my sense of morality, I reached for the back of his shirt and slid it over his head and off his body. He unbuttoned my blouse, removed my bra, and exposed my breasts. The grey hairs on his firm chest softly landed on top of my nipples. I pulled him closer, digging my fingers into the flesh of his back. This time it was his turn to make a sound. It was deep and guttural, very primal. I knew there was no turning back. With his knees, he expertly spread my legs, exposing me to whatever his next intentions were. With his hand, he lifted my skirt. Once again he was on top of me, and through his clothing I could feel his excitement. I needed to have him. Reaching underneath with my hand, I found his zipper. Undoing his pants, I reached inside and brought him out. He was warm and hard. When I squeezed him my hands became damp from his liquid. He whispered in my ear, "Let me please you."

My answer was a soft, "Yes." His fingers found me first. I clung to him as if he were my last hope for happiness. I rocked with the motion of his movements, lifting my hips in the air, until suddenly he was inside me. Upon entering, we both let out a groan of satisfaction. I grabbed the fleshiness of his backside to push him further in me. I wanted him to stay there forever. Lifting my body at an angle I had never participated in before, he was able to affect me in areas I didn't know I had. He searched my expression to confirm it was where it should be. My eyes widened with surprise and pleasure to encourage him. He smiled and continued on this way, until I was out of my mind. Kissing his neck in a series of rapid movements, I called out, "What is happening to me?"

He replied, "Just wait, my sweet, relax, be patient." My toes began to tingle, and my legs felt weak. Without warning, my whole body lit on fire. I had never felt this before, and I didn't know what was happening. My insides were squeezing him in a convulsing manner making my body lose control. My heart exploded with a combination of fear, excitement and tenderness. All the anguish, pain, and frustration I had experienced over the last few years were being lifted from me. My body began to descend into a soft place of peace and comfort. I closed my eyes, I was spent. With one final thrust, he grabbed me at my shoulders and pushed deep inside me. I felt the throbbing of his juices reach my far recesses. He let out a call of complete satisfaction and collapsed my arms. I stroked his hair caringly. When he regained his composure, he rose on to his elbows and looked me in the eyes, smiling. He gradually lowered his lips to mine and kissed me ever so soothingly. Still inside me, he held me close for a long, silent while. I threaded my fingers through his hair, bringing his ear to my mouth and whispered, "Thank you." After a while, feeling the guilt of what had just happened, I gently pushed him away. I said, "Maybe I should go."

"Can I see you again before you go stateside?" "I don't know if that is a good idea. I can't start a relationship until I first dissolve the one I am in."

"I don't want to ask you to enter a relationship you are not ready for. But I must tell you I desire you and would like to see where this could take us."

I stood up and began buttoning my blouse. I looked him tenderly in the eyes and replied, "I'm sorry." He smiled and said he understood. He drove me back to my apartment. The entire way we were silent. He held my hand and stroked my knuckles with his thumb. I looked at him and smiled. I wanted him desperately, but my head was telling me it wasn't right. My heart was aching. When we pulled up in front of my apartment, the place was dark. Only the hall light was on to welcome me. It was going to be a long and lonely night, after what I had just experienced a short while earlier; when I turned to say good bye, he saw the isolation written on my face.

"Can we at least spend one more night together before you go? I promise I will respect you. I just want to be with you. We can have dinner together, maybe see some sights?"

It was the most he had ever said to me at once, and for a moment, he sounded vulnerable and not anything like the man I had come to know, who was always in control.

"Meet me at the Danube Bridge tomorrow night at nine," was all I said as I got out of the car and made for the path that led to my back door. I listened to the sound of his powerful engine fade away in the distance, and he was gone.

The next night before we met, I had it straight in my head that I would only be with him if it were in public places. It wasn't that I was afraid of him or that I didn't trust him...I didn't trust myself. I didn't know why this was such an issue for me. Bobby and I had agreed on a divorce and were not living together. I was staying in the apartment as long as he was at Cass Site. It was agreed that when he got back, I would be gone. I think the real reason for my caution was because my marriage to Bobby was somehow damaging to me. Bobby confused me on a daily basis, being so unpredictable and unreliable; having had two years of that, I was afraid to trust. I was protecting myself. I called my mother that night; we talked for a long time. We never fought when we were on the phone. We talked mostly about the different things we were both experiencing, living in places other than Salem. I never mentioned the separation from Bobby or the time I had spent with William. I wasn't sure how she would handle it, and I didn't want to make her worry. Our relationship was improving, and I wanted it to stay that way. She was always concerned about me, when I lived in Germany.

William was there when I arrived at the bridge. He was out of uniform and looked very handsome. I wondered if I could keep the promise to myself that I had been so convinced an hour earlier was best. I surmised that what I was feeling was physical, a chemical reaction to him, and, therefore I should view it accordingly to help me be strong. There was no way I could be in love with this man; I didn't even know him. He took me out to eat at the most expensive restaurant in town. He talked more freely to me now and told me a lot about himself and growing up in Iowa. I had never been to Iowa, and what he described to me sounded beautiful. Then he spoke to me about his property in Oregon. He told me about the redwood trees and the countryside. I told him my mother lived in Washington state and that we talked to each other once a month on the phone, but I had never been there. We became very comfortable with each other, although I was a little intimidated about telling him about my upbringing. When he asked, I just said, "It was boring." I didn't want him to know anything about me. It wasn't that I was embarrassed by my upbringing and where I had lived, it was more that I didn't want to break the spell. I didn't tell him I was from Salem, only saying it was a city north of Boston. He could tell I didn't want to talk about it, so he didn't push it any further that night. I did tell him that I had lived on the coast, and the one thing I missed was the ocean. He understood how that might be the case, if you had been so used to seeing it every day. Throughout the night, between our conversations, he told me I was beautiful at least a dozen times. After awhile, I asked him to please stop saying it. He asked me what he was supposed to do if it just popped into his head. I said, "Just smile at me instead." He agreed. He smiled at me the rest of the night.

I couldn't help myself; we saw each other every night after that. He took me on long drives through the Black Forest to places I had never seen. I always meant to ask him why they called it black, but the magic that was between us never gave me the chance. It was beautiful to be alone with him in the woods on dirt backroads. We always saw deer on those nights when we drove. Our conversations, during those drives, were about the beauty we had seen. Because of his rank, he didn't have to put up with a lot of the military craziness that Bobby had to... or, at least he never let on that he did. He never spoke about his job. As far as I was concerned, it was as simple as if he had worked in an office. I wouldn't let him take me to his house, and he never saw the inside of mine. I felt it would have been disrespectful to Bobby if I had brought him there. In my eyes, it was never an option.

One day, when he was off work, he took me to Neuschwanstein. It was not far from where he lived, and he told me it was only fitting that I see where Disney had gotten his inspiration for Cinderella's castle. We took a horse-drawn carriage up a long, winding road. The castle sat on the peak of a beautiful mountain. We shared a blanket on our laps the whole way to the top. It was intimate and the closest our bodies had been together since that first encounter. It felt warm and comfortable. When we reached the apex, the view was spectacular. I had never been up so high in my life and still had my feet on the ground. The buds were now opening with the first signs of spring. The air was still and thin; all that could be heard were birds chirping in their new nests below us. He took me in his arms, and he embraced me with a kiss. Two days later I left for Massachusetts.

CHAPTER: 41

Doug picked me up at the airport. It felt like our relationship had turned for the better since that day I lost the baby. We were closer than we had ever been before, and I took this as a good sign. He told me my mother was moving back to Massachusetts with her new husband, John. He said she would be arriving in two days, so he was living in a two bedroom apartment with a guy he had met through a friend. He told me I could stay at Mom's and discuss further plans with her, when she got back. To his surprise, I told him my stay was only temporary, that I was planning on moving back to Europe without Bobby. He asked me if there were another man. I told him that there was someone I was interested in, but we had not gotten to the point of being serious yet. He asked me who he was, and I told him he was an American non-commissioned officer, but that I wasn't sure if it were going anywhere. I tried to hide my true feelings, to play it down.

I had arrived in the morning. Two hours after I was home, I went looking for a part-time job. I was walking up Lafayette Street to the Ivy Manor, when I passed a help wanted sign in the window of a store. It was called "The Frame Shop" and sold frames and art supplies. Walking up to the counter, I inquired about the position. The owner's name was Dan. Although we had never been introduced, it was the store I had always bought my art supplies in as a kid, and I was familiar with what they did. I was hired on the spot and was to start the next day. When I left The Frame Shop after the interview, I went to two other places that day. The first was to a lawyer's office that I had also passed that morning. I had managed to save a few thousand dollars when I had been in Germany, so I hired him to handle my divorce. It was going to be easy, because there were no children or property involved. He assured me it was just a matter of signing papers. How sad I thought, that my divorce was going to be easier than my wedding. The last place I went to that day was to sign up for a math class at Salem State College. Their summer program would be starting in a few weeks, and I wanted to make sure I was enrolled. I figured, this was the only choice I had for college...picking off one course at a time. I didn't care if it took me a lifetime; I was going to get it done.

It had been a busy day. The evening before I had been in Germany, and now, by the following afternoon, I was back in the States, had a job and was enrolled in school. I bought myself a dinner to go from a restaurant downtown and looked forward to having the house to myself for the night. The first thing I did was pour myself a glass of wine and a bath. I sat in the tub for three hours and read a book. I went to bed early and slept like the dead.

The next morning I got up at 7:00 AM. I had to be at work by nine. I knew that the walk to work would take me at least forty minutes. I had not needed the use of my cane for over a month, but I still had to wear flat ballet slippers because of the incision. It was a beautiful day, and I headed downtown with the anticipation of my new employment. I stopped at Dunkin Donuts and bought two large coffees. I wanted a coffee and felt I had a better chance of drinking it if I brought the boss one too. It was a good decision. Dan was a big coffee drinker. The job was not as easy as I had thought. I had to measure each piece of artwork that came in and help the customers choose frames and mats. As each layer of the framing order was added, the calculations of the size also expanded. With my math skills, I was really nervous. In a short time, I was able to do it all visually. Dan was always perplexed by this method I had for figuring framing and was always checking my calculations. But they were never wrong.

Dan was Italian and married to a beautiful woman. He was average in height and build and had black hair that was always perfectly kept. Dan was a sarcastic comedian. He joked with me constantly, and it was a pleasant environment to work in. He was extremely funny and always made me laugh. One day a friend of his came in to the store. They were the same age, both men in their forties. He had brought us all coffee. He was dressed in a leather jacket and under his arm was a helmet. His name was Jack.

I liked Jack a lot. He visited almost every day. Every time he came, he always had coffee. He was an artist, although we never framed his work. Without anyone telling me, I understood that he was a "real" artist. He was the kind who works to make art for himself and no one else. I had heard from Dan that he was married to a very successful woman, an editor for a national magazine. He said she was a real brain and that she made a lot of money. He also said that he didn't care for her much.

I never saw the paintings Jack made while I worked there, but he drew on scraps of mat board every time he visited. His drawings usually consisted of odd looking people who were slightly contorted. Their faces often showed the world in which they lived. Mostly, that world looked hard and convoluted. I liked looking at his drawings; they fascinated me. Despite the twisted looks of the people he drew, it was evident that Jack understood everything about anatomy. One day I asked him where he had gone to school. He told me he had graduated from Boston University.

The thing that stuck in my mind the most about Jack, when I first met him that summer, was that he was the first person I had ever met who knew how to listen to people. He didn't just hear the words that were coming from your mouth; he really tried to understand what the meaning was that you were trying to convey. He did this to everyone, not just me. He would comment on everything that someone said. He wasn't trying to add to the conversation; it was more a way of him helping you add to the conversation. He was genuinely interested. When he spoke, his voice was always soft and caring. He looked in your eyes and made sure that everyone else in the room was doing the same. He was a master at communication.

The other thing that stood out about him was that he was very educated. His vocabulary was at a much higher level than anyone I had ever met. It wasn't that he used big words, it was more in the way he constructed his sentences. To myself, I wondered why he and Dan were so close. These were not traits that Dan shared with Jack. In many ways, they were complete opposites. One had to question who Jack was inside, someone who understood these imaginary tortured souls he drew. He intrigued me. Unfortunately, Jack and I never became that close that summer. I never got the chance to ask him such an intimate question.

One Friday after work, Dan asked me if I wanted to join him and Jack for a drink at the pub next door. It was a neighborhood "townie" bar that I had been to before. Away from all the tourist attractions, anyone who grew up in Salem was familiar with it. I accepted, and we all went in and found a seat in the center of the room. It was crowded. There was cigarette smoke filling the room and depositing pockets of tar in every orifice, manmade and otherwise. Some guys were in the corner playing darts. The Boston Red Sox were on the TV, losing yet another game of baseball, and a group of patrons was sitting at the bar screaming at them for it. A gaggle of overly made-up and scantily clad girls were giggling against the wall, drinking Bailey's. The juke box in the corner was playing Bob Seger's "Still The Same." The atmosphere was a symbol of life here in this small town. It was a comfort to know that some things never changed. Dan was talking to me about a customer's work that we had taken in that day. It was a large, complicated order, and he wanted to make sure I understood how it was going to come together. Jack sat quietly, while Dan and I were talking. Eventually, he picked up a napkin from the table and began to draw me as we spoke. In a few minutes, interrupting Dan and me, Jack said, "Do you know how beautiful you are?" He said this as if he were noticing it for the first time and couldn't believe he had never noticed it before.

I laughed and said sarcastically, "Yes, Jack, I'm a real head turner."

Dan replied in dry, humorous way, "Well, not quite like Linda Blair, but I don't think that's what Jack meant."

We all laughed. Dan was great for off the cuff comments like that. "No, really," said Jack, "look at her. I never noticed it before. Look at that face; it's so symmetrical."

I put a smirk on my face and said, "That's because you are over forty. All women in their twenties look beautiful to men over forty."

"No, all kidding aside, you have an amazing face. It is perfectly aligned with no flaws," he said. Fortunately, Dan jumped in again, "Jack, enough already, you're embarrassing her." I looked at Dan and exasperatedly said, "Thank you."

Jack said, "I didn't mean anything by it. I was just stating a fact." He handed me the napkin drawing he did of me. I studied it quietly. Unlike most of Jack's work, he had drawn the features perfectly and untortured. Only the eyes showed the truth. Behind them laid the pain and longing of a girl thrown into womanhood much too early. I tucked the drawing into my purse. It's reality was too much for me to look at.

My mother arrived home the next day. I was genuinely glad to see her. When I met John, her new husband, I realized that I actually remembered him from when I was little. As was always the case with my mother, she was happier when she was with a man. I was happier for her too; if I could only stay out of her way and not aggravate her, then everything would be fine. I tried to make this my mission. I was, however, beginning to develop anxiety. I had never felt quite like this before, and I was certain it was because of the impending divorce. My stomach had a chronic nervousness to it. It felt jumpy all the time. No matter what I took, it wouldn't go away. I also started dropping weight like crazy, and my hair appeared to be thinning. When I left Germany my weight had been 135 pounds; now, three weeks later, it was 125. This was a first for me. I was always someone who had had to watch her weight. In high school I had dropped to 108 pounds, but I was also not eating. This time I was. One night I talked to my mother about it, because I was concerned. She told me not to worry, that all women lose weight when they get a divorce. It was an intimate conversation we were having. I was asking her motherly advice, and she was enjoying it. It was nice. She made me feel confident that the weight loss was nothing to worry about.

I started my night class. It was college level Algebra One. To most people, this class would have been a breeze. But I had a history with math that wouldn't leave me alone. After the end of the first class, I went to the teacher and explained my dilemma. He was a kind man who was very patient. He told me that his experience was that students who had done poorly with math in high school had been more than likely the consequence of bad math teachers. He said, "Don't worry, Mrs. McCleary. I will make sure you understand. I won't leave you out in left field." I felt confident that he wouldn't.

I spent my days working. When I was not working, I was studying. This teacher was right; I was able to understand what he was teaching me. I was thrilled that on my first test I got 100%. I also wasn't surprised. I was confident before I took it. When the teacher passed it back to me, he smiled and said, "Congratulations." I had never had a math teacher say that to me before. Usually I had gotten looks of sympathy.

I went to visit my old boss at the coin shop. He said that if I ever needed a job, he would hire me back. I told him that I would keep it in mind but that I really wanted to get myself back to Germany. At night I spent time with my mother and John. We would all watch TV, and I did my needlepoint at the same time. I found that working on mindless projects like that calmed my nerves. John was a nice man. He was good for my mother. I didn't see the sparks of love like I had when she was younger and with Gil, but they seemed to get along and enjoy each other's company. I knew she had married him because she was lonely, and I couldn't help but wonder if she had just settled. I knew she would always be in love with Gil and, for the first time, thought what a shame that they couldn't have made it work.

John and I got along fine. He was quiet mostly, but he did like to talk about his time in the Navy. He was with the first deep sea diving expedition that the Navy had ever sent underwater in suits. He had a picture of himself in that big, clunky, metal helmet, and he was proud of it. I thought it looked like a scary thing to agree to do and was amazed that the Navy had just sent these guys under the water in them, not knowing if they were going to work. Meanwhile, my relationship with my mother was changing. She didn't have the sour look as much anymore, now that John was around. With myself being older, I could now see that although I had always thought I was the source of her sour look, it was really a result of her loneliness. I always knew it was hard for my mother to be alone with three kids. Even as a young child, I often felt guilty about it. Now for the first time, I wondered if she had ever regretted it. I was beginning to see her as a person who was separate from my mother, who had a life. It was a life she hadn't always had a choice with, a life I would have hated to have had.

The court date for my divorce was coming up. I called Bobby in Germany and told him when it was. True to form, he acted like he didn't know what I was talking about. I would like to say I was surprised by this, but I wasn't. He asked me why I wanted a divorce and if we couldn't just talk about it first. I felt like he was living on another planet and wanted to throttle him through the phone, but I knew that anger was not going to make it better. I wanted him to sign those papers, so I decided that reasoning was probably best. I said, "Bobby, you deserve someone who can give you children, someone that you really love. You have had a difficult time with the loss of your mother and the hard time the Army has always given you. Do this for yourself." I was trying to play into his selfishness. It worked. He told me he would be home in a week and not to worry, that he would sign the papers. Meanwhile, the whole time I had been on the phone, my mother was in the background saying, "Don't be nice to him. Tell him to go to hell."

When I got off the phone, I used the same tactic on her. I said, "Mom, I'm a big girl now, and I can handle this. I don't want you to have to worry about it. There are no children or property involved. It is not going to be a big deal, like it was when you divorced Dad. All we have to do is sign some papers." Then I added, "The last thing I want to do is get you upset." This calmed her down. It was a pivotal point in our relationship. I was either learning how to deal with her, or being in Germany had actually made me grow up. Either way, I felt confident that everything was going to be fine on all fronts.

Bobby came home a week later. He called me to let me know he was in New Hampshire. I asked him how his flight had been, and he asked me how I was doing. We were civil to each other, and I wanted to keep it that way. I told him when the court date was, and he said he would be there. A few days later he showed up at The Frame Shop and said he wanted to talk to me. Meanwhile, I had told Jack and Dan earlier about my phone call to Germany, when he had acted like he didn't realize we were getting a divorce. When he walked through the door, I said, "Oh no, there's Bobby." Dan and Jack immediately got up from their seats and walked over to him. When he said that he wanted to speak to me, Dan put his chest in Bobby's face and said, "She doesn't want to see you." Jack stood there quietly next to Dan. I went out front and said, "Wait a minute. I'll talk to him." Dan looked at me and said, "Are you sure?" I said, "Yeah, its ok." Both men left the front room yet stood in the large opening to the back to make sure I was ok. Their protectiveness was sweet, but I was confused about where it came from. Bobby started in again, asking me if I felt I was doing the right thing. I told him I was. When he kept harping on it, I told him that he wasn't going to change my mind and to please let me get back to work. When he didn't leave right away, Dan came back and threw him out.

When the day finally arrived, I had such anxiety that the ever-present trembling that I got when I was scared was the first thing to greet me when I woke up. I'm sure the fact that I hadn't been able to eat breakfast or dinner the night before had something to do with it. The shakiness began with my hands that morning, when I tried to drink my coffee. By the time I was ready to go, it had worked its way through my body. My legs felt weak, and my stomach was in knots. It literally felt like my knees were knocking together. I was an emotional mess. It was obvious that this was difficult for me; anyone with eyes could see that. My mother, however, didn't ask if she could come with me. I was disappointed by her lack of concern but knew in my heart that I more than likely would have turned her down anyway. I was afraid she might have made a scene in the halls of the courtroom, if Bobby acted up. They were both so unpredictable. I didn't want to have to play referee between them, even if I knew it was going to be for the last time.

I walked the mile to the court by myself. Fortunately my joints had been cooperating. With every step I took, I felt I was heading towards freedom. Unlike my walk down the aisle for my wedding, I had no doubts whatsoever that what I was doing was right. But for some reason, other parts of my body were reacting strongly to the events that were about to unfold. And by the time I was sitting on the courthouse steps, waiting for my lawyer to arrive, I had difficulty breathing and my face had a butterfly rash across my nose and extending to both cheeks. I made a mental note to mention it to the next doctor I saw.

I tried so hard not to let anyone see my trembling, but it was impossible. Sitting on the cold, stone wall, I placed my hands between my knees. I felt that everyone who looked at me saw a person who was ready to have a nervous breakdown. I didn't meet anyone's gaze who passed by me. Instead, I just looked at my feet and prayed to God that my lawyer would arrive before Bobby did. With Bobby's history of being late, I knew the odds were in my favor. Looking across the street to a dark alley I saw Shadow Man lurking. I gave him a nod with my head in recognition.

When my lawyer finally arrived, Bobby was still nowhere to be seen. A panic grew inside me; I was thinking that maybe he wouldn't show. He wasn't having representation. I told him he could, but he chose not to. I had my lawyer with me, and Bobby was to be alone. A few minutes later, he walked through the door. From the start, he was difficult. He began asking the judge what a lot of the legal words meant on the documents, and I think the judge was a little angry that he hadn't read them ahead of time with a lawyer. But that was Bobby; he always had a way of antagonizing people. All the papers had said was that I was taking back whatever I brought into the marriage; basically that meant my clothes. I gave Bobby everything we had acquired in Germany, such as the couch and stereo. We never did get a TV. I always had my own bank account when we were married; Bobby knew I had taken that money with me when I left. It was what I was using to pay for the divorce; Bobby didn't have to pay a dime. As a matter of fact, he didn't have to pay alimony either. This was an arrangement to be free from me financially and emotionally. It was an ideal divorce that any man would have been thrilled to have.

As he asked each question, I was getting more uncertain he was going to go through with it. When he finally picked up the pen to sign the papers, I held my breath without realizing it. When he finished, I inadvertently let out a huge sigh...everyone turned to look at me. I just smiled. Walking out of the courtroom, Bobby stopped me on the steps. He said, "Let's go for some coffee." I said, "OK."

I didn't have anyone to celebrate with when it was all over. I felt bad about this and wished I could find Cherri. Unfortunately, she had moved away. Her family had also moved, and I had no way of getting in touch with them. That summer that I first came home from Germany, I had no friends whatsoever. One day, I went to the Willows with my mother and ran into a girl I knew from high school. She was working at one of the food stands, and I had gone up to order a slice of pizza. When I saw her, I said, "Hi Kerri." Her face paled when she saw me. I asked her what was wrong. I was confused by her reaction.

In a frightened low voice, she said, "I thought you were dead." I said, "WHAT!"

She commented, "Everyone thinks you're dead. You were hit by a car in Beverly. I read it in the paper myself, a year ago."

I was stunned for a moment. Then I laughed and said, "No, I'm very much alive."

I later learned that a girl my age, with the same name, did in fact get hit by a car and die. If that wasn't weird enough, my Social Security number came up "deceased," when I tried to file some papers after the divorce. It had never been an issue when I started working for Dan. The mix up must have happened more recently, when I changed back to my maiden name. When I went to the office downtown to straighten it out, they wouldn't believe that I was who I said I was. I told them about the other girl, but they wouldn't give me any information as to whether my problem was connected to that. It was a big mess, filled with bureaucratic complications. In the end, they just gave me a new number. I wondered if it would resurface as a problem in my life when I retired; would I ever see the money I had earned with the old number? I never could get a straight answer on that question. Finally, after dealing with one person after another at the Social Security office on this issue, I just gave up and accepted the new number.

CHAPTER: 42

It had amazed me how easy it was for me to jump back into my life in Salem, even though I knew in my heart it was only temporary. Then when I thought there were no more surprises for me, the unthinkable happened. It was a Monday morning; my mom and John had gone out to breakfast, and I was home alone. With my hair pulled up in a French twist, I was trying my best to emulate Audrey Hepburn as I was ironing a dress. Standing in the kitchen in white fuzzy slippers, wearing a white lacy, silk slip and a thin, sheer white bathrobe, I was startled when a knock came from the front door. Walking into the living room, I went to see who it was. Because of the way I was dressed, I cracked the door only a little to peer out. When I saw who it was, I was in such shock that I threw the door open wide and just stood there with my mouth open in disbelief. Standing in my mother's hallway in Salem was William! Wearing his dress greens uniform, he looked wonderful. He was smiling and holding an airline ticket in his hand. I couldn't believe it. My first question was, "How on earth did you find me?"

He asked, "Can I come in?" And then he said in a provocative voice, as he stepped past me and into the living room, "I like the outfit."

Looking down, I realized that I was basically in my underwear. "Hold on," I said, as I ran back to the kitchen, shut off the iron and put on the dress.

When I returned I asked him again, "How did you know where I lived? I don't think I ever told you I was from Salem." I was remembering how many times I had avoided his questions about my childhood.

He said, "My job for the military is to run the Top Secret Document Department." "My address, I'm sure, is not top secret information," I said, smiling and thinking he was joking.

"Actually, you do have a file. When Bobby got top secret clearance to work on the coding for the missiles, you got a file too." Then he added, "I couldn't stand to see you go. After you left, I pulled your file." He was looking to me for reassurance that I wasn't upset. Again, I felt I had a power over him.

I put my arms around his neck and said, "I'm glad you did." Then I kissed him.

"Let's go out to breakfast," he said, "I have been flying all night." I grabbed my purse, and we went out the door.

"I don't have a car," I said, "We'll have to walk." "No we don't; I rented one. It's not as nice as the Porsche, but it will do."

We got into the rented car and headed down town to Red's Sandwich Shop. I assured him it was the best breakfast in Salem. When we were seated at the restaurant, I couldn't believe he was sitting across from me. I kept looking at him with a big grin on my face that I couldn't control. He pulled out the plane ticket, "I bought you something."

"But, William, I still have a week of classes before I can leave. When is it for?"

He said. "That's ok; I rented a room at the Salem Bed and Breakfast for two weeks." I wanted to throw my arms around him and scream with delight. Instead, I said in a seductive, low voice, "Nice place."

He returned my comment with the similarly seductive, "Maybe if you're a good girl, I'll show it to you later." I just smiled and looked away, afraid to meet his gaze. I felt my face go flush. My body wanted him, but my heart was scared.

"You look like you have been through a lot. You seem thin." "Yeah, divorce is a wonderful diet," I said, laughing it off. I had dropped another five pounds. "Well, we will just have to do something about that now, won't we?" he said. "Let's go shopping." I said, "You're kidding, right?" "No, you need new clothes, and I want to buy you something." Then I said the only thing that any red blooded American woman would have said, "Let's go!"

He took me to practically every store in town. Back then, there were quite a few. He bought me pants, dresses and tops. Then he bought me sexy underwear. With our arms full of packages, he said, "There is one more thing I want to get you." He steered me in the direction of Dexter's Furs, and he bought me a waist length grey fox fur coat. I felt like Cinderella and told him so. He said, "You are. Why do you think I showed you the castle?" It felt good to have someone spoil me. I had never experienced this before. Even still, there was a little voice in my head that said, "Don't get caught up in this emotionally, Barbara. You will only get hurt."

When we were done, we were exhausted, so we headed home. We were walking into my mother's house with our arms loaded with packages and bags. Despite the fact it was summer...I was wearing the coat. We were laughing and so excited to be together that we didn't notice my mother, at first, when we came through the door. She was standing there in shock at the spectacle we made. John was sitting quietly in a chair and rose. The first thing he did was shake William's hand; after all, he was a fellow soldier. I saw a million questions cross my mom's face in a split second. All I could muster to say was a sheepish, "Hi." "What is going on here?" was all she could ask.

I hadn't thought about the fact that my mother knew nothing about William. I hadn't even thought of it the whole time we had been shopping that day. I was so caught up in the moment; the entire issue completely slipped my mind. It is a funny thing that happens to a person who has been on his own for so long; he no longer thinks about his parents' approval of daily events. Besides, I had had no idea I would ever see William again, never mind having him show up at my front door like that. Since the slow death of my marriage, I had gotten into the habit of trying not to think too far ahead. Until that moment we had walked through the door, my mother had never known he existed. I had a lot of explaining to do.

"Mom, this is William. We knew each other in Germany and have been dating." She politely said hello. The fact that he was dressed in uniform, with a chest full of medals, helped a lot. The fact that he had obviously just spent a lot of money on me helped even more. She told him to sit down and, in her ever crafty way, gave him the third degree. I was too scared to watch it. I said, "I'll make us some coffee." John, the dutiful husband who also knew the power my mother could have on a helpless soul, said, "I'll help." When we got into the kitchen, John asked me who this man was. I said, "I told you. We were dating in Germany." Then I added, "Don't worry; Bobby and I were already separated." He seemed to be relieved.

Walking into the living room, I heard William say, "I'm sorry; I couldn't just let her go. That's when I made it my job to find her." It sounded like he was telling her everything. I wondered if he had told her about the many months we spent just staring at each other.

My mother said, "I just have one question. Where was Bobby when all this was going on?"

I said, "Bobby and I were separated." I just let the words sit heavily in the air. I was afraid she would think I was lying; she had a history of not believing what I said.

Instead, she said, "That's good, but you know Aunt Flo won't believe it." I said, "Aunt Flo is not a part of my life, and, quite frankly, I don't care what she thinks."

I was surprised that it had come out of my mouth so fast. I was afraid it would start a fight. I didn't want William to witness this, so I added, "Mom, we can't be governed by fear of Aunt Flo. Haven't you put up with enough trouble from that woman?"

She said quietly, "You're right." It was one of those pivotal moments I had rarely shared with my mother.

Then she said, "William, what do you want for dinner tonight?"

We spent the evening with my parents. William felt it was a good idea to help reassure them. He and John talked about the military, as my mother and I listened. I learned more about William's job and the fact that he also was the custodian of the documents on the missiles. I asked him if it was dangerous to have such a job. He said, "Only if I talk about it in public in Germany. That's why I try and keep a low profile there." Everything was starting to make sense to me.

That night, I had to broach another subject with my mother. I needed to tell her I was going to spend the night with William, and I needed to tell her alone. He had asked me when we were shopping if I would do this, and I had told him I would. While my mother and I were clearing the dishes, John poured William a Scotch. They were two men who seemed to get along immediately, and I was glad for the distraction. No one had mentioned the age difference, surprisingly, since he was well over twenty years my senior, and he was older than my mother. Once in the kitchen, it was my mom who opened the subject. She said, "Where is William staying tonight?"

I said, "He has a room at the new Salem Bed and Breakfast." She then asked me where I was sleeping. I simply said, "With him." I waited for the other shoe to drop, but it never happened.

Once I had her unspoken approval, I couldn't wait to get out of there. My body was speaking for my heart again, and I wanted desperately to be in his arms. We politely chatted for twenty more minutes, until, finally, I said, "William, you must be tired, seeing that you haven't slept since you've gotten here, even with the time change and all. Why, it is actually 4:00 AM for you." I tried so hard to make my comment sound light and natural. I don't think it worked, but it was as good an excuse as any, and in no time we were out the door.

The bed and breakfast was beautiful and quaint. The building was a three story brick federalist house. The outside had black shutters on the eight paned windows and black iron banisters on the front steps. The inside was done up in old New England period furniture. The sheers on the widows were white lace. The rooms were huge and inviting. The one where we would sleep had an antique canopy bed. The white tiled bathroom had a ball and claw tub. William said the first thing he wanted to do was take a bath. I thought, instantly, that he was a man after my own heart. The tub was huge, and, when he saw it, he cunningly said, "It looks like there's room for two." I excitedly replied, "I'll get the bubbles." We sat soaking in its warmth. I was cradled in his arms, neither of us saying a word. My hair danced delicately on the surface of the water. The flowery fragrance of the soapy bubbles lingered lightly in the air. It was the first time I had ever shared this luxury with a man, and I knew I could get used to it. I closed my eyes and drank in his embrace. Periodically he would lean over and kiss my ear. His hands would find their way through the bubbles to my breasts. I could feel him getting hard up against me. We lounged this way for quite some time, refilling from the tap twice. When it was finally time to get out I stood there naked in front of him as if for the first time. Bubbles were sliding slowly down my belly and landing in the soft hair between my legs. Taking his right hand he caught them before they hit the white marble floor. I let out an exhale at his touch. A pant escaped from his lips as well, as he moved closer to me, pressing his wet body up to mine. We started to kiss. The fire inside us began to burn hot, as each of our mouths struggled to devour the other. My hands roamed desperately up and down his spine before landing comfortably at the back of his head. Quickly, backing me up against the cold tile, his hands passionately explored my body. The slipperiness of the bubbles only enhanced my desires and caused my feet to slide on the floor and my back on the wall. His forcefulness told me he wanted me right there, in the bathroom, up against the tiles. Lifting my leg up onto his hip, he found his way in. He lifted my remaining leg, until I found I was no longer on solid ground. The only thing keeping me from falling was the inertia of his thrust. He was exerting such force, the next thing I knew, I was riding up and down the wet tiles. The wall was being painted with slick bubbles. My long hair was the brush. I grabbed him around the shoulders, so as not to fall and hung on for dear life. The angle he was catching me was the perfect spot he had found the last time. In an instant, my world began to spin, sending me into an explosion of wet, passionate lust that wouldn't stop. When it finally did subside, I collapsed onto him, spent from the energy that had just been released. Holding my lifeless body, he gently lifted me into his arms. My head rested on his shoulder, as my damp hair trickled down his bare back. Carrying me to the bed, he slid me under the covers and cradled me in his arms. As I began to drift off, I thought, "What a wonderful dream. I hope I never wake up."

The next day, we went into Boston. We walked down Newbury Street, and I refused to let him buy me any more gifts. I told him I just wanted to be with him; that was gift enough for me. He thought I was crazy, but, eventually, he complied. Inside I knew I had never believed in fairy tales. What I felt for him was a raw instinctual lust. It wasn't love. I was afraid of love. After what I had gone through with Bobby and other men in my life, I wanted something different. I needed the control. I knew that I would eventually have to talk to him about my real feelings and my intentions. I didn't want to lead him on.

We had a picnic at the Public Garden and fed the ducks. I had to go to school that evening; watching the swans, he helped me study for my class. I had two classes left; that night was my final exam, which I would find out if I had passed that Thursday. I wasn't worried about it; I had gotten "A's" on all my work so far.

On the way home from Boston, we talked about my plans. I wanted to go back to Germany. He said I could stay with him until I had secured a place of my own. And if living together worked out, then I could just stay with him. I wished there were other options for me, but there weren't. A lack of options had always plagued my life, and this time was no different. I knew I was on the rebound, but I also knew I wanted to get back to that beautiful place. I felt comfortable with him. He made me feel safe. I had been extremely attracted to him from the moment I had laid eyes on him. He felt the same for me.

He told me there would be only one glitch. He had to go to Cass Site when he got back. That meant I would be alone, if I left the States when he did. He didn't like the idea of me being there alone, despite the fact that Frau Hirsh and her family were downstairs. Terrorism was at an all time high in the area, and he would have felt better knowing he could be there for me. At first, I didn't mind the idea about being alone, but then, the more I thought about it, the more it made sense to stay in Salem, working for Dan for three more months; then I would have more money to help me get on my feet. I could take care of any last minute things here, and I also wouldn't feel like I was jumping from the frying pan into the fire. It would be a "step back" time for me. I knew that being impulsive was an area of weakness for me. Since childhood, important transitions in my life were filled with split second decisions; first made by my mother and then later on by me. He was right; I should wait until he was back from the missile base.

It was at this time that I had the first conversation with him that was, on my part, a true explanation of what I felt would be my ideal relationship with a man. It would end up being something that I would never have. I told him I was not looking for another husband, no matter how he made me feel physically. I told him I wanted to be up front with him; I enjoyed being with him. We had had a lot of fun for the month or so before I had left Germany; we seemed to have fun here as well. I needed fun right then, I felt, after all I had been through in my life. I deserved it. "I don't ever want you to tell me you love me...don't make any future plans with me. I want to just live each day to the fullest. I want to have fun with no strings attached. I am a loyal person, and I would never do anything to hurt you. But I have done a lot of growing, and the one thing I have come to know about myself is that I like who I am, and I don't need a man to have an identity." Then I told him I wouldn't be a good wife anyway, that I might never be able to give him children.

Before he could even digest what I had just told him, I continued with my rant. "For years I have had to do what others have told me to do. I'm finished with that. I know how to work hard, and I am a survivor. I will always be able to support myself and be happy. I have dreams of someday finishing college, and, if I am old and grey, and I find that I didn't do just that, it will be because something else came along in my life that was a better decision. When I can look back on my childhood without anger, I'll tell you the whole story so that you will know why I feel this way."

He looked at me without saying a word. I had just dropped a lot of information on him about myself, without having given him any details. I could see he had questions, but he wasn't asking them of me. He simply said.... "Ok" and smiled.

When it was time for me to go to class, William drove me to the campus. When I got out of the car, he jokingly asked me if I wanted him to carry my books. I laughed and said, "Thank you anyway. I'll see you at nine." My mind was focused on the test. The exam was easy for me. I had been studying for it for a month. Every week I had reviewed what I was taught, so that when this day arrived, I could do well. I was surprised, when I realized that I was the first one done in the class. I looked up at my professor, who was quietly sitting at his desk reading a book. He had helped me after class, whenever I had needed it. He checked on me weekly to make sure I was getting everything. He was the best math teacher I had ever had; inside, I thanked him.

When Thursday night rolled around, all I had to do was get my grade, and I could leave. When I walked in, there were still a few others talking to the professor, so I quietly waited until they were through. When it came my turn, I approached his desk and was met by his huge smile. I was smiling too; I knew I had done well. He told me that the grade on my report card was actually going to be incorrect. He said that it would be an "A" and the only reason he had given that to me was because he wasn't allowed to give me an "A+."

It took me a minute to register exactly what he was saying. When I got it, tears came to my eyes, and I thanked him. I handed him a thank you note showing my appreciation, as he handed me back my test. As I left his class, I put him in a different scrapbook in my mind. He sat on a page that also held Mrs. Buras.

The next day I had to work. I only worked on Fridays and Saturdays, so this would be the first time that Dan would meet William. I also had to give Dan my notice. Even though it was three months away, I still didn't feel comfortable about it. I knew he would be mad. He had gone through a lot of weekend employees before he had had someone that was as reliable as I was. Dan considered me a friend, and now I, too, was letting him down. I told William not to go with me, that I would first talk to Dan in the morning. Then he could meet me for lunch, and I would introduce them once he came. He thought it sounded like a good idea and stayed at the bed and breakfast that morning to read.

When I arrived, Jack was already there with coffee. Dan seemed in a great mood, and I thought the gods were being good to me yet one more time in this glorious week. Before I could even put down my purse to begin, Dan said he had something he wanted to tell me. He said that he was giving me a raise, because I was such a good employee, and then asked me what I thought of that.

I looked at the floor and said, "I can't accept it."

"Why?!" was all he could respond.

I said that I was moving back to Germany, and I would be leaving in three months.

He hit the roof! He started yelling at me about the time it had taken to train someone. With the arrival of the Christmas season, I was leaving him high and dry.

All I could say was, "Dan, I told you I was going back eventually."

"Yeah, but I didn't know it was going to be so soon!"

I told him I was sorry.

Meanwhile, Jack just stood there. Finally, he wished me good luck.

"Good luck...good luck...is that all you can say?" said Dan. "I'll bet it's because of a man. You women are all alike."

"Actually, there is a guy that I was seeing there, who has come to bring me back." "See...I knew it! I've been around long enough to know what insane creatures women are...Jesus."

"Dan, you can't ask me to put my life on hold because you have framing to get done. This isn't a career for me."

"I know, but, Jesus Christ, couldn't you wait till after Christmas?" He seemed to be calmer now.

"No, I'm sorry; I can't. William is coming by at noon to pick me up for lunch; I want you to be nice to him."

Dan asked if he were German. I said, "No, he is military." "What rank is he?" Dan had also done some time in the service. I said, "He is an E-8." Dan said, "Well, that's good; at least he's not a kid. Wait a minute...how old is he?" I said, "He's a little older than you guys." They were both shocked. "Jeeesus Christ, girl; he's old enough to be your father!" I said, "Just be nice to him." "I can be nice to him, but it doesn't mean I'm going to like him." "Dan, you're the one acting like my father." "Yeah, now that I know you like that." It broke the tension in the room, and we all laughed.

At lunch time, when William came into the store, I introduced him. Jack was still there, and he and Dan were looking at him through scrutinizing eyes. I could tell that William felt he was being judged, and it bothered me. Jack kept asking him random questions about Germany and the opportunities there. I wondered if he were just being polite or sizing up William's educational status by paying attention to his vocabulary. Jack had a way of doing that. Dan was quiet for probably the first time in his life. He just glared at William the whole time. More than likely the things that were popping into his head were things he couldn't say. I quickly ushered William from that arena, and we left.

The two weeks I had with William went by fast. I worked at the store and spent time with my mother. Our relationship was better than it had ever been. She told me she liked William and was glad I was with him. When Mom was happy, we were all happy. She said that she would send me copies of the Salem News. She had noticed I bought one daily and read it at lunch. I told her I would like that; it was the first time my mother ever acknowledged an aspect of my personality in a positive way. She was paying attention to who I really was.

CHAPTER: 43

When I finally left, I flew Iceland Air. That airline allowed me to have a round trip fare that was good for a year. It was the ticket that William had brought me months before. It was the end of November, and it was very cold. I flew from Boston to New York at six in the evening; the plane bound for Iceland left at eight. Initially, I considered it to be the first air travel I had taken alone that had a connecting flight. Then I thought about the trip back with Bobby after his mother had died, and wondered if I could count that. My plane was to land in Iceland first; after a short wait, it would continue on to Luxemburg. William had said he would pick me up at the airport there. When I first boarded the plane in New York, I was surprised by how small it was. It had only one aisle with three seats in rows on either side. It reminded me of the propeller plane that we had taken that had never made it to Virginia. I tried to put those thoughts out of my mind; after all, I wasn't a child anymore. I had with me some needlepoint and my customary bottle of Amaretto. Amaretto had become my staple now, whenever I flew. I always smuggled a bottle on board; it took that much for me to endure a seven hour flight. If I were ever to go down in a plane again, I was going to be sure I didn't feel a thing. I sat with two Icelandic men who were approximately my age. They were both very handsome with chiseled features. I couldn't get over the beauty of their faces. After I had had a few glasses, I asked them if they were Vikings. They laughed at me. Embarrassed, I said, "I mean your ancestors." They never did give me a straight answer. Instead, they just teased me the rest of the way.

Right before we landed, the pilot announced over the loud speaker that there was a very large snow storm that was hitting the airport, and the landing would be rough. I thought, "Here we go again," and poured myself another drink. The pilot was right. The landing was rough. We hit the ground hard, and it felt like the plane was having trouble staying in a straight line. Sitting at a window seat, I saw snow flying past me in the air. It wasn't falling from the sky; it was coming from the runway. I turned to the Icelandic men and said with a tipsy voice, "Didn't your people even know we were coming? The airport was not even plowed." When we finally stopped, it felt like it was the snow that had stopped us.

We were all told to get off the plane. They said that we had damaged a tire, and it needed to be fixed. They said there was a terminal at the airport that we could warm up in, where there was something to eat.

Heading to the door, wearing a dress with nylons and heels, I was stunned to see that there was no portable ramp that attached to the plane. Instead, we had to walk across the runway in the snow up to our knees to the building that was supposedly warm. It was several yards away, and I was sure I would freeze before I got there. I hoped they at least had a Saint Bernard dog to find my shoes, once they got lost in the drifts. The two Icelandic men walked in front of me plowing my way with their feet. The warm terminal had to be at least a balmy forty degrees. It was one large room, with chairs that looked like they had been taken from a school that was condemned. Sitting in one, I watched as a young child across from me tried to make smoke rings with his breath. The food that they had spoken of was from a snack machine. I resisted the temptation. After thirty minutes of this pleasant experience of Iceland, we were told we could board the plane. I think they were more worried about frozen casualties in the terminal, because we were in no way ready to take off. Next they spent another forty minutes loading the plane with fish that was bound for fancy restaurants in Paris, while plows slowly made zigzag tracks across the runway. The only thing I could think of was that I hoped everything worked out for me in Germany, because I couldn't see myself ever flying Iceland Air again.

When we landed in Luxemburg, we were late, and once again there was no portable ramp to assist us to the terminal. It was early in the morning now, and, although there wasn't as much snow as in Iceland, I was freezing cold and wet. It was the same kind of cold I had felt on my first day in Germany, when I had been lost and the policeman had helped me home. Walking across the runway, I looked up at the glass windows of the terminal and saw a man in uniform waving in my direction.

He was holding a bouquet of flowers when I saw him, and he was wearing a huge smile. He kissed me for a long time, as others pushed their way past us. We gathered my luggage and loaded it in the Porsche. Driving down the street, he said, "I have some friends who live around here, just over the border of Germany. They have invited us for breakfast." Their names were Katrin and Matthias, and they were German. I really just wanted to go home, but that was still many kilometers and several hours away.

William told me that Katrin and Matthias owned the largest chain of drugstores in Germany. They were his age and didn't have any children. He said their house was like no other that he had ever seen: huge, with a beautiful balcony that overlooked breathtaking views. He said it had been built a few years earlier and added it was less than a half mile away from a missile site that was similar to Cass Site. I was surprised. I asked him why they would ever want to build a house so close to nuclear missiles. He said that they figured nuclear war was inevitable and that when the time came, they wanted it to be quick. A chill ran down my spine. For the first time I realized how protected and naive our lives were in America.

William was right; their house was impressive. It looked like a three story German chalet, complete with balconies on the top two floors. The outside was German stucco with exposed beams. Behind the house were mountains and the Black Forest. It was astounding. There were no other houses to be seen. At the end of the road, far into the distance, was a barbed wire fence. William didn't have to tell me; I knew what it was.

When we pulled up in front, the sun was shining, dancing delicately on the hand carved scroll work that lined the balconies. Katrin met us at the big glass door that led to the entrance of their home. She was so tiny that it felt like if there had been even the slightest of wind, she would have been blown from the stoop. She seemed dwarfed in front of this massive backdrop that was their home. In her forties, with blonde, kinky, curly hair that sat on her shoulders, one could sense she was a woman with class. Matthias, who was standing behind her, was physically her opposite. He was over six feet, an abnormality for German men, from what I had experienced. He was extremely thin, a usual German male trait. And he had dark straight hair. Both of them were delighted to see us and greeted us with perfect English.

The first level of their house was an open floor plan. We were standing in a large living room that took up the entire bottom half of it. There were approximately eight wooden pillars standing in the middle of that room, supporting the rest of the floors. They were made from weathered wooden beams, and when I asked about it, they told me they had come from old German buildings in town. You could still see the chiseling that had been made by century old hands. The room had at least four couches with expensive fabrics, along with a half dozen chairs and tables. A bearskin rug was hung on one wall; on another was a floor to ceiling bookcase, filled with books written in several different languages. The hardwood floors were scattered with the most beautiful Turkish rugs I had ever seen. They were earth tone in color and went well with the eclectic array of objects in the room. The back of the house, which overlooked the mountains and German countryside, was solid glass. Throughout the room were large ferns and eight foot fig trees. The whole scene was like a picture out of Architectural Digest. The kitchen that was off to the right had the only full size American refrigerator I had ever seen in Germany. That entire room had floors and walls tiled with grey and black granite. Their white marble canister set read cannabis, hashish, and cocaine instead of sugar, coffee, and flour. I assumed it was a pharmacist's joke.

Breakfast was set up in the dining room/greenhouse that overlooked the mountains. It was a smorgasbord of wurst, cheese and eggs. Espresso was served in tiny, beautiful cups. The display was pleasant to the eye and looked as if it should be painted. Every meal I had ever eaten in German households was set up like this. I loved the style of these feasts.

We spent the day with Katrin and Matthias. We mostly talked about mutual friends that they shared with William and about car racing and Porsches. I learned that day that William not only drove a custom Porsche, but the world known owner of the custom shop, Louis was his best friend. Louis owned the biggest custom Porsche Company in Germany. He had been featured many times in Road and Track Magazine and had a professional racing team. He also had a personal one, made up of mostly friends; this was the one that Katrin, Matthias, and William belonged to. Several times a year, they all raced to Monte Carlo for the weekend. I asked them if they did this on the street. I could only imagine how dangerous it was. Matthias, confused by my question, asked, "How else would you get there?" I felt stupid by my inquiry. As a matter of fact, I was beginning to feel very uncomfortable and out of my league among these people. The Germany I was experiencing with them was very different from the one I had left. I sat quietly with these personal thoughts, as William was telling Katrin and Matthias about Louis's plans for expansion into the American market.

The time we spent at their house went long into the night, with a lot of expensive French wine. At ten in the evening, when William said that we should go, they offered us a guest room instead. The drive back to William's house was at least two hours long; he was tired, and I was practically comatose from traveling. When they offered it to us again, we said yes. We slept that night in a feathered king size bed. The minute my head hit the pillow, I fell fast asleep.

The next day, when we woke up, the house was empty. The table was set for breakfast with a sweet note that said, "Enjoy yourselves. Our home is yours. Love, Katrin and Matthias." After we ate and cleared the table, we were on the road again, heading for our home. William drove very fast and expertly. Now that I knew he raced, I found myself purposely looking at the speedometer. It was in kilometers, which were always difficult for me to figure. The dial said 150. I later learned that it was approximately 95 miles per hour. Despite the speed, the car handled as smoothly as if we were on glass. I wasn't frightened at all. William sat confidently with his hand on my thigh, when it wasn't on the shift.

When we pulled up in front of our apartment, we were met by the entire Hirsch family: all seven daughters, mother and father. They were all standing on the sidewalk by the time it took us to park the car. Frau Hirsch approached me first, as I stepped from the vehicle. She was the woman I had met at that first encounter at William's house. She was laughing and crying when she saw me. She greeted me like her long lost daughter. I immediately fell in love with her. The girls were all smiling at me as well. They were cordial and polite; they took my bags from my hands. The two oldest ones spoke a little English, but only a little. Herr Hirsch was disabled. I thought perhaps he had had a stroke. He was trying his best to talk to me and hug me. Parading up the stairs, the girls left my luggage at the door. Frau Hirsch had a strudel and a spaetzle casserole for us. We thanked them and walked in to our apartment.

When we got inside, we placed my luggage in the bedroom. William took me in his arms, and kissed me lovingly. Then he tenderly removed my clothing. We were finally together. The chemistry that we had first felt over a year before this was still strong. It would be the only time in my life I would experience the magic of love at first sight, although, at the time, I was unwilling to admit it. Afterwards, we lay in each other's arms. I played with the hair on his chest; he gently stroked my bare shoulder. His body was different from men I had known in the past. It was older and softer. I rested my head on it. We weren't saying a word. We were at that quiet place that we had first visited in the tub.

For lunch, I heated the food that was given to us by Frau Hirsch. When I went into the kitchen, I realized that all his pots and pans were solid copper. At first, they looked as if they weren't meant to be used, because they were so shiny. Then I saw a half-used bottle of copper cleaner next to the dish soap at the edge of the sink. It was another sign of how particular he was. The next surprise I got was seeing his set of gold plated silverware. After lunch, we made love again. That evening we watched "Casablanca" on TV.

The next morning, 4:00 AM arrived very quickly; at first I wondered if the previous day had been a dream. Seeing William go about his morning routine made me smile at how set he was in his ways. He was dressed in his fatigues and carrying a cup of hot coffee, when he kissed me goodbye and was out the door. After he left, I sat at the table holding my own coffee. I was so happy. My mind was reeling with all that had happened in the last day. I couldn't believe this poor girl from Salem was sitting here without a single responsibility. My life had been so filled with anticipation of the next misfortune that I had never realized that life could be so welcoming. And to add to the entire scenario, I had a man who was handsome and thoughtful. In a short while, when I came out of my dream, I went into the other room to make the bed.

German beds were different from American ones. They were usually lumpy, because most were made out of feathers and goose down. None of them were an American standard size. The blankets were a similar story; they were feather duvets. In most cases, German beds were easier to make. The sheets had buttons to keep them in place, and the duvets sat neatly on top. That day, however, William had an American sheet on the bed. American sheets were slightly larger and often pulled out from under the mattress. This had happened, so I tried to fix it. I lifted the mattress slightly to tuck it back in, when I was taken by surprise. Sitting perched near the top of the bed and looking back at me was a hand gun. I dropped the mattress down hard in astonishment. I walked into the living room as far away from it as possible. I was too afraid to see if it was loaded. I couldn't believe we had slept and made love with it underneath us. I wasn't completely naive; I figured he had it because of his job. The issue was that I wasn't sure I could ever sleep comfortably knowing it was there. What if it ever went off when we rolled over? Was that even possible? All these thoughts were going through my head, when I decided it was best that I ignore them until he came home and then asked him these questions myself. I went back into the room and made the bed as best I could without disturbing it.

At two in the afternoon, it started to snow. My experience with storms in this country was that they were never much to worry about. This one turned out to be no different. I decided to go for a walk and see what was available in this tiny town in the way of business. As I was leaving, I remembered what William had told me; he had said that the door should be locked at all times, because Tiegar, his cat, knew how to hang on the latch and open it. Tiegar was watching me as I tried to figure out how it worked. He was sure I would make a mistake and therefore give him the opportunity to go see Frau Hirsch for some table scraps.

When I stepped onto the sidewalk, I turned left and started walking down the street. The first retail store I saw was a drugstore. It was seated between two residential homes; there was nothing else in the form of retail around it. I wondered if it belonged to Katrin and Matthias. I went inside and had a look around. I was pleased that it had all the essentials, including my allergy medication. I walked further down the street and saw a flower shop. Because it was winter, all the pretty blooms were inside; only evergreens and holly were left on the sidewalk. It also stood by itself. Two houses down, I could detect mooing sounds. I thought it must be where the neighborhood milk lady lived, it seemed every town had one. I was right. Hanging over the fence was a group of cows. I went over and gently patted them. They seemed happy to see me and welcomed me to the neighborhood.

As I was standing with the cows, I heard a jingling sound coming from another direction. It came from the door of a store that I could see at the intersection at the end of the street. I turned and headed in that direction. It was a small German grocery store that carried everything except meat and bread. Those things I could purchase next door, where the butcher and bakery sat. I went into all three to purchase the ingredients for a special dinner for William when he got home that evening. I was excited to please him and thrilled that I would have something to occupy my mind before he arrived. Passing the flower shop again, I bought some pretty blooms. Somehow this relationship was feeling more like a marriage than Bobby and mine ever had. And we had only been together for less than a day.

I went home and fixed the apartment up pretty with flowers and music. William had said he would be home at six; I made sure he would be greeted by wonderful aromas. When I was pouring the wine, the clock in the living room chimed. It was six in the evening, and I heard his key in the door. He was home exactly when he had said he would be (another thing I had not been used to).

After our dinner, William joined me in the kitchen to help with the dishes. "William, I can do these, why don't you go and pour us some wine, and I will be through in a minute." "Barb, I didn't bring you here to be my housekeeper." He said laughing.

"Hmmm, maybe not, but I am willing to be your concubine," I said, as I grabbed his backside with a wet, soapy hand. Scooping up a handful of lather from the sink, I added..."ooo bubbles." I smiled and lightly blew them into the air.

Grabbing me around the waist, he lifted me in the air and laughed; placing me on the counter he cupped my butt and slid me closer to him. I wrapped my legs around his back. We held each other tenderly, his head on my chest, mine cradled against his head. Breaking the spell he said, "I have a surprise for you. I signed us up for a weeklong ski trip at the Winklmoos, in the Alps. When I told him I knew nothing about skiing, he said not to worry, because he had also signed me up for a week long ski class for beginners. William was an expert skier and said that he wanted me to eventually learn to ski the slopes that he did. I thought about the skis I had gotten as a kid and my pathetic attempt to ski the hills at Mack Park.

I said, "Can I rent skis when we get there?"

He said, "We'll do better than that. After dinner, I'm taking you into Ulm, so we can buy you a set of your own." I had always been athletic, so I wasn't worried about not being able to do it. What surprised me was how quickly I caught on to the sport and loved it.

CHAPTER: 44

The ski trip was organized by William's unit at work. It was the first time his troops had met me. I was surprised that I didn't recognize them from Karen's party. Apparently none of them had been there that night. Karen was back in the States by then and so was Felicia. I made a mental note to try and call Connie and Sara when we returned from our trip. The bus ride was a long one. There was only one other woman besides myself. She was a pretty enlisted girl. I tried to talk to her, but she was very shy, and, besides, I was dating her boss. The other men on the bus were funny and joked the whole way there. William let them have their fun and didn't say a word. I caught him laughing a few times, but I could see that there was a definite line drawn between the ranks. They always referred to him as "sir" and showed him a great respect. The whole weekend, I was the only one who called him William. I, on the other hand, was the mystery woman to them. They had never seen William with a girlfriend. I was polite and wanted to show them that I was approachable. It was the first time I had seen William with his men; he was more like a father figure.

When we arrived at the mountain, it was the first time I had ever been to the Alps. Having only seen them from a distance in the past, it felt like I was gazing upon a majestic God. They stood there so regal, beautiful, and intimidating all at once. They were ominous and quiet. Looking up at the top of them, I thought that it would have to take at least a day's journey to get up there. Fortunately, the beginners were not going up that far, at least not on the first day. We signed in and went to our rooms in the German chalet that was at the base of the mountain. It looked like Katrin and Matthias' house only bigger. The rooms were sided with wide pine. Ours had a bathroom with a hot tub and a huge, comfortable bed. A sitting room was off to the side, stocked with a full bar, along with an espresso machine and the morning paper. There were three large picture windows that looked out onto the slopes. It looked like a honeymoon suite.

The classes didn't start until later that day, so William and I went into the guest house for some hot cider. A guest house is a German pub. The guys we had come with were there too, and we sat with a few of them. I learned that many of them had never skied before either and that they would be in my class. I was glad about that, because I didn't want to be with people I didn't know. The shy girl was also a part of our group, but, for some reason, we never saw her again after the first day.

One of the guys was a black man by the name of Morgan. (Soldiers always called each other by their last names.) He chained smoked and was quiet. When he did talk, he was poignant and comical. I told him that Morgan was a name in my family too. He said we must have been long lost relatives; he called me "sister" the whole weekend. Another guy by the name of Walker was from New Orleans and looked like John Cusack, the actor. He was pleasant, and you could tell he was homesick, because he talked about New Orleans a lot. He was a gentleman and made sure that I had everything I needed when we were in class. The third guy I remember was shorter than I and always cracking jokes. You could tell his humor was a way to compensate for his lack of height, so he would fit in with the others. I found him to be annoying. He spoke constantly in a Popeye voice and was always monopolizing the conversation. I was pleasant to him but tried not to encourage him. I was surprised by the patience the other men had with him. You could tell that they knew why he was that way and just let him be himself. I don't remember the rest of the men that well. There were twelve of us in the beginners' group.

After lunch, we all went to the parking lot to be split up into our level of classes. Everyone had a group, including William. He was with all the expert skiers. Our instructor was a small man who reminded me of Dudley Moore. He was a least six inches shorter than I and had as much energy as a preschooler at a Valentine's Day party. He was in his mid-thirties with a thick, Austrian accent. His name was Philipp. He made us line up in full gear in the parking lot. Philipp started by telling us that we shouldn't be intimidated by the size of the mountains. He knew that most of us had never skied before, and I could tell he was preparing us for the sights we would see. He did a good job. He was like a coach, pumping us up for the big game against the undefeated team. As he did this, he moved up and down the line of us on his skis. They seemed like an extension of his feet, as if he had been born with them. We, on the other hand, were slipping and sliding just standing in one spot. The entire time he was talking to us, every German ski bunny who passed by him gave him a flirtatious hello or a nod. He responded in kind. He was not a handsome man. If anything, he looked like a middle aged man in a child's body. I knew that it was easy for women to be attracted to a man who was an expert at his craft, yet that wasn't the total picture with Philipp. He had something more. It was a magnetism that would have been there regardless of where he was. In no time, we all realized that he had a reputation with the ladies and enjoyed it.

I assumed the first run he had planned for us would be on the children's slope that could be seen from where we were standing. I was wrong. He started leading us to the first Palmer lift off to the right. The Palmer lift was a one person ski lift, with a round disc that you placed between your legs and sat on. In the center of the disc was a long metal rod that was attached to a long cable. With this type of lift, the skier's legs never left the ground. It was basically a tow line that brought you to the first level of the multi-level slopes. I thought, "This is good. I can handle this." My biggest fear with skiing had always been the lift and not the slope. Even though the Palmer lift was the easiest type of lift to deal with, you still had to pay attention so that you didn't fall. Grooves were set in the snow by so many previous skiers. If your skis, for some reason, fell out of those grooves, then there was no escaping it...you were down for the count, and everyone else coming up behind you was as well.

"Ok, everyone line up and, as the tow seat comes around in front of you, grab it and place it between your legs. It is most important to stay in the tracks and don't let go."

It was a bit tricky, yet we somehow managed. Sliding slowly around the bends and straight-aways of the first slope, we came upon the main guest house, where we had been earlier. There were several people lined up inside looking out the window at the spectacular view. Walker, always a kind hearted soul, decided to wave. Then without warning, the tip of his ski got caught on the edge of the groove. In the middle of a wave and big smile, he did a face plant right into the snow. It was the domino effect set in motion. With no time to react, everyone behind him landed on top of him, and each other, until someone alerted the lift driver, who stopped the tow. I was the fourth man down out of seven. We looked like a knotted ball of human carcasses, with arms, legs, skis, and poles protruding from every angle. The pile-up was awkward yet icebreaking. We were wet and embarrassed. With our skis on it was almost impossible to stand up. I am sure from the guest house we must have looked like a silent movie with slapstick comedy. We were quite the sight to see, all these beginners piled up in a heap. Everyone in the guest house was pointing and laughing. In the end, it was actually fortunate that it had happened. There's nothing like collective embarrassment to get a group to warm up to each other. We were the "newfers," the underdogs, the ones whom the others made fun of and, after a day of falling and helping each other up, we were truly a team. It's a good thing too, because we were also informed by the end of that day that we would have to participate in a slalom racing event at the close of the week.

A quarter of the way up the mountain, Philipp stopped us at a clearing that was somewhat level. He wanted to teach us how to "snow plow," an essential element to learning to stay upright when you are first on a pair of skis. Morgan was the funniest at this. He was tall and lanky and completely bow- legged, and, with the cigarette that was ever-present in his mouth and his hat sitting five inches high on his head, he was a spectacle to see. Despite this visual he was cool and calm. I found snow plowing to be very easy. In two runs, I had it down. Philipp came over to me on the second run and congratulated me by throwing his arms around me in a big, boisterous hug. Being the only woman on the team, I quickly looked around to see if the other men had noticed. I was afraid if they did that they might think ill of me, because they knew I was William's girlfriend. If they did notice, it didn't seem to bother them.

Along with learning to snow plow, we also were taught how to stop safely. Philipp taught us how to turn and follow each other in a line that snaked its way down the slope. At first, we looked like a child's train that kept falling off the track. Once one would go down, we would find ourselves again in the snow like a heaping pile of colorful debris. This didn't deter us, although, I did find it hurt my knees and hips a bit. I didn't care and pushed on. By the end of the day, I was so pumped up by this enjoyable activity that I couldn't contain my excitement when I saw William. He was sitting in the guest house drinking cocoa by the fire when I walked in with the others. We all sat together, and I was talking a mile a minute about how much I had enjoyed it and now understood the allure of the sport. He put his arms around me as I sat on the floor between his legs. He was smiling at me and told me he was glad I liked it, because we would be skiing every weekend. I thought to myself... "What a life," and closed my eyes as I leaned my head against his chest.

The next day, Philipp took us to the second level on the slope. After we got off the Palmer lift we approached another one that was a T-bar. He told us that it was important to find someone who weighed the same as you on this lift. Although it wasn't really crucial with this particular slope, there would be others for which it was extremely important. Philipp paired me up with Popeye, to my disappointment. All the way to the next level, he kept saying, "So, Olive, where have you been all my life?" I just smiled and tried not to inspire any hope in him.

When we reached the landing, Philipp reviewed what we had learned the day before. Then he taught us how to turn on small moguls. Moguls are small mounds in the snow; sometimes they are natural and sometimes man-made. Either way, I saw them as extremely fun. I loved the way my body naturally contoured to the rise and fall of each one. When my skis rode the crest to the top of one, I would find my knees at my chin. When I was traveling down the other side, they straightened out again all by themselves. It was as if Mother Nature had complete control of my body and was just letting me come along for the fun. It was better than any carnival ride I had ever taken. No one told me ahead of time how enjoyable skiing a mogul was...I hadn't even heard of them until five minutes before I was to experience my first one.

At lunch time we skied down to a guest house that was actually a pub, halfway up the mountain. It wasn't the one that had our rooms in it. There were at least four of these buildings along the trails from the top. We were going to the one that was second from the bottom. It had been snowing lightly all morning. Sticking our skis into the snow outside, we headed for the door. By the time we were entering the guest house, we were all soaked; unfortunately, so were the fifty other people who had entered ahead of us. On the shellacked hardwood floor at the door was a puddle of water. Morgan was first. When he started to fall, he grabbed hold of me, just behind him. I grabbed Popeye, and it went down the line of people from there. There were a total of five of us in all that were involved in this chain reaction of slipping, sliding beginners. After this ceremonious dance we were all doing to try and stay on our feet...we fell in a pile into the huge puddle on the floor. I was so embarrassed. But I was more embarrassed when I looked up and saw William standing there with a group of other people gawking at us. They lifted their glasses and toasted us with laughter. All except William; he had the decency to come to our aid.

Our team was definitely getting the reputation of being the comedy show to watch. We were so inexperienced in every aspect of skiing the Alps, including how to walk into a wet guesthouse. A woman in a dirndl handed us towels. When we got to our seats at William's table, I was so cold I couldn't believe it. He ordered me a cup of goulash soup and hot cider, which instantly warmed me. Periodically, while we were eating, other skiers came up and patted us on the back. I think it was their way of saying thank you for a good laugh. I, on the other hand, was ready for the next run down the slopes.

After thirty minutes, Philipp stood at the door and called us like a kindergarten teacher calls her class in from recess. We all got up and dutifully headed to line up. He told us that he had a treat for us that afternoon. He said we were heading to the top! We turned around and looked at each other in fearful disbelief. He was excited, but we were a bit hesitant. I wondered what kind of lift was going to get us there. The snow outside was falling a little heavier now. Our skis, being right where we left them, beckoned to us from their refuge. Putting them on, we plodded through the snow like death row inmates walking to the chair. When we arrived at the lift, I was met with my biggest skiing fear. This was a bubble lift that went straight up the mountain and crossed over a ravine. Popeye was once again my partner. The bubble lift was an enclosed two-seater chair. The enclosed part was made from plexiglass, and when you were in it, you felt like you were in a reverse snow globe, especially with all the snow that was whirling around us. I was really afraid to take this lift. I kept forcing Popeye to wait, because I wasn't ready. When we were the last ones left, I closed my eyes and allowed myself to be led to the chair. This would later prove to be a bad decision. Getting on it was tough. Like all the lifts, it didn't stop. Sliding on my skis I had no choice but to lightly jump up in order to have my butt reach the seat. The chances of falling under the lift were great, but somehow I managed to do it without too much embarrassment. The views we saw from this height were spectacular. We were cresting the tops of the trees so closely, I felt I could reach out and touch them. Popeye kept saying…"Olive, have you ever seen such a sight?"

I just responded in a soft, awed voice, not taking my eyes off it, "No, Popeye, I haven't." It was extremely quiet, and my ears needed to pop from the altitude. There were no birds or animals up that high. Other than Popeye doing his routine, the only sound you heard was an occasional grinding of the cable. That towering piece of metal and cable was the only thing between us and the hereafter. Looking down, I saw that we were so high in the air that it would be impossible to judge the distance. It was like looking out the window of an airplane. Half way to our destination, there were large signs attached to the metal poles that held the cables. They read "Avalanche Zone No Talking" in seven different languages. There were no longer any trees, instead they were replaced by jagged rocks rising above us like spirals of a cathedral. On either side of us were heavy crusted walls of snow the weight and threat of which we could feel. We instinctively held our breath. I turned to Popeye and held a finger to my lips in a quiet gesture. He smiled and pretended he locked his with a key. The minute we reached the avalanche zone, the wind picked up. Suddenly the chair started rocking from side to side. It wasn't a violent rocking, but it wasn't a gentle one either. Popeye and I simultaneously grabbed each other's arms and looked each other in the face, doing our best not to say a word. The avalanche zone was a short area through the ravine. In ten minutes we were out of it. Afterwards, when we felt it was safe to speak, we looked at each other, and all we could say was... "Jesus." It was a whispered acknowledgment.

When the lift got to its final destination, the others were there waiting for us. Our team was the only one on the mountain that I could see, and I wondered why. I was also surprised to see that there was still more mountain left to climb. When Popeye and I skied over to the others, Philipp looked at us with eyes of relief. He said, "I'm glad you made it. Our plans have been changed." He said that he had been radioed from below that a storm was heading in the direction of the slopes and that it was probably a good idea to bring everyone off the mountain. He was speaking rather urgently, and, at first, I wondered if it was an act, and he was just trying to teach us another lesson. He told us that storms hit fast up there, and we could have white-out conditions. A white-out, I knew from driving, is when the visibility is so poor you cannot see past the hood of your car. I've experienced that a few times in the long winters of Massachusetts. Philipp, however, was saying that on a mountain, the sky and ground becomes one wall of white, with no distinction between the two. Then he informed us of the necessary precautions a skier must take in case he finds himself in that situation. Basically, as beginners in a school such as this, we should stop where we were and wait for the ski patrol. If you were skiing alone, it was important to also stop and wait for the storm to pass over you, before you headed back down the slope. Walker raised his hand and asked why stopping was so important; wouldn't the chances of freezing or being snowed in be greater? Philipp's response was simple... "So you don't ski off the mountain." His words hung in the swirl of snow that was beginning to gather around us.

Popeye looked at me and whispered, "This could be bad, Olive." I just looked at him and, for the first time, was grateful for his humor. Philipp, bringing us all back to reality, said, "So are we all ready? We are going to ski down the mountain in a line formation. Stay with the group please." Lining up behind one another, the twelve of us did as he said. I was last, with Popeye in front of me and Walker in front of him. I felt bad that we had to get off the mountain. This part of the run looked fun. Although the visibility was getting really poor, I was certain it was beautiful as well. The snow started to pick up more now, and if I were back home, I would have been sure we were in a Nor'easter. Snaking down the mountain single file, I was amazed at how, collectively, we were so much better at this sport than we had been the day we had first arrived. Being the last person in the line, I had a perfect view of the gracefulness we were displaying as a group. I smiled to myself and felt pride at how we had worked together to accomplish this task. When we had started out, we were all falling and frustrated. After the shy girl dropped out, when one person showed signs of wanting to quit, we got him through it as a group and helped him persevere. I was wishing William could see how well his men worked together and how they went out of their way to make me feel like one of them. I thought to myself, I must tell him this when we get down from this run.

Suddenly, a reality hit me. Where was William skiing? Was he on a dangerous side of this mountain with the same threat of white out conditions? I knew wherever he was, it was a more dangerous side than where we were. I began to worry about him. All these worries were whirling though my head. There was no distinction between the storm that was raging inside me and the one that was swirling in front of me. I tried to concentrate on Popeye, who was directly in front of me, but it was getting more difficult. The snow was getting even worse. I could now only make out Walker as a dark silhouette. No longer could I see the insignias on his ski clothes. I couldn't see any of the others ahead of him. I no sooner had thought this, that he disappeared altogether into the snow.

Apparently, Popeye had realized this at the exact same time I had. He abruptly stopped, causing me to ram into his back. We collided and found ourselves on the ground in a pile of snow. We had to use all our might to keep from sliding down the mountain head first. One of my skis came free from the binding. Holding each other, we both watched as it disappeared out of sight into the white. Together, we helped each other up. Holding on for fear of falling again, I realized that all I could visually make out were the dark goggles on his face. All around us was a wall of snow. If I didn't know I had feet at the end of my legs, somebody would have had to tell me, because I couldn't see them or feel them. We tried to communicate with each other, but the wind was loud and carried our voices to destinations unknown. I saw that his mouth was moving, but his words hit me as if on a dubbed delay, like a foreign movie, only giving me fragmented words from his sentences. In the thickness of the air, a sentence was carried back to me, "Don't worry, Olive, They --- come---get us." I could tell he was scared too. I tried not to panic.

It started to get bitter cold. The temperature felt as if it had dropped ten degrees in the short time we had been there. When I had looked at the thermometer before we had left that morning, it was 28 degrees Fahrenheit. Now I was certain it was 18. I wondered how long this snow condition could last. I prayed it wouldn't get any colder. A stronger gust of wind hit us, and we grabbed each other tighter. With the cold we instinctively hugged to keep warm. Despite all that was happening to us, I couldn't help but wish Popeye were taller. His head was buried in my chest. I did the best I could to cradle my face into his shoulder, to protect it from the wind.

I don't know how long we were up there in that position. I know it felt like a lifetime. My face felt as if the skin on my cheeks was frozen. At first they hurt, and then they burned really badly. After awhile, I couldn't feel them at all. My joints from my neck to my ankles were throbbing. I knew that Shadow Man was with us. I could feel him. With the whiteness all around us, I couldn't see him. I am not sure how long we stood there, but the snow seemed to lessen as time went on. I was so disoriented by having no vision, that I doubted my own eyes when it first started easing. It is strange what happens to your other senses when you are faced with conditions such as this. My lungs, for the first time in my life, felt like they could freeze. I knew in my head this was bad. I was wondering if Popeye felt it too, but we had stopped trying to talk to each other long before that.

Suddenly, as quickly as it had come, the snow started to dissipate. I noticed, for the first time, that we were actually at the crest of the tree line. In the distance, I saw two headlights heading our way, making me think of the night Felicia and I had been on the fussganger with the mopeds in front of us. Popeye and I were standing in that same position. This time, I knew that the lights were two snowmobiles with the ski patrol. When they got into view, I noticed one of them had my ski. I wondered if they had picked it up as a way of identification, if they got back without having found us. A different chill went down my spine. Popeye asked where the Saint Bernard dogs were who held the barrel of booze. I couldn't help but laugh. I admit I was wondering the same thing.

I had never been on a snowmobile before. I was grateful the drivers spoke English. With all that had happened, there was no way I could have remembered my German. I thanked them for my ski and put it on. They told us to keep our heads tucked in low and to hang on tight. Popeye and I did as they said, and, the next thing we knew, we were zooming down the mountain in record time. I was surprised at how fast we got to the next guest house. I was so cold, all I could think about was hoping I could see William sitting by the fire. I asked the patrol if anyone else had been stuck up there. He told me not to worry, that everyone else had gotten down safely. I was surprised, considering how fast the storm had come in. When I mentioned this later to Popeye, he reminded me that we had been the last off the lift that day.

When we stepped into the guest house, I was surprised by what I saw. The entire place was waiting for us with anticipation. Walking into the door, we were met by the applause of about fifty people. This time it was of relief. William was at my side in seconds. He grabbed me and held on as tight as he could. I thought, at first, he wasn't going to let go. The warmth from his body felt so good. We were ushered to the fireplace and met with blankets and hot cider. I asked the girl in the dirndl to please bring me a cup of black espresso. Then I added, "Two, please," in German. When I took off my goggles and looked in the large mirror next to me, I noticed my face was all wind burned. Only the goggle area was white. I looked over at Popeye, who had the same raccoon look as I did. We had received first degree frost bite on our faces.

Philipp came over and sat with us, as did the rest of the team. He said we had done exactly what we should have done, and he was proud. I told him we had had a good teacher. I started another kind of scrap book. This one was of people who had shared unusual experiences with me that only they would understand. Looking at Popeye captivated in comic monologue with the rest of the guys, unaware of my thoughts, I smiled and put him on the first page.

There was one storm after another coming in that day. The near crisis situation of Popeye and me caused the school to decide to close the slopes. I was relieved to hear this, since I wasn't sure I would have been brave enough to go back up there, not to mention ride on the bubble lift again. When I heard the news, I whispered in William's ear, "Would you like to join me and some bubbles in the tub?" I was cold and wanted to warm up. I also wanted to be in his arms again in silent relaxation. William looked at me with that smile I had come to know so well and provocatively said, "Absolutely."

That evening we met a few of the guys for supper. It was in the guest house attached to our chalet. We were late arriving, and when we got there, I was pleased to see that they had saved us a seat. The place was packed, and it was standing room only. The smell of knockwurst and goulash soup took over my nasal passages, when we opened the door. William stopped a dirndl girl and ordered a bottle of champagne. When we sat at the table, I glanced around the room. There was a group of German men and women singing prousting songs at the fire. A mean game of chess was being played off to the side. There were at least ten people huddled around the chess table, just watching. On the other side of the room, there were people having a dart game tournament. In the corner was a couple kissing, unaware that there was anyone else in the room. The atmosphere felt like a scene out of an old German movie. If it weren't for the modern dress we all had on, no one would have guessed it was 1983. There was not one electronic device in the whole place, not even a stereo, and all these people were collectively having a great time.

The next day, the sun was shining in a cloudless sky. Meeting Philipp at the second guest house on the slope, we were going to continue with what he had originally planned the day before and head to the top. Without saying anything, Popeye and I quietly teamed up for the lift. I have to admit I was still nervous about the bubble lift, but we found it didn't rock as much this time. When we got to the spot that had been our highest destination the day before, Philipp had us ski about fifty yards to the left to meet another lift. Looking around at the site of the white-out from the day before, I was struck by how high up we were and how lucky we had been. When we all had arrived, I noticed there was a wooden pole in the ground with handmade signs all nailed in a line, one on top of the other, which read Italy, France and Switzerland. Each sign was painted on a piece of wood that was in the shape of an arrow. When I asked Philipp about them, he said that if you skied in the direction that each pointed, you would find yourself in that country.

With the sky now clear, I could see the breathtaking sights that we had missed the day before. As far as I could see were snow covered mountains and valleys below. The air felt so thin that it left a different taste in your mouth. It took me a minute to identify it. It was the taste of purity without pollution, the way air is supposed to be. The thing I couldn't get over the most was the lack of sound around us. I couldn't put my finger on it at first, but the one thing that was missing were background noises we hear every day and take for granted: the hum of a refrigerator, the chirp of a bird, tires rolling down a wet street, or the engines of a passing plane. When we stood at the edge of the mountain in awed splendor, none of us said a word. All you could hear was the sound of our breathing. The quietness would be the one memory that stayed with me the most about that view near the peak.

After giving us time to enjoy the view, Philipp told us it was time to see the summit. He had us ski back from where we had just come to a t-bar lift that was at a vertical angle to the side of the mountain. The length of the lift and, subsequently, the rest of the way to the top were only about twenty feet. It was essentially the distance from the ground to the top of a second story window. Despite its length, this lift was by far the scariest for me. With primitive technology it hoisted you to the top. The skier had to keep his skis flat against the vertical face of the mountain in the snow, in order to avoid getting the tips caught. Your knees were at your face when you were in this position. As I was watching the first set of skiers scale the side of the mountain, one did get his tips caught in the snow and fell. He took everyone below him in his wake. The drop was only about ten feet, but with all those skis, it looked like it hurt. When I saw that, fear gripped me like a wild bear. I grabbed Philipp and said, "There is no way in hell I am getting on that thing." My face got flush, and my eyes began to well up in panic. I was about to cry, and he could tell my fear was real. If it weren't for the fact that ten feet in every direction around us was wide open air and not ground, I don't think I would have been as scared, but falling, even from that short distance, felt to me like falling into oblivion. The chances of falling right off the mountain was also evident in my eyes. He reassured me by what I had just seen that it wasn't so. If you fell, it would be straight down, and you would land at our feet. I still wasn't having anything to do with it and told him so. The guys who were on my team spoke up and told me they would help me. I turned to them and said, "You are as new at this as me, it will be like the blind leading the blind." Morgan said, "Barbara, we have to scale heights like this all the time in training maneuvers. We can help you."

It was Philipp who spoke next. "She has to have someone the same weight. This is the lift I was talking about when I told you that there would come a time when it would be extremely important to be of similar weight and height. Barbara, how much do you weigh?"

"128 pounds," I said. "Well, that's a little less than I weigh," said, Philipp, "so I'll get you up there." "Can we go last so that we don't take anyone with us if we fall?" "Yes."

He helped the others get into position two at a time. When it came to be my turn, he put his arm around me and spoke softly to me, "Barbara, you are a strong skier, the best in the class. If I didn't think you could do this, I wouldn't have brought you this far."

I then said something I hadn't thought about until that point, "What is the slope like at the top?"

He said, "Like nothing you have ever seen before. You can reach up and touch the heavens. This is a once in a lifetime opportunity; you don't want to miss it." Then he smiled at me with reassurance, just as I heard Walker say from above, "Oh, my God, this is amazing."

Philipp took my hand and led me to the lift. Standing next to me with his arm around my waist because the lift had no back, he only let go of me for a second, as the bar automatically positioned itself under our butts. He told me to let the skis do the work of getting into place, that my knees would naturally come to my chin like they did on the moguls. I did as he said, and it worked. With his hand around my waist again, he held me the whole way to the top. We didn't fall. To my surprise, the lift brought us to an upright position again, and all you had to do was gently ski away from it. The guys were all waiting for me and cheered when I got there. Popeye came over to me and said, "I'm glad you made it, Olive. It wouldn't have been the same without ya."

When I looked around, I realized that no matter how hard I would try, words would never describe what I was seeing. The width of the peak was only seventy-five yards. We all grouped together to take in the experience. I tried to lock the image in my brain, to have it with me until the day I died. I came to the conclusion that the world that I had known until that point was merely a grouping of people and places to live. I was now on top of it all. Philipp came to my side, putting his arm around me and said, "I told you it was worth the lift."

All around me were mountains and valleys as far as my eyes could see. I took off my goggles to get a better look. It was more than the view that captivated you, it was the sense of spirituality that grabbed at your heart unexpectedly that you couldn't deny. I wanted to stay there the rest of my life and never ski down.

William and I spent that evening alone. I told him about my experience on the mountain, and he was thrilled that I had enjoyed it. He told me that he had gotten a letter from his uncle before I had arrived back in Germany, who had said that he would be visiting and wanted to go skiing for a weekend. I asked William if we could come back to this place, because I loved it so much. He said we could.

The rest of the week, Philipp prepared us for the slalom race. He brought us to the top every day; I was no longer afraid of any of the lifts. As we skied down, he gave us pointers on turning and cutting the slope. Every afternoon, he set up gates like they have in the Olympics and had us race against each other and timed us. I was the best in the class and won every run. I was more flexible and more agile than the guys, not to mention younger and shorter than most of them, and it paid off. When William and I got to the guest house for dinner, the guys couldn't wait to tell him how well I was doing in the races. They were excited and told him I was their secret weapon. Our team was scheduled to compete with another beginner group, and they were sure I was going to win for them. William looked at me with pride, and I felt that there was nothing that could ever go wrong in this relationship. We went back to our room, shared a bath and made love. My life was complete.

The day of the race it was snowing. It was more sleet than snow, and the conditions on the slope were icy. "This should make for an interesting day," said William, as he looked out the window from our room. I became nervous and told him. There were a lot of hopes riding on me, and I had never skied in icy conditions before. Seeing the concern on my face, he told me not to worry, that I would do just fine. He told me the other beginners had never skied in this type of weather before either. His words were reassuring, but I was still scared.

The location of the race was set halfway up the mountain. It looked just like the Olympic races I had seen on TV. The gates were set up on two separate runs, next to each other. The same course would be used for all levels. I learned quickly that the beginners were to go first. I wondered for a brief moment why this was so but quickly turned my thoughts to the moment at hand. Our team was all pumped up. We had worked hard to get to this point, and we were reassuring each other that we were going to do well. The guys were pinning all their hopes on me, because it was to come down to the best skier on each team racing against each other for the title. They were sure that person was me. I wanted so badly to win it for them.

The process of elimination went quickly. It was really slippery, and one guy on our team slid right off the course and down the hill. He was ok, but his ego was bruised. We gave him a pat on the back when he joined us at the top. Both teams had started with the worst skiers first, to reserve the energy of the best ones. I was last. When they got to the best skiers, it would be a best two out of three runs. When it was finally my turn, all the guys were cheering, as I positioned myself at the starting gate. I looked over at William, and he gave me that knowing smile and a wink. It was hard for me to stay on my feet at the gate; I knew my time would be compromised because of it. Despite the reality of the conditions, I was pumped and ready to go.

The skier I was up against was also a woman. I could tell by her build that she was an athlete. She was beautiful and lean, but all I saw of her at that point was that she was the enemy. When the gun sounded, we took off with record speed. The snow under my skies made a scratching sound, like two pieces of glass rubbing against each other. The surface vibrated under my feet, as I hit hard little ice mounds. My balance was difficult to maintain; it felt as if I had no control whatsoever of the slope. I struggled to keep my center of gravity over the middle of the ski, something nearly impossible since the slope had become my master, and I was merely its slave. The previous skiers had cut grooves into the turns that I was unprepared to handle. There were approximately twelve gates. The poles were flexible, and points were taken off if you hit any of them. The turning was the hardest. Every time I made one it felt like I was going to go flying in the air and land on my face. This was a very different feeling from what I had had with the practice runs I had done the previous days, when I always felt in control.

We were head to head the whole way down the mountain. When I would get even a little bit of a lead, she would then regain control and be ahead of me a second later. At first, I thought it would be a tie. But with seconds on the clock, I had the luck of being the one who was ahead as we crossed the finish line. I knew it had been only luck that I won the first run, but the guys were all screaming about a glorious victory at the top. I looked up at William just as he was blowing me a kiss.

Our second run was similar to the first, only this time the conditions around the pole were even worse. The grooves our skis had made in our first run only added to the poor conditions and had iced over more. I was amazed that either of us could stay vertical at all. As the edges of my skis bit into the snow and ice, I could feel the weight of my body straining on my ankles, knees and hips at a forty-five degree angle. At one point, I was so close to the ground with my left shoulder that I had to put my hand down to stop myself from falling over completely. My opponent won that run a split second before me. I felt I had let all the guys down and was afraid to look at them at the top of the slope. It was Popeye's voice that gave me courage; I heard it carry in the air, "Don't worry, Olive, we'll get them on the next one!" I skied slowly to the lift that took me back to the top.

I knew the third run would be the most difficult. I now understood why they had had the beginners go first. With every run, the course became more treacherous, and, for the first time, I was worried I might get hurt. Ice was now forming in my hair. I was warm from the exertion but found that by the time I got back to the top for a new run, I was freezing cold. I tried to put these thoughts out of my mind, and when the gun sounded, I didn't care if the run killed me, I was going to win this race.

Right from the start, I knew I was in trouble. My turns were sloppy and more out of control. It was hard to keep my skis together on the turns; one would cut in while the other rode the crest of the groove. The turns at certain gates provided worse conditions than others, and I was trying my hardest to acknowledge which ones they were. When I got to the third flag down, I hit it hard with my shoulder. It bent way over to the side, and I knew this would be a point lost that could only be gained by more speed. Pushing myself even harder, twisting one way and then the next at the waist as I headed to the fourth flag, I began to feel a pain in my hip joint that I knew was from taxing it to its limit. When I arrived at the flag, I had mixed up in my head which turns were the iciest. I had thought it was the fifth one, but it was actually the fourth. Cutting the edges of my skis into the snow as hard as I could in order to make the turn, I got the front tips stuck in the ice and found myself airborn and disoriented. I flipped over backwards, as if I were flying over the handlebars of a bicycle. My skis came free from their bindings, leaving one stuck in the snow in a vertical position, while the other one made a solo voyage down the bumpy slope. I landed square on my back with a hard, icy thud. I laid there with pain shooting up my entire spine; the back of my head and neck were killing me. I was afraid I couldn't get up. With my eyes closed in private humiliation, I heard the roar of victory from the other team, as their skier crossed the finish line to the sound of swooshing ice. Like the Olympic commercials I had seen on TV for so many years, I was in my own agony of defeat.

My entire team, including William and Philipp, was at my side when I finally opened my eyes. They told me not to let it get me down; in their eyes, I was the best. A doctor was with them, and he examined me before they let me rise to my feet. With his ok, they helped me stand and try to regain my composure. It was the first time I had ever hurt my back, and walking was nearly impossible. I was determined I would walk off that slope and not need the ski patrol to bring me down. It took William on one side of me and Morgan on the other to help me to the hot tub, where I would stay for most of the night and the next day. William never did get to compete that day. He sat with me the whole time I was in the tub. The only time he left my side was to bring back a bottle of champagne to celebrate, as he said, my victory over fear.

CHAPTER: 45

The day after we returned home from the ski week, I called Sara. I was glad to hear she had gotten a car, because I didn't know how to take a bus to the base from this new apartment. She was shocked I was back in Germany and wanted to know who the hell William was. I told her to go to the MP station on base and get directions to my house, and I would explain the whole thing when she got here. She did and was knocking at my door two hours later. She was three weeks shy of delivering Danny and brought the ultrasound pictures to show me.

"Girl, do you realize how far you are from the base?"

"Not really. It is all so new here, I can't seem to get my bearings I don't go to the base because I am not eligible to pass the gates. Without a government service job and no longer married to a service man, I exist even less than I did before." I was now one of those girls that Felicia loathed; I would have to wait for my American soldier at the gate. I was mostly concerned about getting to see Sara and Connie. That day, Sara drove me around to help me figure out the bus system. We became very close again and saw each other daily after that.

Before we knew it, the Christmas holidays were upon us again. I had been painting a lot of various German scenes, when one day William told me that one of his men had inquired if I could paint a female nude for him. I said yes, and it was a hit at the barracks. With the help of Walker, the man I had met on our ski week, I soon began selling paintings of tasteful nudes to the GI's on base. For a percentage of the profits, Walker did all my selling and delivering for me. All I did was the painting. I also did portraits of children for the numerous moms who were on the base and quaint German scenes. I was selling, on average, one painting per week for $100 to $200 per painting. Walker got twenty percent. He didn't have to work that hard at it. Because of the close knit circumstances of a military base, the paintings practically sold themselves. William usually brought Walker the finished product, and all Walker did was have to pick up the cash, from which he took his cut. It was quite a racket we had going, and I made a lot of money doing it. I liked the feeling of independence it gave me, and the whole time I lived with William, I didn't have to ask him for money.

For Christmas, I bought William another train for his collection. There was a store in downtown Ulm that was exclusively for model train collectors. I was surprised by how much the tiny things cost, basically the same as one of my paintings. I also bought him a really nice hat. It was a stylish fedora that reminded me of the hats that men wore in the old movies he had. Finding the store that he bought his porcelain tea balls in, I bought him one of those, too. The rest of his gifts were just the usual Christmas stuff, necessities for daily living. The last thing I bought was a set of wine glasses that were similar to William's, except the stems were all green; I sent those to my mother. She and I were still talking on the phone a lot. We were getting along great, and I told her how happy I was. She was genuinely happy for me. For the first time in my life, I missed her.

The day we picked out our Christmas tree was fun. The Germans have Christmas tree lots like we do, but, unlike ours, their trees are wrapped in stretchy nylon mesh. This was meant to help in the transporting of them to one's house. What is interesting about this concept is that you never really got to choose what your tree looked like. When you brought it home and unwrapped it, it was always a surprise. The Germans enjoyed the wonder of this, and we did as well.

William was a popcorn fanatic. He actually had popcorn kernels shipped to him on a monthly basis from the States. Popcorn was a staple that could not be found in a German market. That night we strung popcorn into garlands and watched "Gone with the Wind." When it came time to decorate the tree, I took out my camera and took pictures of us. It was such a happy night; I wanted to remember it forever. The next morning, when I opened my gifts, I found that William had bought me an expensive gold watch and my own porcelain tea ball. He bought me clothes and shoes and accessories. Under the tree were numerous art supplies from France. It was a quiet day filled with a feeling of peace. We had dinner alone that afternoon. We had been invited to have it with the Hirschs downstairs, but William wanted to cook for me. After we ate, we sat on the balcony. It was unusually warm, and William said it was because of the foehn, a warm air current that blew up from the south, off the coast of the Mediterranean. That day, the Alps could be seen clearly from where we sat on the balcony. It was a wonderful Christmas.

A week later it was New Year's Eve. This was a holiday that was also celebrated differently from the ones I was used to back in Massachusetts. On this night, there were parties in the street with wild, costumed people. At the stroke of midnight, everyone went to his balcony and set off fireworks. These weren't firecrackers as much as they were actual fireworks. The explosives were easy to purchase, and the stores all sold them for the event. Looking down at the town stretched out below us, it was an incredible sight to watch. With the whole town lit up in all directions; it amazed me that nothing caught on fire. It was scary and exciting at the same time. William bought us some of our own, and, after our New Year's kiss, he set them off.

We had settled into a comfortable routine of domestic life during the week combined with luxurious weekend getaways. Then William received a call from the States that his uncle would be in the area and had been wondering if we would like to join him on a ski weekend. His name was Tom. We met him at the train station in Stuttgart. Stuttgart was as close to us as Munich but in the opposite direction. The first thing I noticed about Tom was that he was so young. I expected him to be a man of sixty odd years, but instead he was only a few years older than William. He was handsome and obviously very wealthy. The clothes he wore were of expensive wool. He treated us to lunch at the best restaurant in Stuttgart and filled William in on the people back home. He was originally from Iowa but lived in Texas and was in Germany on business. I'm not sure what he did for work, but I quickly learned that whatever it was, he owned it. He traveled a lot. He was very polite and tried to include me in his conversations as much as possible. I knew immediately that this was a man who knew how to attract women. He had the same magnetism as William, and I wondered if it ran in the family.

We went skiing together for the weekend. We went back to the Winklmoos. It was different this time, skiing without the school. Because it was the weekend, we didn't see any of the instructors we knew. Tom and William were skiing at the same skill level. I had it in my head that by the end of the weekend, I would be skiing intermediate. But I didn't tell them this. William gave me a map of the slope, so I wouldn't get lost. There were a lot of nice, green runs that I hadn't tried with the school. The slopes were color coordinated, to help the skier distinguish the different levels; the green runs were the easiest. The intermediate levels were split up into two categories, blue and red, with red being more difficult. The expert was marked by black diamonds. Those trails were on the other side of the mountain, and there was little chance that you could accidentally end up on one.

The map was very simple to follow with the trails clearly marked by flags. I felt confident to use it and was excited to get started. The first run I decided to take was a green run that looked like it went through the woods. I thought that sounded pleasant, so I kissed William at the base of the slope and headed to the lift. It was a different lift from the other ones I had been on, but it was similar in that it was a t-bar. There were fewer people at the lift line, but, as luck would have it, I was standing next to a German girl who was similar in stature to me. When I got to the run, I saw a few people take off in the direction I wanted to go. At first, I skied slowly, because it felt strange for me to be up there all alone. But once I got started, I felt very comfortable. This run was beautiful. It would turn out to be the most serene experience of my life. I was glad that I was alone and could take it all in. It started at the tree line and wound its way down the mountain in a curved path through the woods. The width of it was intimate; it was only about fifteen feet wide. It had the same, quiet feeling as the top. Every once in a while, a bird would fly across my path and light on a branch of a nearby tree. The forest was all pine, and the smell reminded me of Christmas. Halfway down the slope, I came across a small, wooden bridge. It was covered with packed snow, so that you could ski over it. I stopped on the bridge and noticed it was over a tiny stream. Taking off my glove, I reached down and cupped some water in my hand to taste it. It was the coldest and purest water I had ever had.

Continuing on my way, I found small moguls that were easy and fun. I was in heaven and thought no one would believe the beauty that my eyes were feasting on. In a short while, I stopped dead in my tracks as a small doe happened to cross the path and freeze at the sight of me. I had never been this close to a deer before. It was five feet away from me. I could have reached out and touched it, but I chose to let it have its way. After all, this was her home, and I was merely a guest. I stood and watched her for a long time. I now understood the meaning of doe eyes. They were large and had a look of enticing beauty. She was tall and graceful. Her back stood maybe four and a half feet from the ground. In an instant, she leaped into the woods, as if she were a ballerina doing a final farewell from the stage. I stood there for a second longer and wondered how anyone could shoot such a peaceful creature. A little while later, I came across squirrels. They were red and busy with their daily routine. I realized that with this first run, I now understood the levels of habitats that the mountain provided for its creatures. If I were seeing squirrels, then I was close to the bottom. When I came to the clearing, which was the place that I had started from, I looked at my watch. I had been skiing for forty-five minutes. Getting back on the lift, I made that run several more times. At noontime, I went to the guest house to meet William and Tom. I was excited to tell them what I had seen.

When I got to the guest house, they were not there yet. The place was crowded, and I chose a seat that was near a window, so that I could see when they were coming. The tables were long, cafeteria style, and everyone was sitting together. I was sitting with a group of Swedish men, and they struck up a conversation with me in German. They were talking about the mountain and skiing conditions. This was the first time they had ever been there, and I was telling them about the spectacular views from the top. I was keeping up with the conversation very well. To anyone who was listening, I might have been speaking the German language for many years. After a while, they asked me where I was from. Always afraid to say I was an American, especially to young people, I asked them to guess. They knew my accent was something they were not familiar with, and at first, they thought I was from South Africa. At one point, among all the guessing, I said, "Ne." "Ne" is German slang that is only used in southern Germany. It means, no. At the Winklmoos we were in the central part of the Alps. The minute they heard that word, they felt victory. They said, "You can't fool us. You are Schwabisch!" Schwabisch is what the Germans call people from the south. I laughed and said, "You found me out!" They assumed I was German; they never did find out that I was American. I have to admit, I was convinced by that point that I was German too. After all, this was where I would live for the rest of my life. Glancing out the window, I saw William and Tom heading towards the guest house.

Politely excusing myself, I made my way to the door. They were in a jovial mood, and I felt good that I had been able to give them time alone together. We crossed the room and sat at a different table from the Swedish men. I knew, for sure, my secret would be found out if we hadn't. The three of us ordered some soup and talked about the runs we had had so far. The two of them were insistent that I do a run with them. I became frightened by the thought and told them there was no way I would do a black diamond. They said that they weren't talking about black diamonds; they wanted me to try a blue or red run. I said, "What if I find I can't get down?"

William said, "Barbara, I used to teach skiing. I can get you down from anywhere." "My goodness, is there anything you can't do?" "Did he tell you he also flies?" said Tom. "No." Turning to William I said, "A plane?" They both laughed at the ridiculousness of the question.

I said, "Ok, I'll try it." Right on cue, the trembling began. I tried to hide my fear. If they noticed it, they didn't say anything. Halfway up the mountain, we skied to a side I had never been on. Taking another lift, I found myself on the far side of the mountain. When we got to the top, I was struck by a different view from the one I had seen before. It was just as spectacular, but, because this was now spring skiing, it was much sunnier and warmer. To the left of the lift were lawn chairs, and women were in bathing suit tops, sunning themselves. I had never heard of such a thing and stood there in amazement. William said, "You might want to tie your coat around your waist. You will get really hot before this run is through. Do you have a tee-shirt under your sweater?" He had told me to put one on before we had left the house. I had assumed it was for extra layers, because we would be cold. I had had no idea it was to be able to take everything else off, because I would get warm. Doing as he said, I was surprised that he was right.

Pulling out his map, he showed me the route we would be taking. I was relieved that it didn't just head straight down the mountain. Instead, it wound its way down in a series of plateau levels. They were steep plateaus, of course; after all, this was the Alps. William called them resting spots. He said we would need them, because the run was an hour and a half long; and besides, he wanted me to enjoy the view all the way down. The first part of the run was easy, to my delight. It was similar to runs I had made with the school. We stopped at the peak of a clearing, and Tom asked me if I would take a picture of him and William, so he could send one to William's mother. Handing me a camera, he and William stood about ten feet away from me and posed. His camera looked really high tech. I had never seen one like it before. It was a thirty-five millimeter, but it was all silver and small; he told me it was automatic. I hadn't even known they made automatic thirty-five millimeter cameras and thought it was a waste. Half the fun of a thirty-five was manipulating the depth of field and aperture. I just shrugged my shoulders to myself and took the picture. We were all alone when we were doing this, with no other skiers near us. When I pressed the button, I heard a voice that said, "I'm sorry; you have too much light." Startled by the voice, I looked around me to see where it had come from. Tom started laughing out loud and told me it was from the camera. Looking back at him in disbelief and almost dropping it to the ground, I heard him explain it was a new thing with cameras; they told you how to take a correct picture. Having spent almost three years in a little village in Germany, I suddenly felt, for the first time, how out of touch I was with the outside world. I wasn't sure I liked the idea of a camera telling me what to do, but I followed its commands anyway and took the picture.

When I skied over to where they were standing, I was met with a prospect that put instant dread through my whole body. Two feet in front of them was a ravine that went down at a thirty degree angle for about eighty feet. The other side of it was a hill that rose to the same height as that on which we were standing. The width of the expanse was very wide, at least a New York City block. Skiing down it would be the first problem; getting back up on the other side would be another story.

"How on earth am I going to do that?" I asked with dread.

"There is a trick to it," William said. "You must point your skis straight down the hill, in order to get enough speed to get up the other side. Even if you fall, remember you are on the ground, and your skis will release from the bindings. But if you do fall, that means you have to walk up the hill, and that could be tough. We'll go first and show you."

They made it look so easy. In seconds they were on the other side. I have to admit, it did look like fun. As they rose up the hill, I saw that their skis rose to their chests automatically as well. It was like riding the biggest mogul in the world, and, although I was scared out of my mind, I wanted to try it. It took me a few minutes to psyche myself up for this event. By the time I did, I was really pumped and ready to go. Just as I was pushing myself off the peak, a drunken American soldier came flying up behind me, out of nowhere. He was whooping and hollering like a cowboy and even wore a cowboy hat to prove he was from Texas, just in case anyone misunderstood. He threw my balance off, as he meandered his way, criss-crossing the slope. I got really mad and thought if this idiot made me fall, he would be the one who would carry my skis to the other side. Sure enough, he plowed right into me. We were rolling down the hill together, with skis flying in all different directions. If we had been a cartoon, we would have become a big snowball by the time we landed at the base. When I stood up, the first thing I could think to do was to push him back into the snow and give him a piece of my mind.

"Are you a total moron?" I said, pushing him in the snow again. "You could have killed us both."

I took my ski pole and was waving it in the air at him. "What idiot skis at the top of the Alps drunk? You could ski right off the mountain, you jerk." He was so drunk, he could barely stand and kept saying, "Lady, lady, please, I'm sorry; don't hurt me."

"Hurt you! I'm going to do better than that; you're carrying my skis up that hill!"

With him doing the best he could to gather two sets of skis in his drunken state, we tried to make our way to the top. The whole way, I was poking him in the back with my pole and yelling at him about skiing responsibly and how he could have killed us if we had been on another side of the slope. Looking up at William and Tom, I noticed them laughing and clapping. Wafting down in the spring air, I heard Tom say, "That-a-girl, Barbara, you tell him!"

When we arrived at the top, ten minutes later, the cowboy was all apologies. He drunkenly put his skis back on and wobbled his way to the next slope. I turned to William and said, "He's a good example of why the German people hate Americans." That winter and spring I became a very good skier and loved it. We often went to Ifen. Ifen ski resort was in Austria, closer to us than any other. It was much smaller than the Winklmoos, but just as fun. I was skiing the red trails. William was still doing black diamonds, so we didn't see each other much when we were there, but that was ok; I was having fun anyway. Coming back from Ifen, we often stopped at Louis' house and sometimes spent the night.

One night William got a call from Louis. We had spent a lot of time with Louis that winter. He had had several parties which we had attended. Louis loved jazz music, and he and I would dance. William wasn't a dancer, so he often just watched us. William and I spent the night at his penthouse apartment above the dealership many times. Louis' dealership was a fantastic place for a car enthusiast to see. At the time, the production of these custom built Porsches was done only by a few men who worked for him. Each automobile was handled with kid gloves. The cars sat in each bay of the garage like glowing trophies ready to be engraved; the showroom was a garden of new and antique customized delights. The night that Louis called us, he asked William if we could deliver a car to Nice, France. William did this occasionally for him, so it wasn't unusual. What was unusual was the fact that it had to be done at three in the morning. That way, there would be no cars on the road, and we would get there by daybreak. As we pulled out of the garage and headed for the Autobahn, I could tell we were riding in a machine that had few peers on earth. You could sense its almost limitless power and it was both thrilling and frightening. William tried to drive with care, but it was as if the car were whispering to both of us, faster...faster. This brilliantly crafted machine was like an entity, and while we drove on the Autobahn, it had power over us. Like a great stallion, it was born to run out, and we were along for the ride. As we powered through the night, William couldn't help but let the car run to its limits. I was so mesmerized, that I had to consciously stop myself from wanting to open the door. It wasn't a desire to escape. It was a desire to experience the speed even more. This was a very low-to-the ground sports car that we had to deliver in pristine condition. The car had been sold for approximately $250,000 (about $400,000 by today's standards), and it could not have so much as a scratch on it. William, always a man in control, knew how to play the songs of this magnificent beauty. He synchronized expertly from wheel to shift as the car and road became as one. Every movement of his hands on the wheel was smooth and swift, as the car responded to his touch, and he had a mastery over it, just as he did over me. When we arrived at the home of its rightful owner, we found him waiting for us at the foot of his drive. We slowly drifted her to a stop. Stepping from the vehicle, as spent as two lovers, we gave him no idea of the excitement we had just wrung from his vehicle. We smiled at him pleasantly as we handed him the keys. He drove us slowly with caution to the train station. I wanted to stay in France for a while, but we couldn't. William had to get back to work later that day.

It was a good thing we went back. As I was walking through the door, the phone was ringing. It was Sara's husband, Josh, to tell me she had had the baby, and it was a boy. They, in fact, did name him Danny, like Sara had wanted all along. William drove me to the Frauen Klinik on his way to work, so that I could see her.

When I arrived at the maternity ward, the place was going crazy. Nurses were running everywhere, and I could tell that something was not right. When I saw them running in and out of Sara's room, I began to panic. When I tried to enter the room at first, they wouldn't let me. Instinctively, I lied to them and told them I was her sister. Letting me through the door, I saw Sara and Josh holding each other and sobbing uncontrollably in each other's arms. When Sara looked up and saw that it was me, she began to cry harder. Through her tears, she told me that Danny was dead. I was in shock. Not an hour before that, Josh had been telling me how perfect he was. Somewhere between his phone call and the ride to the clinic, something went terribly wrong. "What on earth happened?" I asked. "I don't know," Sara sobbed. "They are bringing in an interpreter to tell us." I went over to my friends and wrapped my arms around both of them.

When the interpreter came in, she tried to explain what had happened. Sara, apparently, had had a cold. It was a type of strep that had settled in her birth canal, and, because Danny was delivered naturally, it attacked his lungs and killed him within an hour. They told her that it was not an uncommon way for a baby to die, but the doctors should have tested Sara for it at the first signs of illness. He had been a large, healthy baby before the delivery, and the whole story sounded absurd. I immediately became angry and asked to talk to the interpreter outside, when Sara and Josh weren't looking. It was no use; she wouldn't talk to me any further about it. Sara kept saying she was going to sue their ass, but in the end, I don't think she ever did. I stayed with her for as long as the visiting hours would allow. Taking the bus home, I sat in a fog of injustice. Sara had wanted a baby as badly as I had. If there was a God, why would He do this to women like that? I was beginning to think that the answer was simple: there wasn't a God.

The next few days went by like a whirling cyclone. I met Sara at her house, the day Josh brought her home. The Army had given him a few days off, and he was at the base making arrangements for the two of them to be transferred to the States and for Danny's body to be shipped home. I thought about the bodies I had flown with from Frankfort and told Sara how well they respected them. I didn't tell her much more than that. Sara said she wanted me to pick out the outfit that Danny was to be buried in. She didn't have the heart to do it herself. When I was in the baby room, she called me from the living room, where she sat grieving on the couch, "Barbara, make sure it has long pants. I don't want Danny's legs to be cold."

A chill went through my whole body when she said that, and I never forgot it. I wondered if Sara were going to be all right. I went back into the living room and sat with her. I held her hand all day, while she cried. I knew it was the best thing she could have done at that moment. The next day they were gone, and I never saw Sara again.

The next week, William went back to Cass Site. He was to be gone for three months. I found this time alone in Germany to be more difficult than any other before. My feelings were always on the surface, and I cried a lot. I'm sure some of it had to do with the death of Danny, bringing back my own sense of loss for my babies. I began calling my mother once a week. She had started to send me packages of reminders of back home. I think she was worried about me being so isolated and wanted me to stay in touch with the world I knew. In the packages were Salem and Boston newspapers, as well as salt water taffy that she had bought from the Willows and other items she knew I couldn't get, like peanut butter and magazines. Her care packages are what got me through those three months.

One day I was painting, and it wasn't going well. My concentration was off, and I couldn't figure out why. It wasn't that I was thinking about anything else in particular; it was just that I was filled with a feeling of unease. I started wondering if all my past paintings were just temporary flukes; a gift that had been given to me that had disappeared. In frustration, I began pacing around the room. I tried to do other things that would occupy my mind but found that my mind and heart weren't in those either. I couldn't call Sara; she and Josh had left for the States. Connie was at work, and I supposed I could go and see her, but the children at the center had all changed, and none of them knew me. Painting was now my job, and I made twice the money doing it, but for some reason, on that day, I couldn't work.

I knew that what I really needed was a therapeutic bath for about three hours, but, unfortunately, all I had was a shower. Looking outside, I saw that it was raining lightly. Grabbing an umbrella, I went for a walk.

First I went to see the cows. They were in the barn and not taking visitors. Then I went to the store at the end of the street. I bought a kinder egg chocolate and headed up the hill to see what I could see. The houses in Oberelchingen were stretched out on a five block hill. At the top, lined with trees, was a large, grassy expanse free of houses, that always reminded me of the opening scene of "The Sound of Music," the part where Julie Andrews is twirling and singing. There was a bench on the side of the road at the top, looking out over the town. Despite the fact that it was wet from rain, I sat down and tried to figure what it was that had been bothering me that day.

William and I were getting along ok. The newness of our relationship had waned, and we were now into the second stage of living together: finding compatibility. I felt it was going well, but William, I was learning, was not one to express his feelings too much; maybe it was his age, or maybe it was the responsibilities he had at work. I was ok with that. I had learned, at a very young age, from working with children that "everyone has his thing." God knows I had mine, the little things that were mostly bred from fear, like forcing myself to meet new people or driving on the Autobahn alone. Deep down, I had always felt this sense of dread about my own inadequacies. It was a fear that I had developed at a very young age, of expecting too much, because at any given moment, my world could change. I lived in constant expectation of this. Because I had had to learn the ways of living so early, I had also learned to trust my intuition. I always had a strange understanding, when things weren't right. I thought about the day that Bobby's dad had called me with news about his mother. I knew it before he had told me. It's not that I knew the details; it's more that I felt that the balance was off. Sometimes, as was the case with Bobby's mom, I knew who was off. That day, I sat in the rain and tried to zero in on who was the cause. While sitting on the bench, I noticed movement at the edge of the woods. At first I thought perhaps it was a deer. Then I realized it was the form of a man, a man I had come to know all too well, a man who was well-dressed, dark, and quiet. Straining to get a better look, I watched him stop abruptly and turn in my direction. He beckoned me before he disappeared into the haze. Shadow Man was there to tell me to trust my soul. Then, swirling in the mist of the rain, my mother's face came to me. Jumping up from my seat, I ran down the hill.

By the time I got to the house, I was sure it was she. I was in full blown dread, as I burst through the door. Picking up the phone before I even took my coat off, I dialed the number. Calculating the time, I figured it was early morning there, sometime around six. It didn't matter how early; Mom never slept.

John answered the phone on the second ring. At first I thought that was weird, because he was the one who did sleep. I asked him if I had awakened him; he said he had been up for hours. I didn't tell him what I was feeling; instead, I asked to speak to my mother. He told me she wasn't feeling well and couldn't come to the phone. I asked him if she was ok. He said that she was, just a little under the weather. I knew he was lying to me, but I didn't push it any further. I told him to tell her that I would call back later. I spent the rest of the day pacing the house. I tried a second time to speak to her, but a second time John told me she was busy. By the time William got home from work that day, I was a wreck. I had convinced myself that something was wrong and focused on my mother. I told him of my fears, and he tried to reassure me. I told him until I could talk to her, I couldn't be reassured. I called her again, and again John said she couldn't come to the phone. Now I was certain.

The next day was when I was scheduled to receive another package from her. My mother's boxes came like clockwork. She knew how much I looked forward to them, and I knew how organized she was in her life. If the box didn't arrive, then something was dreadfully wrong. I went to bed that night and had nightmares until 3:00 AM, when I finally got up. Sitting in the kitchen with a cup of coffee, I knew this would be a long day. When William got up, he asked me how I had slept. I said I was fine and poured him some coffee. He said, "I have something to tell you. I was going to tell you last night, but you were so upset, I couldn't. I have got new orders to transfer to Oklahoma in a month. We will be living there for three years. Then, after that, I have to do a year in Korea before I can retire."

The information seeped slowly into my brain. I had thought we would be living in Germany forever. I just had assumed this was where he would retire. I asked him how long he had known about this. He said he had known for awhile but had been trying to get the orders changed. He had realized the previous day that it was never going to happen. He said I wouldn't be allowed to live with him in Korea. Wives and girlfriends were not permitted. He said, "I'm sorry to have to tell you this, but we have plenty of time to figure it all out when we are in Oklahoma." As I watched his back disappear beyond the door, I knew I would not be getting any painting done that day.

I put a video on the TV and watched movies all morning. I wanted to escape into a world other than my own. It helped a little, but every twenty minutes, my mother's face would find itself creeping back into the crevasses of my mind. At one o'clock, after the mail had come and gone with no package, I called her again. Again, John answered and said she couldn't come to the phone. This time I was insistent. I began yelling at him and told him I knew something was wrong, and I just needed to hear from her that everything was ok. Hearing the desperation in my voice, he put her on the phone.

The minute she said hello, I could tell she had been crying. I asked her what was wrong. Avoiding my question, she apologized about the box. She said she had been very busy the previous week and hadn't gotten a chance to get to the post office. I knew my mother had been retired for two years already, although she was only forty-two; going to the post office was a highlight of her day. I pressed her further and asked her what she had had to do. She said, "Oh, just stuff." Then she said, "Barbara, I can't talk right now; I'll talk to you another time." And the phone went dead.

Standing in the hall with the receiver in my hand, a strength took hold of me that I had never felt before. Without returning the phone to the cradle, I called the travel agency in town to make arrangements to fly out on Iceland Air as soon as possible with the return ticket I already had. I had the choice of leaving that day or taking the next flight in a week. I chose the latter. The next call I made was to William. I told him what had happened and what my plans were. He was shocked that I had made the arrangements already but said he understood. He said, "Don't worry. You can spend the next month with your mom and meet me in Oklahoma when you're ready." He said we could discuss the details at dinner. Hanging up the phone, I was grateful he was an understanding man and wondered how I had gotten so lucky to have him.

I went from room to room and surveyed my belongings. What would I need, and what could stay that could be shipped with William's things? I packed some boxes with my winter clothes and kept out enough of my summer ones to last me the week. It was the first time in two days that I had been able to even function at all; busy work was good for the soul. The next thing I did was to try and figure out what I could do with the paintings I had just finished. I had completed my last commission, and all that was left were half a dozen landscapes. I decided to call Walker and see if he wanted to try and unload them for me before the end of the week. That call would have to wait until that night. With nothing else left to do, I headed downstairs to tell Frau Hirsch. The scene was reminiscent of the day I had had to tell my last landlord that I was leaving for the States in a hurry. I tried to convince myself that this time was different.

By the end of the week, I had all but two paintings sold. Walker had come through for me and was able to get rid of them. I knew I was leaving the opportunity of a lifetime for my artwork. In the States, it wouldn't be as easy to sell my work. I had never let the fact that I had been so successful with my paintings go to my head. I still had a lot of learning to do as a painter. I knew my success was a matter of being in the right place at the right time. It was easy to sell nostalgic images to people who were so far away from home, as was the case on this military base. I wondered if I would have the same luck in Oklahoma.

William had told me that he owned a plane that was in storage in Oklahoma. He used to fly it when he was last stationed there. I knew he was a pilot, but this was the first time I had heard of a plane. He said it was a Cessna and that once he was settled and could get some leave, he would fly up to Massachusetts to see how everything was going, and we could fly back to Oklahoma together. As usual, he had it all worked out.

On the way to Luxemburg, we stopped off to see Katrin and Matthias. We had our last meal together in Germany at their house and, in the morning, were back on the road. With all the other things done, all I had left to do was worry about my mother. In no time, the shakes began. William had told me not to bring any luggage, so that transferring planes in New York would be easier. A few days before I left, we packed my clothes and sent them on ahead. My mom didn't know I was returning. I wanted to show up unannounced, so that I could see for myself what was going on. When I arrived in Boston, my plan was to take a train to Salem. Not having luggage made this all easier. At the airport in Luxemburg, William wasn't allowed to go as far as the plane with me. Our goodbye was a tearful one, and he was very sweet and held on to me tight. He told me not to worry, that everything was going to be ok and that he would see me in a month. His words were so tender that I hung on to every last syllable he uttered.

CHAPTER: 46

When I got into the terminal, I was surprised that it wasn't that crowded, but after all, this was Iceland Air. When my flight was called, I stood in line with about fifty other people and waited to go through the gate. I was about the twentieth person in line, when a man approached me and asked to see my passport. He was about fifty years old, of average height and a little overweight. He was wearing a uniform and looked like he had been working this job for a long time. He gave the impression that he was in charge. With an expressionless face, he showed me his badge. He was head of security, and I instantly wondered what he wanted with me. Fumbling for my passport, I was surprised that I felt guilty. The movie "Midnight Express" immediately flashed in my head, but unlike the movie, I didn't have anything illegal in my possession. Unhappy with what he apparently saw in my passport, he very abruptly grabbed me by the top of my arm and led me away from the line and into a back room. Looking over at my plane that was now boarding, I wondered if it would take off without me. The hold this man had on me began to hurt, and my fingers were going numb. I knew whatever this was, it was serious, and there was no one there to help me. I became nervous and thought that if they did something to me, there was no one back home expecting me, and I would not be missed. William, I was sure, was on the road and couldn't be reached for hours. I asked the man the reason for my detention. He simply stated, "You will see."

The room he took me to was actually just a space divided off from the rest of the terminal. It had been created by rolling padded dividers that exposed our feet from below. He told me to empty my purse and asked me how long I had been in Europe. Pouring the contents of my purse on the table provided, I was embarrassed that the purse also contained a clean pair of underwear. It had been a last minute decision I made that was prompted by my past experience of trying to fly home with Bobby on emergency leave, the trip that had taken days to complete. I thought to explain this to him but knew it would be ridiculous. Instead, I did the best I could to ignore the underwear. He didn't mention it. He did however ask me why I had never gotten my passport stamped the whole time I had been in Germany. I told him that I hadn't known I had to. He said I should have had it stamped once a month in Munich. I was shocked and said that the military hadn't told me that. Then I wondered to myself if perhaps they had told Bobby, and he had never told me. I thought it was absurd that William hadn't mentioned it but, then again, he never had had a civilian living with him before. I did the best I could to explain my life for the past few years to that man. When I got to the part about William finding me in Salem, I knew it sounded unreal. I tried to stick to the present and told him I was heading home because I felt that there was something wrong with my mother.

He said, "Wait here. There will be a female inspector who will be back to search you."

My first instinct was to run. I'm not sure why; I wasn't guilty of anything, but Hollywood movies can do that to your brain. Before I had time to think my next thought, a stern looking woman entered the room. She didn't tell me her name; instead, she told me to take off my clothes. In protest, I said, "Before I do that, you need to tell me why."

She looked into my eyes with a deadly stare and produced a poster from her back pocket. When she unfolded it, I was in shock, as well as amazed. Looking back at me was a picture of a woman who could have been my identical twin. It was on the front of a terrorist wanted poster, the kind that was plastered all over the train stations and post offices. The only thing I could say was, "Wow, that's amazing."

When I realized that she was convinced that I was this woman, I became really scared. I said, "I know that woman looks like me, and I can understand your concern, but I can guarantee that she is not me." I pointed to the poster. I began rambling on about where I had grown up and where I had gone to school and, if they wanted to make sure I was telling the truth, I could give them phone numbers they could call. I gave them Connie's number as well as the one at the Childcare Center.

"Take off your clothes," was her only response.

Nervously, I removed the pale, pink linen suit I was wearing. When that didn't satisfy her, I removed my blouse and slip. Standing in my underwear, I watched her search the lining of my clothes, while I stood there trembling. I wasn't sure if I was cold or just nervous. The feeling I had at that moment was one of violation. I felt helpless, as if I were being sexually assaulted. I begged her to understand that they had the wrong person and to please let me go. I began to cry. With a cold stone face and voice, she asked me why I didn't have any luggage. I told her that I was moving back to the States and that I had sent it all ahead of me, to make traveling easier. She didn't respond to my answer. Instead, she said, "Wait here, and don't move." I asked her if I could put my clothes back on. She told me I couldn't and took them with her. I think she did this so I wouldn't leave. I felt so exposed in that divided area. There was no door, and anyone could have walked in there and seen me. It was another reminder that I was far from home. I knew no one would have gotten away with this type of violation in the United States. It was well before 9/11, and I had never experienced this type of security. I tried to find a spot as far away from the opening into the terminal as best I could, but there was no place to hide. I was a sitting duck. My first instinct was to curl my body into a small ball to hide my feeling of nakedness. I wanted to sit down, but there were no seats. I wanted to sit on the floor, but with the opening at the bottom of the partitions, everyone would get a clear view of me. Other than my vulnerable form and the table, there was nothing else in the room. After the longest ten minutes of my life, the inspector returned and handed me my clothes. She said, "I'm sorry for the inconvenience" and told me my plane was waiting for me. As she exited the room, she said, as if it were a last minute thought, "You may have a hard time getting back into the United States, because your passport was not stamped. Good luck." In a daze, I dressed and headed to the plane.

The entire plane ride, I couldn't shake what had just happened to me. The words of the customs official kept running through my head. "You may have difficulty getting back into the U.S." I wondered if the problem with my social security number was only going to add to the predicament. In my head, I was going through different scenarios. I was pretty sure they would not send me back; after all I was a U.S. citizen. The thoughts were in the forefront of my mind so that, as is the case with most return trips, the time went by quickly.

Landing in New York, I headed to the customs terminal to show my passport. The line was unusually long, for such an early morning arrival. There was a family in front of me who had just completed a trip to Africa. They were all wearing pith helmets and fatigues and looked quite comical to me. They were waiting to take a connecting flight to Chicago. The family consisted of a mother and father and a five year old boy. The boy was obviously tired and cranky. The parents shuffled him, to his disappointment, from one to the other, because he was heavy, and they were also tired. With every movement they made, he whimpered. In a half hour's time, when it was their turn to declare their treasures, the boy was placed in line in front of them, while the father searched for their passports. Clutched in the hand of the young boy was a film container that he periodically opened and spoke to. The customs lady noticed this odd exchange and asked what it was he had in the container. The young boy proudly held it to her and said, "It is my bumble bee!" A look of horror crossed the face of the woman, as well as anyone in earshot. Subconsciously, we all stepped back. "Don't worry," he said, "it is dead. I am going to add it to my collection when I get home." "You can't bring that into the country," the woman said in a very severe voice. This, of course, made the young boy wail at the top of his lungs and subsequently brought other officers to the first official's aid.

The next thing I knew, there were five people there, trying to explain to the parents that this item could not pass U.S. borders. The parents were arguing, and the child was crying even harder. I couldn't believe all this trouble over a dead bee. I understood the point of the officials; what I didn't understand was the attitude of the parents. It was obvious that this child ruled this household. After ten minutes of this craziness, it dawned on me that this might be the break I needed. I politely leaned over to the customs official who was closest to me and said, "Excuse me, I am going to miss my connecting flight. I don't have anything to declare." I held up my passport, showing my picture and covering the rest with my hand. In exasperation she waved me through. Squeezing my way past the pandemonium, I tried the best I could to act naturally and walk in the direction of my plane. It worked, and in no time I was sitting on another flight bound for Boston.

When I landed at Logan International Airport, I stepped into the warm New England air and felt a sense of relief. I was home, and I had been able to get there all by myself, despite the few curve balls that were thrown my way. I felt empowered and grown up. I knew I could handle anything that I would have to face that day. Hailing a cab, I made my way to North Station. When my train pulled in, it was filled with commuters, arriving in Boston for their daily grind. Looking at the mechanical faces of the passengers stepping from the door, it was hard for me to comprehend that to them, this was just another ordinary day. I wanted to yell to them, "Can you believe I just traveled three thousand miles alone and was dragged out of line for being a terrorist and almost couldn't get back into this country because of a misunderstanding about my passport?!" Smiling to myself, I thought I should end the sentence with ... "and I was saved by a five year old boy and his dead bumble bee." Instead, I just said, "Excuse me," as they pushed past me and went on their way.

The train ride was approximately thirty minutes long. In little less than an hour, I would find out what was wrong with my mother. The safety of the hometown train environment gave way to the anxiety that was now gripping hold of me. I knew my mother was sick. Staring at my feet in thought, I was surprised when I realized that the train had arrived at Salem station. Stepping onto the platform, I looked down and changed my watch. It was 9:00 AM on a Friday morning. My mother's house was a mile away. My first inclination was to walk. It was a beautiful day, and I wanted to see the town that I had come to miss. Then I realized that I didn't have a key to my mother's house. She often went out in the mornings to do errands and sometimes wouldn't be back until noon. I didn't want to wait that long; I called her from the nearest payphone to tell her I was home.

Surprisingly, it was my mother who answered the phone. She wasn't as excited to hear from me as I had thought she would be. I told her I was in Salem at the train station and wanted to make sure she was home before I trekked over to her. She told me she was glad I was home, and, although she had an appointment in an hour and a half, she would come and pick me up. Her voice sounded strained. It was as if she were pretending that everything was going to be all right. A million questions raced through my mind. I had rehearsed them for hours on the plane. Never having had the ability to communicate with my mother in the past, I now found myself struck dumb. I said, "Ok, I'll be out front."

It had been almost a year since I had last seen my mother. The day I had left, we were on better terms than in previous times, although our relationship had never been close when we were face to face. When I was living in Europe, we had found that we could communicate with each other more easily. We became experts at small talk; feelings were generally not discussed. The one time I did let my guard down, when I was desperate and lonely, she did show compassion by the end of the conversation. At first she had scolded me, but I realized that because of the distance, she felt a lack of control in helping me. After that phone call was when the boxes started arriving weekly. I sat there on the curb waiting for her and realized that conversation had been a baby step. I decided that no matter how long it would take, I was going to force communication between us. I knew the only way to do it would be to shed our roles as mother and daughter first. I was certainly willing to do this...I wondered if she would be capable.

I wouldn't have a lot of time to accomplish this great task before I was to leave again with William, so I had to plan it right. I only had one month to fix the dysfunctions of the past twenty-two years. I knew the first thing I had to do was not fall into the role of child again, when I saw her. It was something that had always bothered me. She became demanding, and I would become submissive until it irritated me and then combative until it was a full blown fight. I thought of the communication skills that Mrs. Buras had taught me to use when speaking to children. She had said to take a deep breath and state your case firmly and reassuringly in a non-challenging manner. Never raise your voice and repeat your request if necessary. As long as the person you are speaking to does not feel threatened, then your voice will be heard. If you sound reasonable, the person you are talking to will reason with you. If he still acts defensively, put your own feelings aside and find out why.

Something changed in me at that moment, as I sat on the curb. It was a feeling of understanding, a sense of control of a situation I had never had control of before. I wasn't meeting my mother on the battlefield, like I had so many times in the past; instead, we were heading for the peace table. I was willing to agree to disagree with her and let her have her opinions. When I saw her car heading up the road, I rose to my feet with a big smile and enthusiastic wave; I suddenly felt two feet taller.

When I got into the back seat of the car, I said hello to John and leaned forward to kiss my mother. She politely asked me if everything was ok between William and me. When I said that it was, she asked me why I had come home. Knowing this was my chance to prove my maturity, I said, "Because there is something upsetting you, and you are my mother. I came home to see if you are all right." The car became silent. It was a response I wasn't expecting. I pressed the issue further. "Mom, I just flew three thousand miles. I'm not leaving until you tell me. I was worried." I didn't tell her of my premonitions. She looked straight ahead, out the front window of the car, and stated in a flat tone… "I have a lump in my breast, and I am having a biopsy in an hour."

The blood drained from my head, and I thought I would faint. MaryJane was the invincible one, the matriarch of the family. How could this possibly happen to her, of all people? She was the Head of the War Department! It was the last thing I had expected her to say. I suddenly realized how young and naïve I really was. Who was I fooling? Within the first ten seconds of our meeting, my Mrs. Buras' plan was put into a tailspin…or was it? I placed my hand on her shoulder and gently caressed her. "Mom, it isn't necessarily cancer. Don't worry until after the biopsy. I'm sure it will be just fine." I began to have that feeling again, the instinct I was cursed to be born with. I knew she wasn't going to be ok. I knew the next chapter of our lives had just been laid out before me. She asked me if I wanted John to drop me off at the house. I said, "No, I want to go with you to the hospital." John turned the car around, and we headed that way in silence.

When we entered the hospital, my mother was visibly nervous. I watched her with concern that became mixed with curiosity. I had never seen this look on my mother's face before. I tried to understand just what it was that was different about it. It dawned on me that what I was seeing was her lack of control and vulnerability. It was the first time in MaryJane's life that she could not manipulate a situation. I suddenly felt bad for her; she looked like a helpless child waiting to be scolded. I unconsciously put my arm around her and rested it on the back of the chair where we all sat. She turned to me, gave me a wary smile and patted my knee.

The biopsy seemed to take forever. John and I sat together in the waiting room in an awkward silence. I didn't really know him well enough to talk openly about such an intimate subject; besides, I had been trained over the years to not discuss family issues with others. Even though he was her husband, I found myself following these rules. I asked him if the boys knew she was doing this. He said they did. John told me that Doug had left the hospital and was now working in an antique shop. I was surprised but just nodded my head.

I was feeling a strong sense of culture shock, while I was sitting in the waiting room. Living in Germany, I had unconsciously blocked outside noise, like the conversations between the people on the streets, easy to do because I could just tune out the German language. And I had lived in a small village where background noise just didn't exist. Here was a whole different story. The intercom above my head kept announcing one urgent situation after another every five minutes, asking busy people to become even busier. I heard every conversation between people passing in the halls, talking about what they had done the night before and where they were going that weekend. I even heard a conversation between two nurses about what they were having for lunch and the crazy diet one of them was on. The whole thing kept up a constant chatter in my head. I didn't care about these people's lives. My only concern was for my mother, and I wanted to tune them out and couldn't. It was too much input for my brain to process. I wasn't used to it, and I thought my head was going to explode. It was as if someone turned the volume in my ears up to high. Sifting through this clamor, I heard John's voice. His head was bent down towards his knees, and he was staring at the floor. At first, I wondered if he were talking to me or just thinking out loud. He said, "Jane is scared." I didn't know how to respond. He was in a quiet place with his own thoughts, and I didn't want to violate that sanctuary. As if someone else were controlling my actions, I unconsciously placed my hand on his and didn't say anything. Awkwardly pulling himself back to reality, he stood up and said, "I need coffee and I'm sure you do; how do you take it?"

"Black," I replied. And he left.

He was gone not more than three minutes, when the doctor entered the room. He was walking towards me, and I tried to read his face. He had a file in his hand, and he didn't look pleased. I wanted to scream before he even opened his mouth. I wanted to say to him that I already knew. I didn't want to hear the words. To speak them out loud would physically hurt me. My brain was at the breaking point, and all I wanted to do was run back to the train station and head back to Germany, getting away from it all, as far away as I could.

It was I who spoke first, "How bad is it?"

He wasn't surprised I knew, and I realized he must see this type of intuition all the time. He said, "Not as bad as I thought. It was encapsulated with cysts. But she does have a spot in her nodes under her arm, and that's not good. She will need to have a mastectomy and chemotherapy."

He let the information seep into my brain. How silly of him to think this twenty-two year old girl could comprehend what he was telling me. Then he said something that made me realize he had no idea of how old I was. He stated firmly, "I don't want you to tell her. I want to wait until the long weekend is over. I know she was planning on having a dinner with her entire family on Monday, and I don't want it to be filled with talk about cancer. I want her to enjoy herself. Please keep it to yourself, until I talk to her on Tuesday." He gave me a gentle pat on the shoulder and asked me if I had any questions. I looked at the floor and wondered, what do I ask? The obvious one would be, "Is my mother going to die?" I was afraid to say it. He knew what I was thinking and said, "She has a real good chance of beating this."

I said, "Thank you." And he left.

How on earth was I going to keep this secret? I had never been any good at hiding anything from my mother. I was thinking this, when John walked back into the room with the coffee. I said, "The doctor was just here. He said Mom could go home soon."

"What else did he say? Is it cancer?" Without even having time to think of a plan, I said, "He said he doesn't have the results yet." "Well, I want to talk to him," said John as he approached the receptionist at the desk.

I didn't try to stop him. I was suddenly exhausted and didn't have the strength. I hadn't slept since the previous night in Germany. I knew that in Germany, it was night again. My body was telling me it was time for bed. John spoke to the doctor, and he told him the same thing I had. He said he would have the results on Tuesday and to just go home and try not to think about it. He said we could go and see her, and when she felt well enough, she could leave.

I walked into the recovery room with John. It was brighter than any other room I had ever seen. I was struck by how many women were in there. There were about twelve beds filled with women attached to tubes and oxygen masks. The room was filled with the symphonic beeps of heart monitors. The women all looked so helpless. It felt like I had stepped into an epidemic ward. I learned that day that breast cancer was an illness that was all around us, yet no one seemed to understand just how prevalent it was. It would be another several years before that would be common knowledge. I knew I had just entered a new country filled with a language I didn't understand, with words such as mastectomy and chemotherapy and Tamoxifen. My brain wanted to shut it all out, but I knew if I did, it would prove I was still a child. I had to be strong.

When I saw my mother lying on the gurney, she looked a mess. It seemed that the woman we had brought there that morning was nowhere to be found. I thought of the day when I had been a young child and had searched in the closets and under the couch for the mother I remembered. I wished, as I stood there looking at her, that I could find her again. This time there would be no matching outfits to ease my pain. Her hair was in disarray and her color looked awful. She had dark circles under her eyes, and they were swollen. I couldn't believe that in just a little over an hour, such a transformation could take place. My mother looked like a cancer patient. A weird feeling took a hold of me; I felt that these people had somehow violated her. I felt guilty for having let them do it. I stroked her head and tried to fix her hair. I asked her how she felt. She said she was tired. John told her to rest, that we would sit with her until she felt ready to leave. Suddenly, reality hit her. She said, "What did the doctor say?"

I was about to speak, when John spoke first. "He said they won't have the results until Tuesday."

Mom said, "Then it must not be cancer, because he told me before he started that he can usually tell by looking at it." She was feeling the control she knew she had lost. She smiled and closed her eyes.

I turned around and wouldn't let her see my face. I was on the verge of tears. The lump in my throat was choking me. In a little while, she opened her eyes again and said, "Barbara, you must be tired. We should go home, so that you can rest."

In her drug induced state, her love and concern for me shone through. I know I should have felt a warm feeling inside because of the lack of selfishness that she was showing me, but, instead, it made me feel awful. I was weighed down with a guilt that was so strong, I wondered if I would ever be able to look at myself in the mirror again. I had always felt that my mother had only tolerated me. I then understood why she had sent me those packages when I had been in Germany. All those years I hadn't allowed myself to believe that she had actually loved me... until that moment. I was ashamed that I had misjudged her. The remorse wouldn't leave me; instead, it was united with another type of guilt. It was intertwined with the fact that she was sick, and I was perfectly fine. I knew it wasn't my fault that I was well, but I couldn't dismiss it.

All weekend, my mother made phone calls to the people she was close to. She told them that she was sure it would be ok, repeating what she had told John and me in the hospital, about the doctor knowing what cancer looked like. She reassured them all that life was good. As she spoke to every unsuspecting supporter about the good news, I could hear their words of encouragement travel back to her through the phone line. I sat quietly at the kitchen table, watching. The knowledge of the truth ate at my insides like a cancer of my own.

By the time Monday rolled around, the family gathering had turned into a full blown party. She had invited friends she used to work with and the neighbors who lived next door. Mom was clearly celebrating, and most of us, though afraid to encourage her, were able to see it. Some who had gotten caught up in the revelry were toasting her. It was only me, the youngest of the entire clan, who knew the truth. I tried to keep myself scarce, so that no one could see the look of pain on my face. This was hard to do, considering that I had just returned from a lengthy stay overseas.

At dinner, we were all sitting around the table. People were asking me about my trip, and I laughed to myself when I realized how they all considered my absence. It was so typical for my family to be clueless about how I felt and what was important to me. I wanted to yell at them that it hadn't been a trip; Germany had been my home for the past three years. But then, I decided against it. After dinner, when the sun had started to dip below the horizon, we all gathered in the large room that was a combination living room/dining room. My mother had torn down the dividing wall between them when we had been children and needed the room.

My Uncle Joe and Aunt Martha from New Hampshire were there. Veronica and the boys weren't with them, and I remember feeling disappointed about that. When we had been kids and the family discussions around the dining room table had begun, Veronica and I used to escape to our room to talk about boys. I wished we were that age again and she were there to distract me; especially because I knew what to expect. It never failed; when my family got together after dinner, they would always end up in a huge political debate about one topic or another. In time, the reasonable voices would turn ugly, and, at any given moment, five people would be on their feet trying to out-volume the others with their point of view, theirs, of course, being the only one worth listening to. This day was no exception.

I wanted to go to my room to be away from it, but unfortunately I couldn't. When I had arrived home for the first time after my mother's biopsy, I had walked into my old room and was met, unannounced, by a couch and TV. My mother had gotten rid of my bed and all my belongings and had turned the room into a den. When I asked her what she had done with all my stuff, she told me it was in boxes in the cellar. Looking over at the boys' room across the hall, I noticed it had become her dressing room.

"After Jake got married, I found myself with all this extra space," she said with a look of apology. "It's ok," I said, "I've slept on couches before."

Jake and Justine had married a year earlier. Mom had told me about it when I was in Germany.

A woman by the name of Pat was at the party, Janet's daughter. Janet was my mother's second cousin; my mother and Janet had become very close when I was away. Pat was four months pregnant. She had a young son and was now expecting her second child. My Aunt Flo was talking to her about her pregnancy and, true to form, asking her personal questions. Flo said, "Now that you are three months along, you don't have to worry about a miscarriage." I knew from experience that that wasn't true, but I kept my mouth shut anyway. Instead, I just watched the two of them chatting about gestation. Suddenly, the whole table began to talk about it. The main topic became miscarriages and at what time in gestation a fetus was considered a baby.

I couldn't hold my tongue any longer. I said, in a very quiet voice, "To the mother, it is at conception."

"Well, that's just the mother's own ego!" bellowed Joe. "If that were the case, there wouldn't be a simple thing called abortion."

"Abortion is not a simple thing, whether you're a person for or against it," I said. "Sure it is. If you're for it, it is a simple procedure that takes only a few minutes to have."

"And a lifetime to get over in some cases," I said..."Besides, I always got the feeling that the pro-life people in general had never had to personally face that decision. I bet the majority of the women getting abortions today feel they don't have another option...no matter how many people there are willing to adopt."

"So, now you're an adult, older and wiser than me? Just because, you've "traveled the world" doesn't mean you know what you're talking about! Besides, the question was...Does a woman know when she has conceived? I say no."

"I guess the fact that I have conceived...and you have not means nothing?"

I looked over at Martha, knowing she had had miscarriages, and gave her a wary smile. She acknowledged one back to me in return. It was the same old argument I had heard before, that a woman who has had a miscarriage hadn't lost a child, because she had never had the child in the first place. The ignorance and uncaring response of this type of belief sickened me. It was Flo's turn to speak next. "A woman doesn't know when she is pregnant anyway, not until she misses her period." Her voice was so condescending; she was looking directly at me, when she said it. At first I didn't respond, but she wouldn't let it drop. "Well I'm right, aren't I?" She was still looking at me to respond. The rest of the table became quiet and were looking at me as well.

"If you want to know the truth," I said, in a confident tone, "I have always known when I was pregnant, long before I had gotten any tests."

"LISTEN TO YOU!" she screamed at me from across the table. "YOU HAVE ONE MISCARRIAGE, AND NOW YOU'RE AN EXPERT!" Putting her head down, she laughed into the table top. "Talk about arrogance."

I looked to my mother for help in my defense. She was the only one who knew the truth about me and my pregnancies. When I saw that she was not going to support me, I became angry at her for still being afraid of this horrible person she called family. I knew I couldn't just sit there and be insulted.

"Flo," I said, "How many times have you been pregnant in your life?" "Once," she answered, with a smug looking smile on her face.

"Well, I have been pregnant three times. That is two times more than you, so don't tell me I don't know what I'm talking about. I knew every time I was pregnant! And, as you can see, I have no children to show for it! So I think the only people at this table who can be experts about miscarriages, and if they feel the baby was in fact a life at that time, would be Martha and me!"

I was screaming by the time the last word escaped my lips. The whole table was quiet. No one knew what to say. It was Martha who finally broke the silence. She said in a soft voice, "I always knew, too. Maybe when it's not right, the mother can feel it."

I stood up and headed in the direction of my room. I had had enough of this uncaring family. They would never change. Entering the kitchen, I heard my mother confirm to them that I had, in fact, been pregnant three times. Under my breath I said, "Thanks for the support, Mom." When I opened the door to my room, I was reminded that it wasn't there anymore. Grabbing my purse, I left the house. I slammed the door behind me. Mrs. Buras's plan was going to be tougher than I had thought. I knew that night she would have given me an "F."

The next morning I woke up at 6:00 AM, only to find my mother sitting at the table, having a cup of coffee. Pouring myself a cup from the pot, I sat in the seat across from her. We sat in silence, as I waited for her to scold me for the way in which I had spoken to my Aunt Flo. All she said was, "You know, I never told her about the baby you lost in high school."

"I would have hoped you hadn't," was my only reply. "I didn't want her to ever know, because she would never have let any of us live that down," she said.

"And knowing that, you're not willing to have it be reason enough to get her out of your life? Mom, you're forty-two years old; I think you have done your time with that woman."

"She's my mother's sister; I have to respect her," she said.

"That's funny," I said, "I always thought respect was something that was earned. Don't confuse your respect with your submissive behavior when you're with her."

My mother turned to me and gave me an odd look, perhaps of something dawning on her. We didn't discuss it any further that day.

At exactly 9:00 AM, the doctor called her. John and I were standing next to her in the kitchen as she took the phone. She didn't say a word, the whole time he was talking. Instead, a tear rolled quietly down her face. When the doctor had finished and obviously had asked her if she had any questions, in a hoarse voice she said, "When I think of them, I'll call you," and hung up the phone. She was confused and looking around the room as if she were lost. When she found what she was looking for, she made her way to the chair she had always sat at near the table. I said, "Mom, are you ok?"

She just looked at me and said, "Why did you let me have such hope?" The doctor had told her that I knew.

"Mom, I wanted to tell you, but the doctor insisted that I didn't. We thought it would be best that you had a nice weekend."

"So instead you let me believe that I was ok?"

I put my arms around her and said, "Mom, you are going to be ok; you have to believe that."

I looked over at John. He was dumbstruck. I could tell he was hurting inside. Mom looked at him too. She stood up and put her arms around him and cried. I went to the den, so they could be alone. With the doors closed, I quietly cried to myself.

The next week was filled with blood tests and paper work. Mom's surgery was scheduled in four weeks. She told Doug and Jake individually, in private. We never sat down as a family to try and work out the details. We all knew what was happening and never discussed it with each other. All the people whom my mother knew saw this as her being brave. I saw it as dysfunction. I was frustrated by it and attempted to talk to Jake. The conversation was hopeless. Every question I asked him he answered in a monotonous, short sentence. Every statement I attempted to make, he ignored. I then called Doug to talk to him. I needed my family to rally together. Even though it was my mother who had the tumor, we were all dealing with cancer. Doug got impatient with me. When I told him of the pain I was feeling with this, he said I was being selfish and ought to imagine what Mom was going through.

I was imagining what my mother was going through; that's why I was in pain. It was difficult for me to watch; after all, I was the one who lived with her. I didn't say that to him; his abruptness paralyzed me. Sobbing, I told him I was sorry and hung up the phone.

Later that night, I tried to call William. His phone had been disconnected, and I began to worry about him. I didn't know the exact date he would be heading for the States. In the turmoil of worrying about my mother, I had forgotten to get that one little detail. My mother was sitting in the kitchen next to me, when I made the next call. It was to Frau Hirsch. When I got her on the phone, I said, "Frau Hirsch, wo William ist. Ich habe versucht, ihn anzurufen, aber der Betreiber sagte, es war disconected.."

Her reply was one of confusion. She told me that he had moved to Oklahoma but said she didn't have his new number. She thought I was with him. He had obviously left a few days after I had.

"Danka, Frau Hirsch," I said in a sad voice. "Weidersein, tschuss." Before I hung up, I gave her my new address.

When I hung up the phone, my mother was staring at me with her mouth wide open. "When did you learn to speak German?"

"Mom, I did live there for three years, remember? Besides, it's really not that impressive; to them it sounds like I am nine years old."

"I never thought about the fact that you had to learn a whole new language. I had assumed they all spoke English."

"Yeah, that's a big misconception that most Americans have. It is because we are so isolated here. No one in Germany will speak English to you, unless they have to. Only about ten percent of the people who lived where I lived could."

"What did she say about William?" "She said he moved to Oklahoma." "Did you know he was going to do that?" "Yeah, but I didn't know when. Besides, I think I should be here, anyway."

My mother never brought up the subject of William again. I endured that pain alone, as well. I never heard from him or saw him again. He had never found out what the emergency was that I had come home for. He had never called to ask.

CHAPTER: 47

After my conversations with Frau Hirsch, I had come to several conclusions about my life, the first being that I would no longer be moving to Oklahoma. Mom had come to this conclusion too and told me I would have to go out and find a job, so that I could pay room and board. My second thought was that no matter how hard I tried, I would never be able to truly control the direction of my life. Something died inside me after William abandoned me. With one disappointment after another, it would become more difficult to allow my heart to be that exposed again. All I ever wanted was someone to love and to love me back. I knew that even if I did find someone, they would never have me completely. That was damaged forever. I decided to go for a walk.

Before I realized where I was going, I found myself at Ivy Manor. As I sat on the cold granite steps of that beautiful estate, I watched the traffic roll by and thought of all the wonderful times I had had there. I realized, at that moment, that Ivy Manor had been the only safe home I had ever really had, the only place in my life where everyone had truly loved me. I knew that some of the ladies had passed on. I wondered if perhaps a few might still be there. While I was thinking these thoughts, the door behind me opened. Out stepped Nora for her afternoon cigarette. When she saw me, she shouted in delight, causing others in earshot to come out as well. I suddenly found myself engulfed in hugs, kisses and the smell of Jean Nate. Without hesitation, they dragged me to my feet and into the door.

Martha, the cook, came into the front hall to see what all the commotion was. She gave me a big toothless grin and said, "Welcome home." Picking up the phone that was in the hall, she called Sherry down from the third floor. We were all congregating in the kitchen, talking about my travels, when Sherry walked in. She gave me a big hug and asked me how I was doing. She said she had gotten my German Christmas card, and one of the ladies who spoke German had read it out loud to everyone at dinner. She asked me if I was home to stay. I told her about my mother. She said she was sorry to hear it but to have faith, she had seen survivors from breast cancer. "They are coming up with new treatments all the time." Those were words I needed to hear, and I thanked her.

I said it had been difficult for me to leave Germany, because I had really found the place to be like home to me. She said, "Now that you are here, do you want a job?" I said, "Sure, maybe weekends if you need me."

She said, "Absolutely, when can you start?" I said, "How about right now?" She said, "The bingo game is still in the closet. I'll rally up the girls."

And so I stepped back into my job at Ivy Manor, as if I hadn't left. I never had a concrete job description the whole time I was there. My days were Saturdays and Sundays. The hours changed according to need. If they needed a night shift nurse's aide, I did that. I played bingo with the ladies during the day and read to the ones who were blind. Sometimes my job was to just sit and talk with them and make them feel special. Every weekend I took it upon myself to sweep the floors and dust. It was rewarding work, and I loved it very much. I was sad to see that Sarah was gone, as well as Laila, the woman I used to talk to who was a hundred. I was no longer called Isabella, and I missed the stories about the horses and buggies and gas street lamps. I didn't cry. Death was part of the process at Ivy Manor, and so we never discussed it.

When I got home that evening and told my mother that I had gotten a job at Ivy Manor, she seemed surprised. She asked me why I would ever want to work in such a depressing environment. I said, "It's funny, I never saw it that way," and I dropped the subject. There was no way I was ever going to have my mother understand the rewarding feeling I got from taking care of the lonely women who lived there.

She asked me why I had only gotten a part time job. I told her I thought she might need me around the house. She said, "I'm not an invalid. I want you to work full time; a part time job won't cover your board."

I said, "Ok, I'll look tomorrow," and went to sit in the den that was now my room.

That Monday, I went to the coin shop to see Phil. I brought him coffee, and we talked for an hour. He was glad to see me and filled me in on all that had happened while I was gone. He asked me if I wanted my job back. I told him I was looking for something for Monday through Friday. He said I could start the next day, so I did. When I got home, later Monday afternoon, I noticed a brochure on the counter for the Montserrat School of Art, a private art school in Beverly that had just been accredited. The brochure had arrived a few weeks earlier, and the deadline for the evening class enrollment was the following week. I saw they offered a beginner's class in painting. I grabbed my purse and asked Mom if I could borrow her car. I had never borrowed her car before, so she was hesitant. I told her I wanted to enroll in a painting class and would only go there and right back. She said she would drive me, because she didn't want me to ever use her car. She asked me how I was going to get to the evening classes. I said,

"I guess I'll have to buy my own car, won't I?"

I had some money saved up from the paintings I had sold in Germany. It was enough to enroll in the class, leaving me four hundred dollars to buy a car. After that, I was all tapped out. I would have to start saving again from my jobs. I still didn't know what Mom was going to charge me for room and board. I was hoping it was a flat rate and not a percentage of my pay. Every time she had charged me a percentage, it had made it impossible for me to save money. I made a mental note to come up with a reasonable way to plead my case. I bought a car from a used car lot in Middleton. It was an old Opel Manta, powder blue in color. It was a cute little car, but I was short by a hundred dollars. Mom and John went with me to check it out. She said she would loan me the extra money, and I could pay her back. So I gave her twenty dollars a week until I had paid my debt.

I made my case regarding the percentage rate for room and board. I told her that if she cared about my welfare, then she should encourage me to think to the future and not force me to live week to week. I said I wanted to do something with my life and finish my degree, but I couldn't do that if it would cost me so much to live with her. She said it would cost me more to live anywhere else. I said I understood that, but she was my mother, and I would have hoped that she would want me to secure my future. After a while, she agreed. My room and board was only fifty dollars a week. I only used my car for school and rainy days to save on gas. The insurance, however, was killing me. I knew if I were frugal and didn't buy any extras, in a year I would be in good shape.

Tuesday was a beautiful day. Walking to the coin shop, three miles from my house, I felt my feet were fitting right back into the grooves in the sidewalk that I had made so many times before. It was a comforting feeling, and I had a lift to my step. Even my arthritis seemed to have eased a bit. I made my own lunch from supplies I had bought at the grocery store. I had figured what it would cost for sandwich fixings versus buying lunch out and was shocked at the difference. I also brought a jar of instant coffee and a mug. I figured that the combination of those two things would save me at least thirty dollars a week. Between Ivy Manor and the coin shop, I was bringing home $175, a lot for that time. I was working seven days a week and going to school Tuesday and Thursday nights. I found that keeping busy was a great distraction from the thoughts that would creep into my head about the situation with my mother and the loss I felt about William.

At night, when I was lying on the couch trying to sleep, I would think about him and cry. I felt betrayed and confused. I had told him that I hadn't wanted a serious relationship when we had first met. He agreed and was sticking to his end of the bargain. I, unfortunately, had fallen in love. Those were words I had never spoken to him out loud. He would be the only man who had ever broken my heart. I wished he had been man enough to have talked to me about it, instead of just leading me on.

One morning, when I was opening up the coin shop, Jack walked by. He didn't notice me at first, so I called to him. When he saw me, he came over and walked into the store with me. Sitting down with his ever-present cup of coffee in his hand, he talked with me for hours. He said he had a studio up the street, on the top floor of a brick building, next to the library. I told him I would have given anything to have a studio, and, for the first time, he realized that I was a painter. Jack was easy to talk to. He had a nurturing voice and always was genuine in his advice. He quickly became the father figure in my life that, until that point, I hadn't realized I was lacking. We saw each other almost every day. He gave me pointers in painting that were more understandable than anything I was learning in college. At Montserrat, the exercises they had us do seemed pointless to me. I was frustrated and eager to learn about representational painting. Jack seemed to fill this void for me. In time, I told him about my mother and the loss I was feeling for William. He said he had never trusted William. It was something he had felt the first time he had met him. He said he had seemed too good to be true. Jack's words put my life into perspective.

Jack became the person in my life who knew everything about me. He listened to my hopes and dreams and was always sure to give me solid advice, if it looked like I wasn't seeing things clearly. He was always a gentleman towards me, and I never got that feeling that women sometimes get when they know a man is just interested in getting physical with them. He was married, and when I asked him about his wife, he was very up front with me on the subject. One time I asked him why I had never seen her at his studio. He told me she had a very stressful job as an editor of a national magazine, based in Boston. She worked fourteen hours a day. It was hard for them to have time together. In many ways we both had our own family issues. He was appalled by the manner in which my mother treated me. He told me that in a loving family, that type of behavior shouldn't exist. I had always felt that this was true, but I had never heard it spoken out loud until I met Jack.

At Ivy Manor, things were wonderful. I enjoyed the women very much, and if it weren't for my mother's impending mastectomy, my life would have been perfectly content. I didn't mind working so many hours in the week; as a matter of fact, I thrived on it. I was alone in the world without a man and I was enjoying it.

The surgery was scheduled for early morning. John and I once again found ourselves sitting in another waiting room. This time my brothers were with us. None of us spoke to each other the whole time we sat there. Lost in our own private thoughts, the only thing that linked us together in that room was the mechanical tick of the clock. Our common bond was our mother.

When the doctor finally emerged, he said that it had gone well. He said the only glitch he had had was that the breast was so intertwined with cysts that it had been difficult to lift; at one point, it had fallen back into her chest cavity. He told us she was resting, and, after we got to see her we should probably go home and come back tomorrow. She was too weak to see anyone for a lengthy visit that day.

I decided that I would see her the next day. She was still knocked out cold. All night and that morning, I had been crying at the drop of a hat about the littlest things. There was nothing I could do to ease my mother's burdens, and I was feeling helpless on every front. At a time when I should have been relating to my family, I was feeling very disconnected. I knew my brothers viewed my lack of desire to see her as heartless. My relationship with them had been deteriorating rapidly, since my mother's illness. It had never been a very strong one to begin with, so I wasn't surprised. I was trying desperately to get lost in a different life, away from talk of cancer and life that was slipping away.

The next day I went to see my mother. She was yellow in complexion and looked worse than the day she had had her biopsy. Trying to sound light and struggling with the lump that had lodged itself in my throat, I said, "Boy, you must feel a big relief, having that tumor out of you. How do you feel?"

"I feel awful," she said. "Look what they did to me." Pulling down the covers, she revealed to me a bandage that covered her whole chest and wound around to her back. On one side was an obvious breast; on the other, it was flat.

All I could say was, "I'm sorry Mom."

I didn't stay long at the hospital. She was in and out of sleep, because of the morphine they were giving her. After a few hours, I kissed her on the forehead and told her I would see her later on. Sitting alone at her kitchen table, I wondered what the future had in store for her. At least I lived with my mom and could keep a daily tab on her, although I was not sure what my role in her life was at that point. She never confided in me or talked to me about her fears. I wanted to talk to her about the changes one goes through when losing a breast. She became clinical about it. She explained the procedure and how much it had physically hurt. I wanted to talk to her about it in a different way, in a way a mother could confide in a daughter, the way one woman would talk to the next about such a radical disfigurement. I was sure it must be emotionally difficult as a woman to lose a breast. I was the only woman in the family besides her. I wanted her to know that I was there for her in that way. When I tried to get her to open up about it, she refused to talk.

"Mom, umm, I can't speak for you, but, umm, I feel if this happened to me, I would have to fight the feelings of thinking I am less of a woman. Beauty is so important to a woman's identity. Do you feel any of that? Because you know, it isn't what defines a woman."

"When you find yourself disfigured and looking like you're mauled, then you will have the ability to talk to me about this; until then I don't want to discuss it."

That was the extent of our mother/daughter discussion on the matter. I went back to the den/my bedroom and sat on the couch. I had no idea how important that brief exchange of words, years later, would be in my life.

Jake lived upstairs and was at my mother's beck and call. When something in the house needed fixing, he played that role for her, and now it was more evident. He wanted to fix her, and this was the only way he could. When he would come into the house, he never said a word to me. The only exchange was when I would say "hi" and he would reply back. This was nothing new, cancer or no cancer. Our relationship had always been that way. I had found us back in the same roles we had always had. Jake and I didn't see each other or communicate in any way. Doug and my mother spent a lot of time together. She relied on him a lot to explain things to her since he had a medical background. Both sons had their parts to play. I searched desperately for mine but couldn't find it.

CHAPTER: 48

One day when I arrived at the coin shop, I was surprised to see that Phil was there. He usually worked the evening shift, and I manned the store during the day. He told me that he had some news for me and wanted to tell me in person. He said that he had sold the store to a guy named Jimmy and that he should be there in an hour. I asked him if it meant I still had a job. He told me that Jimmy was going to keep me on and that he wanted to change the store to focus more on the jewelry and gold. I was thrilled to hear that prospect. The collectible business of coins and stamps was changing. When the Hunt brothers cornered the silver market in the early eighties, it caused a lot of old coins to be melted for their weight value. This created a scarcity in coins, making it difficult for the average low-end collector to complete sets, unless they were in mint condition. Because collecting is a phenomenon that runs through the veins of such people, they had turned all their focus to baseball cards. I hated dealing with the baseball cards. This revamped form of collecting drew a lot of children and men who had never grown up. It had been difficult for me to have a serious conversation with a customer about a diamond purchase, when I had impatient kids wanting to give me their change to purchase a pack of cards and gum.

The stamp market was also doing poorly. The majority of our sales were for investment, and the remainder was split up into two categories: low-end collectors, who were of the same caliber as the coin collectors, and tax packages. They were people who would buy sets of rare stamps and donate them to a favorite charity. Because they could buy them at well below market price and donate them for the book value with a tax benefit, they were saving a good amount of money on their taxes without spending a lot. All stamp dealers sold their stamps for below book value. I'm not sure how this started, but the serious collectors knew it. I loved dealing with the stamps. I had collected them as a child and understood the language of perforations, watermarks and hinged verses non-hinged, long before I had gotten this job. I had a great eye for evaluating dye runs, and Phil was always amazed at how I could see these differences. Friday nights were when the serious collectors came, mostly older men who had been collecting for years. Phil was always running around frantically, pulling different binders off the shelves, which held thousands of stamps to accommodate any type of collector. My job, when it came to the stamps, was generally cataloging as well as purchasing. But I found on Friday nights, I enjoyed staying on to supply coffee and snacks for the guys. Phil had never told me to do this; I saw on my own that it was a gratuity that was missing. This end of the business had flowed beautifully for years, that is, until the government stepped in and changed a lot of the tax codes. Overnight, the bottom of the stamp market dropped out of sight and never recovered.

Phil had gotten into the jewelry business when the silver rush occurred. He knew nothing about jewelry but was a quick learner. At first, I knew more than he did and took over the role of teacher for him when it came to diamonds. He understood the equations for converting to pennyweight, and he taught me that. With jewelry, we were a great team. Now he was telling me the team was splitting up. I wasn't sure how I felt about it. I didn't know Jimmy and hoped he wasn't a letch, like most men in the jewelry business. My experience with every jeweler I had met, from the jewelry district in Boston to the little, one man shows in small towns, had always been the same...they wanted to get into my pants. My biggest concern wasn't the new job; it was the new boss.

I soon found I had nothing to worry about. An hour later, a man walked through the door who was in his thirties, slightly overweight and a bit nervous. He also stuttered. I knew if anything happened, I could outrun this man if necessary. I also knew that I would never have to. He was certainly not the smooth, jeweler type that I had become accustomed to. The whole time I was thinking this, Phil was introducing us. He had apparently shown Jimmy around the store at another time, because in less than ten minutes, Phil said good bye and was gone. I never saw him again.

Jimmy knew where everything was. He wanted to sit down with some coffee, so that he could tell me about the changes he wanted to make. The first thing he wanted to do was get rid of the baseball cards. He wanted to do it slowly, so that we wouldn't disrupt the cash flow, considering that was where the biggest chunk was coming from. I then asked him if it would be better to revamp the whole image if he wanted to make this a jewelry store. The problem with this store was that once the baseball cards had come in, no one took it seriously any more. Phil would never let me make changes for the sake of image, but I knew I could fix that. The fact that he had been disorganized hadn't helped either. Jimmy said he wanted to run the store the same way it had been running for a month. He first wanted to see how I handled the customers and how the store flowed. In a month, we would discuss the changes. On the surface, it sounded like a reasonable idea; inside, I knew it really meant he had no money.

"Well, since Phil is gone, I am going to do the one thing I've always wanted to do...clean and organize the back room." I left Jimmy out front, as I went to the back. I was projecting a show of authority that I didn't even know I had, then. Jimmy was pleased.

That first month was very telling about who Jimmy was. He was a man who had probably been picked on in high school and had somehow made it through. When he talked to customers, he had a bad habit of stuttering and rocking back and forth on his heels. He didn't give an impression of confidence, a trait that is important when you are selling something to someone who has to trust that you know what you are talking about, because he doesn't. Many times I would want to help him out, but, unlike Phil, we didn't flow as a team. He was definitely the boss, and I was just an employee.

One day, right before closing, Jimmy told me he had a silent partner in the store whom he wanted me to meet, a friend of his wife and himself. When the man pulled up out front, the first thing I saw was the nose of his shiny, silver Datson 280Z. I didn't realize that this was the man I was to meet. When I saw the car, I felt a pain in my heart for William. Stepping from it was a well-dressed, ethnic- looking man with dark hair and eyes. Sitting perched on his face was a pair of stylish glasses. He had perfect posture and gave an air of confidence. He was wearing a white, freshly ironed dress shirt with white corduroy pants that had ironed creases down the front. His shoes were black. I thought to myself, "Why don't ethnic men look at their feet before they leave the house?" Growing up in a largely Portuguese area, I saw this a lot. It seemed to be a common trait at the time for those men to wear white clothes with black shoes. This had always been a pet peeve of mine. When he walked through the door and Jimmy introduced him to me, I thought...this is a jeweler? When he told me that he owned a leather factory, the picture became clearer. His name was Nick, and when he opened his mouth to say hello, I was struck by the softness of his voice. He also seemed like the nervous type, and I was surprised because of the confidence I was sure I had seen when he had stepped from his car. I never saw that self assured man again, the whole time we knew each other. I would wonder, years later, if the thoughts I was having about William when I first saw Nick's car had somehow influenced my opinions.

One day, Jimmy said, "Christina and I are going out to dinner with Nick; would you like to join us? I thought we could all discuss the changes at the store." Feeling there was no way I could say no, considering he made it sound work related, I accepted.

"Good," said Jimmy. "Why don't you go with Nick in his car and meet me at my house, when I pick up Christina?"

"Hmm," I thought, "This sounds like a set up." I was not interested in a relationship. I had hoped they understood that.

When Nick arrived, he was the perfect gentleman. He was dressed very sharply and smelled real good. Everything on the exterior of this man said confident, educated, and stylish. When he spoke he hesitated. He was very soft spoken and had a habit of clearing his throat. Despite all this, he knew how to treat a woman. He always opened the door for me. He would even lean over to buckle me in the seat belt. Sitting in the low seat of his sports car, I was reminded, once again, about the life I had left behind in Germany. I also wondered if, somehow, I had just been manipulated into going on a date. I wasn't worried; I knew I could out run him, as well. I also knew I wouldn't have to. We went to a local steakhouse on Route 114 in Danvers, only a few miles from the store. Christina and I had met previously and seemed to get along well. The first chance we had alone together, Christina made sure I knew that Nick was not married. Realizing that this was, in fact, a set up, I said, "Christina, I'm not looking for a relationship. I have too much on my plate right now."

She laughed and said, "Barbara, I'm not asking you to marry the guy. We're just going out and having fun. Besides, aren't you tired of being around so many people who are sick? When you're not with us, you're taking care of your mother and working at the rest home. Don't you want a social life?"

She had a point. I had been playing with the idea of quitting the rest home for that very same reason. After several had died, it was hard for me to work there without thinking we were going to lose someone else. I didn't have the strong will that the nurses had. I became too attached.

"Ok," I said, "But I'm warning you, I don't want to get serious."

That night, Nick stared at me the whole time. I felt a little uncomfortable, but I have to admit it also felt good. I had forgotten what it was like to be desired. When he looked at me, it was as if he were a loyal puppy. I knew I didn't feel the same way about him; I was still feeling the effects of the rebound from William; I hoped I wouldn't break Nick's heart. I had feelings for William, and although I was hurt and angry at him, I couldn't change the love that I still felt. Soon the conversation turned to the business at hand, and we talked about the changes Jimmy wanted to make in the store. It was mostly about moving furniture, and I tried to plead my case again about the store's image. I don't think Jimmy got it. I soon learned that this store was his baby, and all ideas were to come from him.

The conversation I had had with Christina about my social life made me realize that I needed to make some changes. I knew that hanging around with women who were so much older than I was not healthy for me. Christina had been right; I needed to be around people my own age. That week I gave my notice at the Manor. It was sad on my last day; the cook even baked a cake. It was a tearful goodbye. After I had walked out the door, I turned back once, as a gesture of thanks to the institution which had raised me. Heading down the street, I knew my life had entered a new chapter.

The painting class I had at school was an introductory course. The teacher made me work with two inch brushes, and the emphasis was on expression. With all the emotions I was dealing with at the time, self-expression was a closed door for me. I didn't do that well in the class. I didn't stand out as talented; I didn't stand out at all. If anything, I wouldn't have been missed if I hadn't shown up. The class wasn't the foundations course that I thought it would be. I wanted to learn how to represent the world I saw in an accurate manner, not interpret the images I saw to mean something else. I was glad when the course ended. I was surprised when I got a "B."

Mom started her chemotherapy. It was twice a week at first and then tapered off to once a week. I asked her if she would like me to drive her. She said she would rather spend that time with John. She made it sound like a private time she wanted them to share. Even though I wasn't at the hospital, I made sure I was home on the days she had her treatment, as often as I could. Jimmy understood, and although it wasn't every day, he would often give me the time off. I felt guilty living at my mother's house and encroaching on her life with John. I was hanging on to her in a strange, emotional way. I wasn't ready to let go, even if the only attention I got from her was negative; it was who she was and all I knew. I was honest with myself about these feelings, but it didn't help. Besides, I also felt I shouldn't leave, because at some point they might need my help. I tried to make myself as invisible as possible, when I knew they could enjoy some time alone.

Mom didn't like talking about the cancer. I always found it difficult to even broach the subject. The few times she did discuss it would be when it was early in the morning, and the two of us were having coffee while John was still in bed. My mother and I were both very early risers, and during this time we shared, we could communicate. She often put on a brave face for these chats. She never cried and was sure she was going to beat the disease. I, on the other hand, wanted to see her show more emotion than just strength. I knew she was scared, and I wanted her to express that to me. When I asked her once to tell me of her fears, she responded with, "I can't." Through the rest of her chemo, I never asked her that again. I only listened to her talk about the future. The treatments made her sick. After every one, she could be heard violently vomiting in the bathroom. On those occasions, I would find myself sitting on the floor outside the bathroom door with my head buried in my knees, often in tears; I was worried that something would happen to her while she was in there. I had this immense feeling of a lack of control of the situation, and it was driving me crazy. When she was finished, I would quickly rise and run to my room, so that she wouldn't see me there. I never knew what to say to her, when she emerged from the bathroom. I was afraid she would feel embarrassed and uncomfortable to know that I had been listening. John would watch me perform this ritual, and he never said a word to her about it. It was an unspoken rule in this house of three that when Mom was finished vomiting, it was John who was to comfort her, and I dutifully complied.

CHAPTER: 49

Nick asked me out on a date the next weekend, after our pseudo date with Jimmy and Christina. I remember it was a warm spring night, and, after a dinner at the Beverly Depot restaurant, we went to a beach. It was the one that was across the street from my house, when I had lived on Pickman Street. I hadn't been there in years, and I wanted to see it. Sitting on the rocks, we talked for hours. I told him the cursory aspects of my life: the fact that I had been married and had lived in Europe, the outline of the pleasant edges of my history. He was completely enthralled with all that I was saying. He was a nice guy who was ready to fall in love and settle down. I, on the other hand, was still recovering from my past two relationships. I was in no condition to feel anything but defensive ...I had learned the hard way. After coming from a situation that I thought was one way and turned out to be another, his sweetness appeared to be naive. He was a man who could be easily led. It was a species I had never seen before. I worried that someday he might find a woman who would take advantage of his easy going behavior. There was one thing that was amazing about him. He was an engineer, so he could do anything. All Nick had to do was sit and look at something for ten minutes, and he could figure out the things that made it work. He was able to do this with anything mechanical, as well as constructed. I had never met anyone like that before, and this talent of his intrigued me.

Sitting on the beach that night, after having spent only a few hours together, I asked him, "Nick how is it that someone as sweet and caring as yourself has never been married?"

"I never got married, because I never met anyone like you." The shock of his statement nearly made me fall off the rock I was sitting on. It also made me upset.

"Nick, please, let's not go there with this conversation. I am never going to get married again, and if that is what you are looking for, we might as well end it right here. I don't want to lead you on."

"I thought you said you wanted to have a child someday?"

"I do, I just don't want a husband." He smiled, because he thought I was joking. When I turned and gave him a serious look, he just dropped the subject.

The coin shop wasn't going well. Jimmy had rearranged the display cases to prominently show the jewelry. It looked beautiful, but he still had the baseball cards, and when business would slow down, there were times he had trouble paying me. I felt bad for him and remained his employee and friend. Every Friday and Saturday night, the four of us would go out together. Nick's proposal didn't deter me. I knew in my heart that no man could make me do something I didn't want to. I kept reassuring him that our relationship was for enjoyment purposes only. Every time I said it, he would just smile.

The treatments that my mother was having were making her very tired. The simple things she loved doing, like food shopping, were suddenly a great burden for her. I offered to do it for her, to ease her load. When I told Jimmy and Christina that I could no longer go with them on Friday nights because of this task, they offered to put the activity into our Friday night routine. That was how it came to be that Nick would drive me to the grocery store every week and walk the aisles with me to perform this very domestic task. We all tried to make the best of this mundane chore. We often joked and pretended we were TV commercials with the products. Nick could be very animated when he wanted to be. He was always trying to bring laughter to my life that was filled with the illness of a parent. Every time we entered the frozen foods aisle, he would hold up a bag of frozen peas and, with a lost puppy dog look on his face, say, "Peas marry me?" It became a ritual, week after week, and I found myself waiting in anticipation for it. I never responded when he asked me this; I just smiled. Our relationship went on this way for a year.

In time, my mother appeared to be her old self again. She was off the chemotherapy treatments, and her cancer was in remission. She kept telling every one, "They got it all." Since both she and John had retired early, they were able to enjoy a simple life together. They could now spend their days shopping and going out to lunch. Jake and Justine were living upstairs from them with a new baby. Her name was Emily. Being a grandmother was a very fulfilling experience for my mother. She babysat Emily every chance she got and thoroughly enjoyed her.

The coin shop was still seeing some hard times. I knew a layoff was around the corner. I told Nick that I didn't want them to hang on to me just out of loyalty; perhaps I should look for another job. I had been trying like crazy to sell my artwork, but nothing was ever going to replace the unusual situation I had had in Germany. Nick was an amateur photographer and suggested I apply at a photo lab in Lynn called North Shore Color Lab. He said they hired artists, and, if I brought them some of my best work, they might see the talent I had and give me a job. It was a long shot, but I didn't have anything to lose.

At 9:00 AM, on a beautiful autumn day, I loaded up my artwork in a portfolio that Nick had bought me the Christmas before, and I headed to Lynn. I was wearing the same pink linen suit I had worn for my trip back from Germany, the day I had been pulled out of line for being a suspected terrorist. It was the only suit I had, and I wanted to look professional. The building was made of brick and looked like a factory. It was shared with another company. The photo lab was on the second floor. Climbing the dusty, old wooden stairs, I made my way to the place that I was hoping would be my future. I was really nervous when I walked through the door. Who the hell was I kidding? I knew a little about black and white photography; I had taken a course in high school, but I knew nothing about color processing. Pushing open the door, the first thing that struck me was the odor of the chemicals. It attacked your nostrils like a skunk and sat at the back of your throat. The taste was metallic, yet familiar. I wondered if this type of exposure was good for the employees and was curious to know if they ever got used to it. The second thing I noticed was the lack of windows. I couldn't see one and knew they must have boarded them up. After all, controlled light would be an issue in a business such as this. I knew in the winter time, if we had a snow storm, no one in this place would know it.

The film machine was the first piece of equipment I saw. It went the length of the room and made a noise that sounded like a conveyer belt. It was completely enclosed, so that the film wouldn't be exposed. A man was running back and forth, through a door on the side of it, with great haste to keep it operating properly. He stopped and looked at me out of curiosity. He was tall and handsome and looked like a model. He was dressed in very tight black jeans and wore a teal colored shirt. I could have sworn he was wearing mascara. Our eyes met for a second before he disappeared back into the darkness. There was a set of drafting tables in the center of the room. People were approaching them with the same urgency as the film man had. They were holding cake pans full of photographs and stacking them on the long banquet tables, next to the artists. There were at least a hundred pans perched precariously this way on top of each other. The two artists I saw were bent over their tables in concentration, neither one lifting his head when I walked by.

I stopped for a second to take in this sight. It was as busy there as any hospital emergency room. Everyone had a job to do and was rushing to get it done on time and accurately. It was a very different environment from the coin shop. I was excited by the prospect of becoming a part of this well-oiled machine. While I was standing there, a man stopped me and asked if he could assist me. He was my height and slight in build, with a mustache. He was handsome, with kind and beautiful blue eyes. He had long hair, and, right away, I knew this man had been a hippie in another life. He projected an air about him that said "crunchy granola." I would have bet ten dollars on the spot that he was a vegetarian. He was very approachable. I told him I was an artist, there to apply for a job. The minute the words left my lips, his face lit up like a Christmas tree. "You must be psychic," he said. "I was just putting together an ad for the newspaper for just such a position. Please step into my office. My name is Geoff, and I am the floor supervisor."

I couldn't believe my luck. I had thought I would to have to sell myself much harder than that. I was sure I would have to convince them they needed another artist; and now, here they were, telling me they did.

Showing Geoff my work of mostly portrait paintings and drawings, I could see right away that he was impressed. He was not a man who hid his feelings very well. If anything, he over-compensated by being extremely enthusiastic. His voice reminded me of a nursery school teacher, trying to encourage her students to put on their own mittens for the first time. I felt pleased yet uncomfortable.

"Do you know anything about photography?" he asked.

"Well, when I was in high school I won a gold key for my photography portfolio in the Boston Globe Show. Here is the certificate I received for it." I handed him the paper. I felt like an actor playing a part for him, although everything I had told him was true.

"For the entire portfolio? That's wonderful. Do you have any of those prints?"

I replied, "Unfortunately, that year an entire crate had been stolen from the show when it reached Chicago in the national tour. My photos were in it."

"Do you still have the negatives?"

"I have a few," I said pulling out a binder and showing them to him. I said, "I have been living in Europe for the past three years and had lost the others somewhere along the way. I have been back now a little over a year."

"What did you do for work when you were there?"

"I was a nursery school teacher at first but had found I could make more money with my art, so I did that instead."

He asked, "Why did you leave?"

I looked him directly in the eye and said, "My mother has cancer." "Do you know how to spot a print?"

I told him I knew what that was, but I had never tried it. Acting thrilled to have the opportunity to explain, he jumped into a full-blown lecture on color dyes and the layering process of color photos. Spotting was the removal of a white dust impression on a print with the use of a sable brush and dyes. He said he had several artists who would be retiring by the following summer, and he would need replacements. He said the training could take up to six months of apprenticing. What he wanted was to have these artists ready to go by this time the following year, because from fall to Christmas was crunch time. He said if I wanted the position, I would have to work on the floor until January in various non-art related jobs, so they could see how I was as an employee. If my work checked out, then I would be promoted to the art department.

I said, "When can I start?" Handing me an application he said, "How does tomorrow sound?" "I'll be here; what time?"

After I had filled out the application, Geoff took me on a tour of the lab. We started at the reception desk, which was in another room that I had failed to see when I had first entered the building. Meandering from department to department, I saw the flow of a well-organized company. The stations were set up to create the least amount of steps for each employee to have to make. What amazed me was the amount of people it took to process, print and distribute one image. It felt like a team, and I wanted to be a part of it. The artists I had seen when I had first entered the lab were the spotters. I asked Geoff if this was the position he had been talking about. He said, "Spotting is something you will be doing, but I have other plans for you. Follow me." He led me down a long, dark hallway, separate from the rest of the lab. Opening a door, a flood of light hit me in the eyes. It was the only room with windows. Sitting at drafting tables were two old men. Lifting their heads to acknowledge us with only their eyes, they quickly went back to work. Their backs were curved from years of sitting in this position. I thought I saw a cobweb that extended from one of them to the floor. Glancing at it a second time, I smiled to myself when I realized it was just dust being caught in a ray of light pouring in the window.

Geoff introduced me to Claudio and Ken, two men who had worked at North Shore Color Lab for thirty years. I learned later that everyone referred to them as if they were one person: Ken and Claudio. Claudio was an Italian man who spoke broken English. All day long, he made beautiful, hand- colored photographs out of sepia-toned pictures. He was pleasant and had a large smile. When he stood up, I was surprised at how small he was. He had a wide chest, and I surmised that the funny posture I had seen upon entering the room was more than likely scoliosis, although I was never sure. When he shook my hand, I saw that his fingers were fixed in a position that could only be caused by years of holding a small pencil or brush, or in this case, a cotton-tipped toothpick. I made a mental note to myself to sit up straight when I worked this job. Claudio was a very warm and open man. I liked him the minute I met him. Ken, on the other hand, was someone who intimidated me. When we were introduced, he didn't look me in the eye. He didn't even raise his head. He mumbled a respectable hello under his breath. He reminded me of a postal worker during the Christmas rush. I made another mental note: stay away from him. Ken was doing something to a photograph I had never seen done before. He was painting out the background of a portrait with a brush and oil paints. Geoff turned to me and said, "Is this something you think you can do?"

I said, "Yeah, the hard part is done for you." "What is that?" he asked. "The likeness," I said.

I started working at North Shore Color the next day. The pay was terrible, but they promised me a raise, when I was promoted to the art department. I was started at $5.35 per hour. The first day, they put me in the quality control room. It was at the back of the lab and was next to the shipping department. When I walked into the room, I saw a large banquet table with four other people with whom I would be sharing this job. My first impression when I saw them was that this job had been reserved for people without skills. There were two very elderly women wearing cobbler smocks with flower prints; one was a young girl who was either just out of high school or had dropped out, wearing a tight shirt and jeans; the fourth was a very flamboyant gay man in his early twenties. He was dressed in grunge clothes, with a ripped concert tee shirt. His pants were ripped purposely in various places; on his feet were black work boots. His hair was what stood out the most; it was cut into a Mohawk that wasn't spiked at the time and dyed red. He had been monopolizing the conversation at the table, when Geoff and I approached. The last words I heard out of his mouth were, "I'm telling you, it was crazy, the floor was covered with naked men!" Everyone else at the table seemed to be listening to him intently, and I thought they were an unlikely crew of people. Here I was being thrown into the mix.

Basically, what we did at this job was to check the orders to see if the correct number of prints corresponded to the negatives. We also had to check for any dust spots that might have been missed by the spotters. It was an easy job, to say the least; it was monotonous, to say the most. I was also struck with other, and often surprising, feelings doing this job. It was strangely violating to be looking into the lives of people I had never met, through their camera lenses. It turned one into a type of voyeur. I found myself glimpsing at moments in strangers' lives that they felt were poignant enough to capture in an image that would be frozen forever in time. There were weddings of scared young couples, vacations that lovers had taken, random revealing shots at outlandish parties, and occasionally there would be a nude. I realized that this was why everyone at the table talked to each other every chance they could, when Geoff's back was turned. These people, doing this mundane job, had enough on the plates of their own often difficult lives; they didn't need to be subjected to the glory of someone else's.

After Geoff left, it was Jai, the young man, who interrogated me first. He asked me my name and where I was from and took it upon himself to introduce the rest of the group. He was animated in his gestures and seemed to genuinely be interested. Despite his mode of dress, he was the perfect "welcome wagon" lady. Everyone seemed pleasant enough, and I settled into the routine easily. The job was so easy, a monkey could have done it. The only problem I had with it was the ache I received in the back of my neck from bending over the table in the same position the whole morning. The chairs we sat in were of hard plastic, the kind found in a school cafeteria. I wanted desperately to get up and stretch. But since no one else seemed to be bothered by this, I didn't.

Jai was an extremely funny person. He entertained us all day. We were an odd grouping of people. I knew if it weren't for Jai, this job would have been hell. Because he was gay, it felt like we were all women, sitting around a table, chatting. With all of us busy doing the same thing, it was not unlike a modern quilting bee. Because Jai was an extreme person in regard to the stories of his life and his take on the world, he would have caused fainting spells in any real quilting bee that had ever existed. I was surprised that the older women rolled with his stories as well as they did. Some of these were epics of all nighters spent at a local gay bar. He always told these stories with an air of disbelief. I know for myself, it was an education handed to me on a platter in the time frame it would have taken to eat a tuna sandwich. Through most of it, I wanted to laugh. Instead I just smiled to myself. Jai made the job fun, and I was enjoying this unusual position I was placed in, especially with the knowledge that I would not have to do this job for the rest of my life.

At lunch time, Jai asked me if I would like to join him and his friend John. He said they usually went to the park across the street and sat on the bench to eat. I said ok, and that was how our trio was formed: Jai, the outrageously funny gay man who was always pushing the envelope, John the very handsome film man who, in fact, did wear mascara and was also gay, and me, the young heterosexual girl who had already lived many lives. It was a wonderful time in my life to work with these two men. We laughed together and complained together. When we felt most vulnerable, we also cried together. The one common bond we had was the balancing act we were all playing with our lives. Living from week to week, both financially and emotionally, we all knew that at any given moment, things could fall apart around us. We never discussed it, yet we were all very aware of it. For Jai, his vulnerability was in the lifestyle he led. He was constantly meeting strange men in Boston gay bars and, on more than one occasion, would come to work having been beaten up or worse than that, having played Russian roulette with a disease that finally had a name...AIDS: it was the same disease that took my childhood friend Aaron in its first year...it was not the type of fame Aaron had hoped to find when he spoke on the bridge about the yachts he would buy...but it would be what he was always remembered for. With John, it would be his dreams of becoming a singer and the cost that it would take for such an undertaking. He lived with a female roommate and found that because of his ambition and its cost, he was forced to live week to week. For me it would be fate: an uncontrollable entity that had always been in my life, leading me from one event to the next. This time, it had its hands around the throat of my mother, and all I could do was sit back and watch.

This company was different from others I had worked for in the past. They had employee incentives that seemed to compensate for the pressure we all worked under. They would often throw parties at Halloween and Christmas, as well as give bonuses. They did have an insurance plan, but I never was a part of it. The employees were required to pay more than half for this, and I couldn't afford it.

At Halloween we had a costume party. A photo lab, in general, seemed to attract creative people, so this event was always fun, but Jai had run out of ideas. Sitting in the break room one afternoon, the girl who was in charge of national sales told him she had a dance outfit he could borrow. She said it was a pink ballerina costume, complete with a netted tutu. It was an outfit she had worn when she was ten, but she was sure he could fit in it, seeing that he was six feet two inches tall and only weighed one hundred and twenty pounds. We all insisted he do it. It would be the hit of the party, and we were sure he would win the prize for most outrageous costume. The guy who ran the spray booth, who usually sat quietly in the back of the break room with a scowl on his face, found himself compelled to add his two cents. He said, "I dare you to ride the train from Boston with it on." At first, the room grew quiet. The thought of Jai exposing himself to a possible gay bashing on the subway was too much to ask of him. But, in true Jai style, he stood up and flatly said, "I'll do it!"

The party was a week away. John and I had tried to convince Jai that he didn't have to take the subway in the costume. John had even told him he could change at his house if he wanted to. Jai insisted that he had said he would do it, so he would. All week, the whole lab was waiting for the day to arrive with anticipation. When it finally did, we all burst into laughter as Jai pirouetted into the break room the morning of the party.

Standing before us was a tall, lanky man in a pink tutu. Because of his long torso, the neckline that was supposed to sit at his shoulders was pulled painfully tight below his navel. The one thing we hadn't expected was how hairy he was. Billowing out from under this tortured, nylon garment were tufts of curly brown hair, screaming to escape, from his armpits to his ankles. His face was covered with the same gaudy make-up we had seen on the faces of the little girls in their dance photos which came through the lab. Jai wore the dance outfit the whole day. At one point, he was asked by Geoff to help the UPS man load all the packages he had into his truck, but the man refused to get in the elevator with him. Watching this scene unfold in front of me, I laughed when I saw Jai's only response to this form of rejection was a bashful bat of his blue-shadowed eyes. He was such a good sport about the whole situation; he did, in fact, win a prize.

Through the Christmas rush at the lab, John, Jai and I helped keep each other's sanity intact. Christmas time at a photo lab was like nothing I had ever seen. Even working a retail job at that time of year had to be easier than what I witnessed. Unlike retail, we had to produce the products we were selling. And, unlike retail, we had to rely on the photographers to take the pictures correctly and get them to us on time. I learned very quickly that although photography was viewed as a rather prestigious profession, photographers were generally not a bright lot. The holiday rush orders rolled through the lab like slow moving molten lava. Everything was marked "Urgent" with multi colored round stickers that were reminiscent of Christmas bulbs. The color of each sticker determined the percentage of the rush. Despite this system, it was difficult to prioritize the orders, when everything was considered a gift for Christmas. The fact that every order had to be checked a million times only made the jobs move more slowly. With the work piling up around us like New York towers, it also became confusing. If a mistake got through the quality control department, we heard about it from one boss. If we didn't get it out fast enough, we heard about it from a different one. We were stuck in the middle of a volleyball game, only we weren't playing. We were the ball. The good thing was that the time at work went by fast, despite the overtime we had to put in. We took comfort in the fact that we were all in the same boat. No one thought that any one job was easier than the next. Somehow, from some act of God, we got it all out. I felt a sense of pride when, on Christmas Eve at eight in the evening, the last order was shipped. When I left with John and Jai to fetch our cars in the parking lot, I expressed the doubt I had had that we were going to get it done. I was surprised when they told me that it was the same scenario every year. I didn't want to think about the next year; I just wanted to get home.

After Christmas break, we had our annual Christmas party, always held at a local restaurant. There was food and dancing, and, at first, the atmosphere appeared to be a happy one. After awhile, I noticed the old-timers of the lab looking solemn. When I asked John and Jai about it, they said it was because it was time for the unannounced slaughter. I would soon find out what they were talking about. Fred, the owner of the lab, was standing at the front of the room, trying to get everyone's attention. He was a large man who was never respected by anyone at the lab, not even the supervisors. He had become the owner by marrying the boss's daughter. He was a letch, and every woman who worked there knew it. He would take any chance he had to try and rub your back. It was a violating and uncomfortable feeling. All the women did their best to stay away from him. As far as the supervisors were concerned, Fred knew nothing about the individual departments and would often step in and screw everything up. They just tolerated him because they had to. Behind his back, they told us not to listen to him.

At the party, when he was standing at the front of the room, Fred had a handful of envelopes, our Christmas bonuses. He was talking on and on about the good job that we had all done and how proud he was. After calling our names, one at a time, we each proceeded to retrieve the gift he held for us. It was reminiscent of a graduation, and I remember feeling embarrassed to go and get mine. I had never liked a room full of eyes on me. When we were all seated, the music started playing again. Looking around the room, I watched as everyone opened their supposed accolade. Some of the faces seemed disappointed. Others began to cry. I asked Jai what was going on. His voice was flat in tone with just a word…"Lay off."

He told me to open mine. He told me quality control was usually the first to go. He said he would be doing other jobs in the lab after the rush, so he never got laid off. I was nervous at first. I knew I had been promised a job in the art department, but I had never said a word to anyone, because I had been sworn to secrecy. I looked around the room again. It was like a scene from "Willy Wonka and the Chocolate Factory," only this time, every one was hoping that their sweet delight didn't hold the golden ticket. Opening my envelope with John and Jai by my side, I peered in. There was a piece of paper in it, a note. It stated: "Report to Geoff on Monday in the art department." My bonus was an additional week's pay. Jai was practically bursting at the seams, wondering what the note said. John, however, just sat there with a big grin on his face. He had known all along of my fate. Geoff was his brother, and he had told him. Lifting a similar slip from his envelope, John handed it to me and said, "It looks like you and I, babe, are going to be the new Ken and Claudio." Jai let out such a squeal of delight that it caused the whole room to look in our direction. They were both smiling from ear to ear. I, on the other hand, was embarrassed by this outburst and did my best to avoid any eye contact with the people I knew had just lost their jobs.

Our apprenticeships were grueling. John was to do all the airbrushing and negative retouching. I was to do all the hand painted photographs. There were several aspects to my job. Sometimes I just had to remove the backgrounds of colored photos, while other times I had to paint over the whole photograph to make it look like an oil painting. Those we called DHO's (deluxe heavy oils). For the black and white department, I had to oil photos also. This consisted of light tints to DHO's as well. I liked doing the black and white work. The photos were all sepia-toned, and my job was to make them as old and wonderful as the original, hand-tinted photo had been. We had six months to be able to pull it together and take over the department. Our jobs were difficult to master. For me, the difficulty was the gentle butterfly touch it took to get just the right amount of oil on the picture without it looking garish. Then, there was a whole process of removing just the right amounts to produce facial features and bone structure. I knew learning the anatomy of the face was going to be the key to my success. I also had to learn the photo color wheel. We were taught spotting on color photos as well as black and white. With the color photos, it was important to understand the neutralization of colored dyes. Sometimes a dust spot on a photo would be over several different colors. We had to mix the dyes on our palettes to produce this complicated array of differences. To neutralize a color, you had to add each dye's compliment. Because photo dyes are not pure primaries, I had to memorize a different color wheel.

Ken was the type of teacher who didn't tell you all you needed to know. He felt the company didn't deserve an easy transition. It was an attitude that had been built up over thirty years of Christmas rush orders and changing young supervisors, trying to tell him how to do his job, when none of them were artists or had the faintest idea of how to do what he did. It was a helpless lack of control that had produced the Ken we met that day, added to the fact that Ken had always gotten his work done on time but had felt he had never been really appreciated for it. Claudio, on the other hand, was like a father figure to us. He took us under his wing and treated us with great respect. He was an Italian immigrant who had taught anatomy, painting and drawing in Rome before he moved to the United States. He had moved here because of the love for a woman he would be married to for more than forty years. It was obvious that Claudio was afraid of Ken, so he often taught us when Ken was out of the room. It was so important to Claudio that we know our stuff that, after awhile, we looked up from our desks in anticipation the minute that Ken left. Claudio never let us down. He would hear the conversations of the morning that had included our questions and would have a slip of paper ready with the answers. The minute the coast was clear, he would tell us. The most important tip that Claudio gave us was that we be our own artists. We could be taught techniques, but ultimately it would be the talent of the artist that pushed those techniques to the limit and beyond. He didn't want us to become clones of them but to develop a new art department of John and Barbara.

Over the course of the next few months, John and I grew closer in the misery of the learning curve that we were both a part of. On more than one occasion, we helped the other through the frustrated tears of our mistakes. Despite all the barriers that were placed before us, we were able to persevere. Our desks were butted in front of each other, and we would whisper our plans of making it better. We were a team who cared for each other in no way I had ever experienced before, something that would become useful for me later in life. Claudio's words were what gave us the strength to move forward every day; when it was time for them to retire, we were ready to take over. In six months time, we had done as he had said. Because we were young and not burnt out by years of stress, together John and I found ways to make the job more enjoyable and efficient. It was an improvement that had been noted by our supervisors, and suddenly, with Ken and Claudio gone, they were in the art room more than ever before, asking our advice about different jobs. We were approachable and willing to try anything that was for the better of the product. This attitude helped us develop better techniques, especially with John and his airbrushing. We gained a type of respect from the other employees around us. We became "John and Barbara" just as Ken and Claudio had; one name that was synonymous with the art department. We found those shoes to be comfortable and fit quite well.

Because of our success with the work we did, the lab started campaigning for more artwork. The department began to grow, and the higher level management was pleased.

CHAPTER: 50

The whole time that I was doing my apprenticeship at N.S.C., I was still attending classes at Montserrat College of Art. So far, I had taken a basic drawing course and basic painting, as well as life drawing. John and I took the life drawing class together, so as to improve our anatomy skills for work. That class was very memorable for me. We had talked about it the whole day at work.

"Barb, what are we going to do if the model is a handsome young stud-like guy?" he said with a giggle. "Don't count on it. From what I hear they are usually overweight, middle-aged women." "But if it is a guy, how on earth are you and I going to hold it together without getting the giggles?" "Oh man, now you've gone and done it. I am going to giggle, no matter what."

Meeting in the parking lot of the college with all our supplies, we looked at each other, and already the laughter began. Putting his arm around me and leading me to the building, John said, "I feel honored that we can experience this together for the first time." Putting my arm around his waist I said, "I am with you on that one, girlfriend."

The room was a well lit open expanse. There were approximately twenty easels lined up around the model stand. We took two that were in the back. I was surprised by how nervous I was. I was so glad that John was with me. Every time I looked over at him, he flashed me his perfect relaxed smile. I then would start to giggle again. The class was made up of an array of different types of people. Most were older than we and looked very serious. They didn't seem to acknowledge anyone else in the class and set up their sketch pads quietly, like a musician setting up his sheet music in an orchestra pit before a concert. In a short while, the teacher entered the room. He was in his forties and seemed pleasant. He went through the syllabus of the class and passed out paperwork that supported it. He then turned on a spotlight that faced the model stand and through the door came the most handsome man I had ever seen. He was wearing a bathrobe. I immediately looked at John, who in turned looked back at me. Without any control whatsoever of our feelings, we both burst out into a fit of laughter, causing the rest of the group to look in our direction. I felt my face flush with their eyes upon us. John was as red as I was. I tried so hard not to look in his direction, but I couldn't help myself. The model, seemingly unfazed by our outburst, stood on the stand and removed his robe. Standing before us was a God with proportions of the likes I had never seen before. I stood in awe at his beauty. John leaned over to me and said, "Barb, put your tongue back in your mouth; you are beginning to drool." I looked at him, forgetting where we were for a fraction of a second, till his words slowly penetrated my brain. The laughter started all over again. That class was fun; every woman should take at least one life drawing class with a gay friend.

The last class I took at that college was figure painting. John did not join me. The class was an evening course with a lot of students who were in their fifties. All these students had been taking this same course for two years running, with the same instructor. I was the only new student attending and the only one taking it for credit. When I walked into the class, all eyes were on me. The teacher asked if he could help me, as if I were lost. When I told him I was enrolled in the class, he said, "Oh, good, another victim." I could tell he was an arrogant man, right from the start. I immediately assumed he was an artist with a huge ego, and I chose to ignore him, staying out of his way as much as possible. This class was in a different room from the one I had taken life drawing in. It was crowded and poorly lit, and the room was not set up well to handle a lot of painters who had to see a model. There were no model stands, and because I was new, I had the worst spot in the room. I could barely see the model through the labyrinth of easels and artists. I could only see her from the waist up. I was at least five people deep in the semi-circle of the class that surrounded her. At the beginning of every class, the teacher did a demonstration of how we were to begin. With a dark wash, he drew the model onto the canvas. The whole time, he was talking about himself and what he found to "work" in the form of drawing. Other than his own opinion, he never gave an explanation of why he was doing what he was doing. I couldn't see his canvas very well because of the crowd, so I was forced to mostly listen. When it was our turn to try our hand at it, I did the best I could with what I understood from the lecture. The results were poor. I had done better paintings at home and thought maybe it was because I was nervous. During the break, it was obvious that this group of people worshiped this man. They gathered around him and hung on every word he said. I just sat in the back and watched. No one talked to me. At the end of every class, there was a critique. He would line the paintings up, best to worst. Mine was always last. He would go down the line of paintings, pointing out different merits in each one; occasionally he would talk about areas of improvement. When he got to mine, he would tear it apart. The class went on like this through the winter semester. Every night I would be humiliated, without any words of encouragement or suggestions for improvement. During the class he barely spoke to me, except one time, when he asked if I were from Lynn (a local town known for its crime rate). The last project we had was portraiture. I thought this would be easy for me, since I had been painting portraits most of my life. The model was a young girl with an interesting face. She was easy to paint, and I captured her likeness right away. But as usual, I couldn't get a clear view of her surroundings, because of the size of the class. After awhile, pondering about what to do with the background, I chose to give her the same type of background that I did on the photos at work. It was a dark, Rembrandt-type background, with a lot of browns and a little yellow ochre thrown in for warmth. I hated the picture, but I hated the teacher too. This would be the last course I would ever take with him. The only thing he taught me the whole semester was how to accept criticism in a large group. At the end of that class, he once again put my painting last. This time he turned to me and, in front of the entire class, laughed in my face. He made a comment about the background and told me I should seriously think of another profession. Then he stopped and said, "Wait, I think there are still some openings for painters to paint Elvis on velvet!" The whole class laughed. I quietly took my things and walked out the door. The last class of the semester was scheduled two days later. I didn't go. When I got my grade in the mail, he flunked me. I talked to Jack about it the next morning. I was devastated and humiliated. Jack was appalled. At first he ranted about the arrogance of the man, then he lowered his voice and was kind and told me the man was an idiot and not to take him seriously. He said I had a lot of potential and not to give up. I asked Jack if he would teach me how to paint. I told him I was tired of throwing my money away on teachers with big egos who didn't know how to teach. He told me that he couldn't possibly teach me, having been cautioned by his own professors that teaching would destroy his own work. I couldn't see how it would do that; teaching was such a rewarding job. I had been a teacher for many years and had found it to be inspiring. He said he would think about it. The next day I enlisted Nick to go with me to Jack's studio and plead my case once again. I wasn't going to let the matter drop or put too much time between our discussions. Jack finally agreed, but he didn't know what to charge. I told him to think about it, and we left. The following evening, we met Jack at a local pizza parlor. I told him that I would pay him what I spent at the college for the same amount of time.

He agreed.

The series of lessons I took with Jack provided one of the most pivotal transitions of my entire life. I wouldn't have become the artist I was, if it weren't for him. I wouldn't have looked at the world the way I did; I would have been a totally different person. Jack molded me in many ways. I often refer to Jack as the man who raised me.

We started with drawing. The first thing he did was stack a bunch of ladder back chairs on top of each other. He taught me to gesture them all together, to get the feel of the confusion of the scene. The gesture was done lightly and quickly with loose and freeing lines. Then with the same drawing, he taught me to measure them by extending my arm out in a way that compares the height to the width of the entire conglomerate, as well as individual chairs. He told me to do all this with just placement points, before I would even consider doing a finished drawing; that way the drawing becomes easier with fewer changes. I did as he said, and the results were fabulous.

"Jack, this is so much easier. Why have I not learned this before in other classes I have taken?"

"I don't know. It seems colleges today want to throw out the traditions of drawing foundations and grow free thinking artists who can only interpret what they feel they are looking at. The reality is, until you understand how something is put together, can you really take it apart...even if it is just emotionally?" For the first time in a long time, I was pleased with something I had drawn. But more importantly, he gave me the reasons for working in this way, and I understood them. They were based on math and science and had concrete merit. He never once told me he liked something just because it was his opinion. Instead he would say, "I like this because the measurements work." Jack taught me more on that first day than I had learned in all the years of classes I had taken. After three hours of drawing the chairs, I stood back slowly and looked at my work. It was the best thing I had ever done. The knowledge of this made me tremble instantly. I walked to the large window that looked down three stories into the rainy Peabody Square. It was an essential moment in my life, and I knew it. I wanted to take it all in inside me and hold it like a precious flower. I was quiet and awed by what I had just learned. Jack knew the secret I had been searching for over the years. I couldn't believe it. With this information, anyone could learn to draw. Talent was no longer a factor. He walked over to me and stood next to me. He knew what I was thinking.

When I turned to look up at him, a slow smile crossed his face. In a whispered voice, I said, "Jack, we have to tell people about this. We can't keep this to ourselves; it would be wrong. There are a lot of people out there who have felt the way I did. I now feel like I have been let into a secret club; I can't keep this to myself. I want to tell the world about this."

"Maybe someday you will, Barb." He smiled as he crossed the room, leaving me there, lost in my thoughts. A seed had been planted at that moment that wouldn't take root until several years later and would affect the lives of many.

Jack had an enthusiasm that was contagious. I found myself jumping up and down, when I knew I had done well. He would get excited, too, and often said what a shame it was that I hadn't gone to Boston University, because I was grasping all this knowledge faster than anyone he had ever gone to school with. We hired models, and he taught me anatomy and how to draw the figure. He was a strict teacher, and, if I hadn't gotten it quite right, he would have me do it again. Nothing we worked on was for displaying on a wall. He wanted me to learn the foundations first. He often would give me assignments with complicated problems dealing with measurement and value, then he would leave me alone in the studio for hours at a time, to see how well I was able to figure them out. It angered me at first, to be left alone, but when I look back on it now, I realize that I had learned so much faster, being forced to do it myself without using his expertise as a crutch. When we moved on to painting, he taught me the six different lights that science tells us exist. He gave me the rules that each of these lights follow. It was a world presented to me that had been in my vision all along, yet I hadn't seen it, until he had shown it to me. It was a new language he was teaching me, and I was becoming fluent in it. This was another key component to representational painting that was so easy to teach, yet no one had taught it to me before. The more I spent time learning from Jack, the more I realized what a waste my other classes had been. When it was time for color, he taught me the scientific theories behind neutralization and warms and cools. He set up still life that consisted of the most unusual objects. Often they were tools with baseball caps and lunch boxes. Sometimes the object couldn't even be identified at all, a piece of plastic or PVC piping. He did this purposely, because he wanted me to just see form and color, without the use of my brain to identify what each object was. He would then pile the objects together, so that one item visually melded into the next. Each painting had to start with a gesture and be measured before the oil was applied. It worked. The results were some of the best paintings I had ever done. They were a visual landscape of color and plateaus. One day, I brought one home to my mother. I was so proud of my achievement. When I showed her the piece, she said, "What is it?" I told her what the objects were, and her response was, "No one would ever hang that on a wall. I think you're wasting your money." I never showed her another piece again.

Next we moved on to portraiture. For this assignment, I enlisted a young guy from the lab to pose for me. John and Jai were busy with their own lives, and this kid needed some extra money. He was handsome and a few years younger than I was. He had an interesting face with a prominent nose. Jack left me alone with him for three hours in the studio, after giving me a pep talk about how to begin. When Jack returned, I had a completed image that looked just like the model. I was pleased with myself, and the model was amazed. Jack, however, cared nothing about likeness in a portrait. He said likeness is something you worry about later. He began measuring the drawing and discovered that two major components were off. Without saying a word to me, he took my palette knife and scraped off the entire painting, to the shock and horror of the model and myself. Jack then turned the painting upside down and said, "If the measurements don't work, it's not good. You did it once, you can do it again," and then he left the room. I stood there with my mouth wide open. I knew he was right, but did he have to destroy the work? The model jumped down from the stand and tried to console me. He called Jack an arrogant son-of-a-bitch, as he patted me on the back. I looked at the model and said, "I've met an arrogant son-of-a-bitch, and that is not Jack. Jack is right; it should have measured." We worked another three hours on the new piece, and it was better than the first. When Jack came back, he was floored. He grabbed me, giving me a big bear hug and said, "I knew you could do it. Never be seduced by your ability to easily get a likeness. It will be your enemy through your whole career. It will always be lurking over your shoulder; keep it at bay." Jack and I painted together for several years like this. The education he gave me was worth twice what I paid him. A bond happened between us like no other I had ever had. He was my mentor, my teacher, a father figure, and my friend.

CHAPTER: 51

Nick and I were seeing a lot of each other. He was a nice distraction in my busy life. On a beautiful, autumn Friday evening, he said he wanted to show me something before we did my mother's food shopping. Taking me to a wooded area off a road near the town line, he brought me to Salem's highest peak. Standing in a clearing, he said, "I own this. I know we joke all the time about me asking you to marry me, but I want you to know that I want to build you a house here. I want to have children with you, and if we can't have children, then we can adopt." Then he pulled out a small jeweler's envelope out of his pocket. Inside was a one carat diamond.

I didn't know what to say. He had been asking me to marry him every week for a year, since practically the day we had first met. He was a perfect gentleman, of high character. He was a hard worker with a stable job. He was in many ways everything a woman would look for in a husband. What did he see that was so fascinating about me? What had I really accomplished up to that point in my life?

His property was located on a beautiful crop of land. You could see for miles. We were high above the city, looking down a huge ravine. As the sun was setting, it glowed on the yellow and orange leaves of the maple trees, which were laid below us like a golden carpet. Just past the trees, in the narrow valley thirty feet beneath us, was a pond. As I was thinking about what he was asking me, an egret gracefully glided across the water's surface and stopped.

Turning to Nick, I said, "We should go. Jimmy and Christina will be wondering where we are."

By the time we had picked them up and driven to the grocery store, I had a headache. I was trying to rationalize marrying Nick. I didn't hate him. As a matter of fact, I liked him very much. I admired the responsibilities he took care of on a daily basis, running his family's leather factory. At the factory, he was the one in charge, and everyone knew it. I was amazed weekly on the success he had with the projects people brought him to fix. I knew he was a man who would always be a provider. He had investments in stocks that had seemed to do well, and he was ambitious. Family was important to him. He was very close to his parents and his brothers. They all lived under the same roof, and every day they ate all their meals together. They were a tightly knit Greek family, proud of their heritage; I wondered how they would feel, having me as a part of it. The only thing missing was that, although I cared for him deeply, I wasn't madly in love with him. I began to wonder again if love even existed. I knew it was certainly over-rated. After all, what had love ever gotten me with William? The prospect of it all frightened me. When we got to the frozen food section, and I was picking out a bag of peas for my mother, he held one up to his face and gave me those pleading eyes I had come to know so well. Before I was even aware of what I was saying, I said, "Yes."

I had always been up front with Nick about how I felt, but he would never know the negotiating and reasoning that was going through my head that night, as we drove to the grocery store. I figured I would grow to love him; how could I not, when he was so perfect in many other ways?

My work at the lab was very fulfilling. My desire to get on with my personal life and try and start a family again was still ever present in my mind. I knew I would have a child, even if I had to adopt.

I had been writing journals to her for many years now, in hopes of her arrival. I was certain I would have a girl.

Nick immediately started making plans for our future. He was very organized in that way. The first thing he did was have the diamond sized to fit my finger. The second thing he did was start to break ground on the house that I had picked out for him to build us. Yes, although he had never done it before, Nick was determined to build the house himself. He realized that he couldn't do the blasting. The site was on ledge. He had also contracted the foundation and framing; from there on, the rest was up to him. We had a tough time with the city. I didn't know then that these types of difficulties are common when building. After a lot of negotiations about a turnaround for fire trucks, we got our permit back and were able to make progress. Nick gave me complete control of how I wanted it to look. We had similar taste and never argued about it. Nick never argued with anyone, and I often wondered what he really wanted in life. When I would ask him this, he would say, "You, Sweetie. I want you." It wasn't the answer I was looking for. I wanted to know who he really was. I realized that he didn't even know that answer himself.

At work, John and I were doing great. With the Christmas rush breathing down our necks, we were scared but confident we could get through it. When I announced to John and Jai that I was getting married, they were both thrilled for me.

On September 23, 1985, Nick and I were married. I was twenty-four, and he was thirty-one. The ceremony was held at a Greek church in Peabody. I begged him to elope. I wanted something simple; his mother on the other hand, wanted to invite her entire family--- all one hundred of them. I put my foot down. I told her it would be improper for me to have another big wedding, and I wasn't going to be distasteful in that way. Besides, my mother had had another recurrence of cancer, and I didn't want to tire her out. This time her treatment was radiation, followed by another round of chemotherapy. She developed fourteen tumors across the incision line on her chest. The doctor said it was more than likely a result of her breast falling back into the chest cavity during the mastectomy. I was torn between my impending marriage and the needs of my mother. Mom told me she was happy for me and not to worry; John would be there to take care of her. It was John who took care of her the first time, so I knew in my heart, he would be there for her again.

The wedding was simple, just as I had planned. I bought a beautiful, white, knee-length dress at Marshalls for twelve dollars. I made my own bouquet with dried flowers. For a veil, I attached a tiny drape of white netting to a white wedding hat I had purchased at a local bridal shop. The entire outfit cost me just under twenty-five dollars. It wasn't my intention to be so frugal with my spending; after all, I had by then seen hundreds of photos which had shown elaborate weddings. Nick was financially well off and could have afforded any wedding I would have wanted. It had been my intention to make this wedding as easy as possible on my mother.

I didn't hire a photographer, a surprise to the people I worked with. I didn't want to be just another set of wedding photos coming down the assembly line. Besides, it was against the rules of the Greek Church to photograph the altar. Instead, I gave a camera to Nick's best man, and asked him to take a few pictures of us in front of the church, after the service. The photos were taken with Nick's professional camera. Nick set up each shot with his best man as my groom and then jumped in right before the picture was taken. They were beautiful. I then asked Jack to do a drawing of us as we said our vows at the altar. He had been sketching courtroom scenes for channel seven, and I thought it would be a great solution to the no camera rules of the church. Jack was still my teacher, and I had been modeling for him as well. He was working on a series of paintings about the Beirut bombings and the effects they had had on its people. Sometimes, in the paintings, he would dress me up as a man; other times I would be a peasant woman; he always put me in contorted poses that showed the twisted form of human pain. I liked those paintings he made. The meaning behind his art made me look at my own work and wonder when I, too, would get my inspiration for self-expression. It wouldn't be until I was much older that I could allow myself the freedom to find it.

Despite insistence to respect my wishes about immediate family attending the wedding, my Aunt Flo showed up at the church to watch the service. This made Nick's mother extremely angry. She refused to talk to anyone and sat with her arms folded across her chest through the whole thing. The look on her face said it all...with this woman, my life was not going to be easy.

After the mass, the plan had been to all meet at my mother's house for a quiet dinner, before Nick and I were to leave for a honeymoon in New Hampshire. When my mother saw the look on his mother's face, she approached her to say that it would be only family at the house. My new mother-in-law, looked right past my mother, who obviously wasn't feeling well and was exhausted; she didn't even acknowledge her presence or that my mother had even spoken to her. My mother turned warily on her heels and walked out the door. I had disrespect for Nick's mother after that, and our relationship never recovered from it.

When we got to the house after the service, Nick's mother refused to come inside. I looked out the window to see what could be taking her so long. She sat in the front seat of her car with the same posture she had had at the church. Her arms were folded as tightly across her chest as her lips were pursed across her face. She looked like a three year old child who had been told she couldn't have a Popsicle. I thought she was the most selfish individual I had ever met. She didn't care if she spoiled everyone's day, as long as we all realized how angry she was. Nick, with the help of his brothers and father, went out to console her. I went to check on my mother to see if she needed any help in the kitchen. When I got there, my mother was fuming. The anger she was feeling from the situation had brought a new found strength to her. I put my arms around her and said, "Ok, so my new mother-in-law is a bitch. Let's try to forget about her. If she doesn't want to come in, then so be it. As far as I'm concerned, I'd rather she had her tantrum out there and not in here."

My mother wasn't buying it. She was going to get that woman in there if she had to drag her by the hair. She told me this as she stormed out of the room. I have to admit, it felt good to see my mother all fired up like that. It was the first time in a year that I had seen the old MaryJane back. My mother walked out to the car and ordered all the men back inside. To my surprise, they obeyed. The two women talked for five minutes. I was dying to look out the window and see what was going on. But I was too afraid. No one else looked either. I don't know what my mother said to her, but it worked. When Nick's mom walked through the door, she even had a smile on her face. I was convinced that my mother had insisted on that bit of detail as well.

Despite the difficulty with the wedding, my biggest challenge was ahead of me. Because the house wasn't going to be ready for a few months, after a quiet honeymoon in New Hampshire, we moved in with Nick's parents and brothers. I never felt at home there. If anything, I felt like an intruder. Nick's brothers and father were fine; it was his mother who seemed to disapprove of my presence. She never said anything openly to me about it. It was the little things that she used to do. She had complete control of that house and wouldn't let me do anything without asking, not even my own laundry. I never let her do my laundry. I went through the ritual every week and told her when I would be doing it. I still did my mother's food shopping. I offered to pick some things up for Nick's mother too. She would only laugh at me and say she was the one who shopped for the family. I tried to make it easier by offering to go with her. She complied a few times and let me go along. She was a shopping machine! She knew where every item was in the store and how long it would take her to get through the aisles.

She would start by going to the deli first and taking a number. She would then calculate the length of time it would take for her number to be called. To my embarrassment, she would leave the deli area and race up and down the aisles, throwing various products in the cart. Anyone standing in her wake would jump out of her way, so as not to be mowed down. Often people would curse at her for her abruptness and the rudeness of her demeanor. I would just smile and apologize for her. I never had to worry about her hearing me; usually by then, she was a few more aisles over. I hated going shopping with her. She had such a different personality from mine. Eventually I stayed behind at the deli to avoid most of the craziness of this ritual.

A month after I married Nick, my own family's tragic life was thrown into another tailspin. My mother had called me at work to say that she needed to see me that night. When I arrived at her house, my mom met me at the door. She said she wanted me to come into the kitchen, because she had something she had to tell me. My immediate concern was for her. I asked if she was ok; did she feel ill? She said she felt fine. It was John who was not well. She said, "He has liver cancer and needs to have an operation." I couldn't believe what I was hearing. What were the odds of both of them getting cancer at the same time? The unfairness of it was too ironic to even comprehend. I knew that they would need me now, but I was no longer living there. I suddenly felt guilty for getting married and moving on with my life. There were two weeks that their chemotherapy overlapped. They were both so sick. Because he was not married with a family of his own, Doug drove them to their treatments. I went to visit them every day after I got out of work. They looked a mess, and I wondered how they were going to get through this. John's operation was scheduled after his first rounds of chemotherapy; the doctor wanted to shrink the tumor first. Once again, I sat outside the bathroom on the floor. This time, I let my mother know I was there. Their perseverance through this difficult time was a testament to the human spirit that I would draw strength from years later.

By November, to everyone's surprise, I was pregnant. I had wanted to try and have a baby on my own again. I had wanted my mother to have another grandchild. It seemed to be the only thing that had made her happy. I used an ovulation test to determine when my best chances were to conceive. I couldn't believe it; it worked on the first try. My doctor put me on the high risk list, and I was going to do everything possible in my power to carry this baby. Once again, I had known the moment I conceived. I thought about the words that Martha had spoken the night I had had the fight with Aunt Flo. "If it isn't right, maybe the mother knows it." I tried not to think about it. I had so much else to worry about.

In a month, John had finished his treatments. He was scheduled for surgery right away. It was to take place in Boston instead of Salem. Doug was working at Mass General again and had heard of a new type of operation that was being performed for liver cancer. It was discovered that the human liver could actually regrow after a piece of it had been removed. This was the beginning stages of this type of surgery; Doug was able to get John on the list. We were all hopeful. John was getting the best care in the world. We knew the recovery time would be long, but we were sure he would pull through. The doctors made it sound so easy: just remove the affected corner of his liver, and the remaining good part would grow a new piece.

The operation appeared to be successful. John was in the hospital for several weeks. He seemed thinner and a little disoriented, the one day I saw him. The day after he had come home, he was to have chemotherapy again as a precaution. He chose to have the treatments at Salem Hospital because of the convenience in location. The afternoon after his first treatment, John had a stroke. The hospital hadn't calculated the reduced size of his liver, the organ that processes everything that travels through the human body. The overload of the injection attacked John fiercely in the short time it took for my mother to drive him home. Basically, his body acted as if he had been poisoned. The overload of the chemo brought on a violent episode of vomiting and disoriented behavior. It was so bad, my mother called an ambulance. He had the stroke in the bathroom only moments before they arrived. It was the only time I was not with them after a treatment. His body had been unable to recover from this assault; he died a few days later.

It was difficult for my mother when John died, but she put on a brave face. With the help of Doug, she went through all the motions of planning his funeral. I wondered how she felt about doing this, knowing that someday in the future, it might be her plans that had to be made. I didn't have to wait long for that answer. She told me that night that she had paid for her own expenses as well. She didn't want us put in the position of having the difficult job of arranging her burial. I never saw her cry, not even once, the whole time she told me this. After the funeral, she began to turn all her focus on her grandchildren. Jake and Justine now had two girls. Anna was born into our family at a time when my mother needed hope and the promise of life.

Unfortunately, two days after the funeral, I had to be rushed to the hospital. I was bleeding and in pain. It was happening to me all over again. This time, I was determined to find a solution to keeping this baby. I was at work when it happened. I told John first. I tried to be strong, but I found myself flooded with tears and rambling on about my history with this type of thing. He helped me to the office, where they let me phone my husband. Nick and I went straight from the lab to the doctor's office. The whole way there, I was silent and stared out the window. He was doing his best to reassure me that this time it would be different. I, on the other hand, found myself in that place where people often go for emotional protection. I became numb and just sat comfortably inside my soul, waiting for the powers that be to take over my life. I wasn't scared. I wasn't nervous. Perhaps what I was feeling was defeat. I had fought this battle many times. I needed to find the strength to go to war again. The doctor saw us right away and ordered an ultrasound. After what seemed like an hour, he sat us down to explain what was happening. He said that this situation was different from the last. He said I had a condition known as "placenta previa." Stated simply, this meant that the placenta was underneath the baby instead of in the reverse. He told us it caused bleeding and early delivery for most women who had it, but they had delivered healthy babies under these circumstances, if they had followed medical advice. In a concerned but confident voice, he ordered me to bed for the remainder of the pregnancy. He said that when the baby grew bigger inside of me, it would become heavy and could cause more serious bleeding. He said the biggest danger was the wear and tear on the placenta. If it were to rupture from the weight, the baby could be in danger and might die. His words were coming at me all at once. Was he saying I would have a chance to save this child myself? It was a strange prayer that was answered that day. I had been bargaining with God from the moment I had found out I was pregnant. I had told him I would do anything that was required to carry this child...now he was answering my call. My role of mother started eight months before my child was born.

Nick took me home, and I immediately got into bed. At first, I was afraid to sit up. Any form of gravity I thought was sure to be the enemy in this battle I was now in. Nick went back to the factory and told his family what the doctor had said. That evening, he bought a TV set for our bedroom, so I wouldn't feel so alone during the day. Nick was good like that. He always took care of everything. I told Nick that night that I felt awful about having to leave work. I was feeling the pressures of my responsibilities, and I wasn't sure what to tell my boss. Knowing it had taken six months to train me, I had now put them in a difficult position. As usual Nick had the answer. He told me he would design and make a table for the bed that adjusted like an easel. He was sure they would let me work from home, considering the circumstances they were in and the complexity of the doctor's orders. He said he would have it built by the following weekend and that he would even leave work everyday to pick up and deliver work for me. I called the lab the next day. I needed a few hours to absorb the complexity of this task. When I proposed what Nick was willing to do, they went for it. Nick was pleased. He was concerned about my state of mind for the next few months and knew this would help me get through them.

The table he made was amazing. It not only had all the essentials for everything I needed, it also had storage for reading materials and my make-up. He even installed a small mirror, so that I could apply it.

At first, the time I had at home alone was great. I watched TV while I worked on pictures. If I got tired, all I had to do was lay my head back and take a nap. I could make my own hours and was enjoying the freedom this gave me. The lab was now paying me by the piece. Because I was so efficient at my job, I was actually making more money. Nick had also installed a phone in the room, so that I could keep in touch with the outside world. At break time, I would receive calls from Jai and John. They would tell me about all the gossip at work. "The dirt" is what they called it, and although I wasn't one for gossip, I found myself looking forward to their calls. The first month, the only time I was out of bed was to go to the bathroom, which was the room next door. Every time I got up, the bleeding would start. I found myself being able to perform this simple task in record speed, out of fear for my child. Doctor visits were worse, but I didn't have a choice. I was scheduled for monthly ultrasounds that were important to track the development of the baby and the placenta.

Alone during the day, I would talk to my baby. I made Nick buy me children's books, so that I might read them out loud. Sometimes I would sing lullabies, only to find the peacefulness would actually put me to sleep. My obsession with holding on to this baby bordered on insanity; a concern started to develop in the other members of the household.

One day at a visit to the doctor's office, I asked him if I should be concerned about the paints I was using. He was uncertain about the hazards and gave me a number of an organization that was based in New York, called Artists Hazard Materials Hotline. When I got home I called them first thing. I got a woman on the phone who told me that I had exposed my unborn child to many different chemicals and should consider an abortion within the next week before it became too late to do so. I was in shock from her words and hung up the phone before I heard any more. Nick was next to me at the time I had made the call, and when I told him what she had said, he called her back. He listened to her warnings of gloom and doom. Politely saying thank you, he hung up the phone. He turned to me and said that being a chemical engineer, he was sure I had nothing to worry about. Besides, many people who volunteer for hot lines have a personal experience that causes them to blow everything out of proportion. He said, "You don't even use turpentine, which would be the only thing that I could think of that would touch the nervous system."

I said, "I don't care if this baby has two heads, I cannot allow myself to voluntarily abort it."
"Sweetie, no one is going to ask you to do that. Have faith."

At dinner time, I overheard the entire family talking about it downstairs. Nick was doing his best to explain the situation, but there was one person who wasn't listening. That was his mother. She was so convinced that there was something wrong with the baby, she was insisting we terminate the pregnancy. My heart sank. I had never seen Nick go against any of his mother's wishes. I was hoping he was man enough to stand up to her. When I didn't hear a protest come from him, I hauled myself out of bed to confront her myself. Standing at the bottom of the stairs with my legs held tightly together in false hope of holding in the baby, I stated my case. I told them that there was no way in hell that anyone was going to force me to have an abortion. Looking at her, I said, "This is your grandchild, I'm going to protect it, even from you if I have to."

Nick was upset that I was out of bed. He led me by the arm and back up stairs. Once in the privacy of our room, I told him that I wouldn't allow her to persuade him to do this. He said I shouldn't worry about it. He was just going to ignore her and let her rant. She would probably make a commotion about it for several days, and then she would be fine. "That's how we all deal with her, trust me." I said, "Nick, this isn't a common daily problem we are faced with, I know she won't let this rest. I can't lie here listening to her." The rest of the night we slipped into a silence that left us with our own tormented thoughts.

CHAPTER: 52

The next day, I called my mother to tell her what had happened. Mom and I could only communicate over the phone. After the wedding incident with Nick's mother, she had refused to step foot in that house. She was also still on crutches by then. The tumor that was embedded in her pelvis was causing a painful pressure on her hips. Because of my mother's illness, I talked to her daily. Our conversations were reminiscent of the ones we had had when I was in Germany. I usually did my best not to worry her. This time, I couldn't hold back. I was worried myself and needed to hear a reasonable and reassuring voice. She told me that she would call Doug. Maybe he knew of a doctor who could give us a more precise answer.

The next day, my mother-in-law came up to talk to me when she arrived home to make lunch for the guys. She said she was very concerned and disappointed in me for being so unreasonable and that I should be ashamed of myself. She said I should reconsider the abortion before it was too late. This was how she operated...divide and conquer. I told her that when it came to my body, no one was going to tell me what to do and to please not bring it up again. When she left the room, I felt helpless. I was trapped in a bed in the home of a woman who wanted me to kill my child. My stomach began to jump with nerves, and I knew this wasn't good for the baby. At lunch when the guys came home, it only got worse. She brought up the subject again with the family. An argument started. I couldn't tell who was on my side and who wasn't. I could tell that she wasn't alone in her thinking. I knew I had to take desperate measures. This family worked together as a unified front on every issue. I began to feel as if I didn't have a chance. I would later find out that Nick was always on my side. I called my mother to ask her what I should do. Without hesitation, she said flatly... "You're coming home!"

Rising from the bed, I walked downstairs. I announced that I could no longer live in this environment, and, with the house way behind schedule, I had no choice but to think of the baby. I told them that I was going to stay with my mother. I turned to Nick and said, "Will you drive me?" Without hesitation, he gathered my things. Within the hour, I was back at my mother's house. Nick retrieved the bed from the cellar, and, by later that afternoon, I was in my old room with my old bed and feeling a sense of control. After he had left, my mother and I talked for hours about the audacity of that woman trying to control my body, without any tests to prove her point. As a matter of fact, all the ultrasounds had shown everything was ok. My mother reminded me of that fact, and we held on to it for the duration of the pregnancy. Later that night, Doug called us. He had spoken to a doctor who was researching chemicals which crossed the placenta. He didn't think I had anything to worry about. When he had received a list of the paints I was working with, he found that none of them contained heavy metals. He did say to stick with the mineral spirits instead of turpentine. Turpentine had the ability to be absorbed through the skin. With this particular job, I had never worked with turpentine, so on that score I wasn't worried. The same doctor asked that I be put on a list for him to retrieve my placenta and cord to further conduct his research. I agreed. The next day, Nick set up my table on the new bed. I called the lab and told them that I wanted to limit the amount and type of work I was doing. I told them what I had just been through. They weren't pleased but didn't have a choice. I only worked on the light oils. I had no idea what they did for a DHO artist. I knew they had hired several replacements, but none of them had seemed to work out.

The time I spent with my mother during my pregnancy will always be a fond memory for me. She was with me during the day, and together we formed an alliance to bring this baby safely into the world. We talked daily about names and the baby necessities that I would need to buy. Nick visited every day after work and stayed with us until it was time for him to go home to bed. He took me to the doctors and saw, with me, the normal development of a human being who was going to become our child. When I was six months along, the ultrasound showed that the placenta had moved a little. The baby was now only sitting on a quarter of it. It also showed that she was a girl. The placenta hadn't moved enough for me to resume a normal life, but it was enough for me to have short visits away from my bed. The bleeding, however, never stopped. I was beginning to feel like I was having a nine month period.

To make up for the bad feelings I had left behind at Nick's parents' house, I announced that I was going to name the baby Alexis. It was Greek tradition to name the first grandchild after the grandfather. Since his name was Alex, I felt this would be an appropriate choice and, at the same time, an offering of peace. In my head, she was to be called Lex, a name I started using when I talked to her at night, long before she was born. My mother also started picking up this obsessive behavior and talked to her as well. She would hold my now swollen belly and speak sarcastically to her of how much a pain in the butt she was. We would both laugh when she did this and found the ritual to be comforting. It took her mind off her cancer and let me have the relationship with my mother that I had longed for so often.

By the time I was eight months along, the placenta moved again. It was still sitting under Lex a little bit, but I could now go for short trips to the store. Doug was doing Mom's grocery shopping, so instead, we shopped for baby furniture. Neither of us were allowed to lift anything, so mostly we would look and send Nick back the next day to purchase it. I knew it was a wonderful gift to be able to do this with my mother. She was often in pain, and we found ourselves sitting more than shopping, but she never complained. She wanted this as much as I did. My bleeding became less and less. The weight I had put on from months of being idle was now my source of discomfort. Strangers would stop me and ask if I were having twins. I was shocked by the openness people seemed to have with pregnant women. There was no topic that seemed taboo. I tried my best to ignore the rude ones. With the others, I was more than pleased to answer their questions. It was the first time I had been out in the world as a pregnant woman. I felt that for the previous eight months, I had been living in a cocoon. For the first time, I didn't worry about gaining weight. I knew the sedentary lifestyle was something I had to do. In the end, the reward would be worth it.

When I was in the middle of my eighth month, the house was finished. It was a beautiful day in April when we moved in. Nick had all the rooms set up for my arrival. He had even put the dishes in the cabinets and sheets on the bed. The house was a gambrel style with an attached, below ground-level garage. Above the garage was a four hundred foot studio, just off the kitchen on the first floor. It had six, eight foot windows that wound around the room. The floors throughout were hardwood. The kitchen had more cabinets than any house I had ever seen. It had a breakfast bar and room for a table that sat in front of a picture window that looked over the entire city of Salem and led out to a porch that spanned the back of the house and included the studio. At the front of the house were the living room and dining room. On this same floor was also a half bath. Upstairs, there were two full-size bathrooms. I had never had more than one bathroom in any house I had lived in and thought of what a luxury it was. Every time I passed it, I would think of all the people I had grown up with, under one roof with one tiny bathroom. Now here I was, soon to be a family of three, and we each had our own. Lex, of course, wouldn't need hers for the first two to three years. Lex was due to arrive on May 24th, a day of anticipation that I seemed to have been waiting for long before the nine months that I carried her. In an odd way, it felt as if she had been a part of my life all along. With the journals I had started for her right after graduation, on those lonely nights when I was hungry and poor, she had kept hope in me. It had been a realization that someday I would make my own family, one that was close and understanding, one in which no one would be afraid to say he loved the other. My whole life that was all I had ever wanted. I had never realized the power Lex had already had. As a fetus, she was able to mend the bond between me and my own mother. I began to picture her in my head. She was dark-skinned like Nick with black hair and dark brown eyes. I knew she was a fighter. After all, she had done what no other baby had been able to do in me before...survive.

When May 24th had come and gone, I was disappointed. I knew that a lot of women don't deliver on their due date, especially with the first delivery, but I had been certain that Lex was going to be different. It was a cruel trick to play on me, after all I had been though. I had even gone into early labor the month before and had to be given a shot to stop it. Now it was time, and she wasn't making any move in the direction of delivery. The next day, I had a doctor's appointment. He said the placenta had moved a little more and my chances of delivering naturally were looking good. He was certain it would move the rest of the way when Lex was ready. I asked him what would happen if it didn't. He said that he would deliver her by C-section, a common procedure for placenta previa. "But," he said, "I don't even know if I would put you in that category any more. Get out of bed and do a lot of walking to help this baby along. She needs to know that it's time." I loved how he talked about her as if she already existed. I did what the doctor had said, and every day I went to the Willows and did laps around the park.

After two weeks with no luck, the doctor said that he was going to schedule a C-section for the following Wednesday. She hadn't dropped into position yet, something that was supposed to have happened at least a week before delivery. He also said that my stress test had showed that she was out of amniotic fluid. I would not experience my water breaking like most women do. He told me the longer she was in there without water, the more the risk of infection. I thought of Danny, Sara's baby who had died, and told the doctor to schedule it as soon as he could. He said, "We have another problem. Because of the time you spent in bed, your body has too much fluid of its own. I'm afraid you might be coming down with toxemia. I want to put you in the hospital today to monitor it." It was a Friday afternoon that he gave me this news. I had driven myself to the doctor's office alone, squeezing into the Datsun 280Z. Nick had adjusted the seat back as far as it could go. That morning, I knew, would be the last time I drove until after Lex had arrived. In another day, I wouldn't fit. Calling Nick, I told him what the doctor had said. I also told him that I was having difficulty getting into the car. He told me to wait there; he and his brother would pick me and the car up and take me to the hospital. The doctor's office was one town away, in Peabody.

By the time I was settled in the hospital and my mother was called, the reality of the up and coming events began to sink in. The last time I had been on the maternity ward was when my baby was dead. I was praying this outcome would be different. The nurses told me to walk the halls as much as possible. They wanted to get that fluid out of my body. They attached me to a monitor and noted any changes they might have seen. The whole weekend, I was getting more and more worried about Lex. I wanted them to take her immediately so that she wouldn't be in danger. My own doctor was off for the weekend, and when I expressed these concerns to his replacement, he thought I was crazy to want him to cut me open. I let him know it wasn't me I was thinking about, it was the baby. Instead, he administered pitosin, a hormone that induces labor. He assured me that this baby could be delivered naturally and that it was time we got the ball rolling. I was skeptical; after all, she hadn't dropped. He told me not to worry; a lot of babies don't drop until right before delivery. The pitosin was given to me early Monday morning. At first, I didn't feel a thing. I continued my walking and was so tired of it; I had counted every tile on the hall floors. I made a game of looking at the gold fleck patterns in the linoleum, just as I had as a child, and wondered if my life had come full circle or if this was a game that just stayed with me. I spoke to Lex about this as I walked. If it weren't for the fact that I was obviously pregnant, anyone witnessing my slow paced stroll with the IV bottle attached to the pole I was dragging around like a dog that didn't want to be walked would be sure I was crazy, especially after witnessing me talking to myself. I didn't care; I knew she could hear me. I was trying to convince her that she needed to see this world and the toys I had for her. I wanted to feel her soft skin against my lips, to smell her baby powdered body, to feel the warmth of her belly against my cheeks. I headed back to my room where I found a nurse to be looking for me. She wanted to monitor my progress.

The monitor said that I was showing signs of labor. The nurse said I should keep walking but to stay close to the nurses' desk. I asked her why I didn't feel it. I thought it odd that I had always felt contractions when I had refused to believe them in the past; now she was telling me I was in labor, and I felt nothing. She said the beginning stages of labor were like that. Maybe I hadn't felt them then either. That thought brought a whole new perspective to my head about my previous miscarriages, meaning that I had been in labor long before I had had the pains. It meant I had been losing my babies almost right from the start. I didn't like having this information and tried to put it out of my mind. The day went on like this without any change. I still wasn't in pain, and they kept insisting I was in labor. Nick took the day off from work, and together we watched the ridiculous shows on TV which comprise daytime television. That night I slept peacefully until 5:00 AM, when I was bolted awake by a pain that shot straight up the middle of me. Getting out of bed, I headed to the bathroom. When I was finished, I knew this was it. I began my routine of walking the corridors again. It was now Tuesday, the day before my scheduled C-section. The halls were dark; a light glow was being cast from the nurses' station desk lamp. Quietly, I made my way down the hall in the opposite direction. Oddly, I wanted to be alone with Lex and begin this process myself. I wasn't alone though, Shadow Man picked up the pace beside me. His hands were clasped behind his back as he walked next to me. I turned to him and said, "Tell me she is going to be ok." He stopped in his tracks and turned to face me, but he didn't say a word. I continued, "If anyone in this world understands how badly I have wanted Lex in my life, it is you. Thank you for always being there for me, even when I was young and didn't understand." He nodded his head in reply. I timed my contractions and noted that they were ten minutes apart. "I have plenty of time," I thought and kept walking.

A short time later, the pains seemed to be coming faster. Riding the rollercoaster of contractions, I dutifully looked at my watch as they rose, peaked and dropped. They were now five minutes apart. I thought that maybe I should be heading for the nurses' station. I was at the far end of the hall, and suddenly, it seemed a million miles away. For the first time, I thought maybe I should have said something to them sooner. Passing the door to the stairwell, I came face to face with a sweet Irish nurse I had met the previous day. Before I could tell her what was happening, I was struck with another pain. Seeing this, she grabbed me with one arm and timed the contraction with the watch she had on the other. "Tell me when it peaks," she said, "and then tell me when it stops." I did as she said, and before she could say another word, I exclaimed, "They're coming again." "Let's get you to the labor room; I think you are going to deliver this baby soon; your contractions are two minutes apart. How long have you been walking the halls?" I couldn't answer her; I was struck with another pain.

By the time she got me upstairs to the labor and delivery floor, it was 8:00 AM. I hadn't realized it, but I had been walking the halls for three hours. My first instinct was to stay in an upright position and not lie down. Maybe it was the birthing chair memory that was telling me this, or maybe it was the natural instincts of my body. Either way, I should have listened, because the minute they laid me down, my contractions stopped. Lying down was also hurting my back. The nurses assured me these were still the pains of labor, but this pain was different. It was a constant, dull ache; I was sure it was Lex sitting on my spine. They started playing with the amount of pitosin they were letting drip into my body. In two more hours, with no signs of the labor I had experienced earlier that morning, I was convinced this baby was not going to be delivered naturally. I tried to keep my spirits up, but as time kept passing, I was getting more and more agitated. Nick had arrived shortly after I had entered the labor room, and, once again, we were watching TV.

At 10:00 AM, a group of nurses came flying into the room, under great duress. All at once, they started shaking me from side to side, as I laid sprawled out on the gurney. I yelled at them and asked if they had gone mad! "Didn't anyone ever tell you not to violently shake a pregnant woman!?" At first, they didn't answer me. They were listening to the nurse who was monitoring Lex's heart beat from the machine in the other room. When that nurse said it was back, I knew something was desperately wrong. In a panic, I demanded to know why they had just done that to me. They said that Lex's heart had stopped, and perhaps she had rolled over onto her umbilical cord. "That's it," I said. "I want to see my doctor." They informed me that he had had a family emergency, and the doctor I had seen over the weekend was still on call. I was disappointed, but this time I wasn't going to take no for an answer. I would insist he take this baby that very day.

In fifteen minutes, he was by my side. His mock calmness irritated me, and in an angry voice, I stated my case. Once again, he said that I had nothing to worry about. He said these things happened, and, as a matter of fact, he saw no reason to keep me there. "Barbara, would you like to go home today and come back when the baby is ready to be born?"

He was so lucky that I was hooked up to so many monitors and tubes. If I hadn't been, I would have grabbed him by the throat, screaming. Instead I gave him a steely-eyed glare and yelled, "This baby is now two and a half weeks overdue; if you don't take this baby right this instant I am going to sue the pants off you when she dies! You and I both know that she is at risk!" Nick was trying to calm me down. He was apologizing to the doctor. I glared at Nick and said, "Do not apologize for me. I am her mother and she needs my help." I was in such a state of hysteria that it caused Lex to roll once more. Once again, the nurses came running into the room, and once again I became a human volleyball. The doctor left the room. His parting words were, "I'll go tell them to get the OR ready."

After the coast was all clear, and Lex's heart was started again, Nick and I found ourselves alone. I was angry at him for not showing initiative, but, instead, I apologized to him for what I had said. He said he understood, that he knew I had been under a lot of pressure. A few minutes later, the gentle, Irish nurse entered the room. She said, "Barbara, you did the right thing. At the desk, we all feel this baby needs to be born. Sometimes doctors feel a mother's instinct starts at birth; we nurses know otherwise." These were reassuring words that I needed to hear. They calmed me down, and I thanked her. I was grateful for her gentle words. I knew that it was important for me to not get upset again, for the sake of my baby.

The whole time I was waiting to be wheeled into the delivery room, I could hear screams and moans coming from other adjoining rooms, women that were in the throes of labor and delivery, while I watched the clock tick slowly by. When I asked a nurse who had come in to check my blood pressure what was taking so long, she told me that there were 21 women all having babies at the same time on the floor. She said the doctors were running from room to room, and there just wasn't any delivery room available. I said "What will they do if this baby needs to come out?" She said, "We will have to play that one by ear. Just try and relax, and we will get you a room as soon as we can."

When Lex rolled over a third time and stopped her heart again, the nurses knew that time was running out. In a short time, the doctor entered the room with a big smile, as if he were rejoining a party he had left an hour earlier. He said, "Ok, Barbara, it is time to have this baby. We still don't have a room, but we are going to administer the spinal outside the one we feel will be available next, so that when it is your turn, we can just roll you right in and get it done." I was trying to understand all that he was telling me, but I couldn't comprehend it. Did he just say my baby was going to be delivered in the hall? I scolded myself for losing my energy, for not staying alert. My mind was reeling with all the stuff that was inside of it; there was no more room to allow outside information to penetrate. As I was rounding the corner out of the room I had been in all morning, I glanced at the desk of the nurses' station, the headquarters of the operation that had saved my daughter three times that morning. To my shock, I thought I saw my mother sitting with them. I was sure I had been delusional; how on earth could she possibly have gotten herself there? She now had to use her crutches all the time, and she certainly couldn't have driven herself. Before I could confirm what I had seen, we took another turn, and I was parked in the hall outside the delivery room, away from the sanctity of the nurses' desk.

I don't' know how long I was in the hall. Time felt different. I kept thinking of the image of my mother at the desk. If she were there, why hadn't she come into the room with me when I was so upset? I asked Nick if he had seen my mother. "When?" he asked. "A minute ago," I said, "sitting with the nurses." "Sweetie, you're under a lot of stress. Just relax." He hadn't seen her? I began to worry about myself for the first time. Was I going out of my mind? I closed my eyes tight and tried to will reasonable sense into me. I wasn't sure if it worked. I know it gave me an awful headache. The next thing I knew, a half dozen other people and I were in the delivery room. Lex's baby doctor was there. We had picked him out three weeks prior to this event. He was a quiet man who reminded me of Jimmy, whom I had worked for at the coin shop. Along with the pediatrician was the anesthesiologist. He was also very serious and only nodded when we were introduced. He was a painfully thin man with glasses. When he did speak to the doctor, his voice was soft and almost apologetic. The rest were interns and nurses. It felt like I was at a party that I was surprised to find myself attending. Nick sat at my head, as a sheet was placed to obstruct my view. When the first cut was made, I was surprised I could feel it. I turned to the anesthesiologist and asked him if that was ok. He said it was ok but not necessary. He gave me a shot, and suddenly the feeling was gone. When they reached in to pull her out, Nick was on his feet and watching from over my head. I kept asking him to tell me what was going on, but instead of answering, he just tightened the grip he had on my cheeks, until the hold he had on me hurt so badly, my teeth began to ache. In a desperate state, through the fish lips that his hold was causing on my mouth, I protested. It took three times to attract his attention. When he realized what he was doing, he apologized to me and kissed me on the forehead. It became a reality that I was merely the vehicle for this magnificent event, and the baby was really the patient.

As they pulled her out, I could feel her kicking from the inside. She was fighting the process every step of the way. It seemed as if she didn't want to leave the warm comfort of my belly that she had called home. Her tiny feet were hitting every organ of mine in range. When it felt as if she had kicked my stomach, I thought I would vomit. I tried to get the anesthesiologist's attention about this matter but couldn't. He was also focused on the complexity of the delivery. I was sure I was going to choke on my own vomit. I thought of Cherri and the lengths I had gone through to keep her alive the night she had had alcohol poisoning. Would anyone care about me today, if I started choking? Would anyone notice? I would be no good to this child if I were a dead mother. I was surprised by the lack of attention I was getting. I tried to figure out why this was so. Surely there were enough people in this room that someone could perhaps glance my way to see if I were Ok. When the nausea got so bad I couldn't take it anymore, I did the only thing I could think to do out of desperation. I grabbed the anesthesiologist by his expensive tie and pulled his face down to within two inches of mine. I looked in his eyes and said, "I'm going to vomit." He then apologized and gave me another shot, and all felt better. I thanked him.

The delivery was taking a long time. I couldn't figure out what was causing the panic that was suddenly rising in the room. When the pressure was finally gone from several pairs of hands inside of me, I waited for the notorious cry from my baby's lips. None came, and I began to panic. "Is she Ok?" I insisted. With my own self feeling as close to normal as it could under such circumstances, my focus immediately reverted to Lex. I felt awful, when I realized that for awhile during the delivery, my worry for her had waned. Now my focus had heightened, and I was demanding answers. No one would answer me. Only Nick spoke. In a whispered voice, he said, "It's a girl."

I knew she was a girl! What I wanted to know was, was she all right? Did she have two heads or one? Did she have the extra digit on both hands, like my father did? He had had them removed at birth. Still, no one would answer me. I heard her cough and gag. I heard the excitement of panic in the delivery room. Then I heard someone on the phone. They were calling an ambulance to transport her to Boston Children's Floating Hospital. My questions suddenly ceased. I didn't want to know. I was afraid to speak a word. My body went into shock, taking my voice with it. It was the pediatrician who broke the silent world I found myself in. He said, "Barbara, Alexis was born with collapsed lungs. We were able to correct it as best we could; she is on oxygen right now. An ambulance is coming to bring her to a hospital in Boston that is better equipped to handle this. Because of the dry birth, she swallowed a lot of maconium, and we collapsed her lungs again with suctioning. Maconium is the residue of her first bowel movement. Because she was so late, she was acting like a full term baby and had had one during delivery. If we hadn't done the suctioning, she could have been brain damaged. I think she is out of the woods for now. There is air outside her chest cavity, so there is the possibility of her lungs collapsing again. We are only sending her to Boston as a precaution. Please don't worry."

The whole time he spoke, I felt like he was talking in a different language. I tried to understand what he was telling me, but I couldn't. In a second, Lex was whisked from the room and out of my sight. I never even got the chance to see what she looked like. A moment later, a nurse was at my side with an out of focus, dark Polaroid of her to show me. My heart sank. At the lab I had worked on many of these types of pictures. The babies were always dead, and this was the only reminder that their parents had been parents at all. How could this be happening to me? I had worked so hard to keep her alive during the pregnancy. I refused to take the picture. The nurse was confused.

A moment later my mother entered the room. It was her; she was here! I began to feel a sense of relief that I hadn't lost my mind. Hobbling up to my bed with her crutches, she grasped my hand. "She's beautiful, Barbara. She has dark hair and eyes just like you said she would." I began to cry. "Is she going to live?" I asked.

"Of course she is! She's a fighter, just like her mom. She was screaming and carrying on all the way down the hall. Didn't you hear her?"

I hadn't, but I believed my mother. "Where is Nick?" I asked.

"He rode in the ambulance. He said he told you before he left." I hadn't heard that, either. The only thing I could think of to explain this lack of awareness was that my mind and body were protecting themselves from the horrors of what I was experiencing. I closed my eyes, as my mother rubbed my forehead. I fell asleep. The next thing I remember was being back in my room on the floor below. It was afternoon, and my mother was still with me. She must have been at the hospital the whole afternoon. No one else was with her. "How did you get here?"

"Jake drove me."

"Mom, tell me again how she looks and what she was doing." It was as if I were a child again, wanting hear a comforting familiar story. I also needed reassuring that our previous conversation had not been just a dream. It hadn't, and the realization that I was finally a mother began to sink in and make me stronger.

I didn't see Nick until later that evening. He told me she was feisty, and all the nurses were in love with her. He said the other babies on her ward were tiny, because they were all premature. Alexis's problem, on the other hand, was just that she had been over cooked, a term the nurses used. She weighed 9lbs. 4ozs. She barely fit in the tiny incubators. Her head touched one end, while her feet touched the other. She hated to be swaddled in blankets, like the others. Her hands and feet were in constant motion. He ended the monologue with, "Barbara, she is going to be just fine. She is perfect."

I cried again, this time with tears of joy. Despite my having had a c-section the day before, a nurse entered my room at 8:00 AM to get me on my feet. It would be the first time my body had been in an upright position without the duty of supporting my child. I was surprised by how quickly it was ready to accept the fact that I was no longer pregnant. Even though my body was telling me everything was getting back to normal, my head wasn't...something was missing. I had never felt that Lex and I were a united soul when she had been inside me. On the contrary, I felt she was an individual who had depended on me for survival from the very beginning. With her in a separate hospital, I felt as if someone else had taken my role, the position I had fought so hard to keep. Grabbing the IV pole that I saw now as my "dog," I went for a walk in the hall. Stopping at the window to the nursery, I longed to have my baby be there...but she wasn't. I wanted desperately to hold her. It was as if the impatience that had been fermenting for nine months was now at the point of explosion. I wanted to see what she looked like. I wished I had had the Polaroid picture the nurse had showed me, even if it were dark. I was certain Lex was going to be fine; now I just wanted to see what she looked like. Turning around, I headed to the nurses' station.

When I got back to my room with the picture, I was disappointed. The image was so poor that all I could make out was the outline of her body. It was virtually a silhouette with no facial features. She looked more like Shadow Man's child than mine. Staring out the window into the warm sunlight of June 11, 1987, I wondered when she would be returned to me. Picking up the phone by the side of the bed, I called Children's Floating Hospital in Boston to find out. When I was connected to a nurse on Lex's floor, I was pleased that she was more than willing to talk to me. She told me Lex was a perfectly wonderful baby and a long overdue gift to the staff who were so used to having to worry about sick babies who might not make it. Unlike those babies, Lex was healthy enough to be picked up and rocked in the chair. She was very alert and seemed to respond when spoken to. She said that she was a fighter and had her own mind about things; she didn't like to be wrapped in a blanket and preferred to sleep uncovered; she also didn't like to eat. She would rather stay awake all day, being carried and sitting with the nurses. "Barbara," she said, "this baby doesn't know she's a baby." And then she started to laugh.

"When can she come home?" I asked.

"She is scheduled to be sent by ambulance back to Salem Hospital in three days." Then she added, "We'll miss her."

I thanked her for the time she had spent easing my mind and taking care of Lex, then hung up the phone. I was thrilled to know that Lex was getting a lot of attention from people who really cared about her. The doctor told me that I would be leaving in three days also; that meant we might be able to leave together. I hoped that Salem wouldn't want to keep her any longer, once she arrived. All this was going through my mind, when the phone rang. It was my mother-in-law; she wanted to see how I was doing. I was still a little guarded whenever I talked to her.

When I said hello, the first thing out of her mouth was, "Barbara, I was sure she wasn't going to make it." I couldn't help myself, I said, "I knew she would, because I have been her mother and protected her from her conception. I never gave up on her." She never apologized or acknowledged the struggle I had had; she just kept saying it was a miracle, a gift from God, and that all our prayers had been answered.

I couldn't listen to her. Her mock sense of relief was making me angry. So I lied, "I have to go. A nurse is here and wants to take my blood pressure." She said ok and hung up the phone.

The next three days dragged on like watching paint dry. I changed the masks of depression and delight as often as the channels changed on the TV that was forever in front of me. The morning programming was filled with talk shows about every fear that women have, including sick babies. Eventually, I just turned it off. The morning Lex was to arrive, I was so excited. I got up at 6:00 AM and took a shower. Dressed in the prettiest nightgown I had, I sat in a chair and waited. She was expected to be there by 10:00 AM, and while I sat there, I thought about this new person I was going to meet. Suddenly, gone were my feelings that I knew her and knew what was best for her. I began to panic and wonder if I was going to be a good mother. I thought about the time I had spent with Felicia and Sophie. I remembered how natural the feelings were that I had for Sophie and how I instinctively knew how to take care of her. That helped ease the doubts a little.

At 8:30 AM, Nick and his father came into my room. They said that they had received a call from Boston Children's, and she should be there by nine. I couldn't believe that she was going to arrive an hour early. When does fate ever work in your favor? We were all so excited and worked up, when a nurse entered the room and told us she was just pulling into the parking lot. A doctor, a nurse and the EMT's were with her when they rolled her into my room. She was still in a special incubator. I was surprised by how many people it took to transport a baby. When I commented on this, Nick told me that was how many there had been with her when they took her too. When I rose from the bed to see her, I laughed at how crunched she looked in her glass bed. Nick was right, her feet touched the bottom and her head was touching the top.

"Can I hold her?" I asked.

"I think she would love that," said the nurse. She smiled at me in a knowing way, and I wondered if she was the woman I had talked to three days prior to this glorious event. They lifted her from the incubator and placed her gently in my arms. Bringing the crook of her neck to my lips, I kissed her. Burying the same area into my face, I held her tight and cried. The scent of her seemed to carry me down a corridor to see all of her future. My dreams had been answered and I was a mother. It was at that moment, the smell of her flesh, we bonded. She lay in my arms, as content as could be, not making a sound. The nurse leaned over to me and said, "We could never hold her that close without her screaming; she must know she's home." I walked over to the chair and sat with her, while Nick thanked her entourage before they left. I was lost in a world I had not thought possible; I never saw them leave.

Talking to Lex, as I had always done, I told her how much I had missed her. Suddenly, it was as if we were alone; Nick and his father were still there, but somehow I don't remember them. I told her about the room I had ready for her and all the things we were going to do together for the rest of our lives. I made a promise to always be there for her and to listen to her whenever she needed me. I told her she was my best friend, and I would do everything in my power to make her life easy and enjoyable. Without realizing it, I was telling her I would give her all the things that I had been robbed of. When I looked into her eyes to say all this, she stared back at me as if she understood. She then closed her eyes again and nestled her head into my chest. The bond was made, and I knew we were going to be ok, no matter what life had in store for us.

The doctor wouldn't let us go home for at least two days. He said she had not eaten in Boston, and they had had to keep her on an IV the whole time. As soon as they saw that she could digest her milk properly, they would let her go. They were going to wean her from the IV over the next few hours and watch what happened. To my disappointment, they also took her from me. She was still considered at risk and therefore could not stay in my room. They put her in the special nursery down the hall. I planted myself in front of the window the rest of the day. She was fun to watch. Every time a nurse saw that she had thrown off her blankets, they would rewrap her. The minute the nurse turned her back again, Lex would thrash her legs to get them off. All the other babies just lay there, unmoving. But Lex was a fireball. I laughed whenever I saw her play this game. I got to hold her a few more times. Every time they put her in my arms, she seemed to cuddle up next to me. The nurse commented on how strong she was. At one point, I looked up at her and said, "Well, technically, considering how late she was, next week she will be a month old."

The nurse just looked at me with a smile and said, "You're right; that is probably why she seems so mature...that and the fact that she is just downright stubborn." We both laughed. I couldn't remember ever feeling so happy. Leaning down to Lex's face, I told her so.

At 2:00 AM, a nurse entered my dark room and turned on the light over the sink. She shook me gently and said, "Barbara, your daughter is calling for you." It was the first time I had ever heard anyone refer to her as my daughter. A pang of excitement gripped my heart. In a flash, I was on my feet and out the door. Practically running down the hall, as best I could with the stitches I still had tearing at my flesh, I showed up at the special nursery. Before I had the chance to knock, the door was opened. They led me to a back room, where a nurse was holding Lex as she cried wildly in her arms. The room was dimly lit. There were monitors and unused equipment lining the floor against the walls. In the center of the room was a rocking chair. Next to it was a floor lamp. It looked like someone had tried hard to make this storage room feel like a home nursery, yet had failed. A new maternity wing was being built at that time, and until it was finished, space was at a premium. Sitting in the rocker, I spoke to Lex gently as they placed her in my lap. The nurse asked if I had ever nursed a baby before. For a second I thought about Sophie and the day she had latched on to my breast. I turned to the woman and said, "No."

"Would you like me to show you how to do it?"

"I think we will be all right," was all I said. Placing the baby to my breast, Lex immediately knew what to do.

"That is amazing," the nurse said. "I have all this paperwork from Boston, saying she refused to eat. They tried many times, but Lex would have nothing to do with it. She must know that you're her mother."

I just smiled. Lex knew I would be the one who she could count on to have what she needed. It was an unspoken rule we had had between us, even when I had been carrying her.

Seeing that we both knew what to do; the nurse left. It was the first time we were alone together. I started talking to Lex again, about how proud I was that she was eating. Every so often, she would pause and look up at me. I felt she was telling me that she was proud of me too. She admired my perseverance through this whole ordeal. Although she couldn't tell me with her words, I knew she was thanking me. I nursed her for ten minutes, and then she fell asleep in my arms. I didn't call the nurse; I held her there for another half hour, until, finally, they came in and put her back in her crib. Kissing her tiny feet, I went back to my room.

CHAPTER: 53

When I brought Lex home from the hospital, I felt my life was complete. I had the child I had longed for since the age of fourteen, a new home and a kind, providing husband. Unfortunately, completeness means nothing without passion, and I wasn't sure if I had room for that anymore.

My days became very busy. It would be the start of a momentum that I would endure for many years to come. Nick had insisted that I continue working; after all, his mother always had. I didn't mind, I liked to work. So the day Lex and I arrived home from the hospital, I went back to photo retouching. I was working from home now, which gave me the freedom to have my daughter with me. I didn't want to put her in daycare. I had seen too many children in that situation to want that for her. I didn't want her to grow up having to share every moment of her day with twenty other children; I wanted her for myself. I looked at her as the family I had been waiting my whole life to have, someone who would appreciate me for who I was and love me despite my faults. We became immediate best friends. Everyday we sat and had breakfast alone. Nick left for work very early in the morning, and that was fine by us. She was funny in the morning. She always woke up grouchy, and we had an unspoken rule that we didn't talk to each other for at least an hour. There we sat, she in her high chair with her apple juice and me next to her at the kitchen counter with my coffee, staring into space. When our hour was up, we would talk. I never talked baby talk to her or talked down. From the beginning, she was my equal as far as respect was concerned. I was determined to raise her differently from the way I had been raised.

During the day, I worked on my retouching, while Lex sat by my side. When she was six months old, I had Nick build a series of cabinets on casters that doubled as a large play area for her. In the center, I put a round table, so that she could lift herself up and travel around it to play with her toys. The back of the cabinets had shelves where the toys were stored. I pushed the cabinets close together to help her be self-sufficient. This was not only to give her a feeling of autonomy but was also helpful to me, so that I wasn't constantly disturbed in my work. My easel was stationed right next to her, so that we could see each other at all times. On a few occasions when she wanted to be picked up, I would put her on my back in a backpack while I worked. I figured if it was good enough for the Native American women, it was good enough for me...I just wasn't picking corn. I began taking my mother grocery shopping once a week. We learned how to get around the inconvenience of her crutches. At times like this it was easier for her to use a walker. She was still a very young woman. She had just turned forty- nine, but she knew that in order to be a part of the real world, these were the things she had to do. It was another unspoken lesson that she taught me that I would need years later.

My relationship with my mother began to improve greatly. We laughed often when we were out. It was mostly about Lex and her unique and strong personality. She was always so happy and was a joy to have around. Lex never gave me any trouble and slept through the night, the minute I brought her home from the hospital. When it was time for bed or an afternoon nap, she was perfectly content to be alone and go to sleep. My mother repeated over and over how lucky I was that she was so good. Although I never said it to her, I knew in my heart that it was because Lex understood the respect I had for her. She was such an advanced baby in so many ways. She walked at just under eight months and was talking in coherent sentences at eighteen months. She was rarely sick and was always good for me when I had to drop off work at the lab. We looked like quite a sight when we did this. She was stationed on my back, with me carrying a portfolio of work as well. The minute I walked into the art room, John and Jai were there to grab her from my arms and play with her. They were completely enthralled, having a baby in the room. She got the nickname Papoose from them, because she was always on my back. At night when Nick came home from work, he didn't spend that much time with her, and this upset me. His usual routine was to take a shower and then a nap...because he had left for work so early in the morning. Later, I would make dinner, and we all ate together. Lex was not a night owl and would often ask for her bed at around six in the evening. I would try to keep her up, so that she could spend time with Nick. It was a useless endeavor. She would get cranky, because she was tired. Having grown up in a house of men, he was a little uncomfortable around babies and often held her awkwardly. She didn't understand this and would cry for me. Eventually, I gave up and just put her to bed when she asked. On the weekends, it wasn't much different. Nick was obsessed with the new lawn he was putting in and spent most of his day outside. Being an engineer, he would often be asked to fix things for family and friends. He was remarkable in this way, and I believe, for him, it was a creative outlet. He often did odd jobs for people at no charge. So when he wasn't doing the lawn, he was doing something for someone else. It was nothing for him to spend four or five hours on someone else's problems. This often irritated me, and I tried to talk to him about it. He didn't understand how important it was for me that he have a relationship with his child and with me. Maybe I was being overly sensitive. I tried to make the best of it. It caused a distance between us. The result of the distance between him and me was that Lex and I became closer.

Once she and I had gotten into a routine, I tried to paint my own work again. I found frustration there, too. Jack and I still talked and were good friends. He had even visited Lex and me in the hospital when she was born. She was the first baby he had ever held, and he immediately fell in love with her. He often came to the house to see her. He would hold her and talk to her so gently. It was a side of Jack I had never seen before. Nick and Jack became friends as well. Together, they came up with a side business of transferring super eight movies to VHS video. Their customers were video stores, and, at first, it looked like it could be a profitable endeavor. Jack did all the selling, as well as the pick-up and delivery. Nick was the mechanic behind the equipment. Every night the three of us would sit and watch a stranger's home movies and eat popcorn. Sometimes it was funny, but most of the time it was boring.

One night while doing this, Lex, who was eighteen months old at the time, became very sick. She ran a high fever, and there was nothing I could do to console her. She kept vomiting the medicine I was giving her to lower her temperature, and I was afraid she would get dehydrated. When I called the doctor and told him of the symptoms, he said she more than likely had Roseola and to expect a rash. I wanted to bring her in for him to see her, but the doctor wouldn't let me. He said she was highly contagious and that it wouldn't be a good idea for the sake of the other babies in the office. Because Lex was a fussy eater, when it came to solid food, and was still on formula, I was greatly concerned that she was depleted of all the necessary nutrients from the vomiting. The doctor told me to give her a teaspoon of Pedialite every half hour, but it was no use; even that was coming up.

With her tiny high pitched voice, trying the best she could to persuade us, she said, "A little water Mommy?" My heart was breaking at her beckoning. "I'm sorry Lex, the doctor said it will be bad for your tummy."

"Just a little water, Mommy." It was more a statement than a question. Picking her up into my arms, I tried to hold her close. She grabbed my face, forcing me to look into her eyes. This time her bottom lip protruded in anguish and her soft voice got caught in her throat, "A little water, Mommy?"

It was tearing me apart, so I called the doctor again. He told me to resist the urge to give it to her, because she would just become more dehydrated when she would ultimately vomit it up. The begging went on all night. I felt hopeless and wanted to cry, but I knew I had to hold it together. Then she began to shiver. She grabbed me by the hand, because she wanted to tell me something, yet didn't know the word for it. I asked her to show me, and the three of us, me, Nick and Jack, followed her to her room. She led us to her closet and tugged on her bathrobe. She was so hot that the air around her felt cold. I was afraid to put it on her, because I wasn't sure it wouldn't raise the fever more. She cried for it so badly that eventually I did. I took her temperature every ten minutes. Every time it showed an increase. When it reached 105 degrees, I placed popsicles under her arms and between her legs to try and reduce it. When the fever peaked at 106.2, I went into a full blown panic. I filled the sink with lukewarm water and placed her in it. The whole time I was doing this, she was thrashing and fighting it.

Jack jumped in and was helping me. Nick, on the other hand, reacted differently to the situation. He seemed to go into a type of shock and was paralyzed with fear. He sat at the kitchen counter the whole time with a blank look on his face. He had lost it, and I knew it. I couldn't hold it back anymore; I began to scream at him. I knew in my heart he felt no control. Lex continued to fight me in the water. Jack took the top half of her under her arms to help me hold her. He began talking softly to her, telling her he loved her and it was going to be all right. I had the bottom half of her and was gently pouring water over her belly. Eventually, with the help of the water, we were able to get the fever down. By the time all was said and done, Jack and I were soaked. I sat in the rocking chair in her room with Lex in my lap. I was saddened that Nick didn't have the ability to take control of the situation. I was grateful that Jack had. With the excitement now over, Jack went home. Nick went to bed, and I held Lex in my arms the rest of the night. I was afraid to go to sleep, because I could have dropped her. I was afraid to put her in her bed, in case the fever came back. I stayed up and watched the moon cross the sky and listened to her breathe. At 6:00 AM, Nick came in before he went to work. He asked me how she was. I said that she was fine. When the door closed behind him, I cried.

One evening, I got a phone call from my brother Doug. He told me the most extraordinary thing. He said our father had called him and said he wanted to see all three of us. He said he was sick with the late stages of diabetes and was dying. What made the call extraordinary wasn't the fact that our father was contacting us after all the years; it was that the news didn't affect me. I felt nothing and was surprised by my lack of caring towards him. When I was four years old and not understanding of the relationship between men and women, I had begged my mother to get back together with him. Now I was a mother myself and had been married twice, and I couldn't feel a thing.

I was surprised to find out that my father was only an hour away from us. He had been living in Hudson, New Hampshire, the whole time. It would be one of a few surprises I would receive that day. He and his wife lived in a trailer park, although she was not there at that time. The inside was filled with dingy gold and brown furniture. I wondered what he and my mother had had in common. He was short in stature. His arms and legs were thin. The skin on them hung from their bones. He stood no taller than me. My brothers towered over his frail frame. He and I looked remarkably alike. My whole life, I had felt different from the rest of my family. I was the only one with stick straight black hair, my brothers both having wiry, light brown and blond curls. My mother's hair was a curly auburn. Looking at this stranger confirmed that I was definitely his. It wasn't just our hair that was similar. We had the same hands and the way that we gestured them; the structure of our faces was also the same. The only difference was his eyes. They were blue like Jake's; mine were light, hazel green. When he spoke, he sounded uneducated with a thick Boston accent. He was nervous and asked us mundane questions about our children. He never brought up the subject of his divorce from my mother. He never apologized for not trying to see us, never gave the answers to questions my brothers and I had in our heads. It was a good thing we had brought the grandchildren. They filled in the gaps of our conversation. Children can be a great buffer in awkward times like that. Looking around the tiny room, I was stunned that there were pictures of us on his walls. They were taken at various stages of our lives...when we never realized he had been there. The scenes in the photos were usually at pivotal gatherings in a crowd. One was of my high school graduation. He also had another one of me and Bobby standing on the steps of the church, after we had been married. I looked like I had just been told I had a terminal illness. When he saw that I was looking at them, he said, "Barbara, you've grown into a beautiful woman, just like your mom." He then pulled out an old Polaroid camera and took a picture of me with Lex on my lap. That morning, before we had arrived, I had been ready to be angry at him. I was afraid I would feel sorry for him. Instead, I was left with confusion and bewilderment. We left an hour later. Driving home, I sat quietly in the front seat and stared out the window. Nick didn't say a word. I folded up all the uncertainty I was feeling, like a prom dress that had done its service and had been tucked away, and never looked back. A month after our visit, my father was dead.

At home, I was finding my struggles with my art to be unnerving. I needed to have live models, and I asked Jack if he wanted to start a guild, so that a few of us could share the expense. I figured with my four hundred square foot studio, it could be held at my house. He thought it was a great idea. Between us, we knew several fellow artists who might also be interested, so we gave them a call. I also had a friend whom I had known as an acquaintance in high school who was willing to model nude. At that time, she worked at North Shore Color as a printer and had offered her modeling services to me many times in the past.

The guild started very small. There were only four of us, and we didn't have a name. The people who were painting were Katherine (an accomplished artist in her own right, who did restorations for the MFA in Boston), my brother Doug (who didn't paint much, but had potential), Jack and myself. We set the model up in long poses for seven week sessions, and we split her fee, which, at the time, was ten dollars an hour. Nick took Lex to his mother's house and spent the evenings with them. I saw this as a great opportunity for them to bond.

We were a great group: the four of us. We helped each other a lot with our paintings. Jack was a natural born teacher, and we all gravitated to him for advice. Eventually, without saying so, every week one person brought wine, while others brought cheese and crackers. The atmosphere was very relaxed, and we all enjoyed each other's company very much. The model fit in well and became a regular part of the ensemble. As with all tight knit units, we became close and eventually began to talk about personal feelings: for Katherine, it was her desire to have a child, but for me it was always about my desire to make good art and my feelings of inadequacy in that area. On one particular night at the end of a seven week pose, I realized that all the measurements of my painting were off ... by a lot. The head was slightly too large for the body, and the arms were too short. The legs were not short enough. It was all fixable, but not in the time that was now left. I knew that I had just spent countless hours on a piece of work that I was going to have to scrap. In total frustration, I quietly went to one of the large picture windows in the room and threw my canvas, brushes and all my supplies into the woods. Falling in a heap on the floor, I began to cry. I didn't care who saw me. I didn't care what I looked like. I was alone in my misery, and I felt I had come to the end of the road for my learning. At that moment, I felt I would never be the artist I had always strived to be. I cried for what seemed like hours. When I eventually pulled myself together and looked up, everyone was gone... except Jack. I had finally given him the tears he felt all artists must shed. He sat on the floor next to me and held me. It was tenderness between two friends that cannot be described. It wasn't sexual; it was pure caring. He told me what I was experiencing was a good thing. He said if that had never happened to me, it would have meant I wasn't passionate enough about my desire to succeed. He said that all art students experience this: all the ones who count, that is. We talked for over an hour. He helped me pull it together. When he knew I was going to be ok, he left. Later that evening, Nick arrived with Lex. He asked me how everything had gone. Taking my sleeping child from his hands, I kissed her tenderly in the crook of her neck and quietly climbed the stairs to her room. Over my shoulder I said, "It was ok," and closed her door behind us. In the dark, I rocked my baby and told her she was the best creation I had ever made and softly cried, so that Nick could not hear me. Somehow, I knew he wouldn't understand. Lex woke only once and reached up to touch my tears out of curiosity. I slept in her room that night on the spare twin bed.

The next week we set up a new pose. Jack said that he would check my measurements of the drawing before I applied the paint. Everyone was very concerned for my feelings. What they had witnessed the week before had been a total meltdown, and they knew it. I could feel the love they had for me, and it was comforting. The other thing the group saw was the true friendship between Jack and me. Over the years we had become a team, long before Nick and I had even met. There was an unmistakable bond that had formed, a respect that was hard to match. In many ways, he was the father I had never really had.

That night, when the wine had had time to relax everyone, we took a break. We talked about what had happened the week before and about the frustration they had all felt at one time or another. Each one of them had experienced a similar breakdown. It was comforting to know. Then it was talk about relationships in general and what makes them work and what doesn't. It was mostly the model, Doug and Katherine, talking among themselves. Jack and I were just listening. The word respect came up and its true meaning. Then my brother said something that floored me. He claimed that the only true respect he had ever seen between two people was the one between Jack and me. He said, "Look at the two of you. You ask nothing of each other, other than friendship. You are always there for each other, and yet it is obvious that you're not involved. How did this relationship come to be, Barb? Why did you marry Nick, when you should have married Jack?" I immediately became flushed. I was speechless. I didn't know what to say. It was Jack who rescued me. He said, "I think you're underestimating Nick. He is a great guy. Why shouldn't she have married him?"

"Because they have nothing in common," said Doug. Everyone in the room joined in and agreed with him, everyone but Jack and me. Jack stood up and said, "Well this conversation is amusing, but I'm afraid I have to go." He awkwardly gathered his things and left.

Doug looked at the rest of the group and asked defensively, "Well, am I right?" I stated flatly, "Doug, Jack is married."

The entire group was shocked. Only I knew that Jack had a wife. I also knew they were as opposite in their relationship as Nick and I were in ours. I chose not to tell them this. Instead, we all packed up for the night...the party was over.

CHAPTER: 54

Lex was growing like a weed. She was talking and walking all over the house. Every day we spent time together. Some days we would walk through the woods; other times I took her to the park or to the Willows. On good days, we brought my mother. I began to solicit customers of my own for retouching. They were photographers who didn't use North Shore Color. A few of them were from out of state and would ship me the work. Meanwhile, my work at the lab was still strong, but, more and more, I found myself at the mercy of new black and white printers, whom they had hired. A few times I would bring photos back to them, because I knew they were too dark to work on. The results would have created a change in the ethnicity of the subject in the photo. After months of this, which caused me to do the work over at no charge, I got angry.

"Fred, can I have a word with you?" "Sure what is on your mind?"

"Well, this past week I did over a hundred photos for you. The hours they took were well over forty. I was only paid for thirty of the photos because the prints were so dark, and I was forced to work on them anyway. I can't go on like this...working for you for nothing."

"Well, I am sorry, but that is not something I can fix. You need to talk to the head of the black and white department."

"I did, she refuses to let me reject dark prints."

"Well, I am sorry, that is her call."

"Oh, really? Well then here...take this art work and shove it up your ass. If you aren't boss enough to run this place properly, then I don't want to be a part of it! Oh, and you are going to be sorry you ever heard my name...that I can guarantee." Turning on my heels, I headed for the door. The entire operation came to a standstill and was looking at me. The last glimpse I saw was John, not far from the film machine, talking to its operator. He reached up and blew me a kiss with a smile that said, "Good for you." Lex was on my back in her pack and kept asking me, "What's wrong? What's wrong?"

I said, "When people treat you unfairly, Lex...that's what's wrong. Don't ever let anyone treat you like you don't know what you're talking about, when you know that you do."

"Ok," she said with a big smile, as I put her in the car. I laughed and buckled her into the back seat of the Datsun 280Z.

The following week I had thirty customers, and Creations in Color was born. A year later, North Shore Color closed their black and white department. They no longer offered oils. Without intending to, I put them out of business in that department. John still did retouching for them in the color department. It was what he had done all along, anyway. Jai was still their jack-of-all-trades. When it became obvious that I needed to do my own printing, Nick built me a dark room. With only what I had learned in high school about printing, I became a full blown black and white lab. I taught myself how to airbrush, and soon I was doing full restorations. John helped me out a lot with the color work. He gave me pointers on color technique. Soon I had more work than I had time and space to do it in. I told Nick I needed to rent a commercial studio. He wasn't crazy about the idea. Nick was always concerned about spending money, but eventually, he agreed. When I talked to the guild about it, they all agreed to go in together. Our group was also growing. We were now up to seven. We rented an entire loft that was 5000 square feet of space in Beverly. It was on the top floor of the old Porter Sewing Machine factory on Rantoul Street. It was wide open and drafty. In the summer, it was hot as hell; in the winter, we had no heat. It was perfect. I hadn't been back to Beverly since my broken-hearted romance with Mark, back in eighth grade. That seemed like centuries ago. The entire experience of returning to Beverly was surreal.

Another person joined our group. Her name was Brenda. She was a photographer, and we immediately got along. She was in the middle of a divorce and had a son the same age as Lex, named Tommy. We often let them play together in the wide open space, while she showed me dark room techniques, and I showed her how to paint. After the first week, she asked me how long Jack and I had been married. I laughed when she said it and told her that we were both married to other people. She then asked me how long we had been having an affair. I told her we weren't. She then said, "Well I think it is time to shit or get off the pot, because you two were meant to be together." The subject of Jack and me became an unspoken issue after the night my brother had brought it up, and Jack had left. I just shrugged it off with Brenda. Inside, I liked Jack a lot. To myself, I'd even admit I loved him, but I couldn't see me uprooting Lex from her father, even if I knew I had never felt the same way for him. Besides, Jack was 19 years older than I, and he was married.

My business began to grow some more. I found myself in the middle of a vortex of work with no way out. Lex was with me all day. She was two years old now and felt very comfortable being in a dark room with me. When I was at my easel, she was beside me at hers. We were a team. Sometimes she stayed with my mother, so that she could play with Jake's kids, who lived upstairs. When I had to work late because of the Christmas rush, Nick had her at home. Eventually, my life outside the house became more real to me than the one I had inside. Communications between Nick and me had collapsed. I wondered if it were because I was my own person, self-sufficient now. In the area of sexual desire, I was alone. We no longer connected in that way or in any other way common between a husband and wife. I didn't feel totally unloved; as long as Lex was with me, I felt complete. It seemed that Nick didn't care if we were there or not. Maybe he was just being his usual, passive self. I had a heart to heart talk with myself after many months of this. Although I hated the idea of disrupting Lex and her home life, I knew that I could realistically last only five more years with this man, and by that time, Lex would be seven. I knew that would be a bad age for a child to experience the breakup of her parents. My reasoning for leaving Nick was very unemotional and logical; it was not unlike the decision making process I had gone through to marry him. My mind was made up. I had to leave him while Lex was still so young. I knew in another year she would remember it, like I had at the age of three. I didn't want that for her; so once again, I closed my eyes and jumped. Meanwhile, my mother had another go around with an occurrence of the cancer. The tumor that was lodged in her pelvis was getting bigger. The ones on her ribs were also spreading. She was in a lot of pain. Once again, I found myself doing things for her. Between work, Lex and my mother, it seemed like the only reasonable thing to do was to go back home. I knew when I was doing it that I was stuck in a pattern of self destruction: leaving men and going back home for more abuse. I was afraid of what it would do to Lex. I made a promise to myself to protect her from all this: the separation and the possible turn around in the relationship between me and my mother. In my heart, I felt if I gave Lex as much love as I felt for her, it wouldn't matter where we lived. And if living with my mother became too much, then I would figure out something else. Meanwhile, I would start saving money, in case that day came.

When I told my mother of my plans, she was worried but relieved, at the same time, for the help she would need. She also said that I was running away again. I told her she was right. That's what I had done when I had married Nick. Now I was trying to correct that before my daughter got too involved. The next day, I packed a few things that belonged to Lex and me and brought them to my mother's house, while Nick was at work. Later that night, I went back to the house to tell Nick in person. I was really scared. After all, we had never really fought. He had been a good provider, even though he had made it clear that I had to work to bring money into the house. I didn't know what to expect. When I told him, he seemed stunned. I tried to point out the realities to him, but I wasn't sure he was listening. I reminded him that he had had to talk me into marrying him in the first place and that we never talked at all now. I also mentioned the fact that we had not made love in two years. I ended with..."You can't possibly be happy in this relationship. Be honest with yourself." He didn't say a word. He let me go, and

I felt like such a terrible person. I didn't mean to mislead him; I had been vulnerable.

I was right. The transition for Lex was much easier. She cried a little when Nick would drop her off after having her for the weekend, but not much. She had never seen much of him when we were living there, so why should this be any different? I felt, in a way, this move could be good for them. It would force him to have a relationship with her. Then I found out that she stayed with his mother and not with him at the house, whenever he had her. It angered me, and I tried to talk to him reasonably about it. No matter what I said, he didn't understand the importance of having a relationship with his daughter. I was surprised to find out he was suing me for custody. At first, his grounds were that I wouldn't be able to support her, a stupid claim in the eyes of the court, since he made so much money and, up to that point, had refused to give me any. I was not surprised to find out that it was his mother who had really been behind it and wanted Lex for herself. I had walked away from everything. I had given him the house and all the furniture. All I asked for was eighty dollars a week to get us on our feet. He refused. I felt I was being more than reasonable. I even told him he could be with Lex whenever he wanted. That is, until one day he took her and refused to give her back. At first, he had made it sound like everything was normal, and he was doing things with her. They were having fun. After four days that felt more like a week, I told him if he didn't bring her back that instant, I would call the police. He eventually complied and only took her for weekends after that. One day after her return, I was running an errand for my mother. I was driving down the street with Lex in the back seat. Suddenly, she began to scream as if she were in pain. I pulled over to the side of the road, because I thought, perhaps, the buckle of her seat belt had become hot from the sun. By the time I had pulled her from the car and we were both sitting on the sidewalk, she was clinging to me so strongly that if she could have crawled into my skin, she would have. When I asked her what was wrong, she said, in between tears, "I don't want Yia Yia to be my mommy. I want you." "Who told you that Yia Yia was going to be your mommy?" She said, "Yia Yia did." (Yai Yia is the Greek word for grandmother.) Sitting on the ground, as curious onlookers passed us by, I made her look me in the eyes. I reassured her that only I was her mommy and no one else. Then I held her close, until we both stopped crying.

By the end of the year, it was evident the landlord was not going to put the heat on in the studio. It wasn't just our space that was suffering from this fate; the entire building, filled with artists, was too. Together, we tried to do something about it. We called meetings and signed petitions. We presented them to the landlord as a group. He knew we couldn't afford a lawyer. It didn't work, so the whole building moved out. Most of us went to the United Shoe Building that was a few blocks over. For me it was tough, because it was right in the middle of the Christmas rush. Once again, Jack came through. He stayed with me all day and night, setting up my new dark room and art room. This time, I had a studio to myself with three rooms and a large hall. I couldn't have done it without Jack. My mom watched Lex while we were setting it up. Somehow, we got it all done and informed all my customers and pulled it off without a hitch. We had been up for over twenty-four hours that day, but we had done it. I didn't realize it, but my true life was just beginning. Jack and Brenda had their own separate studios upstairs. The other three artists that shared with us also found other studios. John and Jai were becoming fed up with North Shore Color and said that they would come and set up shop with me, if it got too bad there. Lex, once again, was with me in my studio. Other than the always impending illness of my mother, things were looking up. But most importantly, I felt a feeling of independent strength I had never felt before in my life. I was a single woman raising my child and running my own business .At the time I was twenty-seven. With the help of the big brown eyes of my daughter looking me in the face, I felt I could take on the world. Little did I know that divorcing Nick would be just as much of a struggle. Shadow Man made himself at home and available in my old room. I smiled at him when I saw him the first night. He nodded at me in return.

That spring, my mother went to see her first religious healer. She had become more connected to God and was going to church again. Her neighbor next door had told her about Father McDonough coming to the La Salette church in Ipswich. Father McDonough was known, at least locally, as a healing priest. She didn't ask me if I wanted to go. She didn't tell anyone she was to be attending. I wouldn't have gone anyway. To me, the whole idea was too scary to even think about witnessing: people falling in the aisle and speaking in tongues and all. When she came home that night, she was all worked up. She had pep in her ambling stride and a glow on her face. She was still walking with crutches because of the large tumor that had lodged itself in the iliac crest of her pelvis. It was the size of a grapefruit. This night, however, she had a look on her face that I had never seen before. It was as if she were hiding something. When I asked her where she had been, she just grinned with a devilish look at me and said, "I can't tell you." It was too good to pass up, so I pressed her even further. She was bursting at the seams with excitement, so I knew it would only be a matter of time before she gave up her secret. After two hours of begging, she finally told me what had happened. She and her neighbor had gone to La Salette to see Father McDonough. She said the church had been packed with people in all stages of cancer and terminal illnesses. Some, she said, were blind. I sat there with my mouth hanging open. The woman talking to me did not sound like the mother I grew up with. She was filled with hope and desire and youthfulness. I wondered if that alone was the power of Father McDonough's healing. She continued her story. She said the priest had been walking down the aisle, chanting and throwing holy water. I asked her where she had been sitting. It had been four rows down from the altar and five people deep. As he sprayed the people with the holy water, several were falling to the floor. He passed her at first and then stopped dead in his tracks. She knew he was coming back to her; she could feel it. She said he backed up and looked past all the people in her pew and directly into her eyes. He then tossed a handful of holy water right in her face, and her world went black.

"What happened?" I asked, my voice elevating with fear and excitement.

"Jenny said I fell in the pew, and she was afraid I had hurt myself. She said that when I was on the floor, I started speaking Latin. I was down for five minutes. When I woke up, there were several people helping me to my feet. When I stood up, the pain was gone!" Then she looked at me and said, "Barb, I don't know how to speak Latin! I never had it in school. I never participate in it at church."

I sat there, not knowing what to say. Then I said, "I don't want you to stop taking your medicine." She agreed that would be foolish.

"I have an appointment in a few weeks to have an x-ray of my hip, to see if the tumor has gotten any bigger. Won't the doctor be surprised?!"

I was in a slight predicament. I didn't want to destroy the new found hope she had. It was the first time in awhile I had seen her happy. At the same time, I was afraid of the letdown if her hopes got too high, and the tumor was still there. I just smiled and said, "Think positive thoughts and don't be foolish about your treatments." For the next few weeks, she was a changed woman. She went out with her friends and talked about the future. She told my brothers what had happened. We purposely avoided eye contact when she did. I think we were all afraid to break this magical spell. The day of her x-ray, she was like a kid. She couldn't wait to go. I was surprised that she seemed to have no doubt in her mind. I tried to talk to her to say something wise to protect her from possible defeat. When I opened my mouth, nothing came out. Doug took her to the appointment. Lex and I went to work. I couldn't concentrate on my orders. Making people beautiful for their photos seemed uninspiring at a time of such expectation of life and death. John and Jai were with me. They had left North Shore Color and set up desks next to mine in my studio. I told them what had happened. John was fascinated. Jai had the same frightened feeling I had. We all agreed it could be a huge set back emotionally for her, if it weren't true. When I called her later that day to see what had happened, we were all huddled next to the phone receiver. Lex was jumping up and down; she knew something exciting was happening. When I got Mom on the other end, she practically screamed into the receiver. The tumor was gone. John, Jai and I looked at each other in amazement, afraid to say a word. I was still skeptical, but I told her I would talk to her later. When I put down the phone, I went back to work in silence. John said, "Jai, if I were you I would throw myself at the mercy of God's feet and stop seeing those strange men in the middle of the night." Jai said, "I was just thinking that." We all looked at each other, not knowing how to react. Then with the images in our heads of Jai planted at the feet of the Lord, we all burst out laughing.

Every day, Jack took Lex and me to lunch. To anyone who saw us together, we were a family. In reality, he had never made any inappropriate moves on me. Sometimes I wondered what it was that drew him to us. One day at lunch, he told me that he and his wife had split up. I asked him, "When?" He said, "Six months ago." I asked him, "Why?" He said that she had been practically living at work anyway. Sometimes she didn't come home for days. He said she never had wanted children, and she was more married to her work than she had ever been to him. He said they had talked about it very honestly, and, without a fight, they had decided to part. I thought, "How civilized." I asked him if they were planning on divorcing. He said, they were going to do it without lawyers, that it was just a matter of signing papers at the courthouse. I was amazed. My divorce was costing me thousands of dollars, and so far it had been almost two years, and it was still not settled! I then asked him how he felt about it. He said he felt good. He told me his elderly father, who lived with him, was pleased about it. Jack's wife had always fought with his father, and Jack had hated to witness it. He felt in the middle and torn. The relationship Jack had with Lex was suddenly made clear to me. His doting over her with gifts and the playful ways in which he talked to her were evident. She was the child he had never had and probably never would have. But where did I fit into the picture? I didn't press him further. My world was spinning too rapidly.

After that conversation, Jack and Lex and I began spending even more time together. We ate all our meals together, and he often cooked for my mother and us at her house. He and my mother always got along. After all, she had known him almost as long as I had. It was strange in a way...they were closer in age than he and I were; every once in a while, when they were talking about old music or movies, I felt this difference. Jack genuinely cared about my mother. He often did things to ensure her comfort. Every Saturday night we had movie night. Because she was still not very mobile (despite the healing), Jack brought videos over for us to watch. These movies were often accompanied by dinner that he had picked up on the way.

Jack and I personally were taking it slow. When we took Lex to the beach or the Willows, we did hold hands or, more often than not, we both had hold of Lex's hands. Lex was a child who would run the minute she smelled freedom. It was kind of funny. If she got away from us, we would laugh and yell, "Prisoner escaping!" and make pretend alarm sounds. This always caused her to laugh and try to get away even faster. She was also fascinated with the telephone. Whenever my back was turned, she would immediately grab it and start dialing. That also brought screeching words from our lips... "She's calling Hong Kong!" She was definitely a handful. The minute this girl learned to walk ...she was running. People would often ask me how it was that I wasn't exhausted all the time. The truth is, I was. But I tried never to show it. I didn't want my daughter to have a mother who always looked tired. The way I dealt with Lex's energy and discipline was mostly with humor. This was something that Jack, inadvertently, was teaching me. I still talked to her as if she were my equal in many ways. I never told her that we were going to do something ...I would often say, "I was thinking we should do this today. What do you think? Would that be fun?" Fortunately, she was a child who was agreeable and always ready for adventure and would often go along with it. When it was nap time, it was she who told me she was tired. She would say, "I think I should lay down for awhile." I would then agree, and that is how we lived our life...with communication right from the start. My mother, however, thought that this was strange. She would often argue with me that Lex had too much control. My retort was that if she didn't have any discipline issues, what was the problem? Still my mother couldn't accept it. She was sure that someday this type of parenting was going to backfire on me. I felt that respect for another human being could never backfire.

One day in early spring, I was helping Lex get dressed. Lex always picked out her own clothes, and I was usually there to help her get them on. To make this process less embarrassing, when we went out, I made sure all her outfits went together. On this particular day, she had asked me if it was ok that she didn't wear a tee shirt. Although she couldn't express it to me directly, I knew she was expressing that feeling of freedom we all get when we have our first taste of spring and want to shed our winter clothing. I smiled to myself, because I was feeling the same way that day. I said, "Ok, but I think it is a good idea to still wear our coats, because it could get colder in the late afternoon." It was agreed, and we got dressed. This entire conversation happened when my mother was not in the room. When Lex was putting on her shirt, my mother came in and asked her if she had forgotten to put on her tee shirt.

Lex proudly looked at her and said, "We decided that it was warm enough to just have our shirts today." I laughed to myself about the grown up way in which she had said this. After all, she was only a little over three. My mother, on the other hand, looked at me and said, "Put a tee shirt on that girl." I stood up for what Lex wanted, because I felt that if she got cold, this would be the best way for her to learn this lesson. My plan was to put an extra tee shirt in my bag, just in case. Besides, Lex was the type of person whose temperature was always on the warmer side of normal, and she was a better judge than I of her comfort factor. I told all this to my mother, who just rolled her eyes and left the room. I thought that was the end of it, until later that evening, when she had a big blow out with me on the way I was raising my child. She wasn't just angry about the tee shirt. She also didn't like the fact that Lex call me by my first name. It was a habit she had picked up from being with me at work and hearing everyone else called me Barbara. To me, it was just a name and no big deal. It didn't help matters much that everyone around me always thought it was cute. The tension between my mother and me now stemmed from the way in which I was raising Lex. I knew, in my heart, I wanted to do a complete about face from the way in which I had been raised. I often wondered if my mother understood this, but I never asked her. My mother's cancer seemed to be under control. She was in remission and was seeing her friends again socially. If it weren't for the numerous pills and the crutches, you wouldn't have known she was sick. Although the tumor in her hip appeared to be gone, it had left a large gaping hole that had made the possibility of breaking her hip very great.

My divorce with Nick was going slowly. My lawyer wanted me to ask for more than I wanted. I couldn't take that beautiful house away from him. He had built it with his own two hands. In my eyes, it was his masterpiece, and as an artist, I understood that. Besides, I wanted to be Lex's provider. I didn't want to be dependent on anyone. I paid a lot of money to live with my mother, so even that didn't feel like dependency. Occasionally, my mother would watch Lex if I had to work late, but other than that, Lex was my responsibility, and I liked it that way. Besides, I always paid her to watch Lex. All I wanted from Nick was eighty dollars a week. I felt he was her father and should provide this money so that I could buy her extra things that I couldn't normally have gotten. Everyone told me I was crazy because of the amount of money he had, including my mother. Only Jack understood how I felt and told me to stick to my beliefs. Nick, on the other hand, didn't even want to give me the $80. I was sure he was being fueled by his mother. He fought me all the way on every agreement that was presented to him. My lawyer said it was going to eventually backfire in his face; the courts would see how compliant I was being. I wasn't worried about the money, it was the process that was driving me crazy. It was just taking forever, and I wanted this part of my life over. I was still feeling a strong guilt that I had led this man on; even though it was he who had talked me into it at a time I was most vulnerable.

The tension between my mother and me was getting to the boiling point. With her renewed sense of wellness, she was back to her old self again. She tried to control every aspect of my life. I desperately tried to hold on to my independence, but the walls of that fort were caving in. Jack began to see a change in me, whenever my mother and I were together. I often found myself appeasing her by letting her discipline Lex her way. It bothered me, but I felt helpless in her presence. One time, she wanted to put Lex down for a nap. Lex wasn't tired, and she looked at my mother and said, "No, later." My mother calmly called Lex to her side and, without warning, hit her with the back of her hand on Lex's mouth. She said, "You never talk to me that way." This was shocking for Jack and me, who were in the room, not to mention Lex. I suddenly saw my childhood pass before me on the face of my own child. I picked Lex up and said, "Come on, let's go for a ride." This, of course, angered my mother more, and she started yelling at me about my responsibilities as a mother, as Jack, Lex and I closed the door. When we got outside, I turned to Jack and said, "I have to get Lex and me out of there." I was afraid that if I stayed any longer, all I believed so strongly about raising my child would eventually be destroyed. Jack agreed.

I started scanning the newspapers for an affordable apartment but was having no luck. Then, one day a few months later, Jack came over and said he had a surprise for Lex and me. Lex was all excited, just the word surprise used to send her into a torrent of leaps and screams. We piled into the car and strapped Lex into her seat. Jack drove us to Marblehead, down by the water. We pulled up in front of an old house with light blue shingles and a large wrought iron arch that led to the back yard. At the back of the house was a stairway that led to the third floor. When we got to the top and Jack opened the door, I was hit with a flood of light that was streaming through the front windows that surrounded the entire, empty living room. "It's yours, if you want it," he said. "I put down the first month's rent and a security deposit." Lex was squirming in my arms; she wanted to get down. When I let her go, she started running around, making echoing sounds in the room. I thought of that time many years before when Jake and I had done the same thing. I thought about the universality of children and how much we are all alike. Jack assured me I could afford this apartment. He said, "Don't worry, I won't let you two down. You have to be brave, Barbara, and do this for Lex." We went to the landlord, and I signed the lease. That night, when I told my mother, she seemed relieved. I wondered if I actually had moved in to help her, or was I just being a coward when I did it? It didn't matter anymore; I was going to be on my own now.

The day I moved in was rather pathetic. I had no furniture to speak of. Lex didn't even have a bed. I figured she would sleep with me, until I could afford one. In the living room were only the cushions of an antique Beidermeier that I had purchased years before that. The rest of the couch didn't fit up the narrow stairs. I bought a few bean bag chairs and a lamp. My canopy bed and dresser were in my room. Lex's room, at that moment, housed only her toys and a small dresser. I was planning on using my drafting table as a kitchen table, but Jack surprised us with a used one he had found at a yard sale. It was metal and Formica. It looked very similar to the one I had in the sixties when I was growing up. After we were finished moving all the stuff (which we did by ourselves), I said I needed to go food shopping so that we would have something for dinner and breakfast. Jack just smiled and said, "Look in the refrigerator." When I did, I was shocked to see that it was completely stocked. He must have done it the night before, after he had left.

CHAPTER: 55

I was in the final lap of the divorce. My business was going well, but because of the legal expenses, money was tight. Nick was given a court order to pay me the eighty dollars a week, and that helped. I still wanted to get out of my financial rut. Jack said he would help, but I refused. Instead he bought our groceries every week and put them in the refrigerator when I wasn't looking. I had given him a key in case of emergencies. Our relationship had gone to the next level, when I moved into the apartment. We were now a couple and more and more felt like a family. It was obvious that he wasn't just dating me... he was fathering Lex as well. Jack started shooting wedding videos for the photographers that I did retouching for. He was very talented with this and soon had more work than he could handle. Every time he tried to hire another shooter, the photographers were not satisfied. This caused Jack to have to do it all himself. The videos were a lot of work. He was away most weekends. During the week, he had to edit them, but he seemed to enjoy it. He still made time for Lex and me. With the responsibility of his father, I'm sure he felt he had no time. He stopped painting, and that made me feel bad. When I tried to talk to him about this, he would just shrug it off. The day Lex and I met his dad, John Henry, we immediately got along. He was delighted to have Lex in his life, and I instantly felt a fondness for him. The attachment that Jack had felt for Lex from the beginning was mirroring itself for me with John Henry. He was a very tiny, unassuming man. His manners were impeccable, and I realized that Jack learned to nurture from this incredible individual. He told wonderful stories of his childhood and growing up in West Virginia. The stroke that he had had at the age of 84 had left him with limited mobility. When I met him, he was 90. He dragged his right foot when he walked, and his hands shook terribly. His voice was a very deep baritone that always seemed out of place with his stature. His speech was a little slurred. Over the next few months, I learned that he was actually Jack's adopted father. He had married Jack's mother when Jack was nine years old. Jack's birth father had died right before he was born. No one had ever told Jack how. Jack's mother died the year Jack graduated from high school. Over the years, all that Jack and John Henry had for family was each other.

John Henry was a scientist. He had worked many years in the leather industry, when Jack's mother had been alive. He was the head of the research department of the United Shoe Machinery Corporation, the tenth largest corporation in the world. As a defunct institution, it was the place we now had our studios. In the late fifties he was asked by a group of scientists at MIT to work on a project that was being funded by Massachusetts General Hospital. This work involved understanding the structures of the biological elements in the skin. Because he had been working with hides for years that helped the tanning process run more smoothly, he was the perfect candidate. This group of three men was the scientific team that identified the first molecular structure and catalogued it. They called it collagen. John Henry got immediate, worldwide attention from the scientific arena. This type of research had never been done before, and they were recognized greatly for it. For their work, they were considered on the short list for the Nobel Prize for the next ten years. A humble man by nature, he rarely discussed his successes and preferred to talk about the innocence of life and growing up. He was truly an inspirational man, and when I listened to him, I couldn't help but think in every way he was a perfect human being. Having Lex around brought those feelings of innocence in him much closer to the surface.

John Henry naturally became a new member of my family with Jack and Lex. We ate dinner together almost every night, and after dinner, we drove to the ocean's edge to watch the evening sailboat races. After that, Jack, Lex and I would usually go to check on my mother and see if she needed anything. Mostly, all she needed was some company. After our visit with my mother, Lex and I would go home and Jack would stay until he was sure we were safe and in bed, then he would go home, to tend to his father and put him down for the night. Our life was very full, but satisfying.

In many ways I had all that I needed, until I realized that for several weeks, my suspicions of feeling that I was being followed were true. At first, it was an uncomfortable feeling I had when I left my apartment and headed to the car. A man was parked across the street and watched me that morning, as Lex and I were walking to the parking lot. I tried not to make eye contact with him and locked the doors the minute we were in the car. By the time I got to my destination, I had convinced myself that I was being silly and went on with my day. I saw the man several more times. He was in the parking lot of United Shoe when I got out of work. He was across the street from my house when I left in the morning. I knew it was Nick having me followed. What I didn't understand was why. There were several reasons he could have been doing this. One could have been that he was obsessed by every move I made. That didn't sound like Nick. The other reason might have been that he was serious about taking Lex from me and wanted to catch me in an act that was un-motherly. I concluded that this was probably the case, and I was sure his mother was behind this as well. My reputation as a mother was impeccable. Every day people commented on my patience and the wonderful relationship we had. All a judge had to do was see Lex and me together to know this. Not to mention, I had a list as long as my arm of photographers, who were respected members of the local chamber of commerce, who could be called as character witnesses, if I needed them. They all knew Lex and adored her. I did, however, feel that it was in my best interest to do a few things in preparation for this fight. The next weekend, Jack, Lex and I went to yard sales to find her a good used bed. At first, I thought we were not going to have any luck. Then, after a few hours, we found one. It was a walnut, four poster junior bed. It was obviously for a child; it had a ship carved in the headboard, and it was a twin. All we had to do was buy her a new mattress, which we did that same day. It reminded me of the beds my brothers had had when they were little. Lex was all excited when she saw it. I took her with us to find it, because I wanted to make her part of the process. I knew if she helped pick it out, it would be easier to get her sleeping in her own room again. It worked like a charm. She couldn't wait to go to bed that night.

Lex and I lived in that house a total of two and a half years. Lex loved it. Every day we had our coffee and juice at the beach, which was just steps from our front door. Jack joined us almost every morning. He took pictures of Lex often and recorded her growth. He marked in pencil, on the molding in the kitchen, how tall she was getting. Every time there was a marked difference, he praised her at how big she was. She delighted in these simple rituals, and I enjoyed watching them. My divorce took three years to get to court. Nick had taken it right to the top. He wouldn't let a magistrate resolve our differences; instead, he wanted a judge. I think if he could have had a jury, he would have. When we stood before the judge, he made a lot of comments to him that were inappropriate in the judge's eyes. He said he wanted to have Lex so that he wouldn't have to pay child support. I just smiled to myself...I knew he had hung himself right there. He then said that I had nude models in Lex's presence and that I had taken her to the Museum with Jack in the middle of the day. The judge just looked at me and said, "Barbara, you are an artist, right?" When I said yes, the judge blew up at Nick and told him to stop wasting his time. Then Nick took out his trump card. He claimed I was having an affair with Jack and was sure it had been going on for some time. He said he had had me followed and that Jack had slept there overnight. What Nick didn't know was that Jack had been divorced and that he went home to John Henry every night. When I explained this to the judge and added that Jack and I hadn't started our relationship until after the separation, the judge was really angry with Nick. Nick didn't have representation. I'm not sure why. Perhaps his lawyer had been fed up with him and had dropped him as a client. So the whole time that Nick was rambling on, he had no one to stop him. When the judge asked him how he was going to take care of Lex, Nick said, "I'm going to give her to my mother." He probably meant while he was at work. But it didn't come across that way. I thought the judge was going to throttle him. The judge then looked at the support he was giving me and the income he made and asked me why I was asking for so little. He advised me that with the assets and the income, I should be getting a lot more. I said that I didn't want Nick to have to sell his house. I wanted Lex to always know that home and that he had built it himself, and I hadn't had the heart to take it away. He said, "Barbara, in these cases, my job is to protect the welfare of children. Nick, the physical custody of Alexis is awarded to Barbara, and you must now give her $200 a week." He then looked at Nick and said, "You don't know how lucky you are. She could be given a hell of a lot more than that." He then hit the gavel on his desk, and it was over. When I stepped out of the courthouse the sun was shining, and it felt as if I was reborn. I walked to my car alone with this feeling of relief. I had been holding my breath for three years, and for the first time I could breathe. I raced to my mother's house to get Lex. All I wanted to do was hold her in my arms.

A short while after the court hearing, I got a phone call from my mother...her cancer was back. This time, she had tumors in her skull and jaw. The one on her pelvis had never returned, a mystery we will all take to our own graves. More and more, Lex, Jack and I were spending time at my mother's house. Her pelvis was very weak because of the large hole, and her mobility was once again deteriorating. She still walked with crutches when she was outside. But inside, she now used a walker. She was 52 years old. It killed me to see her this way. This illness was going to take her, one little piece at a time. I had never realized that breast cancer killed you slowly like this. I was beginning to resolve myself to the fact that she would never see Lex grow up. She was, too, and it saddened her. She spoke about it often. She was now ready to have the conversations about her feelings that I had longed to have with her at the start of all this. Now that Lex was older, and it was evident that my way of parenting couldn't be all that bad, my mother eased up on me. She had other things on her mind. Jake's children, who still lived upstairs from her, kept her very busy. He now had four girls. Lex loved going over there to play with them. They were all so cute when they were together. The older girls were a big help to my mother. They would sit with her and help her get things, so she didn't have to get out of her seat. They were four and six years of age, so it didn't feel like a chore to them. Altogether, the girls brought a life to my mother's home that otherwise wouldn't have been there. The time I spent at my mom's house was usually Friday through Sunday. I would arrive around noon and stay until eleven at night, after I was sure she was ok and in bed. When we were there, we would put Lex in her bed to sleep, wrap her up in a blanket to go home, and she would wake up in her own bed the next morning. She never woke up when we did this, and I always thought it was funny that she never questioned it the next morning. But Lex was like that. She was a "go with the flow" kind of kid, and as long as she was with people who loved her and she loved them, she would go along with anything. I decided to put her in preschool two mornings a week. I was concerned that with our busy life she wouldn't get the academic stimulation that I knew in my heart was important for a child that age. She was also sounding more like an adult than a child, and I wanted her to converse more with children her own age than with the people she saw at my studio. I enrolled her at The Children's Center. She didn't like this at first and clung to me. Or was it me clinging to her? There was one teacher that she grew attached to eventually; her name was Susan, and we both liked her very much. She helped both of us with this transition. For years, when I was younger, I had been the teacher helping the parent; now the roles were reversed, and for the first time, I understood the difficulty of this process.

It was a real learning experience for me, which I didn't realize at the time would help me in years to come. The first few weeks, I called the school a couple of times a morning to check on Lex. Considering she was dropped off at eight and picked up at one, it was almost as if I kept tabs on her every hour. She was always fine. It was I who was having the difficulty. John and Jai helped me through it. They missed her too. She was a great presence around the studio. She often answered the phone for us and helped me as an extra pair of hands in the darkroom. When I was printing a large image of a bride and groom, she was what we called the artful dodger, because she was often the extra pair of hands I needed to dodge the light that was exposing part of the image. She was the perfect height and loved to do it. The photographers missed her too; when they arrived, they usually brought her lollipops and treats. The first week she wasn't there, they felt it. When I picked her up at one in the afternoon, Jack and I would take her to the Willows and let her ride the carousel. We became real regulars there and got to know the owner of the ride. His name was Manny, and Lex loved him as well as he did her. Eventually, he let her ride as long as she wanted for no charge. Manny and the Willows became the distraction we all needed to get through this busy life we were leading. He and Jack became good friends, and Jack talked to him about setting up his own wedding video business. Ironically, Manny was the brother-in-law of one of the photographers I did work for. The wedding photographers were a tight knit community; everyone knew everyone else. No one was getting rich from it. Jack was also making TV commercials at the time, and I was his voiceover. We did mostly local stuff. At one point we made the security tape for Logan Airport. This, of course, was before 9/11. When we played my mother the tape, she had no idea that the voice on it was mine. It was strange for me to comprehend that my own mother couldn't recognize it. It saddened me at the time. In Lex's third year, I decided that I wanted to give her the best Christmas I could. I had been buying new looking toys all summer for her at yard sales. Jack would distract her, while I made the purchases. I also had been saving up all year for a doll house. It was the large, wooden, Victorian kind with the tower room. It was a kit, and I had the store put it together for me. Jack picked it up in October and said it was almost impossible to get out of the mall with it, because everyone was stopping him to admire its beauty. He brought it to my studio, when Lex was in school. Every free chance I had, I worked on painting it and finishing the inside. John and Jai thought it was beautiful. John said he would have killed to have had one when he was little. We all laughed. When Christmas came, Jack and I put Lex to bed in my room. She was not sure about this Santa Claus thing, a strange man coming into our house. She asked if she could sleep with me that night. We read her a half dozen Christmas books and set out hot chocolate and cookies for Santa. We trimmed the tree beautifully with the German Christmas ornaments I had bought so many years earlier. It was part of my divorce decree that Nick had had to return them to me, along with Lex's tricycle. I remember the judge saying to Nick, "Give the poor girl her bike," as he rolled his eyes. Once Lex was asleep, Jack and I sat in the living room and talked about the Christmases we had had as children. I told him about the presents I had received, as he described a world to me and a time and place I had never known. It was filled with happy gatherings and an abundance of toys. The joys of being an only child in a family that never had to worry about money or alcohol sounded so magical, I wanted to be there just to see it. I told him this as I fell asleep in his arms. He put me to bed next to Lex and went home. At 6:00 AM he came back. He shook us gently to wake us. Lex was so cute; she bolted straight up to a sitting position and in a soft voice said, "Santa Claus." It wasn't a question; it was a declaration. I hugged her close and said, "Are you ready?" Jack said, "Wait, let me see if he is gone." He went into the living room, as Lex and I huddled together on the bed. She was trembling, so that at first, I thought she was scared. I wrapped my arms around her as she whispered in my ear over and over, "Santa Claus...Santa Claus." Suddenly, we heard jingle bells! Then we heard his voice. It was Santa talking to Jack. He said, "My, Jackie, you have grown to be a big boy." Then we heard Jack's response, "Yes, Santa, but it is Lex that you have come to give presents to today." When Lex heard this, she put her finger to her lips and in a whisper said, "SHHHHH, he has presents." The love I felt for her at that moment was so great, I thought I was going to explode. Then we heard Santa again. He said, "Yes, Lex has been a very good girl this year. I have lots of wonderful things for her. Tell her I am proud of her." "I will, Santa," said Jack, and we heard him leave. Returning to the room, Jack said, "Santa was just here. Did you hear him?" I said, "We did; is the coast clear; is he gone?" "He's gone," said Jack. Gathering Lex in my arms, I headed for the living room. The whole house was dark, because it was still so early in the morning. At the end of the kitchen, the only light we could see was from the glow of the Christmas tree, coming from the closed French doors that led to the living room. Jack swung open the doors, and inside was the most spectacular sight I had ever seen. The tree appeared to have twice as many lights on it than it had when I had left it a few hours earlier. The effect was almost blinding. Christmas music was playing softly on the radio across the room. Something else was also different. There were three times as many presents under the tree. They spilled out to at least fifteen feet from its base. Standing at attention to the side was the doll house. It even looked grander than it had when I had left it. For a split second, I was convinced that the voice we had heard really was Santa. I was three years old again. When I came back to reality, I laughed at myself for the thought. I threw my arms around Jack and whispered in his ear, "What did you do?" He just smiled and whispered, "It wasn't me, it was Santa." Lex was so excited; she didn't know what to open first. Reading the tags for her as she opened all the gifts, it took us over an hour to get through them all. There were at least six more gifts for me, as well. A lot of them were things we needed for the house and art supplies. One was my very first computer. It was the most magical Christmas I had ever experienced, because for a split second, for the first time ever in my life...I believed.

CHAPTER: 56

The following spring, my mother's weak pelvis was no longer able to support her. We were all grateful the tumor was gone, but the hole it had left was a horrible compromise to have to accept. She now needed a wheelchair, which depressed her terribly. In her eyes, she could no longer go outside. Although she was determined as ever to be self-sufficient around the house, my brothers and I still kept a careful watch over her. The sour look on her face had turned to one of self-pity. I only saw this when she didn't know I was looking. The only time she seemed happy was when her grandchildren were with her. We all made certain that it was often. Lex and I continued to sleep at her house from Friday to Sunday. We never left her side, the whole time we were there. For Lex, it wasn't all that bad. She had her cousins to keep her company, and once again, the two apartments melded into one. This time it was the grandchildren making the decisions about which floor they would eat on and what TV they would watch that night. I always stayed down stairs with my mother. She was no longer talking about beating the illness. She was in the stage of acceptance. I, on the other hand, wasn't at that stage with it. Sometimes I was angry; other times I still had hope. I knew one thing for sure. I wasn't going to let her deteriorate in that chair without living a normal life. One day I said, "Come on. We are going to go shopping." At first she was reluctant. But after having spent over a week in the house, she was also going stir-crazy. I decided to use this element to get her out the door. It worked. It wasn't physically easy for me, but we did it. I couldn't lift her completely, because she was my height and heavier than I. I was, however, able to support her under her arms. I wondered if at some point she would become as small and frail as my father had. I knew when that time came, it would be physically easier but emotionally more difficult. I was able to get her out the door. The hard part was the steps. With some maneuvering and supporting her with all my might, we were able to do it. I made a mental note to have Jake build a ramp. When I told her this, she simply replied, "We would only need it for such a short time; it's not worth it." I didn't know how to respond, so I just dropped the subject. We drove to the grocery store like escaped convicts. Lex was in the back seat, clapping her hands and singing; she was feeling the lightness in the air that was suddenly surrounding my mother once again. When we got to the store, I had no problem maneuvering my mother into her chair, as Lex waited patiently in the back seat. Mom sat there, listening intently to the commands I was giving her to make the task easier. The reversal of our roles was now complete. She was dependent on me, and I was now the one who had control. When we got into the store, I felt assaulted by the crowds and blinding lights. The announcements of produce specials were being broadcast for all to hear. Looking around, I realized that pushing a wheelchair through the narrow aisles was not going to be easy. We were suddenly thrown into the world of the handicapped. I had never realized it was so difficult and cumbersome; two worlds existing on the same plane, the people around us unaware of our difficulties. The one thing we hadn't thought about was who was going to push the grocery cart. Because of the unhealed broken ribs caused by the tumors a year earlier, she found it difficult to push herself for any distance on her own, and wheelchair grocery carts hadn't been invented yet. We had no other choice than to make a rolling train with the wheelchair and the carriage. I pushed Mom; she pushed the cart. Lex loved it. She was seated inside the cart where the food went and was making train imitations. I kept telling her to stop, because I was embarrassed. It didn't help that it made my mother laugh, and she joined Lex in chorus. People were looking at us as we passed. Some laughed, while others just stared in disbelief. I wanted to crawl under a rock and never come out again. Because the whole situation was making me nervous, I was looking around to see if people were still watching us. And that's when it happened. I mistakenly judged the next corner and hit the bottom of a display rack that was neatly stacked with paper towels. They all came crashing down on us like a house of cards: on the floor, in the cart on top of Lex and all over my mother in the wheelchair. One even hit me on the top of the head. We were stunned by the impact. I was grateful they weren't canned soup. Everyone around us who was shopping ran to our aid. Lex was laughing, as was my mother. I was apologizing to the stock boys, who were now there to help. They just gave us pathetic smiles and stacked the towels back up. It took us three times as long to do the shopping that day.

When we were finished and it looked like we were actually going to escape with some dignity, I didn't realize the worst was yet to come. It was tough pushing the cart and my mother at the same time over the rough terrain of the parking lot. Some areas were flat, while others had slight hills that you would never realize were there if you hadn't been in this predicament. That day I developed a new respect for people in wheelchairs and what they had to deal with in the ambulatory world they were no longer a part of. When we finally got to the car, I told my mother I was going to put Lex in first, because I was afraid she might run. The minute I lifted Lex from the cart, I stood there in disbelief, as my mother and groceries started rolling away into oncoming cars that were trying to park. I had apparently stopped her on a slight decline and hadn't realized it. I had also forgotten to apply the brakes on the wheelchair. I was faced with that old saying, "Who would you save first... your mother or your child?" I screamed, and fortunately, a woman who was a few cars down ran out and grabbed my mother, as cars were slamming on their brakes. She was shaken but ok. The woman helped my mother and her chair to the side of my car and locked down the brakes. Holding Lex tight in my arms, I thanked her a million times. My heart was beating a mile a minute. My hands were trembling, as I fumbled with Lex and her car seat. I turned to help my mother next. I felt like such a failure. How could I forget to lock down the wheels? I couldn't even look my mother in the face. Some role reversal this was. I had been passed the golden crown, and in less than an hour it had fallen from my head. At the tender age of twenty-eight, I knew I had already lived the life of someone much older. I was disappointed and was scolding myself inside. We were all quiet during the ride home. Even Lex was just looking out the window, watching the world fly by in the stillness of the moment. Then suddenly, out of the silence...my mother burst out laughing.

The people who lived downstairs from Lex and me were from Russia. With their new found freedom, the Russian immigrants were suddenly everywhere. It was an exciting time in history. The cold war was over, and the world seemed a little closer and more at peace. We couldn't communicate with our neighbors, but we always greeted each other with a smile. One day, my landlord, who lived in the next house, knocked on my door. She said that she had received complaints from the people downstairs about me moving furniture in the middle of the night across my living room floor. I laughed when she said this for three reasons: the first because the night before was a Sunday, and I was sleeping at my mother's house, the second because we practically had no furniture to speak of and the third because I was curious about how she had been able to understand a complaint from our neighbors. I assured her that we were doing no such thing, and I could prove it. Bringing her into my apartment, I showed her that my furniture in the living room consisted of bean bag chairs and cushions and a floor lamp. I then asked her if she thought it was the new kitten that I had bought for Lex. She said, "No, the cat is too small." She felt that maybe she had misunderstood them and told me to forget about it, which I did. That evening after Lex was in bed, I was reading a book in the living room, when I heard my front door open. The front door was actually a door that opened into my bedroom. I then heard heavy man's footsteps as they crossed the room. Next they stepped down into my kitchen where the floor board was rotted and always made a creaking sound. A wall divided the kitchen from the living room. Getting closer to me, I stood up in the living room as I mimicked the steps in the same direction from the other room. At the end of the living room where it met the kitchen were the French doors. Assuming it was Jack, I got up and said, "Hi!" But no one was there. I stood there in fear, as a chill went down my spine. My first thought was that it must be Shadow Man. Looking around desperately in every dark corner I could see, I couldn't find him. My next thought was someone was in the house. After that, all I could think of was getting to Lex. From the living room doorway, I looked across the kitchen to Lex's room. Her door was slightly opened, but I couldn't see her in there because it was so dark. Without thinking, I made a mad dash for it to see if she were ok. She was fast asleep with her pouting lips and her damp hair. I then checked the rest of the house, but no one was there. When I returned to the living room, the cat was acting strangely. He was staring into a corner with his back hunched, like he had trapped a mouse...but there was no mouse. There was nothing there. I then picked up the phone and called Jack. He was just finishing up with his father and said he would be right over. By the time Jack got there, I had the radio on for distraction and was pacing the floor.

"Jack I am telling you, it was someone or something in this house. It wasn't a question in my mind. The footsteps were so loud, I thought it was you."

"Well, Barb, there is no one here at the moment. I checked the whole apartment and even in the closets."

"I need to put Lex in my bed tonight. She is too far away from me in her room when I am in mine."

"Ok, I will go get her for you." Hanging on to his shirt, I went with him and got Lex. She only stirred a little as Jack spoke softly to her and then laid her next to me in bed. He stayed with me that evening, until I fell asleep.

The noise I heard that night I would hear again many more times in the course of the two and a half years we lived there. The house was very old. It had been built in the 1700's. The people downstairs complained constantly about me moving heavy furniture. I never heard the furniture, just the footsteps. They were always at the same time in the late part of the night. Lex slept with me the whole time we lived there. Every time the neighbors complained about the furniture, I reassured my landlord that it wasn't me; most of the time it happened when I was staying at my mother's. It got so bad that I would make it a point to say good bye to the landlord on Friday, before I left. I would then tell her that I would see her upon my return on Monday. She knew it wasn't me, so she never forced me to resolve it. Instead, she thought it was the neighbors being crazy. Eventually the neighbors moved out because of it. I thought the whole situation was over, until a girl my age by the name of Amanda moved in. Amanda and I got along great. She loved Lex and would let her play with her new puppy, Cody. Amanda was always concerned about Cody barking and disturbing us, but I reassured her not to worry. I think that is why Amanda came to me before she talked to my landlord about the furniture she heard being moved around in the middle of the night. When she said the words, my heart sank and goose bumps covered my body. I, too, had convinced myself the old neighbors were just crazy. Now I knew they weren't. I told her that they had heard it too, but that I was not home. I then told her about my mother and the time I spent there. I asked her if it could be the cat. Tyke was getting bigger now, and maybe he was getting a little wild when we were gone? She said, "No, it definitely wasn't Tyke. It was very heavy furniture." I said, "Amanda, you have seen my house. Other than my bedroom, I don't have heavy furniture." She said, "It wasn't coming from the bedroom. It was coming from the living room." I laughed, because all I had in there still were two beanbag chairs, a few cushions from my couch. I didn't even have a coffee table. My drafting table and easel were down at my studio in Beverly. We went into my living room to investigate the possibilities but couldn't find any. I said, "Well, it isn't me, so do me a favor. It looks like I am going to be staying at my mother's every weekend from now on until the end. I don't know when the end will be, so could you keep an eye on the place while I'm gone? Maybe someone else also knows I'm not home and is taking advantage of it." I didn't know what else to say; I couldn't tell her about the footsteps. She would think I was crazy! After all, I didn't hear them every night. A few more weeks had passed. My mother's condition was unchanged, yet her spirits were going downhill rapidly. That weekend she had taken me aside when everyone left and said, "This is it Barbara. The doctor said that we are going to stop all treatments." I was devastated by her words. I said, "You can't give up!" I immediately broke into tears. Even though, in my head, I had been trying to introduce the idea of losing her for some time now, it was as if I were hearing it for the first time. "I'm not ready to give up, but I can't be strong and hold on if you are," I was on the verge of hysteria. She didn't hug me or try to console me; she just looked at me and said, "Barbara, it wasn't me who came up with the idea. It was the doctor." I said, "Don't you understand? I am not old enough to take your place, to be the daughter who becomes strong enough to walk in your shoes. I always figured when the time came, and you were gone, that I would be a mature woman who was as strong as you are. Not a girl of twenty-nine...I'm not there yet." She just looked at me. I think it was the most intimate conversation we had ever had. I know, for me, it was the most honest. Then composing her words carefully, she said, "Well, you have to be strong, because this is going to be difficult," and left the room. I stood there alone in the kitchen with my thoughts. I was paralyzed with grief; I couldn't move. Then Lex came bouncing into the room like a ray of hope... "Can we go to the Willows today?"

That weekend I was able to leave early. My Uncle Joe had come down from New Hampshire unannounced to visit with my mother. She must have told him the news, too. They had been in touch almost every week since her illness. Often when he came down he would only stay for a few hours. Now he was going to stay a few days. He wanted to be with her. We were all grateful for the break. On Sunday evening, as the sun was going down, Lex and I were in the backyard of my apartment, heading for the door, when Amanda stopped us. She seemed upset and frightened. She grabbed me by the arm and without saying a word led me into her apartment. Cody was in her kitchen, and Lex immediately ran to pet him. When Lex was out of ear shot, I said, "What's the matter, are you all right?" After the emotional rollercoaster I had just been through that weekend, it felt funny to be asking someone something that should have been asked of me. "Barbara," she said, "something really strange is going on in your apartment."

"What?" I asked as a chill went up my spine.

"I was with you when you left on Friday. I saw you lock the door. We walked down the stairs together and we were talking about your photo retouching business, remember?"

"Yeah, what about it?"

"Well, last night I got home late. I was at the bar down the street with some friends. I was home for only a few minutes, when I heard the furniture again. I remembered what you said about someone being in there when you weren't home, so I decided to investigate."

"What, are you crazy? I meant call the police!"

"I know I should have, but something told me that the police would find nothing. I went to the back hall that leads to your apartment. When I got upstairs, the door was wide open. Everything looked exactly as you left it. The light was on."

"I leave the light on when I'm gone for the weekend, but I know I locked the door."

"I know; I was with you when you did it. That's why I thought that maybe someone was in there."

"What did you see?"

"That's just it, nothing. The cat was in the corner with its back hunched, but everything was fine, and there was no noise."

"Did the cat acknowledge you when you entered the room?"

"Only to look at me; he didn't move from his spot. I felt really scared, so I ran back downstairs. I didn't even shut the door. When I realized that the door was still open, I was too afraid to go back up there. I figured I'd do it in the morning."

"When you went up there in the morning, was anything moved?" "I didn't have to go back up; the door was closed!"

We just looked at each other in disbelief. I said, "Come with me." I yelled to Lex to stay with Cody; that we would be right back. Climbing the stairs together, we didn't say a word. Since the door had to be locked with a key, and I had the only one, I assumed it would just open when I turned the knob. It didn't; it was locked. Turning the key, I opened the door slowly. Tyke came running to me all excited, and the living room was just as I had left it. The book I had been reading was still opened to the last page I was on and laid on the floor next to the beanbag chair, where I had been sitting before I had left on Friday.

Amanda said it first. "Barbara, this place is haunted." She then turned on her heels and ran back down the stairs. I was not far behind her.

When we were back in her apartment, I turned to Lex and said, "Come on, Lex, let's go find Jack and go to the Willows."

That night, Jack came back to the apartment with us. I was afraid to go alone. Lex had been sleeping with me since the night I had first heard the footsteps, but until this point, I wasn't ready to face the possibilities of what Amanda was suggesting. I told Jack that I didn't want him to leave us. We went to settle John Henry for the night. Jack told him he would be back very early in the morning, before he was up, and we left. At one in the morning, the three of us were still in the living room. Lex was sleeping on the couch cushions, and Jack and I were each on a bean bag chair. Everything was quiet, and then we heard them...the footsteps. We both heard them at the same time. The bedroom door opened and closed and the steps were walking through the kitchen, getting closer. They stopped at the French doors like before, and Jack went to investigate...but no one was there. I could see he was disturbed by this but tried to act like it was nothing. I, on the other hand, kept saying, "See, I'm not crazy am I?"

He picked up Lex and said, "Come on, it's getting late. Let's go to bed." When I woke up at 6:00 AM, he was gone.

I never did hear furniture moving in that house. All I ever heard was the footsteps. After awhile, when I realized that whatever it was, it wasn't going to hurt us, I just ignored it...but Lex never slept in her own bed the entire time we lived there, after the first episode.

One day at work, while trying to order some retouching pencils from Kodak, I was told that the line of supplies had been discontinued. Pressing the man further, I couldn't get any more information other than that. When I hung up the phone and told the guys, we couldn't believe it. Those pencils were vital to our work. John said, "I bet it's because of Photoshop. That computer program is eventually going to put us all out of business."

"That program costs thousands of dollars. How can photographers possibly justify it, not to mention the learning curve it takes to use it?"

Even though I was trying to dismiss it, in my heart I knew he was right. I had been thinking for some time now about this possibility. I knew that I couldn't afford it, and I had no desire to sit in front of a computer all day. John's brother, on the other hand, had the program. He would show him what it did, every time he visited. Over a period of three months, the work load in the lab started to drop off. We went from taking in five hundred orders a day to two hundred. John and Jai were on contract work and also had clients of their own. They were feeling it the most. When the work was dropping even more, and we were down to the nubs on our pencils, John announced he was thinking about moving to California in a few months. Jai said he was thinking about applying at Tech Color, a rival of North Shore. I had already gotten a second job, the only one I could find and still keep up the pace of my responsibilities: delivering newspapers at three in the morning. Lex and I now went to bed at 8:30 PM. I was too tired to care about any furniture or footsteps. We got up at 2:00 AM, and I drove her to my mother's house and put her in bed with her. I then went to the Herald office and picked up the papers. The job was every day. The hours were grueling. I had two routes that took me three hours to deliver. I took home three hundred dollars a week in cash. I hated to have to get Lex up so early and disturb her sleep, but just as she always had, she went with the flow. One morning as I was buckling her into her car seat, she looked up, smiled at me and said in a happy voice, "Good morning, Mommy." I smiled back, and I told myself that someday, when she was old enough to understand, I was going to thank her for being such a great kid. She finally started calling me Mommy when she was about four. Jack also thought it was weird that she only called me Barbara. He figured out a solution. Without discussing it, he started calling me Mommy. It was only natural, after that, for Lex to mimic him.

On one particular morning in January, Lex and I were stepping out the front door and were met by a beautiful sight. It had rained in the night, and then the temperature had dropped suddenly, causing everything around us to freeze. She was wrapped tight in a snowsuit and blanket, so I wasn't concerned about her being cold. The view that was in front of me was so beautiful; I had to wake her to see it. I said, "Look, Lex, the fairies have frosted the trees with ice while we were sleeping." Every bare twig on every tree was coated. It was as if it were a gift to me from Germany, so many years ago, when every winter I would see the trees like this.

She opened her eyes, smiled and said, "Fairy trees," in a soft voice. Walking to the car that was parked around the corner in the parking lot, we listened, as the only sound that could be heard was the crunching of our feet.

"It's so quiet, Mommy, are the fairies sleeping?"

Stopping in front of the Barnacle, a restaurant that sat on the ocean, I said in a puzzled voice, "They must be, Lex." The reason I was confused was because normally you could at least hear the ocean. After all, it was only ten feet away. Standing quietly at the sea wall, I noticed that there was also a full moon. "Look, Lex, the man in the moon is saying good morning."

"Good morning, moon," she said back in a sleepy voice.

This peaceful exchange was suddenly broken by what I can only describe as a loud noise that sounded like someone was trying to tune in a short wave radio. The sound came from the direction of the ocean. Lex and I looked at the same time to figure out what it was. The moon cast a bright light on the water's surface. Scanning the horizon, I realized that there were no boats in the harbor. Of course, there wouldn't be any in January, and the diehard fishermen who worked all winter moored their boats further down the harbor. I knew that was too far for it to be the source; besides, no fisherman in his right mind would be out on the ocean at 2:00 AM in January.

"What is it?" said Lex, confused by what we were hearing.

Before I could answer her, I heard a scream from a woman. She was shouting the word "no" very loudly. Her voice was vibrating, making me think she was running, yet I couldn't hear any footsteps. The odd thing was that I could swear the sound was coming from the middle of the harbor, out on the water. My first instinct was to try and help her. I leaned over the sea wall to see if I could find her. But no one was there. Then we heard it again. Seeing my hesitation, Lex decided to take charge. She grabbed both of my cheeks and forced me to look in her eyes. She stated very matter of factly, "Run, Mommy!" So I did. It was difficult with all the ice under our feet. The voice was agonizingly calling from behind us. Fumbling with the keys, I got us into the car as quickly as I could. Driving down the street, we headed to my mother's. Lex kept asking me, "Who was that lady, Mommy, and why was she scared?"

I simply said, "I don't know, honey, but when we get to Grammy's house, I will call someone to go and find out. Don't worry." When we entered my mother's house, she was still asleep. Tiptoeing into the kitchen, I placed Lex on a chair, as I dialed the Marblehead Police. I told them what we had heard and where we had heard it. I was sure there was someone in trouble down by the sea wall and added that it really had sounded like it was coming from a boat in the harbor. I told them about the radio sounds. He told me that they didn't respond to what I had heard anymore.

"What are you talking about? There is a woman being brutally hurt out in the harbor." "Lady, there are no boats in the harbor in January." "I know, but there must be one now, because I heard it. My daughter heard it too."

"What you heard was the screaming lady. It is reported a lot in that area. Legend has it she was raped and killed on the beach by pirates, back in the late 1600's. We get calls from newcomers to the area about three times a year. All the locals and old time Marbleheaders just ignore her." Then he added, "Consider yourself lucky. A lot of people flock to that spot at night, in hopes of hearing her and don't." I couldn't believe what he was telling me. I said, "You must be mistaken. This woman was really in danger. I was at the edge of the beach, but she wasn't there. I think she is in a boat. This isn't just a legend; you have to go and check it out."

His reply was stoic, "Lady, we no longer do that. Besides, there are no boats at that end of the harbor, and back then the center of the harbor was the beach." Then he said in a softer tone, "Listen, I do have a car downtown. I'll see what I can do."

When I hung up the phone, Lex asked me if someone were going to help the lady. I just looked at her and smiled, "Yes, Lex, don't worry." I put her in bed next to my mother.

The entire route, I couldn't get out of my head what I had heard and what the officer had told me. I knew that Marblehead was one of the oldest towns in the country, but between the happenings at my house and now this, I thought I was losing my mind. Why was I experiencing this? I wondered if it was because I had been dealing with the thoughts of life and death since my mother's illness had begun eight years before. Was I bringing this on myself? I knew one thing. I wasn't the only person who was experiencing it. Everyone around me was, too: the Russian neighbors, Amanda, Jack and now Lex.

CHAPTER: 57

Jack and I were beginning to feel the effects of taking care of so many people. I, personally, felt I had lived three lifetimes, and I still hadn't turned thirty. Between John Henry, my mother, Lex and the two businesses, not to mention my paper route, something was sure to give. For most people, it would have been a strain on the relationship. For Jack and me, it forged a stronger bond. Somehow, the individual responsibilities we had began to meld as one. I'm not sure when or how it happened, because it was a gradual blend. I found myself checking on John Henry, when Jack was shooting a wedding. He was with my mother, if I had to work late. Everyone who met us, assumed we were married. At an afternoon lunch in November, it all came together.

"Jack, when we first met nine years ago, did you ever think our relationship would be what it is today?" "What is it today?" he asked with a grin. "You know," I said smiling, "best friends. Two people helping each other get through this crazy life."

"Well, now that you mention, it I have thought about it a lot. And maybe it is because I am old fashioned but I was thinking, you should move in with me for the sake of Lex. She would be able to live in a house instead of an apartment, have a back yard to play in, and a room you aren't afraid to put her in at night to sleep."

"Are you asking me to marry you?"

"Hell, everyone thinks we are married anyway, so why not? Seriously, what would be the difference? We have known each other for nine years. We have been together as a couple for almost three. We see each other every day. We eat every meal together. We take care of each other's parents. The only difference is I will be able to share my bed with you; which I want to do."

"Ok, let's do it. You make a good point. I have to admit you are the best friend I have ever had." Our decision to get married was not based on romance. It was more like a mutual agreement. It took us no more time than it did to place our orders with the waitress, when she came to our table. We decided that we weren't going to make a big deal about it. We wanted it to be our day alone. I wanted Lex and John Henry to stand in as our witnesses. It seemed fitting, since the result would affect all of us. We were going to be a true family, under one roof. The only problem we had was that Lex had to be able to write her own name. If she couldn't do this, then legally she could not be my "maid of honor." I spent as much time as I could with this task, but it was no use. It would be the first time the alarms would go off in my head about her learning abilities. Over the years, I had worked with many children and taught them how to write their names. When Lex tried to do it, she could trace the letters when I dotted them on the page, but when left to do it herself, she just made straight line marks all over the paper, with an occasional circle thrown in, because she liked to make them. I didn't tell her why we were practicing this, although she did know that Jack and I were going to get married. As a matter of fact, when she talked to me about it, she would say, "When are we going to marry Jack?" It seemed so honest and truthful a question. In her eyes, this union of marriage was very much a union for her as well. We stuck to the plan and didn't tell anyone except John Henry. When it became evident that Lex was not going to learn to write her name in time, we included my mother. We got married on a Monday evening, November 18, 1991. I wore a dress that I had borrowed from a female photographer. One of the town historians of Marblehead was also a justice of the peace, and she performed the ceremony. She was very good at what she did. It was the most special wedding I had ever had. Gone were the confines of religious doctrine and in their place were truth and love. For the first time in this situation, I cried. They were tears of absolute joy. John Henry stood next to Jack, looking so dignified in his suit. He had a bandage on his head from a growth that was developing from his daily visits to the backyard to sit in the sun. My mother stood next to me. She had come in a wheelchair, but for the ceremony, she insisted on standing with her walker. Lex was between Jack and me and was holding our hands. The JP included Lex in the service, as part of the union, without me even asking her to. It was the wedding I had always wanted.

With no time for a honeymoon, the next day we went to work. We had moved all our things into Jack's house the week before. When we woke up on Tuesday, it was business as usual; Lex went to preschool, while we went to work. When I dropped Lex off, her teacher told me that she had to ask me something. She said Lex had been obsessing all Monday that she was getting married that night. She had talked about it the entire day. Susan said she had never seen a child be so adamant about one subject for so long and was concerned. I told her not to worry. Lex and Jack and I had gotten married the previous night. She wasn't lost in a fantasy world; it was real.

When I got to work, I had a lot of deadlines that had to be met. I immediately went into the dark room and didn't emerge until lunch. When I did, I joined John and Jai with a sandwich. Sitting there, we listened to Jai's latest adventure with a man he had met the night before. It was an intriguing story, and for a while, I forgot about the news I had. It was just one more thing that proved to me that marrying Jack was the most natural thing I had ever done. When Jai was finished, I said, "Oh! Guess what? Jack and I got married last night!"

"What! Why didn't you tell us?" The only thing I could think of was the truth... "I forgot." "I don't believe you," said Jai,"Let me see your driver's license." "What, you think I have had time to change it? It happened last night."

"She has a point, Jai." "Why didn't you invite us? We would have loved to have been bridesmaids in tuxes." "Actually I had the wedding I always wanted, I eloped."

Living with Jack and John Henry was as natural as walking, for Lex and me. John Henry was thrilled to have a child running around. It was an image he had been sure he wouldn't ever see in his lifetime, when Jack had been married to his first wife. There was a small room on the second floor of the house that had been Jack's, when he was a child. Because the room had not been needed for a long time, it was used as extra storage for Jack's video equipment. Cleaning out the room, I painted it bubble gum pink with white molding. On one wall, I painted a mural of the Disney version of the little mermaid. Lex was thrilled. At first, I was afraid she would not understand that Jack and I now shared a room, and she had one of her own, but the issue never came up, and, once again, Lex easily adapted. John Henry's bedroom was next to hers; ours was down the hall. At night, we would all retire to our rooms and read. John Henry had his favorites. The book he looked at most every night was titled, "Three Men in a Boat, Not to Mention the Dog," It was written around 1918. He had difficulty reading by then. His eyes had deteriorated tremendously over the previous five years. He had developed cataracts. Jack refused to have them checked. He felt that every time a doctor had touched this man, he had come back with fewer abilities than when he had left. This was how John Henry had suffered his stroke, during a minor surgery. Because of his eyes, Jack and I would read to his father. Some times Lex would listen with him; other times she just waited patiently for us to finish, so we could read her stories. In many ways, the needs that John Henry had were similar to what Lex needed. In my heart, I felt I had two children. I loved them both equally.

The major difference with John Henry was the amazing, intellectual mind that was still intact within his frail body. After Lex went to bed, if I didn't have any obligations with my mother, the three of us would sit together and talk. John Henry always had a highball when we did this. He often talked to us about the time he had met President Taft, when he was just nine. His memory was incredible. When I asked him what his first job had been, he told me that he had delivered groceries for a local food store in his home town of Greensburg, West Virginia, as a teenager. He said he had done it on a donkey, because cars had not been invented. He remembered the first automobile and knew a time when telephones were not in every household. He had seen all the major achievements of the 20th century. When he did get his driver's license, he had to tape a quarter to a postcard and send it to an office of motor vehicles in Ohio. There were no tests, road or otherwise. It came in the mail a month later. He met his wife in New York, when he was first working research in the late 1940's. She was a research librarian, and the two hit it off right away. She was widowed with a nine year old son named Jack. Never having met his real father, Jack became very close to him, right from the beginning. That was when John Henry transferred to Massachusetts to become the research director of the United Shoe Machine Corporation. Eight years after they had married and moved to Massachusetts, Jack's mother had died, and the two men were alone.

Shortly after we were married, John Henry's "growth" that had appeared on his forehead began to get bigger. I begged Jack to bring him to the doctor, but, as usual, he didn't want anyone to touch him. Jack was overly protective in that way with his father. He never asked for outside help in taking care of him. Jack cut his hair and trimmed his nails. He didn't even take him to the doctor for checkups, other than every so often to get his blood tested. John Henry was on Coumadin, a drug to thin the blood. Jack knew all the signs that indicated the medication had to be reduced and consulted with his own doctor, who was a family friend and a long time contemporary of John Henry, for his medication monitoring. Jack had witnessed, at a young age, what discomfort the treatments can create for a person who is ill, when his mother was diagnosed with lymphoma. Chemotherapy was in the beginning stages of testing then. Although his mother did receive it, insurance didn't cover it. It almost ruined his family financially. Because John Henry's job relied on research grants, he had never really taken home the normal doctor's salary to begin with.

Other than his blood needing to be thinned, John Henry was in perfect health at the age of 92. When the growth went from the size of a dime to the size of a golf ball in one month, I began to get very concerned. Jack, however, was still not budging on the idea of sending him to the doctor. He did talk to his family physician. That doctor said that as long as it wasn't bothering him, he shouldn't worry about it. If it were cancer, John Henry would refuse treatments anyway. In another month, it became the size of a tennis ball and began to bleed. In an argument with Jack, I laid out the realities. I stated that someday we would come home and find he had bled to death on the floor, because of his medication and the fact that we couldn't get this growth to heal. It was because of my continued persistence that Jack finally complied and took his father to see a local dermatologist to have it examined. That doctor said that it was not cancer and could be easily removed. He wanted to put him in the hospital because of his age; otherwise it could have been done on an outpatient basis. Jack was not thrilled by this. He kept saying, "They're going to kill my father." I, on the other hand, was relieved that something was going to be done about it and had full faith in the hospital and doctors. The day that John Henry was going into the hospital, my mother took a turn for the worse. She was in a lot of pain and couldn't get around. She called me at 8:00 AM and asked if I could stay with her that day. Though I was torn between the two responsibilities, Jack assured me that it was ok. It was a decision I wish I had never made. Jack had been right; the hospital killed his father.

The day John Henry died, I kept Lex out of school, and together we went to my mother's house. Jack dropped us off, since we only had one car at the time. My mother wasn't as bad as I had thought she would be. Mostly, she was scared of the obvious. She now realized she would die. The entire day I sat with her, and we talked. She went through stages like this, when the thoughts in her head totally consumed her. This was one of those days. Having Lex around seemed to help. It was because of this that I stayed for the entire day and night. By the time Lex went to sleep, Jack was still with his dad at the hospital. He wasn't ready to hand over the responsibility of getting him ready for bed. When John Henry fell asleep at 11:30 PM, Jack drove to my mother's house to get us. John Henry's surgery was scheduled for the next morning. When we got home, I was thoroughly exhausted. I asked him how his dad had been, and Jack said, "Right now, he is fine; it is tomorrow I'm worried about." I told him not to worry, because he was in good hands, and we went to bed.

At 4:00 AM, we awoke to the ringing of the telephone. Stumbling for the receiver that was in our room, Jack sat naked on the chair, as I watched him be given the information he knew he would get. He had a look of absolute anguish on his face. In the middle of the night, John Henry had fallen out of bed, trying to go to the bathroom. He had hit his head and lacerated the growth. He had bled to death on the floor. Jack let out a primal scream that shook the house and caused Lex to run to our room. He stood up and started throwing objects around that were in reach. Lex ran to my arms, and I turned on the light. I still didn't know what had happened, but I was certain of the outcome. I didn't know what to do. I was frightened by Jack's behavior. When I looked at him, he seemed like a madman, ready to kill someone. Placing Lex in my bed, I went to Jack to try and comfort him. He looked me in the eye and just kept screaming, "THEY KILLED HIM...THEY KILLED MY DADDY!" It was like he was Lex's age emotionally, with the rage of a grown man. Lex kept saying, "What's the matter, Mommy? What's wrong with Jack?" I didn't answer her. Instead, I went downstairs and pulled all the dishes out of the cabinets and started to rewash them. I don't know why I was doing this; I know I was crying hysterically, too. Lex followed me downstairs and tried to talk to me, but I wasn't hearing her. I wasn't hearing anything, except the guilty echoes in my own head: "This is your fault. Jack was right. He never should have been left in someone else's hands." Upstairs could still be heard the moans of grief. Jack was walking from room to room in a state of confusion. Lex, four at the time, was the only person in the house in her right mind, and somehow she knew it. She climbed the stairs to help Jack. She went into his dresser and got him something to wear. She handed him each article of clothing, while the whole time she kept saying, "It's going to be all right, Papa; Mommy and I are here." She had started calling Jack "Papa," when we had gotten married. After she had helped dress Jack, she came back to the kitchen and tried to reason with me. By this time, I was expressing the words in my head out loud. Over and over, I kept repeating, "John Henry is dead, and it is my fault he's gone." Hearing my words, Lex pulled at my nightgown to bring me down to her height. When I lowered my face to hers, she said, "Mommy, John Henry is not gone. He's in your heart." These were words my mother had used with her just the day before, when she had tried to explain that at some point she would be gone. She took Lex aside and said, "You never have to worry, because I will always be right here." She then touched Lex's chest and pointed to her heart. It was this gesture that Lex was now making to me. It brought me back to reality, and I knew that this house, with all its grief and lack of parental control, was not good for her. I went to the phone and called her father...it was 4:30 AM.

Nick was there in ten minutes. When I opened the front door, the uncontrollable sobs coming from upstairs could still be heard. I told Nick that he needed to take Lex for a few days, until we could sort things out and find out what had happened. He was very sympathetic and told me he would do whatever we needed, to call him for anything. I kissed Lex a long time, and they left. Turning around, I climbed the stairs to comfort my husband. The strong person I had never thought existed in me emerged.

By the time I was dressed, Jack was sitting in the chair and quietly staring into space. He was a million miles away, running through the scenes of his childhood with the man whom he had loved and learned to call Dad. When I gently lifted him from his seat, he didn't fight me. I led him out to the car and placed him in the passenger seat. The whole time, he said nothing. I was afraid to speak myself, so instead I drove to Dunkin Donuts and bought us both strong, black coffees and then headed to the hospital. When we got there, I pulled into a parking space and turned off the engine. We sat there for awhile...Jack in a daze and me waiting for his cue that he was ready. I was concerned for him. I quietly prayed and told God not to take him from me too. Eventually, his despair turned to anger, and he looked at me and said, "Those bastards have some answering to do." He then got out of the car.

We went to the floor where Jack had left his father. The nurse there stopped us and ushered us to a room. Jack insisted on seeing his father's body. It was something I knew I couldn't do. Jack must have known it too. He turned to me and said, "I want to be alone with him." It was a stern statement, and I didn't say a thing. While he was gone, a woman entered the room. She was dressed in a suit and looked like she was in charge. We never found out who she was. She said she wasn't sure how it had happened but wondered why John Henry would not have asked for assistance in the middle of the night. She said these words very directly, and I knew she was trying to place blame on him. The look on her face was not that of concern for our loss, instead it was more of irritation for the mess this had caused her. I wanted to reach across the desk and grab her by the neck, but at that moment, Jack walked into the room. Jack started asking her all sorts of questions. Through the course of the interview, she let slip that John Henry had never been admitted properly and that the nurse's call button was out of reach from his grasp. She started asking Jack why he had never informed the nurses that he was there. I said, "Who would think that one had to do that?" I was yelling at her, with my face close to hers, when I said this, and she immediately told me that if I didn't calm down, she was going to call for someone. Jack asked her if they had taken his father off the Coumadin. She had no record of him being on the drug and said that they hadn't. Jack said, "I had been reducing it for twenty-four hours before I brought him here, but he was still taking some." Then Jack said, "So the reality is, he would have bled to death on the operating room table if this hadn't happened." She then got all fired up and said, "This meeting is over," and handed us John Henry's things, one of which was his cane. We stormed out of there and swore to each other we would never go back there for any medical emergencies.

Over the course of the next few weeks, we discovered from our neighbor, who had just retired from being a nurse there, that the hospital had just been bought out and was downsizing. The floors were half-staffed, and the admissions office had been completely revamped the week before John Henry's scheduled surgery. The place was in disarray as far as functioning was concerned. She advised us to sue. Jack and I knew that John Henry wouldn't have wanted that, but after numerous people told us to seek council, we decided to see what could be done. The hospital was sending us bills to cover his short stay, and I think that was the final straw that made Jack want to seek justice. We talked to several different lawyers, and they all said the same thing. John Henry was too old for us to have a suit. In the eyes of the courts, a man is only worth what life he would have had left. They also said that you can only sue a hospital for $20,000, and that wasn't enough for any lawyer to take it on. They said the only thing we could do was sue the nurses personally who were on staff that night. We felt the nurses were being treated unfairly by the work load as it was...why bring more misery to their lives?...so we did nothing and endured the pain of the loss for many years to come. Jack closed the door to John Henry's bedroom and refused to let anyone go in there. It would be five years before it was opened again.

My mother's condition was stable. She was still in her wheelchair, and her spirits were low. In essence, she was waiting to die. Lex went off to kindergarten, and I closed my business and started working as a preschool teacher. Jack was still shooting video. John moved to California, like he had said he would, in search of a singing career. Jai got a job in New Hampshire, working for Tech Color as an airbrush artist. Life was going on, but Jack and Lex and I were waiting for the last ball to drop...the death of my mother. While still in the wheelchair, with the impending thoughts of having to soon be in a bed for the remainder of her life, my mother called in a family therapist from hospice. I didn't want to have anything to do with it. I felt there was too much water under that bridge to be dredging it up in the final hours. My brothers, on the other hand, seemed to think it was a good idea. We still weren't communicating...we never had, but that wasn't what they felt it would be for. They were sure that it would help Mom get over the hurdle of facing death. I wondered how we were all going to discuss this delicate subject, when we couldn't even discuss politics without fighting. The meeting was scheduled for an evening at my mother's house. The woman they sent over was a mousy, thirty year old, who looked too emotionally weak to handle what was ahead of her. She didn't exude any sense of control or confidence. My first thought was, "This is such a joke." The people who attended were Jake, Justine, Doug, Jack, me and my mother. Right from the start, we sat there not saying a word. We were all in the living room; I sat in a recliner with my hands folded across my chest. Jack sat next to me, rubbing my leg. Jake and Justine shared the couch; Doug was in a chair next to Jack. My mother was in her wheelchair with the counselor to her right. We were all facing each other in a circle. Eventually, Jake spoke first. Or, I should say, he cried. Through his sobs, he said, "I have always fixed things my whole life for you, I'm sorry I can't fix this." It was an admirable admission on his part. It was the first time in my life I had ever seen him shed a tear. The counselor talked to him at length about his feelings of guilt. My mother consoled him as best she could. Doug was next. He talked about the endless doctor visits he had taken her to and about the stall it had put on his career. He was also doing her shopping now, as well, because I was now working at the Children's Center, the same school I had sent Lex to preschool. My teaching schedule no longer allowed the shopping time with my mother. The discussion about Doug and his feelings went on for an hour. I admit, he did hold the burden of all the technical aspects of her illness. But he was also the one in the family who understood the medical jargon and knew more than we ever would. What wasn't brought up was the fact that I was with her during the night, the fact that I left my home for days and didn't return until I had relief. Doug wasn't living away from his house to take care of her. And Jake and Justine split up their duties between themselves. Besides, they lived upstairs. I knew it wasn't any use bringing it up. They would just verbally knock me down anyway, like they had for so many years in the past. The counselor never asked me any questions. I just sat there quietly, not saying a thing. When she felt we were finished and stood up to leave, she then realized that I, too, was a child of this family. She seemed embarrassed by this oversight and sat back down and asked me why I hadn't contributed. I looked at her flatly and said, "Because it wouldn't have done any good. My opinions have never mattered much in family discussions." The room went quiet. I naively expected someone to express that I was wrong. I realized my statement was more a question, and the silence was my answer. I stood up and began to gather my things. I realized the truth of my role in this awful situation. I was as good as hired help. In my head I thought, "When this is all over, I'm closing the door to this chapter of my life. I will never talk to them or have to see them again. I will be free." Before I could leave, my mother stopped me with her comment. She stated very flatly, "It is true. We have all disliked Barbara...including myself. She was always making poor decisions and following every pipe dream she ever had, leaving us to pick up the pieces. But now that I have been able to spend some time with her, I can see that she is not the selfish person we had all made her out to be." The words cut in my chest like a knife. I often would scold myself, when I had thought that my family didn't love me. I had thought I was being childish with these feelings. Even Jack didn't know the extent of the torment I had felt with this. And now I knew the truth. I had an admission, and no one had denied it. A lump developed in my throat, and I couldn't speak. I could hear the counselor asking me how this made me feel. Her words sounded distant, as if a TV had been left on in the other room. I didn't say anything; I stood up with Jack holding my hand, and we left.

CHAPTER: 58

In the late spring of 1993, MaryJane was confined to a bed. She had a hospital bed delivered to her home, and it was placed in the living room. She wanted to be able to still see what little was left of her world. I was still staying at her house with Lex from Friday to Monday. Jack was with us until the early hours of the morning, when he would go home to an empty house, without his father and without Lex and me. My mother's dependency was great. She could no longer leave her bed. It was where she bathed and where she went to the bathroom. I slept on the couch next to her bed, when I stayed with her. She got me up every two hours to help her try and go to the bathroom. The pressure in her pelvis always made it seem like she had to go. There was no reasoning with her about this. Soon after that, she slipped into a coma. A week before she had slipped into a deep sleep, she had had a long discussion with me. It was two o'clock in the morning. She was exhausted and asked me to make it all stop right then. She wanted me to overdose her, to put her out of her misery. At the time, Dr. Kervorkian was all over the news. They were trying to arrest him for assisted suicides. I looked at my mother and said, "I can't do that; I have to think of Lex." She agreed that I was right and dropped the subject. The meds she was on were administered intravenously by a tube and the assistance of a small computer. There was a code that had to be typed in, a different one for every hour. I was never any good at these types of gadgets and often found myself fumbling with the numbers. That next morning, I accidentally typed in the wrong amount of medication. I realized it, when my mother went from talking to me to having her head fall back on the pillow in mid sentence. I panicked and tried to wake her but couldn't. I started pacing around the room and talking to myself. I didn't know what to do. Who would believe that I had accidentally killed my mother? I searched for a pulse but couldn't feel one. Suddenly, a feeling of calmness came over me. I thought of Ivy Manor and Sherry. The words "do not resuscitate" rang in my head. I remembered asking her what they had meant. I heard her voice that morning I had done this to my mother. She said, "You go make a cup of coffee." So that is what I did. After an hour had passed, I went back into her room. I felt for a pulse, but there still was none to be found. I then called my brother Doug at work and told him what I had done. He raced home and was at her side in forty minutes. I sat in the kitchen, as calm as could be. In my head, I was coming to terms with the fact that her prayers had been answered. A moment later, Doug came into the kitchen and said, "She's still alive; she's just in a very deep sleep." She woke up later that evening. She didn't ask why it was so late, and I never told her what had happened. The next day, she had an unexpected visitor. Gil knocked at the door. We hadn't seen him since he had left, many years before that. When my mother saw him, her face lit up. She cooed, "Gil, I missed you so much." She was highly medicated and slurred her words.

He knelt down beside her bed and, without saying a word, he embraced her. I left them alone and went to sit on the front porch to give them some privacy. I was happy he was there. I knew she was, too.

The hospice nurses had been coming to her house twice a week by then. They checked on her meds and took over my job of giving her a bath. Now they also tended to her bed sores. They were all kind, and any help they could give was greatly appreciated. They didn't, however, stay through the night. They wouldn't do that until they were sure she only had two weeks left to live. My mother knew when the morphine pump was to be put in that her time on this earth was going to be short. The day that time arrived, we were all at her side. When the nurse put it in, my mother, who had been in a coma, woke up. She realized what they were doing and cried out, "OH, NO, NOT YET!" My heart sank, and I burst into tears and had to leave the room. She was only awake for a short time.

A few days later, the nurses said they could stay through the night. We had all been taking turns staying with her. Joe and Martha also helped out. Now being told I no longer had to stay, I found it difficult to leave. One morning when I arrived, I found my brothers already at her house. They told me that the day had come...she should be gone before nightfall. I went to her side and kissed her gently. She was sweaty, and her breathing was labored. I told her she had put up a good fight and that I would see her in heaven. I then turned to Doug and said, "I don't want to witness this. I don't want to have it be my last memory." He understood and told me it was probably not going to be peaceful, and maybe I should go. I told him I was going to go over to my friend Carol's house. Carol was a woman in Marblehead whom I had befriended when my mother's condition started to deteriorate. She had a child who was Lex's age, and they played together. Carol became that person in my life I would go to when life was too much for me to handle. She never asked me any questions; she just let me sit with her in silence. During this time, she was my angel. I had had Nick pick up Lex a week prior to this event. I remembered how out of control I was with John Henry's death and wasn't sure how I would react with this one. I called Carol, and she said to come over. It was a beautiful day, the last day in July. When I got to Carol's house, it was 11:00 AM. She was working in her garden. I sat on her back steps and watched her. Ordinarily I would have been grateful for the distraction and joined in with her. But on this day, my grief was too strong, and I alternated from silence to uncontrollable sobbing. I wasn't crying as much for the loss of my mother, as I was for the loss of a relationship that I had never come to terms with, a woman who chose not to understand me, until it was too late. Some would say that it was just in time, that resolving differences are important, no matter when they arrive. I, on the other hand, knew differently, because of the years we had lost...the resentment I still felt. I sat on Carol's step all afternoon, until at 5:36 PM, I stood up and said, "I have to go...my mother is dead." Looking over my shoulder, I saw Shadow Man in the dark corner of Carol's garden. He nodded to me in kind. Carol was thrown by the calmness in my voice and thought that perhaps I was having a breakdown. She said, "Barbara, your brothers said they would call you. Jack said he would pick you up. I think you should wait until we hear from them."

I said, "Jack is out front (although I couldn't see him), and my brothers will be calling soon." I stood up from my perch and started walking into the house. I was heading for the front door with Carol on my heels trying to stop me, when Jack pulled up out front, as her phone began ringing. My mother died at exactly 5:36 that evening, ending a lifetime of suffering.

CHAPTER: 59

For years I was angry; what a wasted relationship my mother and I had had. It could have been so much more. I would never refer to it as abusive, just a lack of understanding of our differences. Who was at fault? I don't know. It was probably somewhere down the middle. The night she died I woke up in the middle of the night, screaming for Jack. When he asked me what was wrong, I said, "Mom is downstairs with her wheel chair; you need to help her up the stairs." I was wide-awake when I spoke these words to him, and although she was never at my home in a wheel chair, I was dead serious. He looked at me and said, "Barbara, your mother died today." I looked at him with the face of a helpless child and said in a sorrowful whisper, "Oh, no." I cried myself back to sleep.

The first year she was gone, I remember feeling like an orphan. Strange, I know, but it was an honest feeling just the same. Many times I found myself picking up the phone and dialing her number to see how she was. It wasn't till the disconnected recording came on that reality hit me. You never feel like you are an adult until the death of a parent, when that daughter/son title is severed completely. Once the wounds have been licked clean and the holes have been properly patched, it is time to move on. With the death of a parent comes a new found freedom as well as fears: the passing of the torch, the awkwardness of the shoes. For me, after the dust settled, what emerged was a strong woman ready, for the first time, to show the world who she really was. I was no longer afraid or doubted my character or abilities. This was with the help of Jack. I had decided from that day on, no one was going to misjudge me. Eventually, I realized that being misjudged was part of life. So instead, I opted not to care. In the long run, that type of attitude produced less anxiety and more focus as to what was really important in my life.

In the spring of 1995, I was asked, by a fellow teacher if I could teach her shy, nine year old daughter how to paint. I said yes, and in my garage, which was my painting studio, Acorn School of Art began.

We chose this name from the Celtic proverb, "mighty oaks from little acorns grow." It ended up being a befitting name, considering how far this little school would go. I found working with this young girl to be very rewarding. It brought me back to an age of innocence and wonder. She, in turn, opened up to me, showing me how intelligent and talented she was. After my success with her, another teacher asked me to help her dyslexic twin boys. They were age eleven at the time and were having a lot of difficulty expressing themselves verbally. She felt perhaps painting would unlock their dark world of language. Jeffery and Jason were polite and happy boys who were very dependent on each other for every aspect of their communication. Singularly they could not complete a sentence. Together they seemed to get each other's points across. It was fascinating to watch. I chose not to separate them, as I felt this codependency was much too strong. The results I got from these boys were amazing. What they lacked in verbal communication was not lost in comprehension. They understood fully what I was teaching them about drawing and painting. I taught them how to see an object, in the real world, for the first time; how the light falls across it and the names for those individual lights and their rules. I showed them how to measure the ratios of the objects, so that they could render them in proper proportion on their canvases. I taught them color theory and how to put it all together into a piece of art. The last thing I taught them was how to use their natural thinking as artists: to express themselves and get their ideas out there. If they felt a warm feeling about something...then choose a subject that reflects that and use warm light and color. If they felt dark about a subject...then follow the same theory with cools and deeper shades. It would turn out to be the missing piece to their puzzled existence in communication. We would talk about their work, and in turn I would show them my paintings. I spoke to them about why I was painting a particular subject. This exchange that we had not only increased their understanding of art at a very young age, but it also developed a respect between us as individuals and as artists looking for common ground. Through these new techniques, their verbal skills improved dramatically. They began to become independent of each other for speech. Soon word got out about the success I was having with them, and I was asked by others to teach their children as well. Most of these newer students were children who just needed to feel better about themselves. In time I had more students than I could handle. That is when Jack joined in and taught as well. A lot of referrals began to come from local child psychologists and occupational therapists. Eventually, they came from the public and private schools. The children we had were ones with verbal and reading issues, as well as difficulty with fine motor tasks. I taught each of them to the level of their needs and used art as the vehicle. Drawing and painting requires the use of verbal communication as well as hand to eye coordination. All were quite successful in the work they did with me, and as a result they did much better in school. Our life began to evolve around our students and their needs.

While art was what we taught, it shared a focus with giving kids a sense of accomplishment and dignity. I found that the key to teaching a child anything was encouraging self-respect and giving them a positive sense of autonomy. It was easy to give this to children. I often found myself simply saying, "Good job" and meaning it from the bottom of my heart. Mrs. Buras would have been proud of me. I had hoped my mother was watching as well. In time, our student base grew too large for our tiny studio. Jack gave me the courage to rent a space downtown on the ocean. It was a place we had been looking at for years. We had sat on a bench across the street several years earlier and looked at it when I was moving my photo business. Jack said to me, "Wouldn't that place be a nice spot for a business." Looking at the "FOR RENT" sign, I replied, "In all my wildest dreams, I could never afford that spot." Little did we know then that in a few years time we would be renting the back half of it. It was a small place, but with Jack taking over some of my older students and me still teaching at the studio at home, we were able to accommodate everyone's needs. I was still working at the preschool, and Lex was attending the after school program there.

Our life was very full and rewarding. We were in that small space for a year. When the space in front became available, we rented it and moved my students from the house to the larger space downtown. The studio was set in an old turn of the century building on the harbor in Marblehead. Being on a corner, two sides of the room were floor to ceiling windows. The light was warm and inviting. There was an array of objects in the center of the room for still life paintings, with easels encircling it. When the classes were in session, not only could the children see each other at all times, but anyone walking on the sidewalk could look in and see the cheerful atmosphere.

We were, in a sense, entertainment for the people walking by, and soon the success of our program was becoming well known. Happy children were seen going in and out of the small studio on Front Street. The neighborhood townies and the older men who occupied the bench out front approved greatly. We often heard them saying to passersby, "That is the best thing that has ever happened to this corner."

Our own needs got tangled in the mix of helping children, as well as consulting with their parents, teachers and sometimes psychologists. Lex was with me every day and often played in the neighborhood of the gallery after school. She was now in third grade. She became a "wharf rat," a term often used for children in the area. The other businesses around knew her well and would often participate in scavenger hunts I would set up for her. The ocean and all its wonders of tide pooling became her back yard. And although it was difficult at first, she learned to share me as an only child with many "siblings." It was at this time that we began to realize she had learning difficulties of her own. Always an active girl, I was not surprised when the school system told me she had attention issues. What did surprise me was the fact she had a hearing problem and auditory processing concerns. I immediately felt like the cobbler whose children didn't have shoes. I jumped full force into getting her services and hiring an advocate and having outside testing performed. It was a fine line I walked to make her take lessons from me, but she eventually did that also. We were in the throes of all this when, one day, the landlord told us he had to sell both units. He was a good man, an honest guy who cared about us greatly. Then he said," It is hard for me to do this, and I can't imagine this corner without the kids. Let's go to the bank and see what you can afford, and if I can, I will sell it to you for that."

At the time, we had approximately thirty students through the course of the week, as well as some on a waiting list. Once again, Jack stepped forward and gave me the courage I needed. We bought both units. In a month's time, our student base rose to eighty. Ten years later, it was in the hundreds. The success our students were having was astounding. With their newfound assurance, they were succeeding in school as well. We had integrated non-learning challenged children into the same classes as our learning challenged ones. We found the integration to be helpful on both ends. Because art is a subject that doesn't discriminate and with each child still working on his own individual projects, there was no way of telling who had learning difficulties and who didn't. It became a place where children grew and felt good about themselves. What they didn't know was that I was developing my self esteem right along with them, bringing truth to what Mrs. Buras had told me many years before, "One never grows up, one just keeps on growing." As the studio rounded its eighth year, and our students were getting older, so were their needs. We found assisting them in the college process a natural next step. We never doubted the children who were challenged. We included them in this process and found the right college that fit for them. As they learned about art and worked hard to learn very difficult lessons, the life lesson they learned from the art lesson was that there is direct connection between hard work and accomplishment, and it defined who they were. It clarified. Along with portfolios they made with us, we supplied them with scholarship applications and letters of recommendation. We took them on tours of various colleges and advised them about their choices. In eighteen years time, the amount given to our students for college scholarships exceeded five million dollars.

Lex was also growing as both an individual and a student. We were able to get her enrolled in the local charter school for fourth through eighth grades. It was the best decision I had made as a parent. They taught her to read and how to overcome her difficulties. She graduated from there with an award as the student who achieved the most in learning.

Acorn became a pulsating living thing. Its main components still stayed the same, and yet we allowed the needs of both the children and the school to grow. I taught the younger children to paint, and I told them stories, and we had fun. For the teenagers, I was there to hear all their woes and help them with relationships with their peers and parents. I was giving to people all that had been lost for me. Losing a parent is an opportunity to reflect on one's life. Despite all our grievances, my mother had done her job. I was the strong woman that I told her I was afraid I'd never be...and my life was full. My classroom had always been my sanctuary. As if I were "Dorothy" in Munchkinland, I felt protected. Children never judge; they trust that you are in control. That trust gave me a self-assurance that I was. It was a positive energy that worked well for everyone. At that moment it was the best place I could be.

Everyone always commented on the good I had done for their children. No matter how hard I tried, I could never explain the joy they were for me. Children face the world with a blind trust that it is a good place, free from harm and pain.

The first time this theory was put to a test for me was 9/11. It was Lex's first week of high school. Having forgotten her lunch that morning, Jack was at the school office dropping it off. I was getting ready for a ten-mile bike ride with my field easel on my back to paint a landscape. We didn't own a TV. We had made a conscious decision not to get one due to Lex's difficulty with reading. Instead we read together at night as a family. As I was pulling out of the driveway that morning, on my bike, Jack pulled up in the car and stopped me. "The World Trade Center was just hit by a plane!" he exclaimed.

"Oh my god!" was all I could say. We went to a neighbor's house to watch on her TV the images that would be etched forever in a nation's eyes.

When the towers fell and it was obvious that the planes were from Boston, I turned to Jack and said, "The public schools will probably have an early dismissal. We better get to the studio; I think the kids will show up and need us." It was the teenagers I was most concerned for. Even though their classes with us weren't scheduled until 7PM, I knew they would come to us directly from school. I was right. What I didn't expect was to be greeted by Shadow Man as I opened the door. I hadn't seen him in years. I knew immediately that this wasn't a good sign. Ignoring him I walked past and headed to the back door to open it and let the cool ocean breeze flow through the classroom like an old fashioned New England cleansing serum. I was a different person since I had last seen him. I was more confident and in control. I wanted him to see that side of me. Although something told me he knew...that he had been here all along.

The studio was packed with kids in an hour. The teenagers showed up first. Their questions were filled with fear and anguish. Some had known people who were on the planes and were upset. Jack and I went into crisis mode to comfort them, but how can you explain such a heinous crime? They kept asking why it had happened. Why would anyone do that?

I said, "Why would someone kill John Kennedy? It is part of history. That was Jack's history as a young man, and although I was just a small child, it was mine too. History is filled with war and acts of violence and is forever repeating itself. As odd as it seems, most wars are started over religion and beliefs. I'm not sure why something that is so powerful and good can turn people into such zealots. I guess when you live in a country that has only seen war, it just becomes a way of life. The world around you is filled with such pain that the promise of an afterlife that is filled with such peace and comfort becomes appealing. In their twisted minds, they are the victims.

The events that happened today are now your history, as well as ours. Everyone in this room right now will remember that you were here." Each one looked around as if to engrave in their minds the roll call of the room. After a bit, the questions subsided. The room had a somber air of quiet. Jack and I tried to reassure them that they were safe. When the dust settled, I said to them, "The little ones will be here in a short while. I am counting on you guys to work with us and help them deal with this. They will be looking to you as you looked to us. It is your time to shine. Let's get through this together." I knew that this simple act would give the teenagers the power they needed to feel in control again. I was saddened that they had to deal with such a grown-up issue. I knew that not only would they be "changed" by this, but also the entire country would never be the same. No longer would we be living in the blissful reality of a nation that was unaffected by the daily goings on overseas. The ocean could no longer protect us.

When the younger ones arrived, the setting they had all just come from had obvious affects on them. I didn't know what they had been told. The plan of action was to only answer questions as best we could when they arose. The first parent I met asked me not to let the subject be brought up in front of her child.

I turned to her and said, "Then maybe you should bring her home, because this is an avalanche I'm not sure I can hold back. These kids are frightened. It would be irresponsible for me to brush it under the rug and not try to comfort them." She decided to leave her child in my care. There were approximately ten teenagers in the studio that day. When half a dozen younger kids showed up, I turned to the teenagers and saw a look of care on their faces. No longer were their own feelings as important as their need to help and protect the younger ones.

The first class was filled with elementary school children. The energy was quiet, but no one asked anything. It was a presence I had never felt in a classroom before. It was an issue I had never had. I decided to play it by ear. They were curious as to why the older kids were there. I just said they were here to help me that day. The minute I said it, all the teenagers got up and chose a child to sit next to and work one on one with. My breath got caught in my throat at the sight. By the time the first class was over and the next was arriving, the teenagers were showing a confidence I had not seen in them before.

I told them the second class was with slightly older kids and where the questions would begin. "Let's stick to our plan, now that we will have middle school kids here." Within ten minutes it began. One girl, without saying a word, began to cry. Although I didn't learn this until later, her friend's father was on the plane, and she had never known someone who had died before. I went to her and put my arm around her. No one asked why she was crying; everyone in the class knew.

Another child said, "Barbara, are the bad guys going to come to Marblehead and get us?"

Before I could respond, Tyler, a big kid of 17 with a gentle heart, walked up to that little girl and put his arm around her. With a quiet yet firm voice he said, "You know I have lived here my whole life. My family goes back many generations, and I have never seen a bad guy here, and neither has anyone I know." He ended with, "Besides, Acorn is a magical place and always protected. We won't let anything happen to you." After he said these words, several of the teenagers cried quietly to themselves. Tyler was right. Acorn is a magical place, a place that creates more than just art. It molds peaceful souls.

As I thought it would, 9/11 did change us all as individuals and a nation. But as with many life-changing events, life still goes on. By the time Lex graduated from high school with honors, she was a healthy and poised woman, going off to college with a full scholarship. She was only a little more than two hours away, yet for me it felt like my heart had been torn from my chest.

Lex and I did have a time when things between us were not always perfect. When she was away at college, I began having health issues. To make matters worse, she was dating a man whom we did not approve of, a fact most women experience early in their lives, myself included. She couldn't understand why we disapproved of him. We didn't understand her love for a man who didn't believe in her as we did, a man who would insist she take care of him, because he was emotionally unable to. In that way, he reminded me of Bobby, and that scared me the most. We had caught him in several very large lies. They gave me reason to believe he was not who he claimed to be. With the help of her friends, we tried to explain these misgivings. She wouldn't listen to us and estranged herself from us, as well as from her friends. When Lex did come home, she fought with us, like a person dangling on the end of a rope. She was trying to hold on to that last bit of childhood she had. Yet at the same time, she was trying to be an adult. She was living a dual existence. I didn't want to repeat the issues with her that I had had with my mother, so I kept 50% of what I was feeling inside. That would be the trigger that was pulled on the gun that I hadn't realized had been pointed at my head. It was the third week of April, 2006, and I was doing what I always do that week. I was working in my garden. Ten years before, I had begun rebuilding the garden. It was Japanese, and it was in my back yard. A large area with a lot of potential, I viewed it as an enormous canvas, and my plantings were the paint. Textures of green with an occasional splattering of colored flowers spread from one end to the other. There was a hush to the place, not unlike a church. When anyone entered my garden, they were immediately transported to another time. It was as if they had entered Shangri-La. I needed a place like this in my life. Having done a lot and seen so much, it was important to me to settle down and create. I had had the career of an artist. I had shows

531

around the world including New York City. That life seemed artificial to me. When I realized it was no longer important to get that kind of notoriety, I pulled out from all the galleries. As I was comfortably sliding into my forties, I found my garden to be the outlet that pleased me the most.

I would sit out there every chance I got. It had overhanging trees, like great druids watching over their territory. These trees had been planted seventy years ago by my mother-in-law, the original owner, an avid gardener in her own right. I had never met her. She had died a few years after I was born. Somehow this garden always felt like hers, too. It would have been unfair for me to take all the credit. Her presence was always there. Like the secret garden in the story, I had merely awakened it.

With a pond tucked in a far corner, there was a waterfall and plantings. It was a place the birds drank and splashed for their daily bath. The sound of the water cascading over the rocks brought instant soothing to a hard day's work. It was hypnotic and wonderful. Wildlife was abundant in this spiritual existence. Squirrels ran rampant, followed by an occasional woodchuck or raccoon. Sometimes they would stop and look at me, surprised that I was sitting there. It was at those times I realized that this was their world, and I was fortunate to be allowed in it, just as the small doe had taught me so many years ago in Germany. Away from the hum of traffic and noise, I would often play soothing instrumental music as I weeded and planted. It always had to be instrumental. Somehow, adding words to this visual oasis changed it in a way that was no longer sacred.

On that particular day in April, I was weeding between the rocks of the dry riverbed and cleaning out the debris from under them. It was a task that started simple, and then slowly grew to a time consuming endeavor. Because of the scope of the area, I was resolved to the fact that it would take a week to accomplish. With every four foot section, I removed all the rocks, sifted them and cleared out any soil that had gathered there, then replaced the rocks as before. I enjoyed doing this chore, because it was brainless and allowed me to be in my own thoughts. Also, because of the bending and hauling, I was sure I would be left alone. No one would think to volunteer to help. After the first few days of working with the rocks, my fingers started to ache. Not being afraid of physical labor, I figured it was just from overuse. I had had arthritis for approximately thirty-five years. I learned early on that pain was just a fact of life. That is why, on that day in the garden, I ignored the familiar dialogue my joints were giving me and kept on working.

Then, towards the end of that week, I developed strange symptoms. The first thing was an odd, painful non-muscular sensation in my right glute. Although I had never usually talked to him over the years about the pains I had with my arthritis, one morning I spoke to Jack about this odd new feeling. Making light of it, I laughingly said to him, "I think my butt is broken."

Jack said quizzically, "What do you mean your butt is broken?" "Every time I sit or stand, I get a stabbing pain in the butt."

"I've always said you were a pain in the butt." he stated, smiling at me. As much as I hated to admit it, I loved when he teased me. I had always said it was because he had been an only child. Now he saw me as the little sister he never had. After our laughter subsided, we agreed it was most likely from all the work I was doing in the garden, and maybe I should leave the rocks as they were. But of course, I didn't. The thought of leaving a job half done was not something I could handle.

The pain in my backside lasted for days. I found that my joints, too, were revolting. I soon started walking with a limp again. The images of Germany and the difficulty I had had with my mobility came flooding back to me. I was hoping that this was not a recurrence. Jack and I were now thinking that it was another round of shingles, which I had had the year before. We waited for the infamous rash on my back, but it didn't come.

There was a part of me that was disappointed in myself. Prior to this, I had been very athletic, always riding my bike and lifting weights. Three days a week, I had attended a dance class. I had stopped weightlifting three years before, because of knee pain that I had summed up as age and my old joint pains. Since then, I had slowly cut all that activity from my life. In my head, I deserved this. I did it to myself. I had never been a person in denial before.

I wasn't completely without exercise. I did walk three times a week with my Aunt Tina. Usually, we walked around the Salem Common. It was a charming place that hadn't changed since I had lived near there as a child, with a bandstand in the center. It still had the clay path along the outer edge of it, with overhanging trees that dated back many years. Surrounding it was the familiar old Victorian wrought iron fence. It was still ornate and beautiful. The squirrels were so tame there, they would eat peanuts from your hands. An old fashion popcorn cart sat at its entrance. A true New England setting, it had been protected and preserved over the years.

I visited this place often. I had photographed the trees at odd angles for many of my paintings in years past. Every time I had painted these trees, the artwork would sell. It was the place that held fond memories of my childhood: the trees I had climbed, the park instructors who had always yelled at me for doing it. Tina and I had been walking the perimeter of the Common for about a year and had averaged a mile or two each time. But soon my feet started acting up, making that more and more difficult.

"Barb, I have noticed you have been limping the last few days. Are you ok?"

"My feet seem to be bothering me. My knees and hips aren't much better. But my feet really hurt. I must have some kind of virus, because I noticed I have some plantar warts developing on them. I am wondering if I am aggravating them with this walk. Let's stop; I need to sit for a minute."

"Is it your arthritis? When was the last time you saw a rheumatologist?"

"It has been a long time. But my insurance, that I pay a thousand dollars a month for, won't cover it. And rheumatologists like to see you on a regular basis, at two hundred dollars a visit."

"I think you need different insurance." "I know. I keep meaning to look into it. But it is all so confusing for me."

Shortly after this conversation, I woke up one morning, and I found my feet to be so swollen that my shoes no longer fit. That day I wore slippers to work and sat whenever I could. The next morning, I could only walk if necessary; they were throbbing too much. I began teaching from a chair. The day after, that my hands swelled as well. My ring size went from an eight to a ten. Gripping things was impossible. I began to drop everything I picked up. Always having had slender hands with long fingers, this was equally disturbing to me. My condition was getting worse. It had been three weeks since I had first felt the pain in my backside, and now it was all over my body. Both my hands and my feet were swollen to unbelievable sizes. I had resolved to wearing slippers all the time and sitting whenever I could. I had lost the palms of my hands. My hands became two balls at the ends of my arms. The toughest part was the pain and weakness. With every beat of my heart, I throbbed. I assumed the pain was from the swelling, but the weakness I didn't understand. Everything was happening so fast. It had only been a few weeks since my first symptom.

Work was almost impossible. With the lack of proper health care, I felt helpless. For those three weeks, for the first time in twenty-five years, my painting stopped. The odd thing was that by mid-day, the symptoms seemed to subside a little. I was able to keep the worst of it from all who knew me. Because I always got up early and we worked different shifts, I was even able to keep it from Jack.

Eventually one Sunday, Jack picked up on the seriousness of what was happening to me. He immediately became very concerned. He kept telling me I should see a doctor. I was insisting I was ok, making up one excuse after another as to what was happening to me. I was still feeling it was my own fault and I didn't want to admit that to him. I also knew that new insurance would have a waiting period to be covered. I found myself paralyzed with the thought of the paperwork, not to mention the information I might receive from a doctor. I was convinced it would eventually correct itself. I told little to Lex at first. When we did speak, it usually ended in an argument. I found myself jumping back and forth, between wanting to help her ease her pain about this relationship she refused to admit was bad and wanting to yell at her; because I was in so much physical pain, I was not of my right mind. As a mother, I wanted to comfort her. As a fellow woman who had been there, I wanted to warn her. But she didn't want my comforting or my warnings. Instead, she would argue with us about the tumultuous relationship between us and her boyfriend. She was convinced that was the root of the problem. It was an all too familiar picture I was seeing on the wall of my own history. I hated to do it, but I had to turn it off in my head and tackle the battle I was dealing with at home, the war my body was now raging.

After canceling our daily walks, it was Aunt Tina who stepped up to the plate. Behind my back she made an appointment with a podiatrist and paid for it in full. I will never forget that simple act of kindness. When I needed a mother, she was there, despite the fact that I was now forty-five.

By the time I went to the podiatrist a week later, my elbows, shoulders, ankles, knees, and hips were involved. Sleeping became impossible. Every pressure point and nerve ending on my body was cranked on high.

The morning the appointment finally arrived, I was having a particularly bad day. To walk, I needed to use John Henry's old cane. Sitting in the low chairs of the office, I suffered in silence. When it was my turn to be examined, it took me several minutes to stand. I was embarrassed in this cramped office, with all the eyes on me. The doctor stood in the doorway and watched me struggle to my feet and compose myself. As I made my way slowly to the examining room, he acted concerned and asked me how long I had been in this condition. When I told him three weeks, he looked shocked and without hesitation he said, "You need to see a rheumatologist; I believe you may have a systemic joint disease. This can't be ignored." The room began to spin for me. Grabbing the door jamb, I tried to steady myself. Disease, what did he mean, disease? The realizations of my denial hit me like a wave cresting the top of my head. My heart started to beat faster and breathing became difficult.

"I do have arthritis, could it be that?" "I think it is something more. You need to get this checked out right away."

After checking the warts on my feet, he said he didn't think he should touch them. He was very concerned for me and spoke to me slowly, as he looked me directly in the eye. It was as if we didn't share the same language. "Why is he acting this way?" was all that I allowed to go through my head. In that same slow and concerned voice, he said he was afraid if he treated my feet, there was a chance of possible infection, because of my edema. He called a local rheumatologist and made me an appointment. Because he was so booked, the rheumatologist couldn't see me for another week.

By the time that day arrived, I was beside myself. Alone with my thoughts, I wondered what it all meant. I had been afraid to look anything up online all week. I wasn't ready for the information. In the mornings, I could no longer do simple daily routines. Jack now washed and dressed me. Opening a jar or turning a doorknob became an impossible task. My motor skills reverted to those of a toddler.

Nighttime was the worst. It felt like all the demons came out at night. The setting sun and impending nightfall were like a bell tolling, waiting for my torture to begin. At eleven o'clock, I would begin to get ready for bed. I waited until then, so I could fool myself into thinking the night was shorter. Eventually, that time would be pushed back to twelve or 1:00 AM, depending on how tired Jack was. Many nights, he would wait up with me. We never talked about it. He never complained, but I knew he was exhausted. The more I became dependent on him, the more I feared what would happen to me, if I were to lose him. As it was, I could no longer sleep with him, it would hurt too much to do so. I took over Lex's old room. The bed in there also had a better mattress. This was the room that had been John Henry's bedroom when Jack and I got married. When it became Lex's room, it was filled with all the things that kids love: favorite stuffed animals and wishing dust. It was the first time a little girl had been in the house, and the room took on a different life. As she grew and became a teenager, always a creative child, I let her cover the walls with magazine cut outs of stars. At first it started out to be the usual idol photos, but then it grew to be something more. She began to cut out photos of anyone that struck her fancy: pretty girls, adorable children and, of course, cute boys. They were all pictures of people interacting in some sort of movement. As she spent hours cutting and pasting this world she was creating, I saw it as a magnificent work of creative outpouring. It took her three years to complete this wonderful piece of art; her collage brought the images together in an interactive visual symphony on her wall. As a child, she had never liked being alone. I think she was comforted by this illustrated display of a random crowd. By the time she left for college, there were thousands of pairs of eyes staring at her. They had become her friends and bade her farewell. She no longer needed them. The summer before she left, she took it all down and painted the room a warm, inviting yellow.

Now it was my room. Isolated and lonely, I never thought I would wish to see those thousands pairs of eyes again. That room had a rich history. It was filled for so many years with laughing and giggling. But now it was a place I retreated to every night to face my pain alone.

Even with Jack helping me, it would take us approximately fifteen to twenty minutes to remove my clothes and get me ready for bed. Putting my pajamas on was like trying to dress a baby the size of a full-grown woman. A simple sock created a painstaking endeavor that would bring tears to my eyes. I had to give up certain things, as well. I could no longer wear a nightgown, because I would get tangled in it. For a cover, I could only have a sheet. A blanket was too heavy for me to lift, caging me like a mouse in a trap. By the time the entire ordeal was over, I was as exhausted as if I had just run a marathon. Jack wasn't far behind me. We learned quickly what worked and what didn't. Positioning each of my five pillows to relieve as many pressure points as possible took us awhile to learn. When we realized that a travel pillow around my neck, as I lay on top of a curved pillow, suppressed some of the pain in my shoulder, we rejoiced together. It was one of our all too few triumphs, during those early weeks. Once I was settled, Jack would sit in a chair next to my bed, until I fell asleep. We never talked at these times. We secretly both knew we were too vulnerable to discuss it: what it all meant... what the future would be. Alone in my thoughts, I felt guilt. First, he had had to take care of his elderly father, then my dying mother, and now me. This could not be what this wonderful and talented man's life was meant to be. Why would God be so cruel to him? Alone in his thoughts, he silently prayed that he would not lose me. In the middle of the night, I would wake up alone and scared. That first week, Shadow Man came back to me like an old friend. I spoke these words to him as he sat across the room at Lex's desk: "Shadow Man, what is happening to me? Why does life always have to be so difficult? I feel, for some reason, I have been put in this situation, because I need to slow down and reflect. Is this true? Please answer me and tell me what it all means." He sat there with his legs crossed and his arms draped over his knees. Leaning forward so as to hear me more clearly, he reminded me of a nursery school teacher, poised and relaxed, as her charges spoke of their misgivings. It was a posture that was familiar to me. Unlike the teacher in me, he didn't respond. Eventually, I fell back to sleep.

My sleep those first weeks, if you want to call it that, would last for 1 1/2 hours, if I was lucky. When my luck ran out, it would be twenty minutes. My REM sleep ceased at this point and wouldn't return for two years. The deepest I could go was to doze. Other than Shadow Man, my only companion through that misery was my cat. Her name was Boogie. Boogie sensed that I was ill, and from that time on, she slept at the head of my bed. We were like two cats taking a nap together, except mine was filled with anguish. On several occasions, when I did wake, I found myself alone and scared and up against a corner of the wall. I was trapped in my bed and could no longer ignore my demons. After a few nights like that, I began sleeping at the foot of the bed instead. In that position, I could look out the window and still feel a part of the world. Shadow Man remained where he was, across the room. I spoke to him every night. I often talked of the history that we shared. He had been in my life longer than anyone, including my parents. He was always there at my time of most need. He was good in that way. In all those years, I had never seen his face. A mere outline of protection was how I viewed him now, something I could rely on to always be there for me. Once the shadowy demon of my childhood, he now held the title of friend.

After a short time of lying down, I couldn't take the aching any longer. It felt as if every joint and muscle in my body was trying to hold itself afloat in mid air on its own. My body couldn't relax, no matter how hard I tried. In simple terms, I was being tortured. Through trial and error, I learned to sit up alone. I would ask Shadow Man to help me, but he just sat there. I began running ideas by him, in hopes of a response.

"Shadow Man, if I can lift my legs over my head and with my own weight bring them back down to the bed, I think I can bring the upper half of my body to a sitting position. I just have to remove the covers with my feet first." Although he did not speak, I could feel his questions and answered them appropriately." I don't know what I will do after that. When I am sitting, I will figure it out. I know it is going to hurt, but being in one position hurts worse. I need to move around." Was it him questioning me or was that voice in my head? I could no longer tell; the pain was taking over my brain. In one awkward yet swift motion, I did it. The pain shot through my body like a fiery poker. I let out a scream in the darkness that landed on sleeping ears. Next to my bed was a heavy treadmill. I grabbed on to it to steady myself. "If I can swing my legs over the side of the bed, I can use this treadmill to help me stand." Looking in his direction for Shadow Man's approval was to no avail. He didn't move. Grabbing on to the treadmill, I lifted myself to a standing position. That first step onto the floor sent radiating pain through my legs. Another scream escaped my lips. Again, there was no response.

"What do you mean, what am I going to do now? I am going to walk. I need to move my legs, just like when I was little. Do you remember Shadow Man? Every night, you watched me pace the room." Tina had bought me a walker a few days before. It sat in the corner like a distant beacon on a dark sea. Somehow I had to wade my heavy legs over to it. "Stop antagonizing me! I know I should have left it near the bed! I just wasn't ready to admit I needed it." Sliding one foot at a time across the floor with my arms raised in the air, I looked like a tight rope walker, uncertain of the distance below me. It took me an agonizing solid five minutes to get a mere ten feet. Grabbing the handles of the walker, I couldn't help but let out a "YES!" Turning to Shadow Man, I said, "See, I told you I could do it. Never underestimate me." Pushing the walker ahead of me, I exited the door to the hallway, to freedom. It was at this time I began my nightly ritual of walking the hall. I couldn't lift my feet, so my walking was more like shuffling. Twenty minutes walking, twenty minutes sitting in a raised chair... if I were lucky, I dozed when I sat. I repeated this mantra of events all night long, until dawn.

When the day finally arrived for me to see the rheumatologist, I felt hopeful. Someone would finally help me escape from this hell I was in. After waiting in his office for over an hour in chairs that were too low to sit on, I realized how wrong I was. His office was outdated. Faded posters of Monet's lilies hung in cheap metal frames. The color of the room was a pasty array of dusty mauve and mint green. When I entered the examining room, it, too, looked like a throwback to another time, with antiquated scales and examining tables that still used a crank to adjust. I had hoped his medicine, unlike his office, had kept up more with the current times.

He was an arrogant man of about fifty, tall and thin with stark white hair and an air of distraction on his face. He droned on for an hour, asking me questions in a monotone voice, not showing any form of feeling. He pressed my joints in certain places, and after seeing the nodules growing on my knuckles and elbows he clinically diagnosed me with rheumatoid arthritis. I thought, "Tell me something I don't know."

He said it was systemic. He called it an autoimmune disease. All I heard was "cripple." In my head I wondered if I would ever be able to paint again. I thought of Renoir and the difficulty he had had with this disease. And although I had never been fond of his work, it was all I had to hold on to. I was immediately put on prednisone, vitamins and a very strong prescription strength Advil. He also put me in arm braces to protect my wrists. He asked to see me in another week.

When I went back to him, I was worse. The arrogant questions persisted. He kept asking me to rate my pain on a scale of one to ten. With it elevating every time I saw him, this was a difficult task for me. If the previous week was ten, then the next week was a twelve. He became impatient with me and would roll his eyes. I didn't fit neatly in the "little box" of rules he expected of his patients. For some reason, he couldn't accept the concept that a patient could get worse with time, not better. All he would do would be to change my meds again and ask to see me in another week, as my medical bills began to mount. Every time I left his office, I felt beaten and worse than when I had arrived. This scenario went on for months.

With all the jargon I was hearing from this doctor, I no longer trusted my ears alone. I asked Jack to sit in on my exams. This doctor didn't seem to like that idea, but because of my heightened state of pain, all I heard was "blah, blah, blah," not unlike when I would talk to an auto mechanic. Jack, also being who he was, would never have considered me going through this without him. He knew I was only hearing half of what was being said. My brain kept shutting down, when it could no longer accept the information. On one particular day, when Jack couldn't find a parking space in the lot, he had to wait outside. The doctor, noticing that he wasn't there, asked me in a condescending voice, "Where is your bodyguard?" He constantly belittled me, trying his hardest to look superior. He infuriated me week after week, until one day, I made a snide remark to remind him that he worked for me. Our doctor-patient relationship went from bad to worse. I wanted to change doctors, but I couldn't. He was the only rheumatologist in a twenty mile radius who was taking patients. The next closest place would have been to go into Boston. Although I had wanted to do this right from the start, I felt we couldn't afford it; with our tight schedule at work, that would mean canceling some classes. To me, that was a last resort.

This doctor changed my dosage of meds several times. He took me off the Advil, put me on Plaquenil and once again increased the prednisone. Prednisone is a steroid that has many side effects, including kidney damage. I found when I was taking 20mg twice a day that it caused me to bruise terribly. But worse than that, it made me weepy, an aspect of my personality I was not used to. The weepiness was never for my own predicament. I often cried for others. Sometimes it would be as obvious as the morning news, when they were announcing the names of soldiers killed in the war or as silly as a sappy TV commercial. Working with the children caught me emotionally by surprise as well. If a student were doing especially well with his work and I realized he was advancing, I would have to leave the room. My pride for him would well up in my eyes. My empathy "switch" was stuck in the on position, and I couldn't adjust it.

The Plaquenil didn't seem to have an effect. When I inquired about it, he said it would take several months to get into my body. I had to be patient.

Patience...fortunately, it was the one aspect of my personality I was blessed with. For the past twenty odd years I had worked with children, it was the first thing a new parent always commented on: my patience in allowing children to be who they truly were. I knew in my heart I was going to have to call on this facet of my personality as much as I could.

Lex was home with us that first summer. We argued a lot, which was very out of character for our twenty-one year history. Before that, parents would ask me my secret for having such a good relationship with her. I usually told them it was because she was naturally a good kid. At this time though, most of our arguments were about her living with her boyfriend, who now was still not able to function without her. As a person who had little choice of dependency, I couldn't shake my misgivings about that character flaw in him. I kept thinking about the three miscarriages I had had to have Lex. I thought about the nine months I had spent in bed during my pregnancy to not lose her. And now I was losing her to this person that she had to mother. I expected better things for her in life. As a mother, I had insisted on it. As her mother, I also saw the stress on her face from the responsibility. It was for this reason I never asked anything of her in the form of help, when she came home that summer. I was afraid if she realized all she was doing for him and not for me, she would feel awful about herself. Poor self-esteem is the last thing a parent wants for her child. And under the circumstances, her self-esteem would be what I was hoping would eventually get her out of her current situation. I kept thinking of how I had done the same thing, when I had been her age. These thoughts would not escape me. I was hoping she had the strength to see she deserved more.

Despite my trying to keep the true scope of my illness from her, she did help me, when she saw I needed it. Not one to talk to about weaknesses, hers as well as mine, she often took my arm when we were walking outside and helped me with other things that I needed. She did this in silence. She didn't know about my nighttime rituals; at that point it wasn't necessary. With her bedroom having been moved to the first floor, it was easy. Eventually the stress between us was too much for both us. September came and she went back to school. I wouldn't see or talk to her again for almost a year. My emails and messages went unanswered. Once a month, I sent her money. I was grateful she had a full scholarship. At least I didn't need to worry about tuition.

The children became my only source of relief. Watching their jovial antics and their lust for life kept me grounded. My studio classroom had always been a refuge for me. We would relate funny stories about our day, and they would tell me about their hopes and dreams. As if I were Dorothy in Munchkinland I felt protected. Children never judge; they trust that you are in control. That trust gave me a confidence that I was. It was a positive energy that worked well for everyone. At that moment, it was the best place I could be.

Everyone had always commented on the good I had done for them. No matter how hard I tried I could never explain the help they were for me, in this time of great stress. Children face the world with a blind trust that it is a good place, free of harm and pain; they are a medicine to adults, a tonic that we haven't properly explored.

My mornings were difficult and filled with a teetering scale, balancing frustration and determination. The afternoons brought me eases of the symptoms but never completely. My nights were hell. That is when all my emotional weaknesses would emerge. I cried a lot; most of the time it was for the predicament I was putting Jack through. I had resolved myself to the fact that I was going to live a life of torture. I just didn't want to put him through it. That is why I never woke him at night, when I was hurting. He suddenly was doing all the household things I had so easily done, adding to all the things he had had to do to take care of me.

When the afternoon would hit and I could reason again with my own thoughts, I found a new strength. I began to develop a stubbornness I didn't realize I had. The one thing I refused to give up was teaching. I was afraid to. I felt that if I gave in to this completely, it would consume me, and I would never get back. In the distance of my mind, I saw this as a great dark hole with no way out. The kids became helpful. If I needed something picked up off the floor, several would come to my rescue at once. They were wonderful. They allowed me to be who I was now. It brought out the best in them. It proved to me that all children are born with an inherent instinct to be good and caring. Because my classes consisted of mixed age groups, suddenly the older ones were helping the younger ones. The teenagers began to arrive early for their classes. Jumping in, they would sometimes sit with the younger kids and give them one on one attention. As much as I had felt we were always a community there, never had it shown itself more evident than during those years. They rallied together, bringing out the best of humanity. These were the things I thought about at night and took comfort in. I learned to supply myself with what I needed at night. I had a heating pillow I used on my shoulders. There was a microwave in my room that I used to prepare it, three times in the course of the night. When I could no longer lie down, I would walk the hall. When I could no longer walk, I would sit with the walker and stack it with pillows to try and rest my head on it. When even that didn't work and I could no longer sit, I did the most incredible thing. I learned to sleep standing supported between my walker and the door jam. A whimper was always just rising to the top of my throat. Yet I would never let it out. I had approximately ten to fifteen minutes, before my body would be too heavy, and I would falter. Shadow Man, ever present with me now, was always there when I opened my eyes. I never could go back to bed. That was something I couldn't do without the help of Jack. Once I was up, I was up. In total, I "slept," if I was lucky, three hours a night. It was an issue that was concerning everyone, an issue that impeded my healing process. It was late at night, during this ritual, that I first started thinking about adversity and the human spirit. I had to look as deep as I could to find mine. It was like rummaging through a cereal box as a child, only to pull up a cheap, plastic toy.

"Shadow Man, do you think I am being punished? Is this a trial of sorts that I am being put through? Am I taking a test? How will I know if I pass, and what do I gain if I do? What does this all mean? Only you really know what I am going through, and I know only you have the answers. All I have ever wanted in life, was to do a good job." Once again he said nothing, leaving me to fend for myself.

Fortunately, along with patience, I was also blessed with the ability to be content with being alone. Isolated in my own thoughts was often my playground as a child, and now it was this facility that I was calling on to get me through.

I kept thinking of the phrase, "Everyone dies alone." Although I knew I wasn't dying, I felt it could also be stated, "Everyone suffers alone." My thoughts went to my mother many times. A part of me ached that she was no longer there to comfort me. Another part of me was glad she hadn't lived to see this. She and I had never really gotten along, yet for some reason, when I was in pain, it was the child in me that would cry for her. I thought to myself, "Only I can make this work." It would be my decision if I gave into this or not. I knew that my physical mobility was limited, and there was not much I could do about that. What I did have full control over was my spirit, a part of the soul that I witnessed in my mother, when she was faced with such personal torment. It was her final lesson to me in a class I hadn't realized I was attending. All things happen for a reason, and now I knew why.

These thoughts made me stronger. I had a choice. I could think of things such as this and feel better about them, or I could be swallowed up by my own despair. Nothing could take my will to beat this, if I chose to fight. If you think you can do something, then you can. I was also practical. I knew that my movements needed help. Arthritic aids, for lack of a better word, would help me lead a semi-normal life again. I craved my independence back. The next day, I told Jack that I needed to handicap the house and to buy some tools to help me.

CHAPTER: 60

We purchased all sorts of gadgets: ones that opened jars, another that helped me put on my socks, rails in the bathroom, an aid to help me buckle my seat belt (as a passenger, since I could no longer drive), shoelaces that were elastic, a grabber to pick things up off the floor, and my all time favorite, a back scratcher that Lex won for me at the Willows Amusement Park.

I began trying to dress myself in the morning. I didn't shower myself, I knew better; I waited for Jack to help me with that at night. My bathroom rituals were similar. In the mornings, when the pain was at its worst, he had to help me with that as well. With the meds I was on, my digestive system was also out of whack.

While Jack was asleep, at around 5:00 AM in what still felt like night, I would start. I learned quickly that there had to be a system to dressing, or I couldn't do it. First, having laid my clothes out the night before, I would use my grabber to pick them up and separate them on the bed. The grabber became an awkward extension of my arm. I bought some bras that clasped in the front. I no longer had the ability to put my arms behind my back or the strength to clasp the old ones in front and then rotate them. I was shocked that my arms could no longer reach behind me. To put the new bras on, I had to bend at the waist, with my arms in the holes of the straps. Slowly standing upright with my arms lifted as high over my head as I could, the straps would slide down my back and land on my shoulders. Unfortunately, I would sometimes get stuck in this position and looked like a prisoner shackled in the gallows. It would take me another ten to fifteen minutes to untangle myself. If I couldn't, I had to wake Jack, who would look up at me and laugh at the sight. It made me laugh as well, even in the midst of it all. Laughter was beginning to be the first drug that was working in my favor. My underwear was just as difficult. I had to buy sizes that were too big for me. Placing them on the floor with my grabber, I would use the same tool to carefully try and separate the leg holes on the floor, just below my feet. Stepping into them gingerly, I would then use the grabber to slowly raise one side to, hopefully, my knees. One day I noticed that while doing this, my face made contorted gestures. Usually my tongue was sticking out in determination. That, too, made me laugh. I could never do this task in one try; it usually took about four or five. The tricky part was retrieving the other side without then losing the first and having to start all over again. Next were my shorts. That was done in the same fashion as my underwear. My shoes were easy, if my feet weren't swollen. But that was rare. Jack usually had to help me with those. Until I found the elastic ties, he had to tie them too. The funniest was my shirt. Since it was summer, I wore t-shirts. As with my bra, I couldn't help getting tangled in one. I would then shuffle into

Jack's room again, looking like a mummy, trying to unravel from my confines with only my eyes showing.

"Barb, why don't you just let me dress you? This looks ridiculous and painful."

"NO! I want to do it myself."

"But you never seem to be able to. You always show up in here twisted, contorted, and shackled."

"But someday I will be able to. If I just give in, what do I have to look forward to?" Somehow this felt like independence for me, a state I grabbed on to, no matter how small the victory.

I had been seeing the rheumatologist for a year now. The Plaquenil didn't seem to be helping much. It was true that I had slight improvement. Some days were better than others. But when it was bad, it was really bad.

One night I did the impossible. I tried to roll over in my sleep. The result was a loud snap coming from my right elbow. Having broken at least six bones in my life, I knew the feeling. It was 3:00 AM, and I struggled with the thought of waking Jack. I had to. It was too much pain for me to bear. Passing Shadow Man as I exited my room, I said, "What are you looking at? Some help you are!" With tears streaming down my face, I went to Jack. I was amazed with the swiftness he wakened and was on his feet. "What's wrong ...what's wrong?" was all he kept saying.

Through my sobs, I told him, "I think I broke my arm."

"How did you do that; did you fall?" he said in a panic.

"No," I said, "I just rolled over." My crying became more intense. Once the flood gates opened, there was no stopping it.

"Barb, I don't think you can break your arm rolling over." When he realized I hadn't fallen, he took a logical stance towards the situation. After all, one of us had to have a level head.

I, on the other hand, was on the verge of hysteria. "But, Jack, I can't rotate my arm!" I began to hyperventilate. The breathing thing was weird. I found myself doing the Lamaze method of childbirth, whenever the situation was too much for me. Unlike in childbirth, in this case, it only made things worse.

Jack got up and sat with me. He kept asking if he should take me to the emergency room. Having broken my elbow at the age of forty and remembering the awful experience I had had there, I said, "No, just sit with me." Every once in awhile, he would forget and reach to rub my back. Even that was no good. A week before that, the hair follicles on my whole body had become sensitive. I was no longer able to be touched. At one point, I looked him in the face with such despair, he asked me what I was thinking. I stated in a childlike voice through my tears, "I want my Mom." With a look of pure love, he reached over and gently touched his pinky finger to mine. No words were necessary.

This pain was different from what I had experienced so far. It was as if a knife had lodged in the joint of my elbow, with another one halfway up my arm into the bicep. My arm was now fixed in a bent position, with my hand resting on my chest. I used my other hand to support it, but even that started to ache after awhile, being locked in one position. There was nothing I could do. I started to drift away to a place I had never been before. My mind disconnected itself from my body, and I was floating. I started rocking back and forth and humming softly to myself.

Without any pain-killing meds, leaving my body behind was the only recourse I had. We did not laugh that night. Jack just sat with me until dawn. The next day was a Saturday. Jack called the doctor to see what we should do. The pain was still as intense, and I found myself "going inside" more and more. "Going inside" was what I now referred to as a type of meditation, although in reality it appeared to look like a mild shock. Concerned that I was in shock, Jack was constantly trying to pull me back into the real world, to talk to me. He was always able to do it, but the real world would hurt too much, and soon I was gone again.

He begged to take me to the hospital. With already $8000 in medical debt, I was insistent that all I needed was a pain killer. I figured the emergency room with x-rays would be another $2000 we couldn't afford. I realized that I had to do something about the insurance. I could no longer be afraid. I had to face this reality. Jack sat on the couch, as I continued to rock and hum, waiting by the phone to get word from my rheumatologist, to tell us what we should do. But the doctor never called back.

Saturday turned into Saturday night. My arms were now fixed in an upward position against my chest. My hands were inadvertently clenched into fists. My body's motor skills were reverting back to infancy. I no longer thought the arm was broken; now I feared it would just stay that way. We had tried to reach the doctor so many times that the answering service knew our voices before we stated our problem. All they kept telling us was that the doctor had been informed. They no longer listened to our pleas for help. Jack still wanted to take me to the hospital, but I held my ground. I always assumed the doctor would call. At 1:00AM Sunday morning, I had to face the fact that he wasn't going to, and I had to go to bed. It had been two days since either of us had slept. Still in fits of pain, I laid in bed while Jack read me a book in hopes that I would be calmed and fall asleep. It was John Henry's book he had loved so much: "Three Men in a Boat, To Say Nothing of the Dog." The words brought me back to our nightly reading sessions, a time in our lives that was so busy, yet that night I longed to have those days back. His voice soothed me, and we both fell asleep.

On Sunday, the pain began to subside a little. I questioned whether I was just getting used to it and wondered if this was what my life would be like till the end. I was certain, at that point, I would die. I was beginning to be fearful that I wouldn't. Although I still couldn't rotate my arm, I was able to stabilize it with a sling Jack had bought the day before.

On Monday, I was furious. We had called the doctor at least a dozen times the entire weekend, and he never returned our calls. I felt this man had done nothing for me in the course of the past year, and this was intolerable. I decided to get a different doctor. Jack's friend, David, had been trying to get me to call the Brigham and Women's hospital in Boston for months. I was afraid I couldn't afford such a prestigious place. I now realized I didn't have a choice. I needed a doctor who cared.

Monday, despite the pain, I wrapped my arm and went to the studio to teach. Working that day was, as you can imagine, impossible. I was merely an entity in a chair, and the kids tried to cheer me up. Jack had long since hired extra staff to help me. I was there in reality but not in spirit. Jack didn't argue with me about going to work. He felt it was better that I was with someone all day. My spirits became top priority, to him since he couldn't help me medically. He knew my years of teaching would kick in, and I would be able to control my feelings in front of the children. It was difficult, but I did the best I could. A few parents called me at home later that night to see if I was ok and if there were anything they could do. It was a warming feeling to have them reach out to me like that.

On Tuesday, I had an appointment with the doctor who had left me stranded. My first question was obvious.

"Did you get any of my messages this past weekend?" "Yes, I did. Did you get the Darvocet I called in for you?" "I never heard back from you; how was I suppose to know you called anything in?" "My nurse was supposed to have called you."

"Well she didn't, and quite frankly, when I call my doctor in an emergency, I don't wish to speak to a nurse." He still didn't show empathy to the situation, only a defensive attitude. I then added, "I don't think this pain and all these weird symptoms I am having is rheumatoid arthritis. I have been doing some research, and I want to be tested for lupus."

"So now you have a medical degree?" "No, but I am smart enough to know that what you are giving me isn't working."

He said, "The test is very expensive, and why don't we start with x-rays." I was defeated. Without his ok, I couldn't get the test.

When I got home, I called a friend with MS. Telling him about all that I had been through, I asked him if he knew of any organization that I might turn to for financial aid, so I could get the test. He told me about an insurance person he felt might help. It was the most important phone call I made. Within a week, I had better insurance.

I couldn't believe how easy it was. But to do it required a balancing act. Jack was now old enough for SSI and went that route; Lex got picked up by her father. The final outcome was that I was spending $500 less per month and was now fully covered. I immediately called the doctor and demanded the test for lupus, as well as my medical records. Making an appointment with a new rheumatologist at Brigham and Women's, I felt my first real sense of control over my health and future.

A few months later, it was all over the news that the insurance company I had belonged to was involved in a large class action suit. The suit alleged overcharges and little coverage. I was too overwhelmed with my present situation to get involved.

Summer hit again with a vengeance. I found the heat to be unbearable for me, even when everyone else was ok. For some reason, my body temperature would skyrocket, and I couldn't stop it. Having had a partial hysterectomy at forty-one, I was certain it wasn't hot flashes. Besides, it didn't happen unless I was at work, which is where I expended the most energy. I believe part of it was also nerves. It was embarrassing to have the parents of my students seeing my physical downfall. To reassure them, I had to tell them what was happening to me and that I would soon be seeing a new doctor.

Although I had my bad days, I was beginning to have good ones as well. Dressing became easier. Sometimes I had the strength to be able to pick up a dish. Washing dishes became oddly comforting. The warm water on my hands was relaxing. But usually on my good days, I would overdo it, and the next day would be bad again. Being an active person by nature, it was hard for me to find a balance.

Before I had become ill, every morning I had brought Jack his coffee; placing it by the bed its aroma was always the first thing that woke him. It was a ritual we had practiced for ten years. For the past year, I had been unable to do this, because the coffee pot was downstairs in the kitchen. One night, at 3:00 AM, frustrated and determined, I decided I could do it, if I put my mind to it. Carefully and quietly making my way to the stairs, I began my slow descent, one step at a time. We had fourteen stairs in our house. Half way down, I realized I was in trouble. The strength in my legs left me. My feet became as heavy as twenty-pound bags of cement. With no way up and no way down, I became frightened. I didn't know what to do. I wanted to sit but that was impossible. I knew in ten minutes my legs were going to give way and I would fall. Although I was perfectly quiet, Jack somehow knew I was in trouble. Calling out in the night, he shouted, "BARB, WHERE ARE YOU?"

"I'm on the stairs," I called back, "I can't get down."

Running to my aid he scolded me. Wrapping one of my arms around his shoulder and supporting my back with his arm, he helped me back up and to the den. Sitting next to me in his nakedness, he told me he had been dreaming. When he called to me in the midst of his dream, I had been missing. He was searching for me in a cloud of mist and rain, but he couldn't find me. If he hadn't had a nightmare, he never would have heard me. The whole situation made me pause and reflect. How is it he had had that dream at a time I was most vulnerable? I was convinced there had to be a power stronger than us. Then I saw Shadow Man emerge from Jack's bedroom down the hall. He stood there quietly and acknowledged me. That night Jack brought the coffee pot upstairs.

When summer arrived, JM came to take Lex's place as a teacher in our summer camp. Lex was having difficulty dealing with my illness and the arguments about her boyfriend, so she stayed away. Having had to watch a mother die of breast cancer when I was young, I understood what she was feeling. As a mother who was now sick, I didn't want it to cause her such anguish. With the stress I was feeling for the situation Lex was in, I also knew it was best for me. JM's mother was Canadian and had named him JeanMarc, but everyone called him JM. He had been a friend of Lex's since childhood. He had been a student of ours for the same amount of time. He was more than that. To me, he was a son. He had always done what a son should do. Over the years, when my grass needed cutting, he would show up and do it. If he were at our house on trash night, he took it out for us. When he was heartsick over a girl, it was me he came to for advice. An intellectual, he was often a contributor to the art discussions that Jack and I shared. He had a wonderful mother and father, and I would forever be grateful to them for sharing him with us. It takes a very secure relationship with your child to be able to do this without jealousies. It was yet another testimony to their parenting skills.

JM was an amazing person. He could draw, paint, act, dance, and he got great grades in school, not to mention, he could build or put together anything he set his mind to. Freshman year of high school, he put a floor in our attic. Before that, there hadn't been one. Balancing on the rafters with a nail gun, he was in his element. He was a boy with an engineer's mind and an artist's heart. I called him my renaissance man. His biggest problem was that he did everything so well, he was unsure of which direction to take for college. He ended up going to the University of British Columbia in Vancouver, Canada, 4000 miles away. I was heartbroken.

That summer, like Lex, he was finishing his sophomore year. We kept in touch through email the whole while he was away. He understood what my needs were. It killed me to see the concern on his face, when he would come home and visit on break. I would do my best to reassure him. I would tell him what my next plan of action was concerning my health, and he would amaze me by having already done the research on my behalf. Adding that to the school work he had been doing, it was then I realized he loved me as much as I did him. It was another wonderful moment in my life stirred into the soup of my despair.

The first thing JM did when he got home was to make sure my entire house was safe. He installed more railings and raised more seats for me. He even spent an entire day building a platform for my garden rocker so that I could sit. He knew the garden was the most important place in the house for me. He knew it was where my spirit lived. He worked it for me all summer, weeding and cutting the lawn. Watching him made me want to cry. I wanted to be down on my knees with him in the dirt. It was difficult for me to sit there and not be able to work the soil. He adjusted doorknobs to make it easier for me to turn them. He placed an extra step out the back door. Then he put a lock on our front door, because he felt it was time we had one.

The best part about JM was his spirit and constant joking around. Whenever we were together, we would laugh with humor befitting of children in middle school and were proud of it. It was funny to see others around us not joining in. We would look at each other and just laugh some more. It was that sense of camaraderie that I needed. It was better than any prescription.

When the day finally arrived for me to go to BWH to see my new doctor, I was nervous about what I would learn. Walking into the room, we found the receptionist was expecting me, and the waiting room was empty. Among the regular seating were also some raised chairs. It was a warm and welcoming room that was already addressing my needs. I wasn't there for more than five minutes, when the doctor came out to gather me himself.

He was a shy, unassuming Asian man by the name of Shon; as soon as he spoke a bit, you realized how smart he was. With his soft and concerned voice, he made me feel at ease the minute we met. He was a resident. Because the BWH is a teaching hospital, I had several resident doctors reviewing my case as well. The thought of that many minds concerned about me was comforting.

After our introduction, he went straight to business. He told me he had received my test results but wanted to ask me some questions first. I was to answer them yes or no. The first one took me off guard. He asked, "How many miscarriages have you had?" This wasn't a question of "if" I had but instead "how many." In an instant, the burden of fault I had carried for so many years lifted. I was not a bad mother, unable to protect my children.

Then he began a list of words: hypoglycemia, low blood pressure, sun rashes, red mask on the face, Reynaud's, hair loss, hysterectomy. There were eleven in all, and I answered yes to each one. When he saw I had a daughter, he seemed pleased and said, "Do you realize how special that is?"

My answer was a simple statement, "Every day."

He then put down the folder and paused. Looking at me with care in his eyes, he faltered ever so slightly.

Taking the lead, I said, "Its lupus, isn't it?" It was a statement more than a question. Suddenly, my entire life made sense.

He said, "The tests were positive. In combination with the eleven responses, I have no doubt. In reality, it only required a yes answer to four of the questions. I'm surprised that you hadn't been tested for it before."

"I actually had been tested for it as a child. Back then, it always came back negative. Until I did the research online, I had no idea I could get a positive after all these years. When it became a possibility, I insisted on the test with the other physician."

He said, "That was smart; you were right." Even though neither of us spoke it, we both knew we were all thinking the same thing, "Why didn't the first doctor see this right away?" After all, he had my medical history and had asked me most of the same questions. I looked over at Jack. I saw a look on his face that was both anger and concern. When our eyes met, all we could think of was Effi.

Fifteen years ago, Effi had been a friend of ours. She had lupus. Over the course of the five years that we knew her, we saw her struggles: her difficulty standing, the obvious pain she was in. Until finally she was yellow from a malfunctioning kidney, and she couldn't fight anymore. In a short time she was gone.

Afraid to ask, it took all the strength I could muster, "Am I going to die?"

Without a definitive answer, he replied, "There is a lot of new research, and everyday more and more people are living longer, some into old age." It is hard to say what I was feeling. It was a wide variety of emotions. The first was the anger at the care I had received from my original doctor: the arguments, the snide remarks, not to mention the expense and torment I went through.

He paused, so the information he had just given us would sink in. Next, he invited one of the senior residents into the room. Dr. Newton was an older man with a gentle face. With years of experience and compassion, he told me what to expect and our next course of action. I asked him if I would ever be myself again. I was grasping for any sense of hope. Dr. Newton couldn't exactly answer that. He told me that it was all about controlling flares. "In many ways lupus is similar to rheumatoid arthritis, which you also have, only with lupus, there is no joint damage." My thoughts went to my paintings. Jack and I sighed in unison. "Unfortunately," he said, "it can sometimes go to soft tissue. But with all the new advances, we are better able to control it." He explained to me the Plaquenil I had been taking was actually an anti malaria drug, which is also used for lupus and arthritis; but since it wasn't working that well, we would back it up with methotrexate. Methotrexate had been around for many years and is a form of chemotherapy used to fight cancer. Unfortunately, it also takes a few months to kick in. He said we would still use the prednisone to bridge it, but we really needed to get me off the steroids.

The ride home from Boston took forty minutes. After the first ten, I turned to Jack and said, "Let me see if I have this right. The arthritis will cripple me but not kill me, and the lupus could kill me but not cripple me."

"I believe that's right," he said.

"And I have both."

"Yes, you do."

The rest of the way home we rode in silence; when we arrived, JM was waiting for us at the door. We added the new medicine to my growing arsenal of drugs.

I went online to better understand what it all meant. The first thing I did was look up the meanings of all the jargon I had just heard: letters and numbers relating to tests. The first was ANA (antinuclear antibody). This is a representation of the substance against the cell nucleus. I remembered from high school that the nucleus is the control center of the cell. ANA can damage or destroy good cells. In other words, my body was attacking itself. It is kind of like having the armies of white blood cells in your body getting confused, the same ones that help you fight infection or heal a cut. Now imagine them looking for something to fight and thinking that your good cells are spies.

ANA is a tricky test. It is based on how many times the lab has to dilute your blood, in order not to find ANA. Because of the dilution processes, the test fluid is doubled every time. The titer number refers to this process. 1:80 means one divided by eighty. Anything that is 1:80 or lower is a negative test. 1:160 doesn't necessarily mean a huge jump. It is in fact only one jump. It is because of this and other factors that a test alone doesn't diagnose this disease. A positive ANA is present for many other diseases, such as Arthritis and MS. It is because of this that they also look under a microscope for a pattern, when the antibodies are attacking the nucleus. There are four different types. For lupus there is a rim pattern, shown strongly around the outer edge. This is the most specific for detecting lupus. In addition, they also look to see which antigen is causing the positive ANA. Antibodies to DNA (the protein that makes up the body's genetic code) are found primarily in lupus SLE. What's more, antibodies Sm are originated almost exclusively in lupus patients. After digesting all this information, I tried to not think about it too much, especially since the prickly sensation in my joints that felt like hundreds of little people were consuming me, in fact was just that.

The best thing about hiring JM to work the summer camp classes was his strength. Not only could he drive the large van, but he also lugged all the gear. He even included lifting me in and out of the car as part of his job description. From the first day forward, it also became his number one priority to make me laugh. His first test with this was loading me into the van. The van was a fifteen passenger. The running boards were high off the ground. He would help me by placing my arm on the arm pull and my left foot up on the step. To pull me up, he had to grab me by the waist band on the back of my shorts and lift as I was pulling as best as I could. Imagine pulling a sack of sand out of the ocean. It was like that, only not as wet. It was a trial and error effort, and after the first few times of laughing and cringing, we had it down. By the third time, he said, "I feel our relationship has risen to new heights!" Unfortunately, I was half way in the uplift position, when he said it. Laughing, I immediately fell backwards into his awkwardly waiting arms, like a clumsy cannon ball dive into a pool. After a few weeks of that, lifting my leg to the running board became impossible. Never wanting to experience that again, I thought of a great idea. I bought a small, Rubber Maid step stool and attached a dog's leash to a corner of one of its legs. When JM saw me leaving the house one morning with a cane in one hand and dragging this contraption with the other, he said, "What the hell is that?"

I smiled with a triumphant grin, "It's my dog!" So excited to show him, I walked proudly to the van: not proud like a peacock, more like Quasimodo off to work. Stubbornly insisting on doing it myself, with one awkward move, I dumped myself into the front seat. "Wait," I said, "You need to see the best part." I then pulled on the leash and lifted the whole thing into the car. "That is genius!" he said. Smiling, I looked to Jack who was next to me. He was grinning proudly.

CHAPTER: 61

The Salem Willows hadn't changed much since I was a child. It was where I played as a teenager. It was the place I took Lex when she was little. And now I was teaching painting there with my classes up on the hills. An amusement park on the water, it is visited by children and adults alike. A throwback from the late 19th century, it was once a place for summer fun and entertainment. The old photographs displayed there showed women finely dressed in floor length dresses and carrying parasols, strolling along the promenade. Today, it isn't quite so formal. The promenade (or line, as we called it) has arcades, fast food restaurants, miniature golf, and, sitting like a dinosaur on the end, one of the original ice cream and popcorn establishments: Hobbs. The buildings are mostly original. Adjust your easel at just the right angle in front of Hobbs, and you can paint a picture so close to what it used to be that one could question the date of the painting's origin.

Across from the line is the harbor. Between the line and the harbor is a grassy knoll, housing a concert shell and gazebos. That is the spot we set up camp. We chose this area under the gazebos for several reasons, the first being rain. There is nothing worse than painting outside and having it start to pour, especially when you're with children. The second reason is that there are visual options. From that vantage point, a painter has many choices of scenery: a seascape, a landscape or buildings. It is also handy that there are restrooms with running water there as well.

Our enrollment consisted of ten children, ages nine and up, plus three teachers. Jack, JM, and I filled that criteria. Sometimes my daytime class would show up, adding three or four more adults. Although it was called a camp, it was certainly not "camping." We didn't set up tents and fish for lunch. No, this was a day camp for art. It was a "plein air" class for painting landscapes. We talked about what it was like painting outside and the issues that could arise: bugs, changing light, and, more annoying than that, people coming up to you and telling you about a relative they have who paints. Always the business woman, I tried to coach the kids at how to seal the deal and possibly sell their work. This had happened more than once with the children, and they were thrilled every time. It was their validation as artists.

I would do a demonstration for fifteen minutes every morning. The students would then disperse to their chosen spots to paint. Then the teachers roamed from student to student with help and advice. I found the kids would be less whiny about their work in this type of setting. Maybe it was because they were in public.

At the end of the painting time, JM would pack up the van and get it ready for the next day. Twenty minutes before we left, we let the kids play games in the arcade. At the end of the week, we had a critique and pizza party. After dropping the kids off to their parents, JM and I would go back to the studio and teach the afternoon classes. Jack taught the evening ones. The whole program worked very well and was extremely popular. Year after year, we would work out any kinks and revise it for the next. Without any advertising, we were filled every week in the summer.

As my illness progressed throughout the school year, the impending summer camp became a concern for me. No longer would I have the morning or the even ground of the studio to work out the kinks. The children would have to see me at my worst, not to mention, that some of them had never met me. I didn't have a choice. As always, honesty proved to be best, especially with children. On the first day of every week before we left, I would sit them down and, without going into too much detail, I would tell them why I walked the way I did and not to worry, it was only temporary, until my medicine kicked in and my joints "got oiled." By the end of my speech, I always finished with the happy note, "Hey, but we can park in the handicap zone!" That usually brought cheers and laughter. By the end of the week, children, being who they were, were either helping me or wanting to use my cane.

Of course, the children loved JM. He was a big goof ball who loved to joke around with them. He could even make the visually difficult fact that he had to lift me in and out of a chair comical. That, of course, made some of them want to try it; and of course, that is where I drew the line. The stairs to the gazebos were the most difficult, even on a good day. As part of the original structures of the park, only one was handicap accessible. All the restrooms, however, were. The gazebos were approximately spaced anywhere from fifteen to twenty-five feet apart. Climbing the stairs and walking that distance with a cane on uneven ground made Jack and JM very nervous for me. It was a comfort to know that they always had an eye on me. Being who I was, I insisted I do as much as I could myself. My knees were my worst problem. Every time I sat or rose, it would feel as if someone were stabbing hundreds of needles in my knee caps. Sometimes it would be so bad that it would make me fall back into my seat. It was at that point that JM, with both arms under my armpits, would lift me to take the pressure off. Sometimes he would do this to suspend me in the air, because I found that to relieve the most pain. To someone who didn't know the situation, we must have looked like we were always in an embrace. Once we were standing, he would ask me if I wanted to dance. Unfortunately, every twenty minutes we had to perform this ritual. He never once showed irritation about it or complained. When he saw that it made me feel bad, he would just crack another joke. A few times, the pain would be so bad that, out of view from the children, I would cry. At those times, he would sit quietly holding my hand and let me do it.

Most of the summer went on like this, with very little change. There was one day, however, that the pain grabbed a hold of me, and no matter how much coaxing from JM, I couldn't shake it. Jack kept insisting I stay home, but my sense of responsibility was too overwhelming. There was a particular little girl that day at the camp who was insecure, a condition that we referred to as "fragile." The main reasons some kids are like this can fall into two categories. The first is trauma. The trauma can be anything, but it is almost always visual. Included in this category is divorce. The second is an overprotective parent who had made the poor child paranoid by the time he was four. Those are always the toughest, because not only are you dealing with the child, but also the parent. In essence, you are dealing with two children, because a parent's paranoia often stems from something in his childhood that he has not addressed. The thing that always baffled me about this was the fact that a parent would announce it to me. They would say, "I'm sorry I'm an overprotective parent who's paranoid about leaving my child." To them, it defined them as a good parent. Usually this statement was said in front of the kid, and that's when I cringed. Let me announce it here; it is never appropriate to put fear into a child. In the growing process to adulthood that "fear" changes and evolves into many things. It becomes an entity in and of itself, like a mean dog just within reach, always waiting to attack.

On that particular day, that was what I was dealing with. I had to strategize my game plan. How was I going to teach as well as keep an eye on that child so she wouldn't feel unsure of her work, not to mention deal with my limited mobility? Another form of fallout from an overprotective parent is that it squashes the initiative in children. The only choice I had was to put her in the large gazebo with several others, with a chair not too far away. I was close enough to make her feel secure, yet far enough for it to not be noticeable. Doing this without anyone knowing took some finesse. The other issue that day was that I couldn't use my cane. It wasn't sturdy enough to hold me. I needed both my arms for support that day. It was a difficult decision, but I had to do it; I took my walker.

That was the part that was most difficult for me. When we arrived at the studio, I stayed in the car while Jack and JM loaded up the gear and kids. When we got to the park, JM knew how I was feeling and walked with me slowly up the hill, until I was settled in a chair under a gazebo. As much as I wanted to cry that day, I couldn't. I was too much in view of the children, it was best that I was there. What would I have done if I weren't---stayed at home isolated and sobbing? I never allowed that to be an option. When I think back on that summer, and I think of the difficult times, that day is the first one that comes to mind. Somehow we were able to manage, and the child was happy and so was her mother. By the end of the morning, I was out of my mind in pain. I had pushed myself too far physically. Jack insisted I not do my afternoon classes.

He sent me home after the camp. I was reluctant, because without splitting the afternoon classes, that would mean he was working 9:00 AM to 9:00 PM. I knew this would tire him out. He had so many things he had to do for me now, so the last thing I wanted was to give him more. He was firm about it and suddenly I didn't have a choice. Helping me into bed, he kissed me on the forehead and said he was a phone call away if I needed him. Smiling back at him, I said, "Don't worry, I'll be ok." Lying in my bed, looking out the window, I watched as he drove away. Within ten minutes, a slow panic set in. I realized I was trapped beneath my sheet. Somehow we had forgotten to arrange them so that I could get out. One side was inadvertently tucked under my body. Without the ability to roll over or even turn slightly, I felt as Gulliver must have when he woke up tied to the ground with all the "little people" around him. I called out to Boogie. I knew she couldn't help me escape; I just wanted the company. When she didn't respond, I wasn't concerned. She often camped out in the cellar on hot summer days, and then someone would accidently close the door and trap her as well. I had learned early on with this disease how to remove my covers with my feet. That day, however, it was impossible. My knees were in too much pain. All I could do was lie there and take it. I wondered how long it would take before I went "inside." In this position, rocking and humming would be impossible. Trapped in my bed, I started thinking about all I had been through, a thing I only allowed myself to do if I knew it was useless to stop it. I wanted to cry, but I had no more tears left. The burning of my joints was setting in, and I had no fire hose to stop it. I realized then that the power of my mind and strong will to get through it was my only defense. A strange peace came over me that I had never felt before. It was internal yet all around me, and I feared it was the first sign of going mentally insane. At least if I were to cry, it would be a form of resistance. I told myself, "Maybe it was because I was too tired to cry."

Looking at the trees across the street I watched as the patterns of familiar faces in the leaves blew in the gentle breeze. I was reminded of my time as a child in Greenlawn Cemetery, when I spent hours sitting under the branches and finding pictures. It was then that I realized what this sensation of peace was. It was spiritual. The faces in the leaves were comical and eased my loneliness. For months now, the lights and darks among the leaves blowing in the wind visually transported me to different places, a setting that was not filled with pain and anguish. They were virtual paintings in my mind. Sometimes I saw faces while other times I saw gestures of figures interacting. Many people have done this as kids. It is the game where you try and find animals in the clouds. I was surprised by how easy it was to let my imagination take over. It was hypnotic, and when I played this game, time as we knew it would go on fast forward, the same feeling I would get when I actually was painting.

I tried more and more to see other patterns I had not yet noticed. When I looked to my right, there was a street light just several feet away. It was always in a direct line of my view. Hearing some birds singing the joys of summer, I realized that they were living in the top section of the lamp above the bulb. They were building a nest. They were sparrows, a male and a female. Each had a job to do and was quite good at it. As the male gathered the twigs, the female took them and arranged the nest from inside. Their working together reminded me of how Jack and I were. I was fascinated by this raw and natural cohabitation that was happening just a few feet from my window.

The light seemed like a perfect place for a home. During the day, it was hidden and protected from any possible predators; at night, it was warmed from its bulb. I imagined how cozy it must be in there, two little birds huddled together, waiting for their brood. It gave me hope in this world that was filled with so much violence and war. I began to cry. I could not cry for my pain, yet somehow when it came to beauty, the tears flowed. I felt this was a gift given to me by God, and I thanked him. I felt if it hadn't been for lupus, I never would have had this experience. I was surprised to realize that several hours had passed.

I watched the birds the entire day. I dozed on and off, and when I awoke, they were still there, and so was my pain. If I could just move my legs even a fraction of an inch, maybe it would relieve some of it. It was useless. The covers were too tangled around me. I began to feel like an Egyptian mummy in a crypt. I went back to watching the birds. They were my only solace. They became my friends, two creatures that were there for me to enjoy their company. I watched them throughout the afternoon, as they busied themselves with their task.

As the light of day turned to dusk and the fifth hour arrived, I found it difficult to focus my eyes in the darkening room. The birds settled themselves in, and sadly, I bade them goodnight. It was then the pain became excruciating. Having been in one position for so long, my legs were not only throbbing and burning, but now they had pins and needles running up the length of them, like electric shock treatments. Despite all this, I couldn't help but be awed that the birds had distracted me in such a way. I was sure there was something more to this that should be explored further. With those final thoughts, I dozed off until later that night. Suddenly I awoke from a noise in the distance. It was a car door being closed. Looking at the watch I had placed on my windowsill, I read the dial; it was 8:00 PM. The light switch was across the room, and now I was in total darkness. I knew that by the time Jack cleaned up after the classes, it would be 10:00 PM. If I were lucky, I would see him at 10:30. Having slept more than I had in over a year, I was no longer tired. I wondered, too, if this were a gift from God or my long since deceased mother who could still watch over me. It gave me a feeling that I wasn't alone and made me feel comforted. I had now been in this position for six hours. Going "inside" had now become a tool I could use at will. It would be a strategy I would use often from then on. With the realization I now had of time, it became more and more difficult to hold back the demons.

Along with the pain, I was now feeling restless. I felt my bed was a deserted island and myself a castaway. I looked to the light in hopes of seeing some activity, but all was quiet. The silence I felt was as encompassing as my now damp sheet.

Without any electrical devices to let me know I was in the real world, the stillness only added to the darkness that surrounded me. Looking around the room, I saw Shadow Man sitting quietly. This time he had a companion. Sitting at his feet was a wolf.

"Shadow Man, won't you please talk to me? Why is that wolf here? What does it mean? Am I going crazy? Why is it I seem to always see you at times like these? Have I been crazy all along? Are you just a vision in my head? Perhaps you are my conscience, my fears...my strength? Please talk to me." He didn't speak. The wolf growled softly. Shadow Man turned his head and looked towards my window. I turned away from him and followed his gaze. The light outside the window was my only connection to life. I searched frantically for something to distract me from the pain.

In a short time, I became aware of another family that lived in the street light. At night, it had become a different society with dissimilar activity. Spiders had spun webs throughout the intricate telephone and cable wires that connected from my house to the pole, wires that ironically as it was could bring communication to me from all over the world. (Yet there I was, unable to even call to my cat.) How ingenious, I thought, for spiders to build webs there. After all, the street light was where the moths gathered for their nightly dance. Being responsible parents, these spiders were merely feeding their young. Not knowing a whole lot about the life of spiders, I watched them intently as they rappelled from one wire to the next like great mountain climbers. They are Mother Nature's most talented engineers and talented artists. I was certain daVinci had watched spiders. Suddenly, my own art felt inferior. This left me with a newfound respect for spiders. In the past, I would just run when I saw one and call for Jack. This time they were far enough away: besides, running had long been out of my repertoire. I watched those spiders as if they were tigers in a zoo, barred from hurting me. In this case, it was the screen to my window and ten feet of space that was the barrier. Hours had passed, until finally I heard the front door open. "Barb," Jack called out in a panic, "Are you ok? Why are all the lights out?" Eight and a half hours I had lain in that position. I found a strength that night that made me realize that no matter how difficult the pain, I could endure this.

I simply replied, "I'm fine, but I think I need to move around a bit."

For weeks after, I watched the birds and spiders, thinking a lot about this universe so few people knew existed, a place in this world where insects and animals learned to adapt to their environment. It made me think of my life and how I had handled the adversity of my existence.

It made me realize that anything is possible. It was a true turning point in my growth as a handicapped person, as an individual. Then one day as the cold winds from the north settled into my bones, my furry and feathered friends were all gone. It was ok; they gave me what I needed at a time when I most needed it: my spirit.

From that night forward I had changed. Things that had mattered to me in the past were no longer important. Life became a precious gift to me that I no longer took for granted. I made it a point to enjoy the little things: the birds feeding in my back yard, the patterns I saw in everyday life, the smile of success I witnessed on a child's face. I no longer felt I was disabled and apart from things. I now felt I was lucky, because I was more in the real world than most. So many of us go through life without feeling; I, too, had been one of those people. I now felt everything, in my body as well as my heart. My tolerance for pain grew at the same time that my medicine began to take hold; or was it that my heart was so filled with the wonder of life that it overruled? The peaceful feeling I felt when I went inside from pain could now be accessed at anytime that I needed it. With this newfound ability, I began feeling better. As with stress having the ability to make me feel worse, I now knew that peace made me heal. Strapping the brushes into my braces, I began to paint again.

Another thing started to happen to me. It was slow at first, yet I found like the peace, I could turn it on at will. It was my sense of intuition. It was as if someone had turned up the dial, and now I felt all the things that concerned people around me. I always had a strong sense of intuition. But this was different. It was as if I could see pictures in my head of people I had known in my past. When I would contact them, inevitably something important was going on in their lives. It was as if my soul could pick up the happenings in theirs.

In my heart, I knew if my attitude could control how well I did to a certain extent, then what ever part of my brain was doing that was also controlling my "visions," for lack of a better word. When I say visions, what I mean really are visual thoughts. No, I was not like one of those scary movies that had people seeing things right before their eyes. It was more like a spontaneous thought. Being an artist and therefore a visual person, my thoughts are more like flashes of pictures. I had always been this way. The difference was that with my heightened sense of my own self, I no longer brushed them off. When a person is aware of all the functioning aspects of her body, as I had been over the past few years, wouldn't it make sense that she would be highly tuned into the functioning of her brain? If I could feel every joint and muscle, every beat of my heart and expansion of my lungs, every hair follicle in my skin, then why would I not feel the processes of my brain? These were the thoughts that were on my mind. To fully explain the road that led me to this, I must first tell you another story. This was not something I did personally but something that was done for me.

One Sunday, I was watching a baseball game. Being an avid Red Sox fan, I had been watching the games since I was a young girl. That day, while watching the game, I was cutting rags for the next day's classes. This was a brainless yet painful chore I forced myself to do during every game. I was always afraid of my muscles atrophying and knew that using them, even when it hurt, was necessary. My fingers, as usual, were aching. I was aware of every joint in my body. What I mean by that is that I was throbbing all over. I had resigned myself to this fact, and it was becoming a way of life. I had bouts of relief from the extreme pain I had been in, but it never fully went away. Modern medicine was helping me there. A short while into the game, I looked at the clock. It read 4:00 PM. I continued cutting. The whole time, I was coaching myself through the pain; not unlike Terry Francona, who was coaching his team. Then the most remarkable thing happened. In an instant, all my pain was gone. The throbbing had stopped and my fingers were fine as well. I quickly stood up; something I hadn't been able to do fast for awhile. I looked at the clock again. It read 4:37. In my head, I tried to rationalize it. I convinced myself it must be the methotrexate. It had finally kicked in. No matter... I was absolutely free of pain. I immediately began doing all the things around the house that I couldn't before. I never would have thought carrying laundry would give me such pleasure. My first thought was to have it all done before Jack came home, to surprise him. This feeling of wellness lasted through the next day. Monday afternoon, I literally ran to Jack in the parking lot of the school. He, of course, scolded me for it, but I didn't care. In my eyes, modern medicine was a miracle. That is until Tuesday morning at 3:00 AM. I woke up with a start. The pain was back, and I had to get out of bed and walk the hall. The disappointment grabbed me like an antagonist just waiting around the corner. When I entered the darkened hallway, Shadow Man and his new companion, the wolf, were there. I nodded to them in acknowledgment and continued on my quest. I was angry at myself for having let myself get carried away so. I wondered if maybe I had done too much. Deep down, I knew it was something that was unexplainable, something spiritual. It had been too abrupt when it had happened. I kept referring to it to Jack as a switch turning on; funny, that I had never thought of it as a switch shutting off.

Tuesday morning, I had an adult class at 9:00 AM. I hobbled into the studio and positioned myself near a table; a short while later, one of my students arrived and asked how I was feeling. After telling her about my weekend, a large smile came across her face. She said that when she retired from nursing, she had joined a group of Buddhist healers. She said she did this because, with all the years of nursing, she had seen too many things that had convinced her there was something more to the brain and healing than just what we know. She was certain that the ancients were onto something. The previous Sunday, her group had chosen me to heal. She said the ceremony started at 4:00 PM. It took a half hour and was finished by 4:30. (I felt "zapped" at 4:37.) She also said it was common for it to only last about a day and a half. I stood looking at her with my mouth wide open. I didn't know what to say. My thoughts were racing.

The first thing I thought of was the fact that it wasn't my medicine. That was disappointing. The second thing that flashed through my mind was my mother, and the healing she had had that resulted in the disappearance of the tumor in her pelvis. After I processed all that my student had told me, my thoughts reverted to the inevitable. If she could do that to me...then I could do it to myself. As with most new concepts, I had to mull it around in my head for awhile. To be honest, I was afraid.

One night, I was in an awful state and desperate. That night I had more difficulty than usual getting out of bed to walk the hall. As a matter of fact, I couldn't. I was so tired, all I wanted to do was sleep. All I could do was sit on the side of the bed and cry. Shadow Man and the wolf were there, not moving, not making a sound. The pain had started that afternoon. Like a contraction when you're in labor, it began to peak. Sitting there on the side of the bed, I hit "the wall." It is a term used often when you feel the pain has peaked and can't get any worse. I like to refer to it as falling down the other side of the hill. It is different from "going inside." When I fall down the hill, I am no longer aware of my surroundings. I become part of a void. Time gets lost. That night, before I fell down the hill, I thought of my student and her healing. Although she didn't tell me how it had been done, I did the only thing I knew how to do. I pictured all the people in my life who loved me, my students past and present as well as my family. I called on their help and strength. I put them in a circle around me in my mind and saw their love projecting from their hearts to me, standing in the middle. I then asked them to please just help me sleep. The next thing I knew, it was three hours later, and I was lying down in bed, having slept the whole time. The thing that was most remarkable about this was that for two years, I had been unable to put myself back to bed, once I was in a sitting position. Pillows and sheets always had to be arranged by someone else. I have no idea what helped me that night. I feel I'm not supposed to know. Was it a healing? Is love really that strong? Or maybe our brains are a useful tool we need to explore further; like with the birds, I had found peace. Either way, it worked, and that was all I cared about. My mind became more open after that, and I started paying attention to the visions as well. I opened a door in my brain that night. Through extreme pain, I found the knob.

I believe it is through these experiences that I never saw the world as black and white. And it is through these experiences that I feel blessed, having been given the gift of spirituality. Never following any specific religion, I couldn't help but wonder if the heart, the head, and the hand are somehow connected. As an artist, I'm sure of it. As a person with a chronic illness, it gave me hope.

I never did stop taking my medicine. That would have been irresponsible and crazy. For me, my meds are like insulin to a diabetic. Without them, my body can't function. If my brain is misfiring and telling my white blood cells to fight and attack my good tissue, I wonder if it can do other things.

As the summer was coming to a close, so was our camp. I was feeling better and getting used to the fluctuation of good days and bad days. Jack still insisted I use my cane at the Willows. He was always concerned with the uneven ground under the grass. On the last day of our last week, we were all exhausted. With the day's heat, we all looked like we had just climbed a mountain instead of painted a landscape. As we headed to the van, JM dragged all the gear on a dolly, and Jack tried to rally the troops.

"Why don't you take the kids to the pizza parlor?" I said. "JM and I will load the car." Loading the car meant I watched as he struggled with the ten field easels. The only thing I could do was open the side door. JM had the keys. Turning to him, I said, "It's locked."

"Oh," he said, "Sorry." He pressed the button, making that annoying beeping sound. I tried the door again. Again it was locked. Turning to him again, being too tired to realize it was intentional on his part, I said, "It's still locked."

"Really?" he said so innocently, with a straight face. He pressed the button again. After the third attempt, I realized what he was doing.

Laughing, I said, "Don't do this to me, I'm too tired." He did it again; this time when I looked at him, he was smiling from ear to ear. He looked so funny standing there with that stupid grin that I could no longer control myself. Looking past his shoulder, I noticed a lot of people standing outside at a fast food restaurant, waiting for their meals to go. Staring at us, I was sure they were wondering why this young boy was teasing this handicapped woman. They were the lunch crowd of construction workers, annoyed by our antics. They were greasy and sweating. Some were landscapers covered in mowed grass. They were hot as well and probably only had a few minutes for a meal. Scattered among them were the occasional grandparents. Retirement brought them a day at the park to sit in the sun and eat. It was a tough audience, and, for some reason, their confused glares made me laugh more. It was the kind of laughter one shared with a best friend in eighth grade math class, when you were supposed to be listening. It was the type of moment that was now only a memory for most, the kind that adults no longer indulged in. I was sure no one else saw it as funny, and that just made us laugh more. Between gasps of air, I said, "Don't you know you should never make a woman over forty who has had a child laugh this hard? The consequences are too great." That made JM roar and everyone look more intently. I begged and pleaded with him to stop, as I tried desperately to cross my legs. With all the energy we could gather to control ourselves, we both took a deep breath and pulled it together. "Ok," I said, "Unlock the door."

"Ok," he said, "I'm sorry." With a stone look on his face, he made the sound again. I tried to pull open the door, and again it was locked. Crouching down as far as I could, laughing, my statement was a defeated one, "Too late!"

Two days later, JM left. He went back to Canada, and Jack and I were alone again. At night when the house was quiet and I walked the halls, I missed him so. Reflecting over the summer, I realized how laughter had begun to heal me. I was selfish. I wanted more of it. My joking around and storytelling had always been a part of who I was as a teacher before my illness. It was what my young students craved from me now. Late at night, I realized I yearned for it too. JM had taught me something that summer, something that had always been there, yet I had been too involved in my own situation to see it. Everything pointed to the same thing. With my attitude, I could lead a productive and happy life. I would still have obstacles, but I would be strong enough to hurdle them. The emotional hurdles would always be the most difficult, but now I knew I could do it. When JM left for school I removed my braces.

September arrived, and with the help of three and four teachers per class, I was able to work again. Because of vomiting and more hair loss, my methotrexate was now taken by injection that I had to give myself once a week. It was strange, at first, but not impossible. Lex broke up with her boyfriend and started calling me every day. Our relationship had come back even stronger than before. The way that came about was also with the help of JM. On Christmas break, he was so sick of the situation she was in, he drove to Connecticut to speak to her about it. She was ready for a change. She was just frightened and needed support. He helped her make the move. He packed her things for her and drove her home. The act of having my daughter back healed me more. It would be another thing I would always be grateful to him for. My relationship with Lex grew stronger than it had ever been. Maybe she had needed that time away from me to separate. Maybe we had been too close to begin with. After Lex graduated from college with a BFA in fine arts, she worked alongside me as a teacher. And again, we were a great team. Our relationship has been exactly what I had said it would be.

I decided to do something more with my life. I began writing for a magazine about lupus. With an online circulation, I was able to reach people across the globe. My life was moving in a positive way. Some would even say I hadn't started living until I realized I could die. I say, I was given a different life. I was just fortunate enough to see it.

I had always known struggle. Now I wondered if it were just to prepare me for what was to come. I laughed in the face of lupus. I teased it whenever I could. But in the end, I always knew I would lose. I just wasn't going to go down without a fight. Then, the day of the final round began. It would be my last dance with the wolf.

It started as a cold. With all the immune-suppressing drugs I was taking, I was not surprised. Jack insisted I stay home, so I did. A few weeks and several rounds of antibiotics later, I found it was getting worse, not better. It had developed into full blown pneumonia. A few days after that, I was placed in the hospital. My time spent there, I was in and out of consciousness, living a life in a dream world that faded into reality. I found myself in a great forest, surrounded by wolves. This time, I walked with the pack freely, unafraid of them and accepting. The times I was aware, I found myself reflecting on my life. Would I have changed anything, if I could? Maybe I would have wanted the relationship with my mother to have been different, but never my spirit. The men in my life slowly walked in front of me. One at a time, I thanked them. They all had helped to mold me to be the woman I had become. I loved to love, and I did it openly and with conviction.

Shadow Man joined me with the wolf and sat vigil the entire time I was in the hospital. Sometimes I would speak to him; other times we just sat in quiet contemplation, two individuals who had spent a lifetime together when the words seemed to run out. My family would often come and sit with me, every chance they got, bringing me stories of the kids and trying to make me feel I was still a part of the real world. I didn't have the heart to tell them that I had already left. On one particular night, my world became watery. The fluid in my lungs seemed to reach the rest of my body. Suspended in this watery world, I waited. My eyes, that were once the access road to the information that flowed through my brain, were now mere slits, trying to keep out the pain I saw on the faces of the ones who loved me. The only real sense I had was of the wolf, occasionally licking my face. Turning to Shadow Man, I yelled in my delirium, "Talk to me! Tell me it is going to be ok!" This brought my family closer to my bed, in desperation adjusting my covers and rubbing my head. I smelled them when they came close to me.

Familiar and pleasing, it smelled like the crook of my baby's neck, that first time we met. Feeling their anguish over my outburst, I lowered my voice and spoke to Shadow Man again. "Did I just win the lottery? I didn't know I bought a ticket." There was silence. The room began to darken. I felt the wind pick up outside, or was that inside? I could no longer tell. Shadow Man, sitting on the edge of a chair across the room, seemed to mock me. Lifting my head I called to him, "Did I die eight years ago, when I was working the rocks in my garden? Have I been in Hell? Who are you? Are you Lucifer?" Still there was no answer, as the pillows got adjusted again, and the fragrance returned. After a period of time, I became quiet; my voice was now a whisper. "Shadow Man, when we walk this earth, do we leave a piece of ourselves behind in every step, or are the people we meet our only footprints?" Standing up from his chair, he came closer. In the distance, I now heard," Mom, it is ok to let go, we will be ok." It was a familiar voice; I felt it as love in my heart.

Shadow Man now at the end of my bed, touches my foot. I ask him, "Will my mother recognize me in heaven or will I be a mere glimpse of the child she once knew, a human existence that gets watered down as every generation's DNA gets thinned through the plasma of their offspring? Come to me Shadow Man, this is my last chance to see you. I need to know who you are. Show yourself to me...please." Upon hearing my last plea, the wolf backed slowly away and disappeared into the mist.

Shadow Man glides slowly to the head of the bed, as his cold hand travels up my legs and rests heavily on my heart, my body seems to disengage. Opening my eyes, I see him for the first time. He is beautiful and full of pure, white light. He is the most magnificent thing I have ever seen. He lifts me from the bed to stand next to him. We start heading for the door. In the distance, I hear sobs, yet in front of me, I feel love. I ask him, "What does this mean? Did I do it right?" His reply was soft and simple, "Good job."

ABOUT THE AUTHOR

Debra Freeman Highberger is a professional painter and writer. She owns the Acorn School of Art In Marblehead, Massachusetts, which she currently operates with her husband and daughter.

Cover: Oil, 30x40, Debra Freeman Highberger

Author painting: Oil, 14x18, Self-portrait, age 40

Photo credits: Jennifer Shore Photography

Made in the USA
Middletown, DE
20 April 2019